THE COLLECTED SHORT STORIES OF CHEKHOV

契诃夫短篇小说选

〔俄罗斯〕契诃夫 著　童道明 等 译

上海三联书店

图书在版编目（CIP）数据

契诃夫短篇小说选 ／〔俄罗斯〕契诃夫（Chekhov,A.P.）著；
童道明等译．－上海：上海三联书店，2009.5

ISBN 978-7-5426-3048-3

Ⅰ.契... Ⅱ.①契...②童... Ⅲ.短篇小说-作品集-俄罗斯-
近代 Ⅳ.I512.44

中国版本图书馆CIP数据核字（2009）第054032号

契诃夫短篇小说选

著　　者／〔俄罗斯〕契诃夫

译　　者／童道明　等

责任编辑／戴　俊　叶　庆

特约编辑／张　迪

装帧设计／**metis** 灵动视线
　　　　　 TEL:010-85983452

监　　制／研　发

出版发行／上海三联书店

　　　　（200031）中国上海市乌鲁木齐南路396弄10号

　　　　http://www.sanlianc.com

　　　　E-mail:shsanlian@yahoo.com.cn

印　　刷／三河市汇鑫印务有限公司

版　　次／2009年5月第1版

印　　次／2011年10月第5次印刷

开　　本／640×965　1/16

字　　数／190千字

印　　张／15.5

ISBN 978-7-5426-3048-3/I·426

定　价：23.00元

编者的话

　　谁能解开契诃夫心中永恒的孤独？谁能在浮世中品尝他忧郁的陈酿？谁又能体会到他的笔下人性的暖光？契诃夫为什么能铭刻在每个深刻懂得活着意义的人心上，成为永恒？因为契诃夫的作品包涵着人类永恒的思索、永恒的困顿和永恒的希望。

　　"人的一切都应该是美丽的——无论是面孔、还是衣裳，还是心灵，还是思想。"人生在契诃夫的笔下是忧伤的。《苦恼》中马车夫姚纳的儿子死了，丧子之痛，无人可诉，他只好孤单单一人，寂静和苦恼向他袭来，而且变本加厉地折磨着他的心胸。"小母马嚼着草，倾听着……姚纳讲得出了神，把所有要说的话，统统讲给了它听。"如此安静的结局，却仿佛轻轻敲打着每一个为之动容的人的心。《带小狗的女人》中"只是到了现在，到了他的头发开始变白的时候，他才爱上了；认真地爱，真正地爱，有生以来第一次。"在这里，契诃夫好像看到了当年的自己，第一次体会到真正的爱，而此时鬓已斑白。这迟来的爱情令人哀叹、伤痛之余，反心生慰藉，如果没有沉痛的过往，怎会有而今刻骨铭心的相遇？《忧伤》中"镟工哭了起来。他又是忧愁，又是烦恼。他想，这个世界上的一切，过去得多么快呵！"他的妻子死了，可为什么这样快呢？什么都来不及……道尽人生最大的憾事：没有为你做到的时候，你却已经离去。死亡在契诃夫的笔下简单、纯净，然而这种单纯反倒牵动了生者之隐痛。契诃夫笔下的各种情感的源头都是忧伤，而这忧伤来自于一个孤独、神圣的人性深处所发出的光芒，它照射到每一个人的身上，如阳光一样自然，是他让我们看到人生中的现实，现实中的哀伤，忧伤中的平淡，平淡中的希望。

当漫步在亲手建成的花园之中的时候，当徜徉在落日的金色余晖下的时候，当行进在俄罗斯广袤的草原和漂流在波涛滚滚的阿穆尔河上的时候，契诃夫体味着与大自然亲近所带来的幸福，因而，他的文字质朴而宁静。然而契诃夫还有另外一重身份，他是一名医生。他注视着国民那灰色、可怜却又不思改进的生活，忍不住以笔作刀，犀利精准地解剖国民的麻木与奴性。他带着忧郁而痛心的微笑，告诉人们：生活不能再这样继续下去了。

高尔基曾说："我们读安东·契诃夫的小说时会有这样一种印象：仿佛在一个悒郁的晚秋的日子里，空气十分明净，光秃的树木，窄小的房屋和带灰色的人都显得轮廓分明。一切都是奇怪地孤寂的，静止的，无力的……他的心灵跟秋天的太阳一样，用一种残酷无情的光明照亮了那些坍塌的道路，曲折的街道，窄小潮湿的房屋，在那里面一些渺小可怜的人给倦怠和懒惰闷得透不过气来……"

契诃夫离开我们已经一个世纪了，而他在我们眼中，宛如夜空中闪烁的星辰一样遥远。当我们宁静下来仰望星空的时候，想到那些曾经感动过契诃夫的永恒的问题，如今他又用静静的文字，静静的灵魂抚慰我们的心灵，此刻，契诃夫离我们是最近的。

2009年5月

目　　录

套 中 人

　　在米罗诺辛茨基村的尽头，在村长普罗柯菲耶家的板棚里，误了点的猎人准备留宿过夜。他们只有两个人：兽医伊凡·伊凡内奇和中学教师布尔金。伊凡·伊凡内奇有个很古怪的复姓——奇姆沙－吉马拉耶斯基，这和他显然不匹配，所以省里的人干脆叫他的本名和父名，他住在城郊的养马场，这次出来打猎，是为了呼吸呼吸新鲜空气。中学教师布尔金则每年夏天都要到伯爵家做客，他早就是这个地区的熟人。

　　他们没有睡觉。伊凡·伊凡内奇是个瘦瘦的高个子老头，留着长须，坐在门口抽烟，明月照亮了他。布尔金躺在屋里的干草堆上，人影消失在黑暗中。

　　他们说了很多故事，顺便也说起村长的老婆玛芙拉，一个很健康也不笨的女人，这一辈子她竟然没有出过这个村子，她既没见过城市，也没有见过铁路，而最近十年她整天守着灶台，只有到了夜间才上街去走一走。

　　"这有什么可惊奇的！"布尔金说，"那种生性孤独，像寄生蟹或蜗牛那样拼命躲进自己的外壳里的人，在这个世上并不少。也许，这是隔世遗传，又回到了我们老祖宗的时代，那时的人还不是群居动物，而是单个生活在自己的洞穴中，或许，这不过是人的性格的一种变异，——有谁知道呢？我不是自然科学家，我不研究这些问题，我只是想说，像玛芙拉这样的人，决不是少有的现象。也是，不必往远了找，两个月前，我们城里死了个叫别里科夫的人，希腊语教师，是我的同事。想必你也听说过他。他名声在外，是因为他即便在阳光灿烂的日子出门，也穿上套鞋，带上雨伞，而且还一定要穿着暖和的棉大衣。"

　　他的雨伞装在套子里，他的怀表也装在皮套子里，而当他掏出小刀削铅笔的时候，那小刀也放在一个小套子里，他的脸似乎也装在套子里，因为它总是藏在拉起的衣领里。他戴墨镜，穿绒衣，耳朵塞上棉花，要是坐马车出行，一定吩咐把车篷支起。总而言之，这个人有一种恒久的、不可抗拒的心愿，力图用外壳把自己包围起来，就好比给自己制造一个套子，好让他与世隔绝不受外界影响。现实生活刺激了他，惊吓了他，使他总是处于恐慌之中；也许是为自己的胆怯和对现实生活的憎恶作辩解，他不遗余力地赞美过去，赞美从来也不存在的东西；他讲授的古代语言，对于他来说，实际上也是一双套鞋，一把伞，借助它们回避现实生活。

　　"噢，希腊语多么悦耳，多么美妙！"他带着甜美的表情说道，为了证明自己说得有道理，他眯缝着眼睛，举起一个手指，念道："安特洛普斯！"

　　别里科夫也极力把自己的思想藏在套子里。对于他来说，有发布什么禁令的政府告示和报纸社论，才是一目了然的。当有份告示禁止中学生在晚上九点过后上街，或是有篇报纸的文章鼓吹禁止性爱，他就觉得一清二楚，发出禁令———了百了。他认为在一切的开禁和允许里，都包含着某种可疑的，说不清道不明的因素。而当有关部门批准在城里成立剧社，或是开设阅览室和茶座，他就摇摇头轻声说道：

　　"这，当然，好倒是好，但怎么会不闹出点乱子来。"

　　一切偏离章程，有点出格的事，都会让他垂头丧气，尽管，这与他有何相干呢？如果有个同事没有准点参加祷告仪式，或是听说中学生调皮捣蛋，或是看到女教师晚上和军官在一起散步，他就会激动起来，反复说，这怎么会不闹出点乱子来。在学校的教务会上，他用自己的谨小慎微，神经过敏，以及他那类套子式的议论压迫着我们，他认为男校和女校的年轻人都行为不轨，教室里闹得不成体统，他说，这怎么会不传到上司的耳朵里去，啊喔，这怎么会不闹出点乱子来，他还说，如果把二年级的彼得洛夫，四年级的叶果洛夫开除了，倒是很好。结果怎么样？他用他的一声声叹息和哀怨，用他那副贴在小白脸上的黑眼镜——您知道，他的小脸活像黄鼠狼的脸——来压迫我们，我们只好让步，我们把彼得洛夫和叶果洛夫的操行分数压低，给他俩关了禁闭，而最后还是把彼得洛夫和叶果洛夫开除了事。他有个奇怪的习癖——常来我们宿舍走动。他到了一位教师家里，坐了下来，一言不发，像是要侦探什么似的。就这样一言不发地坐上一、两个小时，然后走了。他把这称作"与同事们保持友善关系"，但很明显，来看望我们，枯坐一两个小时，在他是件痛苦的事，他来探望我们仅仅是因为他觉得这是在尽一份同事的义务。我们这些教师都怕他，甚至校长也怕他。您倒是想想，我们教师都是有头脑的人，他们的品行受过屠格涅夫和谢德林的熏陶，而这个总是穿着雨鞋打着雨伞的人，却整整十五年把整个学校捏在自己的手心里！学校算得了什么？整个城市都被他捏在手心里！我们的妇女到了星期六不敢举办业余戏剧演出，因为怕他知道，有他在场，神父不敢吃肉，不敢打牌。在像别里科夫这类人的影响下，最近十年到十五年的时间里，我们这个城市的居民变得害怕一切。害怕大声说话，害怕邮寄书信，害怕结交朋友，害怕阅读书籍，害怕接济穷人，害怕学习文化。

伊凡·伊凡内奇咳嗽了一声，想说点什么，他先吸了口烟，看了看月亮，然后才抑扬顿挫地说道："是啊，有头脑、有品行的人，读着谢德林的书、屠格涅夫的书，还读勃克尔等等名家的书，可是却忍气吞声，服从管制……事情就是这样。"

"别里科夫和我是邻居。"布尔金继续说。同一层楼房，门对门，我们常常见面，我知道他的家庭生活。家里也是这一套：睡衣，睡帽，门闩，百叶窗，种种禁忌，种种忌讳，还有——这怎么会不闹出点乱子来！吃素有害，而吃荤又不行，因为怕别人说别里科夫不持斋，于是他要吃用奶油炸过的小鲈鱼，这虽然不是素菜，但也不能说是荤腥。他不用女仆，怕别人说他闲话，就雇了阿法纳西来当厨子，这是个六十岁的老头，爱喝酒，头脑不清醒，以前当过勤务兵，多少能烧点菜。阿法纳西经常站在门口，手臂交叉在胸前，总是唉声叹气，反复嘟囔这样一句：

"现在像他们这样的人有的是！"

他的卧室很小，像个木头匣子，床上挂着蚊帐。他上床睡觉总是用被子裹着脑袋，房里又热又闷，风吹打着紧闭的房门，炉子也嗡嗡作响；从厨房里传来叹息声，那是不祥的叹息声……

他躺在被子里头感到恐惧。他担心会闹出点什么乱子来，担心阿法纳西会宰了他，担心会有小偷破门而入。于是他做了一夜的噩梦，早上我和他一起去学校，一路上他脸色苍白，郁郁寡欢，看得出来，他要去那所人声鼎沸的学校，让他恐慌与厌恶，和我结伴同行，对于他这个生性孤僻的人也是件苦事。

"我们学校的教室里太闹了"，他这样说，像是要为自己的沉闷心情找到原因，"太不像话。"

您倒是想一想，这位希腊语教师，这位套子里的人差一点结了婚。

伊凡·伊凡内奇迅速瞅了瞅板棚说道：

"您是在开玩笑！"

真的，差一点结了婚，不管这有多么奇怪。我们学校来了一位新的史地教员，名叫米哈依尔·萨维奇·柯瓦连克，是乌克兰人。他不是一个人来的，他的胞妹瓦莲卡也跟来了。他年轻，皮肤黝黑，个头很高，手掌很大，从他的长相就能猜想他用低音说话，他的嗓音的确像是从木桶里传出来的："嘟嘟嘟"……而她已经不年轻，有三十岁了，但身材也很高，长得丰满，黑眉毛，红脸蛋，——一句话，不是女人，是水晶软糖，她是那么活泼、机敏，总是哼唱乌克兰民歌，总是笑声朗朗。她动不动就发出爽朗的笑声："哈哈哈！"和柯瓦连克兄妹的第一次真正相识，是在校长的命名日聚餐会上。在一群严肃的、老气横秋的、把参加命名日聚餐都看成应付差事的教师中间，我们突然看到一位新的阿芙罗基黛爱神浮出了水面：她两手叉腰来回走动，她笑着，唱着，跳着……她带着感情唱了《风之歌》，然后又唱了支歌，然后又是一支歌，她把我们所有的人，甚至包括别里科夫在内，都迷住了。别里科夫坐到她跟前，堆着甜蜜的笑容，说："乌克兰语的柔和与悦耳能让人联想到古希腊语。"

这话满足了她的虚荣心，于是她开始带着感情，用肯定的口吻对他说起她家在加德雅契县有个庄园，她妈现在就住在庄园里。那里有多么好的凤梨，多么好的甜瓜，多么好的卡巴卡呀！乌克兰人管南瓜叫卡巴卡，管小酒店叫什恩卡，他们用红颜色的甜菜和青菜熬出来的菜汤"非常好吃，简直是好吃死了！"

我们听着听着，突然间在我们脑子里浮现出一个相同的念头。

"让他们结成夫妻，倒也很好。"校长太太轻声对人说。

我们大家终于想到，我们的别里科夫还是个单身汉，我们开始感到奇怪，我们到现在为止竟然没有发现，完全忽略了他生活中如此重要的一个细节。他对女人有什么样的基本看法，他如何为自己解决这个终身大事？早先这样的问题完全不会让我们感兴趣，我们甚至不会产生这样的想法：一个不管什么天气都要穿雨鞋上街，天天都挂着帐子睡觉的人会谈恋爱。

"他已经四十开外，而她三十岁……"校长太太说明自己的想法。"我以为，她可以嫁给他。"

在我们外省，由于寂寞无聊什么样的事情都做得出来！有多少不应该做的荒唐事！这是因为完全不做正经事！就说这个别里科夫吧，我们甚至无法想象他是个未婚夫，可我们突然间为什么要操心替他做媒？校长太太、训导主任太太和所有我们学校的女士们全都活跃起来了，甚至变得标致了，好像一下子看见了生活的目标。校长太太在戏院里订了个包厢，瞧——在她的包厢里坐着瓦莲卡，她扇着扇子，喜形于色，她旁边是别里科夫，他蜷着身子，小得可怜，像是有人用钳子把他从家里夹到这里来的。我要举办游艺晚会，女士们便要求我务必把别里科夫和瓦莲卡请到。总而言之，机器开动了。而且发现，瓦莲卡也不反对嫁人。她和哥哥住在一起并不愉快，就知道整天争吵与对骂。您瞧这样一个场面：柯瓦连克在街上行走，是个高个儿壮汉，穿着绣花衬衣，一缕头发从帽檐落在额头；他一手拿着一包书，另一只手拄着一根多节的粗棍。妹妹走在他身后，也拿着一包书。

"米哈依里克，你没有读过这本书！"她大声争辩，"我敢向你发誓，你压根没有读过！"

"而我要对你说，我读过了！"柯瓦连克大声喊道，用木棍敲打着人行道。

"米契克，我的上帝！你干吗发火，我们是在进行原则性的对话。"

"而我要对你说，我读过了！"柯瓦连克喊得更响了。

而在家里，即便当着外人的面，也会互相吵骂。大概，这样的生活让她太厌倦了，她想要有个自己的家，而且也不能忽略年龄；现在已经不好挑三拣四，能嫁个人就行，甚至嫁给希腊文教师。对于我们大多数妇女来说，嫁给谁并不重要，要紧的是嫁出去。不管怎么样，瓦莲卡开始对我们的别里科夫表现出明显的好感。

而别里科夫呢？他也常常去柯瓦连克家里，就像常常来看我们一样。他一到那里，就坐下来，一言不发。他一言不发，瓦莲卡则给他唱《风之歌》，或是用她那双黑眼睛瞧着他，要不就突然大笑起来：

"哈哈哈！"

在情爱方面，尤其是在婚姻上，诱导能起很大作用。所有的人——无论是同事们还是同事的太太们——都试图让别里科夫相信他应该结婚，除了结婚之外，在他生活中再没有什么要紧的事。我们都向他道喜，都用严肃的口吻讲着各种无聊的套话，不外是婚姻是终身大事，况且瓦莲卡长得不错，也有品位，她还是五品文官的女儿，还有一处庄园，而更重要的是，她是头一个对他态度亲切的女人，——他终于昏了头，觉得自己的确应该结婚。

"应该把他的雨鞋、雨伞拿走才对。"伊凡·伊凡内奇这样说。

你要知道，这是不可能的。他把瓦莲卡的照片放到了自己的书架上，他照样来我这里，谈论瓦莲卡，谈论家庭生活，谈婚姻是终身大事，他也常去柯瓦连克家里，但他的生活方式依然如故。甚至相反，结婚的决定好像对他产生了负面的影响，他人变瘦了，脸色更加苍白，他像是更深地陷进了自己的套子里去了。

"瓦尔瓦拉·萨维什娜我喜欢，"他苦笑着轻声对我说，"我也知道，每个人都应该结婚，但……您要知道，这一切来得过于突然……应该好好考虑一下。"

"还考虑什么？"我对他说，"结婚就完事了。"

"不，结婚是终身大事。应当首先估量一下眼前的职责和义务……免得以后出什么乱子。这太让我担心了，我现在天天失眠。我得承认，我心里害怕：她和她哥哥的思想很奇怪，他们的言论，知道吗，也很离奇，性格也很张扬。结婚了，然后少不了会遇到什么麻烦。"

他没有求婚，一味地拖延，这让校长太太和我们的其他女士深感遗憾。他一直在估量眼前的职责和义务，与此同时他几乎每天与瓦莲卡出去散步，可能他以为处在他的地位必须这样行事。他也来看我，谈论家庭生活。如果没有出现一场轩然大波，很有可能他终于会求婚，从容不迫地完成一桩无聊而愚蠢的婚事，在我们这里，由于寂寞和无所事事而造就的这类婚事数以千计。应该指出，瓦莲卡的哥哥柯瓦连克从认识别里科夫的第一天起就憎恶他，忍受不了他。

"我不明白，"柯瓦连克耸耸肩，对我们说，"我不明白，你们怎么忍受这个告密者，这副讨厌的嘴脸。哎嘿，先生们，你们怎么能在这里生活！你们这里的空气太压抑、太恶浊。你们难道是教书先生？你们是群小官僚，你们这地方不是科学的殿堂，而是衙门，而且散发着只有在警察局里才能闻到的臭气。不的，兄弟们，我和你们再相处一阵就回自己的庄园，我将在那里捕鱼捉虾，教乌克兰的小孩读书识字。我会走的，让你们和自己的犹大留在这里，一起倒霉。"

有时他哈哈大笑，笑得流出眼泪，或是粗声粗气，或是细声细气，或是用尖利的嗓音，两手一推问我："他到我家来干什么？他需要什么？他坐着，瞪着眼睛看着。"

他甚至给别里科夫起了个外号："名副其实的蜘蛛"。可以理解，我们避免和他说起他妹妹正想嫁给这只"蜘蛛"。但有一次校长太太向他暗示说，要是能促成他妹妹和别里科夫这样体面、受人尊敬的男人结为夫妻也不失为一件好事，他便阴沉下了脸嘟囔说：

"这不关我什么事。哪怕她嫁给一条蟒蛇。我不爱干涉别人的事。"

现在请听以后发生的事。有个淘气鬼画了一幅漫画：别里科夫在走着，穿着雨鞋，卷着裤腿，打着雨伞，旁边走着瓦莲卡，俩人手挽着手，下边有一行字："恋爱中的安特洛普斯。"画家可能干了不止一个通宵，因为不管是男校或是女校，或是师范学校的教师们，以及各种官员们，人人都收到了这样一份漫画。别里科夫也收到了一份。这幅漫画使他苦不堪言。

我们一道出了门，这天是礼拜日，恰好是五月一日，我们所有的老师和学生都约好在校门口集合，然后步行出城到一个树林子去，我们走出来的时候，他脸色铁青，比乌云还要阴沉。

"竟然有这样良心不好的恶人！"他说，嘴唇在发抖。

我甚至对他产生了怜悯。我们走着，突然间，您倒想想，柯瓦连克骑着自行车过来了，瓦莲卡在他身后，也骑着自行车，她满脸通红，很疲劳的样子，但兴高采烈，情绪极好。

"我们，"她喊道，"在前面走！天气太好了，好得要命！"

两个人影消失了。我的别里科夫的脸色由铁青变成惨白，人像是一下子僵住了。他停下来看着我……

"请问，这是怎么回事？"他问道，"也许，是我的眼睛欺骗了我？难道中学教师和妇女骑自行车也合体统？"

"有什么不合体统的？"我这样说，"就让他们骑个痛快好了。"

"这怎么可以？"他大声吼道，惊讶于我的平心静气，"您在说些什么呀？！"

他受到那样的震动，以至于不想再往前赶路，便返回了家中。

第二天，他不住地搓手，身子也神经质地抖动着，从脸色看得出来，他也没有吃午饭。尽管还是夏天的天气，但晚间他穿得暖暖的，缓步来到了柯瓦连克家。瓦莲卡不在，他只是碰到了她哥哥。

"请坐。"柯瓦连克皱起眉头，冷冷地说；他睡眼惺忪，午饭过后刚打了盹儿，情绪极坏。

别里科夫默默地坐了十分钟之后，说：

"我到您这儿来，是为了减轻我心中的负担。我很痛苦，很痛苦。有个爱造谣的家伙给我和一位你我都熟悉的女士画了幅漫画。我以为有责任向您申明，这与我毫不相干……我没有做出什么可以让人如此嘲弄我的事情。相反，我一直是像一个正派人的样子行事的。"

柯瓦连克坐着，沉默着，心里火冒三丈。别里科夫停顿了一下，然后继续轻声地、伤感地说道：

"我还要对您说几句。我教书已有不少年头，而您才刚刚开始，所以我作为一个老教师认为有责任提醒您。您骑自行车，这种娱乐对于一个青少年教育工作者是绝对不合适的。"

"为什么呢？"柯瓦连克压低了嗓子问。

"这难道还需要解释，米哈依尔·萨维奇，难道这还不明白？如果老师能骑自行车，那么学生应该干什么？他们就可以两脚朝天，拿着大顶走道？既然行政当局没有颁布告示允许做，就不能做。我昨天真是大惊失色呵！当我看到您妹妹的时候，我眼前一片漆黑。一个妇女或者是一位姑娘骑在自行车上——这太可怕了！"

"您究竟是想要什么？"

"——我就需要做一件事——给您提个醒儿，米哈依尔·萨维奇。您是年轻人，您前程万里，您应该非常谨慎行事才对，可您的行为是那样的不检点，那样的不检点！您穿着绣花衬衣出门，常常抱着些什么书本上街；现在又是骑上自行车。校长早晚会知道您和您妹妹骑自行车的事，然后再传到督学那里……这会有什么好结果！"

"我和妹妹骑自行车，不关任何人的什么事！"柯瓦连克说，脸孔涨得通红，"而谁要是干涉我的家庭私事，我就让他滚得远远的。"

别里科夫脸色煞白，站起身来。

"如果您用这种口吻与我说话，那我就不再往下说了。"他又说："但请您以后永远不要当着我的面这么议论上司。对待上级行政当局您应该有所尊敬。"

"我难道说了什么行政当局的坏话？"柯瓦连克问道，用憎恶的眼光瞧着他，"我是个正大光明的人，我不想跟像您这样的先生交谈。我不喜欢爱告密的小人。"

别里科夫张皇失措了，他急匆匆地穿上大衣，脸上露出惊恐的神情。要知道他这是平生第一次听到这样粗鲁的话。

"您可以想说什么就说什么，"他这样说，一边走出门厅朝楼梯口走去，"我只是需要预先向您申明一下，可能有什么人偷听了我们的谈话，为避免有人曲解我们的谈话，再闹出什么乱子来，我应该把我们的谈话内容向校长如实报告……主要的内容。我必须这样做。"

"报告？去吧，去报告呀！"

柯瓦连克从身后一把抓住他的衣领，猛地推了一下，别里科夫便连同他的雨鞋一起带了响声滚到了楼梯下。楼梯又高又陡，但滚下楼梯的别里科夫安然无恙，他站起身来，摸摸鼻子：眼镜是否完整无损？但就在他顺着楼梯往下滚动的时候，瓦莲卡带着两位女士回到了家里；她们在楼梯下站着，看着，这在别里科夫是最最可怕的了。看来，他宁肯摔断颈脖子和两条腿，也不当别人的笑柄。要知道，现在这件事会传得满城风雨，会传进校长和督学的耳朵里，啊嘿，这怎么会不闹出点什么乱子来！然后会有人画新的漫画，最后只有奉命辞职了事……

当他站起身来，瓦莲卡认出了他，瞅着他可笑的面孔，他的皱巴巴的大衣，他的一双雨鞋，她不了解事情的原委，还以为这是他自己不小心摔下了楼去，便忍不住大笑起来，她的笑声响彻整个屋子：

"哈哈哈！"

这一串银铃般的"哈哈哈"的笑声把一切都了结了：了结了这门婚事，了结了别里科夫的人世生活。他已经听不见瓦莲卡说了什么，他也什么都看不见。回到自己家里之后，他做的第一件事是从桌子上撤去瓦莲卡的照片，然后躺下，从此再也没有起来。

过了三天，阿法纳西来找我，问我是否应该去请医生，因为他主人的情况不妙。我去看望别里科夫。他躺在帐子里，蒙着被子，一声不吭；有话问他，他仅仅以"是"与"不是"作答，其他的话一句也不说。

他躺着，愁眉不展的阿法纳西在他床边走来走去，深深地叹气，从他身上散发出像是从下等酒馆里散发出的酒气。

一个月后别里科夫死了。我们所有的人——两所中学和一所神学院的人，都去给他送葬。现在他躺在棺材里，他的神情祥和、爽朗，甚至喜庆。好像他很高兴，终于被人放进了一个他永远不会从中走出的套子里。是的，他实现了自己的理想！天气也仿佛要对他表示尊敬，出殡的时候乌云密布，下起了雨，我们都穿着雨鞋，打着雨伞。瓦莲卡也参加了葬礼，当棺材送进墓穴的时候，她哭了几声。我发现，乌克兰女人要么哭泣要么欢笑，处于这二者之间的情绪状态是没有的。

我要承认，埋葬像别里科夫这样的人是件十分愉快的事。从墓地归来，我们的脸色凝重；谁也不想表露这样愉快的心情——这样的心情我们很早很早以前就体验过，那时我们都还是孩子，大人出门了，我们可以到花园里去跑上一、两个钟头，尽情享受那完全的自由。啊嘿，自由，自由！甚至仅仅是对自由的某种暗示，甚至是对自由的微小希望，都能给灵魂插上翅膀，难道不是这样？

我们从墓地回来时的心情是舒畅的。但没有过去一个星期，生活又回到了老路上，它还照样的严酷、沉闷、无序，这是没有明令禁止，但也没有完全开放的生活。生活没有变得好起来。也是的，别里科夫是被埋葬了，但像他这样的套中人现在还有多少，将来还会有多少！

"问题就在这里。"伊凡·伊凡内奇说，他抽起烟来。

"将来还会有多少！"布尔金又重复了一句。

中学教师走出了板棚。这人个头不高，已经发福，完全歇顶，长长的黑须几乎齐到腰间；两只狗也跟他一块儿走了出来。

"月亮呵，月亮！"他这样说，两眼看着天空。

已是午夜。右边，可以看见整个村子，一条长街伸得很远，约莫有五里地。一切都沉浸在静静的、深深的梦里。没有动静，没有声音，甚至不能相信大自然会这样的宁静。当你在月夜里看到农村的长街，看到它的茅舍、草堆、入睡的垂柳，你的心也会变得平静。农村的长街笼罩在夜色苍茫之中，疏离了劳苦、忧愁和苦痛，在这份安宁里，它显得温柔和凄美，好像，星星也在温存地看着它，好像，恶已经从大地上消失，天下已经太平。左边，田野从林子的尽头伸展开去，远远地一直伸展到天边，这宽阔的田野沐浴在月光里，同样是没有动静，没有声音。

"问题就在这里，"伊凡·伊凡内奇又重复了一句，"而我们住在城里，空气污浊，拥挤不堪，写着无用的文章，玩着无聊的纸牌，这难道不也是套子？而我们终生周旋于俗人、庸人、蠢人和懒散的女人中间，自己说着和听着各种废话，这难道不是套子？好了，如果您有兴趣，我给您讲个很有教益的故事。"

"不，该睡觉了，明天再说。"布尔金说。

两人走进板棚，躺在干草堆上。他俩已经蒙上被子，昏昏欲睡，突然间听到了轻轻的脚步声：嗒普，嗒普……有个人在板棚旁边走动，走了一会儿停住了，过了一分钟又是嗒普嗒普地响起来……狗也汪汪地叫起来。

"这是玛芙拉在走路。"布尔金说。

脚步声消失了。

"看着和听着人家说假话，"伊凡·伊凡内奇翻了个身说，"人家骂你是傻瓜，就因为你容忍了这些假话；面对侮辱与委屈，你忍气吞声，不敢直言自己是正派的自由人中的一员，你自己也说假话，还面露笑容，这全是为了一块面包，一个温暖的角落，为了分文不值的一官半职，——不，不能再这样生活下去！"

"得了，您这是在借题发挥，伊凡·伊凡内奇，"教师说，"睡吧。"

过了十分钟，布尔金已经入睡。而伊凡·伊凡内奇还在不停地翻身，叹气，后来他站起身，又走到门外，坐在门口，抽起烟来。

（童道明　译）

灯　火

　　门外，一条狗猖猖地叫着有点恐怖。工程师阿纳尼耶夫，他的助手——大学生封·什登贝格和我走出工棚，看看狗是在向谁吠叫。我是客人，可以留在工棚里的，但得承认，我喝了点酒，头有点晕，我也想到外边去透透新鲜空气。

　　"没有人……"我们走出门外，阿纳尼耶夫说，"阿卓尔卡，你为什么骗我们？蠢货！"周围阒无一人。蠢货阿卓尔卡，是一条黑色的看家狗，也许是想了为自己的无缘无故的吠叫表示歉意，它扭扭捏捏地走到我们跟前，摇晃着它的尾巴。工程师弯下身去，抚摸着两个耳朵之间的狗头。

　　"坏家伙，你为什么无缘无故地叫唤？"他用好心的成年人与小孩和狗说话时通常用的口吻说道。"做噩梦了？"他又转过身来对我说："大夫，我请您注意，这是一条非常神经质的狗！您倒是想想，它受不了孤独，总是做噩梦，被梦魇折磨，而当你朝他大声吼叫，他简直会歇斯底里大发作的。"

　　"不假，是一条感情丰富的狗……"

　　大学生补充说。

　　阿卓尔卡想必知道人们是在议论它，它抬起头来，悲哀地叫唤了一声，像是想说："是的，有时我忍受不住痛苦，但还请你们多多包涵！"

　　这是一个八月的夜晚，天上有星星，但夜色昏黑。先前我从未有过在如此的非常环境中的经历，我是偶然地闯入这片生活的，因此这个有星星闪烁的夜晚，比真实的它更让我感到萧索、沉郁与黑暗。我身处于一条刚刚开工修建的铁路线上。那高高的才完工一半的路基，那些砂粒堆、泥土堆、碎石堆，那些土窟窿，那些随手扔在一边的手推车，那些住着民工的简易工棚的平顶——所有这些乱七八糟的东西，被黑暗染成一种最单调的颜色，给这片大地平添了一种奇怪的、野蛮的图像，让人联想到那混沌初开的洪荒时代。在我面前呈现的一切是那样的杂乱无章，以至于在这支离破碎的、面目全非的大地上立着的人的侧影和笔直的电线杆也似乎有点奇形怪状。因为它们都破坏了画面的和谐，好像不属于同一个世界。周遭很静，仅仅能听到在我们头顶上的某个很高的地方，电报机在哼唱着单调的歌。

我们爬上了高高的路基，俯视大地。离我们五十丈远的地方，那些坑坑洼洼，那些土堆已经消融在黑黑的夜色中，却有一个昏暗的灯火在闪烁。在它后边还有一个灯火，再后边还有一个灯火，再往后过去一百步的样子，有两只红色的眼睛并排地在闪光——想必是简易工棚的窗子——，这样的灯火排成一长串，愈远愈密，愈远愈暗，一直延伸到地平线的尽头，然后往左转了半个圈，消失在黑暗的远处。灯火是静止不动的。在这些灯火中，在这夜晚的宁静中，在这电报机的歌声中，似乎能感受到某种特别的东西。似乎有某种秘密被掩埋到了路基下，只有灯火、夜色和电线杆才知道似的……

"啊，上帝，这多么美好！"阿纳尼耶夫感叹道，"多么宽广，多么美丽，太棒了！这是什么样的路基啊！我的爹，这简直不是路基，而是整整一条阿尔卑斯山的山峰！价值几百万……"

微醺的，也微微伤感的工程师，在赞美灯火与价值几百万的路基的同时，拍了拍大学生封·什登贝格的肩膀，继续以调侃的口吻说道：

"怎么的，米哈依尔·米哈依雷奇，想得出神了吧？欣赏欣赏自己双手干出来的成果是很愉快的吧？去年，这个地方还是个荒凉的草原，看不见一个人影，而现在您瞧，生活，文明！真的，这是多么美好！我和您在修铁路，而在我们之后一百年或两百年，将有一批批善良的人在这里建造工厂，学校，医院——机器就会转动起来！是不是这样？"

大学生纹丝不动地站着，把双手插进衣兜，眼睛凝望着灯火。他没有听工程师说的话，他独自在思考着什么，似乎是处于一种既不想说什么也不想听什么的精神状态之中。在长时间的沉默之后，他转过身来小声对我说：

"您知道这些无穷无尽的灯火像什么吗？它们让我想起某些存在于几千年前但现在已经灭绝了的东西，比如类似阿美里凯特人或非列士人的帐篷这样的东西。好像是《圣经》里的某一个部落已经安营扎寨，枕戈待旦，准备跟《圣经》里的索尔或大卫打仗似的。要使这种幻觉完满起来，就差号角的声响，和哨兵操阿比西尼亚方言喊出的几句口令。"

"有道理……"工程师表示同意，好像是故意似的，一阵风沿着铁路线呼啸而过，送来了近似刀剑交接后发出的声响。然后是沉寂。我不知道现在工程师和大学生在想些什么，而我已经感觉到，好像在我的面前当真出现了某种早已灭绝的部族，甚至好像听到了哨兵在用我们听不懂的语言说话。我的幻想迅速描绘出了这些帐篷，这些奇怪的人形，他们的衣服，盔甲……

"是的，"大学生在沉思中喃喃地说，"阿美里凯特人和非列士人从前曾在这个世界上生存过，打过仗，扮演过他们的角色，而现在呢，他们已无影无踪。我们的命运也将是如此。我们现在在这里修铁路，站在这里说大话，但两千年之后，无论是这些铁路路基，还是这些一天劳累之后正在酣睡的修路民工，都会灰飞烟灭，不会留下一点痕迹。认真说起来，这是可怕的！"

"您必须把这些想法丢掉……"工程师用严肃的、教训的口吻说道：

"为什么？"

"因为……人应该用这样的思想来结束而不是开始自己的生命。拥有这样的思想，您还过于年轻。"

"为什么呢？"大学生重复自己的问题。

"所有这些关于人生如梦，人生无常，人生无目的，人必有一死，关于阴曹地府等等的思想，我亲爱的，我对您说，这些思想对于老年人来说是精彩的，也是自然的，因为这是他们长期的精神生活的成果，是用苦难换来的，的的确确是一笔精神财富，但对于刚刚开始独立生活的年轻人的头脑，这些思想会变成灾难！灾难！"阿纳尼耶夫挥舞了一下手，重复了灾难这个字眼。"以我之见，在您这个年岁，与其有这类想法不如在您的肩膀上不长脑袋。男爵，我这是认真地对您说话。我早就想跟您谈这个问题，因为打从我认识您的第一天起，就发现您热衷于这些歪门邪念。"

"上帝，为什么这算是歪门邪念呢？"大学生微笑着问道，根据他的嗓音与脸色可以发现，他作出反应完全是出于普通的礼貌，而对于工程师挑起的这个争论，他完全不感兴趣。

我都睁不开眼睛了。我希望在我们散步回来之后立即互相说一声晚安，然后上床睡觉，但我的这个希望没有很快实现。我们回到工棚之后，工程师把空酒瓶放到了床底下，再从一个很大的柳条箱里取出两瓶装得满满的酒，把瓶盖拧开，坐到自己的办公桌前，显然是准备继续喝下去，说下去，干下去。他呷了几口酒后，用铅笔在图纸上描画着什么，继续在向大学生证明，他的那些想法是要不得的。大学生坐在他旁边，在查阅什么账单，也一言不发。他像我一样，既不想说，也不想听。为了不影响他们工作，我坐在离桌子稍远的工程师那张弯腿的行军床上，随时等待着吩咐我上床睡觉，我无精打采地坐着。已经是深夜一点钟。

因为无事可做，我开始认真观察这两位我新交的朋友。无论

是阿纳尼耶夫还是大学生，我先前都没有见过，我是在这个晚上
才有缘与他们相识。晚上，我骑马从市集赶往我作客的那位地主
家，在暮色中迷了路。绕着铁路线转着圈子，看着夜色已深，我
想起了专门打劫各种行人的"铁路上的赤脚汉"，我害怕了，便
去敲开了我首先看到的这个工棚的门。阿纳尼耶夫和大学生在这
里热情地接待了我。就像常常发生在萍水相逢的人身上的情形一
样，我们很快亲热起来，先是喝茶，继而喝酒，彼此已经感觉到
好像双方已经相识多年。过了一个时辰，我已经知道，他们是什
么样的人，是什么命运把他们从首都抛掷到这个遥远的荒原，而
他们也知道，我是什么人，我从事何种职业，我有什么念想。

　　阿纳尼耶夫工程师，尼古拉·阿纳斯塔谢耶维奇，是个宽肩
的壮汉，已经像莎士比亚笔下的那个奥赛罗一样，"掉进了岁月
的谷地"，身体有点发福。他正处于媒婆通常称之为"标准男人"
的黄金时段，也就是说，既不年少也不年老，爱吃美食，爱饮点
酒，可以吹嘘一下光荣的过去，路走多了也会微微喘气，睡着了
鼾声如雷，平时待人接物却表现得老成持重，正派的男人一旦当
上校级军官，而且开始身体发福，都有这个派头。他的须发远没
有发白，但他已经不由自主地把年轻人称作"我亲爱的"，已经
自以为有权好意地指责他们的思想方式。他的动作与嗓音都很平
稳，很流畅，很自然，这样的人一般都是因为清清楚楚地意识到，
自己已经走上了人生的正道，已经拥有一个可靠的工作，已经有
了一份可靠的面包，已经对世事有了一定的思想见解……他的黝
黑的、长着一个大鼻子的脸盘，他的肌肉丰富的颈项似乎在诉说：
"我健康、富足、知足、到了将来，你们这些年轻人，同样会健康、
富足和知足……"他穿一件歪领的印花布衬衣，穿一条肥大的麻
布裤子，裤脚管塞在高皮靴里。从一些很小的细节，比如从他那
条用粗绒丝编织的腰带上，从他那绣花的衣领上，以及从他那衣
服肘部的那块补丁上，我可以猜到他已经结婚，而且很可能被自

己的妻子温柔地爱着。

　　男爵封·什登贝格，米哈依尔·米哈依洛维奇，交通学院的大学生，还很年轻，约莫二十三四岁光景。只有他的浅褐色的头发，稀疏的胡子，还有他的脸孔轮廓中显示出的某种粗犷与冷漠，才能让人意识到他是波罗的海地区男爵家族的后代，其他的一切——名字，信仰，思想，举止神情，都纯粹是俄罗斯的。他和阿纳尼耶夫一样，穿一件印花布衬衣，不塞进裤腰里，也脚蹬高皮靴，他有点驼背，好久没有理发，脸孔黝黑，这神态不大像大学生和男爵，倒是像一个普通的俄罗斯技工。他很少说话和移动身子，喝酒也喝不出兴致来，他神情呆滞地翻阅着账本，好像心里一直在想着什么事儿。他的动作和嗓音也很平稳，流畅，但他的平稳与工程师的平稳迥然不同。他的被太阳晒黑了的、略带嘲讽与沉思状的脸孔，他的略微皱起眉头瞧人的眼睛，他的整个身躯都表现出了精神的疲软，智能的懒散……从他的眼神看得出，在他的面前灯火是否亮着，葡萄酒是否好喝，账本是否有误，于他全都无所谓……在他的聪明的、平静的脸孔上我读到了他的思绪："我看不出在这一个可靠的工作、一份可靠的面包和一定的思想见解里有什么好的东西。我以前住在彼得堡，现在坐在这工棚里，到了秋天我又要返回彼得堡，而开春之后还要回到此地……这种生活究竟有什么意义，我不理解，看来也不会有人能理解……所以，也没有必要去讨论它……"

　　他无精打采地听工程师说话，显出一种勉强的无动于衷的神情，就如同士官学校的高班生听情绪激动的好心肠叔叔的宣讲一样。好像工程师所讲的这一切对于他都不是什么新鲜的东西，如果他不是自己懒得开口，他会讲一些更新鲜更智慧的东西出来。但阿纳尼耶夫还在滔滔不绝地说话。他已经放弃了轻松愉快的腔调，而是说得特别严肃和执著，这与他的平静的表情完全不相协调。看来，他对一些抽象思辨的问题也很有兴趣，他喜欢谈论这类话题，但又不善于、不习惯谈论它们。这样的不习惯严重地影响了他的语言表达，以至于我不能马上明了他想说什么。

"我全身心地仇恨这类思想！"他说，"年轻时我也迷恋过这类思想，直到现在我也还没有完全从它们的束缚中解脱出来。我跟您说，也许是因为我太愚笨，那些思想不是我的精神食粮，它们只能给我带来害处。这是显而易见的！关于人生无目的，人生无常，所罗门式的'万事皆空'的思想，直到今天还被视为人类思维的最高的终极的层次，思想家一旦达到这个层次，机器就停止了转动！前边已无路可走。正常的头脑的思维活动就到此结束，这是很自然的，也是合乎逻辑的。我们的不幸是，我们竟然从这思维活动的最后结局开始我们的思维。我们在正常人结束的地方开始。我们从脑子刚刚能独立活动的时候，就跳到了思维活动的最高的、终极的层次，完全不想知道还有一些更低的层次存在着。""这有什么不好呢？"大学生问。"您要明白这是反常！"阿纳尼耶夫高声喊道，几乎是用一种愤怒的眼光逼视着他，"如果我们找到了一个不需攀登任何阶梯一步登天的办法，那么整个这个长长的阶梯，也就是我们的整个人生，连同它的色彩、音响、思想，对于我们便失去了所有的意义。您可以从您在自己的理性的独立生活中迈出的每一步，理解到这类思想在您这个年岁是有害的和荒唐的。打个比方，您现在坐着读达尔文或莎士比亚的某一部著作。您刚读完第一页，有害的念头就冒出来了：对于您来说，无论是您的漫长的生命，还是达尔文和莎士比亚，都是荒谬的玩笑，因为您知道，您难免一死，莎士比亚和达尔文也都死了，他们的思想没有拯救了他们自己，也拯救不了大地和您，而如果生活本身失去了意义，那么所有这些知识，这些诗歌和高尚的思想，只不过是些无用的消遣，供大小孩娱乐的玩具。于是您不会再去读第二页书。再比方说，现在有人走到您这个聪明人跟前征求意见，比方，问您对于战争有什么看法：战争是有道德的、值得欢迎的，还是不道德的、不值得欢迎的？回答这样一个可怕的问题，您也只需耸一耸肩膀，或是说几句不痛不痒的话，因为对您来说，按照您的思想方式，上百万人的死于非命还是寿终正寝都没有区别，无论哪一种死法都是一种结果——灰飞烟灭。我和您现在在修铁路。有人会问，既然这条铁路两千年后也会化为灰烬，那么我们今天何必要为它绞尽脑汁，突破陈规，创造发明，整顿纪律，关心工人？诸如此类，一言难尽……请您相信，有了这样可悲的思维方式，便不可能产生任何的进步，任何的科学，任何的艺术，任何的真正的思想。我们自以为比大众比莎士比亚高明，而实际上我们的思维方法在导致虚无，因为我们不愿意走下底层重新起步，我们也无力向上攀登，我们的头脑也冻结在了一个冰点上——顽固不化……我有将近六年的时间就处于这种思想的压迫之下。我以上帝的名义向您起誓，在这几年中，我没有读过一本正经的书，我的智慧没有长进一寸，我的思想库里没有增添一个字母。这难道不是不幸？而且，问题不仅仅在我们自己受了毒害，我们还把自己身上的毒素扩散到了我们周围的人身上。要是我们带着自己的悲观主义放弃生活，隐居洞穴或赶紧结束自己的生命，那也还说得过去，可是我们照样屈从于公共社会法则。我们照样活着，照样在喜怒哀乐，照样在和女人谈恋爱，在教育孩子，在修建铁路！"

"我们的思想既不能给人带来温暖，也不会给人带来寒冷。"大学生很不情愿地说了这样一句话。

"不，啊嘿，您别来这一套！您还没有好好生活过，等到您活到了我这把年纪，您就能品尝到生活的痛苦了！我们的思想并不像您想象得那样无辜。一旦接触实际生活，一旦和人打起交道，形成冲突，这套思想只能把人引向灾难和荒诞。我就经历过一些这样的灾难，即使是可恶的鞑靼人，我也不希望他们遭受这样的灾难呀。"

"举个例子行吗？"我问。

"举个例子？"工程师反问。他想了想，微笑着说："就举这件事情吧。更准确地说，这不是一件事情，而是一部完整的既有开端又有结局的小说。是个再好不过的教训！啊，那是什么样的教训呀！"

他给我们和他自己都斟满了酒，喝了酒，用手掌抚摸着自己宽宽的胸膛，继续往下说，这回他主要是对我，而不是对大学生说：这发生在一八七……年的夏天，战争刚刚结束，我也刚刚毕业。我去了一趟高加索，在沿海的 N 城逗留了五天。应该对你们说明，我是在这个城市长大成人，所以 N 城让我感到特别的舒适、温暖和美丽便也不足为怪，尽管任何一个从首都来的人住在这里，就像住在任何一个类似丘赫洛姆或卡希尔这样的偏僻小城一样的感到乏味与不舒坦。我怀着忧郁的心绪走过我曾经求学过的中学，我怀着忧郁的心绪在一座著名的城市公园旁散步，我怀着忧郁的心绪，试图就近观察久违了的同乡……一切都染上了忧郁的色彩……

想起来了，在一个夜晚我坐马车去了一个称作检疫站的所在。这是一片不大的稀疏的树林子，在好久以前的一个鼠疫流行的年代，这里当真有过检疫站，但现在住着一群避暑客。从城里到这里要走四里地，那都是松软的好路。坐在马车上放眼看去：左边是蔚蓝色的大海，右边是无边的、沉郁的草原；可以轻松地呼吸，可以舒畅地远眺，小树林就坐落在海边。我放走了马车夫，走进了熟悉的大门，首先想到的，是顺着林荫道，走向那座我童年时代就喜欢的石砌的亭子。在我看来，这座圆形的、笨重的，支撑着几根不匀称的柱子的石亭，结合着古代陵墓的抒情与萨巴凯维奇[①]的粗笨，是全城一个最有诗意的所在，它立在海岸的陡坡之上，

---

①　萨巴凯维奇是果戈理小说《死魂灵》中的一个人物。

整个海景尽收眼底。

我坐在椅子上，探身栏杆外，朝下边张望。从亭子往下有一条陡峭的山路穿过，两边布满了大块的黏土与一丛丛牛蒡。山路的尽头，已是远处的沙滩，不高的海浪在懒洋洋地吞吐着泡沫，温柔地发出声响。大海还像七年前一样的庞大、无边和冷漠，那时我中学毕业，准备离开故乡到首都去。远处有一条黑烟的长带，是一条轮船在航行。除了这条隐约可见和静止不动的长带，以及时而在海石上出现的海鸟，没有任何东西给这海和天的单调的画面添加些许生趣。亭子的左右两边伸展着凹凸不平的黏土山壁……

您知道，要是一个心情忧郁的人单独地面对大海或面对什么他以为是很宏大的风景，不知为什么总会使他在忧伤中产生一种想法，他会在无声无息中活着和死去，于是他本能地拿起一支铅笔，在随手碰到的一张纸上写下自己的名字。也许这就是为什么，在像这个亭子一样孤零零的僻静的角落，总是布满铅笔的笔痕和用小刀刻字的刀痕。我记得，就在那个时候，我瞧了一眼亭子的栏杆，就读到了这一行字："伊凡·柯罗里柯夫 1876 年 5 月 16 日到此一游。"就在柯罗里柯夫的名字旁边，有本地一位幻想家的涂鸦，还添加了一句："他站在荒凉的海岸上，心中充满了伟大的思想。"他的笔迹是充满幻想的、软弱无力的，像一条潮湿的丝绸。还有一个叫克罗斯的人，想必是个微不足道的小人物吧，他是那么深切地意识到了自己的渺小，以至于使出狠劲，将自己的名字用小刀往亭子栏杆上刻进去一寸深。

我也下意识地从口袋里掏出一支铅笔，在一根柱子上涂抹起来。这当然与我要讲的故事没有什么关系……请原谅，我不会简明地讲一个故事。

我忧伤，也有点烦闷。烦闷，宁静和海浪的低语逐渐把我引向了我们刚刚说到的那种思想。那是在七十年代末，这种思想已经在大众中流行起来，而到了八十年代初，这种思想又从大众渗透到了文学、科学和政治之中。那时我还不过二十六岁，但我已经清楚地知道，人生是没有目的和没有意义的，一切都是欺骗和幻觉，无论是就其本质还是就其结果而言，萨哈林岛上的流放生活与尼斯城里的生活毫无区别，哲学家康德的脑子与苍蝇的脑子的区别没有实质意义，在这个世界上没有是非曲直可言，一切都是扯淡，一切都见鬼去吧！我生活着，好像这是屈从于逼着我一定要生活下去的某种力量，好像是要对这个力量说："其实我真瞧不起这生活，但我还是要生活下去！"我的思路是一条方向固定的思路，但形态上也可以花样翻新。这就好比一位精巧的美食家，可以用一个土豆做出上百道可口的小菜来。毫无疑问，我有点片面，甚至有点偏激。但我那时以为，我的思维的领域没有开端也没有结尾，我的思想像大海一样辽阔。现在，根据我自己的经历可以作出判断，刚刚说到的这种思想，就像烟草和吗啡一样，是具有诱人的麻醉力的。它变成了一种习惯，一种需求。您可以利用每一个孤独的时刻，利用每一个合适的机会，遐想生活的没有意义和阴曹地府的没有阳光。当我坐在亭子里的时候，林荫道上正有一群长着大鼻子的希腊少年在规规矩矩地散步。我瞧着他们，利用这个机会展开了这样的想象：

"干吗生养这一帮孩子？他们的存在有什么意义？连他们自己都不知道为什么要在这个偏远的地方长大成人，然后再死去……"

这些希腊孩子开始让我感到气恼，因为他们走道循规蹈矩，还像模像样地在谈论着什么，好像他们当真很看重自己的小小的、没有光彩的生活，知道自己为什么活着……我记得，在林荫道的尽头出现了三个女人的身影，都是少女，其中一位穿着粉红色的裙子，另外两位穿着白裙。她们手挽着手，并肩而行，面露笑容，谈论着什么。我看着她们，一面想："既然这么烦闷，在此地找个女人谈两天恋爱岂不是件好事！"

　　我同时想到，我最后一次与彼得堡的情妇幽会已是三个星期之前的事，我想现在闹出点短暂的风流韵事也正是时候，中间那个穿白裙的姑娘好像比她的两个女伴更年轻更美丽，从她的笑声与举止来判断，她该是个高年级的中学生。我不无邪念地瞅着她的胸脯，一边想着她："她会学点音乐知识和社交礼仪，然后，请上帝原谅，嫁给一个希腊人，过一种灰色的、愚蠢的、毫无意义的生活，连自己也不知道为什么要生一大堆孩子，然后死掉。多么荒谬的生活！"

　　总的来说，我是一个善于把自己的崇高的思想与卑下的思想结合到一起去的高手。关于阴曹地府的念想，并不妨碍我欣赏女人的胸脯和大腿。我们那位可爱的男爵大人的思想，也并不妨碍他每星期六到乌科洛夫卡去寻花问柳。说句良心话，就我对于自己的了解，我这个人对于女人的看法是很下流的。现在我回忆起那位女学生，我不免要为当时的想法脸红，但那时我的良心一点没有因此而不安。我，出身于良好的家庭，是个基督徒，受过高等教育，从本质上说，并不恶毒，也不愚蠢，但当我给女人支付嫖资或是用下流的目光盯视女学生的时候，我竟然安之若素……不幸是在于，青春拥有青春的权利，而我们的思想观念从原则上说，不会对这青春的权利表示任何异议，不管这权利是好的还是糟的。凡是认为生活无目的，死亡不可避免的人，对于与自然环境的斗争和对于罪恶的概念都是无动于衷的：斗争也罢，不斗争也罢——反正人都要死去的，都要腐烂的……第二，我的朋友，我们的思想意识早早就把所谓的理智灌输到了年轻人的头脑里。鲜活的情感，灵性，都被繁琐的分析给肢解了。哪里理性十足，哪里就冷若冰霜，而冷若冰霜的人——这有什么可隐瞒的——是不懂得圣洁的。只有热情的人，热忱的人，善于爱的人才理解这种美德。第三，我们的思想理念否定生活的意义，从而也否定了每一个具体的个人的生存意义。这是可以理解的，如果我否定某个名叫纳塔丽娅·斯捷潘诺芙娜的女人的人格，那么她是否受到侮辱与我毫不相干。今天我侮辱了她的人格，给她支付嫖资，而明天就会把她忘得一干二净。

就这样，我坐在亭子里。欣赏着少女。在林荫道又出现了一个女人的身影，她没有戴帽子，头发呈浅黄色，一条针织的白色围巾披在她的肩膀上。她在林荫道上散步，然后走进了亭子，手抓住栏杆，冷漠地向下俯视远处的大海。她走进亭子的时候，对我熟视无睹，好像根本就没有看见我。我从脚到头打量了她（不是像打量男人要从头到脚），发现她很年轻，年纪不会超过二十五岁，很漂亮，身材也好，已经不是小姐，而是属于良家少妇的行列。穿得很随便，但透着时尚与情趣，N城的所有有教养的女士都这样穿戴。"跟她玩玩也不错……"我一边欣赏着她美丽的腰肢和胳膊，一边这样想。"长得挺有味道……应该是某个医生或教师的妻子……"但跟她玩玩，也就是让她充当旅游者们趋之若鹜的一桩即兴浪漫史的女主角，也并非易事，可能完全实现不了。这是我好好端详了一下她的脸孔之后得到的感觉。她有那样一种表情与眼神，好像这大海，这远处的烟雾和天空早就让她厌倦，让她看烦了。看来，她很疲惫，很寂寞，她在想着一些很不愉快的事儿，她的脸上甚至没有显现出局促的、生硬地表示冷漠的神情，当一个女人发现身旁有个陌生的男人，一般都会显露出这样的神情。

这位头发浅黄的女士，匆匆地、淡淡地朝我瞥了一眼，坐到椅子上，想她的心事，我从她的眼神看出，她顾不得我，我的来自首都的派头，甚至没有引起她一点好奇心。但我还是决定与她搭话，我问："夫人，请允许我打听一下，进城的敞篷马车几点钟从这里出发？"

"大概是十点钟或者是十一点钟……"我向她道谢。她看了我一两眼，在她的淡漠的脸上突然现出了好奇的表情，然后这表情变成了惊奇……我赶紧做出漠不关心的样子，摆出一种符合尊严的姿态：等她上钩！她像是被什么狠狠咬了一口，突然从椅子上跳起来，温柔地笑着，急促地看了我一眼，怯生生地问道："喂，您难道不是阿纳尼耶夫？"

"是的，我是阿纳尼耶夫……"——我回答。

"您认不出我了？认不出了？"

我有点不好意思了，我好好地端详着她，你们可以想象，我不是根据她的脸孔，她的身材，而是从她的温柔的、带有倦意的微笑中，认出了她。她是娜塔丽娅·斯捷潘诺芙娜，或者如同大家对她习惯的称呼基索奇卡，七八年之前我曾经热恋过她，那时我还穿着高级中学的校服。那是遥远过去的往事……我记得这个基索奇卡，那时是个十五六岁的娇小的中学女生，她的女生形象，像是上帝特地为了一桩柏拉图式的恋爱而创造出来的。多么美妙的姑娘！白白的，柔弱的，轻盈的——好像轻轻朝她吹口气，她就会像一片羽毛似的飞到天空中去——温情脉脉的脸，小巧的手，柔软的垂到腰际的长发，细如黄蜂的腰肢——通体像月光一样的超然与透亮，一句话，在一个中学高班男生的眼睛里，这是无与伦比的美……我是怎样狂热地爱恋着她的啊！夜不成寐，写诗……晚上她常常坐在城市公园的长椅上，而我们这些中学男生都聚集她的周围，用崇拜的目光看着她……作为对于我们的这些献媚的姿态与叹息的回应，她眯缝起眼睛，甜美地微笑着，由于黄昏的寒气逼人，她的身子不由自主地瑟缩了一阵。在这个时刻她特别像一只可爱的小猫。当我们这样看着她的时候，我们之中的每一个人都想去爱抚她，都想去像抚摸一只小猫似的抚摸她，于是她就得到了一个小名——基索奇卡。

在我们离别的七、八年中，基索奇卡有了很大的变化。她变得壮实了，丰满了，已经完全不像一只柔软的小猫。倒不是说她变老了、枯萎了，而是好像她失去了一些光彩，变得严肃了，头发也变短了，个头长高了，肩膀几乎宽了一倍，而主要的是，她的脸上已经有了母性的、温顺的神情，像她这个年岁的良家妇女都有这种神情，但却是我从前在她脸上没有见到的……总而言之，在这位适合于柏拉图式的恋爱的女中学生身上，完整地保留下来的仅仅是她那可爱的笑容……

我们交谈了起来，基索奇卡听到我已是个工程师，高兴得不得了。

"这多好！"她兴奋地凝视着我的眼睛，说，"啊，这多好！你们都是好样的！你们班出来的人里没有一个是倒霉蛋，个个都有出息。有的是工程师，有的是医生，有的是教师，还有一个，据说现在成了彼得堡的著名歌手……你们全都是好样的！啊，这多好！"

在基索奇卡的眼睛里，闪烁着真诚的快乐与善意。她像一位大姐姐或是过去的女教师一样地欣赏着我。而我瞧着她的可爱的脸蛋儿，却在想："今天能把她弄到手也很好！"

"娜塔丽娅·斯捷潘诺芙娜，您还记得吗？"我问，"有一次我在公园里给您送了一束花，上边还附有一张纸条？您读过这张纸条后，脸上露出了犹豫不决的表情……"

"不，我记不得这件事了。"她笑笑说，"但我记得，有一回您为了我想要和弗洛伦斯决斗……"

"唷，这件事，我记不得了……"

"是的，过去的事都过去了……"基索奇卡叹息道，"以前我曾经是你们的偶像，而现在轮到我来仰视你们了……"

从此后的谈话我了解到，基索奇卡中学毕业两年之后嫁给了本地的一个小市民，此人一半希腊血统，一半俄罗斯血统，在一家银行，或是一家保险公司做事，同时也做点粮食生意。他的姓名很古怪，大概是叫帕鲁拉基，或是叫斯卡拉道普洛……鬼知道呢，忘了……总的来说，基索奇卡很少说自己，不喜欢说。话题全围绕着我展开。她问我上的那所大学的情况，问我的同学怎么样，问彼得堡怎么样，问我有什么样的计划。而我所讲的一切都能激起她的兴奋之情与赞美："啊，这多好！"

我们下到海边，在沙滩上散步，当海风吹来了晚间的湿气，我们又上了山。我们一直在谈论我以及我们的过去。我们一直在漫步，直到晚霞的余晖在别墅的窗户上完全消失。

"到我家里去喝点茶。"基索奇卡向我建议，"茶炊大概早已摆上桌了……家里就我一个人。"她说，这时透过树的绿荫已经可以看到她家的别墅。"我的丈夫老是在城里，深夜才回家，而且不是天天回家，我寂寞得很，快寂寞死了。"

我跟在她后边走，欣赏着她的背和肩。她已经结婚，倒让我宽心。对于短暂的浪漫史而言，有夫之妇比未婚少女更加适合。还让我宽心的是，她的丈夫不在家……但同时我也感到，这浪漫史未必能圆满……

我们走进了房子。基索奇卡的房间不大，天花板不高，别墅式的家具（俄国人喜欢把弃之可惜又无处摆放的大而无当的家具塞到别墅里来），但从一些细微处还是能看出，基索奇卡和她的丈夫生活很宽裕，一年估计得有六、七千卢布的开销。我记得，在那间被基索奇卡称作餐厅的房间中央，放着一张竟然支有六条腿的圆桌。桌子上摆着茶炊和几个茶杯，而在桌子的边上放着一本打开了的书，一支铅笔和一个笔记本。我瞅了一眼那本书，认出是本由马列宁和布列宁合著的算学书。我现在记得，打开的那一页正好是"利息分配表"。

"您在教谁做算术题？"我问基索奇卡。

"不教谁……"她回答，"我这是……因为无聊，因为无事可做，就想起了以前的学校生活，做起了算术题。"

"您有孩子吗？"

"生过一个男孩，但生下来一个星期就死了。"

我们开始喝茶。她欣赏着我，又说起她喜欢我的工程师职业，她如何为我的成就感到高兴。她这样说得越多，她的笑容越真诚，我就越坚信我将会两手空空地从这里溜之大吉。那时我已经是个情场老手，我可以准确地判断出自己在情场角逐中的获胜概率。如果您猎取的是一个蠢货，或是一个像您一样追寻情感刺激的女人，或是一个您完全陌生的浪荡女人，您就可以稳操胜算。而如果您遇到一位女士，她不笨，人也正派，她的脸孔呈现出一种温顺的倦意和善意，她真诚地欢迎您，主要的是——她尊敬您，遇到这样的情况，您就可以一无所得地打道回府了。在这种情况下要获得成功，一天的工夫是远远不够的。

在暮色中，基索奇卡比在日光下更加妩媚动人。我越加喜欢她，看来，她对我也有好感。而且环境也适合于调情：丈夫不在家里，仆人不在跟前，四周静悄悄……尽管我对成功不抱太大的希望，但我还是转入了进攻状态。首先要把谈话引向玩世不恭的调调上去，把基索奇卡的抒情而严肃的心情调转到更轻浮的……

"娜塔丽娅·斯捷潘诺芙娜，让我们换个话题。"我开始说，"谈点轻松愉快的……首先请允许我像过去那样叫您基索奇卡。"

她同意了。

"基索奇卡，请您告诉我，"我继续说，"此地的女人怎么变成这个德性啦？她们怎么啦？从前她们都是规规矩矩的淑女，而现在呢，不管问起哪一位，听了都能让您吓一跳……有个小姐跟一个军官私奔了，另一位勾引了个中学生，也跑了，第三位是个少奶奶，离开了丈夫与一个演员私奔了，第四位离开了丈夫与一个军官私奔了，诸如此类……这简直是一场瘟疫！这样下去，在你们的城里很快就剩不下一个纯粹的少女和少妇。"

我是操着粗俗的，挑逗性的语气说这些话的。如果基索奇卡报之以笑声，我便会用同样的口吻再往下说："嘿，基索奇卡，您瞧好了，否则会有一个军官或演员在这里把您拐走的！"她听了也许会垂下眼睛说："有谁愿意来拐走我这样的女人呢？要是我再年轻一些，漂亮一些……"那我就会对她说："基索奇卡，别这样说，我就会头一个高高兴兴地把您拐走！"要是谈话照这样的态势进行下去，我的目的便最终会达到。但基索奇卡没有用笑声作答，相反，她露出了严肃的脸容，还叹了一口气。

"人家说的这一切都是事实……"她说，"我的堂姐索尼娅就是离开丈夫与一个演员私奔的。当然，这不好……每一个人都要忍受命运给予的安排，我不会责怪她们……环境有时会把人压垮。"

"是这样，基索奇卡，但究竟是什么样的环境导致了这一场瘟疫呢？"

"这很简单也容易理解……"基索奇卡扬起眉毛，说，"我们的有文化修养的姑娘和女人在这里毫无出路。不可能让她们全都像男人那样的上大学深造，当教师谋生，为理想生活。只好嫁人……那么嫁给什么人呢？你们男生读完中学，到外地上大学，从此不再返回故乡，你们在首都结婚成家，而女生都留在了本地！……那么让她们嫁给什么人？因为没有正派的优秀男士，就只好嫁给各色各样的经纪人和希腊人，他们就知道喝酒，在俱乐部里闹事……姑娘们就这样草草结了婚……那会是什么样的婚后生活？您自己也明白，有文化教养的女人和粗野的男人生活在一起，后来她遇到了一个有文化的男人，一个军官，一个演员和一个医生，就爱上了，原来的生活她就不能再忍受，她就逃离了丈夫。不能责备这样的女人！"

"如果是这样，基索奇卡，当初她为什么要嫁人呢？"我问。

"问得当然有道理。"基索奇卡叹了口气，"但要知道，每个姑娘心里都这样想：有了丈夫总比没有丈夫强……尼古拉·阿纳斯塔谢耶维奇，总的来说，这里的生活很糟糕，很糟糕！不嫁人的姑娘苦闷，嫁了人的女人也苦闷……人们嘲笑索尼娅，因为她私奔了，而且还是和一个演员私奔的，但如果人们了解了她的内心，也就不会嘲笑她了……"

阿卓尔卡又在门外吠叫起来。它恶狠狠地朝什么人嚎叫着，然后发出了一声哀鸣，用整个身子顶撞着工棚的墙壁……阿纳尼耶夫的脸孔因为怜悯而起了皱，他中断了自己的故事，走出门去。有两分钟的时间，听到他如何在门外安抚爱犬："可爱的狗！可怜的狗！"

"我们的尼古拉·阿纳斯塔谢耶维奇喜欢聊天。"封·什登贝格笑笑说，"他是个好人！"稍作停顿后他又补充了一句。

回到工棚之后，工程师把我们的杯子都斟满了酒，微笑着抚摸自己的胸膛，继续说自己的故事：

"就这样，我的进攻没有取得成功。没有办法，我只好把我的不干净的思想留到更好的机会去发挥了，我承认了自己的失败，俗话说，'只好挥手了之'。不仅如此，在基索奇卡的嗓音、晚间的空气和寂静的影响下，我自己也逐渐地沉进了那静静的、抒情的情调。我记得，我坐在一张椅子上，旁边是一扇敞开着的窗户，我看着外边的树木和幽暗的天空。槐树和菩提树的轮廓还像八年前一样，也还像我的少年时代那样，从远处传来从一架破旧的钢琴上发出的弹奏声，人们还是保留着在林荫道上来回散步的习惯，但人已经不是以前的人了。现在在林荫道上散步的，已经不是我，不是我的同学，不是我所暗恋的对象，而是陌生的中学生，陌生的少女。我感到了忧伤。而当我打听我的旧日的朋友时，从基索奇卡嘴里五次听到了这样的回答：'他死了。'我的忧伤便变成了参加给一个好人开的追悼会时产生的心情。我坐在窗子旁，看着在林荫路上散步的人群，听着杂乱的钢琴弹奏声，有生以来第一次亲身体验到，一代人是如何怀着急切的心情取代另一代人的，甚至就在这七八年的时间里，人的生命里也能发生如此致命的劫运！”

基索奇卡在桌子上放了瓶红葡萄酒。我喝了酒，失去了自持力，滔滔不绝地发表议论。基索奇卡依旧欣赏着我和我的智慧。而时光在流走。天空已经黑得分不清槐树和菩提树的树影，林荫路上的游人看不见了，钢琴声听不见了，能够听到的仅仅是大海的均匀的喘息声。

年轻人都是一个德行。您只需要对他说几句好话，请他喝酒，让他知道他很可爱，他就会坐下来不动窝，忘了该是他告辞的时候了，他不停地说，说，说……主人已经睁不开眼睛了，他们该睡觉了，而他还坐着，说着。我也是这样。只是偶尔看了看钟：已经十点钟了。我准备告辞。

“上路之前再喝一杯。”基索奇卡说。我又喝了一杯送我上路的酒，又滔滔不绝地说下去，忘了该走了，坐了下来。这时传来了男人的说话声，走道声和马刺的碰击声。有人在窗外走过，停到了大门旁。

“大概是丈夫回来了……”基索奇卡一边侧耳倾听，一边说。

大门吱嘎一声打开了，人声已经在门厅里响起，我看到，有两个人从通往餐厅的门旁走过：一个黑发男子，很胖，长着鹰钩鼻，戴着草帽；另一个是穿着白色制服的年轻军官。他们走过房门的时候，都漫不经心地朝我和基索奇卡扫了一眼，我以为他们都喝醉了。

“这么说，她骗了你，而你信以为真！”这一回听到了一个洪亮的带有鼻音的说话声，“第一，这件事情发生在大俱乐部而不是在小俱乐部。”

“你，爱神丘比特，你生气了，但你说得不对……”另一个人说，他大概是军官，一边笑着，一边在咳嗽。“我能在你这儿过夜吗？你说实话：我不会妨碍你吗？”

“什么话？不仅是可以，而且是必须在我这儿过夜。你想喝什么，是啤酒还是葡萄酒？"

那两个男人坐了下来，坐在与我们隔开了两个房间的地方，他们说得很欢，显然对基索奇卡和她的客人毫不在意。而一当丈夫回了家，基索奇卡的情绪却发生了明显的变化。她先是脸红了，然后露出了一种羞怯的近似于负疚的表情：她心里产生了不安，我意识到，她不好意思把丈夫介绍给我，她希望我走开。

我起身告辞。基索奇卡把我送到门廊。我清楚地记得她的温柔的、感伤的微笑和温顺的、亲切的眼睛，当我们握住了手的时候，她说："大概，我们以后再也不会见面了……好吧，让上帝给您幸福。谢谢您！"

没有一声叹息，没有一句多余的话。在分别的时候，她手里拿着蜡烛，蜡烛的光影在她的脸上和颈项上跳动，像是在追逐她的感伤的微笑；我想象着当年的被我们当做小猫可以抚摸的那个基索奇卡，我直视着现在的基索奇卡，不知为什么立即想起了她的这句话——"每一个人都要忍受命运给予的安排"——我的心疼痛了起来。我是敏感的，我的良心在与我作耳语，告诉我，站在我这个幸福而淡漠的人面前的，是一个爱着又痛苦着的好人儿……

我鞠了个躬，向大门走去。天很黑。七月的南方，入夜很早，天也黑得快。到了晚上十点钟，就伸手不见五指了，我摸索着走到大门口，一共点燃了二十根火柴。

"马车夫！"走出大门，我大喊一声，但无人应声……"马车夫！"我重复地喊道："哎，马车！"

但既不见马车，也不见马车夫。坟墓一般的寂静。我只能听到睡意蒙眬的大海的喘息声和我自己的酒醉之后的心跳声。举头望天空，不见一颗星星。黑沉沉，阴沉沉。显然，天空被乌云覆盖了。我无意识地耸了耸肩，傻笑着，再一次呼叫马车夫，但声音不再那么坚定。

"嘿什!"听到了回声。

步行四里地野路,而且还在黑暗之中——这个前景令人丧气。在决定是否步行回城之前,我考虑了许久,然后耸耸肩膀,毫无目的地走回了那片小树林。树林里黑得可怕。在某一个树的空隙处偶尔从别墅的窗子里透出昏暗的红光。一只乌鸦被我的脚步声惊醒了,被我的用来照路的火柴光惊吓了,它从一棵树飞到另一棵树上,在树叶里发出埋怨的叫声。我既懊恼,也害臊,乌鸦像是懂得了我的心思,竟也"哇哇"地叫了起来。我懊恼的是,我得步行回家,我害臊的是,我竟像个孩子一样在基索奇卡家说个没完。

我走到了亭子上,摸到一个椅子,坐了下来。在下边很远的地方,在浓密的黑暗后边,大海在低沉地怒吼。我记得,我像个盲人一样,既看不见大海,也看不见天空,甚至看不见我正置身其中的亭子,我觉得这个世界仅仅有两样东西存在:在我的醉醺醺的头脑里游荡的思想,和在下边单调地轰鸣着的一种看不见的力量。而后来睡意向我袭来,我便觉得,在轰鸣的并不是大海,而是我的思想,全世界仿佛就是我一个人。就这样,我把全世界集中到了我一个人身上,我便忘记了马车夫,忘记了城市,忘记了基索奇卡,完全沉浸到了我自恋的那种情绪里。这是一种可怕的孤独的情绪,这时您觉得,在整个黑暗的、无形的宇宙中就存在您一个人。这种骄傲的、恶魔式的情绪只有俄国人才会具有,他们的思想感情像他们的平原、森林和雪野一样的辽阔,无涯与严峻。如果我是个画家,我一定会画出一个俄国人的这样的脸部表情,他纹丝不动地盘腿坐着,两手捧着头,沉浸在一种情绪之中……而与这种情绪同在的,是关于人生的无目的,关于死亡,关于阴曹地府的思想……这些思想分文不值,但那脸部表情,该是很美的……

我坐在那里打盹,没想站起身来——我很温暖、很安宁、——

突然在大海的均匀的单调的声响中，响起了另外的一个声音，吸引住了我的注意……有一个人在林荫路上急促地走着。这个人走到亭子旁边，停住了脚步，像个小姑娘似的呜咽起来，用小姑娘般的哭腔说道：

"我的上帝，何时才能熬出头呀？上帝！"

从嗓音和哭腔判断，她应该是个十一二岁的小姑娘。她迟疑不决地走进亭子，坐下来，半是祈祷半是诉苦地说着……

"上帝！"她拉长了声调哭诉，"这无法忍受的呀！任何的忍耐都忍耐不下去的！我忍耐着，不出声，但你要明白，我也要生活呀……啊，我的上帝，我的上帝！"吐了一大堆这样的苦水……我想看看这个姑娘，和她说说话。为了不把她吓着，我先出声地叹了口气，干咳了一声，然后小心翼翼地划了一根火柴……火柴在黑暗中闪光，照亮了那个哭泣的姑娘。这是基索奇卡……

"天下奇闻！"封·什登贝格一声叹息。"漆黑的夜晚，大海的轰鸣，万般痛苦的她，而他呢，怀着宇宙般孤独的心绪……要知道这是什么！就差几个手持匕首的粗汉了。"我给你们讲的不是童话，而是真事！""就算是真事……这也没有什么稀罕的……"

"别忙着挖苦，让我讲完！"阿纳尼耶夫懊恼地挥一下手，说："请您别干扰我！我不是说给您听的，我是说给大夫听的……是这样的。"他面对着我继续说，也斜眼瞟了大学生一眼，大学生正埋头在查账，他为能刺激一下工程师而颇为得意。"是这样的，基索奇卡看见了我，并不感到惊讶，也不害怕，似乎她早就知道她能在亭子里见到我。她吃力地喘着气，全身发抖，像是在发高烧，而她的被泪水浸湿了的脸，在我的一根接着一根划亮的火柴的照耀下，让我看到的已经不是原先的那张聪明的、温顺的、疲倦的脸，而成了另外一种我直到今天也无法理喻的状态。这张脸既不表现痛苦，也不表现忧虑，也不表现苦恼，她的言语与眼泪表现出的一切，在她脸上都没有反映……也许，正因为我理解不了她的这张脸，因此我觉得它是没有意义的，是糊里糊涂的。"

"我忍受不住了……"基索奇卡用姑娘的哭腔呢喃道，"我受不了啦，尼古拉·阿纳斯塔谢依奇！请原谅，尼古拉·阿纳斯塔谢依奇……我不能再这样生活下去了……我要进城找妈妈去……您送我去……看在上帝分上，送我去……"

看见了流泪的人，我既不会说话，又不会沉默。我发了慌，胡乱地说了几句安慰的话。

"不，不，我要去找妈妈！"基索奇卡说得很坚决，她站起身来，神经质地拉住了我的手（她的手和衣袖都被眼泪弄湿了），"请原谅，尼古拉·阿纳斯塔谢依奇，我要去……我受不了啦……"

"基索奇卡，但现在一辆马车都没有呀！"我说，"您怎么去？"

"没有关系，我可以步行……不远。我再也忍不住了……"

我发了窘，但没有受感动。对于我来说，基索奇卡的眼泪，她的颤抖，她的麻木的脸部表情，给人留下了的印象像是一部浅薄的法国或乌克兰式的言情剧，在那里每一个微不足道的痛苦都会酿造成泪雨滂沱。我不理解她，我也知道我不能理解她，我原本应该保持沉默的，但不知为什么，也许是不想把我的沉默理解为愚蠢，便以为有必要劝她别去找妈妈，而是留在家里的好。哭泣的人是不希望有人看见她的眼泪的。但我却一根接一根擦亮火柴，直到把火柴匣里的火柴全部点燃完。我为什么要这样不友善地照亮她的泪脸，我到今天还弄不明白。一般来说，心冷的人常常会做些不恰当的傻事。

最终基索奇卡拉住了我的手，我们上路了。走出大门，向右边一拐，不慌不忙地走在松软的土路上。天很黑，待到我的眼睛慢慢地习惯了这个黑暗，开始能看清路旁那些又老又细的橡树和菩提树的轮廓。很快，在右侧影影绰绰地显现出一条黑带，那是参差的峭壁,有几处被不大的深谷与水沟切断。在峡谷旁边生长着一堆灌木丛,像是有一群人坐着。有点恐怖。我斜眼看了一下峭壁。那大海的声响与土地的沉寂反常地刺激着我的想象。基索奇卡不说话,她还在颤抖,还没有走出半里地,她便气喘吁吁了。我也不说话。

在离检疫所一里地的地方,立着一座被废弃的四层楼房,有一个很高的烟囱,这座楼房以前曾经是一个磨粉厂的厂房。它孤零零地站在悬崖上,白天的时候,从海上或从平原上远远地就能看到它。因为是一座废弃的楼房,楼里无人居住,路人的脚步声和说话声都能从楼里传出回声,因此很有点神秘感。你们可以想象一下,在那样一个漆黑的夜晚,我挽着一个逃离丈夫的女人的胳膊从这个庞然大物旁边走过,我的每一个步子都有回声传响,上百个窗口就像上百个黑眼珠紧盯着我。一个正常的年轻人在这样的情景下一定会坠入浪漫主义中去的,而我瞅着这些黑窗子却在想:“所有这一切都能对人有所触动,但再过若干年之后,无论是这座楼房,还是这位基索奇卡以及她的痛苦,还是我和我的思想都会化为灰烬……一切都是虚妄的,一切都是无意义的……”

当我们走到磨粉厂的旁边,基索奇卡突然停住脚步,抽出自己的胳膊,不是用女孩的声音而是用自己的声音说道:

“尼古拉·阿纳斯塔谢依奇,我知道,这一切您会觉得奇怪。但我非常的不幸!您甚至想象不到我是多么的不幸!想象不到!我不告诉您,因为说不出口……这样的生活,这样的生活……”

基索奇卡没有说完,她咬着牙,轻轻呻吟了一声,好像在竭尽全力不让因为痛苦而大声叫喊。“这样的生活!”她惊恐地重复了一遍,拖长了尾音,带有一点南方的近似乌克兰口音的腔调,这种腔调出之于女人之口,便给激情洋溢的话语带来了音乐感。“这样的生活!啊,我的上帝,我的上帝!这叫什么生活?啊,我的上帝,我的上帝!”就像是为了猜透自己人生的秘密,她莫名其妙地耸动着肩膀，摇晃着脑袋，拍打着巴掌。她像唱歌一样地说着话，举止优雅而漂亮，让我觉得她简直像一个著名的乌克兰女演员。

"上帝，我像是掉进了一个深坑！"她拧着手指，继续说，"哪怕有一分钟的时间让我过一过人生的快乐时光也好呀！啊，我的上帝，我的上帝！我居然活到了这种丢人的地步，我像个放荡的女人那样，当着外人的面深更半夜从丈夫身边逃走。从此还能有什么好的指望？"

我欣赏着她的肢体动作和嗓音，我突然感到了一种满足，因为她和丈夫不和。"与她玩玩倒也不错！"——这个念头闪现在我的心头，在往前走的一路上，这个邪念一直盘踞在我的脑海，越来越让我心花怒放……

走过磨粉厂一里半路，需要向左拐弯，顺着墓地直奔县城。在墓地的转弯处，立着一个石质的风车，风车旁也有个小屋，屋里住着风车的主人。走过墓地和小屋，再向左拐，就到了公墓的门口。在这里基索奇卡停住了脚步，说道：

"尼古拉·阿纳斯塔谢依奇，我要回去了！您自己走吧，我自己回去。我不害怕。"

"这算怎么回事！"我慌张了起来，"既然要走，就走好了……"

"我不必这么冲动的……没有什么大不了的事。您的话语让我想起了过去，让我想了很多……我很伤心，想了哭，而丈夫当着那个军官的面对我说了粗话，我就受不了啦……我为什么要进城去找妈妈呢？我这样就能幸福吗？得回去……得了……咱们继续走！"基索奇卡笑笑说，"反正都一样！"我记得，在公墓的门上刻有一行字："总有一天，躺在坟墓中的人会听到天使的声音。"我清楚地知道，早晚有一天，无论是我，还是基索奇卡，还是她的丈夫和那个穿白色军装的军官，都会躺在墓地的黑色树荫下的。我清楚地知道，在我旁边走着的，是一个不幸的，受到侮辱的人。所有这一切我都知道得一清二楚，但与此同时，有一个沉重的、恼人的恐惧攫住了我，基索奇卡要回家，而我还没有把该说的话说给她听。从来没有像这个夜晚那样，高尚的思想和卑下的思想如此紧密地缠绕在一起……真是可怕！

在墓地附近我们雇到了一辆马车。到了基索奇卡母亲居住的那条大街，便把马车夫打发走了，我们沿着人行道走去，基索奇卡一直沉默不语，而我看着她，恨起了我自己：“你为什么还不开始进攻？是时候了！”在距离我下榻的那家旅馆二十步远的地方，基索奇卡停在了路灯的旁边，哭了。

“尼古拉·阿纳斯塔谢依奇！”她哭着，笑着对我说，用她那被闪光的眼泪浸润了的眼睛瞧着我。“我永远不会忘记您对我的体贴……您是个多么善良的人呀！你们都是好人！诚实的、善良的、热心的、聪明的人……啊，这多么美好！”

她把我看做是一个有教养的优秀人士，在她那潮湿的笑脸上流露出悲伤的神情，因为我这个人已经引起了她的感奋，而她难得见到像我这样的人，上帝没有让她成为像我这样一类人的妻子。她喃喃地说：“啊，这是多么美好！”她脸上的天真的快乐，她的眼泪，她的柔和的微笑，她的从头巾下滑落的细软的头发，以及那块随便地搭在头上的头巾，在路灯的照耀下，又让我追忆起了那个基索奇卡，那个我们想象抚摸小猫地抚摸的基索奇卡……

我忍耐不住了，开始抚摸她的头发，肩膀和手……

“基索奇卡，你想要什么呢？”我轻声地说，“你想让我和你走到天涯海角去吗？我要把你从这个深坑中拉出来，给你幸福。我爱你……咱们走吧，我的好人儿？是吗？好吗？”

基索奇卡的脸上显出迷惑不解的表情。她从路灯旁退后了几步，她惊恐地睁大了眼睛瞧着我。我紧紧地抓住了她的手，接连不断地吻她的脸，颈项，肩膀，不断地向她发誓和许愿。在恋爱中，发誓和许愿几乎是必不可少的。没有它们办不成事。有时明知你是说谎，但照样要发誓和许愿。惊恐万状的基索奇卡还是在往后退，还是睁大了眼睛看着我……

"不要这样！不要这样！"她用手挡住我，喃喃地说。

我紧紧地拥抱住了她。她突然间号啕大哭了起来，她的脸孔呈现出一种迷茫的麻木的表情，我在亭子里擦亮火柴的时候，就看到了她这种表情……我不许她说话，也不征得她的同意，便硬是把她拉往我住的旅馆走……她呆若木鸡，我抓住她的手，几乎是拖着她走……我记得，到我们上楼梯的时候，有个戴着镶有红帽檐的制帽的听差，奇怪地看着我，向基索奇卡鞠躬……

阿纳尼耶夫涨红了脸，不说话了。他默默地在桌子周围踱步，烦恼地挠挠他的后脑勺，好几次神经质地耸动着他的肩膀，一阵阵寒战顺着他那宽大的后背溜过，使他的肩胛骨也因此抖动起来。他黯然自伤，这个回忆让他痛苦，他在自己和自己较劲……

"不好！"他喝了一杯酒后，摇摇头说，"人家说，老师在对医学院的大学生讲第一堂妇科学的时候，就要对他们说，在你解去女病人的衣服抚摸她之前，要想一想你们中的每一个人都有母亲，姐妹，未婚妻……"这个忠告不仅适合于医生，也适合于所有在生活中要和女人打交道的男人。现在，我已经有了妻子和女儿，啊，我太能理解这个忠告了！我的上帝，我太能理解这个了！但是，请你们再往下听……基索奇卡成了我的情妇之后，便不同我一样地思考问题了。首先，她热烈地、深深地爱着我。在我看来是一桩平平常常的风流韵事，在她成了生活中的一场革命。我记得，我那时觉得她像是发了疯似的。她第一次感到了幸福，她年轻了五岁似的，一脸的喜庆，幸福得不知道该如何是好，她时而笑，时而哭，不断地说出她的梦想，明天我们要去高加索，秋天再去彼得堡，然后再安排如何生活……

"至于丈夫，你不必担心！"她这样宽慰我，"他必须同意我离婚。全城的人都知道，他和柯斯托维奇家的大女儿在同居。离婚之后我们再结婚。"

女人一旦爱上了，特别能适应环境，跟人很快就亲热起来，像猫一样，基索奇卡在我的房间里才躺了一个半小时，就已经有了像是在自己家里的感觉，把我的家当看成是她自己的家当。她把我的东西装进手提箱，埋怨我没有把自己贵重的新大衣挂在钩子上而是胡乱地把它像一块抹布似的扔到了椅子上。

我看着她，听着与感受着疲倦和困惑。我一想到一个正派的、痛苦着的妇女这么轻易地在三、四个小时之内就成了遇见的第一个男人的情妇，内心不免产生厌恶之感。我作为一个正派的男人，当然不喜欢这样子。其次，像基索奇卡这样的女人，既不深刻，也不严肃，太热衷于世俗的生活，甚至把对于一个男人的爱情这样的生活小事，也抬高到了幸福、痛苦和生活变革的高度，这也让我不高兴……除此之外，这时我已经得到了满足，我反倒觉得自己处境不妙，我有点傻，竟然被一个原本想玩一玩了事的女人缠住了身……而我应该指出，尽管自己有些玩世不恭，但也不能忍受欺骗。我记得，基索奇卡坐在我的大腿旁边，把脑袋枕在我的膝盖上，用她那闪光的、含情脉脉的眼睛看着我，问："柯里亚，你爱我吗？很爱吧？很爱吧？"

她幸福地笑了……我觉得这过于煽情，有点做作，也不得体，与此同时，我当时已经处于一种这样的精神状态，我想在一切事物中追寻"思想的深度"。

"基索奇卡，你该回家了，"我说，"否则你家里人会满世界地找你。而且你大清早到你妈妈家去也不合适……"

基索奇卡同意了。分手之前我们说定，明天中午在公园见面，而后天我们一起去五山城。我上街去送她，我记得，我一路上用真诚的温情爱抚着她。有一个时刻，我突然因为她对于我的极度的信任而感到内疚，我决定当真要带她到五山城去，但一想到我口袋里只剩六百卢布，而且到了秋天再跟她分手会比现在分手更加困难，我就立刻打消了这个念头。

我们走到了基索奇卡母亲的家门口，我按了门铃。当听到了门后的脚步声，基索奇卡的脸孔突然变得严峻起来，她看看天空，急促地像给一个孩子祝福那样地在我的胸口画十字，然后把我的手放到她的嘴唇上。

"明天见！"她说了这句话就进了门。我走到街对面的人行道上，观察那所房子。窗子原先都是漆黑的，后来有一扇窗子里由一支点着的蜡烛泛出了淡淡的蓝光，这光亮在扩大，我看到随着烛光的移动有人影在移动。

"他们没有想到她会来！"我想。

回到旅馆的房间，脱去外衣，喝了一杯酒，吃了点今天在市场上买来的新鲜鱼子，不慌不忙地躺到床上，像一个游倦的旅行者一样地酣睡了。

一觉醒来，头痛，心绪也很坏。有什么东西让我不安。

"这是怎么回事？"为了弄清楚自己的不安，我问自己，"是什么使我不安？"

我把自己的不安解释为害怕基索奇卡现在就来找我，让我不得脱身，让我只好说谎话，在她跟前出洋相。我很快穿上衣服，收拾好行李，走出了旅馆，吩咐听差在晚上七点钟之前把行李送到火车站。整个白天我都在一个医生朋友家里度过的，而到了晚上就坐车离开了这座城市。你们看，我的思想并没有妨碍我作一次可耻的、背信弃义的逃亡……

在我坐在朋友家里和后来到火车站去的整个时间里，不安始终折磨着我。我害怕与基索奇卡相遇，害怕闹出轩然大波。到了火车站，我故意躲在洗手间里直到响了第二遍铃，而当我走向我的那列车厢时，竟然有这样一种感觉在压迫着我，我好像周身上下装满了偷来的赃物。我是怀着何种急迫与恐惧的心情等待那第三遍铃声的呀！

　　救命的第三遍铃声终于响了，列车启动了，火车驶过了监狱，兵营，驶进了田野，令我十分惊异的是，不安还是纠缠着我，我依旧感到自己像是个拼命想着出逃的小偷。这多么奇怪？为了让自己平静下来，我开始往车窗外张望。列车沿着海岸行驶。大海波浪不兴，碧绿的天空几乎有一半被柔和的金色晚霞所覆盖，霞光静静地映照在海面上，有一些渔船和木筏成为一个个星点散落在海面的四周。耸立在悬崖上的城市，清洁而美丽得像一个玩具，也被晚间的雾霭所笼罩。几座教堂的金色拱顶，窗子，树丛映衬着夕照，它们像金子一样，在燃烧着熔化……田野的芳香与从大海吹来的温柔的湿气混合在一起。

　　火车在飞奔。听得出旅客与乘务员的欢笑声。全都喜气洋洋，而我的莫名的不安情绪在不断增长……我看着笼罩着城市的薄雾，我想象着，在教堂与屋舍近旁，在雾霭里，有一个脸色茫然的女人在寻找着我，她在用姑娘一般的声音，像一个乌克兰演员的歌唱般的嗓音在呻吟着："啊，我的上帝，我的上帝！"我记起了她的严峻的面孔，她的心事重重的大眼睛，那是她昨天像为自己的亲人祝福一样地在我胸前画十字的情景，我下意识地瞅了瞅我的手，她昨天曾经亲吻过这只手。

　　"我是爱上了，是吗？"我挠挠手，问自己。

　　只是到了夜里，旅客们都睡着了，我可以单独地和自己的良心面对面，我明白了以前无论如何明白不了的道理。在车厢的黑暗中，基索奇卡的面影我挥之不去，我已经明白，我做了一件相当于谋杀的坏事。良心折磨了我。为了压制住这难以忍受的感觉，我让自己相信，一切都是虚无的，无论是我还是基索奇卡都会死去，腐烂，与死亡相比，她的痛苦算不得什么，等等，等等……归根结底，自由意志是不存在的，因此，我没有过错。然而所有这些推理只是更加使我气恼，它们很快就淡化在其他的思想里了。

那只被基索奇卡吻过的手在隐隐作痛……我时而躺下，时而坐起，在车站喝伏特加酒，拼命地吞食三明治，再一次让自己相信，生活是没有意义的，但无济于事。有一种奇怪的，甚至可以说是互相矛盾的思想在我的头脑里翻腾。最五花八门的想法，纷至沓来，互相挤压，而我这个思想家被这一堆有用和无用的思想搅得晕头转向，无所适从。原来，我这个思想家还没有掌握起码的思维技术，我就像不会修理钟表那样地不会使用自己的头脑。平生第一次我如此努力地、紧张地思索，而且让我感到错愕，我想："我要发疯了！"那些平时不用脑子，临到艰难时刻才动脑筋的人，常常会想到发疯。

就这样，我白白熬过了一个白天，两个夜晚，我明白了，我的思想对我没有多少帮助，我终于看清了我是个什么人。我懂得了，我的思想分文不值。在和基索奇卡相遇之前，我还没有开始思想，甚至对于严肃的思想毫无概念；现在，当我经过了这次磨难之后，我懂得了我既没有什么信念，也没有一定的道德观念，也没有心灵，没有理智；我的全部的心智的财富来自专业知识，无用的记忆断片如别人的思想，我的心理活动像土著人一样的简单和幼稚……如果我不爱说谎，不偷窃，不杀人，不干明显的坏事，并不是因为我的信仰在起作用（我没有信仰），是因为奶妈讲述的童话故事和教科书上的道德教条捆住了我的手脚，这些道德教条已经进入了我的血液，尽管我认为它们是荒谬的……

我明白了，我不是思想家，不是哲学家，而不过是个半吊子式的假行家。上帝给了我健全的俄国式的脑子和天赋。你们想想看，一个二十六岁的年轻人，他的脑子没有经过训练，像是一张没有任何色彩的白纸，只是悄悄沾染一点工程技术方面的零星知识，他年轻，有旺盛的求知欲，追寻着什么，突然间有一个很迷惑人的关于生活无目的和阴曹地府的观念无意中击中了他。他贪婪地把这个观念吸收过来，让它横行无阻，开始玩弄起它来，像猫玩弄耗子一样，他的脑子里既无渊博的知识，也没有完整的体系，但这没有关系。他以自学成才者的天生的力量来运用宏大的思想，不出一个月，他就有了用一个土豆烹制一百道味美小菜的本领，而且自以为是思想家了……

我们这--辈人把这种玩弄严肃思想的技艺，注入到了科学、文学、政治，以及其他一切它可以渗透进去的领域，与这技艺一同注入的还有冷漠、无聊与片面性，我以为，它已经成功地给大众灌输了一种全新的对付严肃思想的办法。

因为这一桩不幸的事儿，我明白了自己的反常和无知。我现在想来，我的正常的思想是从我想从头做起开始的，也就是良心把我赶回到 N 城，我老老实实地在基索奇卡面前忏悔，像一个孩子那样地恳求她原谅，和她一起痛哭流涕……

阿纳尼耶夫简要地描述了他与基索奇卡的最后一次会面，便不做声了。

"是这样……"当工程师讲完之后，大学生从牙缝里挤出了一句话。"在这世界上有这样的事！"

他的面孔照样显出无动于衷的样子，看来，阿纳尼耶夫的故事一点也没有感动他。只是当工程师停顿片刻重新阐发他的思想，重复他原先已经说过的那些话的时候，大学生生气地皱起眉头，从桌旁站起，走到自己的床前。他铺好了床，开始脱衣服。

"您现在这副样子，好像您当真把什么人说服了似的！"大学生气恼地说。

"我把什么人说服了？"工程师问，"亲爱的，我难道有这样的奢望？上帝保佑您！说服您是不可能的！只有通过自己的生活经历与苦难，您才能恍然大悟！……"

"再说，这是多么奇怪的逻辑！"大学生一边穿睡衣，一边嘟囔道，"您非常厌恶的对青年十分有害的思想，按照您的说法，在老年人那里都是合理的。好像这决定于头发是否花白……这是哪来的老年人的特权？它有什么根据？如果这些思想有毒，那么对所有人都应该是有毒的。"

"不，我亲爱的，别这么说！"工程师狡黠地眯缝着眼睛，说，"别这么说！首先，老年人不是半吊子式的假行家。他们的悲观主义不是外在的，不是偶然的心血来潮，而是来自他们大脑的深层，是经过了对于黑格尔、康德等大师的作品的研读，是经历了许多的痛苦，犯下了数不清的错误之后，一句话，是从低层到顶端爬完了整个的楼梯之后才产生的。他们的悲观主义的背后有他们个人的经验和其他的哲学修养作支撑。其次，老一辈的思想家的悲观主义不是像你我这样的表现为空泛的议论，而是体现为一种世界性的悲悯和痛苦；他们的悲观主义有基督教义的底蕴，是植根于对人的爱，是来自于以人为本的思想，和半吊子式的假行家的利己主义毫不相干。您厌恶生活，是因为生活的意义和目的恰好欺瞒了您，您仅仅为您自己的死亡担惊受怕；而真正的思想家之所以痛苦，是因为生活的真理欺瞒了所有的人，他为所有的人担惊受怕。比方说，离这里不远住着一位名叫伊凡·阿历克桑德雷奇的林务官，是个好老头。曾经在什么地方教过书，写过文章，鬼知道他有过什么职业，但他肯定是个智者，懂得哲学。他读过很多书，现在还手不释卷。好了，前不久我在格鲁佐夫斯基工区见到了他……那个工区当时正好在铺设枕木和铁轨。这个活儿其实并不复杂，但在不懂工程技术的伊凡·阿历克桑德雷奇看来，这简直像是魔术。一个有经验的技工，铺上一根枕木，再在枕木上固定一条铁轨，用不了一分钟的时间。工人们精神抖擞，干起活来灵巧而快速。有个家伙更是大显身手，他挥臂一锤敲下去，就把钉帽咬紧了，尽管那锤把几乎有一丈长，每个钉子也有一英尺长。伊凡·阿历克桑德雷奇久久地凝望着工人，受到了感动，眼眶里闪着泪花对我说：'多么遗憾，这样的人才也要死的呀！'我能理解这样的悲观主义……"

"所有这一切既不能证明什么，也不能说明什么。"大学生拉过被单，说，"所有这一切都是无效劳动。没有人能明白这一切，无法用言语来证明这一切。"

他从被单里探出头来，气恼地皱起眉头，加快了语速说道：

"只有很幼稚的人，才会相信言辞，才会对人类的语言与逻辑赋予决定性的意义。人们尽可以用言语来证明或否定他想证明或否定的东西，很快人们将把语言技巧完善到如此地步，可以用数学计算般的精确来证明二乘二等于七。我喜欢听人说话，我也喜欢读书，但要我相信，对不起，我办不到，也不想办到。我只相信一个上帝，至于您，那么即便您给我讲到基督再世，即便您再诱惑五百个基索奇卡，也办不到，要我相信您，除非我什么时候失去了理智……晚安！"

大学生把头藏到被单里，把脸转向墙壁。他想用这样的动作表示，他已经不想再听什么，说什么。争论也到此结束。

在上床睡觉之前，我和工程师走出了工棚，我又一次看到了灯火。

"我们的闲扯让您听烦了！"阿纳尼耶夫打着哈欠说，眼睛看着天空。"唉，有什么法子！在这个鬼地方只有喝酒和神聊才能解闷……这样的路基，上帝！"当我们走近路基，他激动了起来，"这不是路基，而是大山。"

沉默了片刻之后，他又说：

"男爵以为那些灯火让人联想到古代的阿美里凯特人，而我倒觉得这些灯火像人的思想……您知道吗，每个人的思想也是像这样的散乱无序，顺着一条线路在黑暗中伸向某一个目标，没有照亮什么，也没有让黑夜明亮起来，便消失在什么地方了——远远地跟着年华一齐老去……得了，别海阔天空了！该睡觉了……"

我们回到了工棚，工程师殷勤地劝我一定要睡在他的床上。

"请！"他双手放在胸口，恳求道，"请您上床！别为我操心。

我哪都能睡，而且我也不忙睡觉……给个面子吧！"

我答应了，脱衣睡觉，而他坐到桌子前，开始画图样。

"我们这种人没有觉睡，"他低声说，我已经闭上了眼睛睡下，"谁有了老婆孩子，谁就休想睡觉。这时要想到穿衣吃食，想到日后的积蓄。我有两个孩子，一个儿子一个女儿……儿子长得很漂亮……还不到六岁，但有出众的才华，这我是要对您说的……我有他们的照片……哎，我的孩子，孩子！"

他在文件堆里搜寻，终于找出了照片，凝视着它们。我睡着了。

阿卓尔卡的吠声和人的叫嚷声把我惊醒。封·什登贝格只穿一条衬裤，光着脚，站在门口与一个人大声说话。天亮了……一束蓝色的晨光射进房门、窗户和工棚的缝隙，微微照亮了我的床铺，堆满纸张的桌子和阿纳尼耶夫。工程师躺在地板上，身下垫着斗篷，头枕着一个皮制的枕头，挺起了他那壮实的、毛茸茸的胸膛，鼾声如雷，我对那位每天都要和他睡在一起的大学生动了恻隐之心。

"我们凭什么要收下这些东西？"封·什登贝格大声嚷嚷，"这与我们没有关系！你去找恰利索夫工程师！这些铁锅是从哪来的？"

"从尼基丁那儿……"一个沙哑的声音回答。

"那么去找恰利索夫……这不关我们什么事。你站着干什么？赶你的马车走吧！"

"老爷，我们去找过恰利索夫先生了！"那个沙哑的声音更低沉了，"昨天我们顺着铁路线整整找了一天，工棚里的人说，他们都到迪莫科夫斯基工区去了。老爷，行行好，收下吧！我们把它们要拉到什么时候！我们顺着铁路线拉呀，拉呀，没完没了……"

"怎么回事？"阿纳尼耶夫醒来了，很快抬起头来，干哑着嗓子问。

"他们从尼基丁那儿运来了铁锅。"大学生说,"要让我们收下。我们凭什么要收下?"

"把他们轰出去!"

"老爷,行行好吧!马两天没有吃东西了,东家会发脾气的。难道让我再运回去不成?既然铁路上订购了铁锅,就该把它们收下……"

"你要明白,蠢货,这不关我们的事!你去找恰利索夫!"

"怎么回事?谁在那里?"阿纳尼耶夫干哑着嗓子又一次发问。"见了鬼了!"他骂了一声,站起身来,往门口走去,"怎么回事?"

我穿上衣服,两分钟后也走出了工棚。阿纳尼耶夫和大学生都穿着衬裤,光着脚,急切地在和一个庄稼汉解释着什么。那个庄稼汉站在他们面前,没有戴帽子,手里拿着马鞭,显然他听不懂他们说话的意思。两个人的脸上都呈现出被琐事苦恼的神情。

"我要你的铁锅干什么?"阿纳尼耶夫大声喊道,"我把它顶在脑袋上,还是怎么的?如果你找不到恰利索夫本人,就去找他的助手,而别来打扰我们!"

大学生看着我,想必是记起了昨天晚上的谈话,烦恼从他的迷茫的脸上消失了,取而代之的是心智懒散的神情。他朝庄稼汉摆了摆手,带着自己的心事走到了一边。

这是个天气阴沉的早晨。沿着夜晚有灯火闪烁的铁路线,刚刚醒来的工人们聚集起来了。人声鼎沸,手推车咯吱作响,又一个工作日开始了。一匹小马套着绳索已经吃力地爬上路基,伸长脖子,竭尽全力,拉着一车沙子……

我开始告别……晚间说了很多话,但我不能从这里带走一个得到了解决的问题,现在已是早晨,在我的记忆中,就像经过了滤器筛选之后,仅仅留下了灯火和基索奇卡的形象。坐到马上,我最后一次看了看大学生和阿纳尼耶夫,看了看醉眼蒙眬的那只神经质的狗，看了看隐显在晨雾中的工人，看了看路基，和抻长脖子拉车的小马，心里想："这世界上什么都明白不了！"

我鞭打着马儿，沿铁路线飞奔，不久，我能目及的仅仅是无边的、忧郁的平原和阴沉的、冷峻的天空，我想起了昨晚讨论的那些问题。我想，这被太阳灼伤的平原，这辽阔的天空，这远处一大片黑色的橡树林和雾气重重的地平线，似乎都在告诉我："是的，这世界上什么都弄不明白！"

太阳开始高高升起……

（童道明　译）

变 色 龙

　　警监奥丘梅洛夫身穿新大衣，单手提着包袱。穿过集市广场。他身后跟着一个棕红色头发的警士，双手端着筛子，满满当当地装着没收来的醋栗。四周一片寂静……广场上一个人也没有。小铺和酒馆敞开的大门，凄凉地注视世间，像是一张张饥饿的大嘴；它们附近甚至连乞丐也见不到一个。

　　"你敢咬人，可恶的东西？"奥丘梅洛夫突然听见说话声。"伙计们，别放跑它！现如今可不兴咬人啦！逮住它！哎哟……哎哟！"

　　听见狗的尖叫声。奥丘梅洛夫寻声望去，看见：从商人皮丘金的木柴场里，有一只狗三条腿跳着跑出来，还不住地回头看。在它后边，一个穿浆硬印花布衬衫和敞襟坎肩的人紧追不舍。他跑动中身子往前一跃，扑到地上，抓住了狗的两只后爪。又一次听见狗的尖叫和人的喊声："别放跑了它！"从各小铺探出一些睡眼惺忪的面孔，很快在木柴场的周围聚拢起一群人，仿佛从地里冒出来的一样。

　　"好像出事了，长官！……"警士说。

　　奥丘梅洛夫做了个向左转的动作，迈步朝人群的方向走去。在木柴场的门前，他看见，站着刚才描写的那个穿敞襟坎肩的人高举起右手，让人们看他那个满是鲜血的手指头。他半带醉意的面部表情似乎在说："我要剥你的皮，混蛋！"甚至那个手指头也成了胜利的象征。奥丘梅洛夫认出这人是首饰匠赫留金。在人群中央的地上，叉开前腿，浑身颤抖地爬着肇事者———一只白色的小猎犬，尖脸，背上有一块黄斑。它泪水汪汪的眼睛充满了忧郁和恐惧。

"这是怎么回事？"奥丘梅洛夫闯进人群，问道。"为什么围在这儿？你举着那根儿手指头干什么？……是谁在喊叫？"

"我在走路，长官，谁也没招……"赫留金一边捂着嘴咳嗽，一边说。"正和米特里·米特里奇谈木柴的事儿，——突然这个可恶的东西平白无故地咬我的手指头……请您原谅，我是个干活的人……我干的是细活儿。这得赔我钱，因为——我没准儿一星期都不能动这根手指头……就法律上，长官，也没规定人可以受畜生的欺负呀……要是人人都挨咬，还不如别活在这世上呢……"

"嗯！……好……"奥丘梅洛夫说着，咳嗽几声，微微挑了挑眉毛。"好……谁家的狗？这事我非管不可。我让你们看看，放狗出来有什么后果！到了该收拾这帮不愿遵守法令的老爷们的时候了！罚他的款，这个恶棍，我要叫他知道，放狗和别的什么畜生出来闲逛意味着什么！等我给他点儿颜色瞧瞧！……叶尔德林，"警监把脸转向警士。"查查是谁家的狗，要做记录！这只狗需要消灭。马上就办！它没准儿是只疯狗……这是谁家的狗，我问一声？"

"这像是日加洛夫将军家的！"人群里有人说。

"日加洛夫将军家的？嗯！……把大衣，叶尔德林，从我身上脱下来……真不得了，热死啦！多半是要下雨了……只有一点我不明白：它怎么会咬你呢？"奥丘梅洛夫把脸转向赫留金。"难道它够得到手指头？它这么小，瞧你那么老高！你的手指头也许是让钉子扎的，后来打起诈钱的鬼主意。瞧你……这号人！我知道你们，无赖！"

"他，长官，用烟头烫狗嘴取乐，那狗——不是傻瓜，就咬了一口……他是个爱胡闹的家伙，长官！"

"你胡说，独眼龙！没看见，凭什么胡说八道！长官是位聪明人，他知道谁胡说，谁像在上帝面前一样说良心话……我要是胡说，就让治安法官判我好啦。他那儿的法律上有……现今人人平等……我本人有个弟弟就是当宪兵的……要是你不知道的话……"

"不准吵闹！"

"不对，这狗不是将军家的……"警士颇有见解地说。"将军家没有这种狗。他家差不多全是大猎狗……"

"你说的这事儿准吗？"

"准，长官……"

"我自己也说嘛。将军家都是名贵的纯种狗，而这只——鬼知道是个什么东西！要毛色没毛色，要模样没模样……完全是个下贱货。怎么会养这种狗呢？！你的脑子哪去啦？这种狗要是在彼得堡或者莫斯科，你们猜会怎么样？那儿才管法律呢，一下——就得要它的狗命！你，赫留金，受了苦，我对这事非管不可……是要教训一顿！到了该……"

"没准儿也是将军家……"警士喃喃自语地想。"它脸上又没写着……前两天我在他家的院子里就见过一只这样的。"

"那还用说，是将军家的！"人群里有声音说。

"嗯！……把大衣，叶尔德林老弟，给我穿上……有点儿起风了……挺冷的……你把狗牵到将军家问问。就说是我找到的，派你送去……再告诉一声，别放它出来了……没准是只好狗呢，要是每个混蛋都拿烟头戳它的鼻子，用不了多久就把它毁啦。狗是娇贵的动物……你，笨蛋，把手放下来！用不着展览你那根儿破手指头！都是你自己的错！"

"将军家的厨师来了，我们问问他……嘿，普罗霍尔！到这儿来，亲爱的朋友！看看这只狗……你们家的？"

"瞎说！我们从来没有这种狗！"

"那就用不着多问啦，"奥丘梅洛夫说。"这是只野狗！用不着多费口舌……说它是野狗，就是野狗……弄死它，就是了。"

"这狗不是我们的，"普罗霍尔继续说。"这是将军哥哥家的，他不久前刚来。我们将军不喜欢这种小猎犬。他哥哥倒是喜……"

"他哥哥真的来了？弗拉基米尔·伊万诺维奇？"奥丘梅洛夫问，整个脸上充满了感动的笑容。"咦，天啊！我还不知道呢！来住一阵子？"

"住一阵……"

"咦，天啊……准是想弟弟啦，瞧我还不知道呢！那这是他的狗啦？非常荣幸……牵它走吧……小狗还不错……真够机灵的……照这家伙的手指头就是一口！哈—哈—哈……喂，你干吗发抖？来来来……来来……小滑头生气了……真是只好小狗……"

普罗霍尔叫着小狗，带它离开了木柴场……人们对赫留金哈哈大笑起来。

"我还会收拾你的！"奥丘梅洛夫威胁他说，然后用大衣裹紧身体，继续沿着市集广场走他的路。

（王景生　译）

玩　　笑

一个晴朗的冬日，中午时分……刺骨的严寒，纳金卡挽着我的胳膊，她的鬓发与上嘴唇的毫毛上都蒙上了一层银霜。我俩站在一座高山上。从我们立足的山顶到山下的平地，伸展着一面斜坡，太阳照着它如同照着镜子。我们身边有个小巧的雪橇，一条鲜红的绒布蒙盖在雪橇上。

"纳杰日达·彼得洛芙娜，咱们往下滑吧！"我恳求着说，"就滑一次！我向您保证，我们肯定完好无损，不会受伤。"

可是纳金卡害怕。从她穿着的那双小套鞋到冰山脚下的这个空间，在她看来简直是一个可怕的无底深渊。我请她坐到雪橇上去，当她往山底下看了一眼，便吓得魂不附体了，如果她当真冒险向深渊飞去，将会是什么结果！她会丢了性命，她会发疯。

"求求您了！"我说，"不必害怕！要知道，这是没有勇气，这是懦弱！"

纳金卡终于让步了，但我从她的脸色看出，她这回是冒着生命危险作出这个让步的。我把她扶上了雪橇，她面色惨白，浑身发抖，我用手把她搂紧，与她一起滑向那深渊。

雪橇像子弹一样地飞行着。被撕裂开来的空气击打着我们的脸，在我们的耳朵里呼啸着，咆哮着，愤怒地撕扯着我们，想要把我们的脑袋从肩膀上揪掉。

强劲的风，让我们喘不过气来。好像有个魔鬼用魔爪抓住我们，呼啸着把我们送进了地狱似的。周遭的一切都幻化为一条长长的，奔腾着的带子……好像再过几秒钟，我们就会命丧黄泉！

"纳嘉，我爱你！"我轻轻地说。

雪橇的滑行逐渐平稳下来，风的吼声和雪橇滑板的声响也不再那样可怕，呼吸也顺畅了一些，我们终于到了山下。纳金卡像是命悬一线似的，她面无血色，上气不接下气……我帮助她站起身来。

"我说什么也不滑第二次了，"她睁开充满恐惧的大眼睛瞧着我，说，"我再也不滑了！我差点儿死去！"

过了一会儿，她恢复了常态，便用疑惑的眼神盯视着我：纳嘉我爱你，这五个字究竟是我说的，还是这不过是她在狂风的怒号中的幻听？我站在她的身边，抽着烟斗，端详着自己的手套。

她挽着我的手臂，我们久久地在山脚下散步。看来，这个谜不能让她心安。这句话到底是说了还是没有说？说了还是没有说？说了还是没有说？这是个有关自尊的问题，有关荣誉的问题，有关生命、有关幸福的问题，这个问题是天底下最最重要的问题。纳金卡用她那锐利的目光，紧紧地、苦苦地盯着我的脸，答非所问地说着话，她期待着我说明真相。噢，她那张可爱的面孔上的表情何等丰富，何等丰富！我发现，她在进行着自我搏斗，她想要说点什么，问点什么，但她找不到恰当的语言，她不好意思，有点害怕，又因为喜悦反倒张不开口……

"这样好吗？"她说，眼睛没有看着我。

"怎样？"我问。

"咱们再滑一次……"

我们顺着阶梯爬到山顶。我又一次把脸色惨白、浑身发抖的纳金卡扶上了雪橇，我们又一次飞向可怕的深渊，又一次听到风的咆哮和滑板的喱喱作响，又一次在雪橇呼啸着飞行的最为紧张的时刻，我轻声地说：

"纳嘉，我爱你！"

雪橇停住之后，纳金卡朝我们刚刚滑行的山坡看了一眼，然后久久地瞅着我的脸，听着我的平淡又平静的话语，整个的她，甚至是她的手笼和帽子，整个她的娇小的身子都显示出她那极度的疑惑。她的脸上好像写着：

"这是怎么回事？是谁说了这句话？是他说的，还是我的幻听？"

这个迷惑折磨着她，使她无法忍受。

这位可怜的姑娘一言不发，愁眉紧锁，甚至要哭。

"咱们回家去吧？"我这样问道。

"我……我喜欢滑冰，"她红着脸说，"咱们不能再滑一次吗？"

她"喜欢"滑冰，然而，一坐上雪橇，她照样面色惨白，浑身发抖，吓得喘不过气来。

我们第三次往下滑行，我发现她在看着我的脸，盯着我的嘴唇。但我假装咳嗽，用手帕捂住了嘴，而当我们滑行到中途，我及时地发出声来：

"纳嘉，我爱你！"

疑问依旧是疑问！纳金卡沉默着，想着什么……我送她回家，一路上她尽量把步子放慢、放轻，一直等着我把这句话说给她听。我看到她的灵魂在痛苦着，她在极力控制自己，不要说出这句话来："风不可能说出这句话！我不希望这句话是风说的！"

第二天一早，我收到一封短信："如果你今天去滑雪橇，务必把我带上。纳嘉。"

从此我天天和纳金卡一起去滑冰场，每次坐在雪橇上往下飞行的途中，我总要轻声地说一句同样的话："纳嘉，我爱你！"

很快，纳金卡听这句话听上了瘾，就如同对美酒或吗啡上了瘾一样。听不到这句话她简直无法生活。当然，从山顶往下飞行照样恐怖，但现在这恐怖反倒给这句情语增加了特殊的魅力，尽管这句情语依旧是个谜,依旧折磨着她的灵魂。怀疑的对象依旧是两个:我和风……这二者之中究竟谁会出来向她坦陈爱情,她不知道,而且看来,她已经并不在乎;从哪个杯子里喝酒都是一样的,只要能喝醉就行。

有一天中午,我独自去滑冰场,我混杂在人群中间,看到纳金卡正向冰山走去,用眼睛搜寻着我……然后她小心翼翼地顺着台阶往上攀登……她独自一人登山是会感到恐怖的,噢,多么可怕!她的脸色白得像雪,身子在发抖,她朝前走去就像是走向刑场,但她走着,头也不回地走着,坚定不移地走着。毫无疑问,她终于决心做个试验:在没有我在场的情况下,是否也能听到这句甜美的情语?我看到面色刷白的她,因为恐惧而张大了嘴巴,坐上雪橇,紧闭双眼,开始滑动,那神情像是要与人间永别……"喔喔"……滑板喔喔作响。纳金卡是否听到了那句话,我不得而知……我只是看到当她从雪橇上站起来的时候,已经精疲力竭。从她的脸色判断,连她自己都不知道是否听到了那句话。往下滑行的恐惧,剥夺了她倾听话语的能力,分辨声音的能力,理解的能力……

早春三月终于来临……太阳变得温和起来。我们的那座冰山变黑了,失去了耀眼的光泽,最后融化了。我们不再去滑雪橇。可怜的纳金卡已经再也听不到这句话了,也是的,谁也不会再说这句话了,因为风已经消歇,而我也准备去彼得堡——要去很久,可能一去不复返。

动身前两天,我坐在自家的小花园里,已经暮色四合。这小花园与纳金卡家的院子由一道高高的上边布满钉子的篱笆墙隔开……天还有几分寒意,粪堆下还有积雪,树木毫无生气,白嘴鸦在聒噪着安顿过夜的鸟窝。我走近篱笆墙,通过缝隙久久地往那边张望。我看到纳金卡走到门廊上,用愁苦的目光在凝望天空……春风直接吹在她那雪白的、忧伤的脸孔上……这风让她联想到了冰山上的曾朝我们呼啸而来的风，在风声中她听到了那五个字，她的面孔变得更加忧郁，眼泪顺着脸颊流了下来……这可怜的姑娘把双手伸展开来，像是在祈求这阵风再给她捎来那句情语。我等到有阵风吹过来，便压低了嗓门说：

"纳嘉，我爱你！"

我的上帝，纳金卡的情绪顿时变了！她满脸笑容，大声喊叫，迎风高高地举起双手，她是那样的兴奋，那样的幸福，那样的美丽。

我抽身去整理行装。

这是很久以前的事了。现在纳金卡已为人妻，嫁给了一个贵族协会的秘书——到底是父母之命还是自由恋爱，这并不重要，她已经生了三个孩子。但当时我们是如何一起去滑冰，风是如何把"纳嘉，我爱你"这句话传进了她的耳朵，则是不可忘怀的，对她来说，这是她生命中最幸福、最感人、最美好的记忆……

我现在也已经上了年纪，已经无法说清，当年我为什么要说那句话，为什么要开这样的玩笑……

（童道明　译）

在 别 墅 里

"我爱您。您是我的生命，我的幸福，我的一切！原谅我的直言不讳，我无法再这样痛苦下去，沉默下去。我并不企求您给我同样的爱，我只求您给我点同情。求您务必今晚八点钟到老亭子里……我以为写上我的名字是多余的，但也请您不必害怕我的隐名埋姓。我年轻，漂亮……您还希求什么呢？"

避暑客巴维尔·伊万内奇·维赫采夫，一个循规蹈矩的有妇之夫，读完这封信，耸了耸肩，疑惑不解地挠挠额头。"什么鬼名堂？"他想，"我是有妇之夫，结果来了这么一封莫名其妙的……愚蠢之极的信！这是谁写的？"

巴维尔·伊万内奇把信纸在眼前晃动了几下，又念了一遍，啐了口吐沫。

"我爱您……"他做了个鬼脸，"把我当三岁小孩了！当是我会随随便便跑到那个亭子里去跟你幽会！……我，这种风流勾当早就不干了……嗯！写这信的肯定是个轻浮的女人……嗯，这些女人呀！她真是昏了头啦，居然把这样的情书写给一个陌生的男人，而且还是一个有妇之夫！简直是道德败坏！"

在八年的婚姻生活中，巴维尔·伊万内奇已经远离细腻的浪漫情怀，除了逢年过节的贺卡，他没有收到过任何信札；因此，尽管他表面作了那一番不为所动的硬汉表演，那封来信还是让他不知所措，慌了手脚，动了心思。接到来信之后过去了一个小时，他躺在沙发上，想道："当然，我不是小孩子，我不会随随便便跑去跟个陌生女人幽会的。不过呢，要是能弄清写信的人究竟是谁，倒也蛮有意思。嗯……看笔迹，肯定是一位女士写的……这信写得还蛮有感情，所以不大像是在开玩笑……大概是个有点神经质的女人，再不然就是寡妇……总的来说，寡妇都有点头脑简单，行为怪异。嗯……这能是谁呢？"

要弄明白这个问题也不容易，因为在这个避暑山庄里，除了自己的妻子外，巴维尔·伊万内奇不认得其他任何一个女人。

"见鬼了……"他很困惑，"'我爱您'……她什么时候开始爱上我的？奇怪的女人！也不认识，也不了解我这个人究竟怎么样，就把我爱上了……如果能这样一见钟情，想必她一定是个年轻的、生性浪漫的女子……可是她究竟会是谁呢？"

巴维尔·伊万内奇蓦地想到，昨天和前天，当他在避暑山庄周围散步的时候，好几次遇到过一个穿浅色裙子、鼻子微微翘起的金发女郎。这位金发女郎总要朝他多看几眼，当他坐到一张长椅上，她也坐到了他旁边……"是她？"维赫采夫在想，"不可能！像她那样一个娇小姐能爱上我这么个糟老头？不，这不可能！"

吃午饭的时候，巴维尔·伊万内奇呆呆地瞅着妻子，想自己的心事：

"她说她年轻、漂亮……这说明她不是个老太婆……嗯……说良心话，我也不算老，我也还能招人爱……我老婆就很爱我！更何况，俗话说得好，爱情是个瞎子——逮到谁就爱谁——"

"你在想什么？"妻子问他。

"嗯……头有点痛……"巴维尔·伊万内奇撒了个谎。

他想明白了，把这封破信当成情书来看待是愚蠢的，他对这封信和写这封信的人嗤之以鼻，可是，唉！人性的魔力强大无比。午饭过后，巴维尔·伊万内奇躺在床上，不睡觉，想心事："要知道她指望我应约前往呢！多么傻！我想象得到，她一走进亭子，不见我人影，她会失望得浑身发抖的！……我偏不去……气气她！"

　　然而，我要重复一句，人性的魔力强大无比。

　　"不过，出于好奇心，也不妨去一趟……"半个小时之后，这位别墅客又这样想。"从远处看看，她究竟是个什么样的女人……看看她的长相，也怪有趣的！逢场作戏罢了！不过，遇到合适的机会，为什么就不能寻寻开心呢？"

　　巴维尔·伊万内奇起床，穿衣服。

　　"这打扮得漂漂亮亮要上哪去？"妻子见他穿了件干净的衬衣，换了条鲜亮的领带问。

　　"嗯，出去散散步……头有点痛……嗯……"巴维尔·伊万内奇打扮完毕，等到八点钟，便走出了房门。在落日余晖照耀着的翠绿色的背景中，来此地消夏的红男绿女在他眼前晃动，他的心剧烈地跳动起来。

　　"她是他们中的哪一个呢？……"他想，羞涩地扫视着一张张女士的脸孔。"没有金发女郎……嗯……如果照她信上写的推测，她应该已经坐在亭子里。"

　　维赫采夫走上林荫道，在林荫道的尽头，透过一行高大的椴树的枝叶，可以看见那个"老亭子"……他悄悄地走近亭子……

　　"从远处看看……"他这样想，迟疑不决地往前挪动脚步。"唷，我有什么好害怕的？我又不是去和女人幽会！好一个……傻瓜蛋！大胆地往前走！我到亭子里去怎的？嗯，嗯……无所谓！"巴维尔·伊万内奇的心脏跳动得更加剧烈了……他情不自禁地突然间想象到了影影绰绰的亭子……在他的想象里，出现了一个身材修长的金发女郎，穿着浅色的衣裙，鼻子微微翘起……他想象着，她因为爱而羞怯，浑身发抖，她忸怩地走近他，大声喘息着……突然间她把他拥进了怀里。

　　"要是我还是个单身汉，那就毫无顾忌了……"他这样想，把厌恶感从脑子里赶了出去。"再说了……一辈子经历这么一次，倒也说得过去,否则到死也不知道这种事是啥滋味。那么老婆……嗨,这与她有什么关系?感谢上帝,这八年来我没有离开过她一步……做了整整八年的守法公民!别管她……甚至有点腻味了……今天我索性造她的反!"

浑身发着抖,屏住了呼吸,巴维尔·伊万内奇走到了亭子跟前,这个亭子上爬满了野葡萄的藤蔓,他往亭子里瞧了瞧……扑鼻而来的是夹杂着霉味的湿气……

"大概,没有人……"他想,当他伸脚跨进了亭子,却在角落里发现了一个人影……是个男人的影子……定晴一看,巴维尔·伊万内奇认出此人是自己的妻弟,大学生米佳,就寄住在他的别墅里。

"哦,原来是你?……"他很不满意地说着,摘下帽子,坐了下来。

"对了,是我……"米佳回答。

沉默了两分钟……

"巴维尔·伊万内奇对不起,请您离开这里,行不行?……我正在构思我的硕士论文……有别人在我跟前,就会妨碍我思考……"米佳先开始发难。

"你还不如到黑黑的林荫道上走一走的好……"巴维尔·伊万内奇温和地回应,"在露天里,容易来灵感!况且……我想在这儿的长椅上打个盹儿……这儿不太闷热……"

"您要打盹儿,我可是要做论文……"米佳嘟囔道,"论文更重要……"

又是沉默……维赫采夫神不守舍,不断地听到脚步声,猛地站起身来,用哀求的声音说道:"好了,米佳,我求求你了!你比我年轻,你应该体谅体谅我才对……我不大舒服……想打个盹了……你走开吧!"

"这是自私自利……为什么您非得待在这儿,却不让我待在这儿？说啥我也不走……"

"得了，我求求你啦！就算我是个自私自利的人，霸道的人，愚蠢的人……可是我还是要求你走开！我这一辈子就低三下四地求你这一回！体谅体谅我！"

米佳摇摇头。

"真是个畜生……"巴维尔·伊万内奇想，"我总不能当着他的面与女人幽会！得把他支走！"

"米佳，你听我说，"他说，"我最后一次恳求你……你该做一个通情达理的文化人才对！"

"我不懂，您为什么老缠着我？……"米佳耸了耸肩，"我已经说了，我不走，不走。说啥我也不走……"

在这个时候，突然有个鼻子微微上翘的女人探头朝亭子里看了看。

看到了米佳和巴维尔·伊万内奇，这个女人皱了皱眉头，走开了……

"她走了！"巴维尔·伊万内奇想，愤怒地瞧着米佳，"她一看到这个坏蛋，就走了！全都泡汤了！"

又等了一会儿，维赫采夫站起身来，戴上帽子，冲着米佳说："你是畜生，坏蛋！是的！畜生！卑鄙，而且……愚蠢！我和你从此绝交！"

"好得很！"米佳喃喃地说，也站起身来，戴上了帽子，"您要知道，您方才在这里赖着不走，坏了我的好事，我活着一天，就决不会饶恕您！"

巴维尔·伊万内奇气呼呼地走出亭子，快步向自家别墅走去……摆上晚餐菜碟的桌子也不能让他宽心。

"一辈子就出现过这么一次机会，"他激动地想着，"也给搅黄了！她现在想必受了委屈……伤透了心！"

吃晚饭的时候，巴维尔·伊万内奇和米佳都盯着自己的碟子，保持着阴郁的沉默，他们彼此憎恶对方。

"你笑什么？"巴维尔·伊万内奇向妻子表示不满，"只有傻瓜才会这样无缘无故地傻笑！"

妻子瞅着丈夫阴沉的脸，扑哧一笑……

"今天早上你接着什么信了？"她问。

"我？……我没有接着信呀……"巴维尔·伊万内奇慌张起来，"你胡诌个什么……""嗨，说吧！坦白交代吧！要知道那封信是我写给你的！千真万确，是我写的！哈哈！"

巴维尔·伊万内奇脸涨得通红，把头埋进了碟子里。

"愚蠢的玩笑。"他嘟哝道。

"可我有什么办法！你自己说说……我们今天要打扫房间，怎样才能把你从家里请出去呢？只有这个办法才能把你请走……但是，你也别生气……为了让你在亭子里不觉得寂寞，我也给米佳写了封同样内容的信！米佳，你也到亭子里去了吧？"

米佳龇牙一笑，不再恶狠狠地瞪视自己的情敌。

（童道明　译）

薇 罗 奇 卡

　　伊凡·阿历克谢耶维奇·奥格涅夫记得，在那个八月的夜晚，他是怎样地当的一声打开了玻璃门，走到了凉台上。那时他披着一件薄薄的披风，头戴一顶宽边草帽，现在，这顶草帽连同那双军靴都沾满灰尘地扔在床底下。他一只手抱了一大捆书和笔记本，另一只手拄着一根长着很多节疤的粗手杖。

　　房子的主人库兹涅佐夫站在门后，举着灯，给他照明，这是一位秃顶的老人，留着长长的花白胡子，穿一件用凸纹布做的上衣。老人友善地微笑着，频频点头。

　　"老人家，再会了！"奥格涅夫向他喊道。库兹涅佐夫把灯放在一张小桌子上，也走到了凉台上。两个窄长的人影通过台阶往花坛方向挪步，摇摇晃晃，脑袋顶着了椴树的树干。

　　"再会了，再一次道一声谢谢，亲爱的！"伊凡·阿历克谢耶维奇说，"谢谢你们的殷勤好客，谢谢你们的亲切关照，谢谢你们的爱心……我永远不会忘记你们的款待。您是个好人，您的女儿也是个好人，你们全都那么善良，那么开朗，那么坦诚……遇上这样一群难得的好人，我都不知该说什么好了！"因为感情冲动，再加上喝了点酒，奥格涅夫说话的声音像教堂唱诗班歌手的声调，他是那样的情绪激动，与其说是在用语言，毋宁说是在用自己的眼光的闪烁和肩膀的耸动在表达自己的感情。库兹涅佐夫也有几分醉意，他情绪有点激动，他向这位年轻人探过身子去，和他接吻。

　　"我像条小狗与你们难分难解了！"奥格涅夫继续说，"我几乎每天到你们家来消磨时光，在你们家一住就是十天，究竟喝了你们多少果子酒，现在想起来都有点后怕。而最最重要的，加夫利尔·彼得罗维奇，我是要感谢您对我工作的帮助。如果没有您的协助，我的统计工作怕是要拖到十月份去。所以我会在统计报告的序言里写上一笔，认为我有义务向 N 县执委会主席库兹涅佐夫的友善协作深表谢意。统计学前程似锦！请您代我向薇拉·加夫利洛芙娜致意，也请您向那几位医生、法官和您的秘书转达我的谢意，就说我永远不会忘记他们的帮助！"

　　无精打采的奥格涅夫再一次与老头子接了吻，便走下台阶。当他走到最后一个台阶的时候，转过身来，问：

　　"我们将来还能见面吗？"

　　"上帝才知道！"老人回答，"大概，无缘再会了！"

　　"有道理！你们不会有兴趣去彼得堡，而我也未必再有机会到这里来。好吧，告别吧！"

　　"您把书留下好了！"库兹涅佐夫朝他背后喊道，"您何必拿着这样重的东西上路？明天我差人给您送去就是了。"

　　但奥格涅夫已经快步走开，听不见了。

　　他的心被葡萄酒温暖了，他感到快活、温馨，也有点惆怅……他一边走着，一边在想，在一生中能见到多少好人呀，遗憾的是，这些美好的相逢，除了回忆之外，留不下任何痕迹。常常有这样的情形，一群大雁在天际飞过，微风送来了它们的既含哀怨又是欢畅的叫声，但过了一分钟之后，不管你怎样的凝神远眺蓝色的远方，你既看不到它们的影子，也听不到它们的声音——人也是这样，他们的音容在生活中闪现一刻，然后沉入我们的过去，遗留下来的不过是些许记忆的点滴。从春天来到 N 县起，伊凡·阿历克谢耶维奇几乎每天都来拜访好客的库兹涅佐夫一家，伊凡·阿历克谢耶维奇对他们视若亲人，他和老人，和他的女儿、女仆都处得很熟，对房子的布局了如指掌，那舒适的凉台，那曲径通幽的林荫道，那厨房和澡堂上方的树影。但当他一跨步走出门外，所有这一切都变成了记忆，失去了现实的意义，而再过一两年，所有这些可爱的形象都会在你的意识中变得模糊不清，就好比是凭空幻想出来的幻影一样。

"在生活中再没有比人更可宝贵的了！"

深受感动的奥格涅夫这样想，他正在沿着林荫道向院门走去。"再也没有了！"

花园里很安静很温暖。木犀草、烟草和天芥草散发着芳香，这些花草在花坛里还没有凋谢。在灌木丛与大树相隔的空间，弥漫着柔和的被月光浸润着的薄雾，这雾霭像幽灵般穿行于林荫小道上，静静地，但看得很分明，这景象会在奥格涅夫的记忆中长久地存留。月亮高高地挂在花园上方，在它的下方有一团团透明的雾状物在向东方飘浮。整个世界似乎就仅仅为这些黑色的倒影和浮动着的雾状物所构成。而奥格涅夫几乎是平生第一次观赏到在八月夜晚的月光下出现的雾霭。他寻思，他看到的也许不是大自然的本色，而是一台舞台布景，并不高明的烟火技师躲在灌木丛的后边，想用白色的孟加拉烟火来照亮花园，却把白烟与白光一起投向了空中。

正当奥格涅夫走近花园门口的时候，一个黑影离开不高的围墙，向他迎面走来。

"薇拉·加夫利洛芙娜！"他兴奋地说，"您在这儿？我找了您好久，想向您辞行……再会了，我要走了！"

"这么早就走？才十一点钟。"

"不，该走了！要步行五里地，还要收拾行装。明天要早起……"

在奥格涅夫面前站着的是库兹涅佐夫的女儿薇拉，一位年方二十一岁的少女，照例有一副愁容，穿着随便而又有情调。大凡耽于幻想，成天懒洋洋地躺着，读读随手抓到的书籍的少女，都是烦闷和忧伤的，她们的穿戴也都很随意。对于她们中的一些天生丽质的姑娘，这种穿戴的随意反倒增添了楚楚动人的魅力。至少奥格涅夫后来一想起美女薇罗奇卡，总会想到她那一件宽大的短上衣，在腰口有很深的褶子，但并没有束住腰身，总会想到那一绺从高高梳起的秀发上垂到额头的卷发，总会想到她那条红色的毛线披巾，周边绣有毛茸茸的小圆球，一到晚上，这披巾毫无生气地搭在薇罗奇卡的肩上，像是一面在无风吹拂的天气里的旗帜，而到了白天，这披巾被随便地丢在前厅的男人们的帽子旁边，或是丢在饭厅的木箱上，那只老猫就会毫不客气地躺在上边。从这条披巾和这件短上衣的皱褶里，散发着一种自由的慵倦，恋家与温顺的气息。也许，正是因为奥格涅夫爱上了薇拉，他就能在她身上的每一个纽扣里，每一个皱褶中寻找到某种温存的、舒心的、纯真的、美好的和富有诗意的东西，而这些恰恰是在那些虚伪的、缺乏美感和冷冰冰的女人身上找不到的。

薇罗奇卡身材很好，侧面轮廓端正，还有一头漂亮的卷发。奥格涅夫平常很少与女人交往，在他眼里，薇拉便是个美女了。"我要走了！"他在门口与她告别，"别记住我的坏处！谢谢您为我做的一切！"

他依旧用与老头子说话时的近似于唱诗班歌手的声调在说话，依旧眨动着眼睛，耸动着肩膀，感谢薇拉的殷勤与温存。

"我在写给母亲的每一封信上都提到您。"他说，"如果所有的人都像您和您父亲，那么我们就生活在极乐世界里了。你们太好了！都是一些纯朴的，热情的，真诚的人。"

"您现在准备上哪去？"薇拉问。

"我现在先去奥寥尔城，在母亲那里住两个星期，然后去彼得堡工作。"

"然后呢？"

"然后？我要在彼得堡工作整整一个冬季，开春之后还要到某个县里去搜集资料。好了，祝您生活幸福，长命百岁……别记住我的坏处。今后我们再也没有可能见面了。"

奥格涅夫弯下腰去，亲吻薇罗奇卡的手。然后在默默的情感冲动中整了整自己的风衣，把那包书拿得更顺手一些，沉默片刻之后说道：

"好大的雾呀！"

"是的，您没有在我家遗忘了什么东西？"

"会是什么东西呢？大概，没有什么东西……"

奥格涅夫默默地站了一会儿，然后笨拙地转过身去，走出了花园。

"您等一等，我把您送到我家的森林边上。"薇拉说，跟在他身后走出来。

他们顺着大路走去。树木现在已经挡不住眼前的广阔空间，已经可以看见远处的天边。整个大自然像是被蒙上了面纱，藏到了透明的、暗淡的雾气里，透过这雾气，才能呈现出大自然的美丽。这时而更浓，时而更白的雾霭不均匀地点缀在干草堆和灌木丛的周边，或是聚成棉絮状贴近地面，越过大路，像是尽可能地不要遮挡住广阔的空间。透过雾霭可以看见通往森林的道路，路的两旁有黑色的水沟，水沟里长出的细小的灌木挡住了棉絮状薄雾的渗透。走出院门半里路的光景，库兹涅佐夫家的黑色森林地带就呈现在了眼前。

"她为什么要和我这么走一路？我还得把她送回家！"奥格涅夫这样想，但当他看了一眼薇拉的侧面，他便露出了亲热的笑容，说："在这么好的辰光，真不想离开！真是个浪漫的夜晚，有明月，有宁静，应有尽有。薇拉·加夫利洛芙娜，您知道吗？我在世上已经活了二十九年，但我在生活中还没有拥有过一个情人。从来没有过一桩风流韵事，什么幽会啦，林荫道上的叹息啦，拥抱接吻啦，我只是听说过。这不正常！要是在城里，单独住在斗室里，倒还意识不到这个缺失，但在这新鲜的空气里，便尖锐地感觉到了……这是多么让人难受！"

"您为什么会是这样呢？"

"不知道。可能是因为整天忙于工作，也许是因为一直没有碰上中意的女人……我熟人很少，也很少到外边走动。"

两个年轻人默默地往前走了三百步的样子。奥格涅夫瞧了一眼薇罗奇卡的没有戴帽子的头和那条披巾，春天和夏天的日子便接二连三地在他的心中重现了。那时他远离彼得堡的灰暗的寓所，享受着好人们的殷勤款待，享受着大自然的美景，和自己钟爱的工作，他竟然没有留意早霞是如何地变成了晚霞，各种鸟类是如何用叫声的停歇来预告夏天的结束，先是夜莺停止了歌唱，然后是鹌鹑和秧鸡不再鸣叫……时光不知不觉中飞过去了，这说明日子过得轻松愉快……他开始出声地回忆他这个寒酸的，喜欢独处不善交际的人，是如何很不情愿地在四月底来到了这个 N 县，他原来以为等待他的将是无聊、孤独和人们对于统计学的漠不关心，而在他看来，统计学是一门最重要的科学。在一个四月的早晨，他来到了 N 县小城，落脚在旧教徒梁布兴开的客栈里，以一天二十戈比的房钱租得一间窗明几净的房间，条件是不准在室内抽烟。稍事休息之后，探听到了县执委会主席的相关信息，便立即拜访加夫利尔·彼特洛维奇。他是步行去的，要走四里地路，得在茂盛的牧场和幼林中穿行。云雀在云层下抖动翅膀，让银铃般的声音弥漫在空气中，而白嘴鸦高傲地扇动起翅膀，掠过绿色的田野。

"上帝！"奥格涅夫那时很惊奇，"这里的空气一直是如此清新，还是因为我今天的到来，才散发出这样的清香？"

奥格涅夫期待着不冷不热的公事公办的接待，他走进库兹涅佐夫的家门的时候，很是拘谨，不敢正眼看人，羞怯地摆弄着自己的胡子。老头子一开始也紧锁眉头，他不明白这位年轻人和他的统计学为什么需要求助于县地方执委会。但一当年轻人向他详细说明了统计材料的功能以及要在什么地方搜集这些材料，加夫利尔·彼特洛维奇就来了精神，脸上浮起笑容，而且怀着孩子般的好奇心去翻阅他的笔记本……那天晚上，伊凡·阿历克谢依奇已经留在库兹涅佐夫家吃晚饭了。浓烈的果子酒很快让他有了醉意，他看着新朋友们的平静的面容，慵倦的动作，感觉到自己身上也有了一种甜美的、昏昏欲睡的倦意，真想躺下来，伸展一下腰腿，微微一笑。而新朋友们也友善地看着他，问他父母是否还健在，他月薪多少，是否常常进剧院看戏……

奥格涅夫回忆起自己参加的郊游、野餐、垂钓，参观修道院，拜访修道院院长玛尔法的情形，当时她给每个客人送了个用玻璃珠子串成的钱包。他也回忆起了激情洋溢的、没完没了的、纯粹俄罗斯式的争辩，争辩双方唾沫四溅，用拳头敲击着桌子，还没有听懂对方的意思，便打断对方的发言，自己的谈话又前后矛盾，还常常变换话题，争吵了两三个小时之后，才笑着说："鬼知道我们是在争论什么！先是为活人祝寿，到后来竟是为死者招魂了！"

"您还记得有一次我、您和一位医生骑马到什斯托沃去的情景吗？"快走到森林的时候，伊凡·阿历克谢依奇对薇拉说，"那回还碰上了一个癫狂的修道士，我给了他一个五戈比的硬币，他在胸前划了三次十字，便把这硬币扔进了麦地里。上帝呀，我要从这里带走多少有趣的印象呀，如果我把它们好好地揉成一团，就会变成一块金子了！我就弄不明白，那些聪明的，敏感的人为什么要挤在首都而不到这里来呢？难道在涅瓦大街和城市的潮湿的房子里较之这里有更大的空间与真理？真的，在我住的那座备有家具的公寓楼里，从上到下挤满了画家、学者和记者们，我总以为这是一种不理智的现象。"

距离森林二十步远的地方，有一座不大的窄桥越过大路，桥的一角立着一个台柱，是供库兹涅佐夫一家人和他家的客人晚间散步到此地休息准备的。在这里，要是谁有兴致，可以朝森林大喊一声，倾听随之传来的回声。而一进入森林，大路便不复存在，变成了一条黑色的林中小路。

"看，小桥到了！"奥格涅夫说，"您可以往回走了……"

薇拉停下脚步，喘了口气。

"咱们坐一会吧，"她坐到了一个台柱上，说，"远行之前，通常总是要坐着道别的。"

奥格涅夫挨近她坐到了自己的那捆书上，继续说着话。她走累了，艰难地喘着气，也没有看着他，而是把目光投向了旁边的什么地方，所以奥格涅夫看不清她的脸孔。

"要是过了十年我们突然间相遇了呢？"奥格涅夫说，"那时我们将成了什么样子了呢？您已经是个受人尊敬的家庭主妇，而我呢，成了一个谁也不需要的统计学大部头著作的作者，篇幅之大让人咋舌。将来我们重逢，我们回忆过去……现在呢，我们感受到的是今天的现实，它充实着我们，激动着我们，而当我们日后重逢的时候，将记不得我们在这个桥头最后一次聚会究竟是何月何日，甚至连哪一年都记不起来。您，到时会变样的。您说，您会变样吗？"

薇拉的身子抖动了一下，朝他转过脸来。

"什么？"她问。

"我现在问您……"

"对不起，我没有听见您刚才说了什么。"

这时奥格涅夫才发现了薇拉的异常。她脸色苍白，呼吸急促，这呼吸的颤抖传导到了双手、双唇和头部，原本垂到额头的卷发只有一缕，现在是两缕……看得出来，她在躲避他的眼光，为了掩饰自己的激动，她时而平整一下自己的领子，好像它磨痛了她的颈项，时而将红色的披巾从一个肩头拉到另一个肩头……

"您好像有点受寒，"奥格涅夫说，"在雾气里不能久坐。我现在送您回家。"

薇拉默不做声。

"您这是怎么啦？"伊凡·阿历克谢依奇笑道，"您不开口，不回答我的问题。您是身体不舒服还是生我气了？说呀？"

薇拉把手掌紧贴在朝向奥格涅夫的面颊上，立即又猛地把手掌移开。

"可怕的处境……"她轻声说道，脸上现出痛苦的表情。"可怕！"

"可怕在哪里？"奥格涅夫问，他耸了耸肩膀，没有掩饰自己的惊奇。"究竟是怎么回事？"薇拉依旧在抖动着双肩，痛苦地喘着粗气，她背对着奥格涅夫，凝望了一会天空，然后说：

"伊凡·阿历克谢依奇，我需要跟您谈谈……"

"我听着。"

"您也许会觉得奇怪……您会大吃一惊，但我也还是要说……"

奥格涅夫再次耸动了一下肩膀，准备洗耳恭听。"是这样……"薇拉开始说，她低着头，用手指摆弄着披巾上的珠子。"我想要……向您说的……您会觉着很奇怪和很愚蠢……可是我……不得不说了。"

薇拉的言语渐渐变成了含糊不清的喃喃细语，而且突然之间又被哭泣中断。姑娘用披巾盖住了脸面，身子弯得更低了，哭得很伤心。伊凡·阿历克谢依奇尴尬地清了清嗓子，慌乱得不知该说点什么，做点什么，只好无助地环顾四周。他见不得别人哭泣、流泪，以至于自己的眼睛也觉着痒痒的。

"怎么会是这样！"他嘟囔道，手足无措，"薇拉·加夫利洛芙娜，为什么要这样？亲爱的，您……不会是病了吧？或者是有人欺侮了您？您倒是说呀，也许我还能……有所帮助……"

当他想好好安慰她的时候，他竟然敢于小心翼翼地把姑娘的手从她的脸上移开，她终于透过眼泪朝他微笑了，说了一句："我……我爱您！"

这是一句很普通很平常的话，是一句由一个很普通的人从嘴里说出来的话，可是奥格涅夫却大为慌张，他躲开薇拉，站起身来，跟在慌张之后的感觉是恐惧。由告别和果子酒诱发的淡淡的、甜甜的忧伤顿时消失了，取而代之的是尖锐的、不快的尴尬。他好像经历了一次灵魂出窍的过程。他斜着眼睛看了看薇拉，现在，她对他说出了这句求爱的话之后，她便丧失了能给女人增添美感的那种可望而不可即的神秘感，她在他的眼睛里变得矮小了，平常了，暗淡了。

"这算怎么回事？"他惊魂未定地自问。

"我到底对她……是爱还是不爱？这才是问题的关键！"

而她呢，一旦把最重要的、最严肃的话说出来之后，反倒呼吸顺畅自如了。她也站起身来，两眼盯视着伊凡·阿历克谢依奇的面孔，开始快节奏地、热烈地、滔滔不绝地说起话来。

就好比一个突然受到惊吓的人，事后记不起大祸临头时前后都出现了些什么声响，奥格涅夫现在也记不得薇拉刚才具体说了些什么话。他仅仅记得她说的大概内容，和她说的这些话给予他的触动。他记得由于激动，她的嗓音似乎有点喑哑，但音调中却洋溢出了不平常的音乐性与激情。她说话的时候，时而哭，时而笑，泪珠在她的眼睫毛上闪烁，她对他说，从彼此相识的头几天，他的出众的风度，学识，善良的透着智慧的眼睛，他的职业，他的生活目标就强烈地把她吸引住了，她强烈地、疯狂地、深深地爱上了他；夏天的时候，当她从花园里走回家去，见到门廊里挂着他的风衣，或是从远处听到他的声音，她的心里就沁出一阵清凉，生出了幸福的预感；有时甚至他的几句普通的玩笑都能引起她哈哈大笑，在他笔记本上记着的每一个数目字里，她都能看出某种极为智慧的和意义非凡的内涵；而他的那根带有节疤的手杖在她眼里比树还要美丽。

那片森林，那缕缕轻雾，那路边的黑水沟，好像都在静静地听她说话，而奥格涅夫听着她的说话，却在心中发生了怪异的、不祥的变化……在倾诉爱情的时候，薇拉妩媚动人，话语甜美而热烈，但他感受到的并不是他期望得到的陶醉与快乐，而仅仅是对于薇拉的怜悯，和心中的遗憾及隐痛，因为由于他的缘故让一个好姑娘受了伤害。只有上帝才知道，这在他身上起作用的，是他的书生意气，或是那种对于所谓客观性的习惯性适应，以至于常常使人不能好好生活。然而薇拉的或喜或悲的情感流露，在他看来是不合常理的，不够严肃的。他自己的情绪也激愤起来，在提醒着他，他现在所看到和听到的一切，从天地自然与个人幸福的角度来看，要比所有的统计学、书本道理都要更有分量……他开始怒火中烧，责备自己，尽管他并不明白，他到底错在哪里。

除了尴尬之外，他还完全不知道该对薇拉说点什么，而他必须说点什么。他自然没有勇气直截了当地说"我不爱您"，然而他也不能说"我爱您"，因为他不管怎样地审视自己的灵魂，也找不到一点情感的星火……

他沉默不语，而她倒打开了话匣子，说对她而言最大的幸福，莫过于能见到他，能跟他走，哪怕是现在就跟他走，不管走到什么地方，做他的妻子和助手，而如果他离她而去，那么她将在痛苦中死去……

"我不能再在这里住下去，"她绞着手，说："这里的房子，森林和空气都让我觉着厌烦。我忍受不了这种一成不变的安宁和浑浑噩噩的生活，我忍受不了这里的毫无个性的、苍白的人群，他们像两滴水珠一样的毫无区别！他们都很客气，都很从容，因为他们都饱餐终日，没有痛苦，不想奋斗……而我真正向往那些潮湿的大房子，那里有人在痛苦，有人在劳动与贫穷中苦苦挣扎……"而这些话在奥格涅夫听来也是不合常理，不够严肃的。在薇拉说完这些话之后，他仍旧不知道该说点什么，但又不能再继续沉默，于是他喃喃地说道：

"薇拉·加夫利洛芙娜，我非常感谢您，尽管我觉得我担当不起……您对我的这份感情。再有，作为一个诚实的人，我应该指出，幸福……应该是建立在平等的基础上，也就是说应该两厢情愿……彼此相爱……"

但刚一说完，奥格涅夫就为自己喃喃地说出的这些话感到羞愧了。他觉得在这个时刻，他脸有愧色，而且显得笨拙，呆板，那脸容一定紧张，不自然……薇拉突然之间也变得严肃起来，脸色发白，垂下了头，想必她已经从他的脸孔上看出了他的真意。

"请您原谅我。"奥格涅夫受不了无语的静场，又嘟囔道，"我非常尊重您，所以……我心里很难过！"

薇拉急促地转过身去，快步往回家的路上走去。奥格涅夫跟在她身后走。

"不，不必了！"薇拉向他摆了摆手，"您别送我，我自己走回去……"

"不行……不送您回去不好……"

不管奥格涅夫说了什么话，最后说出口的话没有一句不让他感到平庸和可憎。他每走一步，他的负疚感就增长一分。他握紧拳头，埋怨自己的冷若冰霜，不会与女人保持热络的关系，他真正在生自己的气了。为了竭力使自己激动起来，他欣赏着薇罗奇卡的美丽的身材，她的头发，她的纤小的双脚在尘土里留下的足迹，他想起了她的话语和眼泪，但所有这些仅仅能使他心软，却不能让他怦然心动。

"唉，总不能强迫自己去爱吧！"他说服了自己，但同时他又想："到什么时候才能不受强迫地去爱一个人呢？要知道我已经是个快三十岁的人了！我还从没有遇到一个比薇拉更好的女人，而且将来怕也遇不到更好的女人了……噢，该死的未老先衰！才三十岁就已经衰老！”

薇拉在前头越走越快，低着脑袋，眼睛不向旁边张望。奥格涅夫觉得由于痛苦她变得瘦了，肩膀也变得窄了……“我能够想象，她此刻的心情！”他从背后瞧着她，心里这样想。“想必她现在羞愧和痛苦得简直会有死的念头！上帝，在这种情感中包含着多少生命、诗情、意义。连顽石都为之动容，而我……我是多么愚蠢，多么不通情理！”

走到篱笆门口，薇拉瞟了他一眼，弯着身子，用披巾把肩膀裹紧，加快脚步沿着林荫路走去。

就剩伊凡·阿历克谢依奇独自一人了。他转身向森林走去，他走得很慢，不时地停下脚步，回头看看篱笆门，他的整个身躯呈现一种奇怪的姿势，好像对自己失去了自信。他用眼睛搜寻着薇罗奇卡在路上留下的痕迹，他无法相信，这位他所钟爱的姑娘，这位刚刚还向他倾诉过爱情的姑娘，竟被他如此生硬和笨拙地“拒绝”了！他生平第一次依据自己的亲身经历体会到，人的行为很难受到自己的善良意志的控制，体会到一个正派的好心人在违背本意地给亲近的人带来残酷的、理应避免的痛苦之后，自己会是个什么样的心情。

他的良心在疼痛。一当薇拉看不见了，他便意识到他失去了某种很宝贵和亲切的、而且再也无法寻找回来的东西。他觉得自己的一部分青春已经和薇拉一起消失了。他觉得刚刚他坐失良机的那个时刻也一去不复返了。

走到小桥旁，他停下了脚步，陷入了沉思之中，他想要寻找到导致他如此冷若冰霜的原因。他很清楚，这原因不在身外，而恰恰是在他自身。他在自己面前坦诚地承认，这并不是聪明的知识分子常常炫耀的理性的冷淡，也不是自我膨胀的愚蠢之徒的冷

淡，而是心灵的蜕化，是对美的麻木不仁，是由于教育，无序的
生存竞争，单身的公寓生活等诸多因素造成的未老先衰。

他好像很不情愿地从桥头向森林走去。在深黑的、浓密的林
子里，月亮的光点东一处西一处地流泻了进来，除了自己的思绪
之外，他在这里没有其他任何的感觉，他非常希望把失去了的再
寻找回来。

伊凡·阿历克谢依奇记得自己又回去了。他用回忆刺激自己，
强迫自己在想象中勾勒薇拉的形象，他快步走向花园。路上和花
园里的雾霭已经消散，一轮明月，皎洁如洗，从天空向下窥望，
只有东方的天际还有几片愁云缭绕……奥格涅夫记得自己的小心
翼翼的脚步，记得黑色的窗子，记得木犀草和天芥草的浓烈的芳
香。已经和他相熟的小狗卡罗，友好地摇摆着尾巴，走过来嗅闻
他的手……这是唯一的一个活物，看到他如何围着住宅绕行了两
圈，站在薇拉的窗下，然后摆了摆手，深深地叹息了一声，离开
了花园。

一个小时之后，他进了城，已经精疲力竭的他，用整个身子
和发热的脸蛋靠在了旅馆的大门上，用门的把手敲门。在城里的
某个地方，有只睡意蒙眬的狗在叫唤，这吠声像是在回应着奥格
涅夫的敲门声。在教堂的附近有人在敲击一块铁板。

"夜里还出去瞎逛……"旅馆的主人嘟囔着出来开门，他是
个旧教徒，穿着像是女人穿的一件睡衣。"与其出去瞎逛，还不
如做做祷告。"

伊凡·阿历克谢依奇回到自己的房间，瘫坐在自己的床上，
久久地凝望着火光，然后摇了摇头，开始整理自己的行装……

（童道明　译）

邻　居

　　彼得·米海雷奇·伊瓦申的心情坏透了；他妹妹还是个姑娘，竟跟一个已婚的男人弗拉西奇走了。在家也好，在庄稼地里也罢，这种沉重懊恼的心情总是纠缠着他。为了想法摆脱这种心情，他便求助于正义感，求助于自己那真诚与美好的信念——他一向主张恋爱自由嘛！——可是这种求助无济于事。每次求助的结果都是事与愿违，他得出的结论和愚蠢的保姆相同，即认为妹妹做得不当，而弗拉西奇则是拐走了他的妹妹。一想到这里，他就苦恼。

　　母亲整天不出自己的屋，保姆讲话时悄声细语，不断叹气，姨妈天天张罗要走，她的箱子一会儿搬到前厅，一会儿又搬回房间。家里，院里，花园里，静得仿佛屋里停着一个死人。彼得·米海雷奇觉得他姨妈、女佣人，甚至农夫们都带着不可理解的疑惑眼神盯着他，似乎想对他说："您妹妹让人给拐跑了，你怎么也不想个办法？"他责备自己不想办法，可是究竟应当采取什么办法，自己也不知道。

　　如此这般过了六天。第七天——星期日，午饭后——有个人骑着马送来一封信。地址是眼熟的女人笔体："安娜·尼古拉耶夫娜·伊瓦申娜大人敬启"。不知为什么彼得·米海雷奇觉得这信皮、这字体以及潦草的简字，都带有一种挑衅、好斗和自由派的劲头。而女人的自由思想是执拗的、铁石心肠的、残酷无情的……

　　彼得·米海雷奇拿信去见母亲，边走边想："妹妹是宁死也不会向可怜的母亲让步的，是不会请她宽恕的。"

母亲和衣在床上躺着。她见儿子进来，腾地坐起，梳理了一下从包发帽下露出来的花白头发，连忙问道：

"有什么信儿？有什么信儿？"

"派人送来的……"儿子说着，把信递给她。

家里人都忌讳济娜这个名字，甚至连"她"字也不提。谈济娜时总是用无称谓："送来的"、"走了"……母亲认出女儿的笔体，脸色一下子变得难看了，充满怒气，花白的头发又从包发帽下滑了出来。

"不！"她说，双手动了一下，仿佛那封信烫了她的手指头。"不，不，永远办不到！说什么也不行！"

母亲由于悲痛和耻辱而神经质地哭了起来；显然她想看看那封信，可是自尊心阻止了她。彼得·米海雷奇知道自己应该先把那封信拆开读出声来，可是一股从来没有的憎恨突然控制了他；他冲到院里对骑马的人喊了一声：

"你就说，没有回信！没有回信！就这么说，畜生！"

他说着便把来信撕了；泪水涌出眼眶，他觉得自己变得冷酷了，有罪了，不幸了，他带着这种心情，向庄稼地里走去。

他还不满二十八岁，可是人已经发福见胖了，像老年人那样喜欢穿宽松肥大的衣服，还患了气喘症。他全身上下都流露出老单身汉地主的架势。他没有谈过恋爱，没有考虑过结婚，他只爱母亲、妹妹、保姆、园丁瓦西里耶奇；他喜欢美食，喜欢午饭后睡一觉，喜欢议论政事和坐而论道……他当年在大学毕业，如今对那时学业的看法，认为如同十八岁到二十五岁的男青年必须经历的一场不可或缺的服役，现在他脑子里每天想的事与大学、与他所学的各种学问毫无关系。

庄稼地里像雨前似的又热又静。树林里闷热，松树和烂叶散发着浓郁的芳香。彼得·米海雷奇走几步停一下，擦擦汗渗的额头，他查看了自家的越冬作物和春麦，绕过苜蓿牧场，还有两次轰跑了落在丘陵上的鹌鹑和它的小雏鸟。他一直在想，这种无法忍受的局面不能够永远拖下去，总得想个办法把这事了结。不管是用愚蠢的办法还是用野蛮的办法，但非了结不可。

"可是怎么了结呢？应当怎么办呢？"他反问自己，祈求望望天空和树木，好像是向它们求助。

可是天空和树木都默默无语。真诚的信念无济于事，而清醒的理性向他暗示：令人苦恼的问题只能靠愚蠢的办法来解决，今天对待骑马的来者绝非这类做法的最后一次。今后还会发生什么事———想就让人不寒而栗！

他往家里走去时，太阳已经快落下了。现在他觉得问题怎么也解决不了。他不能和既成事实妥协，不妥协又不行，又没有折中的办法。他脱下帽子，挥动手帕，走在路上，离家还有两俄里左右时，听到背后传来一串铃铛声。那是配合得很巧妙很和谐的几种小铃铛发出来的清脆音。只有县警察所梅多夫斯基警长上路时，才会有这种声音。过去他是骠骑兵军官，挥金如土、放纵无度，一身是病，他是彼得·米海雷奇的远方亲戚。他在伊瓦申家里如同自家人，像慈父一般温柔体贴地对待济娜，对她很是赞赏。"我正好去您家，"他说道，马车经过时又对彼得·米海雷奇说："上车吧，我带您回去。"

他在微笑，目光里闪烁着愉快的光芒，显然他还不知道济娜跟弗拉西奇走了，也许有人把这事告诉了他，可是他不信。彼得·米海雷奇觉得自己的处境十分尴尬。

"欢迎光临，"他嘟哝了一句，脸色涨得通红，几乎流出泪来。他不知道应该怎样撒谎，撒些什么。"我很高兴，"他接着说，勉强笑一笑。"不过……济娜走了，我妈在患病。"

"太遗憾了！"警长沉思地望着彼得·米海雷奇。"我本想在您家里待上一个晚上呢！济娜伊达·米海依洛夫娜到哪儿去了？”

"到西尼茨基家去了，她好像要从那儿再去修道院。我也不清楚。"

警长又说了几句话，便调转车头回去了。彼得·米海雷奇往家里走，心惊肉跳地设想，警长一旦知道了真情，他的感觉会是什么样呢。彼得·米海雷奇想象着那种感觉，感受着它，进了家门。

"上帝呵，助我一臂之力吧……"他暗自思忖。

喝晚茶时，餐室里只有姨妈一人坐那里。她脸上的表情和往常一样，仿佛在说自己虽然软弱、没有保护能力，可决不允许任何人期负自己。彼得·米海雷奇在餐桌另一端坐下（他不喜欢姨妈），开始默默地饮茶。

"你妈今天又没有吃饭，"姨妈说。"彼得鲁沙，你应当关照一下。用不吃饭的办法来折磨自己，是减轻不了痛苦的。"

彼得·米海雷奇认为姨妈是狗拿耗子多管闲事，她还把自己的离去与济娜的出走联系在一起，这种做法未免过于荒唐。他本想顶她两句，可是憋住了。就在这憋的过程中，他觉得行动的时机到了，他再不能忍受了。或者是说干就干，或者是趴在地上大喊大叫，用脑袋砸地板。他想象弗拉西奇和济娜，这两个自由派的和自得其乐的人，现在正在某地的枫树下亲吻时，这七天里淤积在他胸中的所有痛苦的愤恨，一下子全都宣泄在弗拉西奇的头上了。

"这个人拐走了我妹妹，"他想。"另一个人就会来谋害我妈妈，再来个人就会放火烧房子或抢劫一空……干这些事时又都披着友情啊、崇高的思想啊、表示同情啊的外衣！"

"不，办不到！"彼得·米海雷奇猛叫一声，拳头敲在桌子上。

他跃身冲出餐室。正好管家人的一匹备了鞍的马在马厩里。他骑上马便向弗拉西奇家驰去。

他胸膛里雷雨交加。他觉得需要干一件非同小可的事、干一件耸人听闻的事，哪怕事后为此后悔一辈子也在所不惜。要不要当面痛骂弗拉西奇卑鄙无耻，要不要给他一记耳光，然后向他提出决斗？可弗拉西奇偏偏不是那号能决斗的人；骂他卑鄙无耻，给他一记耳光，只会让他显得更加不幸，更感内疚。这些不幸的人，一杠子压不出个屁来，——让人最厌恶、最难对付。他们做什么事都不受惩罚。一个不幸的人理应受到责备，可是当他用认罪的深邃目光看你一眼、苦笑一下，然后把脑袋乖乖地伸出来让你去砍，到那时连正义本身也没有足够的勇气下手了。

　　"一不做，二不休。我要当着她的面用马鞭抽他，再损他几句。"彼得·米海雷奇下了决心。

　　他骑马沿着自家的树林和空地走去。他在想象济娜为了表白自己的所作所为，会大谈女权、个性自由，会说在教堂举行婚礼和自由结合并没有什么区别。她会像妇道人家那样来争论自己并不理解的事。最后她大概会问："这关你什么事？你有什么权力干涉？"

　　"是的，我没有权力，"彼得·米海雷奇嘟哝道。"这样更好……越粗暴也就越说明没有权力，事情也就越好办。"

　　天气闷热。成群的蚊子像乌云一般在离地面不高的地方盘旋，凤头麦鸡在旷野里凄切哀叫。一切都预示着雨的来临，可是天空没有一片云。彼得·米海雷奇跨过自家的地界，骑着马沿着平坦的田地驰去。他常走这条路，熟悉路上的每个树丛，每个凹坑。现在，在这黄昏时刻，前面仿佛是一堵黑色的峭壁，其实是座漂亮的教堂，他能想象得出教堂的每个细枝末节，甚至大门上的灰泥和总在院内放牧的几条牛犊。离教堂一俄里的地方，右边是一片黑压压的小树林，那是科尔托维伯爵的领地。小树林后边便是弗拉西奇的田地了。

　　一大片乌云从教堂和伯爵的小树林后边涌了过来，乌云时而亮起苍白的闪电。"情况就是如此！"彼得·米海雷奇心想。"助我一臂之力吧，上帝，助我一臂之力。"

坐骑由于急奔很快就累了，彼得·米海雷奇也累了。夹着雷雨的乌云气势汹汹地望着他，好像要劝他回去。有些让人毛骨悚然。

"我要向他们证实：他们错了！"他给自己打气。"他们会说这是自由恋爱，是个性自由，然而自由在于能够节制而不是放纵情欲。他们的行为是放荡而不是自由！"

眼前到了伯爵家的大池塘，池水在乌云下显得又暗又蓝，从池塘飘来潮气和藻味。木柴铺的路旁长着两棵柳树，一老一新两棵柳树卿卿我我地相互依偎着。大约两周以前，彼得·米海雷奇和弗拉西奇就是在这个地方漫步，还低声吟唱过大学时代的歌曲："如果不恋爱，就会白白糟蹋了年轻的生命……"好悲戚的歌啊！

当彼得·米海雷奇骑着马穿行在小树林里时，雷声不停地轰鸣，树林被风吹得东倒西歪，嗡嗡作响。必须加快赶路。从小树林到弗拉西奇庄园还剩下不到一俄里的草地。这里，道路两旁长着一些老桦树。老桦树活像它们的主人弗拉西奇，忧忧郁郁，样子十分可怜，也像主人一样又细又高。硕大的雨点淅淅沥沥地打在桦树和青草地上；风骤然息了，处处散发出潮湿的土地和杨树的气味。弗拉西奇家的栅栏在前边出现了，栅栏旁边长着一棵黄花刺槐，刺槐也那么细那么高；木桩倒塌的地方可以看到荒芜的果园。

彼得·米海雷奇不再想打耳光和抽鞭子的事了，也不知道自己到弗拉西奇家以后应该干什么。他胆怯了。他为自己也为妹妹感到恐惧，一想到现在就会见到她时心里便紧张。她见哥哥会有什么表现呢？他们俩会谈些什么呢？趁着现在还不迟，是不是回去呢？他一边想一边沿着菩提树的林荫路向房子奔去，绕过一大片丁香丛，他突然看见了弗拉西奇。

弗拉西奇没戴帽子，身上穿着一件印花布汗衫，脚上一双长筒靴子，他正顶着雨弯着腰从房子拐角向门廊走去；一个工友拿着榔头和一箱钉子跟在他身后。他们大概是刚刚修完被风吹得啪啦乱响的护窗板。弗拉西奇上眼瞧见彼得·米海雷奇便停住了脚步。

"是你呀？"他说着，微微一笑。"我看，这挺好。"

"是啊，你瞧，我来了……"彼得·米海雷奇低声地说，用双手抖落身上的雨水。

"是啊，这有多好。我很高兴，"弗拉西奇说道，但没有把手伸过去，大概下不了决心，等待对方向他伸出手来。"这场雨对燕麦很好！"他望了望天空说。

"对。"

他俩没有说话，走进家门。前厅右边有一扇门通向另一间厅，然后便是客厅，右边是一间小屋，管家人冬天住的地方。彼得·米海雷奇和弗拉西奇进了这间小屋。

"你在哪儿赶上雨的？"弗拉西奇问道。

"不远的地方。几乎快到家门口了。"

彼得·米海雷奇在床上坐下。他挺高兴，窗外淅淅沥沥下着雨，屋里黑黑糊糊没有光亮。这样更好，心里不烦，也不必观察对方的脸色。这时他心里已经没有憎恨了，反倒对自己产生了畏惧和厌恶。他觉得这个头开得不得法，所以这次专程来访不会有什么结果。

他俩一言不发地待了一会儿，都做出一副听雨的样子。

"谢谢你，彼得鲁沙，"弗拉西奇清了清嗓子，开了口。"你能来，我非常感激。你做得宽宏大量、行为高尚。这一点我理解，请你相信，我很珍视这一点，请相信我。"

他向窗外瞥了一眼，站在小屋中间，接着说道：

"这事闹得有些诡秘，好像我们成心要瞒着你。一想到我们可能把你得罪了，让你发火了，我们幸福的生活在这些天里就像有了一块污点。现在让我表白一下。我们背地这么做并不是因为我们不够信任你。首先，这发生得突然，当时心血来潮，已不容思考了。其次，这是一件容易招人误解的私情……让第三者，即使像你这样的亲近的人，卷进来也多有不便。最主要的是我们当初在这方面就深深指望你的宽宏大度。你是个最宽宏大度的人，最高尚的人。我对你感激不尽。如果有一天你需要我的命，那就来吧，取走就是了。"

弗拉西奇用一种轻微、喑哑的低音讲话，发出的声音一直是同一个嗡嗡的调调。看来，他很激动。彼得·米海雷奇意识到该他说话了。如果再听下去，再沉默不语，那就等于让自己真正扮演起最为宽宏大度的、最为高尚的傻子角色，而他并非为此来到这里。他迅速地站了起来，叹着气，压低嗓门说道：

"你听着，格里戈里，你知道我过去喜欢你，我没有奢望给妹妹找个比你更好的丈夫；不过发生这件事，太不像话了！一想起来就让人心惊肉跳！"

"为什么要心惊肉跳？"弗拉西奇用颤抖的声音问道。"如果我们做了缺德事儿，那才让人心惊肉跳哪，可是我们并非如此啊！"

"你听着，格里戈里，你知道我这个人没有什么偏见，恕我坦言，我认为你们俩干得太自私了。当然，这话我不会对济娜说，说了会伤她的心，但是你们应当知道：我妈伤心得无法形容。"

"是啊，这是一桩叫人难过的事，"弗拉西奇叹了一口气。"这一点我们估计到了，彼得鲁沙，那我们应当怎么办呢？如果你的行为会使某人伤心，那还不等于行为本身是为非作歹。没办法！你的每一个严肃的步骤必然会使某人痛苦。如果你去为自由而战，也会使你母亲伤心。没办法！谁把自己亲人的安逸摆在高于一切的地位，谁就得完全放弃崇高的生活。"

窗外一道明亮的闪电划过了天空，这道光亮仿佛改变了弗拉西奇的思路。他在彼得·米海雷奇身旁坐下，开口讲起完全不相干的事。

"我呀，彼得鲁沙，全心全意崇敬你妹妹，"他说。"过去我每次去你家，总觉得自己仿佛是去朝圣，我真的为济娜祈祷祝福。如今我的敬仰之情与日俱增。她对于我来说，高于妻子！高于妻子！（弗拉西奇挥了一下手）她是我的神灵。自从她搬过来，每次我走进家门时就如同走进教堂。她是一位少有的、不寻常的、最高尚的女人！"

"好哇，他又弹起自己那套陈词滥调了！"彼得·米海雷奇心里想，他不喜欢"女人"这个词。

"你们二人为什么不明媒正娶地结婚呢？"他问道。"你离婚，你妻子想要多少钱？"

"七万五。"

"多了些。如果讨讨价呢？"

"她一文也不会让。她呀，老弟，可是个非常可怕的女人！"弗拉西奇叹了一口气。"过去我从来没有对你讲过她，一想起她来就恶心，如今趁这个机会，我讲给你听。我是在一种美好的、真诚的感情冲动下娶了她。如果你要知道详情的话，我可以告诉你：我们团里有个营长，他和一个十八岁的黄花大姑娘发生了关系，其实是他勾引了她，和她鬼混了两个多月，便把她甩了。她呀，老弟，处境太惨了。她没脸回家去见爹妈，再说爹妈也不会收留她，让情夫给抛弃了，她恨不得到兵营里以卖身为业。团里的兄弟气愤极了。他们并非圣贤，不过这种卑鄙勾当未免让人看不下去。再说团里的人对这个营长都恨之入骨。为了让他丢人现眼，你明白吗，所有恨他的准尉和少尉们便开始自愿捐献来救济这个可怜的姑娘。对啦，就这样，当我们这些下级军官凑到一个商量，有的捐五卢布，有的捐十卢布，当时我的头脑一热，觉得形势太适合于我干件侠义之举。我风风火火地去找那个姑娘，用一些热情的话表示对她的同情。我去找她的路上，以及后来与她谈话时，我都在热烈地爱着她,把她看作是个被侮辱被损害的人。是的……事情就是这么发展的,过了一周我就向她求婚。长官和同事们都认为我娶这样一个女人和军官的荣誉不相容。这就让我更加发火。于是我写了一封长信,你明白吗,说我这种做法应该用金字载入团的史册中,等等等等。我把信寄给了团长,把抄件分别寄给了战友们。当然喽,我大发雷霆,少不了讲些不中听的话。我被劝导离开团队。我的信稿还放在某处,将来给你看看。我是怀着激情写的。你会看到我经受过何等真诚的、光明的时刻。我提出退役,便和妻子来到了这里。父亲身后留下几笔债务,我没有钱,可是我妻子从第一天起就乱交朋友,专事打扮和玩牌赌钱,我不得不把庄园抵押出去。她呀,你明白吗,过着不好的生活,我的邻居当中只有你一个人不是她的情夫。过了两年,我把抵押所得和当时全部钱财都给了她,于是她就搬到城里去了。是啊……如今,我每年付给她一千二百卢布。她是个非常可怕的女人!老弟,有一种苍蝇把蛆下在蜘蛛背上,怎么也甩不掉;蛆长在蜘蛛的身上,吸吮它心脏里的血。这个女人也同样傍在我的身上,吸我心脏里的血。她恨我,瞧不起我,因为我干了一桩蠢事,也就是娶了像她这样一个女人。她把我的侠义之心看成是卑微之举。她说:'聪明人把我抛弃了,蠢货把我捡来了。'她认为只有可怜的白痴才能像我这样干。老弟,真让我痛不欲生啊!总之,老弟,我附带再说一句,命运太欺压我了,快把我压扁了。"

彼得·米海雷奇在听弗拉西奇倾诉,心里疑惑地反问自己:这个家伙又有什么东西值得济娜如此爱他?他已非青年,四十一岁了,长得又瘦又干瘪,窄胸脯,长鼻子,胡子花白。他说话瓮声瓮气,笑的时候一脸病容,交谈时总是难看地摇晃双臂。他既没有矫健的身体,也没有阳刚之美;既没有上流社会人的风度,又无普通人的风趣。论外表,他无光彩也无定型。他穿戴没有品位,家庭环境没有生气,对诗歌绘画毫无兴趣,因为它们"不能解决当前的问题"，也就是说，他对诗歌绘画一窍不通；音乐打动不了他的心。在经营方面他也是个废物。他把庄园弄得一塌糊涂，而且抵押出去了，第二次抵押他要付百分之十二的利息，另外，他还有一万卢布的欠条。每逢到了付利息或是给他妻子汇款时，他就向所有人借钱，他那副表情仿佛家里失了火，这时他已昏头涨脑，五卢布就把储备准备过冬的全部柴火卖了，一垛干草卖了三卢布，然后用果园的木栅栏或者暖房的木框架来生炉子。他家的牧场被猪给祸害了，农家的牲口在树林的苗圃里乱窜，随着冬天的到来，老树剩下的越来越少；菜地里和果园里乱扔着养蜂的用具和生锈的铁桶。他没有才能也没有天赋，连普通人过日子的能力也没有。他在日常生活中是个幼稚的、软弱的、容易上当、常常受人欺负的人，所以庄稼人不是平白无故地叫他"傻帽儿"。

他是个自由派分子，在县里被视为"左倾"人物，可是他的表现无精打采。他的自由思想没有新鲜玩意儿，也没有激情，无论是气愤、是发火，还是高兴，他的表情都是一个模样，萎靡不振，引不起人们的注意。即使在极度亢奋的时刻，他也不抬头，总是弯着腰。然而最枯燥的莫过于他把自己一些美好的、真诚的想法表达得像是平庸无奇的陈旧过时的东西。每当他带着深思熟虑的样子慢条斯理地阐释真诚而光明的时刻，阐释最美好的年华，或者赞扬过去和现在一向走在社会前边的青年人，或者谴责俄国人到了三十岁就穿起长袍，并把抚养他们的母亲的遗训忘在脑后时，他的话就令人想起某些往事，某些早已从书本上读过的内容。如果你留在他家过夜，他就会把皮萨列夫或者达尔文的书摆到你的床头茶几上。如果你说这本书已经读过，那么他就会再去取一本杜勃罗留波夫的著作来。

这在县城里便被说成是自由派思想，很多人把这种思想视为没有害处的不伤大雅的怪行为，但正是这种思想让他倒了大霉。这种思想对于他来说正像他刚刚讲过的那种蛆：它牢牢地傍在他身上，吸吮他心脏里的血。过去，他办了陀思妥耶夫斯基笔下的那种莫名其妙的婚事，他用拙劣的、难认的笔体写过拖泥带水但颇有激情的信，还保留了抄件，他还一再被误解，一再进行解释，一再遭受失望；然后便是欠债，第二次抵押，给妻子寄生活费，月月借钱——这对任何人，无论是对己还是对人，都没有益处。到了今天，和过去一样，他还是匆匆瞎忙，想立奇功，乱管别人闲事；和过去一样，一有机会便写长信，抄留副本，发表令人厌倦的有关村社、发展手工业，或者创办干酪厂的千篇一律的讲话——谈话雷同，这些话仿佛不是从活人的脑子里想出来的，而是用机器批量生产的。最后，又闹成和济娜的丑剧，还不知道怎样收场呢！

其实，济娜妹妹还年轻——她才二十二岁——长相漂亮，仪表优雅，天生喜闹；她好笑，好说话，好斗嘴，她是个非常喜欢音乐的姑娘；她对穿戴、对读书、对于布置舒适的环境都在行，她家里绝对忍受不了这样的小屋子，满屋臭皮鞋和廉价伏特加酒味。她也是个自由派分子，但她的自由思想里让人感觉到有过剩的精力。有年富力强的、勇敢少女的好胜心，她热烈地渴望自己比别人好，比别人别致……她怎么会爱上弗拉西奇呢，怎么会发生这种事呢？

"他是堂吉诃德，顽固的狂人、疯子，"彼得·米海雷奇心想。"可是她呢，她和我一样是个疲沓的软弱的听话的人……我和她很容易被人降伏，甚至不会抗拒。她爱上了他，不管怎么说，难道我不爱她吗……"

彼得·米海雷奇认为弗拉西奇是个正直的好人，只是目光狭窄，做事片面。在他的焦躁不安或痛苦中，实际在他整个一生中，既看不到近期的也看不到长远的崇高目标，他只看到枯燥和生活无着。他的忘我精神以及被弗拉西奇称之为侠义行为或真诚冲动之举，在他眼中只不过是毫无意义地浪费精力，毫无用处地乱打空枪，而且还耗费了相当多的弹药。至于弗拉西奇狂热地相信自己思维的非凡真诚和一贯正确，在他看来则是幼稚的，甚至是病态的；说到弗拉西奇一生中居然能够把无聊的琐事和崇高的事业混淆起来，如他愚蠢的婚事，他还把这事看成是侠义行为，再如后来和女人们厮混，他认为那是某种胜利，——这些事也实在令人无法理解。

但，不管怎么说，彼得·米海雷奇就是喜欢弗拉西奇，感觉到他身上有一股劲儿，而且不知为什么他从来没有勇气反驳他的意见。

弗拉西奇凑到他身边坐下，想趁着潇潇的雨声和茫茫的昏暗讲讲心里的话。他清了清嗓子，准备大讲一下和自己的婚姻经历一样的事，可是彼得·米海雷奇听不下去了，他一想到马上就会见到自己的妹妹，心里就忐忑不安。

"是啊，你这一辈子总是不走运，"他温和地说。"对不起，不过我们已经离开了主题。我们谈的不是那件事。"

"对，对，确实如此。咱们还是回到主题上来吧！"弗拉西奇说着便站了起来。"我告诉你，彼得鲁沙，我们对得起良心。我们没有在教堂举行婚礼，但我们的婚姻完全合法，——这事不用我证明，也不用你听我解释。你和我一样，是主张自由思想的，谢天谢地，咱们在这方面不可能有分歧。至于谈到我们的未来嘛，你也不必为此担心。我会拼死拼活日夜不停地干活儿，——总之，我会尽心尽力让济娜过得幸福。她的生活会异常美满。你会问我是否能办得到，老弟，我能！当一个人无时无刻考虑同一件事时，他就不难达到所期望的目的。好了，咱们去看看济娜吧！应当让她高兴高兴。"

彼得·米海雷奇的心怦怦跳了起来。他起身跟在弗拉西奇后边走向前厅，从前厅又进了客厅。在这间阴森的大厅里只有一架钢琴和很长一排有铜质装饰的旧式椅子，椅子上从来没有一个人坐过。钢琴上点着一支蜡烛。他俩从客厅默默走向餐室。餐室同样宽敞和不舒适，餐室中央摆着一张圆桌，它是由两个半圆桌组合起来的，有六条粗腿，只有一支蜡烛。座钟摆在红色的大钟盒里，像个神龛，时钟指着两点半。

弗拉西奇推开通向隔壁的门，唤了一声：

"济诺奇卡，彼得鲁沙来咱们家了！"

立刻响起一阵急促的脚步声，济娜走进餐室。高高的个儿，丰满的身材，脸色非常苍白，仍然是彼得·米海雷奇最后一次在家里见到她的样子——穿着黑裙子、红上衣，腰带上有个大扣环。她用一条胳膊抱住哥哥，在他的太阳穴上吻了一下。

"好大的雷雨呀！"她说。"刚才格里戈里出去了，整栋房子里只有我一个人。"

她没有窘态，像在家里一样，坦诚地望着哥哥，彼得·米海雷奇盯着她，也不感到难为情了。

"你可从来没有怕过雷雨呵。"他说着便在桌旁坐下。

"是的，可是这儿房间太大，房子太老，一打雷整栋房子就像摆满盘子碗的立柜似的震得叮当乱响。其实这栋房子很讨人喜欢。"她坐哥哥对面接着说道。"这儿，每个房间都有值得回忆的往事。你设想一下，格里戈里的爷爷就是在我住的房间里开枪自杀的。"

"到了八月，有了钱，我就把果园里的厢房修理一下。"弗拉西奇说。

"不知为什么每逢打雷下雨时我就会想起爷爷来，"济娜接着说了下去。"当年就在这间餐室里，活活把一个人给打死了。"

"这是真事，"弗拉西奇证实了一句，然后用大眼睛看了看彼得·米海雷奇。"四十年代，有个叫奥里维耶的法国人承租了这个庄园。他女儿的肖像我至今还扔在我们的阁楼上。她是个非常可爱的姑娘。据我父亲对我说，这个奥里维耶瞧不起俄国人，认为俄国人不懂礼貌，百般刁难他们。比方说，神甫经过他住的庄园时，他要求神甫在半俄里外就脱帽；又如，当奥里维耶一家坐车穿行在村子里时，教堂要敲钟。对待农奴和小小老百姓，他当然更是飞扬跋扈了。有一天，一个云游四方的俄罗斯善良的青年人从这儿路过。这个人有点儿像果戈理小说中的神学院的学员霍马·布鲁特。他要求在此地借宿，没想到管家人看中了他，就把他留在账房里干活儿了。关于这件事有很多说法。有的人说这个学员煽动农民闹事，另外一些人说奥里维耶的千金好像是爱上了他。我也不知道哪种说法确实，只知道有一天，一个暮色迷人的傍晚，奥里维耶把他叫到这儿来，对他进行了审讯，然后下令打他。你知道吗，奥里维耶本人坐这张桌子后边，洋洋得意地豪饮，而几个马车夫在痛打这个神学院学员。大概对他用了刑。天快亮时，这个学员受尽折磨断了气，他的尸体也不知被藏到哪儿去了。有人说把他扔进科尔托维奇家的池塘了。出了人命官司，可是法国人给了相干的人几千卢布，自己便扬长去了阿尔萨斯了。再说，他的租期也快满了，这个官司也就这么不了了之。"

"这帮混蛋！"济娜骂了一句，身子一颤。

"我爹清清楚楚地记得奥里维耶和他的女儿。说那个漂亮姑娘长得出众，但性子古怪。我估计那学员两样事都干了，既煽动了农民闹事，也迷住了小姐的心。说不定他根本不是什么神学院的学员，而是隐姓埋名的人。"

济娜陷入沉思，看来，神学院学员和法国漂亮姑娘的事使她想入非非。彼得·米海雷奇觉得在这一周里，妹妹的外表毫无变化，只是脸色稍显苍白。她的目光同往常一样，还是那么平静，仿佛是随同哥哥一起来弗拉西奇家做客。不过彼得·米海雷奇觉得自己却发生了一种变化。的确，过去妹妹住在家里时，他和她什么事都能谈，如今他连"你在这儿过得怎么样？"这么普普通通的一句话也不敢问。这个问题会让人难堪，而且没有必要。想必她身上也发生同样的变化。她不急于打听母亲和家里的事，不提自己和弗拉西奇的浪漫史；她不为自己辩解，也不说自由同居比教堂主持的婚礼好，她不激动，她安安静静地在思考奥里维耶的事……怎么会一下子提起奥里维耶来了？

"你们俩的肩膀都让雨淋湿了，"济娜说了一句，莞尔一笑，她为哥哥和弗拉西奇有这么一点点相像的地方而动情了。

彼得·米海雷奇的处境使自己感到十分可悲又非常可怕。他想起自己那栋变得空荡了的家，遮盖起来的钢琴，还有济娜那间如今已无人进去的明亮的小房间；他想起果园的林荫路上再没有她的小脚印了，晚茶前再也不会有人爽朗地笑着去游泳。那从童年时代起越来越眷恋的东西，那往日坐在闷热的教室或大学讲堂里喜欢思考的东西，清晰、洁净、欢乐，那使他的家充满生机和光明的一切，已经一去不复返了，消逝了，并和一个莫名其妙的营长、一个宽宏大量的准尉、一个淫荡的骚娘儿们、一个开枪自杀的祖父；这些粗俗的龌龊的故事搅在一起了……在这个时候若提母亲，或认为过去的日子可以回来，那就是不想理解已经一清二楚的事。

彼得·米海雷奇眼中盈满了泪水，放在桌子上的手抖动起来。济娜猜出哥哥的心事，她的眼睛也红了，闪着泪光。

"格里戈里，你过来一下！"她对弗拉西奇说。

他们两人靠近窗户，悄悄地在商量着什么。彼得·米海雷奇看着弗拉西奇向妹妹弯下身去的样子，看着她望着他的那种眼神。他再次明白了：米已成粥，定局已无法改变，什么话也不用说了。济娜走出屋去。

"情况就是这样，老弟，"经过一阵沉默，弗拉西奇一边搓手一边笑盈盈地开了口。"刚才我听说我们的日子过得幸福，这话不过是借用文学语言的描绘而已。其实我们还没有尝到幸福的滋味。济娜脑子里一直在想念你，想念母亲，她心里难受；我看她那样子心里也难受。她天性我行我素，无惧无畏，可是你要知道，她还是不习惯这种生活，不容易啊，再说她还年轻。女佣称呼她小姐，这本来算不了什么，可是她却坐立不安。情况就是如此啊，老弟。"

济娜端来满满一盘草莓。一个外表老老实实、呆头呆脑的小侍女跟在她身后。她把一罐牛奶放在桌子上，深深地鞠了个躬……她的神态和这里的古老家具有些相称，也是那么僵硬、无趣。

已经听不见雨声了。彼得·米海雷奇吃着草莓，弗拉西奇和济娜默默地看着他。临到该讲些无用的，但又不能不讲的话的时候，他们三个人都感觉到启齿的重量。彼得·米海雷奇的眼眶里又盈满了泪水，他把身边的盘子挪开，说该回家了，否则太晚了，说不定又会下起雨来。这时，济娜出于礼貌问问家人的情况和谈谈自己的新生活。

"家里怎样？"她匆匆地问了一句，她那苍白的脸庞抽搐起来。"妈妈怎样？"

"你知道妈妈……"彼得·米海雷奇回答时，没有看她。

"彼得鲁沙，你对发生的事情考虑过很久，"她抓住哥哥的衣袖，说了一句。他立刻明白了，她是多么难于说出口来，"你考虑了很久，你告诉我，能指望妈妈有朝一日和格里戈里和解吗……和这种状况妥协吗？"

她紧挨着哥哥，面对面地站着，哥哥这时才惊奇地发现，妹妹是这么俊秀，他过去似乎没有注意到这一点，至于妹妹长得像妈，贤淑、文雅，住在弗拉西奇家，而且和弗拉西奇与呆头呆脑的侍女、与六条腿的桌子在一起，住在活活打死一个人的房子里，现在又不会随他一起回家，而留住在这里，——他觉得这一切未免过于荒谬绝伦了。

"你是了解妈妈的……"他没有回答妹妹的问话。"我认为应当顾及……应当采取一点办法，是不是请求她宽恕……"

"若请求她宽恕——那就等于让我们做出假象，表示我们行为不轨。为了安慰妈妈，我可以撒谎，但这样做不会有什么结果。我是了解妈妈的。嗨，顺其自然吧！"济娜说完了，她把最伤心的话已经说了出来，变得轻松愉快了。我们再等五年，十年，再忍受一段时间，到了时候，就听天由命吧！

她挽着哥哥的胳膊，经过昏暗的前厅时她把头紧偎在哥哥的肩膀上。

他们走下门廊。彼得·米海雷奇道了别，上了马，缓缓地走了；济娜与弗拉西奇陪着送他一程。四周静悄悄暖烘烘，一片芳香的干草味；天空云隙之间星星熠熠闪闪。当年见过那么多凄惨世面的弗拉西奇的老果园，现在隐没在黑暗中沉睡，不知为什么穿过果园时让人有点伤感。

"今天午饭后，我和济娜真正过了一段心旷神怡的时刻！"弗拉西奇说。"我给她读了一篇关于移民问题的好文章。老弟，你读一读！你一定要读！那篇论文好在诚实上。我忍不住便给编辑写了一封信，请他们转给作者。我只写了一行字：'谨致谢意并紧握真诚的手！'"

彼得·米海雷奇本来想说："请你别乱管与你无关的事了！"——但他没有吱声。

弗拉西奇走在右边的马镫旁，济娜走在左边，两个人似乎都忘记该回家了，天气潮湿，离科尔托维奇家的小树林已经不远了。彼得·米海雷奇总觉得他们在期待他说什么话，究竟什么话他们自己也不知道。这时他极其可怜他们。现在，当他们俩带着百依百顺的样子，沉思地走在马身旁时，他深信他们并不幸福，也不会幸福，他意识到自己无力相助，他的精神好像一下崩溃了，这时他觉得只要能摆脱沉重的恻隐之心，作任何牺牲他已在所不惜。

"以后我会常来你们这儿住。"他说。

这话好像是表示让步，他感到不满意。所以当他们在科尔托维奇家的小树林附近停下脚步告别时，他向济娜弯下身去，触到她的肩头，说了一句。

"济娜，你是对的。你做得好！"

为了不再多说，也别哭出声来，他拍打了一下马，向小树林驰去。到了暗处，他回头望了一眼，看见弗拉西奇和济娜正走在回家的路上——弗拉西奇迈着大步，济娜紧跟在他身旁，移动着急促跳动的碎步——他们兴高采烈地在谈论着什么。

"我简直是个老太婆了，"彼得·米海雷奇心想。"我来的目的是要解决问题，结果反而被我弄得更糊涂。唉，管他呢！"

他心里很难过。出了小树林时，他让马慢慢地走，靠近池塘时，便停了下来。他想一动不动地坐一会儿，考虑考虑。月亮正在升起，池塘对岸的水面映出一条红色的光影。远处一阵阵响起闷雷声。彼得·米海雷奇的眼睛一眨不眨地凝视着池水，想象妹妹那绝望的样子，那痛苦苍白的脸，还有那双为了在外人面前掩饰自己的屈辱而无泪的眼睛。他想象妹妹怀了孕，母亲逝世，为她举行葬礼，济娜的恐惧……又高傲又迷信的老太太只能悲伤欲绝。未来的种种可怕的画面在他眼前黑黝黝的水面上浮现出来，他在几个苍白的妇女形象当中看见自己：缺乏毅力、懦弱无能、一脸内疚……

离池塘右岸大约百步左右的地方，有一个黑乎乎的东西，一动也不动：那是人还是高大树桩？彼得·米海雷奇想起那个被人打死后抛进这个池塘里的神学院学员来。

"奥里维耶干得没有一点儿人性，但不管怎么说，他毕竟把问题解决了，可是我什么也没能解决，反而弄乱套了。"他死死盯着那个幽灵一般的黑东西，心里想。"他怎么想就怎么做，而我讲的和做的并不是我所想的，其实，我大概也不知道自己究竟是怎么想的……"

（高莽　译）

万　　卡

　　万卡·茹科夫，九岁的男孩，三个月前被送到鞋匠阿利亚欣这儿当学徒，圣诞节夜里没有躺下睡觉。等到鞋匠夫妇和师傅们去做晨课以后，他从老板的柜橱里拿出一小瓶墨水和一只笔尖生锈的笔，把一张皱巴巴的纸在自己面前摊开，写了起来。他在写第一个字母之前，几次胆怯地回头看了看门口和窗户，还斜眼瞟了一下昏暗的圣像，圣像两边各摆着一排码满鞋楦头的架子，于是若断若续地叹了口气。那张纸放在一条长凳上，他自己跪在长凳的前边。

　　"亲爱的爷爷，康斯坦丁·马卡雷奇！"他写道。"给你写封信。祝您圣诞节好，愿上帝保佑你事事如意。我没有父亲，没有妈妈，我就剩下你一个人了。"

　　万卡把目光转向黑暗的窗户，窗上闪动着蜡烛映射出的他的影子，不禁清楚地想起给日瓦列夫老爷家当守夜人的自己的祖父康斯坦丁·马卡雷奇的模样。这是个短小精瘦而又异常活泼好动的老头儿，六十五岁上下，有一张总是带笑的面孔和一双迷糊的醉眼。白天他在仆人厨房里睡觉，还有就是和厨娘们逗笑，夜里呢，裹上宽大的皮袄，围着庄园走来走去，敲打手里的梆子。他身后跟着两条狗，全都耷拉着脑袋，一条是老母狗卡什坦卡，另一条是公狗泥鳅。给它起这个绰号，是因为它毛色骏黑，身子像银鼠一样细长。这条泥鳅显得非常恭顺和温和，不论看自家人，还是看外人，都是一副谄媚的神情，不过，外表往往是靠不住的。

在它恭顺而谄媚的外表下面，隐藏着极为阴险狡诈的用心。谁也不如它那么善于及时潜到人的背后，在腿上咬一口，或是溜进冷藏室偷嘴，或是偷吃农民的鸡。它不止一次让人打伤后腿，有两次还被吊了起来，每星期都会被人打得半死，可他总能死里逃生。

现在，祖父大概正站在大门口，眯缝着眼睛看村里教堂的鲜红色的窗户，同时跺着毡靴，和仆人们逗笑。他巡夜用的梆子就系在腰带上。他冻得直拍手，瑟缩着身子，东掐女仆一把，西捏厨娘一下，发出老头儿的嘻嘻笑声。

"咱们吸点儿鼻烟，怎么样？"他说，把烟盒递到女人们面前。女人们闻了闻鼻烟，不停地打喷嚏。祖父无比开心，快活地哈哈大笑，叫道：

"擦掉，冻上啦！"

又让两只狗闻鼻烟。卡什坦卡打喷嚏，皱鼻子，委屈地走到一边。泥鳅出于恭敬，没有打喷嚏，而是摇晃尾巴。天气好极了。空气清新洁净，没有一点儿风。夜很黑，可是却看得见整个村子和村里的白屋顶、烟囱里冒出的缕缕轻烟、被霜染成白色的树木和雪堆。天空布满了愉快的闪烁的星星，银河显得十分清晰，仿佛节前被雪擦洗过似的……

万卡叹了口气，用笔蘸了一下墨水，继续写道：

"昨天我挨打了。老板抓着我的头发，把我揪到院子里拿做鞋用的皮条狠狠揍了我一顿，因为我摇他们摇篮里的孩子时，不小心睡着了。上星期老板娘让我收拾一条鲱鱼，我先从鱼尾收拾，她就抓起鲱鱼，用鱼头戳我的脸。师傅们老是取笑我，支使我去小酒馆买酒，叫我偷老板的黄瓜，而老板逮住什么就拿什么打我。吃的东西就更没什么啦。早上是面包，中午是稀粥，到了晚上还是面包，而茶和汤什么的，只有老板他们自己才大口地喝呢。他们还让我睡在过道里，他们的小孩一哭，我就一点儿都不能睡了，就得去摇摇篮。亲爱的爷爷，可怜可怜我吧，把我从这儿带回家，带回村子吧，我活不了啦……我给你磕头，我一辈子求上帝保佑你，把我从这儿带走吧，要不我就死啦……"

万卡嘴角一撇，用黑黑乎乎的拳头揉揉眼睛，哽哽咽咽地哭了。

"我给你搓烟叶，"他继续写道。"为你祈祷，要是我做错事，你抽我的筋扒我的皮。要是你觉得我没事可做，那我就求管家看在基督的分上让我去擦皮鞋，要不就让我代替费季科去做牧童。亲爱的爷爷，我活不了啦，就剩死路一条了。我本想靠两条腿跑回村子，可是没有靴子，天太冷，我害怕。等我长大了，我会为这事儿养活你，不许别人欺负你，等你死后，我就祈祷，让你的灵魂安息，就像为我娘佩拉格娅祈祷一样。"

"莫斯科是个大城市。房子都是老爷们的，马很多，却没有羊，狗也不凶。这儿的孩子们不举着星星灯笼走来走去，不让人随便去唱诗班唱歌，有一次我看见一家铺子的窗户里卖鱼钩，拴着线，能钓各种各样的鱼，很值的，甚至还有一种能经得住一普特重的鲶鱼呢。还看见有的铺子卖各式各样老爷们用的枪，每支怕是要一百多卢布……肉铺里有黑琴鸡，有花尾棒鸡，有兔子，可是从什么地方打到的，伙计们是不会说的。

"亲爱的爷爷，等老爷家摆上挂着礼物的圣诞树，给我拿一个包着金纸的核桃，藏到那只小绿箱子里。去跟奥莉加·伊格纳季耶夫娜要，就说是给万卡的。"

万卡猛地叹了口气，又目不转睛地瞧着窗子。他想起，祖父总是去树林里给老爷家砍圣诞树，也总是带着孙子一起去。那是多么快乐的时刻呀！祖父嘴里发出嘎嘎的叫声。每次砍树前，祖父总要先抽一阵子烟斗，闻老半天鼻烟，再嘲笑一会儿冻得发僵的万卡……小云杉披着厚厚的白霜，一动也不动，等待谁先大祸临头。突然，有一只兔子飞快地从雪堆之间跑过去……祖父禁不住喊叫：

"抓住，抓住，抓住！嘿，鬼东西！"

祖父把砍下的小云杉拖回老爷的家里，大家一齐动手装饰它……忙得最欢的是奥莉加·伊格纳季耶夫娜小姐，她是万卡最喜欢的人。当万卡的母亲佩拉格娅还活着，在老爷家做女仆的时候，奥莉加·伊格纳季耶夫娜常常给万卡水果糖吃，因为无事可做，就教他读书，写字，数数，从一数到一百，甚至教他跳卡德里尔舞。而当佩拉格娅一死，孤儿万卡就被送到仆人厨房里和祖父住在一起，后来又从厨房送到莫斯科阿利亚欣鞋匠这里……

"来吧，亲爱的爷爷，"万卡继续写道。"求你看在基督上帝分儿上，带我离开这儿吧。你可怜可怜我这个不幸的孤儿吧，要不他们全都打我，我太想吃东西啦，也快闷死啦，我总是哭。前两天，老板用鞋楦头砸我的脑袋，结果我昏倒了，好不容易才醒过来。我的日子没指望了，连狗都不如……还有替我问候奥莉加·伊格纳季耶夫娜、独眼儿叶戈尔卡、马车夫，我的手风琴谁也别给。你的孙子伊万·茹科夫，亲爱的爷爷来吧。"

万卡把写满字的纸叠成四折，装入前一天花一戈买的信封里……他稍微想了想，用笔尖蘸了蘸墨水，写下了地址：

寄给村里爷爷收

然后他搔搔头，想了想，又补写上"康斯坦丁·马卡雷奇"。他对写信时没人打扰感到满意，于是戴上帽子，没穿皮袄，只穿一件衬衫跑到街上……

前几天他问过肉铺的伙计，他们说，把信放到信筒里，而信筒里的信就会由醉醺醺的马车夫赶着挂有叮当响的铃铛的邮车分送到世界各地。万卡跑到最近处的一个邮筒，把那封宝贵的信塞进筒口……

他陶醉于甜蜜的希望之中，一个小时过后，沉沉地睡着了……

他梦见一个炉灶。祖父坐在炉台上，耷拉着两只脚丫子，给厨娘们念信……泥鳅在炉台旁边走来走去，摇晃着尾巴……

（王景生 译）

坏　孩　子

　　伊凡·伊凡诺维支·拉普庚是一个风采可观的青年，安娜·绥米诺夫娜·山勃列支凯耶是一个尖鼻子的少女，走下峻急的河岸来，坐在长椅上面了。长椅摆在水边，在茂密的新柳丛子里。这是一个好地方。如果坐在那里罢，就躲开了全世界，看见的只有鱼儿和在水面上飞跑的水蜘蛛了。这青年们是用钓竿，网兜，蚯蚓罐子以及别的捕鱼家伙武装起来了的。他们一坐下，立刻来钓鱼。

　　"我很高兴，我们到底只有两个人了，"拉普庚开口说，望着四近。"我有许多话要和您讲呢，安娜·绥米诺夫娜……很多……当我第一次看见您的时候……鱼在吃您的了……我才明白自己是为什么活着的，我才明白应当贡献我诚实的勤劳生活的神像是在哪里了……好一条大鱼……在吃哩……我一看见您，这才识得了爱，我爱得您要命！且不要拉起来……等它再吃一点……请您告诉我，我的宝贝，我对您起誓：我希望能是彼此之爱——不的，不是彼此之爱，我不配，我想也不敢想——倒是……您拉呀！"

　　安娜·绥米诺夫娜把那拿着钓竿的手，赶紧一扬，叫起来了。空中闪着一条银绿色的小鱼。

　　"我的天，一条鲈鱼！啊呀，啊呀……快点！脱出了！"

　　鲈鱼脱出了钓钩，在草地上向着它故乡的元素那里一跳……扑通——已经在水里了！

　　追去捉鱼的拉普庚，却替代了鱼，错捉了安娜·绥米诺夫娜的手，又错放在他的嘴唇上……她想缩回那手去，然而已经来不及了：他们的嘴唇又不知怎么一来，接了一个吻。这全自然而然的。接吻又接连地来了第二个，于是立誓，盟心……幸福的一瞬息！在这人间世，绝对的幸福是没有的。幸福大抵在本身里就有毒，或者给外来的什么来毒一下。这一回也如此。当这两个青年人正在接吻的时候，突然起了笑声。他们向水里一望，僵了：河里站着一个水齐着腰的赤条条的孩子。这是中学生珂略，安娜·绥米诺夫娜的弟弟。他站在水里面，望着他们俩，阴险的微笑着。

"嗳哈……你们亲嘴。"他说。"好！我告诉妈妈去。"

"我希望您要做正人君子……"拉普庚红着脸，吃吃地说。"偷看是下流的，告发可是卑劣，讨厌，胡闹的……我看您是高尚的正人君子……"

"您给我一个卢布，我就不说了！"那正人君子回答道。"要是，不，我去说出来。"

拉普庚从袋子里掏出一个卢布来，给了珂略。他把卢布捏在稀湿的拳头里，吹一声口哨，浮开去了。但年轻的他们俩，从此也不再接吻了。

后来拉普庚又从街上给珂略带了一副颜料和一个皮球来，他的姊姊也献出了她所有的丸药的空盒。而且还得送他雕着狗头的硬袖的扣子。这是很讨坏孩子喜欢的，因为想讹得更多，他就开始监视了。只要拉普庚和安娜·绥米诺夫娜到什么地方去，他总是到处跟踪着他们。他没有一刻放他们只有他们俩。

"流氓，"拉普庚咬着牙齿，说。"这么小，已是一个大流氓！他将来还会怎样呢？！"

整一个七月，珂略不给这可怜的情人们得到一点安静。他用告发来恐吓，监视，并且索诈东西；他永是不满意，终于说出要表的话来了。于是只好约给他一个表。

有一回，正在用午餐，刚刚是吃蛋片的时候，他忽然笑了起来，用一只眼睛使着眼色，问拉普庚道："我说罢？怎么样？"

拉普庚满脸通红，错作蛋片，咬了饭巾了。安娜·绥米诺夫娜跳起来，跑进隔壁的屋子去。

年轻的他们俩停在这样的境遇上，一直到八月底，就是拉普庚终于向安娜·绥米诺夫娜求婚的日子。这是怎样的一个幸福的日子呵！他向新娘子的父母说明了一切，得到许可之后，拉普庚就立刻跑到园里去寻珂略。他一寻到他，就高兴得流下眼泪来，一面拉住这坏孩子的耳朵。也在找寻珂略的安娜·绥米诺夫娜，恰恰也跑到了，便拉住了他的那一只耳朵。大家必须看着的，是两个爱人的脸上，显出怎样的狂喜来，当珂略哭着讨饶的时候：

"我的乖乖，我的好人，我再也不敢了！阿唷，阿唷，饶我！"

两个人后来说，他们俩秘密的相爱了这么久，能像在扯住这坏孩子的耳朵的一瞬息中，所感到的那样的幸福，那样的透不过气来的大欢喜，是从来没有的。

（鲁迅　译）

安娜套在颈子上

一

　　他们结过婚后，连一点点茶食都不曾吃；这一对快乐的人只喝了一杯香槟酒，提起行李，便匆匆地跑到车站来了。他们不曾开喜宴，不曾奏音乐，更不曾举行跳舞会，只是预备坐火车到一百五十里外的礼拜堂里去做祷告，来替代一切繁文缛节。人们都称赞这个做法很对，全说莫德士是德高望重之人，不像一些浮浪子弟，只知道虚事铺张；其实以五十二岁的老头子，而和十八岁的大姑娘结婚，如果是奏起音乐来，一定会发出愁惨之音的。人们又说，莫德士究竟是有声誉的人，就连结婚，也要使他年幼的妻子知道，是以宗教和道德为前提了。

　　人们看到这一对快乐的人上车。一群亲戚和同事，拿着酒杯在手里，预备在车开时欢呼"一路平安！"新娘子的父亲包特戴了一顶高帽子，穿了教员的服装，已经喝过了酒，面色灰白，举起头来向着车窗，拿着杯子在手里，恳求的声音说：

　　"安娜！安娜！安娜！一句话！"

　　安娜攀着窗沿伸出头来向着他，他低声向她说了几句话，一阵酒气便扑到她的耳朵上来——却一点也没有听见——后来他又在她的面孔上、胸上和手上都画了个十字；那时他喘着气，眼泪便在他的眼里莹转着。安娜的两个弟弟，皮亚和安诸夏，都是小学生，从后面扯他们父亲的衣服，困恼地说：

"父亲！喂！……父亲，够了，够了！……"

车开的时候，安娜看见她的父亲跟着火车跑了几步，一面蹒跚地走着，一面喷着酒沫，他是如何的慈爱而且可怜呵！

他欢呼道："一路平安！"

现在这一对快乐的人离开了亲戚同事了。莫德士向四面看了一看，将行李放在架子上，便微笑地坐在他妻子的对面。他是一个中等身材的矮胖官员，一看便知道滋补得很好，生着几根长胡子，没有须。他那刮过汗毛的圆腮看起来好像脚踵一样。他的面部的特点便是没有髭须，肥腮的肉颤动起来，好像搅动着的果子酱一般。他的举止大方，容貌雍和，只是行动迟钝一些。

他微笑着说："我不由地想起一件事来了。五年以前，当哥索罗托夫接受圣安娜二等勋章时，上司向他说：'如今你有三个安娜了：一个系在你的衣服和扣子上，（指二等勋章——译者注）两个套在你的颈子上。（喻哥索罗托夫的妻两手围着他，向他纠缠不清——译者注）'这应该加以说明的，那时哥索罗托夫的妻刚刚回到他身边来，她是个欢喜吵闹、纠缠的轻浮女子，恰恰名字也叫安娜。如果我也接受圣安娜二等勋章，上司总不会拿说哥索罗托夫的话来说我罢？因为你是很温驯的。"

他眯着眼睛笑了起来。她也笑了，但想起她的丈夫无论何时都可以举起湿的厚嘴唇来和她亲吻，她又没有理由可以拒绝，她便懊恼起来。肥人的温柔使她很害怕，甚至于还要作呕。他起身，取下颈上的徽章，脱去外衣和背心，穿上便衣。

"这样好一点。"说时他便挨着她的身边坐着。

安娜记起结婚的时候是很忧伤的，在她看来，仿佛僧侣、宾客以及一切在礼拜堂里的人都忧愁的看着她，问她为什么，为什么这样一个美丽的姑娘却嫁给这样一个老而不死的东西。只有那天早晨，她看见一切东西都预备齐全，心里觉得欢喜，至于在结婚的时候和现在在火车里，她都觉得受了骗，她是无辜的，这件事过于滑稽。她嫁了一个富人，然而她依旧没有钱。她的结婚衣服还是借债买来的，当她的父亲和弟弟和她话别时，她能够从他们的脸色看出他们连一个小钱都没有。那一天他们有晚餐吃么？明天呢？为了某种缘故，她觉得她的父亲和弟弟，今晚正饿着肚皮，坐在那里想念她，仿佛他们的母亲死时的光景一样。

她想："我是如何的不快乐呵！我为什么不快乐呢？"

莫德士只晓得一心情愿的做事，不会体贴妇人的心理。他抱着她的腰，拍着她的肩，而她却在那里默想，她想到金钱，想到父母，还想到母亲之死。她的父亲是小学的图画习字教员，自从母亲死后，父亲便喝上了酒，家境也就一天一天的穷乏起来。孩子们连鞋子都没有得穿，债主在县里告了他，县知事便派人查抄他的家具……这是怎样丢脸的事呵！安娜又要照顾她那酗酒的父来，又要替她弟弟缝补袜子，又要上街，真是忙坏了。她想，人家称赞她年轻，美丽，伶俐，一定看见她那顶不值钱的帽子，穿了洞而透了水的鞋子。晚间她时常落泪，时时刻刻，她生怕学校里因了她父亲年老体弱，将他辞去，那么她的父亲，一定会跟着母亲，一同到死的路上去。他们所认识的妇人，知道他的家境不好，便想替安娜找一个丈夫。找来找去，便找着了莫德士，既不美丽，又不年轻，只是有钱。他有十万存在银行里，还有房子，他把它租了出去。他是一个有力量的人；所以有人劝安娜只要托莫德士写一封信给中学校长或是教育厅长，他的事情便可以牢靠了。

她在冥想她的往事，忽然她听得音乐的调子在车窗前飘荡，跟着便是嘈杂的人声。车停在一个小站上了。在月台外一群人里，有两个人正在奏着手风琴和提琴，又从别墅里传出军乐队的声音，高的桦树和白杨都沐浴在月光里；在这样的情景之下，是最适宜于跳舞的。避暑的城里人，每逢天气晴明，总喜欢专程的坐着火车，到这里来呼吸新鲜空气。此刻在月台上散步徘徊的正是这般人。在他们中间，有一个最富的人，许多别墅，都是他的不动产——

他的面色很黑，身体却是高大壮健的。他的名字叫做阿特罗夫。他的眼睛很是秀丽，好似阿米连人一样。他穿了一身奇怪的服装；他的衬衣不曾扣扣，露出他的胸脯。他穿了一双带着踢马刺的高靴，黑斗篷从他的肩上披下，拖在地上。两条猎犬，尖鼻子触着地，跟随着他。

眼泪依旧在安娜的眼睛里润湿着，但现在她想念母亲、金钱和结婚一类的事了；只是同她所认识的小学生和官员握手，她快乐地笑着，很快地说着：

"你好，你近来怎么样？"

在月光之下，她步出车厢，走到月台上，因此人家都能看见她那一身华丽的新装。

她问："我们为什么停在这里呢？"

"这里是接合点。他们要等到邮车过了以后才开。"

她觉察了阿特罗夫正在偷看她，便转动她的眼睛，卖弄风情，高声的说着法国话。因为她的声音非常和悦，又因为听见音乐而月光是反映在湖里，又因为著名的唐璜、幸运之骄子阿特罗夫正在盯着眼看她，又因为大家都很高兴——她忽然觉得快乐起来。车开的时候，她所认识的官员向她致敬，这时别墅里的音乐声传到她的耳畔，她不由得也微微的哼起跳舞曲来。她回到车厢里来时，还依恋着月台上的乐趣，觉得她就是弃掉一切都是愿意的。

这一对快乐的人在礼拜堂里住了两天，便又回到城里来。他们住在一所新房子里。每逢莫德士出去办公，安娜便奏着钢琴，或者忧伤落泪，否则便是躺在睡椅上读小说，翻阅时装画报。用午餐时莫德士吃得很多，一面吃一面谈到政治，谈到委任、移交和升级，谈到一个人应该劳作，又说家庭生活不是耽乐，只是尽职，你如能聚集小钱，也就能变成卢布，积少是可以成多的，又说宗教和道德是最应该注意的。他举起刀在拳头里，仿佛是剑一样，这时要说：

"各人都有各人应尽的职务。"

安娜听他说话，很是害怕，每每食不下咽，饿着肚皮立起身来，离开了餐桌。午餐以后，她的丈夫要睡一个午觉，鼻息如雷，这时安娜便跑去看她家里人去了。她的父亲和弟弟，望着她同平时有些异样，仿佛在她未进门以前，他们曾经责备过她，为了金钱的缘故，宁可嫁给一个她所不爱的可怕的人；她那窘窄的衣服，宝贵的腕环，以及嫁了人的妇人的神情触犯了他们，使他们感到不快。在她面前，他们觉得有一点点局促，不知该向她说什么好；但他们依旧和从前一样的爱她，用午餐时，没有她来，便感到不快。她和他们一同坐下喝椰菜汤，吃羹和油煎番薯。包特颤抖着从壶里倒了一杯酒，很快的喝干了，以后又倒第二杯，又倒第三杯，心里仿佛有说不出的郁闷。那两个眼大身瘦，面色灰白的孩子，皮亚和安诸夏把酒壶夺了过去，忧伤地说：

"父亲呵！不要这样……父亲呵，够了……"

安娜也很忧伤，劝他不要多饮；他就立刻大怒，拳头敲着桌子说：

"混账，你们居然管起老子来了！坏儿子！坏女儿！我要把你们统统赶出去！"

但是他的声音里有微弱温和的表示，所以没有一个人怕他。用过午餐，他总是穿得很齐整，脸上留有小小的刀痕，是剃汗毛不小心所致。他要歪着脖颈，在镜子面前站半点钟，梳头发呀，捻髭须呀，搽香水呀，系颈巾呀，忙个不停；以后这才戴起手套和高帽，出去教家馆去了。如果是放假的日子，他便坐在家里绘画，或是玩着小风琴，弹得呜呜的响。他想调好音键，使它发声和谐，以便唱歌。如果声音不好，便骂儿子：

"小鬼！没用的东西！你们把小风琴弄坏了！"

晚间安娜的丈夫和他的同事们打纸牌，在衙门里他们是住在一起的。这些贵人的妻子都来了，——这些妇人长得又丑，穿得又不时髦，粗得同女厨子一样——她们谈起话来，平板无味，和她们自己一样。有时莫德士也带安娜到剧院里去。休息的时间内他不让她在他身边移动一步，仅带着她臂挽臂的经过走廊和看客散步场。每逢他和一个人鞠躬，必定立刻低声向安娜说："一个文官……向他见个礼。"或者是"一个富人……他自己有房产。"他们经过食物摊时，安娜极想吃点甜食；她很喜欢巧克力糖和杏仁饼，但她没有钱，又不欢喜向丈夫讨。他拿起一个梨子，用手指捏了一会儿，有意无意地问了一句："好多钱？"

"二十五个戈比！"

他说一声："我说呢，好贵！"便把梨子放下了；但是，一点东西不买，便离开了食物摊总有点难为情。他便要了一瓶汽水，整瓶的自己喝了下去，爱惜钱的眼泪也就流了出来。在这种时候安娜最是恨他。

忽然他面色绯红，赶快地向安娜说：

"向那老妇人鞠躬！"

"我不认识她呀！"

"不要紧的，她是本地财政厅长的妻子！鞠躬，我向你说，头不要低下来。"

安娜鞠了躬，果然不曾低下头来，但却做得很不自然。她的丈夫要她做什么，她就做什么，心里自然是很不高兴，他欺骗她真好似傻偏一样。她只是为了他钱多，才嫁给他；但她现在的钱、反比结婚以前还要少。以前她的父亲有时还给她二十个戈比，如今她连一个小钱都没有了。偷钱讨钱，她都做不出来；她很怕她丈夫，站在他面前就发抖。她觉得她怕他已经有许多年了。在她幼时，学校的监学似乎是世界上最有权威的人，他一发怒，就好像一阵雷雨，或是汽机爆发，要将她炸死的一般；全家谈到都有点害怕的便是校长了；还有许多别的人，稍微不大可怕，其中有学校里的教员，上唇剃光了胡子，庄严可敬；最后便是莫德士，他面孔很有点像那监学。在安娜的幻想里，一切这些力量，都混而为一，变成一个可怕的大白熊，威吓她那微弱，颠蹶的父亲。她不敢说一句反对丈夫的话，终日强笑为欢，她的丈夫很粗卤的拥抱她，她吓得要命，然而却不能不假装作欢喜的样子。

只有一次包特大着胆子向莫德士借五十卢布还债，但却受了一顿教训。

莫德士想了一会说："很好；钱，我是借给你；你如果不把酒戒掉，我便不再借钱给你了。这种酗酒的事是不体面的！你须知道，许多大人物被酒毁坏了身体，因之一事无成；能够做大官的酒鬼，简直很少很少。"

跟着大转弯的短语便来了："所以……""照这样看来……""从以上所说的看起来……"但包特受了屈辱，心里更加热烈的想喝起酒来。

弟弟们去看安娜的时候，总是穿着破鞋子和脱了线的裤子，自然也该受教训的。

莫德士向他们说："各人都有各人应尽的职务。"

他不给他们钱。但却给安娜臂环，戒指，胸针，说是这些东西，将来穷时好拿来变卖的。他时常打开她的抽屉，侦察他给她的东西曾否遗失。

二

转瞬冬天到了。在圣诞节以前许久，本地报上便已登有通告，说是冬季跳舞会拟于十二月二十九日在尊贵堂举行。莫德士每晚打过纸牌后，总要同他同事的妻子低语一阵，又向安娜凝视一阵，以后便在房间里踱来踱去的思索了。终于，有一晚很迟了，他默默地站着，向安娜说：

"你应该替你自己做一件舞衣。你明白么？你可以同马亚和兰特亚商量。"

他给了她一百卢布。她拿了钱，但她做舞衣时，却不同人家商量；她除去父亲，谁也不告诉，竭力想象当日她母亲穿舞衣赴会的光景。她的母亲总是穿的最时髦的装束，对于安娜也用尽心思，将她打扮得好似漂亮的泥人一样，又教给她法国话和波兰舞（在她结婚以前，她曾经做过五年女教员。）安娜像她母亲一样，也善于将旧衣改为新衣，用碳化水素洗手套，租借珠宝；又像她母亲一样，善于眉目传情，并且能够喜怒哀乐，随心所欲，使人无从看破。安娜像她父亲的地方，便是黑头发和黑眼睛，易受刺激的神经，和那自视甚高的习惯。

在动身赴跳舞会的半点钟以前，莫德士匆匆跑到她房里，连外衣也不曾穿，对着她的镜子，将勋章挂在颈子上。他看她穿了一件轻纱一般的衣服，简直被她的美丽迷惑住了。他满足地捻着胡须说：

"你真长得好看，你真长得好看！安娜！"

他带着庄严的调子继续地说："我使你享受幸福，现在我求你也替我做一点事。我求你去和上司的妻子结识。为了上帝的缘故，千万要和她结识呀。因了她，我就可以得着秘书的职位了！"

他们往跳舞会行去。他们到了尊贵堂，门口有人守卫，他们带了帽盒和皮衣进了门；仆人急忙地走来走去，短颈的妇人们举起扇子遮着风。一阵煤和兵士的气味。安娜被她丈夫挽着臂上了堂口。她听见音乐，看见玻璃镜映出她长身玉立的风姿，心里不禁快乐起来，她感到同那一次在小车站月台里一样的欢欣。她很骄傲地走了进去，第一次觉到她不是女孩，已是一个妇人，自然而然摹仿起她母亲的一举一动来。就是丈夫与她同行也没有什么，她一面走过堂口，一面自己明白，年老的丈夫不但不使她减色，反更能引起人们的注意。乐队已经开始奏乐了，跳舞也同时开始了。安娜完全被强烈的灯光、鲜明的色彩、音乐和喧声所激动，四围一看，心里想："呵，真可爱呵！"她立刻在人群中辨别出她所认识的人，这些人是她在宴会或野餐时见过面的——一切的官员，教员，律师，办事员，地主，上司以及阿特罗夫。还有许多大家闺秀，美的也有，丑的也有，聚集在慈善市场的柜台旁边。她们是想卖东西来贩济穷人的。有一个著肩章的军官——她做女学生时，曾经有人将他介绍给她，但现在她已不记得他的名字了——似乎是从地底下跳出来的，求她跳舞，她便撇开了丈夫，好像她坐在船里，一阵狂风将她载走，把她丈夫抛撇在海岸上。她热情的跳舞，跳了许多样式，这一个刚刚离开了她，那一个又捉住了她。音乐和嘈杂声音使得她眩晕了，她的俄国话里夹着法国话，笑着说着，忘记了丈夫和一切。她得着了人们极大的赞美——那是自然，谁也赶不上她。她觉得跳热了，拿起扇子不住地扇她的父亲包特穿了一件皱了的衣服，走到她面前来，给她一盘粉红色的冰。

他高兴地看了看她："今晚你真美丽。我很懊恼你这样早就出嫁了……这是为了什么呢？我知道你这样做是为了我们，但是……"握了握手，他趁便交给一沓钞票说："今晚我已领到薪金，我欠你丈夫的钱，能够还他了。"

她刚刚把盘子交还给他手里，又被一个人拉去跳舞了。她从她舞伴的肩上看过去，她父亲跑下去，也同一个妇人在跳舞室里旋转着。

她想："我父亲如果不饮酒，一定很动人的！"

她又和一个高大的军官跳波兰舞；他动得很慢，仿佛是著了衣服的死尸，缩着肩和胸，很疲倦的踏着脚。——他跳得很吃力的。而她又偏偏以她的美貌和赤裸裸的颈子鼓动他，刺激他；她的眼睛挑拨的燃起火来，她的动作是热情的，他渐渐地不行了，举起手向着她，死板得同国王一样。

看的人齐声喝彩："好呀，好呀！"

但是，渐渐的那高大的军官也兴奋起来了；他慢慢地活泼起来，为她的美丽所克服，跳得异常轻快，而她呢，只是移动她的肩部，狡狯地看着他，仿佛现在她做了王后，他做了她的奴仆。那时她觉得满屋子里的人都在看他们，并且也每一个人都妒忌他们。高大的军官刚刚想感谢她陪他跳舞，忽然一群人分了开来，大家都把手垂着。衣服上有两个金星的上司向着她走来。是的，上司确是一直向着她走来的，因为他带着甜蜜的微笑望着她舔着嘴唇，这是他看见美貌女子的老毛病。

他说："好呀，好呀……我要把你的丈夫关在拘留所里，他有这样一个宝贝，却自己享受。我是我的妻子要我来的。"他继续说，一面伸臂给她，"你应该帮助我们一下……是的……为了你的美丽，我们应该给你奖品，如同美国人一样……是的……美国人……我的妻子急切的盼望你去。"

他领着她到一个柜台前，把她介绍给一个中年妇人，她的面孔的下部很大，与上部不称，好像她的口里衔了一块大石头似的。

她带着鼻音，粗声粗气地说："你应该帮助我们一下。一切美丽的女子都替我们这慈善市场工作，你却只顾自己快乐。为什么你不帮助我们呢？"

她走开了，安娜替代她的位子，拿起杯子和银火壶。她的生意很好。安娜至少要卖一个卢布一杯茶，使得那高大的军官喝了三杯。秀眼的富人阿特罗夫喘着气跑了来。他现在不是穿的奇怪服装，如同安娜夏天在小车站上所看见的，只是穿了一身普通衣服，他出神的看着安娜，喝了一杯香槟酒，给了一百卢布，又喝了几口茶，又给了一百卢布——给了以后，一句话也不说，因为他喘气还不曾止息……安娜招待买主，得到他们许多钱，现在完全明白她的一笑或是一瞬都足以使人颠倒。她现在明白，天创造她，是专要她生活在嘈杂、光明、哗笑里的，是专要她生活在音乐、跳舞者和赞美者之间的。她以前所怕的要将她炸死的力量，在现在的她看来，未免太滑稽可笑了。她现在谁也不怕了，只可惜她的母亲已死，不能欢祝她的成功。

包特现已面色灰白，但仍站得住脚，不至颠蹶，跑到柜台前来要一杯白兰地酒。安娜面孔红了起来,希望他不是来买酒的（她现在觉得有这样平常而又穷苦的父亲是可羞耻的了）；但他喝完了酒，居然也拿出十卢布来，丢在台上，一句话也不说，很尊贵的走了。不一会，安娜看见她父亲又在人群中跳舞，现在他的脚站不稳了，不住的狂叫，使得陪舞的妇人很不高兴；安娜记起三年前，她父亲也是在跳舞场里喝醉酒，东倒西歪，高声狂叫，终于被警察送回家，第二天校长便恐吓他，说是要把他辞掉！想起前情，是多么的不好意思呵！

火壶放在柜台上，疲倦的妇人们将器皿统统还给了口衔石头的中年妇人。阿特罗夫挽着安娜的臂走到大厅，在那里晚餐已经预备好了，凡替慈善市场帮忙的人都可以有份。有二十个人用晚餐，并不多，但却很热闹。上司提议饮酒祝贺成功：

"在这样华丽的餐室里，我们应该为卑陋的餐室祝贺成功，也就是说，今天慈善市场的目的已经达到。"

一个武官也赞成庆祝："他们的力量简直大炮都轰不破。"于是大家同妇人们撞杯共饮。这是非常愉快的。

安娜回家，天已大明，女厨子上街买菜去了。她又是快乐，又是疲倦，充满了新的感觉，倒床便睡，立刻就睡熟了……

下午一点，仆人喊醒了她，说是阿特罗夫来访。她很快的穿起衣服，跑到会客厅里来。在阿特罗夫以后，上司也跑来了，他感谢她替他在市场里帮忙。甜蜜的微笑着，咬着嘴唇，他吻了吻她的手，请求她允许，他下次还要来拜访，说完便告别了，她站在会客厅里，很惊讶的，几乎连自己也不相信她的生活改变得这样快；那时莫德士走了进来……他现在站在她的面前，忽然变成讨好，谄媚，恭敬的样子，这种表情，安娜是看惯了的，每逢他看见有权力的人，便做了出来；她知道骂他两声是不要紧的，便带着欢喜和侮慢，慢慢地一个字一个字地说：

"木头走开些！"

从这时起，安娜便没有一天是闲着的，人家不是请她去野餐、旅行，便是请她去演剧。她每天回家总在半夜以后。她需要许多钱，现在她不怕莫德士了，花他的钱好像是她自己的一样；她也不讨钱，也不请求，只是写一张条子给他："请即付二百卢布交来人带下。"或者是，"请即付一百卢布。"

在复活祭日莫德士接受了上司的圣安娜二等勋章。他跑去感谢，上司放下正在读着的报纸，将他的身体移了一移，使得他自己在椅子上坐得更舒服一点。

他闲逸的看着他的白手和红指甲说："现在你有三个安娜了，一个系在你的扣子上，两个套在你的颈子上。"

莫德士想起以前的事，放了两个手指在唇前，恐防高声的笑了出来，并且他也想说一点同样有趣的话，但是上司已经重又埋头看报，只是点一点头。

安娜和阿特罗夫一同坐着三匹马的马车出去打猎，出去演独幕剧，出去用晚餐，很少和她父亲包特以及弟弟们在一起；他们只有独自用餐。包特比以前更加酗酒了；他没有钱用，小风琴是早就卖掉拿来还债了。现在孩子们不让他独自跑到街上去，看护着他，恐怕他跌倒；每逢他们遇见安娜坐着马车在史特罗街上走，阿特罗夫权充作马夫，包特便脱下高帽，预备喊叫她，但是皮亚和安诸夏用手臂拉他开来，请求地说：

"父亲呵，不要这样。够了，父亲！"

（赵景深　译）

大小瓦洛佳

"放开我，我要自己驾车！我要坐到车夫旁边！"索菲娅·里沃芙娜大声喊着，"车夫，等一等，我坐你旁边。"

她站在雪橇马车上。她的丈夫弗拉基米尔·尼基迪奇和她童年时代的朋友弗拉基米尔·米哈依雷奇拉住了她的手，防她跌倒。三驾马车在飞奔。

"我说过，不能让她喝酒，"弗拉基米尔·尼基迪奇懊丧地对他的同伴说，"你啊，真是的！"

上校根据经验知道：像他的妻子索菲娅·里沃芙娜这样的女人，稍稍有了点醉意，在一阵狂喜之后一定会发出歇斯底里的大笑，随后就是哭泣。现在他担心，当他们回到家里，他非但不能上床睡觉，还得给她上绷带，让她服药水。

"啊！我要自己驾车！"索菲娅·里沃芙娜嚷嚷着。

她当真很兴奋，很有成就感。从结婚之日起，最近两个月她一直被一个想法煎熬着，她觉得自己嫁给雅基奇上校是出于世俗的考虑，是如同俗话所说，出于"赌气"，但是今天在城郊的这个餐厅里用餐的时候她终于确信：她非常爱他。尽管他已经五十四岁，但他还是那样壮实，那样灵敏和麻利，还是那样可爱地说俏皮话，哼唱吉卜赛小曲。真的，现在的老年人比年轻人有趣得多，好像是老年和青春对调了位置。上校比她父亲还要大两岁，但说老实话，他的精力、活力远胜过她，尽管她才二十三岁，这样的年岁差距还有什么意义呢？

　　"噢,我亲爱的! 神奇的! "她这样想。

　　在餐厅里她同样确信,原先在她心中拥有的那份情感现在已经荡然不存。对于她童年的朋友弗拉基米尔·米哈依雷奇,就是那个瓦洛佳,她昨天还爱得要死要活,现在却是毫无感情了。今天整个夜晚,她觉得这个瓦洛佳是那么的萎靡不振,那样的乏味与渺小,而他的通常不肯在餐厅主动付账的沉着这回激怒了她,她几乎要对他说:"如果您穷,就待在家里好了。"只有上校一人结了账。

　　也许是因为在她的眼前,树木、电线杆和雪片纷纷闪过,各种各样的念头也涌进了她的心头。她想:按餐厅的账单要支付一百二十卢布,还要给吉卜赛人一百卢布小费,那么,她明天如果愿意,可以随便挥霍一千卢布,而在两个月前,在结婚之前,她甚至没有三个卢布的私房钱,要买任何一样小玩意,都得向父亲伸手。生活发生了多大的变化!

　　她的思想乱成一团,她回想起,在她十岁的时候,雅基奇上校,她现在的丈夫,是如何追求她的姑姑的,家里所有的人都说是他伤害了她,姑姑也当真常常哭红了眼睛到餐厅吃饭,常常躲到一个什么地方去,人们谈论起她,都说这个可怜的女人在生活中没有找到自己的位置。他那时很漂亮,很得女人的欢心,是全城的名人,据说他那时天天去造访对自己感兴趣的女人,就像医生去探望病人一样。现在尽管头上有了白发,脸上有了皱纹,已经戴上了老花眼镜,他的清癯的面孔还挺好看,尤其是从侧面看过去。

　　索菲娅·里沃芙娜的父亲曾是个军医,和雅基奇在一个团队服役,瓦洛佳的父亲也曾经是个军医。也曾经和她的父亲以及雅基奇在一个团队服役。尽管瓦洛佳有一些爱情纠葛,而且还是很复杂、很烦人的爱情纠葛,但他的功课很好,他以优异的成绩完成了大学学业,现在专攻外国文学,据说正在写一本专著。他住在军营里,和当军医的父亲在一起,尽管已经三十岁,但没有自己的钱财。童年时代，索菲娅·里沃芙娜和他住在同一幢大楼里，不过是房号不同罢了。他常常去找她玩，一起学习跳舞，学习说法语。但当他长大成一个英俊少年的时候，她在他跟前有点害羞了，然后就发狂地爱他，直到她嫁给雅基奇为止。他也是一个很能博得女人欢心的人，几乎是从十四岁开始，那些因为他而背叛了自己丈夫的女人都为自己开脱说，他还不过是个孩子。关于他，最近有个传闻，好像他上大学的时候，曾在大学附近租了间公寓房，每当有人去敲他房门的时候，常常能听到房里响起他的脚步声，然后传来他一句轻声的表示歉意的话："对不起，我不是一个人在房间里。"雅基奇非常欣赏他，就像当年的老诗人杰尔查文提携普希金一样。显然，雅基奇很宠爱他。如果雅基奇坐上三驾马车出游，就一定要带上瓦洛佳，他们两人能一起好几个小时默默地玩纸牌，而瓦洛佳也只把他写书的秘密透露给雅基奇一个人听。当上校还年轻的时候，他们两人常常处于情敌的状态下，但他们从不互相吃醋。在他们常常一起出现的社交场合，人们把雅基奇称为大瓦洛佳，而他的朋友就是小瓦洛佳。

除了大小瓦洛佳和索菲娅·里沃芙娜之外，在雪橇车上还坐着另外一个女人——玛尔加丽塔·阿历克山德罗芙娜，或是依大家对她称呼的——丽达，是雅基奇太太的表姐，是个已经三十岁开外的老姑娘，脸孔很白，眉毛很黑，戴副夹鼻眼镜，不停地抽烟，即使是在凛冽的寒风之中，在她的胸前和膝盖上永远有烟灰。她说话带鼻音，拖长每一个字的尾声。她生性冷淡，饮酒无度，永远喝不醉。她能漫不经心地说一些无聊的笑话。在家里，她能一天到晚地读厚本的杂志，弄得书页上尽是烟灰，她也爱吃冰冻的苹果。

"索尼娅，别胡闹了。"她拖长了声调说，"这太不像话啦。"

因为快到城门口，马车放慢了速度，可以看清楚房屋与行人了，索菲娅·里沃芙娜平静了下来，偎依在丈夫身边，想起了自己的心事。小瓦洛佳坐在对面。现在她的轻松愉快的想法里已经混杂了一些阴暗的思绪。她想，这个坐在对面的人知道她曾经爱过他，当然也会相信她嫁给上校是出于"赌气"的说法。她还从来没有向他表露过自己的爱意，她不想让他知道，她要掩饰自己的感情，但从他的脸部神情可以得知，他对她的心意了如指掌——她的自尊心受到了伤害。但在她的处境中使她最感到屈辱的是，在结婚之后这个小瓦洛佳一反常态地向她献起了殷勤，他或是默默地跟她坐上几个小时，或是跟她聊一些鸡毛蒜皮的小事，而现在坐在雪橇里，他不跟她攀谈，却拿脚来碰碰她的脚，用手去捏捏她的手，很明显，他希望她嫁人，他看不起她，她在他心中激起了一种把她当做一个放荡女人的好奇心。而在她的心中，一当成就感与对丈夫的爱和屈辱与自尊心受到伤害的感觉交织在一起的时候，她便狂躁起来，想坐到马车夫的座位上去，大叫大嚷……

就在马车驶过女子修道院的时候，那口千斤重的大钟敲响了，丽达在胸口画十字。

"我们的奥丽娅就在这个修道院里。"索菲娅·里沃芙娜身子抖动了一下，也开始在胸口画十字。

"她为什么进了修道院？"上校问。

"因为赌气。"丽达生气地回答，她显然是在影射索菲娅·里沃芙娜与雅基奇的婚姻。"现在这个'赌气'很时髦。向整个世界发出挑战。她原本是个嘻嘻哈哈的浪漫小姐，就爱舞会，和舞会上的漂亮男人，但突然间她离家出走了！莫名其妙！"

"不是这样的，"——小瓦洛佳说，一边把大衣的领子拉了下来，露出了自己的俊俏的脸孔。

"那不是赌气，而是一件伤心的惨事。她的哥哥德米特里去服终生苦役了，但到现在还不知道在哪里，而她的母亲因为悲伤而去世了。"

他把大衣领子又翻了上来。

"奥丽娅做得很对，"他轻声补充道，"过养女的生活，而且与像索菲娅·里沃芙娜这样的聪明人一样生活，也需要好好思量的！"

索菲娅·里沃芙娜从他的话里听出了嘲讽的口吻，她想回敬一句重话，但她没有说。她又一次狂躁起来，她站直了身子，用含泪的嗓音大声喊道：

"我要去参加晨祷！车夫，往后转！我要去看看奥丽娅！"

马车往回驶去。修道院的钟声深沉，让索菲娅·里沃芙娜从这钟声联想到奥丽娅和她的生活，这时，其他的教堂的钟声也响了起来。马车夫把马车刚刚停下，索菲娅·里沃芙娜就从雪橇上独自跳了下来，没有旁人的扶持，快步向修道院的门口走去。"快去快回！"丈夫朝她喊道，"时间不早了！"她穿过黑暗的门洞，然后顺着一条通往教堂的路径走去，雪在她的脚下吱嘎吱嘎作响，钟声已经在她的头顶上鸣响，钟声似乎穿透了她的全身。进了教堂的大厅，有三个朝下的梯级，然后就是教堂的前厅，两边分列着圣像，散发着刺柏和乳香的气味，前边又有一道门，一位黑衣人把门打开，深深地鞠了一躬……教堂的礼拜还未开始，一位修女从圣像壁前走过，点亮了烛台上的蜡烛，另一位修女点亮了圣像前的枝形烛台。这里那里，在圆柱与祭坛的两侧，一动不动地站着几个穿黑衣的人。"这么说，她们得照这个样子一直站到早晨。"——索菲娅·里沃芙娜这样想，她觉得，这里很黑，很冷，很寂寞——比墓地还寂寞，她怀着寂寥的感觉向那些纹丝不动的人影张望，心里突然有一阵刺痛袭来。不知怎么的，她从一个个头不高、肩膀瘦削、戴着黑色头巾的修女身上认出了奥丽娅，尽管奥丽娅进修道院之前长得胖胖的，个头也要高一些。异常激动的索菲娅·里沃芙娜迟疑不决地走近那个修女，透过肩膀看清了她的脸，终于认出了奥丽娅。

"奥丽娅！"她喊道，扬起了手，因为激动已经无法说话——

"奥丽娅！"

修女也立即认出了她，她惊异地扬起了眉毛，她的刚刚清洗过的白白的、亮洁的脸孔，乃至她的头巾下露出的白色包头布，统统都因为喜悦而放光了。

"这是上帝差你来的。"她说，用她那瘦瘦的白手拍了拍巴掌。

索菲娅·里沃芙娜紧紧地拥抱了她，吻了她，同时她也怕对方闻出了自己的酒气。

"我们刚好路过，想起了你。"她一边说，一边因为走得太急而喘着粗气，"上帝，你怎么这样苍白！我……我见到你真高兴。怎么样？你感到寂寞吗？"

索菲娅·里沃芙娜回头看了看其他的修女，便开始轻声地继续说道："我们已经有了那么多的变化……你知道吗，我已经嫁给了雅基奇。你大概认识他……我们很幸福。"

"感谢上帝。你爸爸身体好吗？"

"身体很好。他常常想起你。奥丽娅，你过节的时候到我们家来做客，好吗？"

"我会来的。"奥丽娅说，微微一笑，"我明天就来。"

索菲娅·里沃芙娜连自己都不知道，她竟然哭了，默默地哭了片刻，她擦去了眼泪，说："丽达没有看见你，她会很难过的。她和我们在一起，瓦洛佳也在，他们就在门口，如果能见到你，他们会非常高兴的！咱们去看看他们，礼拜反正还没有开始。"

"咱们去。"奥丽娅表示同意。

她在胸前画了三次十字，便和索菲娅·里沃芙娜一起向门口走去。

"索菲娅。你说你很幸福？"当她们走出门去的时候，她这样问道。

"很幸福。"

"感谢上帝。"

　　大小瓦洛佳见到修女，都下了雪橇，恭恭敬敬地向她问好，俩人看见她的雪白的脸孔和黑色的道袍，分明都被感动了；她还记得他们，还出来与他们打招呼，这也让他们感到高兴，为了不让她着凉，索菲娅·里沃芙娜把一条毛毯裹住了她，还用自己皮大衣的下摆披到她身上。早先流下的眼泪已经减轻了她的痛苦，让她的心灵亮堂了，她很高兴，因为这个原本喧闹的、不安的、实际上是并不纯洁的夜晚，出乎意外地变得这样纯洁和温馨。为了把奥丽娅留在自己身边的时间再长一些，她提出了建议："让我们带着她去兜兜风吧！奥丽娅，上车，我们走不远。"

　　男人们以为修女会拒绝的——神职人员是不坐三驾马车的，——但出乎他们的意料之外，她同意了，坐到了雪橇马车上。当三驾马车向城门驶去的时候，大家都默不做声，只是尽力让修女坐得舒服，不受凉，每一个人都在想，她以前曾经是什么样子的，而现在又成了什么样子。她现在的脸是木然的，毫无表情的，冷冷的，白白的，透明的，似乎在她的血管里流淌着的不是血，而是水。而在两三年前，她是胖乎乎的，红喷喷的，会议论追求她的男人，会因为一点小事哈哈大笑……

　　马车驶到城门口就掉头折了回来。十分钟后车子停到了修道院附近，奥丽娅从雪橇上下来。钟声已经此起彼伏地响了起来。

　　"上帝保佑你们。"奥丽娅轻声说，按修女的方式鞠了一躬。

　　"奥丽娅，你常回来看看。"

　　"我会来的。"

　　奥丽娅快步走去，很快消失在黑色的门洞里，在这之后，三驾马车再继续前行，这时不知为什么出现了一种忧伤的情怀。大家都不说话。索菲娅·里沃芙娜觉得全身发软，有气无力。她竟怂恿一个修女坐到雪橇上，和几个醉汉一起兜风，这已经让她感到是那样的愚蠢、鲁莽、近似荒唐。她的醉意连同那自我欺骗的愿望一齐消失了，现在她已经清楚地意识到，她不爱自己的丈夫，也不可能爱，所有这一切都是胡闹。她出嫁是带着私心杂念的，因为就像她的女友们说的那样，他富得流油，因为她生怕自己像丽达一样成为老处女，因为厌倦了当医生的父亲，因为她想气气小瓦洛佳。如果她在出嫁之前能预见到以后的生活是如此的沉重，令人厌恶，那么再大的物质财富也不能诱使她同意结婚的。但现在大错已经铸成，就只好认命了。

回到了家里，躺到温暖而柔软的床上，盖上被子，索菲娅·里沃芙娜回想起了那个黑暗的教堂，乳香的气味和圆柱旁的人影，一想到在她入睡的这些时辰他们要一直一动不动地站在那里，她便心里感到别扭，早祷会是很长很长的，然后是弥撒，然后是礼拜……

"但是要知道，上帝可能是存在的，我早晚会死去的，这意味着，应该像奥丽娅那样，早晚得去思考灵魂，思考永恒的生命。奥丽娅现在得救了，她给自己解决了所有的问题……但如果上帝不存在呢？那么她的整个生活就毁了。是怎么毁的呢？为什么毁了呢？"

一分钟之后，这个想法又涌入了脑海：

"上帝是存在的，死亡不可避免，需要思考灵魂。如果奥丽娅现在看到了自己的死亡，她是不会害怕的。她一切都准备好了，主要的是，她给自己把一切生活的问题都解决了。上帝是存在的……是的……但是，难道除了进修道院之外就没有另外的出路？要知道进修道院就意味着疏离生活，毁掉生活……"

索菲娅·里沃芙娜开始感到有点恐惧，她把头埋进了枕头底下。

"不要想这些，"她喃喃自语，"不要想……"

雅基奇在隔壁的房间里踱步，在想着什么心事，军靴的马刺轻轻地在地毯上发出声响，索菲娅有了个想法：这个男人让她感到亲切仅仅是因为他也叫瓦洛佳，她坐到床上，温和地叫了一声他的名字：

"瓦洛佳！"

"你有什么事？"丈夫回应。

"没有什么事。"

她又躺了下来。钟声重又响起，可能就是那个修道院的钟声，她又想起了那个教堂，那些黑色的人影，她的脑海里又浮现起那些关于上帝和不可避免的死亡的想法，为了听不到钟声，她把脑袋缩进了被子里，她想到，在衰老与死亡到来之前，还要延续一段长长的生活，还要日复一日地忍受这个她并不喜欢的男人的亲热，这个男人现在已经走进房间，躺到床上，　不得不在心中扑灭掉对另一个年轻的、可爱的、在她看来是非凡的男人的爱。她瞧了丈夫一眼，本想向他道声晚安，但却突然间哭了起来。她对自己也不满意。

"好戏又开始了！"雅基奇说，把重音放在了"戏"上。

直到早上九点钟的时候，她才平静了下来，她才不再哭泣，不再浑身发抖，但却开始了剧烈的头痛。雅基奇急着去做弥撒，在隔壁的房里向帮他穿衣服的勤务兵嚷嚷着什么。他回到卧室来了一次，轻轻地发出了马刺的声响，取走了什么东西，然后又回来了一次，这时已经把肩章和勋章都佩戴好了，因为患有关节炎，他走起路来有点不稳，索菲娅·里沃芙娜瞧着他边走边张望的样子，觉得他像一头苍鹰。

她听到雅基奇在打电话。

"请接瓦西里耶夫军营……"他说，过了一分钟又说，"是瓦西里耶夫军营？请让沙里莫维奇医生来接电话……"又过了一分钟，"你是谁？你，瓦洛佳？很高兴。亲爱的，让你爸爸过来一趟，我妻子昨天回来之后很不舒服。你说，他不在家？那好……谢谢。很好……非常感谢……谢谢。"

雅基奇第三次走进卧室，俯身在妻子胸前画十字，让她亲吻自己的手（爱过他的女人都吻他的手，他对此很习惯了），说他午饭之前回家。他走了。

十二点钟的时候，女仆进来通报说，弗拉基米尔·米哈依雷奇来了。因为疲乏和头痛，索菲娅·里沃芙娜身子有点摇晃，她迅速地穿上了那件有毛皮镶边的、丁香花色的新大衣，麻利地做了个发式，她感到心中升起了一种莫名的柔情，由于喜悦，她的身子抖动着，她生怕他会走开。她太想见到他了。

小瓦洛佳前来拜访，照例穿着燕尾服，打着白领结。当索菲娅·里沃芙娜走进客厅的时候，他吻了她的手，对她的身体欠安，表示由衷的关切。坐下来后，他夸奖了她穿的衣裳。

"昨天与奥丽娅见面之后我心里很不是滋味，"她说，"起初我觉得可怕，而现在我竟羡慕起她来了。她像一座推不倒的山。但，瓦洛佳，难道她就没有另外的出路？难道把自己活埋就是解决了生活的问题？要知道这是死亡，而不是生活。"

一想到奥丽娅，在小瓦洛佳的脸上显露出了善意。"瓦洛佳，您是个聪明人，"索菲娅·里沃芙娜说，"您要开导开导我该如何效法奥丽娅。当然，我不信教，也不会进修道院，但总有什么相类似的方法。我的日子不好过。"沉默了一会之后，她说，"开导开导我……给我指点一条行之有效的出路。哪怕就给我说一个词儿。"

"一个词儿？那听着：放荡。"

"瓦洛佳，你为什么这么小看我？"她热切地问道，"您用这种特别的，请原谅，是很不体面的语言与我说话，人们与朋友和良家妇女说话是不能用这样的语言的。您是个有成就的学者，要爱科学，您为什么从不跟我谈论科学呢？为什么？是我不配？"

小瓦洛佳厌烦地皱起了眉毛，说：

"你怎么突然间对科学发生了兴趣？或许，您还需要宪法？或许不过是需要洋姜鲟鱼汤吧？""好了，就算我是一个渺小的，没有主见的女人……我有好多好多错误，我神经错乱，生活不检点，我活该让人瞧不起。但是瓦洛佳，你毕竟比我大十岁，我丈夫比我大三十岁呢，你们是看着我长大的，要是你们愿意，本来可以把我培养成你们所希望的那种人的，甚至可以把我塑造成一个天使，可是你们……（她的嗓音颤抖了）这么残酷地对待我。雅基奇这么大岁数了，还娶了我。您……"

"得了，得了，"瓦洛佳说，一边让身子更加靠近她，吻着她的双手，"让叔本华们去高谈阔论，论证他们想论证的一切。就让咱们吻吻这双小手吧。"

"您瞧不起我，如果您能知道这多么让我伤心！"她迟疑地说道，她早就知道他不会相信她的。"如果您能知道，我多么想改变自己，多么想开始新的生活！我热诚地这样想的，"她这样说，而且当真流出了热诚的眼泪，"我要做一个好人，做一个真诚的人，纯洁的人，不说谎，有生活的目标。""行了，行了，就此打住！我不爱听！"瓦洛佳说，他的脸孔有一种诡异的表情，"真的，这像是在演戏，还是说点人话吧。"

为了不让他生气和走开，她开始替自己辩解，为了讨得他的喜欢而强作笑颜，她又说起了奥丽娅，说起了她想解决自己的生活问题，做一个真正的人。

"放……荡……"他轻声地哼唱着，"放……荡吧！"他突然搂住了她的腰，而她呢，也不由自主地把双手搭到了他的肩上，陶醉地欣赏着他那聪明的、有嘲讽意味的脸孔、额头、眼睛、漂亮的胡子……

"你自己早就知道我爱你。"她向他坦白，脸孔痛苦地泛起了潮红，她感到自己的嘴唇也羞怯得扭曲了。"我爱你，你为什么要折磨我？"她闭上眼睛，使劲地亲吻着他的嘴唇，吻得很久，怎么也终止不了这个热吻，尽管她知道这不合规矩，他可能因此会责备她，女仆可能会闯进来……

"嗯，你把我折磨苦了！"她重复道。

过去了半个小时，他得到了他所需要的一切之后，坐在餐厅里吃点心，她跪在他面前，贪婪地看着他的脸，他对她说，她像一只小狗，等着人家给她扔去一块火腿肉。然后他把她抱到自己的膝盖上，像颤动小孩似的颤动着她，一边哼唱着：

"放荡吧……放……荡吧！"

当他要离去的时候，她用热切的声音问他：

"什么时候？今天？哪里？"

她把双手伸向他的嘴唇，好像是想用双手抓住他的回答。

"今天怕是不行了，"他想了想，说，"也许明天。"他们分了手，午饭之前，索菲娅·里沃芙娜到修道院去找奥丽娅，那边的人告诉她说，奥丽娅到什么地方去给一个临终的人诵经去了。从修道院出来她去找父亲，父亲也不在家，她便换了一辆马车，漫无目的地在大街上穿行，一直闲逛到了黄昏时分。不知为什么在这个时候，她想起了那位姑姑，那位因为在生活中找不到位置而终日以泪洗面的姑姑。

夜间，她又坐上三驾马车兜风，在城外的一家饭馆听吉卜赛人唱歌。当她又走过修道院的时候，她便想起了奥丽娅，她痛苦地想到，对于她这个阶层的姑娘与妇女来说，出路只有不停地坐着马车兜风和说谎，或者进修道院去扑灭肉体生活……第二天有幽会，索菲娅·里沃芙娜又孤身一人坐车兜风，回想起了姑姑。

过了一个礼拜，小瓦洛佳抛弃了她。从此，生活又回到原来的轨道，照样是一种乏味的，暗淡无光，有时甚至是很痛苦的生活。上校和小瓦洛佳依旧长时间地打台球，丽达依旧毫无生气地说笑话，索菲娅·里沃芙娜呢，总是坐着雪橇车闲逛，还请求丈夫雇辆三驾马车带她兜风。

她几乎每天都要去一趟修道院，她向奥丽娅倾诉自己的无法忍受的痛苦，她一边哭泣，一边想到她把车内不洁的、卑琐的东西带到了禅房里来了，而奥丽娅呢，总是机械地，像是背书似的对她说，这一切没有什么，这一切都会过去的，上帝会原谅她的。

（童道明　译）

未　婚　妻

一

　　已是晚间十点钟左右，一轮望月在花园上照耀。在舒明家的房子里刚刚结束奶奶玛尔法·米哈伊洛芙娜所吩咐做的彻夜祈祷。娜佳来到花园里稍待一会儿，此刻她看见：大厅里正在摆桌，准备吃点心，穿着华丽绸衣裙的奶奶在忙碌着。大教堂的司祭长安德烈神甫正在同娜佳的母亲尼娜·伊万诺芙娜谈着一件什么事情。这时候在夜晚灯光下隔窗望去，不知道因为什么，母亲显得很年轻。安德烈神甫的儿子安德烈·安德烈伊奇站在一旁，留心地听着。

　　花园里静悄悄的，挺凉爽，地面上铺着一些昏暗宁静的阴影。可以听到，在远处一个什么地方，大约是在城外，不少青蛙在鸣叫。感觉得到五月的气息，可爱的五月！可以深深地呼吸了，不禁想到：并非在这里，而是别的什么地方，在天空之下，在树木之上，在城市的远郊，在田野上，在树林里，春天的生机正在蓬勃展开，神秘、美好、丰富和神圣的生机，脆弱而造孽的人所不能理解的生机。不知为什么真想哭它一场。

　　她，娜佳，已经三十三岁了。从十六岁起她就热望出嫁，现在终于成了安德烈·安德烈伊奇的未婚妻，他正站在窗子那一边。她喜欢他，已经定在7月7日举行婚礼，可是她并不感到高兴，夜间睡不好觉，快乐心情不知去向……厨房位于正房的地下室，从敞开着的窗户里听得见那儿的人都在忙，笃笃笃地用刀子剁着，而单元屋的房门在嘭嘭作响，飘出一股烤鸡和醋渍樱桃的气味。不知为什么她觉得，现在似乎一生都会这么下去，没有变化，没有结局！

这时有个人从屋里出来，在台阶上站住。这人叫亚历山大·季莫费伊奇，或者，随便一些，叫萨沙，是约莫十天前从莫斯科来的客人。很久以前，奶奶有个远亲玛丽亚·彼得罗芙娜，一个贵族出身的穷寡妇，个儿矮小，瘦弱多病，常来找奶奶请求周济。萨沙就是她的儿子，不知为什么提到萨沙时大家都说他是个出色的画家。他母亲去世后，奶奶为了拯救自己的灵魂把他送进莫斯科的科米萨罗夫斯基学校去读书。两年左右后他转入绘画学校，在那儿待了差不多十五年，勉勉强强在建筑系毕业，可是他并未从事建筑工作，却在莫斯科一家石印厂里做事。他几乎每年夏天都到奶奶家来，总是带着重病，在这里休息和调养。

此刻他穿着一件扣上纽扣的长礼服和一条旧的底边已经磨损的帆布裤，他的衬衫没有熨过，周身上下显出没精打采的样子。他很瘦，眼睛大大的，手指头又长又细，蓄着胡子，皮肤黝黑，但仍旧很漂亮。他已经惯于跟舒明一家相处，就像同亲人在一起似的，在他们家里他觉得像在自己家里一样。他在这儿所住的一个房间早已叫做"萨沙的房间"。

他站在台阶上，看见了娜佳，就向她走去。

"你们这儿真好。"他说。

"当然好啦。您应该在这儿住到秋天。"

"是的，大概会这样。也许，我在你这儿要住到9月份。"

他莫名其妙地笑将起来，在她一旁坐下。

"我坐在这儿看妈妈，"娜佳说，"从这儿看去，她显得多么年轻！不错，我妈妈有许多弱点，"她沉默了一会儿补充说。"但她毕竟是一个不寻常的女人。"

"是的，是一个好人……"萨沙同意说。"您的母亲，就她自己的特点来说，当然，还是一个善良的很可爱的女人，可是……该怎么对您说呢？今天一清早我偶然走进你们的厨房，四个女仆在那儿干脆就睡在地板上，没有一张床，没有被褥，只有一些破烂，气味难闻，还有臭虫，蟑螂……仍是二十年前那种情形，没有丝毫变化。讲到奶奶，求上帝保佑她，她总归是奶奶。可是您的妈妈，她恐怕还会讲法国话，还参加演戏。看来，她似乎是该明白的。"

萨沙在讲话时常常在听话人面前伸出两根瘦长的手指头。

"由于不习惯，这儿的一切总使我觉得奇怪，"他接着说。"鬼知道，这儿任何人都不干事。妈妈整天玩，像个公爵夫人似的，祖母也是什么事都不做，您呢，您也是这样。您的未婚夫，安德烈·安德烈伊奇，也是啥事都不干。"

娜佳去年就听到过这些话，似乎前年也听到过，她知道萨沙不会议论别的东西。以前这些话使她感到好笑，现在呢，不知为什么，她听着却觉得烦恼。

"这都是一些老话，早让人听厌了。"说着她站将起来。"您该想出一些比较新鲜的东西来。"

他笑了，也站了起来，两人一道走向正房。她个儿高高的，美丽，匀称，现在同他并排站着显得非常健康和华丽。她感到了这一点，她可怜他，而且不知为什么感到不自在。

"您总说许多废话，"她说。"喏，刚才您就讲到了我的安德烈，可是要知道，您并不了解他。"

"'我的安德烈'……去他的吧，您的安德烈。我为您的青春感到惋惜。"

他们走进大厅时，那儿人们已经就席吃饭了。奶奶，或者按家里人对她的称呼，好奶奶，胖墩墩的，不漂亮，两道眉毛浓浓的，还有唇髭，说话声音很响。单凭她说话的声调和口气就可以看出，她在这里是一家之长。集市上好几排店铺和一幢古老的有圆柱和花园的房屋都是属于她的，可是她天天早晨要流着眼泪做祷告，求上帝保佑她别破产。她的媳妇，娜佳的母亲尼娜·伊万诺芙娜，是一个长着金黄色头发的女人，她总将腰带束得紧紧的，戴着一副夹鼻子眼镜，每个手指上都戴着钻石戒指；安德烈神甫是个掉了牙的瘦老头，他脸上总有一种表情，似乎他打算说一件很有趣的事情；他的儿子安德烈·安德烈伊奇是娜佳的未婚夫，他丰满、漂亮，一头鬈发，像是一个演员或者画家——这三个人正谈着催眠术。

"在这儿住上一个星期你身体准会复原，"好奶奶转向萨沙说，"不过你得多吃点儿。瞧你像个什么啦！"她叹口气说，"你面色可怕！真的，你真成了一个浪子了。""把父亲赠予的资财挥霍一尽后，"安德烈神甫两眼含着笑意慢慢地说。"该死的他就同一些无头脑的牲口一块儿放牧[1]……"

"我喜欢我的爸爸，"安德烈·安德烈伊奇碰一碰父亲的肩膀说。"他是个可爱的老人，善良的老人。"

大家沉默了一阵。萨沙突然笑将起来，他用餐巾捂住嘴。

"这么说来，您相信催眠术？"安德烈神甫问尼娜·伊万诺芙娜。

"当然，我不能肯定说我相信，"尼娜·伊万诺芙娜作出一种十分认真、甚至严厉的样子回答说。"可是我必须承认，自然界有许多神秘的不可解的东西。"

"我完全同意您的说法，不过我还该加上一句：宗教信仰为我们大家缩小了神秘事物的范围。"

这时端上来一只肥大的火鸡。安德烈神甫和尼娜·伊万诺芙娜继续谈着。钻石在尼娜·伊万诺芙娜的手指上闪光，后来泪水在她眼睛里发亮，她激动起来了。

"虽然我不敢跟您争论，"她说。"不过您会同意，生活里有

---

① 在《圣经》中的《路加福音》里讲到了一个浪子。

许许多多解决不了的谜！"

"一个也没有，请您相信。"

晚饭后，安德烈·安德烈伊奇拉小提琴，尼娜·伊万诺芙娜弹钢琴为他伴奏。十年前他在大学语文学系毕业，可是没有在任何地方做过事，不曾有过固定工作，只是偶尔参加一些具有慈善性质的音乐会，城里人因此就称他为演员。

安德烈·安德烈伊奇在演奏，大家默默地听着。桌上的茶炊在轻轻地沸滚，只有萨沙一个人在喝茶。后来时钟敲了十二下，小提琴上突然断了一根弦，大家笑了，一个个都忙乱起来，开始告辞。

送走未婚夫后娜佳回到了楼上自己的房间。她同母亲都住在楼上（奶奶占用着底层）。楼下大厅里的灯火开始熄灭，而萨沙还坐在那儿喝茶：他喝茶的时间一向很长，像在莫斯科一样，一喝就要喝上七大杯。娜佳解衣上床后好久还听见楼下女仆们在收拾房间，还听见奶奶在发脾气。一切终于都静下来了，只是偶尔可以听见萨沙在楼下他自己的房间里低沉地咳嗽。

二

娜佳醒来时大概是两点钟光景，天开始破晓。在远处一个什么地方有守夜人打更。她不想睡了，躺在床上觉得软绵绵的，不舒服。就像在以往的五月之夜那样她坐在床上思忖起来。可是她想到的还是昨夜想到过的那些事情，单调，没意思，令人腻烦，想到了安德烈·安德烈伊奇追求她、向她求婚的情境，想到了她怎样同意，后来她又怎样渐渐看清了这个善良而又聪明的人的优点。可是现在，离开举行婚礼的日子不过一个月的现在，不知为什么她却开始感到恐惧和不安，像是有什么模糊的艰难的东西在等着她似的。

"滴克——笃克,滴克——笃克……"守夜人懒洋洋地敲着,
"滴克——笃克……"

从古老的大窗户里望出去,可以看见花园以及远处盛开着的
丁香丛,花由于寒冷显得委靡和无生气,白白浓浓的迷雾缓缓地
向丁香丛飘去,要把它遮掩。远处的树上有几只昏昏欲睡的白嘴
鸦在啼叫。

"我的上帝啊,为什么我这么难过?"

也许,每个未婚妻在结婚前都有这种心情。谁知道呢! 莫非
这是受了萨沙的影响? 可是几年来一直说这几句话呀,就像背书
一样,而且他说话时让人觉得他幼稚和古怪。可是为什么萨沙仍
然萦回在她脑际? 为什么?

守夜人早已不打更了。鸟雀开始在窗下和在花园里喧闹,迷
雾已从花园消散。四周的一切都被春天的阳光照亮,好像洋溢着
微笑似的。很快整个花园苏醒过来了,太阳照暖了它,阳光抚爱
着它,钻石般的露珠在树叶上闪光。古老的荒芜已久的花园在这
个早晨显得十分年轻和华丽。

奶奶已经醒了。萨沙粗声粗气地咳起嗽来。可以听见楼下已
经准备了茶炊,还听见搬动椅子的声音。

时钟走得很慢。娜佳早已起床,已在花园里散步好久,而早
晨却还在慢慢地延续。

尼娜·伊万诺芙娜出现了,她泪痕斑斑,手里拿着一杯矿泉水。
她在研究招魂术和顺势疗法,她读了很多书,喜欢谈她易于产生
的种种怀疑。在娜佳看来,所有这一切似乎都含有深刻而又神秘
的意义。此刻娜佳吻了吻母亲,同她并排一起走。

"你哭什么,妈妈?"她问。

"昨晚临睡前我开始看一部中篇小说,写的是一个老人和他
的女儿。老人在某个地方工作,上司爱上了他的女儿。我没有读
完,但小说中有这么一个地方,读了它难以忍得住眼泪,"尼娜·伊

万诺芙娜说，从杯子里呷了一口水。"今天早晨我想起了这一段描写，又哭了。"

"这些天我心里很闷，"娜佳沉默了一会儿说。"为什么我夜里睡不着觉呢？"

"我不知道，亲爱的。而我每逢晚间睡不着觉时，就把眼睛闭得紧而又紧，喏，就是这个样子，想象安娜·卡列尼娜，想象她怎么走动和怎么说话，或者想象古代历史上的某一件事情……"

下午两点钟，他们坐下来吃午饭。那是星期三，是斋日，因此给奶奶端上的是素的红甜菜汤和鲥鱼粥。

为了揶揄奶奶，萨沙既吃他的荤汤，也吃素的红甜菜汤。吃饭时他一直说着笑话，可是他的笑话显得笨拙，总打算劝人为善，所以结果就完全不可笑了。每当他在说俏皮话前举起细长消瘦死人般的手指时，每当想到他病得很重，也许会不久于人世时，人们就会为他难过得流泪。

饭后，奶奶回自己房间休息。尼娜·伊万诺芙娜弹了一会儿琴后也走了。

"啊，亲爱的娜佳，"萨沙开始了例行的饭后闲谈。"如果您能听我的话，那就好了！那就好了！"

她坐在一把古老的深圈椅里，闭上了眼睛。他在房间里慢慢地踱步。

"如果您出去学习，那就好了！"他说。"只有文明的人崇高的人方才是有意思的，而需要的也正是这种人。要知道，这种人越多，天国就会越快地来到人间。到那时，你们的城市就会慢慢地彻底毁灭，一切都会底儿朝天，一切都会变样，"像是施了魔法似的。到那时这里就会有宏大华美的房屋，有奇妙的花园，有罕见的喷泉，有卓越的人……然而这并不是主要的。主要的是，到那时将不会有我们所指望的芸芸众生，像现在这种样子的芸芸众生——这一不幸现象，因为每个人都会有信仰，每个人都会知道他为什么而活着，而且不会有一个人到芸芸众生中去寻找支柱。亲爱的，好姑娘，您走吧！您该向大家表示，对这种一潭死水似的灰溜溜的造孽生活您已经厌恶了。您至少该向自己表明这一点！"

"不行，萨沙。我要出嫁了。"

"哎，算了吧！根本没有必要！"

他们走进花园，在一起溜达了一会儿。

"不管怎么样，我亲爱的，应该好好想一想，应该明白，你们这种游手好闲的生活非常不干净，非常不道德，"萨沙继续说。"您要了解我的意思，就打一个比方来说吧，如果您、您的母亲和您的好奶奶什么事情都不做，那就意味着有别人在为你们干活，你们有吞食着别人的生命，这难道干净吗？难道不肮脏吗？"

娜佳想说："是的，这话实在。"她想说，她明白这一点；可是她的眼睛里涌出了泪水，她突然默不做声了，整个身子瑟缩起来，她回自己的房间去了。

傍晚时分，安德烈·安德烈伊奇来了，他像平常一样拉了很长时间的小提琴。一般说他并不健谈，也许，他之所以喜欢拉小提琴，是因为在演奏时可以不说话。十点多钟了，离去时已经穿上大衣的他抱住娜佳，开始贪婪地吻她的脸、肩膀和手。

"宝贝儿，我亲爱的，我的美人！……"他喃喃地说，"啊，我多么幸福！我高兴得发疯了！"

她觉得，这种话她早已听见过，很早以前就听见过，要不就是书里读到过……在一部旧的撕破了的早就被遗忘的长篇小说里读到过。

大厅里萨沙坐在桌旁喝茶，五只长长的手指托着茶碟；奶奶在用纸牌占卦；尼娜·伊万诺芙娜在看书。火苗在圣像面前的长明灯里爆响，一切似乎都宁静平安。娜佳告辞后上楼回到自己的房间里，她一躺下就睡着了。可是如同昨夜一样，天明破晓，她已经醒了。她不想睡觉，感到心里不安和难过。她坐着，把头放在两个膝盖上，想着未婚夫，想着婚礼……不知为什么她想起，她母亲并不爱已故的丈夫，现在她一无所有，生活上完全依赖她的婆婆，她就是奶奶。娜佳左思右想，怎么也弄不懂：为什么一直到现在她总认为她母亲有什么特别的非凡的地方？为什么她没有看出这是一个普普通通、平平常常的不幸女人？

楼下的萨沙也不在睡觉。可以听见他的咳嗽声。娜佳暗想：他是个古怪和天真的人，在他的幻想里，在他讲的奇妙的花园和罕见的喷泉里，都使人觉得有一种荒唐的东西；然而，不知为什么，他的天真，甚至他的这种荒唐却又非常美好，以致她一想到该不该出去学习就有一股凉爽之气沁透她的整个心胸，使她感到欢悦和兴奋。

"不过还是不想为好，还是不想为好……"她小声说。"不该想这种事情。"

"滴克——笃克……"守夜人在一个远远的地方打更。"滴克——笃克……滴克——笃克……"

三

6月中旬萨沙突然感到无聊起来，他打算回莫斯科去。

"我不能住在这个城里，"他阴郁地说。"没有自来水，也没有下水道！我吃饭感到腻味，厨房里脏得令人不能忍受……"

"再住一阵吧，浪子！"奶奶不知为什么小声说。"婚期就在7号！"

"我不想再等了。"

"你本来打算在我们家住到9月份呢！"

"可是现在我不想再住下去了。我要工作！"

这年的夏天潮湿和阴冷，树都是潮乎乎的，花园里的一切都显得无精打采，单调凄凉，人确实不由得想工作。楼上和楼下的房间里响起了好几个陌生女人的说话声，奶奶的房间里有人在踏缝纫机，——这是在赶制嫁妆。光皮大衣就为娜佳准备了六件，据奶奶说，其中最便宜的一件也值三百卢布！这种忙乱惹萨沙生气，他坐在房间里发怒；可是大家仍然劝说他留下，他答应在7月1日走，不会提前。

　　时间过得真快，圣彼得节那天吃过午饭后，安德烈·安德烈伊奇同娜佳一起上莫斯科大街去，再细看一次租下来准备供新婚夫妇使用的房子。这是一幢两层楼房，可是目前还只装修好了二层楼。大厅里有明亮的地板，漆成了细木精镶的样子，有几把维也纳式的椅子，有一架钢琴，有一个小提琴乐谱架。房内弥漫着油漆气味。墙上挂着一张装在金边镜框里的大油画，画面上是一个裸体女人，她身边有一个断了手柄的淡紫色花瓶。

　　"一幅妙不可言的画，"安德烈·安德烈伊奇说，出于尊敬他还吁了一声。"这是画家希什马切夫斯基的作品。"

　　大厅过去是客厅，厅内有一张圆桌子、一个长沙发和几把蒙着蓝色套子的圈椅。长沙发上方挂着安德烈神甫的大照片，戴着法冠，胸佩勋章。接着他们走进了置有餐柜的饭厅，而后又进入卧室，在这里，在薄暗中并排放着两张床，好像是在布置卧室时人们就认定：将来这儿会永远美满，不可能会是别的样子。安德烈·安德烈伊奇领着娜佳观看各个房间，他一直搂着她的腰；她呢，她感到虚弱、惭愧，她憎恨这些房间、床铺、圈椅，而那个裸体女人更使她恶心。对她来说，已经一清二楚的是：她不再爱安德烈·安德烈伊奇了，或者是她，也许，从来就没有爱过他。可是，这话该怎么说出口，该向谁说，为了什么去说，——对此她并不明白，而且也不可能明白，虽说她整天整夜想着的就是这件事情……他搂着她的腰，说话语气十分亲切、温雅，他在自己这个寓所里走来走去，感到十分幸福；可是她处处看到的却只是庸俗，那愚蠢无知使人受不了的庸俗。就连他那只搂着她腰的手她也觉得像是一个铁箍，又硬又凉。她随时都可能逃跑、号啕大哭并从窗口跳出去。安德烈·安德烈伊奇把她领进了浴室，他在这里用手触动一下安在墙内的水龙头，水突然流将出来了。

"怎么样？"他说着哈哈大笑起来。"依照我的吩咐在阁楼放了个水箱，可以装一百桶水，嗬，我和你现在就有用了。"

他们在院子里散步，然后走到街上，雇了一辆出租马车。路上尘土飞扬，就像浓重的乌云一样，看样子，一场雨就要下来了。

"你不觉得冷吗？"安德烈·安德烈伊奇问，尘土使他睁不开眼睛。

她不做声。

"你记得吧，昨天萨沙责备我，说我什么事也不做，"他沉默片刻后说。"是的，他说得对，及其对！我是什么事也不做，我也不会做。我亲爱的，这是为什么？我甚至在想到有朝一日我会戴上帽徽去机关干差事时心里就会十分厌恶，这是为什么？我一见到律师，或者拉丁语教师或者市参议会委员，一见到就会非常不痛快，这是为什么？啊，亲爱的俄罗斯！啊，亲爱的俄罗斯，你背负着的游手好闲、一无用处的人太多啦！压在你身上的像我这样的人太多啦，多灾多难的俄罗斯！"

他对他什么事也不做这一点作了概括，认为这是时代的特征。

"等我们结了婚，"他继续说。"我们一起到乡下去，亲爱的，我们将在那儿干活！我们买上它一块不大的土地，要有花园，有河，我们将一起劳动，一起观察生活……啊，这会有多好啊！"

他脱掉帽子，风把他的头发吹得飘动起来。她一边听他说话一边想："上帝啊，我要回家！上帝啊！"就在快要到家的当口他们赶上了安德烈神甫。

"瞧，我父亲来了！"安德烈·安德烈伊奇高兴地挥动起帽子来。"我喜欢我的爸爸，真的，"他一边付钱给车夫一边说。"他是个可爱的老人，善良的老人。"

娜佳走进屋子，她气冲冲的，一脸病容，心中想着整个晚上会有客人，她得接待他们，得面露笑容，得听小提琴演奏，得听各种荒诞无稽的谈话，还得专门谈谈婚礼。奶奶在茶炊旁边坐着，她自尊自大，穿着华丽的绸衣，目空一切，在客人面前她好像总是这样的。安德烈神甫走进来，面露费解的笑容。

"看见您非常健康，我深感愉快和宽慰，"他对奶奶说。很难弄明白，他这是在开玩笑还是认真说的。

四

风敲打着窗子和屋顶。不断地响着嗖嗖嗖的声音。家神在火炉里凄婉忧郁地唱歌。是夜里十二点钟了。屋里所有的人都已经躺下，可是谁也没有睡着。娜佳总觉得楼下似乎有人在拉小提琴。听到一下刺耳的声音，该是一块百叶窗脱落了。过一会儿尼娜·伊万诺芙娜只穿着一件衬衫走了进来，手中拿着一支蜡烛。

"是什么东西在碰撞作响，娜佳？"她问。

母亲把头发扎成了一条辫子，她神色怯懦，在这个风雨之夜显得苍老难看矮小。娜佳想起，不久前她还认为她母亲是个不寻常的女人，听母亲说话时她还感到自豪。可是现在她却怎么也想不起母亲说过的话，而还记着的却是一些非常无用和无力的话。

火炉里响起了好几个男低音的歌声，还仿佛听到了"唉，唉，我的上帝！"的声音。娜佳从床上坐起来，突然她牢牢抓住自己的头发号啕大哭起来。

"妈妈，妈妈，"她说，"我的亲妈，要是你知道我怎么啦，那就好了！我请求你，我恳求你，让我走吧！我恳求你！"

"到哪儿去？"尼娜·伊万诺芙娜莫名其妙，她问道。她在床上坐下。"到哪儿去？"

娜佳哭泣了很长时间，一句话也说不出来。

"让我离开这个城市吧！"终于说。"不应举行婚礼，也不会有这个婚礼，你得明白！我不喜欢这个人……我连谈都不愿意谈到他。"

"不，我的亲人，不，"尼娜·伊万诺芙娜吓坏了，她急忙说。"你安静一下，这是由于你情绪不好。这会过去的。这种情形是常有的。大概是你跟安德烈吵嘴了吧，不过，相爱的人吵架只是寻开心。"

"得了，你走吧，妈妈，你走吧！"娜佳痛哭起来。

"是啊，"尼娜·伊万诺芙娜沉默一会儿后说。"不久前你还是个孩子，是个小姑娘，可是现在已经是未婚妻了。在自然界新陈代谢是不间断的。你会不知不觉就成为母亲和老太婆，你也会像我一样有这么一个倔强的好女儿。"

"我亲爱的好妈妈，你聪明，你不幸，"娜佳说。"你很不幸。为什么说这些庸俗的话呢？求求你，告诉我，为什么要说呢？"

尼娜·伊万诺芙娜想说些什么，可是她未能说出一个字来，哽咽一声就回自己房间去了。火炉里又响起了呜呜呜的声音，突然使人感到可怕。娜佳从床上跳下，迅速走到母亲的房间里。泪痕满面的尼娜·伊万诺芙娜躺在床上，盖着一条浅蓝色的被子，手里拿着一本书。

"妈妈，你听我讲完！"娜佳说。"我恳求你好好想一想，恳求你理解我！你得明白，我们的生活多么低级庸俗，多么有损尊严。我眼睛亮了，我现在什么都看得清清楚楚了。你的安德烈·安德烈伊奇是哪号子人呢？要知道，他并不聪明，妈妈！主啊，我的上帝！你得明白，妈妈，他愚蠢！"

尼娜·伊万诺芙娜霍地坐起身来。

"你和奶奶都折磨我！"她啜泣了一声说，"我要生活！生活！"她说着用小拳头捶了两下胸口。"给我自由吧！我还年轻，我要生活，而你们却使我成了一个老太婆！……"她痛苦地哭起来，躺了下去，在被子里蜷曲起身子，以致显得十分弱小、可怜、愚蠢。娜佳回到自己的房间里，穿好衣服，坐在窗旁等待早晨的来到。她坐着想了一整夜，户外有个什么人一直在敲打百叶窗和吹口哨。

早晨奶奶发牢骚，说夜间大风吹落了花园里的全部苹果，折断了一棵老李树。天色灰蒙蒙，阴沉沉，令人觉得凄凉，只好点起灯来。大家都在抱怨天冷，雨点在敲打着窗子。喝过早茶后，娜佳走进萨沙的房间，一句话也不说就在墙角里的圈椅旁跪下，双手蒙着脸。

"怎么啦？"萨沙问。

"我不行了……"她说。"从前我怎么能生活在这种地方，我不明白，我弄不懂！现在我看不起未婚夫，看不起自己，看不起这游手好闲、空虚无聊的全部生活……"

"哦，哦……"萨沙说，他还不明白这是怎么一回事。"这没什么……这挺好。"

"我憎恨这种生活，"娜佳继续说。"在这里我一天也待不下去了。我明天就离开这个地方。看在上帝面上，您把我带走吧！"

萨沙惊讶地看了她一会儿。他终于明白了，像小孩子一样十分高兴。他挥动双手，用便鞋踏起拍子来，高兴得好像是在跳舞似的。

"好极了！"他搓着手说。"上帝啊，这太好了！"

她的两只大眼睛爱慕地看着他，一眨也不眨，像是着了魔似的，期待着他马上会对她说出一些意义无限重大的话来。他什么话都没有说，但她已经觉得，在她面前展开着一种她从前不知道的崭新的远大的情景，她充满期望地看着他，决心面对一切，甚至不惜一切死。

"我明天动身，"他想了想说。"您上车站去送我……我把您的行李装进我的箱子，我替您买好车票，第三遍铃响时您就进车厢，我们就一起走了。您陪我到莫斯科，然后您一人去彼得堡。您有身份证吗？"

"有。"

"我向您担保，您决不会遗憾，也决不会后悔，"萨沙津津有味地说。"到了那里，您将进行学习，往后就听凭命运安排吧。如果您能把您的生活翻个底朝上，那就一切都会改变。主要的是把生活翻个底朝上，其余一切都无关紧要。那么，我们明天一起走？"

"啊，对！看在上帝面上！"

娜佳觉得，她十分激动，她心头从未这么沉重过，她觉得，从现在到起程前她会一直难过，会痛苦地思忖；可是，她刚上楼回到自己的房间里，刚在床上躺下，就立刻睡着了，而且睡得非常香，脸上带着泪痕和笑容，一觉直睡到傍晚。

五

派人去叫出租马车了。已经戴上帽子和穿好外衣的娜佳走上楼去，她要再看上一眼母亲，再看上一眼她自己的一切。在自己的房间里，她在还有着余温的床铺旁站了一会儿，向四周环顾一番，接着就轻轻地走去看母亲。尼娜·伊万诺芙娜还在睡觉，房间里静悄悄的。娜佳吻了一下母亲，理了理她的头发，站了两分钟光景……接着她不慌不忙地回到楼下。

外面下着大雨。支起车篷的出租马车停在门口，上上下下都湿淋淋的。

"你同他一起坐不下，娜佳，"奶奶在女仆开始搬箱子上车时说。"这种天气去送行，何苦呢！你留在家里吧！瞧，雨可真大呀！"

娜佳想说些什么，但没能说出口，这时候萨沙把娜佳扶上了车，用车毯盖住她的腿，接着他自己在她一旁坐下。

"一路平安！求上帝保佑你！"奶奶在台阶上喊道。"你呀，萨沙，从莫斯科给我们来信！"

"好啊！再见，好奶奶！"

"求圣母保佑你！"

"啊，这天气！"萨沙说。

只是在这时娜佳才哭出来。现在她已经清楚：她是走定了，而在她向奶奶告辞和在她看望母亲的时候，她对这一点还是不相信的。别了，这座城市！突然间她想起了一切：想起了安德烈，他的父亲，新寓所，裸体女人画像，花瓶，——所有这一切都已不再使她惊骇和苦恼了，而只是显得幼稚和渺小。这一切都过去了，越离越远。当火车开动，他们在车厢里坐好的时候，过去的一切，原本是那么重大那么严肃的过去，目前已缩成一小团，而一直到目前尚很不显眼的宏大而又宽广的未来却在她面前展示开来了。雨点敲打着车厢的窗子，眼前只看见绿油油的田野，电线杆上的鸟儿都纷纷闪过。突然间一种欢悦的心情使得她喘不过气：她想起她这是在走向自由，是去学习，而这就同很久很久以前人们所说的"外出做一个自由的哥萨克"一样。她既笑又哭又祈祷。

"不——错！"萨沙得意地微笑着说。"不——错！"

六

秋天过去了，随它之后冬天也过去了。娜佳已经忧愁得厉害，她天天想念母亲，想念奶奶，想念萨沙。家里的来信都是平静和善的，似乎一切都已经得到宽恕，一切都已经被忘却。五月间考试完毕后健康而欢乐的她动身回家，中途她在莫斯科逗留了一下，看望萨沙。他还是去年夏天那个样子：留着胡子，头发蓬乱，穿的还是那件长礼服和那条帆布裤子，眼睛仍然很美很大；可是他面色不健康，一副疲惫不堪的样子，又老又瘦，不时地咳嗽。不知为什么娜佳觉得他粗陋土气。

"我的上帝啊，娜佳来了！"他说着快活地大笑起来。"我的亲人，好朋友！"

他们在石印车间里坐了一会儿，那里烟雾腾腾，而浓重的油墨和颜料气味使人气闷。接着他们来到他的房间里，那儿烟雾腾腾，痰迹斑斑，桌上有一个已经凉了的茶炊，旁边摆着一只破盒子，上面放着一小块黑纸，桌子上和地板上有许多死蝇。从这里的一切可以看出，萨沙把他的个人生活安排得十分马虎，他随随便便过日子，不讲究舒适。如果有人同他谈起他的个人幸福，谈起他的个人生活，谈起他的爱，他会一窍不通，只是一笑了之。"没什么，一切都顺当，"娜佳匆匆地说。"秋天妈妈到彼得堡看过我，她说起奶奶不再生气，但常去我的房间，向着墙壁画十字。"

萨沙看上去挺高兴，但他不时地咳嗽，而且说话声音嘶裂。娜佳一直仔细地观察着他，她弄不明白：是他真病得厉害，还是仅仅是她觉得如此。

"萨沙，我亲爱的，"她说。"您该不是病了吧！"

"不，没什么。是有病，可是不太厉害……"

"啊，我的上帝，"娜佳焦急不安地说，"您为什么不就医？您为什么不保重身体呢？我宝贵的亲爱的萨沙。"她说着泪珠簌簌落下。这时不知为什么在她的脑海里浮现出安德烈·安德烈伊奇、裸女画、花瓶以及她的全部过去的生活，而这过去的生活现在看来似乎像童年时代一般遥远了。她哭了，因为她觉得萨沙已经不像过去那么新奇，那么有见识和有意思。"亲爱的萨沙，您病得很厉害。我不知道该怎么做才能使您不这么苍白消瘦。我太感激您啦！您简直想象不出来，您为我做了多少事情，我的好萨沙！实际上您现在是我最贴心最亲近的人。"

他们在一起坐了一会儿，谈了一阵子。现在，自从娜佳在彼得堡度过了一个冬天之后，她觉得，萨沙本人、他说的话、他的笑容、他的整个形象，——都有着一种衰颓、陈腐的味道，他的美好时光早已过去，或许它已经进了坟墓。

"后天我将去伏尔加河沿岸旅行，"萨沙说。"嗯，过一阵后我去喝马乳酒①。我想喝点儿马乳酒。和我同行的还有一个朋友和他的妻子。他妻子是个极好的人，我一直在怂恿她，劝说她，要她出去学习。我要她把她的生活翻个底朝上。"

他们谈了一阵后就去火车站。萨沙请她喝茶吃苹果。火车开动时，他笑吟吟地挥动手帕。就从他那双腿也可看出：他病得很厉害，未必会活得很长了。

娜佳在中午抵达故城。在从车站回家途中她觉得街道很宽阔，房屋却又小又矮，街上没有人，只遇见一个德国籍钢琴调音师，他穿着一件棕黄色的大衣。所有的房屋都好像是蒙上了一层尘土似的。奶奶已经衰老，像以前一样胖胖的，不好看，她伸出双臂搂住娜佳，把脸靠在娜佳的肩膀上哭了好久，不能脱开。尼娜·伊万诺芙娜也老了许多，变丑了，好像消瘦了，可是她仍像从前那样束紧腰带，钻石戒指仍在她手指上闪亮。

"我亲爱的！"她说话时全身颤抖。"我亲爱的！"

后来她们都坐着默默地哭泣。看得出来，奶奶和母亲都感到过去的日子已经一去不复返了：已经没有了社会地位和昔日的荣誉，已经没有资格邀请客人。这情况就像是：在轻轻松松无忧无虑地过日子的时候，警察突然在夜间光临，搜查一通，原来这人家的主人盗用了公款，制造了伪币，于是永别吧，轻松的无忧无虑的生活！

娜佳上了楼，看到了原来的那张床，原来的那些挂着的白窗帘。她摸了摸桌子，摸了摸床，坐下思忖了一会儿。她吃了一顿

---

① 喝马乳酒对患肺结核的人有疗效。

丰美的中饭，喝了拌上可口多脂的凝乳的茶，但总觉得已经有所不足，在房间里觉得空虚，就连天花板也低矮了。晚上她躺下睡觉，盖上被子，可是不知为什么她觉得躺在这暖和柔软的床上挺可笑。

尼娜·伊万诺芙娜走进来稍待一会儿。她畏畏缩缩小心翼翼地坐下，就像是个有过错的人一样。

"怎么样，娜佳？"她沉默了一会儿问道。"你满意吗？很满意，是吗？"

"我满意，妈妈。"

尼娜·伊万诺芙娜站起身来，在娜佳胸前和在窗上画十字。

"你瞧，我成了个信教的人了，"她说。"你知道，现在我在研究哲学，一直在思考，思考……现在对我来说，有许多事都变得清清楚楚，像白昼一样。我觉得，首先要像透过三棱镜那样来度过整个一生。"

"告诉我，妈妈，奶奶身体怎么样？"

"似乎不错。那一回，你同萨沙一起走后，收到了你的电报，奶奶一读完就倒下了；她一动不动地在床上躺了三天。后来她一直祈祷上帝，老是哭哭啼啼。现在她还行。"

妈妈站起身来，在房间里走动。

"滴克——笃克……"守夜人在打更。"滴克——笃克，滴克——笃克……"

"首先应该让一生像三棱镜那样来度过，"她说。"换句话说，那就是应该让生活在意识中分成一些十分单纯的因素，就好像分成为七种原色一样，应该对每种因素分别进行研究。"

尼娜·伊万诺芙娜还说了些什么，她又是在什么时候离开的，——这一切娜佳全都没有听见，因为她很快就入睡了。

5月过去了，6月来临。娜佳在家里已经习惯了。奶奶忙着张罗茶炊，深深地叹气；尼娜·伊万诺芙娜每到晚上就讲她的哲学，而在家里她仍同以前一样，像寄人篱下者似的，每个二十戈比的银币都得向奶奶讨。屋里苍蝇很多，房间里的天花板似乎越来越低了。奶奶和尼娜·伊万诺芙娜都不出门，为的是避免遇上安德烈神甫和安德烈·安德烈伊奇。娜佳在花园里散步，也上街去溜达，她看着房屋，看着灰色的围墙，觉得城里的一切东西都早已衰老，都不过是在等待着结局，或者是在等待着一种崭新的充满活力的生活的开端。啊，让这光明的新生活快些来临吧，到那时人就可以勇敢地正视自己的命运，意识到自己是无辜的，做一个快快乐乐自由自在的人！这样的生活迟早一定会到来！可不是么，总会有一天，到那时奶奶家的房子会不留痕迹地消失，会被人忘掉，没有人会记起它来，而现时那里的情况却是：四个女仆只能住在地下室，住在一个肮脏的房间里。只有邻院的几个小男孩能使娜佳开心，当她在花园里散步的时候，他们就敲打着板墙，笑着招惹她说：

"未婚妻！未婚妻！"

萨沙从拉托夫寄来一封信。他用活泼的歪歪扭扭的笔迹写道：他在伏尔加河一带旅游很顺遂，可是在萨拉托夫他有点儿不舒服，嗓音变哑了，躺在医院里已经有两个星期。娜佳明白这些话的意思，一种近于确定性的预感困扰了她。但她感到不快，因为这预感以及有关萨沙的想法不像以前那样使她激动。她热切地想生活，热切地想去彼得堡，以至她觉得她和萨沙的交往虽是亲切的，但已是遥远的过去！她彻夜没有合眼，早晨她在窗旁坐下仔细倾听。楼下果真响起了说话声音，不安的奶奶开始焦急地询问着一件什么事情，又听见有人哭了起来……娜佳走到楼上时，泪水满面的奶奶正在墙角里祈祷，桌子上放着一份电报。娜佳在房间里来回走了好久，听着奶奶哭泣，后来她拿过电报来读。电报里说的是：亚历山大·季莫费伊奇，或者按小名称呼，萨沙，昨天早晨在萨拉比托夫因患肺痨病去世。

奶奶和尼娜·伊万诺芙娜去教堂安排做安魂祭。娜佳又在几个房间里走了好长时间，边走边想。她清清楚楚地意识到，她的生活已经翻了个底朝上，而这正是萨沙想看到的。现在她在这儿觉得孤独寂寞，格格不入，谁也不需要她，而她也不需要这儿的一切，以前的一切已经同她脱离，好像是烧毁了似的已经消失，连灰烬也随风飘散了。她走进萨沙的房间，在那儿站了一会儿。

"别了，亲爱的萨沙！"她想道。在她面前显现出一种崭新的宽广自由的生活，这种生活，尚模模糊糊神秘玄妙的生活，正在招引她、诱惑她。

她到楼上自己的房间里收拾行李。第二天早晨她告辞了家里人，生气勃勃高高兴兴地离开了这个城市，像她所认为的那样，永远地离开了。

（朱逸森　译）

药 内 奇

一

　　每当外来人在 C 省城里抱怨生活枯燥单调时，当地人就像替自己辩解似的说，恰恰相反，C 城很好，C 城有一家图书馆、一座戏院、一处俱乐部，有时还举办舞会，最后，这儿还有一些头脑机敏、言谈风趣的可爱的人家，尽可能和他们交结来往。于是，他们便推荐图尔金一家，认为他家最有教养、最有天分。

　　这家人住在主要大街上的私人宅第里，距省长官邸甚近。伊万·彼得罗维奇·图尔金本人，体态丰满，相貌俊美，一头黑发，蓄有腮须。有时他筹办慈善性的募捐业余义演，亲自上台扮演年迈的将军，咳嗽起来显得滑稽可笑。他一肚子笑话、谜语和谚语，爱开玩笑，爱逗哏，他脸上的表情使人猜不透他是在开玩笑，还是在谈正经事。他的太太，薇拉·约瑟福夫娜，是位消瘦、娇美的夫人，戴着夹鼻子眼镜，她写中篇小说，喜欢读给来访的客人们听，女儿叶卡捷琳娜·伊万诺夫娜，正值妙龄，会弹钢琴。总之一句话，这家人各有所长。图尔金一家殷勤好客，总是高高兴兴、诚诚实实地展示自己的才能。他们高大的砖石结构的房子很宽敞，夏天凉爽，半数窗户朝向一座古老的绿阴密布的花园，春天那里夜莺歌喉婉转；当客人们坐在这栋房子里时，厨房里菜刀声响个不断，院子里飘着煎葱的味道——每次这都预示着将会有一顿丰盛美味的晚餐。

德米特里·药内奇·斯塔尔采夫被委任为县区地方医生的初期，住在离 C 城九俄里的佳里日镇，那时便有人建议他作为一个有知识的人必须结识图尔金一家。那一年冬天，别人在大街上把他介绍给伊万·彼得罗维奇，他们谈了谈天气，谈了谈戏院，谈了谈霍乱，紧接着就是他被邀请到图尔金家去做客。春天，那是一个星期天，欣逢耶稣升天节，斯塔尔采夫给病人看完病之后，进城去散心，顺便为自己买点东西。他不慌不忙地走着（那时他还没有自己的马车），一路上哼唱着：

我在生活中还没有品尝到泪水的滋味……

他在城里吃了一顿饭，在花园里逛了半晌，后来想起伊万·彼得罗维奇的邀请，便决定到图尔金家去一趟，见识见识这是些什么人物。

"欢迎大驾光临，欢迎大驾光临！"伊万·彼得罗维奇在门廊里迎接了他。"我能欢迎这么一位高贵的客人，太高兴了，太高兴了。请进，我把我的贤内助介绍给您。"他把妻子介绍给医生，接着对妻子说："薇罗奇卡，我对他说，即使罗马法典也没有哪项规定让他待在自己的医院里，他应当把自己的闲暇时间贡献给社会。我的心肝儿，你说是不是？"

"您请坐这儿，"薇拉·约瑟福夫娜招呼客人坐到自己身旁。"您来照顾我吧！我丈夫好妒忌，他是奥赛罗，不过我们的举动可以想法让他什么也看不见。"

"你呀，小乖乖，小淘气……"伊万·彼得罗维奇亲昵地喃喃道，在她额头亲吻了一下。"您来得正是时候。"他又对客人开了口。"我的贤内助完成了一部洋洋大观之作，今天她将为大家朗诵。"

"冉奇克，"薇拉·约瑟福夫娜对丈夫说，"您吩咐一下给我们上茶。"

他们把十八岁的女儿叶卡捷琳娜·伊万诺夫娜引见给斯塔尔

采夫。姑娘长得酷似母亲，身材同样苗条，面目同样可爱。她的表情还带有几分稚气，腰身纤细柔韧；她那少女的乳房已经隆起，美丽而健康，说明青春期已到，名副其实的青春。后来大家喝茶，有果酱、有蜂蜜、有糖果，还有非常好吃的饼干，饼干一进口就化了。随着傍晚的降临，客人三三两两地来了。伊万·彼得罗维奇用笑眯眯的眼睛招呼每一位客人，并说：

"欢迎大驾光临。"

后来大家坐在客厅里，表情非常严肃，薇拉·约瑟福夫娜开始朗诵自己的长篇小说。她是这样开始的："严寒更加凛冽……"所有窗户都大敞着，可以听到厨房里的菜刀声，可以闻到煎葱的味道儿……坐在又软又深的软椅里觉得好舒服，黄昏时刻的客厅里灯光柔柔和和；如今，在这盛夏的夜晚，从街道上传来讲话声、欢笑声，还有从院里飘来丁香花香，很难想象严寒是怎样更加凛冽，落日是怎样用冷丝丝的光照射在雪原和路上孤零零跋涉的旅人；薇拉·约瑟福夫娜读到一位年轻貌美的伯爵夫人怎样在农村里办学校、医院、图书馆，怎样爱上一位浪迹天涯的画家，——她朗读的故事是生活中从来不会有的事，但不管怎么说，坐在软椅里听起来既悦耳又舒服，脑子里浮现的都是这类美好的、平静的想法，——实在不愿意站起来。

"蛮不错嘛……"伊万·彼得罗维奇轻轻说了一句。

有一位客人，听着故事飞向很远很远的地方。他用勉强可以听到的声音说了一句：

"是啊……的确……"

过了一个小时，又一个小时。毗邻的市立公园里乐队在演奏，合唱队在唱歌。薇拉·约瑟福夫娜合上自己的笔记本，大家足足有五分钟一声未吭，倾听合唱队演唱的《可爱的松明》，这支歌唱的是小说中所没有的而生活中常见到的事。

"您在杂志上发表自己的大作吗？"斯塔尔采夫问薇拉·约

瑟福夫娜。

　　"不发表，"她答道，"我在任何刊物上都不发表。我写完了便把它藏在自己的柜子里。何必发表呢？"她解释道："我们又不缺钱花。"

　　不知为什么大家都叹了一口气。

　　"现在请你，猫咪，弹个曲子吧，"伊万·彼得罗维奇对女儿说。

　　钢琴的盖子被掀开了，事先准备好的乐谱翻开了。叶卡捷琳娜·伊万诺夫娜落座，双手敲在琴键上；然后用全力猛敲了一次，又一次，又一次；她的肩头和胸部都在抖动，她顽强地敲着同一个地方，仿佛不把琴键敲进钢琴里去是不会罢休的。客厅里充满了隆隆声，什么都在响：地板、天花板、家具……叶卡捷琳娜·伊万诺夫娜弹的是一首难奏的乐句，正因为难度大、又长又单调它才有趣儿，斯塔尔采夫一边聆听，一边给自己描绘一幅情景：一堆石头从高山上滚下来，滚呀，不断地滚，他希望这些石头尽早别再往下滚了。同时，他觉得他非常喜欢这位矫健的、有力的、脸色紧张得绯红的、额前垂下一缕鬈发的叶卡捷琳娜·伊万诺夫娜。在佳里日镇，在病人和农民当中度过一冬之后，坐在这间客厅里，欣赏这位年轻的、漂亮的，大概是纯洁的少女，聆听这嘈杂的、令人生厌的，但毕竟是高雅的声音，——是那么惬意，那么新奇……

　　"啊，猫咪，你从来没有弹得像今天这么精彩。"当女儿演奏完毕站起来时，伊万·彼得罗维奇两眼含着泪水说。"丹尼斯，你可以死了，你再也写不出比这更好的作品。"

　　大家把她围起来，祝贺她，表示惊讶，都说这么多年没有欣赏过如此美妙的乐曲了；而她呢，含着微笑，一声不响地听着，她的整个身姿都显示出成功的喜悦。

　　"好极了！太好了！"

　　"好极了！"斯塔尔采夫在大家的感染下也这么说了一句。

"您是在什么地方学的音乐？"他向叶卡捷琳娜·伊万诺夫娜问道。
"在音乐学院吗？"

"不是，我只是想进音乐学院，目前我在此地跟扎夫洛夫斯卡娅太太学琴。"

"您毕业于当地专科学校的专修班？"

"啊，没有！"薇拉·约瑟福夫娜替女儿回答道。"我们请老师到家里来教她，在学校里或是学院里——您同意我的看法——可能有不良影响；姑娘正在成长，她只能接受母亲一个人的影响。"

"不管怎么说，我一定要进音乐学院，"叶卡捷琳娜·伊万诺夫娜说。

"不，猫咪爱自己的妈妈。猫咪不会让爸爸妈妈伤心。"

"不，我要去！我一定要去！"叶卡捷琳娜·伊万诺夫娜半开玩笑半撒娇地说，她还跺了一下小脚。

晚餐席上，伊万·彼得罗维奇展示了自己的才华。他眯缝着两只笑眼讲起笑话来，说些逗哏话，提出一些可笑的谜语，又由自己来破谜，他一直用与众不同的语言讲话，这是他老说俏皮话养成的，显然，这些话已经成了他的习惯用语：什么"洋洋大观"呀，什么"蛮不赖"呀，什么"千谢万谢让您受罪了"呀……

其实，还不止这些。当客人们吃饱了喝足了，心满意足地挤在前厅里寻找自己的大衣和手杖时，一个十四五岁的佣人帕夫鲁沙在他们身边忙来忙去，这家人把他唤做帕瓦，留个小平头，鼓着胖乎乎的脸蛋。

"喂，帕瓦，表演一下！"伊万·彼得罗维奇对他说。

帕瓦摆出一个架势，举起一只手，用悲惨的腔调说道：

"你去死吧，不幸的女人！"

大家哈哈大笑起来。

"真逗。"斯塔尔采夫走到街时心想。

他又走进一家餐馆，喝了一杯啤酒，然后徒步回到自己的住处佳里日镇。他一路走一路哼哼着：

你的声音对我来说，又温柔又忧伤……

他走了大约九俄里，上床睡觉时，一点也不觉得疲倦，相反，他恨不得高高兴兴地再走上二十俄里。

"蛮不赖呀……"朦胧中他又想起了这句话，于是笑了起来。

二

斯塔尔采夫总想到图尔金家去，可是医院工作太忙，他怎么也抽不出空闲的时间来。就这样，他在忙忙碌碌、孤孤单单中过了一年多。有一天城里有人给他送来一封信，装在淡蓝色的信封里……

薇拉·约瑟福夫娜早就患偏头痛症。最近，自从猫咪每天吓唬她妈妈说要去音乐学院，她犯病的现象越来越频繁了。全城所有医生都来过图尔金家，最近轮到了这位县级医生。薇拉·约瑟福夫娜给他写了一封动人的信，烦他来一趟，以便减轻她的痛苦。斯塔尔采夫来了，从此便经常造访图尔金家，而且非常勤……他确实为薇拉·约瑟福夫娜减轻了一些头痛，手是她逢人便说这是一位不寻常的、妙手回春的医生。不过，他造访图尔金家已经不是为了医治她的偏头痛症了……

有一天过节。叶卡捷琳娜·伊万诺夫娜在钢琴上弹完了又长又枯燥的练习曲。然后大家在餐厅里坐了很久，品茶聊天，叶卡捷琳娜·伊万诺夫娜讲了一桩可笑的事。这时门铃响了，主人起身到前厅去迎接客人，斯塔尔采夫趁一时的忙乱，非常激动地对叶卡捷琳娜·伊万诺夫娜悄悄地说：

"看在上帝的情面上，我恳求您，别再折磨我了，我们到花园去吧！"她耸耸肩，仿佛对他的要求感到莫名其妙和不知所云，但还是站起来，走了出去。

"您在钢琴上一弹就是三四个小时，"他跟在她身后说："然后您和母亲坐在一起，我根本没有一点儿机会和您谈话。我恳求您，哪怕给我一刻钟的时间呢！"

秋天已临近，老花园静谧萧瑟，幽径上落了一层深色的枯叶。天黑得早了。

"我已经有一周时间没有见到您了，"斯塔尔采夫接着说。"您应当知道，这让人多么难受！我们坐下来。您听我讲。"

他们在花园里有一个喜爱的地方：叶子宽大的老枫树下的长椅。现在他们俩在这条长椅上坐了下来。

"有什么事吗？"叶卡捷琳娜·伊万诺夫娜一本正经地干巴巴地问道。

"我已经整整一周时间没有见到您了，我已经这么久没有听到您讲话的声音了。我焦急地渴望、渴望听到您的声音。请您讲话吧！"

她鲜嫩的气息，她的眼睛和脸蛋的天真神采，都让他神魂颠倒。甚至她身上的衣着也使他觉得楚楚动人，认为它别有一种朴实和天真的风采。尽管她天真，他同时又觉得她绝顶聪明，她的修养超过了她的年龄。他可以与她谈文学，谈艺术，无所不谈，甚至向她抱怨生活，抱怨人，不过有时正进行严肃的交谈时，她会突然不是时候地大笑起来，或者跑回屋去。她和 C 城的所有姑娘一样，读书很多（其实，C 城人很少读书，本地图书馆的工作人员说，倘若没有这种姑娘和年轻的犹太人，图书馆完全可以关门大吉）；这让斯塔尔采夫无限欣喜，每次见面时他都兴奋地问她近日阅读了什么，然后像着了迷似的听她讲述。

"我们没有见面的这一周里，您都读了什么呀？"这次他问道。"您说呀，我请求您。"

"我读了皮谢姆斯基的小说。"

"哪部小说？"

"《一千个农奴》。"猫咪回答说。"皮谢姆斯基的名字多逗，阿列克谢·费奥菲拉克特奇！"

斯塔尔采夫看到她突然站起来向屋子走去，便惊讶地问道："您去哪儿？我必须和您谈谈，我必须向您表明……请您和我再待上哪怕是五分钟！求求您啦！"

她停了下来，像是要说什么，然后难为情地把一张纸条塞到他手里，便跑回到屋里，又在钢琴前坐了下来。

斯塔尔采夫读道："请您今晚十一时到公墓院内杰梅蒂墓碑附近来一下。"

"哦，这种约会够绝的了。"他镇定以后，暗自这么想。"为什么约会到公墓去？为什么？"

显然，猫咪是在捉弄人。约会在某一条街上或在市立公园见面多方便，谁能认真地想约人三更半夜到远在城外的公墓里会晤呢？再说，让他这个县级医生，有头脑有地位的人，竟被折腾得唉声叹气，接受纸条，到公墓里去游荡，干些现在连中学生都会嘲笑的蠢事，这段浪漫史会怎样发展下去呢？同事们一旦知道了，会怎么说呢？脸面何容？斯塔尔采夫在俱乐部里围着桌子转来转去，心中这么想着，可是十时半一到，他突然乘车去了公墓。

他已经有自己的双套马车了，还有个车夫，叫潘捷列蒙，身穿一件丝绒坎肩。明月当空。四周一片寂静，他感到温暖，融融秋意的温暖。郊区，靠近屠宰场的地方，犬吠阵阵。在城边一条巷子里斯塔尔采夫下了车，独自向公墓走去。"人人都有自己的怪脾气。"他心里想，"猫咪也是个怪女人——谁晓得呢？——她也许不是开玩笑，真的会来。"他把希望寄托于渺茫的空虚，并为这个希望所陶醉。

大约还有半俄里路程，他是穿过野地走过去的。远看公墓黑茫茫一片，像树林又像大花园。眼前出现了白石头围栏，大门……

月光下可以读出大门上几个字："极乐时刻降临……"斯塔尔采夫从便门走了进去，他第一眼看见的是宽敞的林荫路两旁白色十字架和黑色物体，还有睡意蒙眬的树木将自己的枝条垂悬在白色的物体上。这儿好像比野地里亮堂一些；枫叶，其形状类似野兽脚掌，在林荫路的黄沙上和石板上显得格外突出，墓碑上的铭文也清晰可见。刚来到这里时，斯塔尔采夫感到吃惊，这是他有生第一次所见，也可能是他一辈子再也没有机会到这儿来了：这是与任何其他地方不同的世界——这个世界如此美好，月光如此温柔，仿佛这儿就是他的摇篮，这儿没有人的生命，没有任何生命，可是使人感觉到每棵墨绿的杨树、每座坟茔都具有一种神秘的力量，它保证给人以安宁、温馨的永恒生命。石板、凋谢的花与树叶的秋天气息，散发出宽恕、悲伤和静谧。

万籁俱寂，繁星深沉温和地从高空俯视着大地，斯塔尔采夫的脚步声显得那么刺耳又不是时候。当教堂里敲起钟声时，他把自己想象成是个已经永远埋葬在此地的死人，这时他觉得有人在盯着他，在那一瞬间他想到，那不是安宁也不是寂静，而是虚无茫茫惆怅和悠悠的窒息绝望……

杰梅蒂的墓碑宛若一座小教堂，顶上有个天使。当年有个意大利歌剧团路经 C 城，团里一位女歌唱家不幸逝世，便被安葬在此地，并修了这座墓碑。城里已经无人记得她了，可是碑前的长明灯映着月光，好像还亮着。

一个人也没有。谁会三更半夜到这儿来？可是斯塔尔采夫在等，月光也像是在助燃他的欲念，他满怀激情在等，在想象中描绘接吻、拥抱的情景。他在墓碑旁坐了大约半个小时，然后沿着两旁的林荫路走了一阵，手里拿着帽子，一边等一边想，想象这些墓穴里不知埋葬了多少妇女、多少姑娘，当年她们是那么那么迷人，她们每夜都在温存中经受爱与激情的燃烧。实际上，大自然这位母亲拿人开这样的玩笑真是不好，意识到这一点又是多么令人寒心！斯塔尔采夫这样思忖着，同时他又想大喊一声，说他渴望爱，不管如何他都在期待着爱；现在浮现在他面前的已不是白色大理石，而是婀娜多姿的肉体，他看见了人影羞答答地向树荫里躲藏，他感受到了她们的体温，这种折磨让他忍无可忍……月亮遁入云后，像是幕布落了下来，周围顿时变得一片漆黑。斯塔尔采夫勉勉强强找到了大门，——天色已经黑了，如同秋夜一般，——然后他足足花了一个半小时东走西窜，寻找他停下自己马车的小巷子。

　　"我太累了，快站不住了。"他对潘捷列伊蒙说。

　　当他舒舒服服地坐上马车时，心想："嗨，不该发胖啊！"

<h2 style="text-align:center">三</h2>

　　第二天晚上，他到图尔金家去求婚。来得不是时候，理发师正在叶卡捷琳娜·伊万诺夫娜的房间里为她美发。她准备去俱乐部参加跳舞晚会。

　　他又不得不长时间里坐在客厅里喝茶。伊万·彼得罗维奇觉得客人有心事，待得无聊，便从坎肩兜里掏出几张小纸条，读了德国籍管家写的一封可笑的信，信中说庄园里所有"矢口抵赖"都坏了，所有"羞耻"都塌了。

　　"娘家总该能给不少陪嫁吧……"斯塔尔采夫心不在焉地听着，心里这样想。

　　一夜失眠弄得他神志不清，好像是被甜甜的迷魂汤给灌醉了；他心里懵懵懂懂，但又觉得喜洋洋暖乎乎，同时头脑里还有一种冰冷冷的沉甸甸的东西在作分析：

　　"趁为时不晚，赶快住手，难道她和你门当户对吗？她娇生惯养，调皮任性，每天睡到白天两点钟，而你只不过是一个教堂执事的儿子，一个县级医生……"

"可是，那又怎么样呢？"他心想。"管它呢！"

"再说，如果你娶了她，"脑子里那块东西接着分析。"她的亲人就会逼你放弃县里的工作，搬进城里来住。"

"哼，那又怎么样？"他心想。"进城就进城。她家会给一些陪嫁，我们就可以安顿自己的家了……"

叶卡捷琳娜·伊万诺夫娜终于走了进来，身穿袒胸露背的舞会纱裙，靓丽，纯洁，斯塔尔采夫只顾欣赏她，惊讶地望着她，一味地傻笑，一句话也说不出来了。

她开始告别，他也没有必要留在此地了。于是站起身来说他也应该回去：病人还在等待他。

"您在这儿既然没什么事，"伊万·彼得罗维奇说。"那么就不留您了。啊，请您顺便把猫咪捎到俱乐部。"

外面落雨点了，天很黑，只能凭潘捷列伊蒙喑哑的咳嗽声才能猜出马车的停处。车篷已经支了起来。

"我走路踩地毯，你走路瞎扯淡，"伊万·彼得罗维奇扶女儿上马车时讲了几句顺口溜。"他走路乱胡言……上路吧！再见喽！"

他们走了。

"我昨天可到公墓去了。"斯塔尔采夫开了口。"您的做法太不慈悲、太不仗义了……"

"您到公墓去了？"

"是的，我去了，在那儿一直等您，等到快半夜两点钟了。我好痛苦啊……"

"您既然不懂开玩笑，痛苦也活该。"

叶卡捷琳娜·伊万诺夫娜想到自己如此巧妙地捉弄了一个追求她的人，想到有人热烈地爱着她，感到美滋滋的，笑了起来。突然，她吓了一跳，大叫一声，是两匹马在俱乐部大门口猛转了一个弯，车身倾斜了。斯塔尔采夫抱住了叶卡捷琳娜·伊万诺夫娜的腰；她惊魂未散，依偎在他身上，而他趁势热烈地吻了她的双唇、她的下巴，并且把她抱得更紧。

"够了。"她冷冷说了一句。

转瞬之间，她已不在马车上了。站在灯火通明的俱乐部大门口的警察用难听的声音朝着潘捷列伊蒙喊道：

"笨蛋，你怎么不动了，往前赶！"

斯塔尔采夫回了家，但很快又返了回来，身上穿着别人的礼服，系着挺硬的白领带，领带总是支棱着，好像要从领子上溜下去。他在俱乐部的客厅里一直坐到深夜，温情脉脉地对叶卡捷琳娜·伊万诺夫娜说：

"啊，没有恋爱过的人，对爱情知道得太少了！我觉得还没有一个人正确地描写过爱情，也未必能把这种温柔的欢乐的痛苦的感情描绘出来。一个人只要体验过一次这种感情，他就不会用语言表达它了。何必要开场白，何必要描述？何必讲些没有用的花言巧语？我的爱无边无际……我请求您，恳求您，"斯塔尔采夫终于说出口来：

"请您做我的妻子！"

"德米特里·药内奇，"叶卡捷琳娜·伊万诺夫娜想了片刻，脸露出极其严肃的表情，说道："德米特里·药内奇，我很感谢您的厚爱，我尊敬您，但是……"她站了起来，立着说下去："但是，请您原谅，我不能做您的夫人。让我们严肃地谈一谈这个问题。德米特里·药内奇，您知道，我一生中最钟爱的莫过于艺术，爱得神魂颠倒，我把音乐奉若神明，我把自己的一生献给了音乐。我希望当一名演员，我希望出名、成功、随心所欲，可是您希望我继续留在这座城里，继续过这种空虚无聊的生活，这种生活我已经不能忍受了。当夫人——啊，不，对不起！人应当朝更高的灿烂的目标努力，而家庭生活会把我永远束缚住。德米特里·药内奇（她莞尔一笑，因为当她说'德米特里·药内奇'时，竟想起'阿列克谢·费奥菲拉克特奇'来),德米特里·药内奇,您是一位善良、高尚的聪明人,您比所有人都好……"泪水涌出了她的眼眶,"我真心实意地同情您,但……您可以理解……"

为了不哭出声来,她转身离开了客厅。

斯塔尔采夫的心不再忐忑不安了。他走出俱乐部,来到街上,首先把硬领带扯了下来,并深深地呼了一口气。他感到有些丢人,自尊心受到了伤害,——他没有想到会遭到拒绝,——他也不相信自己的梦想、苦恼和期望会把他引向如此愚蠢的结局,活像是业余剧团演出的小戏里的情节。他惋惜自己的感情、自己的爱,他是如此的惋惜,恨不得大哭一场或者抄起雨伞在潘捷列伊蒙宽宽的后背上狠狠地抽打一顿。

一连三天,他什么事也做不成,吃不下睡不着,可是当他听说叶卡捷琳娜·伊万诺夫娜去了莫斯科报考音乐学院时,他的心平静了,又恢复了往日的生活。

后来,他偶尔也会想起自己怎样在公墓院内晃来晃去,想起怎样坐着马车满城寻找礼服,那时他就伸伸懒腰自言自语:

"当初操心的事还真不少!"

四

四年过去了。斯塔尔采夫在城里已经有很多向他求诊的患者。每天上午,他在佳里日镇自己的医院里匆匆接待完病人之后,便乘车去看望城里的病人。他乘坐的已经不是双套而是三套马车了,套上还缀着铃铛,到了深夜他才能回家。他胖了,发福了,因为患哮喘病,不愿意走路了。潘捷列伊蒙也胖了,他越往横长越爱叹气,抱怨自己命苦:赶车已赶腻味了。

斯塔尔采夫到过一些不同的家庭,见识过很多人,可是他和谁也不接近。城里人的谈吐、对人生的看法,甚至他们的样子都让他心烦。经验一点一点地让他明白了一些事理：当你和城里人一起玩牌或吃吃喝喝时，那个人还算是个老老实实、平平和和，甚至不浑不傻的人，可是话题一离开饮食，比如说，谈及政治或学术上的事，那时他就不知所云，信口雌黄，既愚蠢又伤人，这时你恨不得拂袖而去。每当斯塔尔采夫试图跟城里的人，甚至是自由派人士交谈时，比方说人类——谢天谢地——在向前发展，随着时间的推移人类可以不用护照，可以取消死刑，那时这位城里人便会斜眼看他，疑神疑鬼地问道："也就是说，到了那时，任何人在大街上都可以随便杀人？"当斯塔尔采夫在社交场合，晚餐或喝茶时，说人应当劳动，不劳动是无法生活的，在场的每个人都认为他是在训话，便大动肝火和胡搅蛮缠地争辩。即便如此，城里人还是什么事也不干，绝对不干，他们也不关心任何事，简直想不出一个能够跟他们谈得来的话题。所以斯塔尔采夫便回避谈话，他只埋头吃东西或玩牌，如果赶上某家操办喜事，留他用餐，他便会坐下来，一声不响地吃，眼睛盯着盘子；这时他感到席间的谈话都没有意思，都是胡说八道，愚蠢透顶，他气愤，他激动，但沉默不语，正因为他总是一本正经地默不做声，眼睛盯着盘子，所以城里人给起了一个绰号"气呼呼的波兰人"，其实他从来不是波兰人。

像看戏、听音乐演出之类的娱乐，他一概退避三舍，但他每天晚上玩牌，一玩就是三个小时，而且玩得上瘾。他还有一种爱好，这种爱好是在不知不觉中渐渐养成的：这就是每天晚上从兜里往外掏出给病人治病所得的纸币，有时这些纸币把所有衣兜塞得满满的，足有七十多卢布，有黄票子、绿票子，有的散发着香水味，有的带醋味，有的有神香味和鱼油味；积聚到几百卢布时，他就把钱送到互助信贷社去存起来。

叶卡捷琳娜·伊万诺夫娜离家这四年里，他先后只到图尔金家去过两趟，还是应薇拉·约瑟福夫娜的邀请。她还在医治偏头痛症。叶卡捷琳娜·伊万诺夫娜每年夏天回家省亲，可是他一次也没有见到她，不知怎么没赶上机会。

如今四年过去了，一个宁静、温煦的早晨，有人把一封信送到医院来。薇拉·约瑟福夫娜在写给德米特里·药内奇的信中说，她很想他，请他无论如何赏光来一趟，以便减轻她的病痛，再说今天恰好是她的生日。信的下边附有一句："我也附和家母的邀请。猫。"

斯塔尔采夫思考了一番，傍晚乘车去了图尔金家。

"啊，欢迎大驾光临！"伊万·彼得罗维奇迎接他，只是眼睛带些笑的样子。然后又用变了腔调的法语表示欢迎："邦如尔泰。"

薇拉·约瑟福夫娜老多了，白发苍苍，她握了握斯塔尔采夫的手，煞有介事地叹了一口气：

"医生，您不愿意照顾我，总也不光临寒舍，对于您来说，我已经人老珠黄。如今年轻的姑娘回来了，也许她会得宠。"

那么猫咪呢？她清秀了，白嫩了，更漂亮更苗条了；不过她已是叶卡捷琳娜·伊万诺夫娜，而不是猫咪了；她没有了过去的鲜嫩和稚气。她的眼神里、举止中，多了点新东西——畏怯和歉疚，仿佛在这儿，在图尔金家中，她已经没有自家的感觉了。

"我们有多少年没有见面了！"她说着把手伸给斯塔尔采夫。看得出来，她的心在紧张地跳动，她好奇地注视他的脸，接着说道："您可胖多了！脸色晒得多黑，多有男子汉风度，总之，您的变化不大。"

即使现在他也觉得她可爱，很可爱，可是她身上缺少了些什么，也许增加了些多余的玩意儿，——他自己也说不清楚究竟是什么，但有种东西在妨碍他重现过去那种感情。他不喜欢她那苍白的衣服，她坐的软椅也不喜欢了。回想起他当年几乎娶了她为妻的往事，也让他不痛快。他想起了自己的爱情，想起了四年前使他坐立不安的幻想和希望，——他感到不自在。

大家喝茶，吃甜饼。后来薇拉·约瑟福夫娜朗读长篇小说，小说中讲的是生活中从来不会发生的事。斯塔尔采夫呢，他在倾听，望着她那满头美丽的白发，等她什么时候把小说念完。

"不会写小说的人，"他心想。"不一定是蠢材，写了小说而不会把它藏起来，那才是蠢材。"

"蛮不赖嘛。"伊万·彼得罗维奇说。

后来，叶卡捷琳娜·伊万诺夫娜在钢琴上弹奏了很长时间，声音很热闹。当她弹完时，大家长时间地感谢她，赞美她。

"幸好我没有娶她为妻。"斯塔尔采夫脑子里一闪念。

她望着他，大概盼望他能提出建议到花园里去，可是他默不做声。

"我们谈谈吧，"她走到他跟前："您的生活怎样？近来如何？忙吗？这些天来，我一直在想念您，"她神经质地接着说。"我本来想给您写封信，想亲自到佳里日镇去看望您，我已经决定出发了，可是后来又改变了主意，——天晓得您现在怎样看待我。今天我等您来，心情很乱。看在上帝的情面上，咱们到花园去吧！"

他们去了花园，那里像四年前一样，他们在老枫树下的长椅上坐下。天色漆黑。

"您的生活怎样啊？"叶卡捷琳娜·伊万诺夫娜问道。

"还可以，过得去，"斯塔尔采夫答道。

他再也想不出什么话来，两人都在沉默。

"我的心很不平静，"叶卡捷琳娜·伊万诺夫娜说，用双手捂住脸，"请您不要在意，我回到家里感觉好极了，见到大家我非常高兴，甚至一时还不能习惯。多少回忆啊！我觉得我们俩会不停地谈，一直谈到天亮。"

现在，他近处看见了她的脸庞，闪光的眼睛，在这儿，在一片黑暗中，她显得比在室内年轻，甚至重现出她过去孩子时代的表情。她确实用天真好奇的眼光望着他，仿佛想更近一些把他看个清楚，理解这位当年那么火热、那么温柔、那么不幸地爱过她的人；她的眼睛正为这种爱向他表示感激。他想起了所有往事，每一个极小的细枝末节：他怎样在墓园里游荡，怎样疲惫不堪地在拂晓前返回自己的家，他突然为往事感到忧伤和惋惜。火苗在心中慢慢燃烧起来了。

"您还记得我是怎样送您去俱乐部参加晚会的吗？"他说。"那天在下雨，天很黑……"

"唉！"他叹了一口气。"您问我生活过得怎样。我们在这里能够过上什么生活呢？没有什么好谈的。越来越胖，一年不如一年。一天又一夜——二十四小时就算过去了，生活暗淡无光，糊里糊涂……白天攒钱，晚上泡俱乐部，都是一群赌徒、酒鬼，一些说话嘶哑的人，我实在无法忍受他们。有什么好说的呢？"

"您有自己的事业，生活中有崇高的目标。过去您是那么喜欢谈自己的医院。那时我有点儿矫情，自以为是个伟大的钢琴家。现在谁家的小姐都会弹钢琴，我也弹钢琴，和大家一样，没有与众不同的地方；我这个钢琴家就和我妈是作家一样。那时我当然不理解您，可是后来，到莫斯科，我常常想念您。我只想念您一个人。当县级医生，这是何等的幸福啊，救死扶伤，为人民服务。这是何等的幸福啊！"叶卡捷琳娜·伊万诺夫娜神往地重复了一遍。"当我在莫斯科想念您时，您在我的心中是那么完美，那么崇高……"

斯塔尔采夫想起自己每天晚上兴致勃勃地从衣兜里掏出来的纸币时，心中的火苗便熄灭了。

他站起来，想回到屋子里去。她挽住他的胳膊。

"您是我一生中所认识的人中最好的人，"她接着说。"我们以后还会见面，还会谈心，对不对？请您答应我。我不是钢琴家，我有了自知之明，我也不会再当着您的面弹钢琴和谈论音乐了。"

　　他们进了屋，当斯塔尔采夫在傍晚的灯光下看清了她的面颊和那双注视着他的忧伤的、感激的、探索的眼睛时，感到一阵迷离恍惚，又一次想到："所幸我当时没有娶她为妻。"

　　他和大家告别。

　　"即使罗马法典也没有规定您有任何理由可以不吃晚饭便走。"伊万·彼得罗维奇送他时说。"您这是一厢情愿了。"他在前厅对帕瓦说："喂，表演一个节目！"

　　帕瓦已经不是孩子了，他成了青年人，还长了胡子。他摆出一副架势，扬起手臂，用凄惨的声音说道：

　　"您死吧，不幸的女人！"

　　这一切都刺激斯塔尔采夫的神经。他坐上马车，望着黑压压的房子和花园，望着当年对他来说是那么亲切可爱的地方，所有的往事一下子涌上心头——薇拉·约瑟福夫娜的长篇小说，猫咪叮叮当当的弹奏，伊万·彼得罗维奇的俏皮话，帕瓦的悲剧架势。他随即又想到，如果全城天分最高的人们如此浑浑噩噩，那么此城本身什么样子就可想而知了。

　　过了三天，帕瓦送来叶卡捷琳娜·伊万诺夫娜的一封信。她写道：

　　　　您不来我家，何故？我担心您改变了对我们的态度；我害怕，我一想到这一点就感到心慌。请您让我放下心来，来吧，并告诉我万事顺遂。

　　　　我必须跟您谈谈。

　　　　　　　　　　　　　　　　　　　　您的叶·图

　　他读完这封信，想了想，对帕瓦说：

　　"亲爱的，你回去说一声，我今天去不成，太忙。你说我大约过三天再去。"

三天过去了，一周过去了，他还是没有去。有一天他乘车路过图尔金家，想到应当进去看一看，哪怕待上一分钟呢，可是他考虑了一下……还是没有进去。

从此，他再也没有去过图尔金家。

五

又过了几年。斯塔尔采夫越发胖了，一身肥膘，喘气也吃力，走起路来头向后仰。这位肥头大耳、红光满面的人坐在铃铛丁零零作响的三套马车上，潘捷列伊蒙和他一样，也是肥头大耳、红光满面，后脑勺肉鼓囊囊，坐在车夫的座位上，把木头一般挺直的胳膊伸向前，朝着迎面的人不住地叫喊："靠……右，靠……右！"那种情景可真够威风，车上坐的仿佛不是活人，而是一尊多神教的神像。他在城里要看的病人相当多，连换口气的工夫都没有了。他已经置了一个庄园，城里还有两栋房产，他正在为自己物色第三栋有利可图的房子。每当互助信贷社里有人告诉他某处正准备出售一栋房屋时，他就大摇大摆地走进那栋房子，到每个房间查看一遍，不管屋里还有几个没有穿上衣服的妇女与儿童，那些人睁大眼睛惊讶地提心吊胆地望着他。他用手杖乱捅所有的门：

"这是书房？这是卧室？这是干什么的地方？"

与此同时，他呼哧呼哧喘着气，擦拭额上的汗珠。

他操心的事很多，但他绝不放弃县级医生的职务；他已经变得贪得无厌，这儿什么事都不想耽误。在佳里日镇，还有城里人，已经简单地称他"药内奇"了。"药内奇这是到什么地方去呀？"或者："要不要请药内奇出席会诊？"

他的喉咙大概被脂肪堵住了，所以嗓音变了，变得又细又尖。他的性格也变了：变得粗暴、容易动怒。接待病人时，他常常不耐烦地用手杖敲击地板，并用他那讨厌的嗓音叫着：

"请您只回答我的问题！少说废话！"

他孤身一个，生活枯燥，什么事也引不起他的兴趣。

在佳里日镇的这些年，他对猫咪的爱恋大概是唯一的也是最后的一次欢乐。每天晚上，他到俱乐部去玩牌，然后一个人坐在大桌旁吃晚餐。伺候他的是这里最受人尊重的老堂倌，给他端上拉斐特17号葡萄酒。这里所有人——俱乐部主任、厨师、堂倌——都知道他喜欢吃什么和不喜欢吃什么，他们都想方设法迎合他，生怕他发脾气，又该用手杖敲地板了。

用餐的时候，他偶尔转过身去，在别人的谈话中插上两句：

"你们谈的是什么呀？啊？谁？"

有时，邻桌人提及图尔金家里的事，他就要打听：

"您指的是哪一家图尔金？是女儿会弹钢琴的那一家吗？"

关于他，能说的也只有这些了。

图尔金一家呢？伊万·彼得罗维奇没有老，丝毫无变，和往常一样爱逗哏，爱讲笑话；薇拉·约瑟福夫娜和往常一样兴致勃勃地、诚心诚意地给客人们朗读自己的小说。而猫咪呢，每天弹钢琴，一弹就是四个小时。她明显地老了，常常闹病，年年秋天随母亲到克里木去疗养。伊万·彼得罗维奇送他们去火车站，火车一开动，他便拭着眼泪喊道："再见！"

同时挥舞着手帕。

（高莽　译）

美　女

　　我记得，还是一个五、六年级的小学生的时候，我曾跟着爷爷坐马车从顿河区的大克列普卡村朝罗斯托夫赶路。那是八月的一天，天气炎热，让人疲惫难熬。酷热和干燥的热风扬起的大片尘埃，朝我们迎面扑来，我们的眼睛睁不开了，口干舌烂，既不想看什么，也不想说什么，思维也停顿了。我们的马车夫是个名叫卡尔波的乌克兰人，他也有了睡意，扬鞭策马时，竟把鞭子刮到了我的帽檐上，我没有提出抗议，也没有吱声，只是从半睡状态中惊醒之后，怅怅地望着远方：透过灰尘能否看到一个村庄？我们在一个亚美尼亚人的大村子巴赫契沙拉停了下来，在爷爷的一个富有的亚美尼亚朋友家喂马。我从没有见过比这个亚美尼亚人更丑的面孔。请你们想象一下他的尊容：一个剃光了头的小脑袋，长着两道耷拉下来的浓眉，一个鹰钩鼻，苍白的胡须长得很长，大嘴巴里叼着一个樱桃木制成的烟斗。这个小脑袋笨拙地安置在一个干瘪的、佝偻的躯体上，服装也古怪：上身是件很短的红色上衣，下身是条肥大的鲜蓝色的裤子，迈着八字步走道，脚上趿着一双拖鞋。说话的时候嘴里还叼着烟斗，摆出一副纯粹的亚美尼亚人的派头：鼓起眼珠子，不露笑容，尽可能地淡待客人。

　　在这个亚美尼亚人的房子里没有风，也没有灰尘，但却像在草原上、大路上一样的烦闷和无聊。我记得，满身都是灰尘，热得喘不过气来的我，坐到了墙角的一个绿颜色的木箱子上。没有上过漆的木板墙，家具和上过漆的地板都散发着被太阳烘烤的干木料的气味。眼睛不管往哪里瞧,到处都是苍蝇,苍蝇……爷爷和亚美尼亚人低声谈论着放牧,牧草和燕麦……我知道,茶炊要等一个小时后才能备好,而爷爷喝茶至少花去一个小时,然后睡上两、三个小时,这么说我得等上六个来小时,然后又是酷热、灰尘和一路颠簸。我倾听着两个老头的低声谈话,我开始觉得,这个亚美尼亚人,这个食品柜,这个被阳光照射的窗户,我好久好久以前就看见过,而且要一直把它们看到遥远的将来,于是一种对于草原,对于太阳,对于苍蝇的怨恨的心绪,袭上了心头……

一个戴头巾的乌克兰女人端来了装有茶具的托盘,然后端来了茶炊。亚美尼亚人不慌不忙地走进外屋,喊道:

"玛莎!来倒茶!你在哪?玛莎!"

随即听到了快捷的脚步声,一个十六岁光景的少女走进屋来,她穿一条简朴的布长裙,戴着白色的头巾。她背对着我在洗茶具和朝杯子里倒茶水,我只是发现她的腰肢苗条,光着脚,而她的赤裸的脚后跟恰好被她的长衬裤所遮掩。

主人请我喝茶。坐在桌子旁,眼睛看着给我递过茶杯来的姑娘的脸蛋,我突然感觉到,好像有一阵风吹过我的心灵,吹走了一天的郁闷和灰尘。我看到了梦寐以求的一张无比美丽迷人的脸孔。站在我面前的是一个美女,我一眼就看出来了,就像一眼看到闪电一样。

我可以起誓:玛莎,或是像她父亲称呼的,玛什雅,是个真正的美女,但我无法证明我的判断。常有这样的情形,云团杂乱地堆积在天边,太阳,藏在云彩的后边,照射着它们,天空变得五光十色:深红色的,橙黄色的,金黄色的,浅紫色的,玫瑰色的;云彩呢,这朵像个修士,那朵像条鱼,第三朵像个裹着缠头的土耳其人。霞光布满了三分之一的天空,照耀着教堂的十字架和地主家的窗户,倒映在河流和水塘里,在树梢上颤抖。在这霞光的衬托下,在远处,有一队野鸭飞过,去寻觅栖息的处所……而赶着牛群的牧童，坐着马车走过大坝的土地丈量员，以及正在悠闲散步的老爷们都凝望着这落日的景色，都觉得这很美，但到底美在哪里，谁也不知道，谁也说不出。

不是我一个人觉得这位亚美尼亚姑娘美丽。我的爷爷，一位八十三岁的老头，平时性格倔强，对女人和大自然的美景都漠然置之，但这回也目不转睛地、温情地瞅着玛莎问："阿维特·纳扎雷奇，这是您的女儿？"

"女儿，是女儿……"主人答道。

"好漂亮的小姐。"爷爷赞美道。画家可能要用古典的和严谨的形容词来说明这个亚美尼亚姑娘的美。这真是这样的美，你静静地欣赏着它，你会确信你看到了最端正的相貌：那头发，那眼睛，那鼻子，那颈项，那胸脯和青春肉体的全部动态，都融合在一个完整而和谐的调子里，造化在创造的过程中连一个最小的细节也没有出错。不知为什么你也以为，一个理想的美女就应该长有玛莎那样直直的、稍稍隆起的鼻，那样又大又黑的眼睛，那样长长的睫毛，那样迷茫的眼神，她的黑色的鬈发和眉毛与她的额头与面颊的柔嫩的白色完全匹配，就像绿色的芦苇与郊区的小溪相匹配一样。玛莎的白色的颈项和年轻的乳房还没有充分发育，但你以为，需要具有巨大的创作才赋，才能把它们塑造出来。你看着她，慢慢地产生了一种愿望，想对玛莎说一些非常愉快的、真诚的、美丽的、像她本人一样美丽的话。

起初我有点懊丧和害臊，因为玛莎总是眼睛看着地面，对我毫不在意。我觉得好像有一种特殊的、幸福而骄傲的空气把她与我相阻隔，嫉妒地把她遮盖住，不让我看见。

"这是因为我浑身是土，脸也晒黑了，还因为我还是个小孩。"我这样想。

但后来我逐渐忘记了自己，全身心地沉醉在美的感受中了。我已经忘记了草原的寂寥，忘记了尘土飞扬，不再听到苍蝇的嗡嗡声，体会不到茶水的滋味，而只是感觉到，隔着一张桌子站着一个美女。

我对于美的感受有点奇怪。玛莎在我心中激起的不是欲望，不是亢奋，不是愉快的享受，而是一种尽管甜美却是沉重的忧伤。这种忧伤是蒙蒙的，像是梦幻。不知什么缘故，我开始为自己，为爷爷，为那个亚美尼亚人，和为那个亚美尼亚姑娘本人感到惋惜，好像我们四个人都失去了一种对于生活是很重要很需要的东西，而且我们再也找不到它。爷爷也惆怅起来。他不再谈论牧场和燕麦，而是默默地坐着，沉思地瞅着玛莎。

喝过茶水，爷爷躺下睡觉，而我走出屋去，坐到了门廊上。这所房子像巴赫契沙拉村的所有房子一样，都是让太阳干晒着，没有树木，没有遮阳的棚子，没有阴凉的地方。亚美尼亚人的大院子，长满了滨藜和锦葵，尽管酷热，却也生趣盎然。这个大院子里横贯着一道一道的矮篱笆墙，在其中一道篱笆墙的后边，正好有人在打谷子。在打谷场的中央，立着一根柱子，围绕着柱子，有十二匹马排成一列，形成一个长长的半径在奔跑。旁边有个乌克兰人在走动，他穿着一件长坎肩和一条肥裤子，挥舞着鞭子，大声叫喊着，像是要刺激这些马儿，显示自己的威风：

"啊——啊，该死的！啊——啊……讨厌鬼！害怕了吧？"

那些马，枣红马，白色马，斑色马，不明白为什么要强迫它们绕着一根柱子转圈子，把麦秆踩软，所以它们并不情愿地跑着，像是已经精疲力竭，生气地摇晃着尾巴，风从它们的蹄子下刮起一团团谷壳扬起的金黄色尘埃，远远地吹到了篱笆墙外。在高高的新鲜的麦秆堆房，聚集着一群手拿耙子的女人，大车在旁边移动。在另外的一个大院里，有另外的十二头马在围着柱子转圈，也有一个乌克兰人挥舞鞭子，戏弄着奔马。

我坐的台阶，烫得灼人；在稀疏的栏杆上，在窗子的框架上，有的木头被烧烤出了树脂；台阶下面和护窗板下的阴影里，蜷缩着一群红色的瓢虫。太阳烤着我的头，我的胸脯，我的背，但我全不在意，我只是感觉到，在我身后的过道和房间里，有一双光脚在木制地板上出声地走动。玛莎收拾完茶具，跑下台阶，朝我吹起一阵风，像鸟儿一般，跑进一间不大的，被烟熏黑了的房子，那大概就是厨房，从里边散发出了烤羊肉的气味，也传出了带亚美尼亚口音的骂人话。她消失在黑暗的门里了，从房门口却走出了一个驼背的亚美尼亚老太婆，她的脸孔通红，穿一条绿色的长裤，老太婆很生气，她在骂着什么人。很快，在门口出现了玛莎，厨房的热气烤红了她的脸蛋，她肩上扛着一个硕大的黑面包，因为面包分量很重，把她的腰压出一条弯弯的很好看的曲线，穿过大院，向打谷场跑去，越过篱笆墙，钻进谷壳的金黄色的雾阵，消失在大车的后边。赶马的乌克兰人，放下鞭子，沉默不语，静静地瞅着大车的方向，等到亚美尼亚姑娘再次出现在马群旁边，跳回篱笆墙的这一边，他就盯视着她，而且大声呵斥马群，他的调门让人觉着他很懊丧：

"你们不得好死！讨厌鬼！"

然后，我不断地听到她两只光脚的走步声，看到她是怎样地带着严肃认真的表情来回穿行在大院里。她时而跑过台阶，给我送来一阵风，时而跑向厨房，跑向打谷场，跑进门去，我都来不及转身看清她的身影。

她越是频繁地带着她的美丽闪现在我的眼前，我的惆怅越是变得深重。我既为自己感伤，也为她感伤，也为那个乌克兰人感伤，每当她穿过谷壳的雾阵跑向大车的时候，他都用忧伤的眼神注视着她。我是否在妒忌她的美丽，或者是我感到了惋惜，因为这个姑娘不属于我，而且永远不会属于我，我对她来说仅仅是个陌生人，或者是我隐约地感觉到，她那少有的美丽，如同大地上的一切事物，是偶然出现的，并非必需的，也不会长久保持的；或许我的惆怅，是一种人在静观真正的美时一定会激发的特殊的情感，这只有上帝能知道!

　　三个小时的等候时间在不知不觉中过去了。我觉得我还没有把玛莎看够,而车夫卡尔波已经在河里给马洗了个澡,把马车套好了。全身湿漉漉的马满意地喷着粗气,用蹄子踏着车辕。卡尔波朝它大喊"往后"! 爷爷醒来了。玛莎给我们打开了吱嘎作响的大门,我们坐上马车,驶出院外。我们坐在车上,一声不吭,像是互相在生着气。

　　两三个小时之后,已经能远远地看见罗斯托夫和纳希契瓦城。一直默不做声的卡尔波迅速回头看了一眼,说:

　　"那个亚美尼亚姑娘长得真俊! "

　　他朝马屁股抽了一鞭子。

　　第二个经历是,我当了大学生的时候。我坐火车到南方去。时值五月。在一个好像是白城与哈尔科夫之间的车站,我走出车厢,在月台上散步。

　　夜晚的阴影已经落到了车站的小花园中,落到了月台上和田野里。车站的建筑遮住了落日,但火车头冒出的烟团的最上端,蒙上了一层柔和的玫瑰色,可见太阳还没有完全落山。

　　我在月台上踱步,发现大部分正在散步的旅客都停在了一节二等车厢旁,从他们的表情判断,好像有一个名人就坐在这节车厢里。聚集在这节车厢旁边的好奇的旅客中,就有我一位旅伴,他是个炮兵军官,一个聪明的年轻人,对人热情,讨人喜欢——我们在旅途上偶然结交的人都是这样的。

　　"您在看什么? "我问。

　　他什么也没有回答,只是用眼神让我注意一个女人的身影。这是一个十七八岁的少女,穿一身俄罗斯的服装,没有戴头巾,只有一块小小的围巾,随意地搭在一个肩膀上。她不是旅客,可能是车站站长的女儿或妹妹。她站在车窗旁边,正在跟一个上了年纪的女旅客说话。还在我没有来得及明白我看到的究竟是什么人，突然之间一种我曾在亚美尼亚村子里体验过的感觉又抓住了我。

这姑娘是个美女，关于这一点，无论是我，还是与我一起在欣赏她的人都不怀疑。

如果像通常那样，单从局部来描绘她的外貌，那么真正称得上美丽的，仅仅是那一头浓密的、呈波浪形的浅黄色头发，头发披散下来，由一条黑色的丝带扎在头上，其他的部位要么不大端正，要么极其普通。她的一双眼睛总是眯缝着，要么这是因为近视，要么是为了做出撒娇的姿态。鼻子稍稍向上翘起。嘴很小。侧影并不轮廓分明。肩膀窄小得不合她的年龄。但即便如此，这位少女还是让人感到是个真正的美女。瞧着她，让我深信，俄国女人的脸孔无需端端正正就能显得美丽；甚至如果她那向上翘起的鼻子换上了另外一个塑造得完美无缺的鼻子，像那个亚美尼亚的姑娘那样，她的脸孔会反倒失去了全部神韵。

这位少女站在车窗旁边说话，因为晚间的湿冷而蜷缩着身子，她不时地瞧我们一眼，时而双手叉腰，时而为了扶正头发，把手伸向脑袋，一边说话，一边笑着，她的脸孔时而表现出惊奇，时而表现出恐惧，我记不得她的身子与脸孔有片刻是处于平静状态的，她的美丽的全部奥秘与神奇，正是在于这些细微的、无限典雅的动作中，在于微笑，在于她脸孔的表情变化，在于她朝我们的迅捷一瞥，在于这些动作的精微的优雅与青春生命的结合，与在笑谈中响彻的纯洁灵魂的结合，而且这种我们在小孩、小鸟、小鹿、小树身上捕捉到的柔弱，是十分让人珍爱的。

这是蝴蝶般的美丽，它与华尔兹舞，与花园里的游荡，与欢歌笑语十分和谐，而与严肃的思想，忧愁和文静就搭配不到一起了。似乎，只需在月台上下一阵雨或是刮一阵风，这个柔弱的身体就会突然凋萎，这个脆弱的美丽就会像花粉一样散落。

"这样……"当我们在响过第二遍铃后朝自己的车厢走去的

时候，军官这样叹息了一声。

而"这样……"是什么意思，我无法判断。

可能，他很忧伤，他不想离开这位美女和这个春天的夜晚而关进躁闷的车厢，可能，他和我一样，不由自主地为这位美女，为他自己，为我，为所有懒洋洋地走回自己车厢的旅客感到惋惜。我们走过火车站的一个窗口，窗里有一台发报机，旁边坐着一个脸色苍白、头发棕红、颧骨突出、鬓发高耸的电报员。军官又叹息了一声，说："我敢打赌，这个电报员会爱上这位美女。在这样的旷野与这么一位天使般的美女生活在一个屋顶下而不爱上她——这是任何一个人也办不到的。而如果自己是一个驼背瘸腿但规矩聪明的男人爱上了这个美丽的俊姑娘，而她对你毫不在意，我的朋友，这该是什么样的不幸和嘲弄！还有更糟的呢，请您想象一下，如果这个电报员已经爱上了这个姑娘，而他已经结了婚，妻子像他一样，也是个驼背瘸腿但也规规矩矩……那简直是灾难！"

在我们的车厢旁边，站着乘务员，他把胳膊肘搁在月台的栏杆上，看着美女站着的方向。他那虚胖的、难看的、因为失眠与旅程颠簸而显得憔悴和疲惫的脸孔，却表现出了一种柔情与深深的忧郁，似乎他在这个美女身上看到了自己的青春、幸福，自己的清醒，纯洁，自己的妻子、儿女，似乎是在懊悔，是全身心地意识到，这个美女不属于他，意识到像他这样一个未老先衰、行动迟钝、脸孔虚胖的人，距离普通人和旅客的幸福，已经像天空一样的遥远了。

响了第三遍铃，哨子吹响，火车懒洋洋地开动了。在我们的窗前闪过的，先是乘务员，站长，然后是花园，带着神奇的孩子般笑容的美女……

我把身子探出窗外，往后望去，我看见她目送列车前行，顺着月台走过里边坐着电报员的窗子，整理一下自己的头发，跑进了花园。车站已经遮盖不住西天的景色，田野袒露在我们眼前，但太阳已经落山，一团团黑烟弥漫在绿油油、丝绒般的麦苗上。在春天的空气里，在夜空中，在车厢里，都笼罩着一片忧伤。

我们的乘务员走进车厢，开始点亮蜡烛。

（童道明　译）

喀 希 坦 卡

一、品行不端

一只红毛的小狗——是塔克撒种和守夜犬的混合种——嘴脸很像狐狸，前前后后地在便道上跑来跑去，不安地向各方面张望。它有时停下来，哭着，忽而抬起一条抖索着的腿来，忽而抬起另一条，竭力想给自己寻出理由：这是怎么一回事，难道它是迷了路吗？

它很清楚地记得，它怎样过了一个白天，最后却跑到这条陌生的便道上来了。

白天是这样开始的，它的主人卢卡·阿列克散得雷支木匠，戴上帽子，腋下夹起一个用红布手巾包着的木头东西，喊道：

"喀希坦卡，我们走吧！"

塔克撒和守夜犬的杂种狗，一听见自己的名字，便从刨案下面跑出来，它是睡在那儿的刨花上的，甜蜜地伸着懒腰，跟在主人身后跑起来。卢卡·阿列克散得雷支的订货人都住得非常远，以致在每到一个订货人家之前，木匠一定要到酒店去几次，提一提精神。喀希坦卡记得，它在路上非常不守规矩。因为把它带出来玩耍，它高兴得乱蹦乱跳，汪汪叫着向铁轨马车的车厢奔去，向人家院子里跑，追逐别的狗。于是木匠终于看不到它，停了下来，气冲冲地喊着它。甚至于有一次，他脸上露出生气的表情，把它的狐狸耳朵揪到拳头里，摇晃着，一顿一顿地说道：

"把……你……饿……死，混账东西！"

卢卡·阿列克散得雷支到订货人家去过，顺便到姐姐家去，在她家喝了点酒，吃了点菜；他从姐姐家出来，又到一个熟识的钉书匠家去，从钉书匠家出来，再到酒店，从酒店出来到教父家去，以及其他等等的地方去。总而言之，当喀希坦卡走到陌生的人行便道上时，天已经黑了，木匠也醉了，好像鞋匠一样。他双手挥动，深深地叹着气，嘟哝着说：

"我的母亲怀胎生下我来，真是罪过！噢吓，罪过，罪过！现在我们是沿街走着，向路灯望着，等到我们一死——就要被投入烈火地狱去焚烧……"

他忽然改换成亲热的声调，把喀希坦卡叫到自己面前来，对它说道：

"喀希坦卡，你是畜生，再也没有什么了。你看待人是一样，就像木工和木匠是一样……"

他正和它用这种腔调说话，忽然一阵音乐声音响起来了。喀希坦卡回头一看，发现有一联队兵，正沿着街道向它走来。它忍受不了这种音乐声，它的神经错乱了，便盘旋着，狂叫起来。它大大吃了一惊，因为木匠不但没有害怕，没有尖声叫和狂吠，而且还大笑起来，身体伸直成一条线，五个手指放到帽檐上行举手礼。喀希坦卡一见主人并不反对，越发大叫起来，连自己都不记得了，穿过马路向另一面的便道奔去。

当它醒过来时，音乐声音已经不奏了，联队也不见了。它又跑上马路，来到主人停留的地方，但是，哎呀！木匠也不在那儿了。它向前奔去，后来又跑回来，又横过马路去一次，但是木匠好像已经钻到地中去了……喀希坦卡开始闻嗅着便道，希望能从主人遗留的脚迹的气味上找到他，不过刚刚有一个废物小子穿了一双新鞋走过去，现在所有的淡薄气味都和刺鼻的橡皮臭味混合到一道了，所以什么气味都辨别不出了。

喀希坦卡前前后后地跑着，遇不到主人，但是天气越来越黑了。街道两旁燃起了路灯，窗子里也透出了火光。下起了鹅毛一样的大雪，把道路，马背，车夫的帽子，都染成白色，空中越发黑暗，地上的东西越发清楚。陌生的订货人（喀希坦卡把全部人类分成了非常不平等的两部分；主人和订货主顾；在这两者之间又有本质上的差别：第一种人有殴打它的权利，而它却有权利咬第二种人的脚踝）走过喀希坦卡面前，遮住了它的视线，用脚踢它，不住地前前后后地走来走去。订货人匆忙地向前走，一点也不注意它。

天气完全黑暗下来的时候，喀希坦卡陷入失望和恐慌中去了。它靠在一家的门上，痛哭起来。它跟着卢卡·阿列克散得雷支跑了一整天，感到疲倦了，它的耳朵和脚爪都抖嗦着，同时它还饿得不得了。这一天，它只吃了两次东西：在钉书匠家吃了一点糨糊，在一座酒店内的柜台旁边吃了一点肠子皮——这就是一天的食物。如果它要是人的话，大概要想："不成，这样可不能活下去！要自杀啦！"

二、神秘的陌生人

但是它什么也不想，只是一味地哭。当柔软的羽毛一样的雪片把它的脊背和头完全遮住时，当它疲倦得想要入睡时，忽然门洞中的门响了，吱纽着，撞在它的肋部。它跳了起来。从开开的门内，走出了一个人，衣服是属于订货人一类的。因为喀希坦卡向他尖声叫起来，向他的脚底上扑去，他便不能不注意到它了。他弯下身子，向它问道：

"小狗，你是哪儿来的？我把你碰伤了吗？噢，可怜的狗，可怜的狗……咳，不要生气，不要生气……对不起。"

喀希坦卡透过挂在眼睫毛上的小雪片，望望陌生人，看见自己面前有一个矮胖的人，一张肿起的脸，刮得光光的，戴着礼帽，穿着一件敞胸的皮袄。

"你哭什么？"他用手指把它背上的雪弹掉，继续说。"你的主人在哪儿？你一定是迷了路吧？啊呀，可怜的小狗！我们现在怎么办呢？"

喀希坦卡在陌生人的嗓音中感觉到了温暖的、亲热的调子，舐着他的手，更伤心地哭起来了。

"你是个很好，很有趣的狗！"陌生人说。"简直像个狐狸！咦，有什么，没有办法，就跟我走吧！也许你还有点什么用处……咦，走吧！"

他咂了咂嘴唇，向喀希坦卡做了个手势，这个手势只能表示出一个意思："走吧！"喀希坦卡走了。

最多不过半小时，它已经坐在一间又大又亮的屋子中间的地板上了，头歪到一旁去，亲热地和好奇地望着陌生人，他正坐在桌旁吃饭。他一面吃，一面携些小块子给它……他先携给它一块麦包和一片绿色的奶油硬皮，后来是一块肉，半个包子，许多鸡骨头，但是它因为饥饿的缘故，把这许多东西都很快地吃完了，连滋味都没有辨别出来。它吃的越多，却越发觉得饿得厉害了。

"大概，你的主人们喂你吃的并不好！"陌生人说，眼看着它露出非常贪婪的样子，把连嚼也不嚼的食物块子吞了下去。"你多瘦啊！只有皮和骨头……"

喀希坦卡吃了很多，但是还没有吃够，只不过吃得有点头发晕了。吃过饭后，它卧在屋中间，伸着腿，觉得全身有一种愉快的倦意，摇晃着尾巴。在它的新主人坐在太师椅中，吃着雪茄烟的时候，它就摇着尾巴，考虑着一个问题：哪儿好点呢——在陌生人家呢，还是在木匠家呢？陌生人家的陈设又可怜，又难看；除了太师椅，沙发床，灯和地毯以外，他什么都没有了，屋子里好像是空的；木匠家里堆满了东西：他有桌子，刨案子，一堆刨花，刨子，斧子，锯，装金翅的雀的笼子，大面盆……陌生人地方一点气味也没有，木匠家里总是有一种雾气，还散发着胶漆和刨花的香味。不过陌生人处有一件最重要的可取之处——他肯给许多东西吃，所以也应当对他十二分忠实，每当喀希坦卡蹲在桌子前面，和蔼地望着他时，他从来不打它，不跺脚，从来不喊叫："滚开去，该死的东西！"

新主人吸完雪茄烟，走出去了，过了一分钟又回来了，手中拿着一个小垫子。

"喂，你呀，小狗到这儿来！"他把小垫子放在沙发床角的附近，说道。"躺到这儿来。睡吧！"

后来他便熄了灯走出去了。喀希坦卡卧在小垫子上，闭住眼睛；听见街上有狗吠声，它想答复这吠声，不过忽然它觉得伤心起来了。它想起卢卡·阿列克散得雷支来了，想起他的儿子菲久希加，想起刨案下面舒适的窠……它记得，在漫长的冬夜，当木匠刨着木头，或者高声读报纸的时候，菲久希加总是和它一道玩耍……他捉住它的后腿，把它从刨案下面拖出来，叫它玩一套套把戏，弄得它眼睛发绿，浑身骨节痛。他强迫它用后腿走路，用它来当做铃玩耍，就是用力抓住它的尾巴，提了起来，叫它尖声叫和狂吠，叫它闻鼻烟……顶顶难过是下面这种把戏：菲久希加用线拴上一块肉，把肉投给喀希坦卡，一等它要吞下去时，他便大笑着把肉又从它的喉咙里拉回去。喀希坦卡的回忆越清楚，哭得便越发响，越发痛了。

但疲倦和温暖很快就克服了忧伤……它睡着了。它幻想着有许多狗跑来跑去：其中有一条长毛的老狗，是它今天在街上看到的，眼睛上生着白点，鼻子附近生着硬毛。菲久希加手中拿着锤子，在老狗后面追，后来忽然他自己也满身生了长毛，停在喀希坦卡身旁，快活地吠叫起来。喀希坦卡和他互相亲热地闻嗅着鼻子，向街上跑去……

三、快活的新友谊

喀希坦卡醒来的时候，天已经亮了，从街上传来只有白天才有的喧闹声。屋子里没有一个人。喀希坦卡伸着懒腰，打着哈欠，生气而又忧伤的样子，在屋子里走来走去。它闻嗅着墙角和家具，向前室望去，什么有趣的事也没发现。除了开向前室去的门以外还有一道门。喀希坦卡想想，用双腿抓着它，门开了，它就通另一间屋子去。这儿的床上，睡着一位订货人，盖着一条粗绸被头，它认出了他就是昨天那位陌生人。

"吱儿儿儿……"它叫着，但是记起了昨天的一顿饭，于是摇着尾巴闻嗅起来。

它闻嗅着陌生人的靴子和衣服，发觉它们都发出了马汗味，卧室还有一扇门，也开着的，不知是通到什么地方去的。喀希坦卡抓着这扇门，用胸部顶上去，门开开了。立刻感觉到一种奇怪的，很可疑的气味。喀希坦卡预感到要遭受一种不快的接待，哼哼着，四顾着，走进一间很小的，壁纸肮脏的屋子，立刻吓得倒退了回来。它发现了一个意外的，可怕的东西。一只灰色的鹅，把脖颈和头伸向地上去，扑动着翅膀，嗞嗞叫着，一直向它奔来。离它不远处的小垫子上，卧着一只白猫；它一看见喀希坦卡，跳了起来，把身体弯成了弧形，卷着尾巴，毛倒竖着，也嗞嗞叫了。狗害怕得不得了，但是不愿表示出自己的胆怯来，大声吠叫着，向猫奔去……猫把身体弯得更厉害了，呜呜着，用爪子向喀希坦卡头上打去。喀希坦卡跳开了，四条腿蹲下去，把脸伸向猫去，发出了响亮的，尖利的吠叫声；这时鹅从后面走近来疼痛地用嘴向它背上啄了一下。喀希坦卡跳起来，向鹅奔去……

"这是什么东西？"听见了响亮的，怒气冲冲的声音，陌生人穿着睡衣，口中叨着雪茄烟走进屋子来。"这是怎么回事？各归原位！"

他走到猫跟前去，搔着它的弓起的背说道：

"菲道尔·琪摩菲依支，这是怎么回事？打架了吗？噢吓，你这个老畜生！卧下来！"

他又向鹅喊道：

"伊万·伊万内支，归位。"

猫服从地躺在自己的小垫子上，闭住了眼睛。从它的脸上和胡子上的表情判断，它是很不满意，自己竟会发怒，引起纷争，喀希坦卡气愤地哭着，但是鹅伸出了脖颈，迅速地、热情地、清晰地说起了什么，不过一点也不明白。

"好啦，好啦！"主人打着哈欠说。"应当和气地和友爱地过日子。"他抚摸着喀希坦卡，继续说："红毛，你不要怕……这都是好人，不会侮辱你的。等等，我们怎样称呼你呢？没有名字可不成，老弟。"

陌生人想了想，说道：

"这样吧……你就叫……姑母吧……明白吗？姑母！"

他把"姑母"这两个字重复了好几遍，走出去了。喀希坦卡蹲下来，开始注视着。猫一动不动地蹲在小垫子上，装着睡熟的样子。鹅伸长了脖颈，在原处不动地踏着步，迅速地和热情地继续说着什么。看来，这是一只很聪明的鹅；每讲完一次长篇大论之后，总要惊怪地向后退去，装作很高兴自己的演讲的样子……喀希坦卡听完它的说话，只回答它："吱儿儿儿……"然后闻嗅起墙角来。一只角落里放着一只小槽，它看见槽内不浸湿的豌豆和发潮的麦皮。它尝了尝豌豆——不很好吃，尝了尝麦皮——开始吃起来了。鹅看见陌生的狗吃它的食，一点都不生气，相反，说得更起劲了，好像是表示自己的心思，也走到槽旁去，还吃了几粒豌豆。

四、笼内的把戏

过了一会儿陌生人又进来了，还带来一只奇怪的东西，很像一扇门，又像数字Ⅱ。这个随随便便造成Ⅱ字形的木架子的横梁上挂着一只铃，还拴着一把手枪；铃铛舌头上和手枪的扳机上，都有小绳子拖下来。陌生人把Ⅱ形架子放在屋子中间，解啊，拴啊，弄了半天，后来向鹅望着，说道：

"伊万·伊万内支，请吧！"

鹅走到他面前来，停下，做成等候的姿势。

"呶，您哪，"陌生人说，"我们最起首开始。首先鞠躬行礼！快点！"

伊万·伊万内支伸长了脖颈，向四方点着头，脚掌转动着。

"很好，好汉子……现在装死！"

鹅仰面躺下去，脚掌向上伸着。又做了几套类似的，不重要的把戏，陌生人忽然抓住自己的头，自己的脸上露出了恐怖的表情，高叫道：

"更夫！失火啦！火烧啦！"

伊万·伊万内支跑到Ⅱ形架子前面来，用嘴咬住绳子，铃响起来了。

陌生人很满意。他抚摸着鹅的脖颈，说道：

"好汉子，伊万·伊万内支！现在你来扮演宝石商人，你贩卖金子和宝石。现在表演吧，你到自己的店内来，在那儿遇到了贼。这时候你应该怎么办呢？"

鹅又用嘴咬住另外一根绳子，一拉，立刻就发出了一声震耳的响声。喀希坦卡很欢喜铃声，它听到枪声，更开心得不得了，围Ⅱ形架子跑，吠叫。

"姑母，归位！"陌生人向它喊。"住口！"

伊万·伊万内支的工作在开枪后还没有完结。陌生人用绳子拴着它，用鞭子赶着它，足足在自己身旁转了有一个钟点，这时，鹅要跳过一道低栏，穿过铁环，人立起来，也就是用屁股坐住，挥动着脚掌。喀希坦卡眼睛不离开伊万·伊万内支，快活得大叫着，有好几次响亮地吠叫着，跟在它后面跑。陌生人把自己和鹅都弄得很疲倦了，把额上的汗擦掉，喊道：

"玛利亚，把哈福洛妮亚·伊万诺芙娜叫到这儿来！"

过了一分钟，听见了猪哼哼的声音……喀希坦卡哼哧着，装着很勇敢的样子，总向陌生人跑近去。门开了，一个老太婆向屋内张望了一下，说了几句什么，放进来一只非常难看的黑母猪。母猪一点也不注意喀希坦卡的哼声，抬起了自己的蹄子，很高兴地哼哼着。看来，它很欢喜看见自己的主人，看见猫和伊万·伊万内支。当它走到猫面前时，用自己的蹄子轻轻地踢了它的肚皮下面一下，后来也不知和鹅讲了些什么，在它的行动上，声音上，以及尾巴的摇摆上，感觉到了很亲热的样子。喀希坦卡立刻明白，向这些家伙们哼哧和吠叫——没有什么用处。

主人把Ⅱ形架子拿开，喊道：

"菲道尔·琪摩菲依支，请吧！"

猫站起身来，懒懒地欠伸了一下，不愿意地，好像故意要迟延的样子，走到母猪面前。

"唉，您哪，我们从埃及的金字塔开始，"主人说。

他也不知解释了半天什么，后来下命令："一……二……三！"说到"三"这个字，伊万·伊万内支振动翅膀，跳到母猪背上去……当它拍着翅膀，伸长脖颈，在生满硬毛的母猪背上站牢时，菲道尔·琪摩菲依支精神不振地和懒洋洋地，露出很明显的轻视样子，它似乎是非常轻视自己的演技，认为一个铜板都不值，跳到猪背上去，然后又不高兴地攀到鹅身上去，用后腿站了起来。这样就成了陌生人所说的埃及金字塔。喀希坦卡快活地尖声叫了起来，但是这时候老猫打了一个哈欠，失去了重心，从鹅身上跌了下来。伊万·伊万内支一晃也跌下来了。陌生人喊叫着，挥着手，又讲了一堆废话。不知疲倦的主人弄了整整一个钟点的金字塔，后来便开始教练伊万·伊万内支骑在猫身上，以后又教猫学吸烟，以及其他等等的本事。

直到陌生人擦了擦额上的汗，走了出去，教练才算完毕，菲道尔·琪摩菲依支憎嫌地喷着鼻子，卧到小垫子上去，闭住眼睛。伊万·伊万内支走到木槽旁边去，老太婆又把母猪带走了。在这样许多新的印象之下，喀希坦卡不知不觉地过了一天，晚间，它已经和自己的小垫子都搬到壁纸肮脏的小屋子里来，和菲道尔·琪摩菲依支和鹅在一道过夜了。

五、天才！天才！

过了一个月。

喀希坦卡对于每天晚上喂它美味的食品和叫它姑母，已经很习惯了。它对于陌生人，以及对于自己的同居者都习惯了。生活像从油上滑过一般地过去。

每天的开始都是一样的。照例是伊万·伊万内支比大家都早醒来，立刻走到姑母面前，或者走到猫跟前，伸着脖颈，开始热情地和肯定地讲说一阵，依然是令人不懂。有时，它抬起头来，讲一串很长的独白。在初认识的那些日子，喀希坦卡以为它说话说的多，是因为聪明的缘故，但是过了不久，它便失去了对鹅的敬仰了；当鹅走过来，讲起自己的长篇演说时，它已经不再摇尾巴，却对它板起面孔来了，像对待一个讨厌的，不令人睡觉的唠叨鬼一样，毫无礼貌地回答"吱儿儿儿……"

菲道尔·琪摩菲依支有许多地方很像绅士。这个家伙醒来之后，一点声音也不发，一动也不动，甚至连眼睛都不睁开。它很愿意不醒来，因为显然它是不欢喜这种生活。不论什么都引不起它的兴趣，他对待一切事物都是无精打采和轻视，甚至轻视自己吃的美味的饮食，憎嫌地喷着鼻子。

喀希坦卡一醒来，便在屋内走来走去，闻嗅墙角。只准许它和猫可以在全部房子内走；鹅是不能越过壁纸肮脏的小屋子的门槛一步的，至于哈福洛妮亚·伊万诺芙娜住在院子里的一间小板棚内，只有在教练时才能看到。主人醒来的很晚，喝完茶，立刻便开始自己的把戏。Ⅱ形架子，鞭子，铁环，每天都要拿到小屋子里来，差不多每天都是做的同样的工作。教练要继续三四个钟点，有时菲道尔·琪摩菲依支疲倦地摇晃着，像醉汉一样，伊万·伊万内支张开口困难地呼吸着，主人的脸也红着，额角上的汗简直擦不完。

白昼因为有教练和吃饭，所以很有趣，晚上却寂寞得很。晚间，主人照例是出去，自己随身带着鹅和猫。剩下姑母一个人，卧在垫子上，开始伤心起来……伤感不知不觉地，悄悄地袭上它来，渐渐地包围住它，好像屋中的黑暗一样。狗开始不愿意吠叫，吃喝，在屋子里跑了，甚至连看都不愿意看了，后来在脑海中出现了模糊的影子，也不是狗的样子，也不是人的样子，面貌很和善，但是一点也不清楚；影子一出现，姑母便摇尾巴，它觉得它曾经在什么地方见过他们和爱过他们……每当它睡去的时候，总觉得这些人身上发出了胶水、刨花和油漆的气味。

当它对新生活已经完全习惯了的时候，从一只瘦骨嶙峋的看家狗变成一只饱饱的、可爱的狗时，一天，在教练以前，主人抚摸着它，说道：

"姑母，到我们干事的时候啦。你的舒服日子过得太久啦。我想把你造成一个女伶……你愿意做女伶吗？"

他开始教练它学习各种学科了。第一课它学习站立，用后腿走路，它非常高兴这样做。第二课，它要用后腿跳，抓住教师高高地在它头上擎着的糖块。以后的功课，是跳舞，跑绳，在音乐伴奏下吠叫，打钟，放枪，过了一个月，它已经可以很熟练地代替菲道尔·琪摩菲依支玩"埃及金字塔"了。它很高兴地学习，很满意自己的成绩；伸着舌头在绳索上跑，在铁环内跑，骑在老菲道尔·琪摩菲依支身上，它感觉到了非常的快乐。它每次表演成功，总要响亮地、快活地吠叫一阵，教师很惊异，也快活了，擦着手。

"天才！天才！"他说。"毫无疑问是天才！你一定会成大功的！"

姑母对于"天才"这两个字也习惯了，每当主人一发出"天才"两个字时，便跳起来，四面张望着，好像这就是它的名字。

六、不安的夜

姑母作了一个狗梦，好像有一个更夫，手中拿着扫帚在它身后追赶，它一下子吓醒了。

小屋子里很安静，很黑暗，又很气闷。虼蚤咬。从前姑母从来不怕黑暗，但是现在不知它为什么开始觉得难过和想吠叫了。主人在隔壁屋子里大声叹气，后来，稍过一歇，母猪在自己的板棚内哼哼了，一切又都沉默了。当你一想到吃的东西时，那么精神上就会轻松起来，于是姑母开始想到，它今天偷了菲道尔·琪摩菲依支一只鸡爪子，把它藏到客室中的立柜和墙中间了，那儿有许多蜘蛛网和尘土。现在最好能到那儿去看看：这只鸡爪是否还完整如旧呢？十分可能，主人已经发觉它，吃掉了。但是在清晨之前，不能从小屋子出去——是这样的规矩。姑母闭着眼睛，想要快点睡着，因为它从经验上知道，你越睡着的快，也越天亮的快。但是，忽然在离它不远处，发出了奇怪的呼叫声，这使它抖嗦了一下，四脚跳了起来。这是伊万·伊万内支在叫喊，它的叫喊声并不是玩笑，很正经，不过很粗野，响亮，不自然，很像开门的吱扭声。姑母在黑暗中什么都看不见，什么都不明白，觉得更加恐怖了，咕哝道：

"吱儿儿儿……"

过了很久时候，差不多有啃一根骨头的时间；呼叫声没有重复。姑母渐渐放心了，打盹了。它梦见了两条大黑狗，屁股和肋上有几块去年的毛片；它们正贪婪地从一只大面盆内吃残羹剩饭，盆内放出了白色的蒸气，喷出了很香的气味；它们不时回顾姑母，呲着牙齿，咕哝道："我们可不给你吃！"但是从屋子里跑出来一个穿皮袄的农夫，用鞭子把它们赶跑了；于是姑母走到大面盆前面，开始吃起来，但是当农夫刚一转到门后去，两只黑狗又吼叫着向它奔来，忽然又发出了响亮的叫声。

"嗨！嗨嗨！"伊万·伊万内支喊道。

姑母醒来了，跳起来，并没有走下垫子来，发出了吠声。它已经觉得这不是伊万·伊万内支在呼叫，而是另外的生人在喊叫了。而且不知为什么，母猪又在板棚内哼起来了。

这时听见了橐橐的拖鞋声，主人穿着睡衣，端着蜡烛，走进了小屋内。闪动的光亮在肮脏的壁纸上，在天棚上跳动，驱退了黑暗。姑母看见屋子里什么生人都没有。伊万·伊万内支卧在地上，并没有睡。它的翅膀张开着，嘴也张开，它的样子很像疲倦得不得了，想要喝点水。老菲道尔·琪摩菲依支也没有睡。它一定是被喊叫声惊醒的。

"伊万·伊万内支，你干什么？"主人问鹅。"你喊叫什么？你病了吗？"

鹅一声不响。主人摸摸它的脖颈，摸摸它的脊背，说道：

"你是一个怪物，你自己不睡，也不叫别人睡。"

主人走出去，把光亮带走，小屋里又黑暗了。姑母很害怕。鹅也不喊叫了，但是它又觉得在黑暗中站着一个陌生人。顶顶可怕的，是咬不到这个陌生人，因为看不见他，也没有形。不知为什么它总想着，在这里一定要发生些什么坏事情了。菲道尔·琪摩菲依支也很不安。姑母听见，它在自己的垫子上翻来翻去，打哈欠，摇头。

街上有人在敲门，板棚内母猪在哼哼。姑母哭起来了，前腿伸出去，把头放在腿上面。敲门声中，在不知为什么睡不着的母猪哼哼声中，在黑暗中，以及在寂静中，它都感觉到一种像在伊万·伊万内支的呼叫声中所感觉到的伤感的和恐怖的意味。一切都惊慌，不安，但是为了什么？这个看不见的陌生人是谁？忽然在姑母身旁出现了两个伤感的绿色火光。这是自从和菲道尔·琪摩菲依支相熟以来，它第一次走到它面前来。它要干什么？姑母舐着它的脚掌，也不问它干什么来的，用各种腔调轻轻哼起来。"嗨！"伊万·伊万内支喊道。"嗨，嗨！"

门又开了，主人端着蜡烛进来了。鹅仍是老样子卧着，张着嘴，张着翅膀。它的眼睛却闭着。

"伊万·伊万内支！"主人喊道。

鹅一动不动。主人坐在它面前的地上，沉默地向它望了望，说道：

"伊万·伊万内支！你这是干什么？你要死吗，怎的？啊呀，我现在想起来了，想起来了！"他抱住自己的头喊道。"我知道这是什么原因！这是因为今天有一匹马踏在你身上啦！我的天，我的天！"

姑母不明白主人说的什么，但是从它的脸上可以看出，他是在等候着什么可怕的事情发生。它把脸向黑暗的窗子探过去，它觉得窗子中有一个陌生人，又吠叫起来了。

"它要死啦，姑母！"主人拍了一下手，说。"是的，是的，要死啦！死神已经到你们屋子里来了。我们怎么办？"

脸色苍白，惊慌失措的主人，叹着气，摇着头，回到自己的卧室去了。姑母在暗中觉得非常难过，它跟在他后面走着，他坐到床上，重复了几次。

"我的天，怎么办呢？"

姑母在他的脚边走来走去，也不明白，为什么它会这样伤心，为什么大家都这样不安，竭力想了解一下，注意着他的每一动作。很少离开自己的垫子的菲道尔·琪摩菲依支，也走进主人的卧室来了，开始在他的脚边徘徊。它摇了一下头，好像是想把自己的难过念头摇晃掉，可疑地向床下望着。

主人拿起小碟子来，从水壶中向里面倒了些水，又走到鹅身旁去。

"喝吧，伊万·伊万内支！"他温和地说，把小碟子放在它面前。"喝吧，亲爱的。"

但是伊万·伊万内支一动不动，眼睛也不睁开。主人把它的头弯到小碟子上，把嘴浸进水去，但是鹅也不喝，翅膀越发大张开来，它的头就这样停在小碟子中了。

"不成，已经一点办法也没有了！"主人叹口气说。"什么都完啦。伊万·伊万内支死啦！"

光亮的水滴，像下雨时的窗子上流下来的水珠，顺他的腮颊爬着。姑母和菲道尔·琪摩菲依支莫名其妙是什么事情，贴到他的脚旁，害怕地望着鹅。

"可怜的伊万·伊万内支！"主人悲哀地叹着气，说。"我还想着春天把你带到别墅中去，我和你在青草地上玩耍。亲爱的鹅，我的好同伴，你已经不在人世啦！我现在失去你怎么办呢？"

姑母觉得它也会发生这样的事情的，就是说，它就这样不知为了什么原因，眼一闭，腿一伸，嘴一张，于是大家便都恐怖地望着它。看来，菲道尔·琪摩菲依支的脑筋里也是转着这种念头。老猫从前向来没有像现在这样忧郁和阴沉过。

天开始亮了，小屋子中的那个看不见的，使姑母非常害怕的陌生人也不见了。等到天大亮下来时，更夫进来，抓住鹅掌，把它拖出去了。过了一会儿，老太婆进来了，又把槽拿出去了。

姑母走进客室去，看看柜子后面；主人并没有吃掉鸡腿，它还放在原处的尘土和蛛网中。但是姑母很难过，很忧伤，很想哭一顿。它简直连闻都不闻那只鸡腿，跑到沙发床下面去，坐在那儿，开始轻轻地哭起来，发出了轻微的声音：

"呜，呜，呜……"

七、失败了的处女表演

在一个晴亮的夜晚，主人走进了壁纸肮脏的小屋子，擦着手，说道：

"咦，您哪……"

他还想说些什么，但是没说出来，又出去了。姑母在受训的时候，仔细研究他的面孔和声调，现在猜想他是很不安，大概还很生气。稍微过了一会儿，他又回来了，说道：

"今天我把姑母和菲道尔·琪摩菲依支带去。姑母，今天在作埃及金字塔时，你代替死去的伊万·伊万内支吧。他妈的！什么都还没有预备好，还没有训练好，练习的次数又少！我们真难为情，要坍台啦！"

后来他又出去了，过了一分钟，穿上皮袄和戴上礼帽回来了。他走到猫面前，抓住它的腿，举起来，把它藏在皮袄的胸前，但是菲道尔·琪摩菲依支好像很冷淡，简直连眼睛都不愿睁开。看来，它觉得什么都是一样：卧着，或者站起来，或者在草垫上，或者藏在主人的皮袄的胸前……

"姑母，走吧，"主人说。

姑母什么都不懂，摇着尾巴，跟在他后面走。过了一分钟，它已经卧在雪橇中的主人脚旁了，听见冻得和不安得缩着脖颈的主人嘟哝道：

"我们真难为情！要坍台啦！"

雪橇停在一座很大的怪屋子旁了，这座屋子很像一只翻倒的汤盆子。这座房子的门口，装着三扇玻璃门，点着非常亮的灯。门响亮地开了，像嘴张开一样，把许多在门口附近蠕动的人吞了进去。人很多，时常有马匹跑到门口来，但是狗却看不见。

主人用手把姑母捉住，也把它塞到菲道尔·琪摩菲依支所在的皮袄胸前去。这儿又暗又闷，但是很暖和。有一瞬间有两块忧伤的绿色火光闪烁了——这是被邻人的又凉又硬的爪子弄得不安了的猫睁开了眼睛。姑母舐舐它的耳朵，想要卧舒服一点，不安地移动着，用又凉又硬的爪子踏着它，忽然从皮袄里把头钻了出来。它觉得看见了一间很大的,光线黑暗的房间里面,充满了怪物；从屋子两旁的栏杆里面，有许多可怕的脸向外张望：马脸，牛脸，长耳朵脸，还有一张肥胖的大脸，没有生鼻子，却生了一条尾巴，两根长长的，啃光的骨头，从口中竖了出来。

猫在姑母的爪子下面，沙声地喵喵叫着，这时皮袄敞开了，主人说了一声："跳！"便和姑母一同跳到地板上去。它们已经来到一间有灰色地板墙的小房间了；这儿除了一张有镜子的小桌子，一张木凳和挂在角落的破布片以外，再没有别的家具了，这儿没有灯或者蜡烛，只燃着一片扇子形的亮火，是从钉在墙上的一根管子中冒出来的。菲道尔·琪摩菲依支舐着自己的，被姑母踏皱了的皮衣，走到凳子下面去，卧下来。主人始终还在不安地搓着手，开始脱衣服了……他和平常在自己家中，要躺到被头中去睡时一样脱衣服，就是说脱得精光，只剩下衬衫，后来坐在凳子上，对镜望着，开始把自己改变成个奇怪的东西。首先向头套了一个头发分开的假发套，上面竖出两条，很像牛角，然后用什么白东西厚厚地涂到脸上，白颜色上面又画出眉毛，胡子，再拍上红腮。打扮并没有这样完结。他涂过脸和脖颈，开始穿上一件特别的，什么样子都不像的衣服，姑母以前在家中，在街上，从来没有看见过这种衣服。请您想想看，一条肥大的裤子，是用一种大花的布做成的，这种布只有乡下人用来做窗帘和家具套，裤子紧到腋下；一条裤腿是用酱色布缝成的，另外一条是用亮黄色缝成的。主人穿上肥裤子，又穿上一件布上衣，上面缝着一个大狗牙边的领子，背上还有些金星，一双花袜子和一双绿色软底鞋……

姑母的眼睛和头内都发花了，白色的脸上，口袋一般的身形上发出了主人的气味，声音也是熟悉的，主人的，但是当姑母一阵疑惑起来时，便想跑，离开这个五色斑斓的身形，吠叫起来。新的地方，扇形的火光，气味，主人的变形——这一切都在它心上播种下了不能确定的恐怖种子，预感到它一定会害怕地遇到类似生着尾巴，没有鼻子的胖脸一类的东西。而且这儿的墙外面的远处还奏着讨厌的音乐，不时听见莫名其妙的吼叫声。唯一可安慰它的——是菲道尔·琪摩菲侬支的镇定样子。它非常安心地在凳子下面盹睡，如果凳子动的时候，连眼睛都不张。

一个穿燕尾服和白背心的人，向小屋子里望了一眼，说道：

"现在米司阿拉白拉上台了。她以后——就轮到您啦。"

主人什么话也没有回答。他从桌子底下拉出一个小箱子，坐下来，等着。从他的嘴唇和手上可以看出，他很冲动不安，姑母听见他的喘气声和抖嗦一样。

"米司特尔乔治，请吧！"有人在门后喊你。

主人站起来，画了三次十字，后来从凳子下面把猫拖出来，把它塞进箱子去。

"来，姑母！"他轻轻地说。

姑母什么都不明白，走到他的手底下来；他吻它的头，把它和菲道尔·琪摩菲侬支放在一并排。以后是黑暗降临……姑母在猫身上踏，抓着箱子壁，吓得一点声音都发不出来，箱子摇晃着，像在波浪中一般，抖嗦着……

"是我！"主人大声的喊道。"是我！"

姑母觉得这声喊叫以后，箱子碰到一个硬东西上，不再摇晃了，听见一阵响亮的浓重的吼声：有人拍手了，这大概是那个脸上生着尾巴，没有鼻子的怪物在吼叫，哈哈笑得非常响，连箱子的锁都震得抖嗦了。主人的透亮的，尖利的笑声，从来在家中不曾听到过这种笑声——回答吼叫声了。

"哈！"他喊叫，竭力想盖过吼叫声去。"尊贵的观众！我是刚从火车站上来的！我的祖母死了，留给一项遗产！箱子里有很重的东西——大概是金子……哈哈！忽然这儿是一百万，马上我们就打开一观……"

箱子的锁响了。亮光照进了姑母的眼睛；它从箱子里跳了出来，被吼叫声震聋了，飞快地绕着主人跑起来，发出了响亮的吠叫声。

"哈！"主人喊道，"菲道尔·琪摩菲依支叔叔！亲爱的姑母！亲爱的亲眷们，原来是你们！"

他肚皮朝下伏在砂土上，捉住猫和姑母，抱住了它们。姑母被主人抱在怀中，迅速看见了命运把它送来的那个世界，大吃一惊，有一瞬间奇怪和高兴得发呆了，后来从主人的怀中挣脱出来，因为印象太刺激，像狼一样在原处转来转去。新世界非常广大，充满了光亮；不论你往哪儿看去，从地上到天花板，到处只看见是人脸，人脸，再没有什么了。

"姑母，请您坐下来！"主人喊道。

姑母记得这是什么意思，跳到椅子上去，坐了下来。它望着主人。他的眼睛和从前一样，严厉地和爱抚地望着，但是脸上，特别是嘴和牙齿上，露出了很难看的，不移动的笑容。他自己哈哈笑，跳跃耸肩，装着在几千人面前很快活的样子。姑母很相信他是真快活，忽然全身觉得这几千人的面孔都在注视它，它抬起自己的狐狸脸来，快活地吠叫了。

"姑母，您请坐吧，"主人对它说。"我和叔叔来跳一次卡马林舞。"

菲道尔·琪摩菲依支等候着强迫它来表演什么糊涂玩意儿，站着，冷淡地向四方望着。它精神委靡地，大意地，忧伤地跳着，从它的举动上，尾巴上，胡子上可以看出，它是非常地轻视人群和光亮，轻视主人和自己……它跳完自己的一套，打了个哈欠，卧下来了。

"咦，你哪，姑母，"主人说。"我先和您唱一套歌，以后我们再跳舞。好吗？"

他从口袋里掏出一个笛子，吹了一阵。姑母忍受不住音乐的催促，不安地在椅子上转动着，吼叫起来。从各方面发出了吼叫声和鼓掌声。主人鞠躬，等到安静下来，又表演……正在吹一个最高门的调音时，上面的观众中有人大声哎呀一声。

"姑母！"小孩子的嗓音喊叫。"这原来是喀希坦卡啊！"

"真是喀希坦卡！"一个酒醉的中音证实了一下。"喀希坦卡！菲久希加，真的，这是喀希坦卡！喂！"

有人在看台上打口哨，两个嗓音———一个是孩子的声音，一个是男人的声音，大声唤着：

"喀希坦卡！喀希坦卡！"

姑母哆嗦了一下，向喊叫的地方看去。两张面孔：一张是生满了毛，醉醺醺的，含着笑容的脸，另一张是胖胖的，红腮颊的，惊慌的脸，钻进了它的眼睛，像从前亮光刺进它的眼睛一样……它想起来了，从椅子上跌了下来，在砂土上挣扎，后来跳起来，发出了快活的尖吠声，向这两个人处奔去。发出震耳的吼叫声，透过吼声还有吹哨子和一个透亮的孩子的叫声：

"喀希坦卡！喀希坦卡！"

姑母跳过了栅栏，又跳过不知是谁的肩膀，停在看台上了；

如果想跳到另一层去，还要跳过一道高墙：姑母跳了一下，但是跳不过去，又顺着墙滑下来了。后来它却从这个人的手中传到另外一个人的手中，舐着人的脸和手，越移动越高，最后到了上层看台上……

过了半小时，喀希坦卡已经在街上跟在人后面走了，他们的身上发出了胶水和油漆味。卢卡·阿列克散得雷支摇晃着，由于经验的教训，本能地竭力避免开水沟。

"我的母亲怀胎生我简直是陷入了罪恶的深渊……"他嘟哝着说。"喀希坦卡，你弄错了。你对于人的看法是一样的，就等于木工是木匠。"

菲久希加戴着父亲的帽子，和他并排走着。喀希坦卡望着他们俩的背后，它觉得它已经跟在他们后面走了好久，很高兴它的生活一刻儿也没有离开他们过。

它想起了壁纸肮脏的小屋子，鹅，菲道尔·琪摩菲依支，美味的食品，训练，表演，但是现在他觉得这一切都好像一个很长的，可怕的，难过的梦。

（金人　译）

苦　恼

我向谁去诉说我的痛苦？

　　暮色苍茫。大块的湿雪懒洋洋地在刚刚点亮的路灯四周飘舞。一层薄薄的、软软的雪覆盖到了屋顶上，马背上，人的肩膀和帽子上。马车夫姚纳·帕塔波夫全身银白，像一个幽灵。他弯着身子，弯到一个活的躯体可以弯曲到的最大限度。他坐在驭座上，纹丝不动。哪怕有块大的雪团落到他身上，他也觉得没有必要把它抖落掉……他的那匹瘦马也是白色的，也一动不动。它的呆立不动，它的骨瘦如柴，它的像棍子一样僵直的细腿，甚至有点像一个不值多少钱的马形蜜糖饼。这马好像陷入了沉思。要是有谁被人从犁地的田间、从熟悉的灰色图景里拉走，被扔到这个五光十色、喧闹不休、川流不息的漩涡中，谁就不可能不想想……

　　姚纳和他的瘦马已经很长时间没有动窝了。他们午饭之前就从车马大院里出来，至今没有拉到一个活。眼看着夜色笼罩了这个城市。惨淡的路灯变得更加耀眼，街头的嘈杂也变得更加喧腾。

　　"车夫，到维堡去！"姚纳听到喊声，"马车夫！"

　　姚纳抖动了一下身子，透过沾满雪花的眼睫毛，看到一个穿着带风帽的灰色军大衣的军人。

　　"到维堡去！"军人重复道，"你是睡着了吧？到维堡去！"

　　姚纳为了表示同意，拉动了马缰。于是，一片片雪花从马的背上、人的肩上落了下来……军人坐上雪橇。车夫哑吧着嘴唇，伸长他天鹅般的颈项，稍稍抬起身子，与其说是出于必要，毋宁说是出于习惯地挥动了马鞭。马儿同样地伸长颈脖子，弯曲了棍子一样的细腿，迟疑不决地往前挪步……

"妖怪，你往哪跑！"姚纳立刻听到从周遭黑簇簇的人影里传出的叫骂声，"鬼东西往哪赶呢？靠右边走！"

"你不会赶车！靠右边走！"军人也生气了。

一个坐在四轮轿式马车上的车夫也在骂娘，而一位正赶路、肩膀碰着了马脸的行人，恶狠狠地瞪视着他，抖落了衣袖上的雪。

姚纳局促地坐在驭座上，像是坐在针尖上，他把胳膊肘向两边撑开，翻转着两只眼睛，像是被煤气熏了似的。他好像不知道他是在哪里和为什么在那里。

"都是些混蛋！"军人打趣道，"他们有的往你身上撞，有的往马蹄上扑。他们好像都是串通好的。"

姚纳回头看了一眼乘客，动了动嘴唇……看来，他想说点什么，但喉咙里只是吐出一些嘎哑的声音。

"什么？"军人问。

姚纳一笑把嘴撇歪了，他让自己的喉咙使出劲儿来，沙哑地说：

"老爷，我的……儿子这个星期死了。"

"噢……得什么病死的？"

姚纳把整个身子转向乘客，说：

"谁知道呢！大概是，热病……在医院躺了三天就死了……这是上帝的旨意。"

"拐转呀，死鬼！"在黑暗中传来喊声，"老狗，你眼睛瞎了？用眼睛看看！"

"赶车走吧，走吧……"乘客说，"照这样我们明天都到不了。快走吧！"

马车夫又伸长脖子，把身子微微抬起，粗中有细地挥舞着马鞭。此后，他几次转过头来看看乘客，但他闭着双眼，看样子，不想再听他说什么。把乘客送到维堡之后，他把马车停在一家饭店旁，坐在驭座上弯着腰，又是一动不动了……湿雪又把人和瘦马染白了。过去了一个小时，两个小时……

人行道上走着三个年轻人——其中两个长得又高又瘦，另一个是个矮子，还有点驼背。他们嘴里骂骂咧咧的，脚上的套鞋踩出一片声响。

"马车夫，去警察大街！"驼子用颤声嚷嚷说。"三个人……二十戈比！"姚纳抖动一下缰绳，咂吧一下嘴唇。二十戈比的车钱太少了，但他对车钱已经无所谓……一个卢布也罢，五个戈比也罢，现在对他都一样，只要有乘客就行……

年轻人互相推搡着，说着粗话，走近雪橇。三个人全都往车座上挤。需要解决一个问题：哪两个可以坐，哪一个只能站着？

经过一番争执、胡闹和责难，终于作出决定：应该让驼子站着，因为他个儿最矮。

"呶，快赶车吧！"驼子沙哑地喊着。他站着，朝姚纳的后脑勺哈气，"快跑！老兄，瞧你这顶破帽子！在彼得堡找不到比这更破的帽子……"

"嘿，嘿……"姚纳笑笑，"就这么顶破帽子……"

"呶，你，就这么顶破帽子，快赶车吧！你就这样走一路？是吗？要给你朝脖子上打一拳吗？"

"脑袋都要炸裂了……"一个高个子说，"昨天我们俩人和瓦斯卡一起在杜克马索夫家喝了四瓶白兰地。"

"我不明白，你为什么要撒谎！"另一个高个子生气地说，"像畜生一样撒谎。"

"上帝惩罚我好了，这是实情。"

"这要是成了实情，那虱子能咳嗽也是实情了。"

"嘿，嘿！"姚纳笑了，"享福的老爷！"

"你见鬼了！……"驼子愤怒地说，"老不死，你到底走不走？难道就这么磨磨蹭蹭？抽它一鞭子！见鬼！呶！狠狠抽它一鞭子！"

姚纳感觉到背后那个驼子的扭动着的躯体和颤抖的嗓音。他听到有人骂他，看到了很多人，他的孤独感逐渐在他心中有所消解。驼子一直骂着，一直骂到他的稀奇古怪的谩骂和连声咳嗽让他喘不过气来。两个高个子说出一个名叫纳杰日达·彼得罗芙娜的女人。姚纳转过头去看了看他们。等到了一个他们说话的短短空隙，他又转过头去，喃喃地说：

"这个星期，我儿子死了。"

"谁都会死的……"驼子咳嗽之后抹了抹嘴唇，叹了口气说。

"呶，快走！快走！先生们，我绝对不能再这样赶路了！他什么时候才能把我们送到？"

"你稍稍刺激他一下……照他的脖子来一拳！"

"老不死，听到了吗？我要揍你的脖子！……和你们兄弟讲客气，还不如干脆下车走路！……你听到了没有，毒蛇？你还是不把我们的话当一回事？"

姚纳与其说是感觉到了，不如说是听到了敲打他后脑勺的啪的一声。

"嘿……嘿。"他笑着说，"享福的老爷……上帝赏赐你们健康！"

"赶车的，你有老婆吗？"高个子问。

"我？嘿，嘿……享福的老爷！现在我只有一个老婆，那就是潮湿的土地……哈哈哈……那就是一个坟墓！儿子现在也死了，就我一个人活着……怪事儿，死神认错了门……该来找我的，奔孩子去了……"

姚纳转过身去，想说说儿子是怎么死的，但驼子轻轻地喘了口气，说，感谢上帝，他们终于到了目的地。姚纳收起二十戈比之后，还久久地眼瞅着那几个去寻欢作乐的乘客，如何地消失在乌黑的门洞里。

　　他又孤单单一人了，寂静又向他包围过来……刚刚平静了片刻的苦恼，又一次向他袭来，而且变本加厉地折磨着他的心胸。姚纳的慌恐的眼睛，痛苦地扫视着顺着街道两旁来回穿梭的行人：在这上千的行人里能够哪怕找到一个愿意倾听他诉说的人吗？但人群在疾行，既看不见他这个人，也看不见他的苦恼……这苦恼是巨大的，没有边际的。要是姚纳的胸膛裂开，从中流出苦恼，那么，这苦恼像是能把整个世界都会淹没的，但这苦恼却偏偏不被人看见。这苦恼装进了这样一个渺小的躯壳里，甚至白天举了火把都看不见……

　　姚纳看见一个看门护院的仆人，手里拿着纸袋子，就决定去和他说说话。

　　"亲爱的，现在几点了？"他问。

　　"九点多……你把马车停在这里干什么？走开！……"

　　姚纳把马车挪走了几步，弯下腰去，任凭苦恼把自己包络住……他知道向别人诉说已经没有用处。但是没有过去五分钟，他直起身子，摇晃着头，像是感受到了一阵剧痛，抖了抖缰绳……

　　他忍不住了。

　　"回大车店，"他想，"回大车店！"

　　那匹瘦马也像是明白了他的心思似的，一路快步小跑了起来。一个钟点之后，姚纳已经坐到了一个又大又脏的灶台旁。倦卧在灶台上，地板上，长凳上的人在打鼾。空气污浊燥闷……姚纳瞅瞅沉睡着的人，搔了搔头，后悔不该这么早就回来……

　　"我连买燕麦的钱还没有挣到呢，"他想，"这就是苦恼的原因。一个人要是能把自己的事情处理得井井有条……他自己不饿肚子，马儿也能吃饱，那他就永远会心平气和……"

　　在一个墙角里，有个年轻的车夫爬起身来，睡眼惺忪地清了清嗓子，伸手去拎水桶。

"想喝水。"姚纳问。

"是想喝点水！"

"喝吧，喝个痛快，可，老弟，我的儿子死了……听到了吗？这个星期死在医院里的……好惨呀！"

姚纳想看看他这番话会有什么效果，但什么效果也没有。年轻人蒙头睡过去了。老头长叹一声，搔了搔头……就如同那个年轻人要喝水那样，人要说话。儿子去世快一个星期了，但他还没有好好地跟什么人说过……应该从从容容、条理分明地说一说……应该说说儿子是怎么得的病，这病是怎么折磨他的，他在临死前说了些什么，他是怎么死的……还应该描述一下给儿子下葬的情形，和到医院去取回死者衣物的经过。在村子里就留下女儿阿尼娅一个人了……也应该说说女儿……他现在想说的事儿难道还少吗？听他说话的人应该哀痛得叫出声来，欷歔不止才对……找婆娘们去说更好。她们尽管痴蠢，但她们听不到两句话，就会号啕大哭的。

"去看看吧……"姚纳这样想，"睡觉总是来得及的……不用愁，能睡个够的……"

他穿上衣服，走到马厩里，他的那匹马就立在那儿，他在寻思燕麦、干草、天气……光是他一人，他不能想儿子……他可以跟一个人说说他儿子，但自己念想他，在心里描绘他的模样．就会觉得十分可怕……

"你在啮草吗？"姚纳问自己的马儿，瞅着它的闪闪发光的眼睛。"唉，吃吧，吃吧……燕麦是没有挣回来，但干草总是有的……是的……我老了……赶车不得劲了……赶车的该是儿子，而不是我……他才是赶车的好把式……要是他能活着……"

姚纳沉默了片刻，又继续说："我的小母马，你听着……库兹马·姚内奇不在了……他一闭眼先走了……说走就走了……这好比说，你生了头小马驹，你就是这头小马驹的母亲……突然之间，好比说，这头小马驹也一闭眼先走了……你照样会难过吧？"

小母马嚼着草，倾听着，朝自己主人的手上喷着热气……姚纳讲得出了神，把所有要说的话，统统讲给了它听。

（童道明　译）

欣　喜

午夜十二点钟。

米佳·库尔达洛夫飞也似的跑进父母的家门，头发蓬乱，神情亢奋。他快速地穿过所有房间。父母已经上床。妹妹躺在床上，正要把一本小说读完。在小学念书的弟弟们都已入睡。

"你从哪来？你这是怎么啦？"——父母好生奇怪。

"嘿，别问了！完全出乎我的意料！真的，完全出乎我的意料！……这简直难以置信！"

米佳咯咯大笑，坐到了椅子上，因为幸福，他已经站不直身子。

"这太不可思议了！你们简直无法想象！你们瞧瞧！"

妹妹从床上一跃而起，身上披了条毯子，走到哥哥跟前。弟弟们也都醒了。

"你这是怎么啦？瞧你神魂颠倒的样子！"

"老妈，我这是欣喜若狂！现在全俄罗斯都知道我了！我名扬全国了！以前只有你们知道，在这个世界上存在着一个十四等文官德米特里·库尔达洛夫，而现在呢，全俄罗斯的人都知道我了！老妈！唉，上帝！"

米佳从椅子上跳起，满屋子走圆场地跑了一圈，然后又坐了下来。

"这究竟是怎么回事？你倒是说个明白呀！"

"你们是一群野人，不读报，不知天下事，而报纸上有很多有趣的新闻！外边不管出点什么事，报上马上公之于众，藏着掖着没有门！我多么幸福！噢，上帝！要知道能上报的只有各类名人，而这回我的名字也上了报纸了！"

"你这是怎么回事？上了哪家报纸？"

父亲的面孔刷白，母亲面朝圣像在胸前画着十字。弟弟们从床上跳下来，就穿一条裤衩，走到哥哥跟前。

"真的！我的名字上报了！现在全俄罗斯的人都知道我了！老妈，您把这份报纸保存好，留作纪念！将来有机会再拿出来读读。请看！"

米佳从口袋里掏出一张报纸，递给父亲，用手指指向那个用蓝色铅笔划出的段落，"读吧！"

母亲面朝圣像在胸前画着十字。父亲清了清嗓子开始读："十二月二十九日，晚十一时，十四等文官德米特里·库尔达洛夫……"

"看到了吧，不假吧？往下读！"

"……十四等文官德米特里·库尔达洛夫从小勃朗纳街的科齐兴大楼一家酒吧走出，处于醉酒状态……"

"这说的是我和谢苗·彼得洛维奇……写得完全准确！再往下读！往下读！你们都听着！"

"……处于醉酒状态，一脚踩空，摔倒在地，恰好碰到一辆停靠路边的马拉雪橇车，马车夫伊凡·德罗托夫是尤赫诺夫县杜雷金村村民，坐在马拉雪橇上的是莫斯科二级行会的商人斯捷潘·洛科夫。失惊的马踩过库尔达洛夫连人带雪橇往前直奔，多亏被几位听差奋力拦住。库尔达洛夫起初昏迷不醒，抬到警察署经医生验伤……确诊为后脑勺受伤……"

"我的头碰上了车辕。再往下读！您往下读！"

"……为后脑勺受伤，所幸伤势不重。有关这次事故，主管当局已记录在案。伤者已送往医院就诊……"

"医生关照我用凉水湿敷后脑勺。现在明白了吧？就是这么回事！现在我名扬全俄罗斯！把报纸给我！"

米佳接过报纸，把它叠好，装进口袋。

"我现在到马卡洛夫家跑一趟，给他们说说……还要给伊凡尼茨基夫妇看看，还要给纳塔丽娅·伊凡诺芙娜，阿尼西姆·瓦西里依奇看看……我得赶紧跑！再见！"

米佳戴上一顶佩有帽徽的大檐帽跑到了街上，神气活现，欣喜若狂。

（童道明　译）

大 学 生

天气原本很好，没有风。鸫鸟在高声叫唤，近处的沼泽地里有个什么活物在悲鸣，像是朝一个空瓶子里吹气。有一只山鹬飞过，有人向它打了一枪，那枪声在春天的空气中，发出清脆而欢快的声响，但一当林子里黑了下来，一阵刺骨的寒风不合时宜地从东边吹了过来，一切都归于寂静。水洼上浮起了一层冰凌，树林变得阴森、荒凉和寂寥，透出了冬的气息。

伊凡·维利柯波尔斯基，这位神学院的大学生，教堂执事的儿子，打完山鹬回家，一路走在被水淹没的草地小路上。他的手指被冻僵了，脸孔被风吹红了。他觉得这突然袭来的寒潮打破了周遭的秩序与和谐，连大自然都感到了恐怖，以至于黄昏也要比往常来得早。满目苍凉，一切都显得特别昏暗。只有坐落在河边的那处寡妇菜园里闪耀着灯火，而四里地开外的村庄全都笼罩在一片阴冷的暮色中。大学生想起，当他离开家门的时候，母亲正光着脚坐在过道的地板上擦拭茶炊，而父亲躺在灶台上咳嗽，这天正是基督受难节，家里没有备餐，大家饿着肚子。现在，大学生冻得瑟缩着身子，他心里在想，无论是在柳里克王朝时代，还是在伊凡雷帝时代，或是在彼得大帝时代，都曾经吹刮过这样的寒风，在他们那个年代照样有过如此的贫穷，饥饿，有过这样的四面透风的茅屋，这样的愚昧，这样的哀伤，这样的满目荒凉，这样的黑暗，这样的压抑，所有这些可怕的灾难，从前有过，现在还有，将来也会有，因此再过几千年之后，生活也不会得到改善，于是他想回家。

菜园之所以称为寡妇菜园，是因为菜园的主人是一双寡妇——母女二人。篝火烧得真旺，不时爆出清脆的响声，把四周远处的耕地照得通明。母亲瓦西丽莎是个又胖又高的老太婆，穿着一件男式的短皮袄，站在一边，沉思地凝望着火堆；她的女儿卢基丽娅是个脸上长着麻子的小个子女人，其貌不扬，正坐在地上擦拭一只铁锅和几把汤勺。显然她们刚刚吃过晚饭。传来男人的说话声，这是此地的工人，在河边饮马。

"您瞧，冬天又回来了，"大学生走近篝火堆说，"你们好！"

瓦西丽莎身子抖动了一下，但立刻认出了大学生，微笑着向他表示欢迎。

"认不得了，上帝保佑你。"她说，"许是发财啦。"

他们开始聊天。瓦西丽莎是个见过世面的女人，以前曾在一家财主家当过奶妈，后来当了保姆，说话很有分寸，脸上一直堆着温柔的微笑。她的女儿卢基丽娅却是个深受丈夫虐待过的村姑，她只是默默地眯缝着眼睛朝大学生瞅着，神态像个聋哑人一样怪异。

"使徒彼得当年也是在这样一个寒夜在篝火旁取暖，"大学生说，一边把双手伸到了火堆旁，"这就是说，那天也很寒冷。啊，老大娘，那是一个多么可怕的夜晚！那是一个无比伤心的长夜呀！"

他看了看漆黑的四周，神经质地摇晃了一下脑袋，问：

"您想必听人读过福音书吧？"

"听人读过。"瓦西丽莎回答。

"如果你记得，在那个神秘的夜晚，彼得对耶稣说：'我就是同你下监，同你受死，也是甘心。'主却回答他说：'彼得，我告诉你，今日鸡还没有叫，你要三次说不认得我！'傍晚之后，耶稣在花园里愁闷异常，不停地祷告，而可怜的彼得精疲力竭，眼睛都张不开了，他无论如何抵挡不住睡意，他睡着了。后来，你也听过了，犹大在那个夜晚吻了耶稣，把他出卖给了折磨他的人。他们把他捆绑起来，送到大司祭面前，还殴打了他。而你也知道，彼得已经累极了，心里很痛苦，还受着惊吓，也没有睡足，他预感到了在这人世间要发生一件可怕的事情，便跟着走去……

"他深深地热爱着耶稣，而现在他远远地看到人家在殴打他……"

卢基丽娅把汤勺放到一边，凝视着大学生。

"他们到了大祭司跟前。"大学生继续讲述着，"他们开始审讯耶稣，而因为天气很冷，他们在院子里烧起了一堆火取暖。彼得也和他们一起站在篝火旁边取暖，像我现在一样。这时有一个妇女看见了他，说：'这个人素来也是同那人（耶稣）一伙的。'就是说，也应该把他一起提去受审。所有那些站在火堆旁边的人大概都用怀疑的目光严厉地盯视着他，他显得有点窘迫，说：'我不认得他。'过了一会儿，又有一个人认出了他是耶稣的一个门徒，说：'你也是他们一党的？'但他又一次否认了。后来又有人第三次对他发难：'今天我看到和他一起在花园里的，难道不就是你吗？'他第三次否认了。而就在这个时刻，鸡叫了。彼得远远地看着耶稣，想到了昨晚耶稣对他说的话……他回想起来了，省悟过来了。便走出花园，伤心地哭泣起来。在《圣经》上这样写着：'他就出去痛哭。'我这样想象：一个静静的、黑黑的花园，在这片寂静中隐隐传来声声低沉的哭泣……"

大学生叹了口气，陷入了沉思。瓦西丽莎虽然还在微笑，但突然间哽咽了一声，大颗眼泪如同泉涌从她脸颊流下，她用衣袖遮住脸，挡住火光，像是在为自己的眼泪感到害羞。而卢基丽娅一动不动地瞧着大学生，脸孔涨红了，她的表情紧张而沉重，像是一个人正承受着巨大的痛苦。

工友们从河边回来了，其中的一个坐在马上，已经走近，篝火的光在他的脸上闪耀。大学生向两位寡妇道了晚安，继续往前赶路。黑暗重新降临，手指冻僵了。刮着凛冽的寒风，冬天当真回来了，想象不到后天就是复活节。

现在大学生想到了瓦西丽莎：如果她哭了，也就意味着，使徒彼得在那个可怕的夜晚所经历的一切与她不无关系……

他回头看了一眼。孤独的篝火在黑暗中静静地闪耀，火堆旁边已见不到人影。大学生又想，如果瓦西丽莎哭泣了，而她女儿惊悚了，这就清楚地表明，他刚才讲述的那个发生在一千九百年前的故事与今天——与这两个女人，大概也与这个荒凉的村庄，与他本人，与所有的人都有关系的。如果这位老大娘哭了，这原因不在于他善于作富于感染力的讲述，而是因为彼得让她感到亲切，她全身心地关心在彼得的心灵中曾翻滚过的波澜。

喜悦之情突然在他的心中激荡起来，他甚至为了喘一口气，在原地站了一会儿。他想，过去与现在是由一连串连绵不断、由此及彼的事件联系起来的。他觉得自己刚才已经看到了这个锁链的两端：只需触动一端，另一端就会震颤。

当他坐渡船过了河，然后爬上了山冈，看着自己的故乡，见到西天的一窄条紫霞在闪光，他想，过去曾经在那花园和大祭司的院子里指引过人类生活的真与美，直到今天还在连续不断地指引着人类生活，而且看来，会永远地成为人世生活中的主要原则。青春的感觉，健康、力量——他才二十二岁啊——还有那对于幸福，那玄妙的幸福的无法形容的甜蜜预感，渐渐地控制住了他，生活让他感到是美妙的，令人神往的，充满崇高意义的。

（童道明　译）

带小狗的女人

一

　　大家都在讲，海滨街上出现了一张新面孔：一个牵小狗儿的女人。在雅尔塔已经生活了两个星期，已经熟悉了这个地方的德米特里·德米特里奇·古罗夫也对一些新面孔感兴趣了。他坐在韦尔奈的售货亭里，看见一个年轻女人在海滨街上走过，这是一个金发女郎，身材不高，戴着一顶无檐软帽。一条白色的长毛小狗跟在她身后跑。

　　后来他又在城市公园里和在街心小花园里遇见过她，一天内遇上好几次。她独自一人散步，总戴着那顶无檐软帽，牵着那条白色的长毛小狗。没有人知道她是谁，于是就随便称她为："牵小狗儿的女人"。

　　"如果她在这里没有丈夫和熟人，"古罗夫暗自斟酌着。"倒不妨同她认识一下。"

　　古罗夫还不到四十岁，却已经有一个十二岁的女儿和两个上中学的儿子。很早就给他娶了妻子，那时他还只是一个大学二年级学生，所以现在他妻子看起来比他的年纪要大一倍半。这个女人身材高高的，长着两道黑眉毛。她直率、尊严、庄重，而且，按她自己的说法，有思想。她读过很多书，书写时不写硬音符号"ъ"，叫丈夫时不叫德米特里而叫吉米特里；可是他呢，他私下里却认为她浅薄、狭隘、不优雅。他怕她，不喜欢待在家里。他对她早已变心，而且不止一次，也许正是因为这个缘故他对女人的评论几乎总是不好的，每逢他在场时谈及女人，他总把女人叫做：

"下等人种！"

他觉得，他已经吃足苦头，可以任意称呼她们，可是话虽如此，如果没有了"下等人种"，他就会连两天也活不下去。同男人在一起，他觉得苦燥无味，觉得不自在；同男人在一起他就沉默寡言，冷冷淡淡。可是，一到了女人中间，他就觉得自由自在，知道该同她们谈些什么，该有什么样的举止与态度；同她们在一起，即使不讲话也觉得轻松自在。在他的相貌、性格和资质中，有一种迷人的、不可捉摸的东西，它使女人对他产生好感，它吸引她们；这一点他是清楚的，同时也有一种力量在引诱着他到她们那儿去。

沉痛的多次经验确实早已使他懂得：对一些规矩人来说，尤其是对一些行动缓慢、犹豫不决的莫斯科人来说，同女人相好这种事情起初可以愉快地使生活多样化，显得是一种轻松可爱的猎奇，但到头来它必然会变为一个十分复杂的大问题，而情况会变得令人难以忍受。尽管这样，每逢他新遇漂亮女人，不知何故他就会忘记这种经验，他会想玩一玩，于是一切又都显得十分简单和趣味盎然。

一天傍晚他在公园里吃饭，那个戴无檐软帽的女人不慌不忙地走过来，要在他的邻桌坐下。她的神情、步态、衣着和发型都告诉他：她来自上流社会，是有夫之妇，是初次来雅尔塔，独自一人，在这儿感到寂寞……关于本地的风气败坏有许多并不实在的闲话，古罗夫不理会这些闲话，他知道，大部分闲话是一些人编造的，这些人只要自己有办法也都会乐于作孽。可是当那个戴无檐软帽的女人在离他仅三步远的邻桌坐下时，他不由得想起了那些关于轻易得手和登山旅游的传闻，于是一个诱人的念头突然控制了他：来上一次昙花一现的同居，跟一个陌生的连姓名都不知的女人干一次风流韵事。

他亲热地招呼长毛小白狗到身边来，但当它走近时，他又用手指吓唬它。长毛小狗吠叫起来，古罗夫又摇动手指吓唬它。

女人瞟了他一眼，但马上就垂下眼帘。

"它不咬人。"说着她脸红了。

"可以给它吃骨头吗？"待她点头肯定后他和颜悦色地问道："您来雅尔塔有多久了？"

"将近五天了。"

"我在这儿已是第二星期了。"

他们沉默了一会儿。

"时间过得真快，而这儿又非常无聊、沉闷！"她并不看着他说。

"这儿无聊沉闷，——这不过是通常说说罢了。一个市侩住在他的什么别廖夫^①——或曰兹德拉^②，他倒不觉得无聊沉闷，可是一到这儿他就说：'唉，无聊！哎，尘土！'你还真会以为他来自格林纳达^③呢！"

她笑了。接着他们又继续吃饭，不说话，像两个互不相识的人一样。可是饭后他们却并排走在一起了。开始了一场快活轻松的谈话，这是在一些感到自由满足、对于去哪儿和谈什么都无所谓的人之间进行的谈话。他们散着步，谈到了海面上的奇异光照、海水显出紫藤般的颜色，柔和、温暖，由于月光的照射，水面上有一条金黄色的长带。他们也谈到，在炎炎的白昼过去后天气非常闷热。古罗夫说他是莫斯科人，在学校里学的是语文学，然而却在一家银行里工作；他一度打算在私人歌剧团里演唱，但后来没有去；还说他在莫斯科有两幢房子……而从她口中他了解到，

_____

① 图拉州的一个小城市。
② 卡卢加州的一个小城市。
③ 西印度群岛国家，位于格林纳达岛和格林纳丁斯群岛。

她在彼得堡长大，但嫁到了 C 城，已经在那里生活了两年，她在雅尔塔还将住上个把月，有可能她丈夫会来接她，他也想休养休养。但她怎么也说不清楚她丈夫在哪里工作，是在省政府呢，还是在省地方自治局，这使她自己也觉得好笑。古罗夫还了解到，她的名字叫安娜·谢尔盖耶芙娜。

分手后他在旅馆的房间里想她。他想，明天她一定会同他见面，一定。躺下睡觉时，他想到她不久前还是一个寄宿女子中学的学生，还在读书，就同他女儿现在在读书一样；他想到，在她的笑声和在她同陌生人的交谈中还有不少胆怯和生硬的东西，大概这还是她生平初次孤身一人处在这种环境里，而有些人心怀一种她不会猜不到的秘密目的在跟踪她、在注意她并同她谈话；他还想到她的细长的脖子和美丽的灰色眼睛。

"她身上毕竟有一点儿可怜的东西。"他想着就昏昏入睡了。

二

他们相识已经有一个星期了。这一天是节日。房间里闷热，街道上飞舞着旋风似的尘土，行人的帽子不时被风吹落。人整天想喝水，古罗夫不时去售货亭，有时请安娜·谢尔盖耶芙娜喝果子露冲的水，有时请她吃冰淇淋。没有什么地方可去。

到傍晚，风稍稍静息，他们去防水堤观看轮船抵达的情景。码头上有许多人在散步，他们聚集在这里接人，手中拿着花束。在这里，讲究穿着的雅尔塔人的两个特点分外惹人注目：一个特点是上了岁数的太太们穿得同年轻妇女一样，另一个特点是有许多将军。

轮船在海上遇到了风浪，到达时太阳已经下山，而在向防水堤靠拢前轮船又花了很长时间掉头。安娜·谢尔盖耶芙娜手执长柄眼镜瞧着轮船和乘客，好像是在寻找熟人似的；在她向古罗夫转过身来时，她的眼睛闪闪发光。她话很多，提出许多不连贯的问题，以致她本人也一转眼就忘了她问的是什么。后来她的一把长柄眼镜丢失在人群中了。

装束讲究的人群散了，已经看不见什么人了，风已经完全停息，而古罗夫和安娜·谢尔盖耶芙娜仍站在那里，好像在等着还有没有人从轮船上下来。安娜·谢尔盖耶芙娜闻着鲜花，她已经不再说话，也不看着古罗夫。"傍晚天气有所好转，"他说。"我们现在上哪儿去？要不要坐车去兜兜风？"

她不作回答。

他凝视了她一下，突然间他将她搂住，吻了吻她的嘴唇，一阵鲜花的香味和水汽向他袭来，他立刻胆怯地环顾四周：是不是有人已经看见？

"我们上您那儿去吧……"他轻声说。

两个人迅速走了。

她住的旅馆房间里既闷又热，弥漫着一股香水味，这香水是她在一家日本商店里买的。瞧着她，古罗夫不禁想到："在生活中你真是什么人都会碰到！"从以往的岁月里留下了他对一些善良的乐天的女人的回忆，爱情使她们高兴，她们感激他带来了幸福，虽说这不过是一种十分短暂的幸福；保留着的还有对另一些女人的回忆，举例说像他妻子那样的女人，她们爱得不真诚，她们说许多不必要的话，不自然，狂热，她们的神情表明，好像她们并非在爱，并非在表露情欲，而是在做着某种重要的事情似的；另外他还记着两三个女人，她们美丽、冷淡，她们的脸上会突然掠过一种凶狠的神情和固执的愿望，想从生活获得和夺取比生活所能给予的多得多的东西，她们都已并不年轻，任性，不善判断，不明达，好发号施令，因此在古罗夫对她们失去兴趣的时候，她们的美貌就在他心中唤起憎恶，而她们衬衣上的花边却使他觉着像鱼鳞。

可是眼前他接触到的是一个涉世不深的年轻妇女的胆怯、生硬和拘束。她还给人一种茫然若失的印象，好像是有人突然敲门似的。安娜·谢尔盖耶芙娜，这个"牵着小狗的女人"，对待已经发生的事情的态度有些特别，她看得十分严重，好像这是她道德上的堕落——她给人的感觉就是这样，而这是古怪的、不合时宜的。她沮丧、委靡，长长的头发忧伤地挂在她脸庞的两侧。她凄凉地沉湎于冥想之中，犹如古画上那个犯了教规的女人。①

"这样不好，"她说。"现在第一个会不尊重我的人就是您。"

房间里桌子上放着一个西瓜。古罗夫给自己切了一块，不慌不忙地吃了起来。至少有半个小时就这么在沉默中过去了。

安娜·谢尔盖耶芙娜神态动人，从她身上散发出一个正派、纯朴、处世不深的女人的纯洁气息。桌子上一支孤零零的蜡烛微微照着她的脸，但可以看出来她心绪不好。

"为什么我会不再尊重你呢？"古罗夫问。"你自己都不知道你在说些什么。"

"上帝饶恕我吧！"她泪水盈眶地说。"这可怕。"

"你好像是在替自己开脱。"

"我怎能开脱得了？我是个糟糕下流的女人，我看不起自己，我也不想开脱自己。我不是欺骗了丈夫，而是欺骗了我自己。不光是现在，我早就在欺骗了。也许，我丈夫是个诚实的好人，可是他是个奴才。嫁给他时我才十二岁，一种好奇心使我焦躁不安，我想过得好一点，我对自己说：'不是有着另一种生活吗？'我很想过逍遥快乐的生活！过一过这种生活……好奇心刺激着我……这一点您是不懂的，可是我，我向上帝发誓，我已经控制不住自己，我变了，已经拦阻不住自己，我对丈夫说我病了，我就到这个地方来了……在这里我走来走去，像是着了魔发了

_____

① "犯了教规的女人"指的是《圣经》中的"抹大拉的马利亚"，一个因受耶稣感化而忏悔了的妓女。

疯……就这样我变成了一个庸俗下贱、谁都会瞧不起的女人。"

古罗夫听着觉得烦闷。这天真的口气、这意外的不合时宜的忏悔惹他生气。如果不是她热泪盈眶,那人家真会认为她是在开玩笑或者是在装腔作势。

"我不明白,"他轻声说。"你到底要什么?"

她把脸埋在他的胸前,紧贴着他。

"请您相信我的话,请您相信,我求求您……"她说。"我喜欢正派纯洁的生活,我厌恶罪孽的生活,我自己都不知道我在干什么。老百姓常说:鬼迷心窍。现在我也可以这么说我自己:鬼迷住了我的心窍。"

"够啦,别说了……"他嘟哝说。

他瞧着她两只呆板惊恐的眼睛,吻她,亲热地轻声说话。她的心情逐渐平静,重又兴致勃勃起来。两个人都笑了。

后来他走出旅馆,海滨街上已经没有一个人影,这座城市连同那些柏树都寂静无声,但海水仍在喧闹和拍击着海岸。一条小汽艇在海浪上颠簸,一只小挂灯在船上懒洋洋地闪烁着。

他们雇了马车去奥列安达。①

"刚才我在楼下前厅里知道了你的姓,在一块牌子上写着:方·季杰利茨,"古罗夫说。"你丈夫是德国人?"

"不,他祖父好像是德国人,然而他本人是一个东正派教徒。"

在奥列安达他们坐在一条长凳上,离教堂不远。他们默默地看着下方的大海。透过晨雾可以隐隐约约地看到雅尔塔,白云一动不动地停留在山顶上。树上的叶子纹丝不动,知了在鸣叫,从下方传来的大海的单调低沉的喧哗象征着安谧,象征着那正在等候我们的长眠。想当初,在雅尔塔和奥列安达都还不存在的时候,海水就在下方这么喧哗了,如今它也在喧哗,将来在我们去世后

_____

① 一个在雅尔塔附近、濒临黑海的城镇,是一个旅游胜地。

它仍在如此冷漠地喧哗。也许，在这种永恒性中，在这种对我们每个人的生与死所持的绝对冷漠态度中，正包藏着一种保证：我们会永恒超度的保证，大地上的生命会不断运行不断完善的保证。同一个在晨曦中显得十分美丽的年轻妇女坐在一起的古罗夫，面对着这童话般的环境、面对着海洋山岳云彩和辽阔天空而感到心旷神怡的古罗夫想道：实际上，如果想得深一点的话，世上的一切都是十分美好的，除了我们自己在忘却了生活的最高目标和人的尊严时所想做的事情之外，一切都是十分美好的。

有一个人，大概是个更夫，走近过来，看了他们一眼走开了。就连这个细节也显得非常神秘和美好。可以看见，一条从费奥多西亚开来的轮船到了，船上的灯火已经熄灭，朝霞照亮着船身。

"草上有露水。"安娜·谢尔盖耶芙娜打破沉默说。

"是的，该回去啦。"

他们回到了城里。

后来他们每天晌午在海滨街见面，一起吃早饭进午餐，一起散步，一起欣赏海洋。她抱怨睡眠欠佳，心神不宁；她忽而因嫉妒而激动，忽而又怕他不十分尊重她，老是向他提出一些同样的问题。在街心花园里或者在大公园里，每逢附近没有人的时候，他常常把她拉向自己热烈地亲吻。十足闲逸的生活，左顾右盼生怕被人看见的光天化日之下的接吻，海水的气息，不时在眼前闪过的闲散、盛装和饱腹的人们，——所有这一切都仿佛根本地改造了他。他对安娜·谢尔盖耶芙娜说，她十分美丽，非常迷人。他的情欲强烈难忍，对她可说是寸步不离。而她却常常沉湎于冥想之中，总求他承认他并不尊重她，丝毫也不爱她，不过是把她看成一个下流的女人。几乎每天夜晚他们要驱车出城，或去奥列安达，或去瀑布所在地。这种闲游是成功的，每次的印象总是美好庄重的。

他们在等她丈夫来到。可是从他那儿来了一封信，他在信中说他害了眼疾，恳求妻子尽快回家。安娜·谢尔盖耶芙娜因此就着忙起来。

"我走了倒好，"她对古罗夫说。"这是命运的安排。"

她坐马车离开雅尔塔，他送她。他们赶了一整天路。当她坐进特别快车的车厢、第二遍铃声响起的时候，她说：

"好，让我再看一看您……再看一眼。好，就这样。"

"我会想念您的……会回忆您的，"她说。"上帝保佑您，祝您幸福留下。别念我旧恶。我们永别了，应该是这样，因为我们本来就不该相遇。好，上帝保佑您。"

火车快速地开走了，车上的灯火很快消失，再过一会儿已经听不见轰隆轰隆的声音了，好像是一切都故意商妥了似的，要尽快结束这种甜蜜诱人的忘乎所以的愚蠢行为。古罗夫只身一个留在月台上，他瞧着黑洞洞的远方，听着蚰斯的鸣叫和电报线的呜呜声，他觉得自己像是刚醒来似的。他想：在他一生中又多了一次猎奇或冒险，而且就连这件事情也已经结束，只剩下了回忆……他感动，忧伤，体验一层淡淡的悔悟心意：可不是么，这个他再也见不到的年轻女人同他在一起并不幸福；他对她温和亲切，但在他对她的态度里、在他的口气和抚爱里，毕竟隐隐露出一种轻微的讥诮，露出一种年龄比她差不多大上一倍的幸福男子的略略粗野的倨傲。她一直说他善良、非凡、高尚，显然，在她心目中的他不是实际上的他，就是说，他无意中骗了她……

在这里，在车站上，已经有了秋意，傍晚已经令人感到凉丝丝的了。

"我也该回北方了，"古罗夫离开站台时想道。"是时候了！"

三

在莫斯科家里的一切都已具有了冬天的样子：生上了炉子，

早晨孩子们准备上学和喝早茶的时候天还是黑黑的，保姆还要点上一会儿灯。严冬已经开始。下了头一场雪，第一天坐上雪橇，看到白茫茫的地面和白皑皑的屋顶，觉得舒服，呼吸起来感到轻松和惬意。在这种时候会回忆起青年时代。蒙上了重霜而变白的老菩提树和桦树有一种温和的样子，比起柏树和棕榈树来它们更加贴心。有它们在近处，就没有心思去想山峦和海洋了。

古罗夫是莫斯科人，在一个晴朗寒冷的日子他回到了莫斯科。在他穿着皮大衣戴着暖和的手套沿着彼得罗夫卡大街散步的时候，在星期六傍晚他听到教堂钟声的时候，不久前的那次旅行以及他所到过的地方对他都失去了全部魅力。他逐渐沉浸于莫斯科的生活之中了，他已经每天贪婪地读三份报纸，可是他还说他原则上不读莫斯科的报纸。他已经倾心于饭馆、俱乐部，倾心于宴会、纪念会，常有著名的律师和演员上他家做客，他常在医师俱乐部同教授一起玩牌，这使他感到挺得意。他已经能够一次就吃完一份——小煎锅——酸白菜炖肉了……

他觉得，再过上个把月，在他的记忆中安娜·谢尔盖耶芙娜就会模模糊糊，她只会偶尔含着动人的笑容出现在他的梦中，就像他梦见其他一些女人一样。可是，一个多月过去了，隆冬已经来临，而在他的记忆里一切都清清楚楚，仿佛他只是在昨天才同安娜·谢尔盖耶芙娜分手似的。这种回忆越来越强烈，无论是他在寂静的傍晚在书房里听到孩子们准备功课的声音，还是他在饭馆听着抒情歌曲或大风琴，还是他听到了风雪在壁炉里的哀叫，一切都会顿时在他的记忆中复苏：在防水堤上的情景，清晨山间的迷雾，从费奥多西亚开来的轮船，亲吻，等等……他久久地在房间里走动，回忆着，面带微微笑容，而后回忆又转化为幻想，过去的事在想象中同将会发生的事混到了一起。安娜·谢尔盖耶芙娜并非出现在他的梦境之中，而是像影子似的处处跟随着他，观察着他的一举一动。他一闭上眼就看见她活生生地站在他面前，而且似乎比过去更加美丽、年轻和温柔，就连他本人似乎也比在雅尔塔时更好一些。每天晚上她从书柜里、从壁炉里和从墙角里瞅着他，他听见她的呼吸声，听见她的衣服发出亲切的沙沙声。走在街上，他常常目送来来往往的女人，寻找着有没有长相同她相像的……

他非常想同一个什么人述说所回忆到的一切，这个强烈愿望折磨着他。然而在家里他是不能谈他的爱情的，而在外面又没有人可以谈心。总不该同房客们谈吧，也不能在银行里谈，再说，又谈什么呢？难道当初他真爱她了吗？难道他在同安娜·谢尔盖耶芙娜的关系中有什么优美的富有诗意的东西？有什么富于教育意义的或者干脆是有趣的东西？他常常只好含含糊糊地谈谈爱情，谈谈女人，因此谁也觉察不出是怎么一回事，只有他的妻子扬扬黑眉毛说：

"你，吉米特里，花花公子这角色同你不相配。"

有一天夜间他同一个朋友——一位文官——一起走出医师俱乐部，他忍不住说：

"您不会知道我在雅尔塔结识了一个多么迷人的女人！"

文官坐上雪橇走了，可是他突然又回头招呼一声：

"德米特里·德米特里奇！"

"什么事？"

"您刚才说得对；那鲟鱼肉啊……是臭烘烘的！"

平平常常普普通通的两句话，可是不知为什么却激怒了古罗夫，他觉得这话是侮辱性的，是龌龊的。粗野的习气，粗野的人！乱七八糟的夜晚，没有意思的平平庸庸的白天！狂赌、贪食、酗酒，一套套老生常谈！无用的事情和老生常谈占用了一个人最好的时光、最好的精力，到头来只有一种狭隘平庸的生活，一种荒唐无聊的东西，好像是待在疯人院或犯人劳动队里似的，想走走不开，想逃逃不脱！

　　古罗夫一夜没有合眼，他气愤，头痛了整整一天。以后几夜他也睡不好，老是坐在床上想心事，要不就在房间里踱步。孩子使他生厌，银行使他心烦，什么地方都不想去，什么话也不想说。

　　在 12 月的节日期间，他做好了出门的准备，对妻子说的是要去彼得堡为一个年轻人张罗一件事，实际上他是要到 C 城去，去干什么？他本人也不太清楚。他想同安娜·谢尔盖耶芙娜见一面，谈一谈，如果可能的话约她相会。

　　他早晨到达 C 城，在旅馆租下一个最好的房间。这房间里的地板全都铺上了灰色军用呢，桌上有一只墨水壶，尘土使壶成了灰灰的，壶上刻有一个骑着马的骑士，他举起的一只手拿着帽子，但他的头已被打掉。看门人向他提供了必要的信息：方·季杰利茨住在老冈察尔纳亚街上的私人住宅里，离旅馆并不远。他生活优裕阔绰，有私人马车。城里的人都认识他。看门人把他的姓念成了"德雷迪利茨"。

　　古罗夫朝着老冈察尔纳亚街慢慢地走去。他找到了那幢房子。在房子的正对面延伸着一道围墙：灰灰的，长长的，墙顶上紧着许多钉子。

　　"看到这种围墙壁准会逃走的。"古罗夫暗想，他一会儿看看窗子，一会儿看看围墙。

　　他斟酌着：今天是不上班的日子，她丈夫大概在家里。再说，他就这么进屋，会使人家难堪，是不懂礼节。如果送一张便条进去，它也许会落到她丈夫手中，那就可能败坏全局。最好还是去碰碰巧吧。于是他就一直在街上和在围墙旁走来走去，期待着巧遇。他看见一个乞丐走进了大门，几条狗向乞丐扑去。后来，过了个把小时，他听见了弹钢琴的声音，传来一阵阵微弱含混的琴声。这该是安娜·谢尔盖耶芙娜在弹琴。突然间正门敞开了，走出来一个老太婆，她身后跟着那条熟悉的长毛小白狗。古罗夫想叫住那条狗，可是他的心突然剧烈地跳了，由于兴奋他竟然想不起长毛小白狗的名字。

他走来走去，越来越恨那堵灰色的围墙。他已经生气地想到：安娜·谢尔盖耶芙娜已经把他忘记，她也许已经在同别的男人相好，这种事在一个年轻妇女的处境里是十分自然的，她从早到晚迫不得已要看到这堵该死的围墙。古罗夫回到了他租住的房间里，在沙发上坐了很长时间，不知道该做什么才好。后来他进了午餐，饭后睡了很久。

"这一切真愚蠢！"他醒来后想道，两眼瞧着黑黑的窗子，已经是黄昏时分。"真令人不快！不知怎么的我睡够了，现在夜间我该做什么呢？"

他坐在床上，床上铺着一条廉价的像是医院里用的灰色被子。他懊恼地嘲弄自己说：

"瞧你，你要找牵小狗儿的女人！瞧你，你要猎奇！……现在你就给我坐在这儿吧！"

这是早晨的事情。他在火车站上看到一张用很大很大的字号写成的海报：首次公演《盖伊霞》。现在他想起了这张海报，就驱车上剧院去了。

"很可能，她会常看首次公演的戏。"他想。

剧院里满座。同所有的内地剧院一样：在这儿枝形吊灯的上方也是烟雾腾腾，顶层楼座的观众喧喧嚷嚷；开演前，当地的一些花花公子站在第一排，双手抄在背后；在省长包厢里坐在首席的是省长的女儿，她围着一条毛皮项巾，省长本人谦虚地藏在门帘后面，能见到的只是他的双手；幕布在舞台上晃动着，乐队花很长时间在调音。观众们进入大厅纷纷坐下，古罗夫的两只眼睛在贪婪地搜索着。

安娜·谢尔盖耶芙娜走进来了。她在第三排坐下。古罗夫瞧了她一眼，他的心抽紧了。他清清楚楚地体会到：现在对他来说在世界上她是最亲近的人。她，这个娇小的在成群的内地人里不受注意的女人，手里拿着一把俗气的长柄眼镜，她，现在竟占据了他的全副身心，成了他的悲哀和欢乐，成了他现在所指望的唯一幸福。听着糟糕的乐队和拙劣的小提琴声，古罗夫想道："她多美啊！"他思忖着，幻想着。

同安娜·谢尔盖耶芙娜一起进来、而且并排坐下的是一个年轻人，他留着小小的络腮胡子，身材很高，微微驼背；他每走一步路就摇一下头，好像一直在向人点头致意似的。这个人想必就是她的丈夫，就是当初在雅尔塔时她心情痛苦中骂之为奴才的那个人。果然，他的细长身材、络腮胡子和一小片秃顶都确实反映出一种奴才般谦恭的习气，他笑起来像谄媚，他的纽扣眼上有个令人费解的徽章在发光，像是一块仆役号牌。

第一次幕间休息时，她丈夫出去吸烟，她留在座位上。也坐在正厅里的古罗夫走到她跟前声音发颤地强笑着说：

"您好！"

她瞧了他一眼，脸色顿时发白，她不信自己的眼睛，又惊恐地瞧了他一眼，双手紧紧地握住扇子和长柄眼镜，显然，她这是在克制自己，以免昏厥过去。两个人都不说话，她坐着，他站着。她的困惑使他失措，不敢在她身旁坐下。几把小提琴和一管长笛开始调音。突然令人觉得可怕起来：似乎所有包厢里的人都在看着他们。这时候她站起身来，快步朝出口处走去，他跟在她后面。两个人瞎走着：一会儿在走廊里、一会儿在楼梯上，一会儿上楼，一会儿下楼。他们眼前闪过一些穿着法官制服、教师制服、皇室制服的人。这些人都佩戴着徽章。也闪过一些女人，挂在衣架上的皮大衣……穿堂风迎面吹来，传来一阵烟味。古罗夫心跳得厉害，他想："主啊！干吗要这些人，干吗要这个乐队！"

就在这时他突然想起，那天晚上他在火车站上送走安娜·谢尔盖耶芙娜后对自己说：一切就此结束，他们永远不会再见面。可是，实际上离结束还远着呢！

在一条标有"通向梯形楼座"字样的狭窄阴暗的楼梯上她站住了。

"您真把我吓坏了！"她脸色苍白，神态惊愕，气喘吁吁地说。"哎，您真把我吓坏了！我差点儿死过去了。您来干什么？干什么呀？"

"可是，请您谅解，安娜，请您谅解……"他匆匆地低声说。"我求您谅解……"

她看着他，脸上现出恐惧、哀求和热爱的神情。她凝视着他，要把他的相貌更牢固地留在记忆中。

"我真苦啊！"她不听他的话继续说。"我一直在想您，只想您一个人，我的全部精力都用在对您的思念上了。我一心想把您忘记，忘记……可是，您干什么，干什么要到这儿来？"

在他们的上方，在梯台上有两个中学生正在吸烟，在朝下面看，可是，古罗夫全不在意，他把安娜·谢尔盖耶芙娜拉到身边，开始吻她的面孔、脸颊和双手。

"您干什么呀！干什么呀！"她惊恐地说着把他从身边推开。"我们两个都疯了。您今天就离开，马上离开……我凭一切神圣的东西恳求您，央求您……有人来了！"

有个人正在走上楼来。

"您一定得离开……"安娜·谢尔盖耶芙娜接着小声说。"您听见了吗？德米特里·德米特里奇？我会到莫斯科去找您的。我从来没有幸福过，我现在悲伤，我永远不会幸福，永远不会！别让我更加痛苦了！我赌咒，我一定会到莫斯科去的。现在我们就分手吧，我的宝贝，我的好人，我的亲爱的！我们分手吧！"

她握了握他的手，开始快步走下楼去。她不住地回头看他。从她的眼神中可以看出，她确实不幸福……古罗夫站了一会儿，留神听了一会儿，后来，在一切都静息下来时，他找到了他那件挂在衣帽架上的大衣，离开了剧院。

四

安娜·谢尔盖耶芙娜开始到莫斯科去看他。她两三个月离开 C 城一次，对丈夫说她这是为妇女病去请教一位教授，她丈夫是既相信又不相信。到了莫斯科，她下榻在"斯拉维扬斯基商场大旅馆"，而且派一个戴红帽子的人去找古罗夫。古罗夫去看她，在莫斯科任何人都不知道这件事。

有一次，他在一个冬天的早晨去看她，因为隔夜传信人来他家时没有找着他。女儿和他走在一起，他想送她上学，正好是顺路。大片大片的湿雪纷纷扬扬。

"现在是零上三度，却在下雪，"古罗夫对女儿说。"要知道，这只是在地面上暖和，在大气的上层就完全是另一种气温。"

"爸爸，为什么冬天不打雷？"

他对这个问题也作了解释。他边说边想：他现在去赴幽会，这件事没有一个活人知道，大概永远也不会有人知道。他有两种生活：一种生活是公开的，它是所有需要看看并知道这种生活的人都看见和都知道的，它充满了虚假的真实和虚伪的欺骗，它同他的熟人和朋友们过着的生活一模一样；而另一种生活是在暗中进行的。由许多情况的奇怪（也许是偶然）凑合，所有在他心目中是重大的、有意思的、不可或缺的东西，所有他真诚地做了而又不欺骗自己的事情，所有构成他生活的核心的事情——所有这一切都是背着他人发生的；所有他的不诚实行为，还有他借以隐藏自己来掩蔽真相的外形，比如说，他在银行工作，他在俱乐部里争论，他说的"下等人种"，他同妻子一起参加庆祝会等等——所有这一切都是公开地进行的。他依据本人的情况判断别人，他不相信他看到的事情，而且他总认为，可能是在秘幕下，就像在夜幕的掩护下一样，每个人都过着他真正的最有意思的生活。每个人的私生活都得靠秘密来维持。所以，也许，多多少少是由于这个缘故，文明人才会十分焦急地谋求对个人隐私的尊重。

把女儿送到学校后古罗夫就去"斯拉维扬斯基商场"。他在楼下脱去大衣，上了楼轻轻敲门。安娜·谢尔盖耶芙娜从昨天傍晚起就在等候他了，她穿着一件他所喜爱的灰色连衣裙。旅行和期待使她感到疲惫，她脸色苍白，看着他并不笑，他刚走进门她就扑倒在他的胸脯上。他们的亲吻很久很长，好像是他们两年未见面了。

"哦，你说说，在那儿日子过得怎样？"他问。"有什么新闻？"

"你等一等，我这就说……我说不出来。"

她哭了，所以她说不出话来。她把脸扭向一旁，将手绢紧贴住眼睛。

"好，就让她哭哭吧，我先坐一会儿。"他想了想就在一张圈椅上坐下。

他按了一下铃，吩咐给他送茶。在他喝茶的时候，他一直站着，脸向着窗户……她哭，是由于激动，由于悲痛地意识到他们的生活十分凄惨，只能秘密地见面，背着人家，像窃贼似的。难道他们的生活不是给毁了吗？

"得啦，别哭了！"他说。

在他心目中事情是明显的：他们这场恋爱还不会很快结束，也不知道何时才会结束。安娜·谢尔盖耶芙娜对他的依恋越来越深，她崇拜他，所以如果要告诉她说这一切迟早都该结束，那会是简直不可思议的事，更何况说了她也不会相信。

他走近她，抚爱她的肩膀，想表示一下对她的亲热，说几句笑话，就在此时他在镜子里看见了自己。

他的头发已经开始发白。他甚至感到奇怪：近几年来会老得这么厉害，会变得这么难看。而他双手正抚摸着的双肩却是暖暖的，它们正在颤动。面对这个生命，这个非常温柔和美好的、但想必也将像他的生命一样开始凋谢和枯萎的生命，他感到怜悯。

为什么她如此爱他？在女人的心目中，他一直不是本来的他；在他身上她们爱的并不是他本人，是一个她们在生活中所热切寻求的人，所以她们在发现了自己的错误时仍然爱他。同他在一起，她们中没有一个人是幸福的。时光在流逝，他同一些女人认识、相好而后又分手，然而他从来没有爱过一次；什么都曾有过，唯独不是爱情。

只是到了现在，到了他的头发开始变白的时候，他才爱上了；认真地爱，真正地爱，有生以来第一次。

安娜·谢尔盖耶芙娜和他相亲相爱，像两个十分贴近的人，像了亲戚，像夫妻，像情投意合的朋友。他们觉得，是命运本身预先安排了他们相遇，令人费解的倒是为什么他已经娶了妻子，而她已嫁了丈夫；仿佛这是两只候鸟，一雌一雄，把它们捉住后硬让它们生活在两只单独的笼子里似的。他们互相原谅了他们过去各自感到惭愧的事情，原谅了目前做着的一切，而且感到他们的相爱使他们两人都变了。

从前古罗夫在忧伤的时候，他总用他所想出的各种各样的推理来安慰自己，现在他已顾不上进行什么推理，他感到的是深切的同情，他一心想使自己不矫饰和有柔情……

"别哭了，亲爱的，"他说。"哭过也就够了……现在我们还是来谈谈，想想办法。"

他们商量了很久，讲到了怎样使自己摆脱目前的处境，这种不得不躲避、欺骗、分居在不同城市和久久不能见面的处境。怎样才能摆脱这些不堪忍受的桎梏？

"怎样？怎样？"他抱住看书的头问。"怎样？"

似乎是再过上一会儿就能找到问题的答案，而且一种崭新的美好生活就会开始；不过，他们俩都清楚：离结局还很远很远，而最复杂和最困难的事情才刚刚开始。

（朱逸森　译）

忧　伤

　　镟工皮屈夫许多年来在格钦斯贺县以技艺出众得名，同时也以脑筋最笨得名，现在他正在载着他的老妻到医院里去。他已经赶车赶了二十里，路上很不好走，哪怕政府里的特派员都奈何它不得，像皮屈夫这样的懒鬼对于这条路当然更没有法子可想。一阵刺骨的寒风直扑到他的脸上来。雪花在各方面团团乱转，谁也说不清雪是从天上落下来的，还是从地底下钻出来的。雪花乱绕，连田亩，电线杆和树林都看不清了。有时一阵非常猛烈的风打在皮屈夫脸上，甚至马头上的横轭都看不清楚。软弱败坏的小马慢慢地爬着前进，它用尽力气在雪地里拔着脚走，头儿向前，用力的拉着车。镟工心里很急，他在前面的座位上不住的耸着身子，鞭着马背。

　　他叽咕着说：“梅朱娜，不要哭……耐着性子一点儿。上帝保佑我们赶快走到医院，一会儿你就可以有救了……白夫尔要给你一点药水，或者叫助手替你放血！或者他要亲自动手，用酒精来替你揉擦——就是这样……你把病状告诉他。白夫尔要尽力替你医治，他要乱喊乱跺脚，但他要尽力替你医治……他是一个好人，多么温柔，上帝给他健康罢！我们到了那儿，他一定要从房间冲出来，喊着我的名字。他要这样喊道：‘怎么？为什么？你怎么不在诊治时间内跑来呢？我又不是狗，整天的等着你们这些鬼。你为什么早晨不来呢？滚开些！不要让我看见你。明天再来。’于是我就要说：‘医生老爷呀！白夫尔老爷呀！’该死的马，走呀，鬼东西，走呀！”

　　镟工鞭着马，也回头看他的老妻，继续的自己叽咕着说：

　　“'老爷！我可以在上帝面前发誓……天没有亮我就爬起来……偏偏上帝……圣母……发怒，降下大雪，你叫我怎么能够按时来到呢？你自己替我设想一下罢……就连头号的马也跑不快，我的马你也看见的，哪里是马，简直是丢人末。'白夫尔一定要皱着眉毛喊叫道：'我们知道你。你总有话说！皮屈夫，尤其是你；我早就把你看穿了。我敢说你曾经在半打酒店里停留过，我就要说：'老爷！难道我是个罪人，是个异教徒么？我的老妻灵魂快要归天，命在垂危，难道我还会在这家酒店停停，那家酒店歇歇么？我说，你这是什么话！该死的酒店！'于是白夫尔就命人把你抬到医院里去，我就跪倒在他的脚下……'白夫尔！老爷，我们异常感激你！饶恕我们这些傻子罢，饶恕我们这些该被诅咒的人罢，你不要跟我们乡下人为难呵！我们应该受踢，而你却非常仁慈，把脚放在雪地里，替我们受罪。'白夫尔看了看我，真像要打我似的，他要说：'你这傻子，你如果不喝酒，可怜你的老妻，也就用不着在我面前下跪了。你该打！''你说得不错——白夫尔，打就打罢！你是我们的恩人，我们的慈父，怎能叫我不对你下跪呢？老爷！我可以在你面前发誓……在上帝面前……我们如果欺骗了你，你可以吐我的口水：如果我的梅朱娜能够病愈，我一定要送你一样你所心爱的东西！要送你一个上等赤杨木制成的雪茄烟盒……几个木球，几个弹子球，我要尽我所能的镟出外国花样来……你要我做什么我就做什么！我不要你一个小钱。'医生一定要笑着说：'呵，很好，很好……我看！可惜你是一个酒鬼……'我的老妻呵，我很能对付绅士。随便什么人我都跟他谈得上来。上帝保佑我们不要迷路罢。吓，好厉害的风！眼睛里都是雪。”

　　镟工叽叽咕咕地说着，没有一个完。他机械的谈着，要想略舒胸中的郁闷。他有许多话到舌尖上，但是脑筋里的念头和问题却更多。镟工不知不觉的，自己也莫明其妙的，竟忧伤起来，现在他忧伤得不能自拔，精神不能复原。以前他所过的生活是平静的，仿佛是在醉酒的半意识状态中，不知道忧愁，也不知道快乐，现在他的心中忽然感到一种可怕的痛苦。马马虎虎的懒惰者现在竟忽然成为忙人了，焦急和匆忙重压着他，这个酒鬼甚至想与大自然抵抗起来。

镟工记得他的麻烦是从昨晚起头的。昨晚他回得家来，与平时一样，有一点醉，拿出老脾气来，对天盟誓，捏紧拳头，他的老妻看着他那种吵闹的神气，好像她从来没有看见过他似的。平常她那老花眼的表情好像是道者，温和得好像一只狗，受人打骂，吃残茶冷菜那样的可怜；这一次可不同了，她严肃不动地看着他，好像宗教画里面的圣人，又好像死人。因了她那眼睛里古怪而又凶恶的神情，麻烦就来了。镟工吓得呆了，问邻居借了一匹马，现在他载着老妻到医院去，希望靠着药粉和药水的力量，白夫尔能够带回他的老妻平时的表情。

镟工叽咕着说："梅朱娜，我说……如果白夫尔问你，我打过你没有，你就说，'没有！'从此以后，我再也不打你了。我可以发誓。我曾否因为蔑视你而打你呢？我总是无缘无故打你的，我很替你伤心。别人就不爱找麻烦了，我却把你载了出来……我已经尽我的力量了。呵，好大的雪！上帝，你的旨意成全了！上帝保佑我们不要迷路罢……梅朱娜，你的腰疼么？怎么你不说话呢？我问你的腰痛么？"

他奇怪起来，老妻脸上的雪并不溶化，更奇怪的是老妻脸上没有一点生气，灰白得像蜡纸一般，更加显得严肃起来。

镟工叽咕着说："你是一个傻子！我把良心话来对你说，在上帝面前发誓……你却不理我……你真是一个傻子！我索性不带你到白夫尔那里去治病了。"

镟工放松了缰绳，沉思起来。他很害怕，不敢回过头来看他的老妻，他又怕问起她的话来得不到她的回音。终于，要想祛除疑惑，他头也不回，背过手去，摸着了老妻冷冰冰的手。手落下来的声音好像木头一样。

"唉，她死了！这是怎么一回事呵！"

镟工哭了起来。他又是忧愁，又是烦恼。他想，这个世界上的一切，过去得多么快呵！他的烦恼刚刚起头，最后的灾害又已经来临了。他在她死以前，竟不能与她快快乐乐地同居，告诉她他是可怜她的。他还没有表明心迹，她就死了。他与她同居了四十年，这四十年像烟雾一般的过去。只有酗酒、吵闹和贫穷，简直没有人生的乐趣。仿佛老天爷故意跟他捣蛋似的，他刚要可怜他的老妻，偏偏她就死了。他没有她就不能生活，以前他是虐待过她的呀！

他记了起来："她时常走遍乡村，是我叫她出去求乞的。唉！这是什么待遇！她也应该再活十年，这个傻东西；现在她以为我是一个坏人，叫我跟谁说去呢？现在不用求教医生，只需埋葬了。回转去罢！"

皮屈夫用力鞭着马往回路走。路是愈走愈坏，现在他一点也看不见车辄了。雪车时常碰着小杉树，一个黑东西抓镟工的手，在他的眼前发光，田亩一白无际，雪花乱舞。

镟工想道："重新生活过罢。"

他记起四十年前，梅朱娜年纪很轻，貌美，愉快，本是好人家出身。他们把她嫁给他，因为他们觉得他手艺好，将来一定是有出息的。他的快乐生活就只靠结婚，偏偏结婚后便酗酒，整天昏昏沉沉睡在床上，一直到现在都还算不曾醒。他婚后的事，一点也不记得，只记得喝酒，醉倒，吵闹之类的事。四十年的工夫就像这样浪费了。

白雪渐渐地变成灰色，天快要黑了下来。

镟工忽然吃惊地自思道；"我到什么地方去呢？我应该想一想埋葬的事情，怎么还往医院的路上走呢？……我难道疯了么？"

皮屈夫又鞭着马回过来。小马筋疲力尽，气喘不已，只得慢慢地踱着。镟工时时鞭着它的背……忽然他后面发出撞击声，他虽是不曾回头，已经知道是他的老妻的头碰着车子。天色愈变愈黑，雪风愈变愈冷，刺入肌肤……

镟工想道："重新生活过罢！我要买一个新车床，生活要过得有秩序一点……拿钱给我的老妻……"

于是他放下了缰绳。他又去寻找缰绳，要想拾起来，却办不到——他的手已经不能动了……

他想："不要紧，马认得路，自己会跑的。我现在不妨打一个盹……在埋葬或是做镇魂祭以前，最好是先休息一下……"

镟工闭起眼睛微睡一会儿。他听见马停了蹄，睁开眼睛，只看见黑漆一团……

他想走下雪车，看看究竟到了什么地方，但他被惰性所克服，觉得与其动腿，还是冻死的好，于是他平平安安地睡熟了。

醒来但见一个大房间，油漆过的墙。灿烂的阳光射过了窗子。镟工看见人们围着他，他第一个愿望就是要表明自己是个善良的人。

他说："请你们告诉牧师，替我的老妻做镇魂祭罢……"

一个声音打断他的话："呵，很好，很好，你请躺下。"

镟工看见医生在他面前，偏偏手脚都不肯听他的指挥。

"老爷，我的脚呢？我的手呢？"

"你的手脚都已冻坏，已经没有用处了……喂，喂！……你哭什么呢？你总算活了一世，应该感谢上帝才对呀！我以为你已经有了六十岁——难道这还不够么？……"

"我很伤心……请你仁爱地饶恕我罢！我要是能够再活五六年就好了呵！……"

"为什么？"

"马不是我的，我一定要还给人家……我一定要葬我的老妻……这个世界上的一切怎么完得这样快呢？白夫尔，老爷！我要送你一个上等赤杨木制成的雪茄烟盒！我还要替你镟木球……"

医生摇了摇手，走出病室。镟工就这样死了。

（赵景深　译）

THE COLLECTED SHORT
STORIES OF CHEKHOV

ANTON PAVLOVICH
CHEKHOV

CONTENTS

THE MAN IN A CASE

AT the furthest end of the village of Mironositskoe some belated
sportsmen lodged for the night in the elder Prokofy's barn. There were
two of them, the veterinary surgeon Ivan Ivanovitch and the schoolmaster
Burkin. Ivan Ivanovitch had a rather strange double-barrelled surname—
Tchimsha-Himalaisky—which did not suit him at all, and he was called
simply Ivan Ivanovitch all over the province. He lived at a stud-farm near
the town, and had come out shooting now to get a breath of fresh air.
Burkin, the high-school teacher, stayed every summer at Count P——'s, and
had been thoroughly at home in this district for years.

They did not sleep. Ivan Ivanovitch, a tall, lean old fellow with long
moustaches, was sitting outside the door, smoking a pipe in the moonlight.
Burkin was lying within on the hay, and could not be seen in the darkness.

They were telling each other all sorts of stories. Among other things,
they spoke of the fact that the elder's wife, Mavra, a healthy and by no
means stupid woman, had never been beyond her native village, had never
seen a town nor a railway in her life, and had spent the last ten years sitting
behind the stove, and only at night going out into the street.

"What is there wonderful in that!" said Burkin. "There are plenty of
people in the world, solitary by temperament, who try to retreat into their
shell like a hermit crab or a snail. Perhaps it is an instance of atavism, a
return to the period when the ancestor of man was not yet a social animal
and lived alone in his den, or perhaps it is only one of the diversities of
human character—who knows? I am not a natural science man, and it is
not my business to settle such questions; I only mean to say that people
like Mavra are not uncommon. There is no need to look far; two months
ago a man called Byelikov, a colleague of mine, the Greek master, died in
our town. You have heard of him, no doubt. He was remarkable for always

1

wearing galoshes and a warm wadded coat, and carrying an umbrella even in the very finest weather. And his umbrella was in a case, and his watch was in a case made of grey chamois leather, and when he took out his penknife to sharpen his pencil, his penknife, too, was in a little case; and his face seemed to be in a case too, because he always hid it in his turned-up collar. He wore dark spectacles and flannel vests, stuffed up his ears with cotton-wool, and when he got into a cab always told the driver to put up the hood. In short, the man displayed a constant and insurmountable impulse to wrap himself in a covering, to make himself, so to speak, a case which would isolate him and protect him from external influences. Reality irritated him, frightened him, kept him in continual agitation, and, perhaps to justify his timidity, his aversion for the actual, he always praised the past and what had never existed; and even the classical languages which he taught were in reality for him galoshes and umbrellas in which he sheltered himself from real life.

"'Oh, how sonorous, how beautiful is the Greek language!' he would say, with a sugary expression; and as though to prove his words he would screw up his eyes and, raising his finger, would pronounce 'Anthropos!'

"And Byelikov tried to hide his thoughts also in a case. The only things that were clear to his mind were government circulars and newspaper articles in which something was forbidden. When some proclamation prohibited the boys from going out in the streets after nine o'clock in the evening, or some article declared carnal love unlawful, it was to his mind clear and definite; it was forbidden, and that was enough. For him there was always a doubtful element, something vague and not fully expressed, in any sanction or permission. When a dramatic club or a reading-room or a tea-shop was licensed in the town, he would shake his head and say softly: 'It is all right, of course; it is all very nice, but I hope it won't lead to anything!'

"Every sort of breach of order, deviation or departure from rule, depressed him, though one would have thought it was no business of his. If one of his colleagues was late for church or if rumours reached him of some prank of the high-school boys, or one of the mistresses was seen late in the evening in the company of an officer, he was much disturbed, and said he hoped that nothing would come of it. At the teachers' meetings he simply oppressed us with his caution, his circumspection, and his characteristic reflection on the ill-behaviour of the young people in both male and female high-schools, the uproar in the classes. Oh, he hoped it would not reach the ears of the authorities; oh, he hoped nothing would come of it; and he thought it would be a very good thing if Petrov were expelled from the second class and Yegorov from the fourth. And, do you know, by his sighs, his despondency, his black spectacles on his pale little face, a little face like a pole-cat's, you know, he crushed us all, and we gave way, reduced Petrov's and Yegorov's marks for conduct, kept them in, and in the end expelled them both. He had a strange habit of visiting our lodgings. He would come to a teacher's, would sit down, and remain silent, as though he were carefully inspecting something. He would sit like this in silence for an hour or two and then go away. This he called 'maintaining good relations with his colleagues'; and it was obvious that coming to see us and sitting there was tiresome to him, and that he came to see us simply because he considered it his duty as our colleague. We teachers were afraid of him. And even the headmaster was afraid of him. Would you believe it, our teachers were all intellectual, right-minded people, brought up on Turgenev and Shtchedrin, yet this little chap, who always went about with galoshes and an umbrella, had the whole high-school under his thumb for fifteen long years! High-school, indeed—he had the whole town under his thumb! Our ladies did not get up private theatricals on Saturdays for fear he should hear of it, and the clergy dared not eat meat or play cards in his presence. Under the influence of people like Byelikov we have got into the way of being afraid of everything in our town for the last ten or fifteen years. They are afraid to speak aloud, afraid to send letters, afraid to make acquaintances, afraid to read books, afraid to help the poor, to teach people to read and write..."

Ivan Ivanovitch cleared his throat, meaning to say something, but first lighted his pipe, gazed at the moon, and then said, with pauses: "Yes, intellectual, right minded people read Shtchedrin and Turgenev, Buckle, and all the rest of them, yet they knocked under and put up with it... that's just how it is."

"Byelikov lived in the same house as I did," Burkin went on, "on the same storey, his door facing mine; we often saw each other, and I knew how he lived when he was at home. And at home it was the same story: dressing-gown, nightcap, blinds, bolts, a perfect succession of prohibitions and restrictions of all sorts, and— 'Oh, I hope nothing will come of it!' Lenten fare was bad for him, yet he could not eat meat, as people might perhaps say Byelikov did not keep the fasts, and he ate freshwater fish with butter—not a Lenten dish, yet one could not say that it was meat. He did not keep a female servant for fear people might think evil of him, but had as cook an old man of sixty, called Afanasy, half-witted and given to tippling, who had once been an officer's servant and could cook after a fashion. This Afanasy was usually standing at the door with his arms folded; with a deep sigh, he would mutter always the same thing: 'there are plenty of them about nowadays!'

"Byelikov had a little bedroom like a box; his bed had curtains. When he went to bed he covered his head over; it was hot and stuffy; the wind battered on the closed doors; there was a droning noise in the stove and a sound of sighs from the kitchen—ominous sighs.... And he felt frightened under the bed-clothes. He was afraid that something might happen, that Afanasy might murder him, that thieves might break in, and so he had troubled dreams all night, and in the morning, when we went together to the high-school, he was depressed and pale, and it was evident that the high-school full of people excited dread and aversion in his whole being, and that to walk beside me was irksome to a man of his solitary temperament.

"'they make a great noise in our classes,' he used to say, as though trying to find an explanation for his depression. 'It's beyond anything.'

"And the Greek master, this man in a case—would you believe it? —almost got married. "

Ivan Ivanovitch glanced quickly into the barn, and said: "You are

4

joking!"

"Yes, strange as it seems, he almost got married. A new teacher of history and geography, Milhail Savvitch Kovalenko, a Little Russian, was appointed. He came, not alone, but with his sister Varinka. He was a tall, dark young man with huge hands, and one could see from his face that he had a bass voice, and, in fact, he had a voice that seemed to come out of a barrel—'boom, boom, boom!' And she was not so young, about thirty, but she, too, was tall, well-made, with black eyebrows and red cheeks—in fact, she was a regular sugar-plum, and so sprightly, so noisy; she was always singing Little Russian songs and laughing. For the least thing she would go off into a ringing laugh—'Ha-ha-ha!' We made our first thorough acquaintance with the Kovalenkos at the headmaster's name-day party. Among the glum and intensely bored teachers who came even to the name-day party as a duty we suddenly saw a new Aphrodite risen from the waves; she walked with her arms akimbo, laughed, sang, danced.... She sang with feeling 'the Winds do Blow,' then another song, and another, and she fascinated us all—all, even Byelikov. He sat down by her and said with a honeyed smile: 'The Little Russian reminds one of the ancient Greek in its softness and agreeable resonance.'

"That flattered her, and she began telling him with feeling and earnestness that they had a farm in the Gadyatchsky district, and that her mamma lived at the farm, and that they had such pears, such melons, such _kabaks_! The Little Russians call pumpkins _kabaks_ (i.e., pothouse), while their pothouse they call _shinki_, and they make a beetroot soup with tomatoes and aubergines in it, 'which was so nice—awfully nice!'

"We listened and listened, and suddenly the same idea dawned upon us all: 'It would be a good thing to make a match of it,' the headmaster's wife said to me softly.

"We all for some reason recalled the fact that our friend Byelikov was not married, and it now seemed to us strange that we had hitherto failed to observe, and had in fact completely lost sight of, a detail so important in his life. What was his attitude to woman? How had he settled this vital question for himself? This had not interested us in the least till then; perhaps we had not even admitted the idea that a man who went out in all weathers in galoshes and slept under curtains could be in love.

"'He is a good deal over forty and she is thirty,' the headmaster's wife went on, developing her idea. 'I believe she would marry him. '

"All sorts of things are done in the provinces through boredom, all sorts of unnecessary and nonsensical things! And that is because what is necessary is not done at all. What need was there for instance, for us to make a match for this Byelikov, whom one could not even imagine married? The headmaster's wife, the inspector's wife, and all our high-school ladies, grew livelier and even better-looking, as though they had suddenly found a new object in life. The headmaster's wife would take a box at the theatre, and we beheld sitting in her box Varinka, with such a fan, beaming and happy, and beside her Byelikov, a little bent figure, looking as though he had been extracted from his house by pincers. I would give an evening party, and the ladies would insist on my inviting Byelikov and Varinka. In short, the machine was set in motion. It appeared that Varinka was not averse to matrimony. She had not a very cheerful life with her brother; they could do nothing but quarrel and scold one another from morning till night. Here is a scene, for instance. Kovalenko would be coming along the street, a tall, sturdy young ruffian, in an embroidered shirt, his love-locks falling on his forehead under his cap, in one hand a bundle of books, in the other a thick knotted stick, followed by his sister, also with books in her hand.

"'But you haven't read it, Mihalik!' she would be arguing loudly. 'I tell you, I swear you have not read it at all!'

"'And I tell you I have read it,' cries Kovalenko, thumping his stick on the pavement.

"'Oh, my goodness, Mihalik! why are you so cross? We are arguing about principles.'

"'I tell you that I have read it!' Kovalenko would shout, more loudly than ever.

"And at home, if there was an outsider present, there was sure to be a skirmish. Such a life must have been wearisome, and of course she must have longed for a home of her own. Besides, there was her age to be considered; there was no time left to pick and choose; it was a case of marrying anybody, even a Greek master. And, indeed, most of our young ladies don't mind whom they marry so long as they do get married. However that may be, Varinka began to show an unmistakable partiality for Byelikov.

"And Byelikov? He used to visit Kovalenko just as he did us. He would arrive, sit down, and remain silent. He would sit quiet, and Varinka would sing to him 'the Winds do Blow,' or would look pensively at him with her dark eyes, or would suddenly go off into a peal—'Ha-ha-ha!'

"Suggestion plays a great part in love affairs, and still more in getting married. Everybody—both his colleagues and the ladies—began assuring Byelikov that he ought to get married, that there was nothing left for him in life but to get married; we all congratulated him, with solemn countenances delivered ourselves of various platitudes, such as 'Marriage is a serious step.' Besides, Varinka was good-looking and interesting; she was the daughter of a civil councillor, and had a farm; and what was more, she was the first woman who had been warm and friendly in her manner to him. His head was turned, and he decided that he really ought to get married."

"Well, at that point you ought to have taken away his galoshes and umbrella," said Ivan Ivanovitch.

"Only fancy! that turned out to be impossible. He put Varinka's portrait on his table, kept coming to see me and talking about Varinka, and home life, saying marriage was a serious step. He was frequently at Kovalenko's, but he did not alter his manner of life in the least; on the contrary, indeed, his determination to get married seemed to have a depressing effect on him. He grew thinner and paler, and seemed to retreat further and further into his case.

"'I like Varvara Savvishna,' he used to say to me, with a faint and wry smile, 'and I know that every one ought to get married, but... you know all this has happened so suddenly.... One must think a little.'

"'What is there to think over?' I used to say to him. 'Get married—that is all.'

"'No; marriage is a serious step. One must first weigh the duties before one, the responsibilities... that nothing may go wrong afterwards. It worries me so much that I don't sleep at night. And I must confess I am afraid: her brother and she have a strange way of thinking; they look at things strangely, you know, and her disposition is very impetuous. One may get married, and then, there is no knowing, one may find oneself in an unpleasant position.'

"And he did not make an offer; he kept putting it off, to the great vexation of the headmaster's wife and all our ladies; he went on weighing his future duties and responsibilities, and meanwhile he went for a walk with Varinka almost every day—possibly he thought that this was necessary in his position—and came to see me to talk about family life. And in all probability in the end he would have proposed to her, and would have made one of those unnecessary, stupid marriages such as are made by thousands among us from being bored and having nothing to do, if it had not been for a _kolossalische scandal_. I must mention that Varinka's brother, Kovalenko, detested Byelikov from the first day of their acquaintance, and could not endure him.

"'I don't understand,' he used to say to us, shrugging his shoulders—'I don't understand how you can put up with that sneak, that nasty phiz. Ugh! how can you live here! The atmosphere is stifling and unclean! Do you call yourselves schoolmasters, teachers? You are paltry government clerks. You keep, not a temple of science, but a department for red tape and loyal behaviour, and it smells as sour as a police-station. No, my friends; I will stay with you for a while, and then I will go to my farm and there catch crabs and teach the Little Russians. I shall go, and you can stay here with your Judas—damn his soul!'

"Or he would laugh till he cried, first in a loud bass, then in a shrill, thin laugh, and ask me, waving his hands: 'What does he sit here for? What does he want? He sits and stares.'

"He even gave Byelikov a nickname, 'the Spider.' And it will readily be understood that we avoided talking to him of his sister's being about to marry 'the Spider.' And on one occasion, when the headmaster's wife hinted to him what a good thing it would be to secure his sister's future with such a reliable, universally respected man as Byelikov, he frowned and muttered: 'It's not my business; let her marry a reptile if she likes. I don't like meddling in other people's affairs.'

"Now hear what happened next. Some mischievous person drew a caricature of Byelikov walking along in his galoshes with his trousers tucked up, under his umbrella, with Varinka on his arm; below, the inscription 'Anthropos in love.' The expression was caught to a marvel, you know. The artist must have worked for more than one night, for the teachers of both the boys' and girls' high-schools, the teachers of the seminary, the government officials, all received a copy. Byelikov received one, too. The caricature made a very painful impression on him.

"We went out together; it was the first of May, a Sunday, and all of us, the boys and the teachers, had agreed to meet at the high-school and then to go for a walk together to a wood beyond the town. We set off, and he was green in the face and gloomier than a storm-cloud.

"'What wicked, ill-natured people there are!' he said, and his lips quivered.

"I felt really sorry for him. We were walking along, and all of a sudden—would you believe it?—Kovalenko came bowling along on a bicycle, and after him, also on a bicycle, Varinka, flushed and exhausted, but good-humoured and gay.

"'We are going on ahead,' she called. 'What lovely weather! Awfully lovely!'

"And they both disappeared from our sight. Byelikov turned white instead of green, and seemed petrified. He stopped short and stared at me....

"'What is the meaning of it? Tell me, please!' he asked. 'Can my eyes have deceived me? Is it the proper thing for high-school masters and ladies to ride bicycles?'

"'What is there improper about it?' I said. 'Let them ride and enjoy themselves.'

"'But how can that be?' he cried, amazed at my calm. 'What are you saying?'

"And he was so shocked that he was unwilling to go on, and returned home.

"Next day he was continually twitching and nervously rubbing his hands, and it was evident from his face that he was unwell. And he left before his work was over, for the first time in his life. And he ate no dinner. Towards evening he wrapped himself up warmly, though it was quite warm weather, and sallied out to the Kovalenkos'. Varinka was out; he found her brother, however.

"'Pray sit down,' Kovalenko said coldly, with a frown. His face looked sleepy; he had just had a nap after dinner, and was in a very bad humour.

"Byelikov sat in silence for ten minutes, and then began: 'I have come to see you to relieve my mind. I am very, very much troubled. Some scurrilous fellow has drawn an absurd caricature of me and another person, in whom we are both deeply interested. I regard it as a duty to assure you that I have had no hand in it.... I have given no sort of ground for such ridicule—on the contrary, I have always behaved in every way like a gentleman.'

"Kovalenko sat sulky and silent. Byelikov waited a little, and went on slowly in a mournful voice: 'And I have something else to say to you. I have been in the service for years, while you have only lately entered it, and I consider it my duty as an older colleague to give you a warning. You ride on a bicycle, and that pastime is utterly unsuitable for an educator of youth.'

"'Why so?' asked Kovalenko in his bass.

"'Surely that needs no explanation, Mihail Savvitch—surely you can understand that? If the teacher rides a bicycle, what can you expect the pupils to do? You will have them walking on their heads next! And so long as there is no formal permission to do so, it is out of the question. I was horrified yesterday! When I saw your sister everything seemed dancing before my eyes. A lady or a young girl on a bicycle—it's awful!'

"'What is it you want exactly?'

"'All I want is to warn you, Mihail Savvitch. You are a young man, you have a future before you, you must be very, very careful in your behaviour, and you are so careless—oh, so careless! You go about in an embroidered shirt, are constantly seen in the street carrying books, and now the bicycle, too. The headmaster will learn that you and your sister ride the bicycle, and then it will reach the higher authorities.... Will that be a good thing?'

"'It's no business of anybody else if my sister and I do bicycle!' said Kovalenko, and he turned crimson. 'And damnation take any one who meddles in my private affairs!'

"Byelikov turned pale and got up.

"'If you speak to me in that tone I cannot continue,' he said. 'And I beg you never to express yourself like that about our superiors in my presence; you ought to be respectful to the authorities.'

"'Why, have I said any harm of the authorities?' asked Kovalenko, looking at him wrathfully. 'Please leave me alone. I am an honest man, and do not care to talk to a gentleman like you. I don't like sneaks!'

"Byelikov flew into a nervous flutter, and began hurriedly putting on his coat, with an expression of horror on his face. It was the first time in his life he had been spoken to so rudely.

"'You can say what you please,' he said, as he went out from the entry to the landing on the staircase. 'I ought only to warn you: possibly some on e may have overheard us, and that our conversation may not be misunderstood and harm come of it, I shall be compelled to inform our headmaster of our conversation... in its main features. I am bound to do so.'

"'Inform him? You can go and make your report!'

"Kovalenko seized him from behind by the collar and gave him a push, and Byelikov rolled downstairs, thudding with his galoshes. The staircase was high and steep, but he rolled to the bottom unhurt, got up, and touched his nose to see whether his spectacles were all right. But just as he was falling down the stairs Varinka came in, and with her two ladies; they stood below staring, and to Byelikov this was more terrible than anything. I believe he would rather have broken his neck or both legs than have been an object of ridicule. 'Why, now the whole town would hear of it; it would come to the headmaster's ears, would reach the higher authorities—oh, it might lead to something! There would be another caricature, and it would all end in his being asked to resign his post....

"When he got up, Varinka recognized him, and, looking at his ridiculous face, his crumpled overcoat, and his galoshes, not understanding what had happened and supposing that he had slipped down by accident, could not restrain herself, and laughed loud enough to be heard by all the flats: 'Ha-ha-ha!'

"And this pealing, ringing 'Ha-ha-ha!' was the last straw that put an end to everything: to the proposed match and to Byelikov's earthly existence. He did not hear what Varinka said to him; he saw nothing. On reaching home, the first thing he did was to remove her portrait from the table; then he went to bed, and he never got up again.

"Three days later Afanasy came to me and asked whether we should not send for the doctor, as there was something wrong with his master. I went in to Byelikov. He lay silent behind the curtain, covered with a quilt; if one asked him a question, he said 'Yes' or 'No' and not another sound. He lay there while Afanasy, gloomy and scowling, hovered about him, sighing heavily, and smelling like a pothouse.

"A month later Byelikov died. We all went to his funeral—that is, both the high-schools and the seminary. Now when he was lying in his coffin his expression was mild, agreeable, even cheerful, as though he were glad that he had at last been put into a case which he would never leave again. Yes, he had attained his ideal! And, as though in his honour, it was dull, rainy weather on the day of his funeral, and we all wore galoshes and took our umbrellas. Varinka, too, was at the funeral, and when the coffin was lowered into the grave she burst into tears. I have noticed that Little Russian women are always laughing or crying—no intermediate mood.

"One must confess that to bury people like Byelikov is a great pleasure. As we were returning from the cemetery we wore discreet Lenten faces; no one wanted to display this feeling of pleasure—a feeling like that we had experienced long, long ago as children when our elders had gone out and we ran about the garden for an hour or two, enjoying complete freedom. Ah, freedom, freedom! The merest hint, the faintest hope of its possibility gives wings to the soul, does it not?

"We returned from the cemetery in a good humour. But not more than a week had passed before life went on as in the past, as gloomy, oppressive, and senseless—a life not forbidden by government prohibition, but not fully permitted, either: it was no better. And, indeed, though we had buried Byelikov, how many such men in cases were left, how many more of them there will be!"

"That's just how it is," said Ivan Ivanovitch and he lighted his pipe.

"How many more of them there will be!" repeated Burkin.

The schoolmaster came out of the barn. He was a short, stout man, completely bald, with a black beard down to his waist. The two dogs came out with him.

"What a moon!" he said, looking upwards.

It was midnight. On the right could be seen the whole village, a long street stretching far away for four miles. All was buried in deep silent slumber; not a movement, not a sound; one could hardly believe that nature could be so still. When on a moonlight night you see a broad village street, with its cottages, haystacks, and slumbering willows, a feeling of calm comes over the soul; in this peace, wrapped away from care, toil, and sorrow in the darkness of night, it is mild, melancholy, beautiful, and it seems as though the stars look down upon it kindly and with tenderness, and as though there were no evil on earth and all were well. On the left the open country began from the end of the village; it could be seen stretching far away to the horizon, and there was no movement, no sound in that whole expanse bathed in moonlight.

"Yes, that is just how it is," repeated Ivan Ivanovitch; "and isn't our living in town, airless and crowded, our writing useless papers, our playing _vint_—isn't that all a sort of case for us? And our spending our whole lives among trivial, fussy men and silly, idle women, our talking and our listening to all sorts of nonsense—isn't that a case for us, too? If you like, I will tell you a very edifying story."

"No; it's time we were asleep," said Burkin. "Tell it tomorrow."

They went into the barn and lay down on the hay. And they were both covered up and beginning to doze when they suddenly heard light footsteps—patter, patter.... Some one was walking not far from the barn, walking a little and stopping, and a minute later, patter, patter again.... The dogs began growling.

"That's Mavra," said Burkin.

The footsteps died away.

"You see and hear that they lie," said Ivan Ivanovitch, turning over on the other side, "and they call you a fool for putting up with their lying. You endure insult and humiliation, and dare not openly say that you are on the side of the honest and the free, and you lie and smile yourself; and all that for the sake of a crust of bread, for the sake of a warm corner, for the sake of a wretched little worthless rank in the service. No, one can't go on living like this."

"Well, you are off on another tack now, Ivan Ivanovitch," said the schoolmaster. "Let us go to sleep!"

And ten minutes later Burkin was asleep. But Ivan Ivanovitch kept sighing and turning over from side to side; then he got up, went outside again, and, sitting in the doorway, lighted his pipe.

LIGHTS

THE dog was barking excitedly outside. And Ananyev the engineer, his assistant called Von Schtenberg, and I went out of the hut to see at whom it was barking. I was the visitor, and might have remained indoors, but I must confess my head was a little dizzy from the wine I had drunk, and I was glad to get a breath of fresh air.

"There is nobody here," said Ananyev when we went out. "Why are you telling stories, Azorka? You fool!" There was not a soul in sight. "The fool," Azorka, a black house-dog, probably conscious of his guilt in barking for nothing and anxious to propitiate us, approached us, diffidently wagging his tail. The engineer bent down and touched him between his ears.

"Why are you barking for nothing, creature?" he said in the tone in which good-natured people talk to children and dogs. "Have you had a bad dream or what? Here, doctor, let me commend to your attention," he said, turning to me, "a wonderfully nervous subject! Would you believe it, he can't endure solitude—he is always having terrible dreams and suffering from nightmares; and when you shout at him he has something like an attack of hysterics."

"Yes, a dog of refined feelings," the student chimed in.

Azorka must have understood that the conversation was concerning him. He turned his head upwards and grinned plaintively, as though to say, "Yes, at times I suffer unbearably, but please excuse it!"

It was an August night, there were stars, but it was dark. Owing to the fact that I had never in my life been in such exceptional surroundings, as I had chanced to come into now, the starry night seemed to me gloomy, inhospitable, and darker than it was in reality. I was on a railway line which was still in process of construction. The high, half-finished embankment, the mounds of sand, clay, and rubble, the holes, the wheel-barrows standing

15

here and there, the flat tops of the mud huts in which the workmen lived —all this muddle, coloured to one tint by the darkness, gave the earth a strange, wild aspect that suggested the times of chaos. There was so little order in all that lay before me that it was somehow strange in the midst of the hideously excavated, grotesque-looking earth to see the silhouettes of human beings and the slender telegraph posts. Both spoiled the ensemble of the picture, and seemed to belong to a different world. It was still, and the only sound came from the telegraph wire droning its wearisome refrain somewhere very high above our heads.

We climbed up on the embankment and from its height looked down upon the earth. A hundred yards away where the pits, holes, and mounds melted into the darkness of the night, a dim light was twinkling. Beyond it gleamed another light, beyond that a third, then a hundred paces away two red eyes glowed side by side—probably the windows of some hut—and a long series of such lights, growing continually closer and dimmer, stretched along the line to the very horizon, then turned in a semicircle to the left and disappeared in the darkness of the distance. The lights were motionless. There seemed to be something in common between them and the stillness of the night and the disconsolate song of the telegraph wire. It seemed as though some weighty secret were buried under the embankment and only the lights, the night, and the wires knew of it.

"How glorious, O Lord!" sighed Ananyev; "such space and beauty that one can't tear oneself away! And what an embankment! It's not an embankment, my dear fellow, but a regular Mont Blanc. It's costing millions...."

Going into ecstasies over the lights and the embankment that was costing millions, intoxicated by the wine and his sentimental mood, the engineer slapped Von Schtenberg on the shoulder and went on in a jocose tone: "Well, Mihail Mihailitch, lost in reveries? No doubt it is pleasant to look at the work of one's own hands, eh? Last year this very spot was bare steppe, not a sight of human life, and now look: life... civilisation... And how splendid it all is, upon my soul! You and I are building a railway, and after we are gone, in another century or two, good men will build a factory, a school, a hospital, and things will begin to move! Eh! "

The student stood motionless with his hands thrust in his pockets, and did not take his eyes off the lights. He was not listening to the engineer, but was thinking, and was apparently in the mood in which one does not want to speak or to listen. After a prolonged silence he turned to me and said quietly: "Do you know what those endless lights are like? They make me think of something long dead, that lived thousands of years ago, something like the camps of the Amalekites or the Philistines. It is as though some people of the Old Testament had pitched their camp and were waiting for morning to fight with Saul or David. All that is wanting to complete the illusion is the blare of trumpets and sentries calling to one another in some Ethiopian language. "

And, as though of design, the wind fluttered over the line and brought a sound like the clank of weapons. A silence followed. I don't know what the engineer and the student were thinking of, but it seemed to me already that I actually saw before me something long dead and even heard the sentry talking in an unknown tongue. My imagination hastened to picture the tents, the strange people, their clothes, their armour.

"Yes," muttered the student pensively, "once Philistines and Amalekites were living in this world, making wars, playing their part, and now no trace of them remains. So it will be with us. Now we are making a railway, are standing here philosophizing, but two thousand years will pass—and of this embankment and of all those men, asleep after their hard work, not one grain of dust will remain. In reality, it's awful!"

"You must drop those thoughts..." said the engineer gravely and admonishingly.

"Why?"

"Because.... Thoughts like that are for the end of life, not for the beginning of it. You are too young for them."

"Why so?" repeated the student.

"All these thoughts of the transitoriness, the insignificance and the aimlessness of life, of the inevitability of death, of the shadows of the grave, and so on, all such lofty thoughts, I tell you, my dear fellow, are good and natural in old age when they come as the product of years of inner travail, and are won by suffering and really are intellectual riches; for a youthful brain on the threshold of real life they are simply a calamity! A calamity!" Ananyev repeated with a wave of his hand. "To my mind it is better at your age to have no head on your shoulders at all than to think on these lines. I am speaking seriously, Baron. And I have been meaning to speak to you about it for a long time, for I noticed from the very first day of our acquaintance your partiality for these damnable ideas!"

"Good gracious, why are they damnable?" the student asked with a smile, and from his voice and his face I could see that he asked the question from simple politeness, and that the discussion raised by the engineer did not interest him in the least.

I could hardly keep my eyes open. I was dreaming that immediately after our walk we should wish each other good-night and go to bed, but my dream was not quickly realised. When we had returned to the hut the engineer put away the empty bottles and took out of a large wicker hamper two full ones, and uncorking them, sat down to his work-table with the evident intention of going on drinking, talking, and working. Sipping a little from his glass, he made pencil notes on some plans and went on pointing out to the student that the latter's way of thinking was not what it should be. The student sat beside him checking accounts and saying nothing. He, like me, had no inclination to speak or to listen. That I might not interfere with their work, I sat away from the table on the engineer's crooked-legged travelling bedstead, feeling bored and expecting every moment that they would suggest I should go to bed. It was going on for one o'clock.

Having nothing to do, I watched my new acquaintances. I had never seen Ananyev or the student before. I had only made their acquaintance on the night I have described. Late in the evening I was returning on horseback from a fair to the house of a landowner with whom I was staying, had got on the wrong road in the dark and lost my way. Going round and round by the railway line and seeing how dark the night was becoming, I thought of the "barefoot railway roughs," who lie in wait for travellers on foot and on horseback, was frightened, and knocked at the first hut I came to. There I was cordially received by Ananyev and the student. As is usually the case with strangers casually brought together, we quickly became acquainted, grew friendly and at first over the tea and afterward over the wine, began to feel as though we had known each other for years. At the end of an hour or so, I knew who they were and how fate had brought them from town to the far-away steppe; and they knew who I was, what my occupation and my way of thinking.

Nikolay Anastasyevitch Ananyev, the engineer, was a broad-shouldered, thick-set man, and, judging from his appearance, he had, like Othello, begun the "descent into the vale of years," and was growing rather too stout. He was just at that stage which old match-making women mean when they speak of "a man in the prime of his age," that is, he was neither young nor old, was fond of good fare, good liquor, and praising the past, panted a little as he walked, snored loudly when he was asleep, and in his manner with those surrounding him displayed that calm imperturbable good humour which is always acquired by decent people by the time they have reached the grade of a staff officer and begun to grow stout. His hair and beard were far from being grey, but already, with a condescension of which he was unconscious, he addressed young men as "my dear boy" and felt himself entitled to lecture them good-humouredly about their way of thinking. His movements and his voice were calm, smooth, and self-confident, as they are in a man who is thoroughly well aware that he has got his feet firmly planted on the right road, that he has definite work, a secure living, a settled outlook.... His sunburnt, thicknosed face and muscular neck seemed to say: "I am well fed, healthy, satisfied with myself, and the time will come when you young people too, will be wellfed, healthy, and satisfied with yourselves...." He was dressed in a cotton shirt with the collar awry and in full linen trousers thrust into his high boots. From certain trifles, as for instance, from his coloured worsted girdle, his embroidered collar, and the patch on his elbow, I was able to guess that he was married and in all probability tenderly loved by his wife.

Baron Von Schtenberg, a student of the Institute of Transport, was a young man of about three or four and twenty. Only his fair hair and scanty beard, and, perhaps, a certain coarseness and frigidity in his features showed traces of his descent from Barons of the Baltic provinces; everything else—his name, Mihail Mihailovitch, his religion, his ideas, his manners, and the expression of his face were purely Russian. Wearing, like Ananyev, a cotton shirt and high boots, with his round shoulders, his hair left uncut, and his sunburnt face, he did not look like a student or a Baron, but like an ordinary Russian workman. His words and gestures were few, he drank reluctantly without relish, checked the accounts mechanically, and seemed all the while to be thinking of something else. His movements and voice were calm, and smooth too, but his calmness was of a different kind from the engineer's. His sunburnt, slightly ironical, dreamy face, his eyes which looked up from under his brows, and his whole figure were expressive of spiritual stagnation—mental sloth. He looked as though it did not matter to him in the least whether the light were burning before him or not, whether the wine were nice or nasty, and whether the accounts he was checking were correct or not.... And on his intelligent, calm face I read: "I don't see so far any good in definite work, a secure living, and a settled outlook. It's all nonsense. I was in Petersburg, now I am sitting here in this hut, in the autumn I shall go back to Petersburg, then in the spring here again.... What sense there is in all that I don't know, and no one knows.... And so it's no use talking about it...."

He listened to the engineer without interest, with the condescending indifference with which cadets in the senior classes listen to an effusive and good-natured old attendant. It seemed as though there were nothing new to him in what the engineer said, and that if he had not himself been too lazy to talk, he would have said something newer and cleverer. Meanwhile Ananyev would not desist. He had by now laid aside his good-humoured, jocose tone and spoke seriously, even with a fervour which was quite out of keeping with his expression of calmness. Apparently he had no distaste for abstract subjects, was fond of them, indeed, but had neither skill nor practice in the handling of them. And this lack of practice was so pronounced in his talk that I did not always grasp his meaning at once.

"I hate those ideas with all my heart!" he said, "I was infected by them myself in my youth, I have not quite got rid of them even now, and I tell you—perhaps because I am stupid and such thoughts were not the right food for my mind—they did me nothing but harm. That's easy to understand! Thoughts of the aimlessness of life, of the insignificance and transitoriness of the visible world, Solomon's 'vanity of vanities' have been, and are to this day, the highest and final stage in the realm of thought. The thinker reaches that stage and—comes to a halt! There is nowhere further to go. The activity of the normal brain is completed with this, and that is natural and in the order of things. Our misfortune is that we begin thinking at that end. What normal people end with we begin with. From the first start, as soon as the brain begins working independently, we mount to the very topmost, final step and refuse to know anything about the steps below."

"What harm is there in that?" said the student.

"But you must understand that it's abnormal," shouted Ananyev, looking at him almost wrathfully. "If we find means of mounting to the topmost step without the help of the lower ones, then the whole long ladder, that is the whole of life, with its colours, sounds, and thoughts, loses all meaning for us. That at your age such reflections are harmful and absurd, you can see from every step of your rational independent life. Let us suppose you sit down this minute to read Darwin or Shakespeare, you have scarcely read a page before the poison shows itself; and your long life, and Shakespeare, and Darwin, seem to you nonsense, absurdity, because you know you will die, that Shakespeare and Darwin have died too, that their thoughts have not saved them, nor the earth, nor you, and that if life is deprived of meaning in that way, all science, poetry, and exalted thoughts seem only useless diversions, the idle playthings of grown up people; and you leave off reading at the second page. Now, let us suppose that people come to you as an intelligent man and ask your opinion about war, for instance: whether it is desirable, whether it is morally justifiable or not. In answer to that terrible question you merely shrug your shoulders and confine yourself to some commonplace, because for you, with your way of thinking, it makes absolutely no difference whether hundreds of thousands of people die a violent death, or a natural one: the results are the same—ashes and oblivion. You and I are building a railway line. What's the use, one may ask, of our worrying our heads, inventing, rising above the hackneyed thing, feeling for the workmen, stealing or not stealing, when we know that this railway line will turn to dust within two thousand years, and so on, and so on.... You must admit that with such a disastrous way of looking at things there can be no progress, no science, no art, nor even thought itself. We fancy that we are cleverer than the crowd, and than Shakespeare. In reality our thinking leads to nothing because we have no inclination to go down to the lower steps and there is nowhere higher to go, so our brain stands at the freezing point—neither up nor down; I was in bondage to these ideas for six years, and by all that is holy, I never read a sensible book all that time, did not gain a ha'porth of wisdom, and did not raise my moral standard an inch. Was not that disastrous? Moreover, besides being corrupted ourselves, we bring poison into the lives of those surrounding us. It would be all right if, with our pessimism, we renounced life, went to live in a cave, or made haste to die, but, as it is, in obedience to the universal law, we live, feel, love women, bring up children, construct railways!"

"Our thoughts make no one hot or cold," the student said reluctantly. "Ah! there you are again! —do stop it! You have not yet had a good sniff at life. But when you have lived as long as I have you will know a thing or two! Our theory of life is not so innocent as you suppose. In practical life, in contact with human beings, it leads to nothing but horrors and follies. It has been my lot to pass through experiences which I would not wish a wicked Tatar to endure."

"For instance?" I asked.

"For instance?" repeated the engineer. He thought a minute, smiled and said: "For instance, take this example. More correctly, it is not an example, but a regular drama, with a plot and a dénouement. An excellent lesson! Ah, what a lesson!"

He poured out wine for himself and us, emptied his glass, stroked his broad chest with his open hands, and went on, addressing himself more to me than to the student: "It was in the year 187—, soon after the war, and when I had just left the University. I was going to the Caucasus, and on the way stopped for five days in the seaside town of N. I must tell you that I was born and grew up in that town, and so there is nothing odd in my thinking N. extraordinarily snug, cosy, and beautiful, though for a man from Petersburg or Moscow, life in it would be as dreary and comfortless as in any Tchuhloma or Kashira. With melancholy I passed by the high school where I had been a pupil; with melancholy I walked about the very familiar park, I made a melancholy attempt to get a nearer look at people I had not seen for a long time—all with the same melancholy.

"Among other things, I drove out one evening to the so-called Quarantine. It was a small mangy copse in which, at some forgotten time of plague, there really had been a quarantine station, and which was now the resort of summer visitors. It was a drive of three miles from the town along a good soft road. As one drove along one saw on the left the blue sea, on the right the unending gloomy steppe; there was plenty of air to breathe, and wide views for the eyes to rest on. The copse itself lay on the seashore. Dismissing my cabman, I went in at the familiar gates and first turned along an avenue leading to a little stone summer-house which I had been fond of in my childhood. In my opinion that round, heavy summer-house on its clumsy columns, which combined the romantic charm of an old tomb with the ungainliness of a Sobakevitch, was the most poetical nook in the whole town. It stood at the edge above the cliff, and from it there was a splendid view of the sea.

"I sat down on the seat, and, bending over the parapet, looked down.

A path ran from the summer-house along the steep, almost overhanging cliff, between the lumps of clay and tussocks of burdock. Where it ended, far below on the sandy shore, low waves were languidly foaming and softly purring. The sea was as majestic, as infinite, and as forbidding as seven years before when I left the high school and went from my native town to the capital; in the distance there was a dark streak of smoke—a steamer was passing—and except for this hardly visible and motionless streak and the sea-swallows that flitted over the water, there was nothing to give life to the monotonous view of sea and sky. To right and left of the summer-house stretched uneven clay cliffs.

"You know that when a man in a melancholy mood is left tête-à-tête with the sea, or any landscape which seems to him grandiose, there is always, for some reason, mixed with melancholy, a conviction that he will live and die in obscurity, and he reflectively snatches up a pencil and hastens to write his name on the first thing that comes handy. And that, I suppose, is why all convenient solitary nooks like my summer-house are always scrawled over in pencil or carved with penknives. I remember as though it were today; looking at the parapet I read: 'Ivan Korolkov, May 16, 1876.' Beside Korolkov some local dreamer had scribbled freely, adding: 'He stood on the desolate ocean's strand, while his soul was filled with imaginings grand.'

And his handwriting was dreamy, limp like wet silk. An individual called Kross, probably an insignificant, little man, felt his unimportance so deeply that he gave full licence to his penknife and carved his name in deep letters an inch high. I took a pencil out of my pocket mechanically, and I too scribbled on one of the columns. All that is irrelevant, however... You must forgive me—I don't know how to tell a story briefly.

"I was sad and a little bored. Boredom, the stillness, and the purring of the sea gradually brought me to the line of thought we have been discussing. At that period, towards the end of the seventies, it had begun to be fashionable with the public, and later, at the beginning of the eighties, it gradually passed from the general public into literature, science, and politics. I was no more than twenty-six at the time, but I knew perfectly well that life was aimless and had no meaning, that everything was a deception and an illusion, that in its essential nature and results a life of penal servitude in Sahalin was not in any way different from a life spent in Nice, that the difference between the brain of a Kant and the brain of a fly was of no real significance, that no one in this world is righteous or guilty, that everything was stuff and nonsense and damn it all! I lived as though I were doing a favour to some unseen power which compelled me to live, and to which I seemed to say: 'Look, I don't care a straw for life, but I am living!' I thought on one definite line, but in all sorts of keys, and in that respect I was like the subtle gourmand who could prepare a hundred appetising dishes from nothing but potatoes. There is no doubt that I was one-sided and even to some extent narrow, but I fancied at the time that my intellectual horizon had neither beginning nor end, and that my thought was as boundless as the sea. Well, as far as I can judge by myself, the philosophy of which we are speaking has something alluring, narcotic in its nature, like tobacco or morphia. It becomes a habit, a craving. You take advantage of every minute of solitude to gloat over thoughts of the aimlessness of life and the darkness of the grave. While I was sitting in the summer-house, Greek children with long noses were decorously walking about the avenues. I took advantage of the occasion and, looking at them, began reflecting in this style: 'Why are these children born, and what are they living for? Is there any sort of meaning in their existence? They grow up, without themselves knowing what for; they will live in this God-forsaken, comfortless hole for no sort of reason, and then they will die....'

"And I actually felt vexed with those children because they were walking about decorously and talking with dignity, as though they did not hold their little colourless lives so cheap and knew what they were living for.... I remember that far away at the end of an avenue three feminine figures came into sight. Three young ladies, one in a pink dress, two in white, were walking arm-in-arm, talking and laughing. Looking after them, I thought: 'It wouldn't be bad to have an affair with some woman for a couple of days in this dull place.'

"I recalled by the way that it was three weeks since I had visited my Petersburg lady, and thought that a passing love affair would come in very appropriately for me just now. The young lady in white in the middle was rather younger and better looking than her companions, and judging by her manners and her laugh, she was a high-school girl in an upper form. I looked, not without impure thoughts, at her bust, and at the same time reflected about her: 'she will be trained in music and manners, she will be married to some Greek—God help us!—will lead a grey, stupid, comfortless life, will bring into the world a crowd of children without knowing why, and then will die. An absurd life!'

"I must say that as a rule I was a great hand at combining my lofty ideas with the lowest prose. Thoughts of the darkness of the grave did not prevent me from giving busts and legs their full due. Our dear Baron's exalted ideas do not prevent him from going on Saturdays to Vukolovka on amatory expeditions. To tell the honest truth, as far as I remember, my attitude to women was most insulting. Now, when I think of that high-school girl, I blush for my thoughts then, but at the time my conscience was perfectly untroubled. I, the son of honourable parents, a Christian, who had received a superior education, not naturally wicked or stupid, felt not the slightest uneasiness when I paid women Blutgeld, as the Germans call it, or when I followed highschool girls with insulting looks.... The trouble is that youth makes its demands, and our philosophy has nothing in principle against those demands, whether they are good or whether they are loathsome. One who knows that life is aimless and death inevitable is not interested in the struggle against nature or the conception of sin: whether you struggle or whether you don't, you will die and rot just the same.... Secondly, my friends, our philosophy instils even into very young people what is called reasonableness. The predominance of reason over the heart is simply overwhelming amongst us. Direct feeling, inspiration—everything is choked by petty analysis. Where there is reasonableness there is coldness, and cold people—it's no use to disguise it—know nothing of chastity. That virtue is only known to those who are warm, affectionate, and capable of love. Thirdly, our philosophy denies the significance of each individual personality. It's easy to see that if I deny the personality of some Natalya Stepanovna, it's absolutely nothing to me whether she is insulted or not. To-day one insults her dignity as a human being and pays her Blutgeld, and next day thinks no more of her.

"So I sat in the summer-house and watched the young ladies. Another woman's figure appeared in the avenue, with fair hair, her head uncovered and a white knitted shawl on her shoulders. She walked along the avenue, then came into the summer-house, and taking hold of the parapet, looked indifferently below and into the distance over the sea. As she came in she paid no attention to me, as though she did not notice me. I scrutinized her from foot to head (not from head to foot, as one scrutinizes men) and found that she was young, not more than five-and-twenty, nice-looking, with a good figure, in all probability married and belonging to the class of respectable women. She was dressed as though she were at home, but fashionably and with taste, as ladies are, as a rule, in N.

" 'This one would do nicely,' I thought, looking at her handsome figure and her arms; 'she is all right.... She is probably the wife of some doctor or schoolmaster....'

"But to make up to her—that is, to make her the heroine of one of those impromptu affairs to which tourists are so prone—was not easy and, indeed, hardly possible. I felt that as I gazed at her face. The way she looked, and the expression of her face, suggested that the sea, the smoke in the distance, and the sky had bored her long, long ago, and wearied her sight. She seemed to be tired, bored, and thinking about something dreary, and her face had not even that fussy, affectedly indifferent expression which one sees in the face of almost every woman when she is conscious of the presence of an unknown man in her vicinity.

"The fair-haired lady took a bored and passing glance at me, sat down on a seat and sank into reverie, and from her face I saw that she had no thoughts for me, and that I, with my Petersburg appearance, did not arouse in her even simple curiosity. But yet I made up my mind to speak to her, and asked: 'Madam, allow me to ask you at what time do the waggonettes go from here to the town?'

" 'At ten or eleven, I believe....' "

"I thanked her. She glanced at me once or twice, and suddenly there was a gleam of curiosity, then of something like wonder on her passionless face.... I made haste to assume an indifferent expression and to fall into a suitable attitude; she was catching on! She suddenly jumped up from the seat, as though something had bitten her, and examining me hurriedly, with a gentle smile, asked timidly: 'Oh, aren't you Ananyev?'

" 'Yes, I am Ananyev,' I answered.

" 'And don't you recognise me? No?'

"I was a little confused. I looked intently at her, and—would you believe it?—I recognized her not from her face nor her figure, but from her gentle, weary smile. It was Natalya Stepanovna, or, as she was called, Kisotchka, the very girl I had been head over ears in love with seven or eight years before, when I was wearing the uniform of a high-school boy. The doings of far, vanished days, the days of long ago.... I remember this Kisotchka, a thin little high-school girl of fifteen or sixteen, when she was something just for a schoolboy's taste, created by nature especially for Platonic love. What a charming little girl she was! Pale, fragile, light—she looked as though a breath would send her flying like a feather to the skies—a gentle, perplexed face, little hands, soft long hair to her belt, a waist as thin as a wasp's—altogether something ethereal, transparent like moonlight—in fact, from the point of view of a high-school boy a peerless beauty.... Wasn't I in love with her! I did not sleep at night. I wrote verses.... Sometimes in the evenings she would sit on a seat in the park while we schoolboys crowded round her, gazing reverently; in response to our compliments, our sighing, and attitudinizing, she would shrink nervously from the evening damp, screw up her eyes, and smile gently, and at such times she was awfully like a pretty little kitten. As we gazed at her every one of us had a desire to caress her and stroke her like a cat, hence her nickname of Kisotchka.

"In the course of the seven or eight years since we had met, Kisotchka had greatly changed. She had grown more robust and stouter, and had quite lost the resemblance to a soft, fluffy kitten. It was not that her features looked old or faded, but they had somehow lost their brilliance and looked sterner, her hair seemed shorter, she looked taller, and her shoulders were quite twice as broad, and what was most striking, there was already in her face the expression of motherliness and resignation commonly seen in respectable women of her age, and this, of course, I had never seen in her before.... In short, of the school-girlish and the Platonic her face had kept the gentle smile and nothing more....

"We got into conversation. Learning that I was already an engineer, Kisotchka was immensely delighted.

" 'How good that is!' she said, looking joyfully into my face. 'Ah, how good! And how splendid you all are! Of all who left with you, not one has been a failure—they have all turned out well. One an engineer, another a doctor, a third a teacher, another, they say, is a celebrated singer in Petersburg.... You are all splendid, all of you.... Ah, how good that is!'

"Kisotchka's eyes shone with genuine goodwill and gladness. She was admiring me like an elder sister or a former governess. While I looked at her sweet face and thought, 'It wouldn't be bad to get hold of her to-day!'

" 'Do you remember, Natalya Stepanovna,' I asked her, 'how I once brought you in the park a bouquet with a note in it? You read my note, and such a look of bewilderment came into your face....'

" 'No, I don't remember that,' she said, laughing. 'But I remember how you wanted to challenge Florens to a duel over me....'

" 'Well, would you believe it, I don't remember that....'

" 'Well, that's all over and done with...' sighed Kisotchka. 'At one time I was your idol, and now it is my turn to look up to all of you....'

"From further conversation I learned that two years after leaving the high school, Kisotchka had been married to a resident in the town who was half Greek, half Russian, had a post either in the bank or in the insurance society, and also carried on a trade in corn. He had a strange surname, something in the style of Populaki or Skarandopulo.... Goodness only knows—I have forgotten.... As a matter of fact, Kisotchka spoke little and with reluctance about herself. The conversation was only about me. She asked me about the College of Engineering, about my comrades, about Petersburg, about my plans, and everything I said moved her to eager delight and exclamations of, 'Oh, how good that is!'

"We went down to the sea and walked over the sands; then when the night air began to blow chill and damp from the sea we climbed up again. All the while our talk was of me and of the past. We walked about until the reflection of the sunset had died away from the windows of the summer villas.

" 'Come in and have some tea,' Kisotchka suggested. 'the samovar must have been on the table long ago.... I am alone at home,' she said, as her villa came into sight through the green of the acacias. 'My husband is always in the town and only comes home at night, and not always then, and I must own that I am so dull that it's simply deadly.'

"I followed her in, admiring her back and shoulders. I was glad that she was married. Married women are better material for temporary love affairs than girls. I was also pleased that her husband was not at home. At the same time I felt that the affair would not come off....

"We went into the house. The rooms were smallish and had low ceilings, and the furniture was typical of the summer villa (Russians like having at their summer villas uncomfortable heavy, dingy furniture which they are sorry to throw away and have nowhere to put), but from certain details I could observe that Kisotchka and her husband were not badly off, and must be spending five or six thousand roubles a year. I remember that in the middle of the room which Kisotchka called the dining-room there was a round table, supported for some reason on six legs, and on it a samovar and cups. At the edge of the table lay an open book, a pencil, and an exercise book. I glanced at the book and recognized it as 'Malinin and Burenin's Arithmetical Examples.' It was open, as I now remember, at the

'Rules of Compound Interest.'

" 'To whom are you giving lessons?' I asked Kisotchka.

" 'Nobody,' she answered. 'I am just doing some.... I have nothing to do, and am so bored that I think of the old days and do sums.'

" 'Have you any children?'

" 'I had a baby boy, but he only lived a week.'

"We began drinking tea. Admiring me, Kisotchka said again how good it was that I was an engineer, and how glad she was of my success. And the more she talked and the more genuinely she smiled, the stronger was my conviction that I should go away without having gained my object. I was a connoisseur in love affairs in those days, and could accurately gauge my chances of success. You can boldly reckon on success if you are tracking down a fool or a woman as much on the look out for new experiences and sensations as yourself, or an adventuress to whom you are a stranger. If you come across a sensible and serious woman, whose face has an expression of weary submission and goodwill, who is genuinely delighted at your presence, and, above all, respects you, you may as well turn back. To succeed in that case needs longer than one day.

"And by evening light Kisotchka seemed even more charming than by day. She attracted me more and more, and apparently she liked me too, and the surroundings were most appropriate: the husband not at home, no servants visible, stillness around.... Though I had little confidence in success, I made up my mind to begin the attack anyway. First of all it was necessary to get into a familiar tone and to change Kisotchka's lyrically earnest mood into a more frivolous one.

" 'Let us change the conversation, Natalya Stepanovna,' I began. 'Let us talk of something amusing. First of all, allow me, for the sake of old times, to call you Kisotchka.'

"She allowed me.

" 'Tell me, please, Kisotchka,' I went on, 'what is the matter with all the fair sex here. What has happened to them? In old days they were all so moral and virtuous, and now, upon my word, if one asks about anyone, one is told such things that one is quite shocked at human nature.... One young lady has eloped with an officer; another has run away and carried off a high-school boy with her; another—a married woman—has run away from her husband with an actor; a fourth has left her husband and gone off with an officer, and so on and so on. It's a regular epidemic! If it goes on like this there won't be a girl or a young woman left in your town!'

"I spoke in a vulgar, playful tone. If Kisotchka had laughed in response I should have gone on in this style: 'You had better look out, Kisotchka, or some officer or actor will be carrying you off!' She would have dropped her eyes and said: 'As though anyone would care to carry me off; there are plenty younger and better looking....' And I should have said: 'Nonsense, Kisotchka—I for one should be delighted!' And so on in that style, and it would all have gone swimmingly. But Kisotchka did not laugh in response; on the contrary, she looked grave and sighed.

" 'All you have been told is true,' she said. 'My cousin Sonya ran away from her husband with an actor. Of course, it is wrong.... Everyone ought to bear the lot that fate has laid on him, but I do not condemn them or blame them.... Circumstances are sometimes too strong for anyone!'

" 'that is so, Kisotchka, but what circumstances can produce a regular epidemic?'

" 'It's very simple and easy to understand,' replied Kisotchka, raising her eyebrows. 'there is absolutely nothing for us educated girls and women to do with ourselves. Not everyone is able to go to the University, to become a teacher, to live for ideas, in fact, as men do. They have to be married.... And whom would you have them marry? You boys leave the high-school and go away to the University, never to return to your native town again, and you marry in Petersburg or Moscow, while the girls remain.... To whom are they to be married? Why, in the absence of decent cultured men, goodness knows what sort of men they marry—stockbrokers and such people of all kinds, who can do nothing but drink and get into rows at the club.... A girl married like that, at random.... And what is her life like afterwards? You can understand: a well-educated, cultured woman is living with a stupid, boorish man; if she meets a cultivated man, an officer, an actor, or a doctor—well, she gets to love him, her life becomes unbearable to her, and she runs away from her husband. And one can't condemn her!'

" 'If that is so, Kisotchka, why get married?' I asked.

" 'Yes, of course,' said Kisotchka with a sigh, 'but you know every girl fancies that any husband is better than nothing.... Altogether life is horrid here, Nikolay Anastasyevitch, very horrid! Life is stifling for a girl and stifling when one is married.... Here they laugh at Sonya for having run away from her husband, but if they could see into her soul they would not laugh....'

Azorka began barking outside again. He growled angrily at some one, then howled miserably and dashed with all his force against the wall of the hut.... Ananyev's face was puckered with pity; he broke off his story and went out. For two minutes he could be heard outside comforting his dog. "Good dog! poor dog!"

"Our Nikolay Anastasyevitch is fond of talking," said Von Schtenberg, laughing. "He is a good fellow," he added after a brief silence.

Returning to the hut, the engineer filled up our glasses and, smiling and stroking his chest, went on: "And so my attack was unsuccessful. There was nothing for it, I put off my unclean thoughts to a more favourable occasion, resigned myself to my failure and, as the saying is, waved my hand. What is more, under the influence of Kisotchka's voice, the evening air, and the stillness, I gradually myself fell into a quiet sentimental mood. I remember I sat in an easy chair by the wide-open window and glanced at the trees and darkened sky. The outlines of the acacias and the lime trees were just the same as they had been eight years before; just as then, in the days of my childhood, somewhere far away there was the tinkling of a wretched piano, and the public had just the same habit of sauntering to and fro along the avenues, but the people were not the same. Along the avenues there walked now not my comrades and I and the object of my adoration, but schoolboys and young ladies who were strangers. And I felt melancholy. When to my inquiries about acquaintances I five times received from Kisotchka the answer, 'He is dead,' my melancholy changed into the feeling one has at the funeral service of a good man. And sitting there at the window, looking at the promenading public and listening to the tinkling piano, I saw with my own eyes for the first time in my life with what eagerness one generation hastens to replace another, and what a momentous significance even some seven or eight years may have in a man's life!

"Kisotchka put a bottle of red wine on the table. I drank it off, grew sentimental, and began telling a long story about something or other. Kisotchka listened as before, admiring me and my cleverness. And time passed. The sky was by now so dark that the outlines of the acacias and lime trees melted into one, the public was no longer walking up and down the avenues, the piano was silent and the only sound was the even murmur of the sea.

"Young people are all alike. Be friendly to a young man, make much of him, regale him with wine, let him understand that he is attractive and he will sit on and on, forget that it is time to go, and talk and talk and talk.... His hosts cannot keep their eyes open, it's past their bedtime, and he still stays and talks. That was what I did. Once I chanced to look at the clock; it was half-past ten. I began saying good-bye.

" 'Have another glass before your walk,' said Kisotchka.

"I took another glass, again I began talking at length, forgot it was time to go, and sat down. Then there came the sound of men's voices, footsteps and the clank of spurs.

" 'I think my husband has come in....' said Kisotchka listening.

"The door creaked, two voices came now from the passage and I saw two men pass the door that led into the dining-room: one a stout, solid, dark man with a hooked nose, wearing a straw hat, and the other a young officer in a white tunic. As they passed the door they both glanced casually and indifferently at Kisotchka and me, and I fancied both of them were drunk.

" 'She told you a lie then, and you believed her!' we heard a loud voice

34

with a marked nasal twang say a minute later. 'to begin with, it wasn't at the big club but at the little one.'

" 'You are angry, Jupiter, so you are wrong ....' said another voice, obviously the officer's, laughing and coughing. 'I say, can I stay the night? Tell me honestly, shall I be in your way?'

" 'What a question! Not only you can, but you must. What will you have, beer or wine?'

"They were sitting two rooms away from us, talking loudly, and apparently feeling no interest in Kisotchka or her visitor. A perceptible change came over Kisotchka on her husband's arrival. At first she flushed red, then her face wore a timid, guilty expression; she seemed to be troubled by some anxiety, and I began to fancy that she was ashamed to show me her husband and wanted me to go.

"I began taking leave. Kisotchka saw me to the front door. I remember well her gentle mournful smile and kind patient eyes as she pressed my hand and said: 'Most likely we shall never see each other again. Well, God give you every blessing. Thank you!'

"Not one sigh, not one fine phrase. As she said good-bye she was holding the candle in her hand; patches of light danced over her face and neck, as though chasing her mournful smile. I pictured to myself the old Kisotchka whom one used to want to stroke like a cat, I looked intently at the present Kisotchka, and for some reason recalled her words: 'Everyone ought to bear the lot that fate has laid on him.' And I had a pang at my heart. I instinctively guessed how it was, and my conscience whispered to me that I, in my happiness and indifference, was face to face with a good, warm-hearted, loving creature, who was broken by suffering.

"I said good-bye and went to the gate. By now it was quite dark. In the south the evenings draw in early in July and it gets dark rapidly. Towards ten o'clock it is so dark that you can't see an inch before your nose. I lighted a couple of dozen matches before, almost groping, I found my way to the gate.

" 'Cab!' I shouted, going out of the gate; not a sound, not a sigh in answer.... 'Cab,' I repeated, 'hey, Cab!'

"But there was no cab of any description. The silence of the grave. I could hear nothing but the murmur of the drowsy sea and the beating of my heart from the wine. Lifting my eyes to the sky I found not a single star. It was dark and sullen. Evidently the sky was covered with clouds. For some reason I shrugged my shoulders, smiling foolishly, and once more, not quite so resolutely, shouted for a cab.

"The echo answered me. A walk of three miles across open country and in the pitch dark was not an agreeable prospect. Before making up my mind to walk, I spent a long time deliberating and shouting for a cab; then, shrugging my shoulders, I walked lazily back to the copse, with no definite object in my mind. It was dreadfully dark in the copse. Here and there between the trees the windows of the summer villas glowed a dull red. A raven, disturbed by my steps and the matches with which I lighted my way to the summer-house, flew from tree to tree and rustled among the leaves. I felt vexed and ashamed, and the raven seemed to understand this, and croaked 'krrra!' I was vexed that I had to walk, and ashamed that I had stayed on at Kisotchka's, chatting like a boy.

"I made my way to the summer-house, felt for the seat and sat down. Far below me, behind a veil of thick darkness, the sea kept up a low angry growl. I remember that, as though I were blind, I could see neither sky nor sea, nor even the summer-house in which I was sitting. And it seemed to me as though the whole world consisted only of the thoughts that were straying through my head, dizzy from the wine, and of an unseen power murmuring monotonously somewhere below. And afterwards, as I sank into a doze, it began to seem that it was not the sea murmuring, but my thoughts, and that the whole world consisted of nothing but me. And concentrating the whole world in myself in this way, I thought no more of cabs, of the town, and of Kisotchka, and abandoned myself to the sensation I was so fond of: that is, the sensation of fearful isolation when you feel that in the whole universe, dark and formless, you alone exist. It is a proud, demoniac sensation, only possible to Russians whose thoughts and sensations are as large, boundless, and gloomy as their plains, their forests, and their snow. If I had been an artist I should certainly have depicted the expression of a Russian's face when he sits motionless and, with his legs under him and his head clasped in his hands, abandons himself to this sensation.... And together with this sensation come thoughts of the aimlessness of life, of death, and of the darkness of the grave.... The thoughts are not worth a brass farthing, but the expression of face must be fine....

"While I was sitting and dozing, unable to bring myself to get up—I was warm and comfortable—all at once, against the even monotonous murmur of the sea, as though upon a canvas, sounds began to grow distinct which drew my attention from myself.... Someone was coming hurriedly along the avenue. Reaching the summer-house this someone stopped, gave a sob like a little girl, and said in the voice of a weeping child: 'My God, when will it all end! Merciful Heavens!'

"Judging from the voice and the weeping I took it to be a little girl of ten or twelve. She walked irresolutely into the summer-house, sat down, and began half-praying, half-complaining aloud....

" 'Merciful God!' she said, crying, 'it's unbearable. It's beyond all endurance! I suffer in silence, but I want to live too.... Oh, my God! My God!'

"And so on in the same style.

"I wanted to look at the child and speak to her. So as not to frighten her I first gave a loud sigh and coughed, then cautiously struck a match.... There was a flash of bright light in the darkness, which lighted up the weeping figure. It was Kisotchka!"

"Marvels upon marvels!" said Von Schtenberg with a sigh. "Black night, the murmur of the sea; she in grief, he with a sensation of world—solitude.... It's too much of a good thing.... You only want Circassians with daggers to complete it."

"I am not telling you a tale, but fact."

"Well, even if it is a fact... it all proves nothing, and there is nothing new in it...."

"Wait a little before you find fault! Let me finish," said Ananyev, waving his hand with vexation; "don't interfere, please! I am not telling you, but the doctor.... Well," he went on, addressing me and glancing askance at the student who bent over his books and seemed very well satisfied at having gibed at the engineer—"well, Kisotchka was not surprised or frightened at seeing me. It seemed as though she had known beforehand that she would find me in the summer-house. She was breathing in gasps and trembling all over as though in a fever, while her tear-stained face, so far as I could distinguish it as I struck match after match, was not the intelligent, submissive weary face I had seen before, but something different, which I cannot understand to this day. It did not express pain, nor anxiety, nor misery—nothing of what was expressed by her words and her tears.... I must own that, probably because I did not understand it, it looked to me senseless and as though she were drunk.

" 'I can't bear it,' muttered Kisotchka in the voice of a crying child. 'It's too much for me, Nikolay Anastasyitch. Forgive me, Nikolav Anastasyitch. I can't go on living like this.... I am going to the town to my mother's.... Take me there.... Take me there, for God's sake!'

"In the presence of tears I can neither speak nor be silent. I was flustered and muttered some nonsense. trying to comfort her.

" 'No, no; I will go to my mother's,' said Kisotchka resolutely, getting up and clutching my arm convulsively (her hands and her sleeves were wet with tears). 'Forgive me, Nikolay Anastasyitch, I am going.... I can bear no more....'

" 'Kisotchka, but there isn't a single cab,' I said. 'How can you go?'

" 'No matter, I'll walk.... It's not far. I can't bear it....'

"I was embarrassed, but not touched. Kisotchka's tears, her trembling, and the blank expression of her face suggested to me a trivial, French or Little Russian melodrama, in which every ounce of cheap shallow feeling is washed down with pints of tears. I didn't understand her, and knew I did not understand her; I ought to have been silent, but for some reason, most likely for fear my silence might be taken for stupidity, I thought fit to try to persuade her not to go to her mother's, but to stay at home. When people cry, they don't like their tears to be seen. And I lighted match after match and went on striking till the box was empty. What I wanted with this ungenerous illumination, I can't conceive to this day. Cold-hearted people are apt to be awkward, and even stupid.

"In the end Kisotchka took my arm and we set off. Going out of the gate, we turned to the right and sauntered slowly along the soft dusty road. It was dark. As my eyes grew gradually accustomed to the darkness, I began to distinguish the silhouettes of the old gaunt oaks and lime trees which bordered the road. The jagged, precipitous cliffs, intersected here and there by deep, narrow ravines and creeks, soon showed indistinctly, a black streak on the right. Low bushes nestled by the hollows, looking like sitting figures. It was uncanny. I looked sideways suspiciously at the cliffs, and the murmur of the sea and the stillness of the country alarmed my imagination. Kisotchka did not speak. She was still trembling, and before she had gone half a mile she was exhausted with walking and was out of breath. I too was silent.

"Three-quarters of a mile from the Quarantine Station there was a deserted building of four storeys, with a very high chimney in which there had once been a steam flour mill. It stood solitary on the cliff, and by day it could be seen for a long distance, both by sea and by land. Because it was deserted and no one lived in it, and because there was an echo in it which distinctly repeated the steps and voices of passers-by, it seemed mysterious. Picture me in the dark night arm-in-arm with a woman who was running away from her husband near this tall long monster which repeated the sound of every step I took and stared at me fixedly with its hundred black windows. A normal young man would have been moved to romantic feelings in such surroundings, but I looked at the dark windows and thought: 'All this is very impressive, but time will come when of that building and of Kisntchka and her troubles and of me with my thoughts, not one grain of dust will remain.... All is nonsense and vanity....'

"When we reached the flour mill Kisotchka suddenly stopped, took her arm out of mine, and said, no longer in a childish voice, but in her own: 'Nikolay Anastasvitch, I know all this seems strange to you. But I am terribly unhappy! And you cannot even imagine how unhappy! It's impossible to imagine it! I don't tell you about it because one can't talk about it.... Such a life, such a life!...'

"Kisotchka did not finish. She clenched her teeth and moaned as though she were doing her utmost not to scream with pain.

" 'Such a life!' she repeated with horror, with the cadence and the southern, rather Ukrainian accent which particularly in women gives to emotional speech the effect of singing. 'It is a life! Ah, my God, my God! what does it mean? Oh, my God, my God!'

"As though trying to solve the riddle of her fate, she shrugged her shoulders in perplexity, shook her head, and clasped her hands. She spoke as though she were singing, moved gracefully, and reminded me of a celebrated Little Russian actress.

" 'Great God, it is as though I were in a pit,' she went on. 'If one could live for one minute in happiness as other people live! Oh, my God, my God! I have come to such disgrace that before a stranger I am running away from my husband by night, like some disreputable creature! Can I expect anything good after that?'

"As I admired her movements and her voice, I began to feel annoyed that she was not on good terms with her husband. 'It would be nice to have got on into relations with her!' flitted through my mind; and this pitiless thought stayed in my brain, haunted me all the way and grew more and more alluring.

"About a mile from the flour mill we had to turn to the left by the cemetery. At the turning by the corner of the cemetery there stood a stone windmill, and by it a little hut in which the miller lived. We passed the mill and the hut, turned to the left and reached the gates of the cemetery. There Kisotchka stopped and said: 'I am going back, Nikolay Anastasyitch! You go home, and God bless you, but I am going back. I am not frightened.'

" 'Well, what next!' I said, disconcerted. 'If you are going, you had better go!'

" 'I have been too hasty.... It was all about nothing that mattered. You and your talk took me back to the past and put all sort of ideas into my head.... I was sad and wanted to cry, and my husband said rude things to me before that officer, and I could not bear it.... And what's the good of my going to the town to my mother's? Will that make me any happier? I must go back.... But never mind... let us go on,' said Kisotchka, and she laughed. 'It makes no difference!'

"I remembered that over the gate of the cemetery there was an inscription: 'the hour will come wherein all they that lie in the grave will hear the voice of the Son of God.' I knew very well that sooner of later I and Kisotchka and her husband and the officer in the white tunic would lie under the dark trees in the churchyard; I knew that an unhappy and insulted fellow-creature was walking beside me. All this I recognized distinctly, but at the same time I was troubled by an oppressive and unpleasant dread that Kisotchka would turn back, and that I should not manage to say to her what had to be said. Never at any other time in my life have thoughts of a higher order been so closely interwoven with the basest animal prose as on that night.... It was horrible!

"Not far from the cemetery we found a cab. When we reached the High Street, where Kisotchka's mother lived, we dismissed the cab and walked along the pavement. Kisotchka was silent all the while, while I looked at her, and I raged at myself, 'Why don't you begin? Now's the time!' About twenty paces from the hotel where I was staying, Kisotchka stopped by the lamp-post and burst into tears.

" 'Nikolay Anastasyitch!' she said, crying and laughing and looking at me with wet shining eyes, 'I shall never forget your sympathy.... How good you are! All of you are so splendid—all of you! Honest, great-hearted, kind, clever.... Ah, how good that is!'

"She saw in me a highly educated man, advanced in every sense of the word, and on her tear-stained laughing face, together with the emotion and enthusiasm aroused by my personality, there was clearly written regret that she so rarely saw such people, and that God had not vouchsafed her the bliss of being the wife of one of them. She muttered, 'Ah, how splendid it is!' The childish gladness on her face, the tears, the gentle smile, the soft hair, which had escaped from under the kerchief, and the kerchief itself thrown carelessly over her head, in the light of the street lamp reminded me of the old Kisotchka whom one had wanted to stroke like a kitten.

"I could not restrain myself, and began stroking her hair, her shoulders, and her hands.

" 'Kisotchka, what do you want?' I muttered. 'I'll go to the ends of the earth with you if you like! I will take you out of this hole and give you happiness. I love you.... Let us go, my sweet? Yes? Will you?'

"Kisotchka's face was flooded with bewilderment. She stepped back from the street lamp and, completely overwhelmed, gazed at me with wide-open eyes. I gripped her by the arm, began showering kisses on her face, her neck, her shoulders, and went on making vows and promises. In love affairs vows and promises are almost a physiological necessity. There's no getting on without them. Sometimes you know you are lying and that promises are not necessary, but still you vow and protest. Kisotchka, utterly overwhelmed, kept staggering back and gazing at me with round eyes.

" 'Please don't! Please don't!' she muttered, holding me off with her hands.

"I clasped her tightly in my arms. All at once she broke into hysterical tears. And her face had the same senseless blank expression that I had seen in the summer-house when I lighted the matches. Without asking her consent, preventing her from speaking, I dragged her forcibly towards my hotel. She seemed almost swooning and did not walk, but I took her under the arms and almost carried her.... I remember, as we were going up the stairs, some man with a red band in his cap looked wonderingly at me and bowed to Kisotchka...."

Ananvev flushed crimson and paused. He walked up and down near the table in silence, scratched the back of his head with an air of vexation, and several times shrugged his shoulders and twitched his shoulder-blades, while a shiver ran down his huge back. The memory was painful and made him ashamed, and he was struggling with himself.

"It's horrible!" he said, draining a glass of wine and shaking his head. "I am told that in every introductory lecture on women's diseases the medical students are admonished to remember that each one of them has a mother, a sister, a fiancée, before undressing and examining a female patient.... That advice would be very good not only for medical students but for everyone who in one way or another has to deal with a woman's life. Now that I have a wife and a little daughter, oh, how well I understand that advice! How I understand it, my God! You may as well hear the rest, though.... As soon as she had become my mistress, Kisotchka's view of the position was very different from mine. First of all she felt for me a deep and passionate love. What was for me an ordinary amatory episode was for her an absolute revolution in her life. I remember, it seemed to me that she had gone out of her mind. Happy for the first time in her life, looking five years younger, with an inspired enthusiastic face, not knowing what to do with herself for happiness, she laughed and cried and never ceased dreaming aloud how next day we would set off for the Caucasus, then in the autumn to Petersburg; how we would live afterwards.

" 'Don't worry yourself about my husband,' she said to reassure me. 'He is bound to give me a divorce. Everyone in the town knows that he is living with the elder Kostovitch. We will get a divorce and be married.'

"When women love they become acclimatized and at home with people very quickly, like cats. Kisotchka had only spent an hour and a half in my room when she already felt as though she were at home and was ready to treat my property as though it were her own. She packed my things in my portmanteau, scolded me for not hanging my new expensive overcoat on a peg instead of flinging it on a chair, and so on.

"I looked at her, listened, and felt weariness and vexation. I was conscious of a slight twinge of horror at the thought that a respectable, honest, and unhappy woman had so easily, after some three or four hours, succumbed to the first man she met. As a respectable man, you see, I didn't like it. Then, too, I was unpleasantly impressed by the fact that women of Kisotchka's sort, not deep or serious, are too much in love with life, and exalt what is in reality such a trifle as love for a man to the level of bliss, misery, a complete revolution in life.... Moreover, now that I was satisfied, I was vexed with myself for having been so stupid as to get entangled with a woman whom I should have to deceive. And in spite of my disorderly life I must observe that I could not bear telling lies.

"I remember that Kisotchka sat down at my feet, laid her head on my knees, and, looking at me with shining, loving eyes, asked: 'Kolya, do you love me? Very, very much?'

"And she laughed with happiness.... This struck me as sentimental, affected, and not clever; and meanwhile I was already inclined to look for 'depth of thought' before everything.

" 'Kisotchka, you had better go home,' I said, or else your people will be sure to miss you and will be looking for you all over the town; and it would be awkward for you to go to your mother in the morning.'

"Kisotchka agreed. At parting we arranged to meet at midday next morning in the park, and the day after to set off together to Pyatigorsk. I went into the street to see her home, and I remember that I caressed her with genuine tenderness on the way. There was a minute when I felt unbearably sorry for her, for trusting me so implicitly, and I made up my mind that I would really take her to Pyatigorsk, but remembering that I had only six hundred roubles in my portmanteau, and that it would be far more difficult to break it off with her in the autumn than now, I made haste to suppress my compassion.

"We reached the house where Kisotchka's mother lived. I pulled at the bell. When footsteps were heard at the other side of the door Kisotchka suddenly looked grave, glanced upwards to the sky, made the sign of the Cross over me several times and, clutching my hand, pressed it to her lips.

" 'Till to-morrow,' she said, and disappeared into the house.

"I crossed to the opposite pavement and from there looked at the house. At first the windows were in darkness, then in one of the windows there was the glimmer of the faint bluish flame of a newly lighted candle; the flame grew, gave more light, and I saw shadows moving about the rooms together with it.

" 'They did not expect her,' I thought.

"Returning to my hotel room I undressed, drank off a glass of red wine, ate some fresh caviare which I had bought that day in the bazaar, went to bed in a leisurely way, and slept the sound, untroubled sleep of a tourist.

"In the morning I woke up with a headache and in a bad humour. Something worried me.

" 'What's the matter?' I asked myself, trying to explain my uneasiness. 'What's upsetting me?'

"And I put down my uneasiness to the dread that Kisotchka might turn up any minute and prevent my going away, and that I should have to tell lies and act a part before her. I hurriedly dressed, packed my things, and left the hotel, giving instructions to the porter to take my luggage to the station for the seven o'clock train in the evening. I spent the whole day with a doctor friend and left the town that evening. As you see, my philosophy did not prevent me from taking to my heels in a mean and treacherous flight...

"All the while that I was at my friend's, and afterwards driving to the station, I was tormented by anxiety. I fancied that I was afraid of meeting with Kisotchka and a scene. In the station I purposely remained in the toilet room till the second bell rang, and while I was making my way to my compartment, I was oppressed by a feeling as though I were covered all over with stolen things. With what impatience and terror I waited for the third bell!

"At last the third bell that brought my deliverance rang at last, the train moved; we passed the prison, the barracks, came out into the open country, and yet, to my surprise, the feeling of uneasiness still persisted, and still I felt like a thief passionately longing to escape. It was queer. To distract my mind and calm myself I looked out of the window. The train ran along the coast. The sea was smooth, and the turquoise sky, almost half covered with the tender, golden crimson light of sunset, was gaily and serenely mirrored in it. Here and there fishing boats and rafts made black patches on its surface. The town, as clean and beautiful as a toy, stood on the high cliff, and was already shrouded in the mist of evening. The golden domes of its churches, the windows and the greenery reflected the setting sun, glowing and melting like shimmering gold.... The scent of the fields mingled with the soft damp air from the sea.

"The train flew rapidly along. I heard the laughter of passengers and guards. Everyone was good-humoured and light-hearted, yet my unaccountable uneasiness grew greater and greater.... I looked at the white mist that covered the town and I imagined how a woman with a senseless blank face was hurrying up and down in that mist by the churches and the houses, looking for me and moaning, 'Oh, my God! Oh, my God!' in the voice of a little girl or the cadences of a Little Russian actress. I recalled her grave face and big anxious eyes as she made the sign of the Cross over me, as though I belonged to her, and mechanically I looked at the hand which she had kissed the day before.

"'Surely I am not in love?' I asked myself, scratching my hand.

"Only as night came on when the passengers were asleep and I was left tête-à-tête with my conscience, I began to understand what I had not been able to grasp before. In the twilight of the railway carriage the image of Kisotchka rose before me, haunted me and I recognized clearly that I had committed a crime as bad as murder. My conscience tormented me. To stifle this unbearable feeling, I assured myself that everything was nonsense and vanity, that Kisotchka and I would die and decay, that her grief was nothing in comparison with death, and so on and so on... and that if you come to that, there is no such thing as freewill, and that therefore I was not to blame. But all these arguments only irritated me and were extraordinarily quickly crowded out by other thoughts. There was a miserable feeling in the hand that Kisotchka had kissed.... I kept lying down and getting up again, drank vodka at the stations, forced myself to eat bread and butter, fell to assuring myself again that life had no meaning, but nothing was of any use. A strange and if you like absurd ferment was going on in my brain. The most incongruous ideas crowded one after another in disorder, getting more and more tangled, thwarting each other, and I, the thinker, 'with my brow bent on the earth,' could make out nothing and could not find my bearings in this mass of essential and non-essential ideas. It appeared that I, the thinker, had not mastered the technique of thinking, and that I was no more capable of managing my own brain than mending a watch. For the first time in my life I was really thinking eagerly and intensely, and that seemed to me so monstrous that I said to myself: 'I am going off my head.' A man whose brain does not work at all times, but only at painful moments, is often haunted by the thought of madness.

"I spent a day and a night in this misery, then a second night, and learning from experience how little my philosophy was to me, I came to my senses and realised at last what sort of a creature I was. I saw that my ideas were not worth a brass farthing, and that before meeting Kisotchka I had not begun to think and had not even a conception of what thinking in earnest meant; now through suffering I realised that I had neither convictions nor a definite moral standard, nor heart, nor reason; my whole intellectual and moral wealth consisted of specialist knowledge, fragments, useless memories, other people's ideas—and nothing else; and my mental processes were as lacking in complexity, as useless and as rudimentary as a Yakut's.... If I had disliked lying, had not stolen, had not murdered, and, in fact, made obviously gross mistakes, that was not owing to my convictions—I had none, but because I was in bondage, hand and foot, to my nurse's fairy tales and to copy-book morals, which had entered into my flesh and blood and without my noticing it guided me in life, though I looked on them as absurd....

"I realised that I was not a thinker, not a philosopher, but simply a dilettante. God had given me a strong healthy Russian brain with promise of talent. And, only fancy, here was that brain at twenty-six, undisciplined, completely free from principles, not weighed down by any stores of knowledge, but only lightly sprinkled with information of a sort in the engineering line; it was young and had a physiological craving for exercise, it was on the look-out for it, when all at once quite casually the fine juicy idea of the aimlessness of life and the darkness beyond the tomb descends upon it. It greedily sucks it in, puts its whole outlook at its disposal and begins playing with it, like a cat with a mouse. There is neither learning nor system in the brain, but that does not matter. It deals with the great ideas with its own innate powers, like a self-educated man, and before a month has passed the owner of the brain can turn a potato into a hundred dainty dishes, and fancies himself a philosopher....

"Our generation has carried this dilettantism, this playing with serious ideas into science, into literature, into politics, and into everything which it is not too lazy to go into, and with its dilettantism has introduced, too, its coldness, its boredom, and its one-sidedness and, as it seems to me, it has already succeeded in developing in the masses a new hitherto non-existent attitude to serious ideas.

"I realised and appreciated my abnormality and utter ignorance, thanks to a misfortune. My normal thinking, so it seems to me now, dates from the day when I began again from the A, B, C, when my conscience sent me flying back to N., when with no philosophical subleties I repented, besought Kisotchka's forgiveness like a naughty boy and wept with her...."

Ananyev briefly described his last interview with Kisotchka.

"H'm...." the student filtered through his teeth when the engineer had finished. "That's the sort of thing that happens."

His face still expressed mental inertia, and apparently Ananyev's story had not touched him in the least. Only when the engineer after a moment's pause, began expounding his view again and repeating what he had said at first, the student frowned irritably, got up from the table and walked away to his bed. He made his bed and began undressing.

"You look as though you have really convinced some one this time," he said irritably.

"Me convince anybody!" said the engineer. "My dear soul, do you suppose I claim to do that? God bless you! To convince you is impossible.

You can reach conviction only by way of personal experience and suffering!"

"And then—it's queer logic!" grumbled the student as he put on his nightshirt. "The ideas which you so dislike, which are so ruinous for the young are, according to you, the normal thing for the old; it's as though it were a question of grey hairs.... Where do the old get this privilege? What is it based upon? If these ideas are poison, they are equally poisonous for all?"

"Oh, no, my dear soul, don't say so!" said the engineer with a sly wink. "Don't say so. In the first place, old men are not dilettanti. Their pessimism comes to them not casually from outside, but from the depths of their own brains, and only after they have exhaustively studied the Hegels and Kants of all sorts, have suffered, have made no end of mistakes, in fact—when they have climbed the whole ladder from bottom to top. Their pessimism has both personal experience and sound philosophic training behind it. Secondly, the pessimism of old thinkers does not take the form of idle talk, as it does with you and me, but of Weltschmerz, of suffering; it rests in them on a Christian foundation because it is derived from love for humanity and from thoughts about humanity, and is entirely free from the egoism which is noticeable in dilettanti. You despise life because its meaning and its object are hidden just from you, and you are only afraid of your own death, while the real thinker is unhappy because the truth is hidden from all and he is afraid for all men. For instance, there is living not far from here the Crown forester, Ivan Alexandritch. He is a nice old man. At one time he was a teacher somewhere, and used to write something; the devil only knows what he was, but anyway he is a remarkably clever fellow and in philosophy he is A1. He has read a great deal and he is continually reading now. Well, we came across him lately in the Gruzovsky district.... They were laying the sleepers and rails just at the time. It's not a difficult job, but Ivan Alexandritch, not being a specialist, looked at it as though it were a conjuring trick. It takes an experienced workman less than a minute to lay a sleeper and fix a rail on it. The workmen were in good form and really were working smartly and rapidly; one rascal in particular brought his hammer down with exceptional smartness on the head of the nail and drove it in at one blow, though the handle of the hammer was two yards or more in length and each nail was a foot long. Ivan Alexandritch watched the workmen a long time, was moved, and said to me with tears in his eyes: 'What a pity that these splendid men will die!' Such pessimism I understand."

"All that proves nothing and explains nothing," said the student, covering himself up with a sheet; "all that is simply pounding liquid in a mortar. No one knows anything and nothing can be proved by words."

He peeped out from under the sheet, lifted up his head and, frowning irritably, said quickly: "One must be very naïve to believe in human words and logic and to ascribe any determining value to them. You can prove and disprove anything you like with words, and people will soon perfect the technique of language to such a point that they will prove with mathematical certainty that twice two is seven. I am fond of reading and listening, but as to believing, no thank you; I can't, and I don't want to. I believe only in God, but as for you, if you talk to me till the Second Coming and seduce another five hundred Kisothchkas, I shall believe in you only when I go out of my mind.... Goodnight."

The student hid his head under the sheet and turned his face towards the wall, meaning by this action to let us know that he did not want to speak or listen. The argument ended at that.

Before going to bed the engineer and I went out of the hut, and I saw the lights once more.

"We have tired you out with our chatter," said Ananyev, yawning and looking at the sky. "Well, my good sir! The only pleasure we have in this dull hole is drinking and philosophizing.... What an embankment, Lord have mercy on us!" he said admiringly, as we approached the embankment; "it is more like Mount Ararat than an embankment."

He paused for a little, then said: "Those lights remind the Baron of the Amalekites, but it seems to me that they are like the thoughts of man.... You know the thoughts of each individual man are scattered like that in disorder, stretch in a straight line towards some goal in the midst of the darkness and, without shedding light on anything, without lighting up the night, they vanish somewhere far beyond old age. But enough philosophising! It's time to go bye-bye."

When we were back in the hut the engineer began begging me to take his bed.

"Oh please!" he said imploringly, pressing both hands on his heart. "I entreat you, and don't worry about me! I can sleep anywhere, and, besides, I am not going to bed just yet. Please do—it's a favour!"

I agreed, undressed, and went to bed, while he sat down to the table and set to work on the plans.

"We fellows have no time for sleep," he said in a low voice when I had got into bed and shut my eyes. "When a man has a wife and two children he can't think of sleep. One must think now of food and clothes and saving for the future. And I have two of them, a little son and a daughter.... The boy, little rascal, has a jolly little face. He's not six yet, and already he shows remarkable abilities, I assure you.... I have their photographs here, somewhere.... Ah, my children, my children!"

He rummaged among his papers, found their photographs, and began looking at them. I fell asleep.

I was awakened by the barking of Azorka and loud voices. Von Schtenberg with bare feet and ruffled hair was standing in the doorway dressed in his underclothes, talking loudly with some one .... It was getting light. A gloomy dark blue dawn was peeping in at the door, at the windows, and through the crevices in the hut walls, and casting a faint light on my bed, on the table with the papers, and on Ananyev. Stretched on the floor on a cloak, with a leather pillow under his head, the engineer lay asleep with his fleshy, hairy chest uppermost; he was snoring so loudly that I pitied the student from the bottom of my heart for having to sleep in the same room with him every night.

"Why on earth are we to take them?" shouted Von Schtenberg. "It has nothing to do with us! Go to Tchalisov! From whom do the cauldrons come?"

"From Nikitin..." a bass voice answered gruffly.

"Well, then, take them to Tchalisov.... That's not in our department. What the devil are you standing there for? Drive on!"

"Your honour, we have been to Tchalisov already," said the bass voice still more gruffly. "Yesterday we were the whole day looking for him down the line, and were told at his hut that he had gone to the Dymkovsky section. Please take them, your honour! How much longer are we to go carting them about? We go carting them on and on along the line, and see no end to it."

"What is it?" Ananyev asked huskily, waking up and lifting his head quickly.

"They have brought some cauldrons from Nikitin's," said the student, "and he is begging us to take them. And what business is it of ours to take them?"

"Do be so kind, your honour, and set things right! The horses have been two days without food and the master, for sure, will be angry. Are we to take them back, or what? The railway ordered the cauldrons, so it ought to take them...."

"Can't you understand, you blockhead, that it has nothing to do with us? Go on to Tchalisov!"

"What is it? Who's there?" Ananyev asked huskily again. "Damnation take them all," he said, getting up and going to the door. "What is it?"

I dressed, and two minutes later went out of the hut. Ananyev and the student, both in their underclothes and barefooted, were angrily and impatiently explaining to a peasant who was standing before them bareheaded, with his whip in his hand, apparently not understanding them. Both faces looked preoccupied with workaday cares.

"What use are your cauldrons to me," shouted Ananyev. "Am I to put them on my head, or what? If you can't find Tchalisov, find his assistant, and leave us in peace!"

Seeing me, the student probably recalled the conversation of the previous night. The workaday expression vanished from his sleepy face and a look of mental inertia came into it. He waved the peasant off and walked away absorbed in thought.

It was a cloudy morning. On the line where the lights had been gleaming the night before, the workmen, just roused from sleep, were swarming. There was a sound of voices and the squeaking of wheelbarrows. The working day was beginning. One poor little nag harnessed with cord was already plodding towards the embankment, tugging with its neck, and dragging along a cartful of sand.

I began saying good-bye.... A great deal had been said in the night, but I carried away with me no answer to any question, and in the morning, of the whole conversation there remained in my memory, as in a filter, only the lights and the image of Kisotchka. As I got on the horse, I looked at the student and Ananyev for the last time, at the hysterical dog with the lustreless, tipsy-looking eyes, at the workmen flitting to and fro in the morning fog, at the embankment, at the little nag straining with its neck, and thought: "There is no making out anything in this world."

And when I lashed my horse and galloped along the line, and when a little later I saw nothing before me but the endless gloomy plain and the cold overcast sky, I recalled the questions which were discussed in the night. I pondered while the sun-scorched plain, the immense sky, the oak forest, dark on the horizon and the hazy distance, seemed saying to me: "Yes, there's no understanding anything in this world!"

The sun began to rise....

A CHAMELEON

THE police superintendent Otchumyelov is walking across the market square wearing a new overcoat and carrying a parcel under his arm.

A red-haired policeman strides after him with a sieve full of confiscated gooseberries in his hands. There is silence all around.

Not a soul in the square.... The open doors of the shops and taverns look out upon God's world disconsolately, like hungry mouths; there is not even a beggar near them.

"So you bite, you damned brute?" Otchumyelov hears suddenly. "Lads, don't let him go! Biting is prohibited nowadays! Hold him! ah... ah!"

There is the sound of a dog yelping. Otchumyelov looks in the direction of the sound and sees a dog, hopping on three legs and looking about her, run out of Pitchugin's timber-yard. A man in a starched cotton shirt, with his waistcoat unbuttoned, is chasing her. He runs after her, and throwing his body forward falls down and seizes the dog by her hind legs. Once more there is a yelping and a shout of "Don't let go!" Sleepy countenances are protruded from the shops, and soon a crowd, which seems to have sprung out of the earth, is gathered round the timber-yard.

"It looks like a row, your honour..." says the policeman.

Otchumyelov makes a half turn to the left and strides towards the crowd.

He sees the aforementioned man in the unbuttoned waistcoat standing close by the gate of the timber-yard, holding his right hand in the air and displaying a bleeding finger to the crowd. On his half-drunken face there is plainly written: "I' ll pay you out, you rogue!" and indeed the very finger has the look of a flag of victory. In this man Otchumyelov recognizes Hryukin, the goldsmith. The culprit who has caused the sensation, a white borzoy puppy with a sharp muzzle and a yellow patch on her back, is sitting on the ground with her fore-paws outstretched in the middle of the crowd, trembling all over. There is an expression of misery and terror in her tearful eyes.

"What's it all about?" Otchumyelov inquires, pushing his way through the crowd. "What are you here for? Why are you waving your finger...? Who was it shouted?"

"I was walking along here, not interfering with anyone, your honour," Hryukin begins, coughing into his fist. "I was talking about firewood to Mitry Mitritch, when this low brute for no rhyme or reason bit my finger.... You must excuse me, I am a working man.... Mine is fine work. I must have damages, for I shan't be able to use this finger for a week, may be.... It's not even the law, your honour, that one should put up with it from a beast.... If everyone is going to be bitten, life won't be worth living...."

"H'm. Very good," says Otchumyelov sternly, coughing and raising his eyebrows. "Very good. Whose dog is it? I won't let this pass! I'll teach them to let their dogs run all over the place! It's time these gentry were looked after, if they won't obey the regulations! When he's fined, the blackguard, I'll teach him what it means to keep dogs and such stray cattle! I'll give him a lesson!... Yeldyrin," cries the superintendent, addressing the policeman, "find out whose dog this is and draw up a report! And the dog must be strangled. Without delay! It's sure to be mad.... Whose dog is it, I ask?"

"I fancy it's General Zhigalov's," says someone in the crowd.

"General Zhigalov's, h'm.... Help me off with my coat, Yeldyrin... it's frightfully hot! It must be a sign of rain.... There's one thing I can't make out, how it came to bite you?" Otchumyelov turns to Hryukin. "Surely it couldn't reach your finger. It's a little dog, and you are a great hulking fellow! You must have scratched your finger with a nail, and then the idea struck you to get damages for it. We all know... your sort! I know you devils!"

"He put a cigarette in her face, your honour, for a joke, and she had the sense to snap at him.... He is a nonsensical fellow, your honour!"

"That's a lie, Squinteye! You didn't see, so why tell lies about it? His honour is a wise gentleman, and will see who is telling lies and who is telling the truth, as in God's sight.... And if I am lying let the court decide. It's written in the law.... We are all equal nowadays. My own brother is in the gendarmes... let me tell you...."

"Don't argue!"

"No, that's not the General's dog," says the policeman, with profound conviction, "the General hasn't got one like that. His are mostly setters."

"Do you know that for a fact?"

"Yes, your honour."

"I know it, too. The General has valuable dogs, thoroughbred, and this is goodness knows what! No coat, no shape.... A low creature. And to keep a dog like that!... where's the sense of it. If a dog like that were to turn up in Petersburg or Moscow, do you know what would happen? They would not worry about the law, they would strangle it in a twinkling! You've been injured, Hryukin, and we can't let the matter drop.... We must give them a lesson! It is high time ....!"

"Yet maybe it is the General's," says the policeman, thinking aloud. "It's not written on its face.... I saw one like it the other day in his yard."

"It is the General's, that's certain!" says a voice in the crowd.

"H'm, help me on with my overcoat, Yeldyrin, my lad... the wind's getting up.... I am cold.... You take it to the General's, and inquire there. Say I found it and sent it. And tell them not to let it out into the street.... It may be a valuable dog, and if every swine goes sticking a cigar in its mouth, it will soon be ruined. A dog is a delicate animal.... And you put your hand down, you blockhead. It's no use your displaying your fool of a finger. It's your own fault...."

"Here comes the General's cook, ask him... Hi, Prohor! Come here, my dear man! Look at this dog.... Is it one of yours? "

"What an idea! We have never had one like that!"

"There's no need to waste time asking," says Otchumyelov. "It's a stray dog! There's no need to waste time talking about it.... Since he says it's a stray dog, a stray dog it is.... It must be destroyed, that's all about it."

"It is not our dog," Prohor goes on. "It belongs to the General's brother, who arrived the other day. Our master does not care for hounds. But his honour is fond of them...."

"You don't say his Excellency's brother is here? Vladimir Ivanitch?" inquires Otchumyelov, and his whole face beams with an ecstatic smile. "Well, I never! And I didn't know! Has he come on a visit? "

"Yes."

"Well, I never.... He couldn't stay away from his brother.... And there I didn't know! So this is his honour's dog? Delighted to hear it.... Take it. It's not a bad pup.... A lively creature.... Snapped at this fellow's finger! Ha-ha-ha.... Come, why are you shivering? Rrr... Rrrr.... The rogue's angry... a nice little pup."

Prohor calls the dog, and walks away from the timber-yard with her. The crowd laughs at Hryukin.

"I'll make you smart yet!" Otchumyelov threatens him, and wrapping himself in his greatcoat, goes on his way across the square.

A JOKE

IT was a bright winter midday.... There was a sharp snapping frost and the curls on Nadenka's temples and the down on her upper lip were covered with silvery frost. She was holding my arm and we were standing on a high hill. From where we stood to the ground below there stretched a smooth sloping descent in which the sun was reflected as in a looking-glass. Beside us was a little sledge lined with bright red cloth.

"Let us go down, Nadyezhda Petrovna!" I besought her. "Only once! I assure you we shall be all right and not hurt."

But Nadenka was afraid. The slope from her little galoshes to the bottom of the ice hill seemed to her a terrible, immensely deep abyss. Her spirit failed her, and she held her breath as she looked down, when I merely suggested her getting into the sledge, but what would it be if she were to risk flying into the abyss! She would die, she would go out of her mind.

"I entreat you!" I said. "You mustn't be afraid! You know it's poor-spirited, it's cowardly!"

Nadenka gave way at last, and from her face I saw that she gave way in mortal dread. I sat her in the sledge, pale and trembling, put my arm round her and with her cast myself down the precipice.

The sledge flew like a bullet. The air cleft by our flight beat in our faces, roared, whistled in our ears, tore at us, nipped us cruelly in its anger, tried to tear our heads off our shoulders. We had hardly strength to breathe from the pressure of the wind. It seemed as though the devil himself had caught us in his claws and was dragging us with a roar to hell. Surrounding objects melted into one long furiously racing streak... another moment and it seemed we should perish.

"I love you, Nadya!" I said in a low voice.

The sledge began moving more and more slowly, the roar of the wind and the whirr of the runners was no longer so terrible, it was easier to breathe, and at last we were at the bottom. Nadenka was more dead than alive. She was pale and scarcely breathing.... I helped her to get up.

"Nothing would induce me to go again," she said, looking at me with wide eyes full of horror. "Nothing in the world! I almost died!"

A little later she recovered herself and looked enquiringly into my eyes, wondering had I really uttered those four words or had she fancied them in the roar of the hurricane. And I stood beside her smoking and looking attentively at my glove.

She took my arm and we spent a long while walking near the ice-hill. The riddle evidently would not let her rest.... Had those words been uttered or not?... Yes or no? Yes or no? It was the question of pride, or honour, of life—a very important question, the most important question in the world. Nadenka kept impatiently, sorrowfully looking into my face with a penetrating glance; she answered at random, waiting to see whether I would not speak. Oh, the play of feeling on that sweet face! I saw that she was struggling with herself, that she wanted to say something, to ask some question, but she could not find the words; she felt awkward and frightened and troubled by her joy....

"Do you know what," she said without looking at me.

"Well?" I asked.

"Let us... slide down again."

We clambered up the ice-hill by the steps again. I sat Nadenka, pale and trembling, in the sledge; again we flew into the terrible abyss, again the wind roared and the runners whirred, and again when the flight of our sledge was at its swiftest and noisiest, I said in a low voice: "I love you, Nadenka!"

When the sledge stopped, Nadenka flung a glance at the hill down which we had both slid, then bent a long look upon my face, listened to my voice which was unconcerned and passionless, and the whole of her little figure, every bit of it, even her muff and her hood expressed the utmost bewilderment, and on her face was written: "What does it mean? Who uttered those words? Did he, or did I only fancy it?"

The uncertainty worried her and drove her out of all patience. The poor girl did not answer my questions, frowned, and was on the point of tears.

"Hadn't we better go home?" I asked.

"Well, I... I like this tobogganing," she said, flushing. "Shall we go down once more?"

She "liked" the tobogganing, and yet as she got into the sledge she was, as both times before, pale, trembling, hardly able to breathe for terror.

We went down for the third time, and I saw she was looking at my face and watching my lips. But I put my handkerchief to my lips, coughed, and when we reached the middle of the hill I succeeded in bringing out: "I love you, Nadya!"

And the mystery remained a mystery! Nadenka was silent, pondering on something.... I saw her home, she tried to walk slowly, slackened her pace and kept waiting to see whether I would not say those words to her, and I saw how her soul was suffering, what effort she was making not to say to herself: "It cannot be that the wind said them! And I don't want it to be the wind that said them!"

Next morning I got a little note: "If you are tobogganing to-day, come for me. —N."

And from that time I began going every day tobogganing with Nadenka, and as we flew down in the sledge, every time I pronounced in a low voice the same words: "I love you, Nadya!"

Soon Nadenka grew used to that phrase as to alcohol or morphia. She could not live without it. It is true that flying down the ice-hill terrified her as before, but now the terror and danger gave a peculiar fascination to words of love—words which as before were a mystery and tantalized the soul. The same two—the wind and I were still suspected.... Which of the two was making love to her she did not know, but apparently by now she did not care; from which goblet one drinks matters little if only the beverage is intoxicating.

It happened I went to the skating-ground alone at midday; mingling with the crowd I saw Nadenka go up to the ice-hill and look about for me... then she timidly mounted the steps.... She was frightened of going alone—oh, how frightened! She was white as the snow, she was trembling, she went as though to the scaffold, but she went, she went without looking back, resolutely. She had evidently determined to put it to the test at last: would those sweet amazing words be heard when I was not there? I saw her, pale, her lips parted with horror, get into the sledge, shut her eyes and saying good-bye for ever to the earth, set off.... "Whrrr!" whirred the runners. Whether Nadenka heard those words I do not know. I only saw her getting up from the sledge looking faint and exhausted. And one could tell from her face that she could not tell herself whether she had heard anything or not. Her terror while she had been flying down had deprived of her all power of hearing, of discriminating sounds, of understanding.

But then the month of March arrived... the spring sunshine was more kindly.... Our ice-hill turned dark, lost its brilliance and finally melted. We gave up tobogganing. There was nowhere now where poor Nadenka could hear those words, and indeed no one to utter them, since there was no wind and I was going to Petersburg—for long, perhaps for ever.

It happened two days before my departure I was sitting in the dusk in the little garden which was separated from the yard of Nadenka's house by a high fence with nails in it.... It was still pretty cold, there was still snow by the manure heap, the trees looked dead but there was already the scent of spring and the rooks were cawing loudly as they settled for their night's rest. I went up to the fence and stood for a long while peeping through a chink. I saw Nadenka come out into the porch and fix a mournful yearning gaze on the sky.... The spring wind was blowing straight into her pale dejected face.... It reminded her of the wind which roared at us on the ice-hill when she heard those four words, and her face became very, very sorrowful, a tear trickled down her cheek, and the poor child held out both arms as though begging the wind to bring her those words once more. And waiting for the wind I said in a low voice: "I love you, Nadya!"

Mercy! The change that came over Nadenka! She uttered a cry, smiled all over her face and looking joyful, happy and beautiful, held out her arms to meet the wind.

And I went off to pack up....

That was long ago. Now Nadenka is married; she married—whether of her own choice or not does not matter—a secretary of the Nobility Wardenship and now she has three children. That we once went tobogganing together, and that the wind brought her the words "I love you, Nadenka," is not forgotten; it is for her now the happiest, most touching, and beautiful memory in her life....

But now that I am older I cannot understand why I uttered those words, what was my motive in that joke....

AT A SUMMER VILLA

I LOVE YOU. You are my life, my happiness—everything to me! Forgive the avowal, but I have not the strength to suffer and be silent. I ask not for love in return, but for sympathy. Be at the old arbour at eight o'clock this evening.... To sign my name is unnecessary I think, but do not be uneasy at my being anonymous. I am young, nice-looking... what more do you want?

When Pavel Ivanitch Vyhodtsev, a practical married man who was spending his holidays at a summer villa, read this letter, he shrugged his shoulders and scratched his forehead in perplexity.

"What devilry is this?" he thought. "I'm a married man, and to send me such a queer... silly letter! Who wrote it?"

Pavel Ivanitch turned the letter over and over before his eyes, read it through again, and spat with disgust.

" 'I love you' ..." he said jeeringly. "A nice boy she has pitched on! So I'm to run off to meet you in the arbour!... I got over all such romances and fleurs d'amour years ago, my girl.... Hm! She must be some reckless, immoral creature.... Well, these women are a set! What a whirligig—God forgive us!—she must be to write a letter like that to a stranger, and a married man, too! It's real demoralisation!"

In the course of his eight years of married life Pavel Ivanitch had completely got over all sentimental feeling, and he had received no letters from ladies except letters of congratulation, and so, although he tried to carry it off with disdain, the letter quoted above greatly intrigued and agitated him.

An hour after receiving it, he was lying on his sofa, thinking: "Of course I am not a silly boy, and I am not going to rush off to this idiotic rendezvous; but yet it would be interesting to know who wrote it! Hm.... It is certainly a woman's writing.... The letter is written with genuine feeling, and so it can hardly be a joke.... Most likely it's some neurotic girl, or perhaps a widow... widows are frivolous and eccentric as a rule. Hm.... Who could it be?"

What made it the more difficult to decide the question was that Pavel Ivanitch had not one feminine acquaintance among all the summer visitors, except his wife.

"It is queer..." he mused. " 'I love you!'... When did she manage to fall in love? Amazing woman! To fall in love like this, apropos of nothing, without making any acquaintance and finding out what sort of man I am.... She must be extremely young and romantic if she is capable of falling in love after two or three looks at me.... But... who is she?"

Pavel Ivanitch suddenly recalled that when he had been walking among the summer villas the day before, and the day before that, he had several times been met by a fair young lady with a light blue hat and a turn-up nose. The fair charmer had kept looking at him, and when he sat down on a seat she had sat down beside him....

"Can it be she?" Vyhodtsev wondered. "It can't be! Could a delicate ephemeral creature like that fall in love with a worn-out old eel like me? No, it's impossible!"

At dinner Pavel Ivanitch looked blankly at his wife while he meditated: "She writes that she is young and nice-looking.... So she's not old.... Hm.... To tell the truth, honestly I am not so old and plain that no one could fall in love with me. My wife loves me! Besides, love is blind, we all know...."

"What are you thinking about?" his wife asked him.

"Oh... my head aches a little..." Pavel Ivanitch said, quite untruly.

He made up his mind that it was stupid to pay attention to such a nonsensical thing as a love-letter, and laughed at it and at its authoress, but—alas!—powerful is the "dacha"enemy of mankind! After dinner, Pavel Ivanitch lay down on his bed, and instead of going to sleep, reflected: "But there, I daresay she is expecting me to come! What a silly!

I can just imagine what a nervous fidget she'll be in and how her tournure will quiver when she does not find me in the arbour! I shan't go, though.... Bother her!"

But, I repeat, powerful is the enemy of mankind.

"Though I might, perhaps, just out of curiosity..." he was musing, half an hour later. "I might go and look from a distance what sort of a creature she is.... It would be interesting to have a look at her! It would be fun, and that's all! After all, why shouldn't I have a little fun since such a chance has turned up?"

Pavel Ivanitch got up from his bed and began dressing. "What are you getting yourself up so smartly for?" his wife asked, noticing that he was putting on a clean shirt and a fashionable tie.

"Oh, nothing.... I must have a walk.... My head aches.... Hm."

Pavel Ivanitch dressed in his best, and waiting till eight o'clock, went out of the house. When the figures of gaily dressed summer visitors of both sexes began passing before his eyes against the bright green background, his heart throbbed.

"Which of them is it?..." he wondered, advancing irresolutely. "Come, what am I afraid of? Why, I am not going to the rendezvous! What... a fool! Go forward boldly! And what if I go into the arbour? Well, well... there is no reason I should."

Pavel Ivanitch's heart beat still more violently.... Involuntarily, with no desire to do so, he suddenly pictured to himself the half-darkness of the arbour.... A graceful fair girl with a little blue hat and a turn-up nose rose before his imagination. He saw her, abashed by her love and trembling all over, timidly approach him, breathing excitedly, and... suddenly clasping him in her arms.

"If I weren't married it would be all right..." he mused, driving sinful ideas out of his head. "Though... for once in my life, it would do no harm to have the experience, or else one will die without knowing what.... And my wife, what will it matter to her? Thank God, for eight years I've never moved one step away from her.... Eight years of irreproachable duty!

Enough of her.... It's positively vexatious.... I'm ready to go to spite her!"

Trembling all over and holding his breath, Pavel Ivanitch went up to the arbour, wreathed with ivy and wild vine, and peeped into it.... A smell of dampness and mildew reached him....

"I believe there's nobody..." he thought, going into the arbour, and at once saw a human silhouette in the corner.

The silhouette was that of a man.... Looking more closely, Pavel Ivanitch recognised his wife's brother, Mitya, a student, who was staying with them at the villa.

"Oh, it's you..." he growled discontentedly, as he took off his hat and sat down.

"Yes, it's me ... " answered Mitya.

Two minutes passed in silence.

"Excuse me, Pavel Ivanitch," began Mitya: "but might I ask you to leave me alone?... I am thinking over the dissertation for my degree and... and the presence of anybody else prevents my thinking."

"You had better go somewhere in a dark avenue..." Pavel Ivanitch observed mildly. "It's easier to think in the open air, and, besides,... er... I should like to have a little sleep here on this seat... It's not so hot here...."

"You want to sleep, but it's a question of my dissertation..." Mitya grumbled. "The dissertation is more important."

Again there was a silence. Pavel Ivanitch, who had given the rein to his imagination and was continually hearing footsteps, suddenly leaped up and said in a plaintive voice: "Come, I beg you, Mitya! You are younger and ought to consider me.... I am unwell and... I need sleep.... Go away!"

"That's egoism.... Why must you be here and not I? I won't go as a matter of principle."

"Come, I ask you to! Suppose I am an egoist, a despot and a fool... but I ask you to go! For once in my life I ask you a favour! Show some consideration!"

Mitya shook his head.

"What a beast!..." thought Pavel Ivanitch. "That can't be a rendezvous with him here! It's impossible with him here!"

"I say, Mitya," he said, "I ask you for the last time.... Show that you are a sensible, humane, and cultivated man!"

"I don't know why you keep on so!... " said Mitya, shrugging his shoulders. "I've said I won't go, and I won't. I shall stay here as a matter of principle...."

At that moment a woman's face with a turn-up nose peeped into the arbour....

Seeing Mitya and Pavel Ivanitch, it frowned and vanished.

"She is gone!" thought Pavel Ivanitch, looking angrily at Mitya. "She saw that blackguard and fled! It's all spoilt!"

After waiting a little longer, he got up, put on his hat and said: "You're a beast, a low brute and a blackguard! Yes! A beast! It's mean... and silly! Everything is at an end between us!"

"Delighted to hear it!" muttered Mitya, also getting up and putting on his hat. "Let me tell you that by being here just now you've played me such a dirty trick that I'll never forgive you as long as I live."

Pavel Ivanitch went out of the arbour, and beside himself with rage, strode rapidly to his villa. Even the sight of the table laid for supper did not soothe him.

"Once in a lifetime such a chance has turned up," he thought in agitation; "and then it's been prevented! Now she is offended... crushed!"

At supper Pavel Ivanitch and Mitya kept their eyes on their plates and maintained a sullen silence.... They were hating each other from the bottom of their hearts.

"What are you smiling at?" asked Pavel Ivanitch, pouncing on his wife. "It's only silly fools who laugh for nothing!"

His wife looked at her husband's angry face, and went off into a peal of laughter.

"What was that letter you got this morning?" she asked.

"I?... I didn't get one...." Pavel Ivanitch was overcome with confusion. "You are inventing... imagination."

"Oh, come, tell us! Own up, you did! Why, it was I sent you that letter! Honour bright, I did! Ha ha!"

Pavel Ivanitch turned crimson and bent over his plate. "Silly jokes," he growled.

"But what could I do? Tell me that.... We had to scrub the rooms out this evening, and how could we get you out of the house? There was no other way of getting you out.... But don't be angry, stupid.... I didn't want you to be dull in the arbour, so I sent the same letter to Mitya too! Mitya, have you been to the arbour?"

Mitya grinned and left off glaring with hatred at his rival.

VEROTCHKA

IVAN ALEXEYITCH OGNEV remembers how on that August evening he opened the glass door with a rattle and went out on to the verandah. He was wearing a light Inverness cape and a wide-brimmed straw hat, the very one that was lying with his top-boots in the dust under his bed. In one hand he had a big bundle of books and notebooks, in the other a thick knotted stick.

Behind the door, holding the lamp to show the way, stood the master of the house, Kuznetsov, a bald old man with a long grey beard, in a snow-white piqué jacket. The old man was smiling cordially and nodding his head.

"Good-bye, old fellow!" said Ognev.

Kuznetsov put the lamp on a little table and went out to the verandah. Two long narrow shadows moved down the steps towards the flower-beds, swayed to and fro, and leaned their heads on the trunks of the lime-trees.

"Good-bye and once more thank you, my dear fellow!" said Ivan Alexeyitch. "Thank you for your welcome, for your kindness, for your affection.... I shall never forget your hospitality as long as I live. You are so good, and your daughter is so good, and everyone here is so kind, so good-humoured and friendly... Such a splendid set of people that I don't know how to say what I feel!"

From excess of feeling and under the influence of the home-made wine he had just drunk, Ognev talked in a singing voice like a divinity student, and was so touched that he expressed his feelings not so much by words as by the blinking of his eyes and the twitching of his shoulders. Kuznetsov, who had also drunk a good deal and was touched, craned forward to the young man and kissed him.

"I've grown as fond of you as if I were your dog," Ognev went on. "I've been turning up here almost every day; I've stayed the night a dozen times. It's dreadful to think of all the home-made wine I've drunk. And thank you most of all for your co-operation and help. Without you I should have been busy here over my statistics till October. I shall put in my preface: 'I think it my duty to express my gratitude to the President of the District Zemstvo of N——, Kuznetsov, for his kind co-operation.' There is a brilliant future before statistics! My humble respects to Vera Gavrilovna, and tell the doctors, both the lawyers and your secretary, that I shall never forget their help! And now, old fellow, let us embrace one another and kiss for the last time!"

Ognev, limp with emotion, kissed the old man once more and began going down the steps. On the last step he looked round and asked: "Shall we meet again some day?"

"God knows!" said the old man. "Most likely not!"

"Yes, that's true! Nothing will tempt you to Petersburg and I am never likely to turn up in this district again. Well, good-bye!"

"You had better leave the books behind!" Kuznetsov called after him. "You don't want to drag such a weight with you. I would send them by a servant tomorrow!"

But Ognev was rapidly walking away from the house and was not listening. His heart, warmed by the wine, was brimming over with good-humour, friendliness, and sadness. He walked along thinking how frequently one met with good people, and what a pity it was that nothing was left of those meetings but memories. At times one catches a glimpse of cranes on the horizon, and a faint gust of wind brings their plaintive, ecstatic cry, and a minute later, however greedily one scans the blue distance, one cannot see a speck nor catch a sound; and like that, people with their faces and their words flit through our lives and are drowned in the past, leaving nothing except faint traces in the memory. Having been in the N——District from the early spring, and having been almost every day at the friendly Kuznetsovs', Ivan Alexeyitch had become as much at home with the old man, his daughter, and the servants as though they were his own people; he had grown familiar with the whole house to the smallest detail, with the cosy verandah, the windings of the avenues, the silhouettes of the trees over the kitchen and the bath-house; but as soon as he was out of the gate all this would be changed to memory and would lose its meaning as reality for ever, and in a year or two all these dear images would grow as dim in his consciousness as stories he had read or things he had imagined.

"Nothing in life is so precious as people!" Ognev thought in his emotion, as he strode along the avenue to the gate. "Nothing!"

It was warm and still in the garden. There was a scent of the mignonette, of the tobacco-plants, and of the heliotrope, which were not yet over in the flower-beds. The spaces between the bushes and the tree-trunks were filled with a fine soft mist soaked through and through with moonlight, and, as Ognev long remembered, coils of mist that looked like phantoms slowly but perceptibly followed one another across the avenue. The moon stood high above the garden, and below it transparent patches of mist were floating eastward. The whole world seemed to consist of nothing but black silhouettes and wandering white shadows. Ognev, seeing the mist on a moonlight August evening almost for the first time in his life, imagined he was seeing, not nature, but a stage effect in which unskilful workmen, trying to light up the garden with white Bengal fire, hid behind the bushes and let off clouds of white smoke together with the light.

When Ognev reached the garden gate a dark shadow moved away from the low fence and came towards him.

"Vera Gavrilovna!" he said, delighted. "You here? And I have been looking everywhere for you; wanted to say good-bye.... Good-bye; I am going away!"

"So early? Why, it's only eleven o'clock."

"Yes, it's time I was off. I have a four-mile walk and then my packing. I must be up early tomorrow."

Before Ognev stood Kuznetsov's daughter Vera, a girl of one-and-twenty, as usual melancholy, carelessly dressed, and attractive. Girls who are dreamy and spend whole days lying down, lazily reading whatever they come across, who are bored and melancholy, are usually careless in their dress. To those of them who have been endowed by nature with taste and an instinct of beauty, the slight carelessness adds a special charm. When Ognev later on remembered her, he could not picture pretty Verotchka except in a full blouse which was crumpled in deep folds at the belt and yet did not touch her waist; without her hair done up high and a curl that had come loose from it on her forehead; without the knitted red shawl with ball fringe at the edge which hung disconsolately on Vera's shoulders in the evenings, like a flag on a windless day, and in the daytime lay about, crushed up, in the hall near the men's hats or on a box in the dining-room, where the old cat did not hesitate to sleep on it. This shawl and the folds of her blouse suggested a feeling of freedom and laziness, of good-nature and sitting at home. Perhaps because Vera attracted Ognev he saw in every frill and button something warm, nae, cosy, something nice and poetical, just what is lacking in cold, insincere women that have no instinct for beauty.

Verotchka had a good figure, a regular profile, and beautiful curly hair. Ognev, who had seen few women in his life, thought her a beauty.

"I am going away," he said as he took leave of her at the gate. "Don't remember evil against me! Thank you for everything!"

In the same singing divinity student's voice in which he had talked to her father, with the same blinking and twitching of his shoulders, he began thanking Vera for her hospitality, kindness, and friendliness.

"I've written about you in every letter to my mother," he said. "If everyone were like you and your dad, what a jolly place the world would be! You are such a splendid set of people! All such genuine, friendly people with no nonsense about you."

"Where are you going to now?" asked Vera.

"I am going now to my mother's at Oryol; I shall be a fortnight with her, and then back to Petersburg and work."

"And then?"

"And then? I shall work all the winter and in the spring go somewhere into the provinces again to collect material. Well, be happy, live a hundred years... don't remember evil against me. We shall not see each other again."

Ognev stooped down and kissed Vera's hand. Then, in silent emotion, he straightened his cape, shifted his bundle of books to a more comfortable position, paused, and said: "What a lot of mist!"

"Yes. Have you left anything behind?"

"No, I don't think so...."

For some seconds Ognev stood in silence, then he moved clumsily towards the gate and went out of the garden.

"Stay; I'll see you as far as our wood," said Vera, following him out.

They walked along the road. Now the trees did not obscure the view, and one could see the sky and the distance. As though covered with a veil all nature was hidden in a transparent, colourless haze through which her beauty peeped gaily; where the mist was thicker and whiter it lay heaped unevenly about the stones, stalks, and bushes or drifted in coils over the road, clung close to the earth and seemed trying not to conceal the view. Through the haze they could see all the road as far as the wood, with dark ditches at the sides and tiny bushes which grew in the ditches and caught the straying wisps of mist. Half a mile from the gate they saw the dark patch of Kuznetsov's wood.

"Why has she come with me? I shall have to see her back," thought Ognev, but looking at her profile he gave a friendly smile and said: "One doesn't want to go away in such lovely weather. It's quite a romantic evening, with the moon, the stillness, and all the etceteras. Do you know, Vera Gavrilovna, here I have lived twenty-nine years in the world and never had a romance. No romantic episode in my whole life, so that I only know by hearsay of rendezvous, 'avenues of sighs,' and kisses. It's not normal! In town, when one sits in one's lodgings, one does not notice the blank, but here in the fresh air one feels it.... One resents it!"

"Why is it?"

"I don't know. I suppose I've never had time, or perhaps it was I have never met women who.... In fact, I have very few acquaintances and never go anywhere."

For some three hundred paces the young people walked on in silence.

Ognev kept glancing at Verotchka's bare head and shawl, and days of spring and summer rose to his mind one after another. It had been a period when far from his grey Petersburg lodgings, enjoying the friendly warmth of kind people, nature, and the work he loved, he had not had time to notice how the sunsets followed the glow of dawn, and how, one after another foretelling the end of summer, first the nightingale ceased singing, then the quail, then a little later the landrail. The days slipped by unnoticed, so that life must have been happy and easy. He began calling aloud how reluctantly he, poor and unaccustomed to change of scene and society, had come at the end of April to the N—District, where he had expected dreariness, loneliness, and indifference to statistics, which he considered was now the foremost among the sciences. When he arrived on an April morning at the little town of N—he had put up at the inn kept by Ryabuhin, the Old Believer, where for twenty kopecks a day they had given him a light, clean room on condition that he should not smoke indoors. After resting and finding who was the president of the District Zemstvo, he had set off at once on foot to Kuznetsov. He had to walk three miles through lush meadows and young copses. Larks were hovering in the clouds, filling the air with silvery notes, and rooks flapping their wings with sedate dignity floated over the green cornland.

"Good heavens!" Ognev had thought in wonder; "can it be that there's always air like this to breathe here, or is this scent only today, in honour of my coming?"

Expecting a cold business-like reception, he went in to Kuznetsov's diffidently, looking up from under his eyebrows and shyly pulling his beard. At first Kuznetsov wrinkled up his brows and could not understand what use the Zemstvo could be to the young man and his statistics; but when the latter explained at length what was material for statistics and how such material was collected, Kuznetsov brightened, smiled, and with childish curiosity began looking at his notebooks. On the evening of the same day Ivan Alexeyitch was already sitting at supper with the Kuznetsovs, was rapidly becoming exhilarated by their strong home-made wine, and looking at the calm faces and lazy movements of his new acquaintances, felt all over that sweet, drowsy indolence which makes one want to sleep and stretch and smile; while his new acquaintances looked at him good-naturedly and asked him whether his father and mother were living, how much he earned a month, how often he went to the theatre....

Ognev recalled his expeditions about the neighbourhood, the picnics, the fishing parties, the visit of the whole party to the convent to see the Mother Superior Marfa, who had given each of the visitors a bead purse; he recalled the hot, endless typically Russian arguments in which the opponents, spluttering and banging the table with their fists, misunderstand and interrupt one another, unconsciously contradict themselves at every phrase, continually change the subject, and after arguing for two or three hours, laugh and say: "Goodness knows what we have been arguing about! Beginning with one thing and going on to another!"

"And do you remember how the doctor and you and I rode to Shestovo?" said Ivan Alexeyitch to Vera as they reached the copse. "It was there that the crazy saint met us: I gave him a five-kopeck piece, and he crossed himself three times and flung it into the rye. Good heavens! I am carrying away such a mass of memories that if I could gather them together into a whole it would make a good nugget of gold! I don't understand why clever, perceptive people crowd into Petersburg and Moscow and don't come here. Is there more truth and freedom in the Nevsky and in the big damp houses than here? Really, the idea of artists, scientific men, and journalists all living crowded together in furnished rooms has always seemed to me a mistake."

Twenty paces from the copse the road was crossed by a small narrow bridge with posts at the corners, which had always served as a resting-place for the Kuznetsovs and their guests on their evening walks. From there those who liked could mimic the forest echo, and one could see the road vanish in the dark woodland track.

"Well, here is the bridge!" said Ognev. "Here you must turn back."

Vera stopped and drew a breath.

"Let us sit down," she said, sitting down on one of the posts. "People generally sit down when they say good-bye before starting on a journey."

Ognev settled himself beside her on his bundle of books and went on talking. She was breathless from the walk, and was looking, not at Ivan Alexeyitch, but away into the distance so that he could not see her face.

"And what if we meet in ten years' time?" he said. "What shall we be like then? You will be by then the respectable mother of a family, and I shall be the author of some weighty statistical work of no use to anyone, as thick as forty thousand such works. We shall meet and think of old days.... Now we are conscious of the present; it absorbs and excites us, but when we meet we shall not remember the day, nor the month, nor even the year in which we saw each other for the last time on this bridge. You will be changed, perhaps .... Tell me, will you be different?"

Vera started and turned her face towards him.

"What?" she asked.

"I asked you just now...."

"Excuse me, I did not hear what you were saying."

Only then Ognev noticed a change in Vera. She was pale, breathing fast, and the tremor in her breathing affected her hands and lips and head, and not one curl as usual, but two, came loose and fell on her forehead.... Evidently she avoided looking him in the face, and, trying to mask her emotion, at one moment fingered her collar, which seemed to be rasping her neck, at another pulled her red shawl from one shoulder to the other.

"I am afraid you are cold," said Ognev. "It's not at all wise to sit in the mist. Let me see you back _nach-haus_."

Vera sat mute.

"What is the matter?" asked Ognev, with a smile. "You sit silent and don't answer my questions. Are you cross, or don't you feel well?"

Vera pressed the palm of her hand to the cheek nearest to Ognev, and then abruptly jerked it away.

"An awful position!" she murmured, with a look of pain on her face. "Awful!"

"How is it awful?" asked Ognev, shrugging his shoulders and not concealing his surprise. "What's the matter?"

Still breathing hard and twitching her shoulders, Vera turned her back to him, looked at the sky for half a minute, and said: "There is something I must say to you, Ivan Alexeyitch...."

"I am listening."

"It may seem strange to you.... You will be surprised, but I don't care...."

Ognev shrugged his shoulders once more and prepared himself to listen.

"You see..." Verotchka began, bowing her head and fingering a ball on the fringe of her shawl. "You see... this is what I wanted to tell you.... You'll think it strange... and silly, but I... can't bear it any longer."

Vera's words died away in an indistinct mutter and were suddenly cut short by tears. The girl hid her face in her handkerchief, bent lower than ever, and wept bitterly. Ivan Alexeyitch cleared his throat in confusion and looked about him hopelessly, at his wits' end, not knowing what to say or do. Being unused to the sight of tears, he felt his own eyes, too, beginning to smart.

"Well, what next!" he muttered helplessly. "Vera Gavrilovna, what's this for, I should like to know? My dear girl, are you... are you ill? Or has someone been nasty to you? Tell me, perhaps I could, so to say... help you...."

When, trying to console her, he ventured cautiously to remove her hands from her face, she smiled at him through her tears and said: "I... love you!"

These words, so simple and ordinary, were uttered in ordinary human language, but Ognev, in acute embarrassment, turned away from Vera, and got up, while his confusion was followed by terror. The sad, warm, sentimental mood induced by leave-taking and the home-made wine suddenly vanished, and gave place to an acute and unpleasant feeling of awkwardness. He felt an inward revulsion; he looked askance at Vera, and now that by declaring her love for him she had cast off the aloofness which so adds to a woman's charm, she seemed to him, as it were, shorter, plainer, more ordinary.

"What's the meaning of it?" he thought with horror. "But I... do I love her or not? That's the question!"

And she breathed easily and freely now that the worst and most difficult thing was said. She, too, got up, and looking Ivan Alexeyitch straight in the face, began talking rapidly, warmly, irrepressibly.

As a man suddenly panic-stricken cannot afterwards remember the succession of sounds accompanying the catastrophe that overwhelmed him, so Ognev cannot remember Vera's words and phrases. He can only recall the meaning of what she said, and the sensation her words evoked in him. He remembers her voice, which seemed stifled and husky with emotion, and the extraordinary music and passion of her intonation. Laughing, crying with tears glistening on her eyelashes, she told him that from the first day of their acquaintance he had struck her by his originality, his intelligence, his kind intelligent eyes, by his work and objects in life; that she loved him passionately, deeply, madly; that when coming into the house from the garden in the summer she saw his cape in the hall or heard his voice in the distance, she felt a cold shudder at her heart, a foreboding of happiness; even his slightest jokes had made her laugh; in every figure in his note-books she saw something extraordinarily wise and grand; his knotted stick seemed to her more beautiful than the trees.

The copse and the wisps of mist and the black ditches at the side of the road seemed hushed listening to her, whilst something strange and unpleasant was passing in Ognev's heart.... Telling him of her love, Vera was enchantingly beautiful; she spoke eloquently and passionately, but he felt neither pleasure nor gladness, as he would have liked to; he felt nothing but compassion for Vera, pity and regret that a good girl should be distressed on his account. Whether he was affected by generalizations from reading or by the insuperable habit of looking at things objectively, which so often hinders people from living, but Vera's ecstasies and suffering struck him as affected, not to be taken seriously, and at the same time rebellious feeling whispered to him that all he was hearing and seeing now, from the point of view of nature and personal happiness, was more important than any statistics and books and truths.... And he raged and blamed himself, though he did not understand exactly where he was in fault.

To complete his embarrassment, he was absolutely at a loss what to say, and yet something he must say. To say bluntly, "I don't love you," was beyond him, and he could not bring himself to say "Yes," because however much he rummaged in his heart he could not find one spark of feeling in it....

He was silent, and she meanwhile was saying that for her there was no greater happiness than to see him, to follow him wherever he liked this very moment, to be his wife and helper, and that if he went away from her she would die of misery.

"I cannot stay here!" she said, wringing her hands. "I am sick of the house and this wood and the air. I cannot bear the everlasting peace and aimless life, I can't endure our colourless, pale people, who are all as like one another as two drops of water! They are all good-natured and warm-hearted because they are all well-fed and know nothing of struggle or suffering,... I want to be in those big damp houses where people suffer, embittered by work and need..."

And this, too, seemed to Ognev affected and not to be taken seriously. When Vera had finished he still did not know what to say, but it was impossible to be silent, and he muttered: "Vera Gavrilovna, I am very grateful to you, though I feel I've done nothing to deserve such... feeling... on your part. Besides, as an honest man I ought to tell you that... happiness depends on equality—that is, when both parties are... equally in love...."

But he was immediately ashamed of his mutterings and ceased. He felt that his face at that moment looked stupid, guilty, blank, that it was strained and affected.... Vera must have been able to read the truth on his countenance, for she suddenly became grave, turned pale, and bent her head.

"You must forgive me," Ognev muttered, not able to endure the silence. "I respect you so much that... it pains me...."

Vera turned sharply and walked rapidly homewards. Ognev followed her.

"No, don't!" said Vera, with a wave of her hand. "Don't come; I can go alone."

"Oh, yes... I must see you home anyway."

Whatever Ognev said, it all to the last word struck him as loathsome and flat. The feeling of guilt grew greater at every step. He raged inwardly, clenched his fists, and cursed his coldness and his stupidity with women. Trying to stir his feelings, he looked at Verotchka's beautiful figure, at her hair and the traces of her little feet on the dusty road; he remembered her words and her tears, but all that only touched his heart and did not quicken his pulse.

"Ach! one can't force oneself to love," he assured himself, and at the same time he thought, "But shall I ever fall in love without? I am nearly thirty! I have never met anyone better than Vera and I never shall.... Oh, this premature old age! Old age at thirty!"

Vera walked on in front more and more rapidly, without looking back at him or raising her head. It seemed to him that sorrow had made her thinner and narrower in the shoulders.

"I can imagine what's going on in her heart now!" he thought, looking at her back. "She must be ready to die with shame and mortification! My God, there's so much life, poetry, and meaning in it that it would move a stone, and I... I am stupid and absurd!"

At the gate Vera stole a glance at him, and, shrugging and wrapping her shawl round her walked rapidly away down the avenue.

Ivan Alexeyitch was left alone. Going back to the copse, he walked slowly, continually standing still and looking round at the gate with an expression in his whole figure that suggested that he could not believe his own memory. He looked for Vera's footprints on the road, and could not believe that the girl who had so attracted him had just declared her love, and that he had so clumsily and bluntly "refused" her. For the first time in his life it was his lot to learn by experience how little that a man does depends on his own will, and to suffer in his own person the feelings of a decent kindly man who has against his will caused his neighbour cruel, undeserved anguish.

His conscience tormented him, and when Vera disappeared he felt as though he had lost something very precious, something very near and dear which he could never find again. He felt that with Vera a part of his youth had slipped away from him, and that the moments which he had passed through so fruitlessly would never be repeated.

When he reached the bridge he stopped and sank into thought. He wanted to discover the reason of his strange coldness. That it was due to something within him and not outside himself was clear to him. He frankly acknowledged to himself that it was not the intellectual coldness of which clever people so often boast, not the coldness of a conceited fool, but simply impotence of soul, incapacity for being moved by beauty, premature old age brought on by education, his casual existence, struggling for a livelihood, his homeless life in lodgings. From the bridge he walked slowly, as it were reluctantly, into the wood. Here, where in the dense black darkness glaring patches of moonlight gleamed here and there, where he felt nothing except his thoughts, he longed passionately to regain what he had lost.

And Ivan Alexeyitch remembers that he went back again. Urging himself on with his memories, forcing himself to picture Vera, he strode rapidly towards the garden. There was no mist by then along the road or in the garden, and the bright moon looked down from the sky as though it had just been washed; only the eastern sky was dark and misty.... Ognev remembers his cautious steps, the dark windows, the heavy scent of heliotrope and mignonette. His old friend Karo, wagging his tail amicably, came up to him and sniffed his hand. This was the one living creature who saw him walk two or three times round the house, stand near Vera's dark window, and with a deep sigh and a wave of his hand walk out of the garden.

An hour later he was in the town, and, worn out and exhausted, leaned his body and hot face against the gatepost of the inn as he knocked at the gate. Somewhere in the town a dog barked sleepily, and as though in response to his knock, someone clanged the hour on an iron plate near the church.

"You prowl about at night," grumbled his host, the Old Believer, opening the door to him, in a long nightgown like a woman's. "You had better be saying your prayers instead of prowling about."

When Ivan Alexeyitch reached his room he sank on the bed and gazed a long, long time at the light. Then he tossed his head and began packing.

NEIGHBOURS

PYOTR MIHALITCH IVASHIN was very much out of humour: his sister, a young girl, had gone away to live with Vlassitch, a married man. To shake off the despondency and depression which pursued him at home and in the fields, he called to his aid his sense of justice, his genuine and noble ideas—he had always defended free-love! —but this was of no avail, and he always came back to the same conclusion as their foolish old nurse, that his sister had acted wrongly and that Vlassitch had abducted his sister. And that was distressing.

His mother did not leave her room all day long; the old nurse kept sighing and speaking in whispers; his aunt had been on the point of taking her departure every day, and her trunks were continually being brought down to the hall and carried up again to her room. In the house, in the yard, and in the garden it was as still as though there were some one dead in the house. His aunt, the servants, and even the peasants, so it seemed to Pyotr Mihalitch, looked at him enigmatically and with perplexity, as though they wanted to say "Your sister has been seduced; why are you doing nothing?" And he reproached himself for inactivity, though he did not know precisely what action he ought to have taken.

So passed six days. On the seventh—it was Sunday afternoon—a messenger on horseback brought a letter. The address was in a familiar feminine handwriting: "Her Excy. Anna Nikolaevna Ivashin." Pyotr Mihalitch fancied that there was something defiant, provocative, in the handwriting and in the abbreviation "Excy." And advanced ideas in women are obstinate, ruthless, cruel.

"She'd rather die than make any concession to her unhappy mother, or beg her forgiveness," thought Pyotr Mihalitch, as he went to his mother with the letter.

His mother was lying on her bed, dressed. Seeing her son, she rose impulsively, and straightening her grey hair, which had fallen from under her cap, asked quickly: "What is it? What is it?"

"This has come..." said her son, giving her the letter.

Zina's name, and even the pronoun "she" was not uttered in the house. Zina was spoken of impersonally: "this has come," "Gone away," and so on.... The mother recognised her daughter's handwriting, and her face grew ugly and unpleasant, and her grey hair escaped again from her cap.

"No!" she said, with a motion of her hands, as though the letter scorched her fingers. "No, no, never! Nothing would induce me!"

The mother broke into hysterical sobs of grief and shame; she evidently longed to read the letter, but her pride prevented her. Pyotr Mihalitch realised that he ought to open the letter himself and read it aloud, but he was overcome by anger such as he had never felt before; he ran out into the yard and shouted to the messenger: "Say there will be no answer! There will be no answer! Tell them that, you beast!"

And he tore up the letter; then tears came into his eyes, and feeling that he was cruel, miserable, and to blame, he went out into the fields.

He was only twenty-seven, but he was already stout. He dressed like an old man in loose, roomy clothes, and suffered from asthma. He already seemed to be developing the characteristics of an elderly country bachelor. He never fell in love, never thought of marriage, and loved no one but his mother, his sister, his old nurse, and the gardener, Vassilitch. He was fond of good fare, of his nap after dinner, and of talking about politics and exalted subjects. He had in his day taken his degree at the university, but he now looked upon his studies as though in them he had discharged a duty incumbent upon young men between the ages of eighteen and twenty-five; at any rate, the ideas which now strayed every day through his mind had nothing in common with the university or the subjects he had studied there.

In the fields it was hot and still, as though rain were coming. It was steaming in the wood, and there was a heavy fragrant scent from the pines and rotting leaves. Pyotr Mihalitch stopped several times and wiped his wet brow. He looked at his winter corn and his spring oats, walked round the clover-field, and twice drove away a partridge with its chicks which had strayed in from the wood. And all the while he was thinking that this insufferable state of things could not go on for ever, and that he must end it one way or another. End it stupidly, madly, but he must end it.

"But how? What can I do?" he asked himself, and looked imploringly at the sky and at the trees, as though begging for their help.

But the sky and the trees were mute. His noble ideas were no help, and his common sense whispered that the agonising question could have no solution but a stupid one, and that today's scene with the messenger was not the last one of its kind. It was terrible to think what was in store for him!

As he returned home the sun was setting. By now it seemed to him that the problem was incapable of solution. He could not accept the accomplished fact, and he could not refuse to accept it, and there was no intermediate course. When, taking off his hat and fanning himself with his handkerchief, he was walking along the road, and had only another mile and a half to go before he would reach home, he heard bells behind him. It was a very choice and successful combination of bells, which gave a clear crystal note. No one had such bells on his horses but the police captain, Medovsky, formerly an officer in the hussars, a man in broken-down health, who had been a great rake and spendthrift, and was a distant relation of Pyotr Mihalitch. He was like one of the family at the Ivashins' and had a tender, fatherly affection for Zina, as well as a great admiration for her.

"I was coming to see you," he said, overtaking Pyotr Mihalitch. "Get in; I'll give you a lift."

He was smiling and looked cheerful. Evidently he did not yet know that Zina had gone to live with Vlassitch; perhaps he had been told of it already, but did not believe it. Pyotr Mihalitch felt in a difficult position.

"You are very welcome," he muttered, blushing till the tears came into his eyes, and not knowing how to lie or what to say. "I am delighted," he went on, trying to smile, "but... Zina is away and mother is ill."

"How annoying!" said the police captain, looking pensively at Pyotr

Mihalitch. "And I was meaning to spend the evening with you. Where has Zinaida Mihalovna gone?"

"To the Sinitskys', and I believe she meant to go from there to the monastery. I don't quite know."

The police captain talked a little longer and then turned back. Pyotr Mihalitch walked home, and thought with horror what the police captain's feelings would be when he learned the truth. And Pyotr Mihalitch imagined his feelings, and actually experiencing them himself, went into the house.

"Lord help us," he thought, "Lord help us!"

At evening tea the only one at the table was his aunt. As usual, her face wore the expression that seemed to say that though she was a weak, defenceless woman, she would allow no one to insult her. Pyotr Mihalitch sat down at the other end of the table (he did not like his aunt) and began drinking tea in silence.

"Your mother has had no dinner again today," said his aunt. "You ought to do something about it, Petrusha. Starving oneself is no help in sorrow."

It struck Pyotr Mihalitch as absurd that his aunt should meddle in other people's business and should make her departure depend on Zina's having gone away. He was tempted to say something rude to her, but restrained himself. And as he restrained himself he felt the time had come for action, and that he could not bear it any longer. Either he must act at once or fall on the ground, and scream and bang his head upon the floor. He pictured Vlassitch and Zina, both of them progressive and self-satisfied, kissing each other somewhere under a maple tree, and all the anger and bitterness that had been accumulating in him for the last seven days fastened upon Vlassitch.

"One has seduced and abducted my sister," he thought, "another will come and murder my mother, a third will set fire to the house and sack the place.... And all this under the mask of friendship, lofty ideas, unhappiness!"

"No, it shall not be!" Pyotr Mihalitch cried suddenly, and he brought his fist down on the table.

He jumped up and ran out of the dining-room. In the stable the steward's horse was standing ready saddled. He got on it and galloped off to Vlassitch.

There was a perfect tempest within him. He felt a longing to do something extraordinary, startling, even if he had to repent of it all his life afterwards. Should he call Vlassitch a blackguard, slap him in the face, and then challenge him to a duel? But Vlassitch was not one of those men who do fight duels; being called a blackguard and slapped in the face would only make him more unhappy, and would make him shrink into himself more than ever. These unhappy, defenceless people are the most insufferable, the most tiresome creatures in the world. They can do anything with impunity. When the luckless man responds to well-deserved reproach by looking at you with eyes full of deep and guilty feeling, and with a sickly smile bends his head submissively, even justice itself could not lift its hand against him.

"No matter. I' ll horsewhip him before her eyes and tell him what I think of him," Pyotr Mihalitch decided.

He was riding through his wood and waste land, and he imagined Zina would try to justify her conduct by talking about the rights of women and individual freedom, and about there being no difference between legal marriage and free union. Like a woman, she would argue about what she did not understand. And very likely at the end she would ask, "How do you come in? What right have you to interfere?"

"No, I have no right," muttered Pyotr Mihalitch. "But so much the better.... The harsher I am, the less right I have to interfere, the better."

It was sultry. Clouds of gnats hung over the ground and in the waste places the peewits called plaintively. Everything betokened rain, but he could not see a cloud in the sky. Pyotr Mihalitch crossed the boundary of his estate and galloped over a smooth, level field. He often went along this road and knew every bush, every hollow in it. What now in the far distance looked in the dusk like a dark cliff was a red church; he could picture it all down to the smallest detail, even the plaster on the gate and the calves that were always grazing in the church enclosure. Three-quarters of a mile to the right of the church there was a copse like a dark blur—it was Count Koltonovitch's. And beyond the church Vlassitch's estate began.

From behind the church and the count's copse a huge black storm-loud was rising, and there were ashes of white lightning.

"Here it is!" thought Pyotr Mihalitch. "Lord help us, Lord help us!"

The horse was soon tired after its quick gallop, and Pyotr Mihalitch was tired too. The storm-cloud looked at him angrily and seemed to advise him to go home. He felt a little scared.

"I will prove to them they are wrong," he tried to reassure himself. "They will say that it is free-love, individual freedom; but freedom means self-control and not subjection to passion. It's not liberty but license!"

He reached the count's big pond; it looked dark blue and frowning under the cloud, and a smell of damp and slime rose from it. Near the dam, two willows, one old and one young, drooped tenderly towards one another. Pyotr Mihalitch and Vlassitch had been walking near this very spot only a fortnight before, humming a students' song: "Youth is wasted, life is nought, when the heart is cold and loveless." A wretched song!

It was thundering as Pyotr Mihalitch rode through the copse, and the trees were bending and rustling in the wind. He had to make haste. It was only three-quarters of a mile through a meadow from the copse to Vlassitch's house. Here there were old birch-trees on each side of the road. They had the same melancholy and unhappy air as their owner Vlassitch, and looked as tall and lanky as he. Big drops of rain pattered on the birches and on the grass; the wind had suddenly dropped, and there was a smell of wet earth and poplars. Before him he saw Vlassitch's fence with a row of yellow acacias, which were tall and lanky too; where the fence was broken he could see the neglected orchard.

Pyotr Mihalitch was not thinking now of the horsewhip or of a slap in the face, and did not know what he would do at Vlassitch's. He felt nervous. He felt frightened on his own account and on his sister's, and was terrified at the thought of seeing her. How would she behave with her brother? What would they both talk about? And had he not better go back before it was too late? As he made these reflections, he galloped up the avenue of lime-trees to the house, rode round the big clumps of lilacs, and suddenly saw Vlassitch.

Vlassitch, wearing a cotton shirt, and top-boots, bending forward, with no hat on in the rain, was coming from the corner of the house to the front door. He was followed by a workman with a hammer and a box of nails. They must have been mending a shutter which had been banging in the wind. Seeing Pyotr Mihalitch, Vlassitch stopped.

"It's you!" he said, smiling. "That's nice."

"Yes, I've come, as you see," said Pyotr Mihalitch, brushing the rain off himself with both hands.

"Well, that's capital! I'm very glad," said Vlassitch, but he did not hold out his hand: evidently he did not venture, but waited for Pyotr Mihalitch to hold out his. "It will do the oats good," he said, looking at the sky.

"Yes."

They went into the house in silence. To the right of the hall was a door leading to another hall and then to the drawing-room, and on the left was a little room which in winter was used by the steward. Pyotr Mihalitch and Vlassitch went into this little room.

"Where were you caught in the rain?"

"Not far off, quite close to the house."

Pyotr Mihalitch sat down on the bed. He was glad of the noise of the rain and the darkness of the room. It was better: it made it less dreadful, and there was no need to see his companion's face. There was no anger in his heart now, nothing but fear and vexation with himself. He felt he had made a bad beginning, and that nothing would come of this visit.

Both were silent for some time and affected to be listening to the rain.

"Thank you, Petrusha," Vlassitch began, clearing his throat. "I am very grateful to you for coming. It's generous and noble of you. I understand it, and, believe me, I appreciate it. Believe me."

He looked out of the window and went on, standing in the middle of the room: "Everything happened so secretly, as though we were concealing it all from you. The feeling that you might be wounded and angry has been a blot on our happiness all these days. But let me justify myself. We kept it secret not because we did not trust you. To begin with, it all happened suddenly, by a kind of inspiration; there was no time to discuss it. Besides, it's such a private, delicate matter, and it was awkward to bring a third person in, even some one as intimate as you. Above all, in all this we reckoned on your generosity. You are a very noble and generous person. I am infinitely grateful to you. If you ever need my life, come and take it."

Vlassitch talked in a quiet, hollow bass, always on the same droning note; he was evidently agitated. Pyotr Mihalitch felt it was his turn to speak, and that to listen and keep silent would really mean playing the part of a generous and noble simpleton, and that had not been his idea in coming. He got up quickly and said, breathlessly in an undertone: "Listen, Grigory. You know I liked you and could have desired no better husband for my sister; but what has happened is awful! It's terrible to think of it!"

"Why is it terrible?" asked Vlassitch, with a quiver in his voice. "It would be terrible if we had done wrong, but that isn't so."

"Listen, Grigory. You know I have no prejudices; but, excuse my frankness, to my mind you have both acted selfishly. Of course, I shan't say so to my sister—it will distress her; but you ought to know: mother is miserable beyond all description."

"Yes, that's sad," sighed Vlassitch. "We foresaw that, Petrusha, but what could we have done? Because one's actions hurt other people, it doesn't prove that they are wrong. What's to be done! Every important step one takes is bound to distress somebody. If you went to fight for freedom, that would distress your mother, too. What's to be done! Any one who puts the peace of his family before everything has to renounce the life of ideas completely."

There was a vivid flash of lightning at the window, and the lightning seemed to change the course of Vlassitch's thoughts. He sat down beside Pyotr Mihalitch and began saying what was utterly beside the point.

"I have such a reverence for your sister, Petrusha," he said. "When I used to come and see you, I felt as though I were going to a holy shrine, and I really did worship Zina. Now my reverence for her grows every day. For me she is something higher than a wife—yes, higher!" Vlassitch waved his hands. "She is my holy of holies. Since she is living with me, I enter my house as though it were a temple. She is an extraordinary, rare, most noble woman!"

"Well, he's off now!" thought Pyotr Mihalitch; he disliked the word "woman."

"Why shouldn't you be married properly?" he asked. "How much does your wife want for a divorce?"

"Seventy-five thousand."

"It's rather a lot. But if we were to negotiate with her?"

"She won't take a farthing less. She is an awful woman, brother," sighed Vlassitch. "I've never talked to you about her before—it was unpleasant to think of her; but now that the subject has come up, I'll tell you about her. I married her on the impulse of the moment—a fine, honourable impulse. An officer in command of a battalion of our regiment—if you care to hear the details—had an affair with a girl of eighteen; that is, to put it plainly, he seduced her, lived with her for two months, and abandoned her. She was in an awful position, brother. She was ashamed to go home to her parents; besides, they wouldn't have received her. Her lover had abandoned her; there was nothing left for her but to go to the barracks and sell herself. The other officers in the regiment were indignant. They were by no means saints themselves, but the baseness of it was so striking. Besides, no one in the regiment could endure the man. And to spite him, you understand, the indignant lieutenants and ensigns began getting up a subscription for the unfortunate girl. And when we subalterns met together and began to subscribe five or ten roubles each, I had a sudden inspiration. I felt it was an opportunity to do something fine. I hastened to the girl and warmly expressed my sympathy. And while I was on my way to her, and while I was talking to her, I loved her fervently as a woman insulted and injured.

Yes.... Well, a week later I made her an offer. The colonel and my comrades thought my marriage out of keeping with the dignity of an officer. That roused me more than ever. I wrote a long letter, do you know, in which I proved that my action ought to be inscribed in the annals of the regiment in letters of gold, and so on. I sent the letter to my colonel and copies to my comrades. Well, I was excited, and, of course, I could not avoid being rude. I was asked to leave the regiment. I have a rough copy of it put away somewhere; I'll give it to you to read sometime. It was written with great feeling. You will see what lofty and noble sentiments I was experiencing. I resigned my commission and came here with my wife. My father had left a few debts, I had no money, and from the first day my wife began making acquaintances, dressing herself smartly, and playing cards, and I was obliged to mortgage the estate. She led a bad life, you understand, and you are the only one of the neighbours who hasn't been her lover. After two years I gave her all I had to set me free and she went off to town. Yes.... And now I pay her twelve hundred roubles a year. She is an awful woman! There is a fly, brother, which lays an egg in the back of a spider so that the spider can't shake it off: the grub fastens upon the spider and drinks its heart's blood. That was how this woman fastened upon me and sucks the blood of my heart. She hates and despises me for being so stupid; that is, for marrying a woman like her. My chivalry seems to her despicable. 'A wise man cast me off,' she says, 'and a fool picked me up.' To her thinking no one but a pitiful idiot could have behaved as I did. And that is insufferably bitter to me, brother. Altogether, I may say in parenthesis, fate has been hard upon me, very hard."

Pyotr Mihalitch listened to Vlassitch and wondered in perplexity what it was in this man that had so charmed his sister. He was not young—he was forty-one—lean and lanky, narrow-chested, with a long nose, and grey hairs in his beard. He talked in a droning voice, had a sickly smile, and waved his hands awkwardly as he talked. He had neither health, nor pleasant, manly manners, nor _savoir-faire_, nor gaiety, and in all his exterior there was something colourless and indefinite. He dressed without taste, his surroundings were depressing, he did not care for poetry or painting because "they have no answer to give to the questions of the day" —that is, he did not understand them; music did not touch him. He was a poor farmer. His estate was in a wretched condition and was mortgaged; he was paying twelve percent on the second mortgage and owed ten thousand on personal securities as well. When the time came to pay the interest on the mortgage or to send money to his wife, he asked every one to lend him money with as much agitation as though his house were on fire, and, at the same time losing his head, he would sell the whole of his winter store of fuel for five roubles and a stack of straw for three roubles, and then have his garden fence or old cucumber-frames chopped up to heat his stoves. His meadows were ruined by pigs, the peasants' cattle strayed in the undergrowth in his woods, and every year the old trees were fewer and fewer: beehives and rusty pails lay about in his garden and kitchen-garden. He had neither talents nor abilities, nor even ordinary capacity for living like other people. In practical life he was a weak, nae man, easy to deceive and to cheat, and the peasants with good reason called him "simple."

He was a Liberal, and in the district was regarded as a "Red," but even his progressiveness was a bore. There was no originality nor moving power about his independent views: he was revolted, indignant, and delighted always on the same note; it was always spiritless and ineffective. Even in moments of strong enthusiasm he never raised his head or stood upright. But the most tiresome thing of all was that he managed to express even his best and finest ideas so that they seemed in him commonplace and out of date. It reminded one of something old one had read long ago, when slowly and with an air of profundity he would begin discoursing of his noble, lofty moments, of his best years; or when he went into raptures over the younger generation, which has always been, and still is, in advance of society; or abused Russians for donning their dressing-gowns at thirty and forgetting the principles of their _alma mater_. If you stayed the night with him, he would put Pissarev or Darwin on your bedroom table; if you said you had read it, he would go and bring Dobrolubov.

In the district this was called free-thinking, and many people looked upon this free-thinking as an innocent and harmless eccentricity; it made him profoundly unhappy, however. It was for him the maggot of which he had just been speaking; it had fastened upon him and was sucking his life-blood. In his past there had been the strange marriage in the style of Dostoevsky; long letters and copies written in a bad, unintelligible handwriting, but with great feeling, endless misunderstandings, explanations, disappointments, then debts, a second mortgage, the allowance to his wife, the monthly borrowing of money—and all this for no benefit to any one, either himself or others. And in the present, as in the past, he was still in a nervous flurry, on the lookout for heroic actions, and poking his nose into other people's affairs; as before, at every favourable opportunity there were long letters and copies, wearisome, stereotyped conversations about the village community, or the revival of handicrafts or the establishment of cheese factories—conversations as like one another as though he had prepared them, not in his living brain, but by some mechanical process. And finally this scandal with Zina of which one could not see the end!

And meanwhile Zina was young—she was only twenty-two—good-looking, elegant, gay; she was fond of laughing, chatter, argument, a passionate musician; she had good taste in dress, in furniture, in books, and in her own home she would not have put up with a room like this, smelling of boots and cheap vodka. She, too, had advanced ideas, but in her free-thinking one felt the overflow of energy, the vanity of a young, strong, spirited girl, passionately eager to be better and more original than others.... How had it happened that she had fallen in love with Vlassitch?

"He is a Quixote, an obstinate fanatic, a maniac," thought Pyotr Mihalitch, "and she is as soft, yielding, and weak in character as I am.... She and I give in easily, without resistance. She loves him; but, then, I, too, love him in spite of everything."

Pyotr Mihalitch considered Vlassitch a good, straightforward man, but narrow and one-sided. In his perturbations and his sufferings, and in fact in his whole life, he saw no lofty aims, remote or immediate; he saw nothing but boredom and incapacity for life. His self-sacrifice and all that Vlassitch himself called heroic actions or noble impulses seemed to him a useless waste of force, unnecessary blank shots which consumed a great deal of powder. And Vlassitch's fanatical belief in the extraordinary loftiness and faultlessness of his own way of thinking struck him as nae and even morbid; and the fact that Vlassitch all his life had contrived to mix the trivial with the exalted, that he had made a stupid marriage and looked upon it as an act of heroism, and then had affairs with other women and regarded that as a triumph of some idea or other was simply incomprehensible.

Nevertheless, Pyotr Mihalitch was fond of Vlassitch; he was conscious of a sort of power in him, and for some reason he had never had the heart to contradict him.

Vlassitch sat down quite close to him for a talk in the dark, to the accompaniment of the rain, and he had cleared his throat as a prelude to beginning on something lengthy, such as the history of his marriage. But it was intolerable for Pyotr Mihalitch to listen to him; he was tormented by the thought that he would see his sister directly.

"Yes, you've had bad luck," he said gently; "but, excuse me, we've been wandering from the point. That's not what we are talking about."

"Yes, yes, quite so. Well, let us come back to the point," said Vlassitch, and he stood up. "I tell you, Petrusha, our conscience is clear. We are not married, but there is no need for me to prove to you that our marriage is perfectly legitimate. You are as free in your ideas as I am, and, happily, there can be no disagreement between us on that point. As for our future, that ought not to alarm you. I' ll work in the sweat of my brow, I' ll work day and night—in fact, I will strain every nerve to make Zina happy. Her life will be a splendid one! You may ask, am I able to do it. I am, brother! When a man devotes every minute to one thought, it's not difficult for him to attain his object. But let us go to Zina; it will be a joy to her to see you."

Pyotr Mihalitch's heart began to beat. He got up and followed Vlassitch into the hall, and from there into the drawing-room. There was nothing in the huge gloomy room but a piano and a long row of old chairs ornamented with bronze, on which no one ever sat. There was a candle alight on the piano. From the drawing-room they went in silence into the dining-room. This room, too, was large and comfortless; in the middle of the room there was a round table with two leaves with six thick legs, and only one candle. A clock in a large mahogany case like an ikon stand pointed to half-past two.

Vlassitch opened the door into the next room and said: "Zina, here is Petrusha come to see us!"

At once there was the sound of hurried footsteps and Zina came into the dining-room. She was tall, plump, and very pale, and, just as when he had seen her for the last time at home, she was wearing a black skirt and a red blouse, with a large buckle on her belt. She flung one arm round her brother and kissed him on the temple.

"What a storm!" she said. "Grigory went off somewhere and I was left quite alone in the house."

She was not embarrassed, and looked at her brother as frankly and candidly as at home; looking at her, Pyotr Mihalitch, too, lost his embarrassment.

"But you are not afraid of storms," he said, sitting down at the table.

"No," she said, " but here the rooms are so big, the house is so old, and when there is thunder it all rattles like a cupboard full of crockery. It's a charming house altogether," she went on, sitting down opposite her brother. "There's some pleasant memory in every room. In my room, only fancy, Grigory's grandfather shot himself."

"In August we shall have the money to do up the lodge in the garden," said Vlassitch.

"For some reason when it thunders I think of that grandfather," Zina went on. "And in this dining-room somebody was flogged to death."

"That's an actual fact," said Vlassitch, and he looked with wideopen eyes at Pyotr Mihalitch. "Sometime in the forties this place was let to a Frenchman called Olivier. The portrait of his daughter is lying in an attic now—a very pretty girl. This Olivier, so my father told me, despised

Russians for their ignorance and treated them with cruel derision. Thus, for instance, he insisted on the priest walking without his hat for half a mile round his house, and on the church bells being rung when the Olivier family drove through the village. The serfs and altogether the humble of this world, of course, he treated with even less ceremony. Once there came along this road one of the simple-hearted sons of wandering Russia, somewhat after the style of Gogol's divinity student, Homa Brut. He asked for a night's lodging, pleased the bailiffs, and was given a job at the office of the estate. There are many variations of the story. Some say the divinity student stirred up the peasants, others that Olivier's daughter fell in love with him. I don't know which is true, only one fine evening Olivier called him in here and cross-examined him, then ordered him to be beaten. Do you know, he sat here at this table drinking claret while the stable-boys beat the man. He must have tried to wring something out of him. Towards morning the divinity student died of the torture and his body was hidden. They say it was thrown into Koltovitch's pond. There was an inquiry, but the Frenchman paid some thousands to some one in authority and went away to Alsace. His lease was up just then, and so the matter ended."

"What scoundrels!" said Zina, shuddering.

"My father remembered Olivier and his daughter well. He used to say she was remarkably beautiful and eccentric. I imagine the divinity student had done both—stirred up the peasants and won the daughter's heart. Perhaps he wasn't a divinity student at all, but some one travelling incognito."

Zina grew thoughtful; the story of the divinity student and the beautiful French girl had evidently carried her imagination far away. It seemed to Pyotr Mihalitch that she had not changed in the least during the last week, except that she was a little paler. She looked calm and just as usual, as though she had come with her brother to visit Vlassitch. But Pyotr Mihalitch felt that some change had taken place in himself. Before, when she was living at home, he could have spoken to her about anything, and now he did not feel equal to asking her the simple question, "How do you like being here?" The question seemed awkward and unnecessary. Probably the same change had taken place in her. She was in no haste to turn the conversation to her mother, to her home, to her relations with Vlassitch; she did not defend herself, she did not say that free unions are better than marriages in the church; she was not agitated, and calmly brooded over the story of Olivier.... And why had they suddenly begun talking of Olivier?

"You are both of you wet with the rain," said Zina, and she smiled joyfully; she was touched by this point of resemblance between her brother and Vlassitch.

And Pyotr Mihalitch felt all the bitterness and horror of his position. He thought of his deserted home, the closed piano, and Zina's bright little room into which no one went now; he thought there were no prints of little feet on the garden-paths, and that before tea no one went off, laughing gaily, to bathe. What he had clung to more and more from his childhood upwards, what he had loved thinking about when he used to sit in the stuffy class-room or the lecture theatre—brightness, purity, and joy, everything that filled the house with life and light, had gone never to return, had vanished, and was mixed up with a coarse, clumsy story of some battalion officer, a chivalrous lieutenant, a depraved woman and a grandfather who had shot himself.... And to begin to talk about his mother or to think that the past could ever return would mean not understanding what was clear.

Pyotr Mihalitch's eyes filled with tears and his hand began to tremble as it lay on the table. Zina guessed what he was thinking about, and her eyes, too, glistened and looked red.

"Grigory, come here," she said to Vlassitch.

They walked away to the window and began talking of something in a whisper. From the way that Vlassitch stooped down to her and the way she looked at him, Pyotr Mihalitch realised again that everything was irreparably over, and that it was no use to talk of anything. Zina went out of the room.

"Well, brother!" Vlassitch began, after a brief silence, rubbing his hands and smiling. "I called our life happiness just now, but that was, so to speak, poetical license. In reality, there has not been a sense of happiness so far. Zina has been thinking all the time of you, of her mother, and has been worrying; looking at her, I, too, felt worried. Hers is a bold, free nature, but, you know, it's difficult when you're not used to it, and she is young, too. The servants call her 'Miss'; it seems a trifle, but it upsets her. There it is, brother."

Zina brought in a plateful of strawberries. She was followed by a little maidservant, looking crushed and humble, who set a jug of milk on the table and made a very low bow: she had something about her that was in keeping with the old furniture, something petrified and dreary.

The sound of the rain had ceased. Pyotr Mihalitch ate strawberries while Vlassitch and Zina looked at him in silence. The moment of the inevitable but useless conversation was approaching, and all three felt the burden of it. Pyotr Mihalitch's eyes filled with tears again; he pushed away his plate and said that he must be going home, or it would be getting late, and perhaps it would rain again. The time had come when common decency required Zina to speak of those at home and of her new life.

"How are things at home?" she asked rapidly, and her pale face quivered. "How is mother?"

"You know mother..." said Pyotr Mihalitch, not looking at her.

"Petrusha, you've thought a great deal about what has happened," she said, taking hold of her brother's sleeve, and he knew how hard it was for her to speak. "You've thought a great deal: tell me, can we reckon on mother's accepting Grigory... and the whole position, one day?"

She stood close to her brother, face to face with him, and he was astonished that she was so beautiful, and that he seemed not to have noticed it before. And it seemed to him utterly absurd that his sister, so like his mother, pampered, elegant, should be living with Vlassitch and in Vlassitch's house, with the petrified servant, and the table with six legs in the house where a man had been flogged to death, and that she was not going home with him, but was staying here to sleep.

"You know mother," he said, not answering her question. "I think you ought to have... to do something, to ask her forgiveness or something...."

"But to ask her forgiveness would mean pretending we had done wrong. I'm ready to tell a lie to comfort mother, but it won't lead anywhere. I know mother. Well, what will be, must be!" said Zina, growing more cheerful now that the most unpleasant had been said. "We'll wait for five years, ten years, and be patient, and then God's will be done."

She took her brother's arm, and when she walked through the dark hall she squeezed close to him. They went out on the steps. Pyotr Mihalitch said good-bye, got on his horse, and set off at a walk; Zina and Vlassitch walked a little way with him. It was still and warm, with a delicious smell of hay; stars were twinkling brightly between the clouds. Vlassitch's old garden, which had seen so many gloomy stories in its time, lay slumbering in the darkness, and for some reason it was mournful riding through it.

"Zina and I today after dinner spent some really exalted moments," said Vlassitch. "I read aloud to her an excellent article on the question of emigration. You must read it, brother! You really must. It's remarkable for its lofty tone. I could not resist writing a letter to the editor to be forwarded to the author. I wrote only a single line: 'I thank you and warmly press your noble hand.'"

Pyotr Mihalitch was tempted to say, "Don't meddle in what does not concern you," but he held his tongue.

Vlassitch walked by his right stirrup and Zina by the left; both seemed to have forgotten that they had to go home. It was damp, and they had almost reached Koltovitch's copse. Pyotr Mihalitch felt that they were expecting something from him, though they hardly knew what it was, and he felt unbearably sorry for them. Now as they walked by the horse with submissive faces, lost in thought, he had a deep conviction that they were unhappy, and could not be happy, and their love seemed to him a melancholy, irreparable mistake. Pity and the sense that he could do nothing to help them reduced him to that state of spiritual softening when he was ready to make any sacrifice to get rid of the painful feeling of sympathy.

"I'll come over sometimes for a night," he said.

But it sounded as though he were making a concession, and did not satisfy him. When they stopped near Koltovitch's copse to say good-bye, he bent down to Zina, touched her shoulder, and said: "You are right, Zina! You have done well." To avoid saying more and bursting into tears, he lashed his horse and galloped into the wood. As he rode into the darkness, he looked round and saw Vlassitch and Zina walking home along the road—he taking long strides, while she walked with a hurried, jerky step beside him—talking eagerly about something.

"I am an old woman!" thought Pyotr Mihalitch. "I went to solve the question and I have only made it more complicated—there it is!"

He was heavy at heart. When he got out of the copse he rode at a walk and then stopped his horse near the pond. He wanted to sit and think without moving. The moon was rising and was reflected in a streak of red on the other side of the pond. There were low rumbles of thunder in the distance. Pyotr Mihalitch looked steadily at the water and imagined his sister's despair, her martyr-like pallor, the tearless eyes with which she would conceal her humiliation from others. He imagined her with child, imagined the death of their mother, her funeral, Zina's horror.... The proud, superstitious old woman would be sure to die of grief. Terrible pictures of the future rose before him on the background of smooth, dark water, and among pale feminine figures he saw himself, a weak, cowardly man with a guilty face.

A hundred paces off on the right bank of the pond, something dark was standing motionless: was it a man or a tall post? Pyotr Mihalitch thought of the divinity student who had been killed and thrown into the pond.

"Olivier behaved inhumanly, but one way or another he did settle the question, while I have settled nothing and have only made it worse," he thought, gazing at the dark figure that looked like a ghost. "He said and did what he thought right while I say and do what I don't think right; and I don't know really what I do think...."

He rode up to the dark figure: it was an old rotten post, the relic of some shed.

From Koltovitch's copse and garden there came a strong fragrant scent of lilies of the valley and honey-laden flowers. Pyotr Mihalitch rode along the bank of the pond and looked mournfully into the water. And thinking about his life, he came to the conclusion he had never said or acted upon what he really thought, and other people had repaid him in the same way. And so the whole of life seemed to him as dark as this water in which the night sky was reflected and water-weeds grew in a tangle. And it seemed to him that nothing could ever set it right.

VANKA

VANKA ZHUKOV, a boy of nine, who had been for three months apprenticed to Alyahin the shoemaker, was sitting up on Christmas Eve. Waiting till his master and mistress and their workmen had gone to the midnight service, he took out of his master's cupboard a bottle of ink and a pen with a rusty nib, and, spreading out a crumpled sheet of paper in front of him, began writing. Before forming the first letter he several times looked round fearfully at the door and the windows, stole a glance at the dark ikon, on both sides of which stretched shelves full of lasts, and heaved a broken sigh. The paper lay on the bench while he knelt before it.

"Dear grandfather, Konstantin Makaritch," he wrote, "I am writing you a letter. I wish you a happy Christmas, and all blessings from God Almighty. I have neither father nor mother, you are the only one left me."

Vanka raised his eyes to the dark ikon on which the light of his candle was reflected, and vividly recalled his grandfather, Konstantin Makaritch, who was night watchman to a family called Zhivarev. He was a thin but extraordinarily nimble and lively little old man of sixty-five, with an everlastingly laughing face and drunken eyes. By day he slept in the servants' kitchen, or made jokes with the cooks; at night, wrapped in an ample sheepskin, he walked round the grounds and tapped with his little mallet. Old Kashtanka and Eel, so-called on account of his dark colour and his long body like a weasel's, followed him with hanging heads. This Eel was exceptionally polite and affectionate, and looked with equal kindness on strangers and his own masters, but had not a very good reputation. Under his politeness and meekness was hidden the most Jesuitical cunning. No one knew better how to creep up on occasion and snap at one's legs, to slip into the store-room, or steal a hen from a peasant. His hind legs had been nearly pulled off more than once, twice he had been hanged, every week he was thrashed till he was half dead, but he always revived.

At this moment grandfather was, no doubt, standing at the gate, screwing up his eyes at the red windows of the church, stamping with his high felt boots, and joking with the servants. His little mallet was hanging on his belt. He was clasping his hands, shrugging with the cold, and, with an aged chuckle, pinching first the housemaid, then the cook.

"How about a pinch of snuff?" he was saying, offering the women his snuff-box.

The women would take a sniff and sneeze. Grandfather would be indescribably delighted, go off into a merry chuckle, and cry: "Tear it off, it has frozen on!"

They give the dogs a sniff of snuff too. Kashtanka sneezes, wriggles her head, and walks away offended. Eel does not sneeze, from politeness, but wags his tail. And the weather is glorious. The air is still, fresh, and transparent. The night is dark, but one can see the whole village with its white roofs and coils of smoke coming from the chimneys, the trees silvered with hoar frost, the snowdrifts. The whole sky spangled with gay twinkling stars, and the Milky Way is as distinct as though it had been washed and rubbed with snow for a holiday....

Vanka sighed, dipped his pen, and went on writing: "And yesterday I had a wigging. The master pulled me out into the yard by my hair, and whacked me with a boot-stretcher because I accidentally fell asleep while I was rocking their brat in the cradle. And a week ago the mistress told me to clean a herring, and I began from the tail end, and she took the herring and thrust its head in my face. The workmen laugh at me and send me to the tavern for vodka, and tell me to steal the master's cucumbers for them, and the master beats me with anything that comes to hand. And there is nothing to eat. In the morning they give me bread, for dinner, porridge, and in the evening, bread again; but as for tea, or soup, the master and mistress gobble it all up themselves. And I am put to sleep in the passage, and when their wretched brat cries I get no sleep at all, but have to rock the cradle. Dear grandfather, show the divine mercy, take me away from here, home to the village. It's more than I can bear. I bow down to your feet, and will pray to God for you for ever, take me away from here or I shall die."

Vanka's mouth worked, he rubbed his eyes with his black fist, and gave a sob.

"I will powder your snuff for you," he went on. "I will pray for you, and if I do anything you can thrash me like Sidor's goat. And if you think I've no job, then I will beg the steward for Christ's sake to let me clean his boots, or I' ll go for a shepherd-boy instead of Fedka. Dear grandfather, it is more than I can bear, it's simply no life at all. I wanted to run away to the village, but I have no boots, and I am afraid of the frost. When I grow up big I will take care of you for this, and not let anyone annoy you, and when you die I will pray for the rest of your soul, just as for my mammy's."

"Moscow is a big town. It's all gentlemen's houses, and there are lots of horses, but there are no sheep, and the dogs are not spiteful. The lads here don't go out with the star, and they don't let anyone go into the choir, and once I saw in a shop window fishing-hooks for sale, fitted ready with the line and for all sorts of fish, awfully good ones, there was even one hook that would hold a forty-pound sheat-fish. And I have seen shops where there are guns of all sorts, after the pattern of the master's guns at home, so that I shouldn't wonder if they are a hundred roubles each.... And in the butchers' shops there are grouse and woodcocks and fish and hares, but the shopmen don't say where they shoot them."

"Dear grandfather, when they have the Christmas tree at the big house, get me a gilt walnut, and put it away in the green trunk. Ask the young lady Olga Ignatyevna, say it's for Vanka."

Vanka gave a tremulous sigh, and again stared at the window. He remembered how his grandfather always went into the forest to get the Christmas tree for his master's family, and took his grandson with him. It was a merry time! Grandfather made a noise in his throat, the forest crackled with the frost, and looking at them Vanka chortled too. Before chopping down the Christmas tree, grandfather would smoke a pipe, slowly take a pinch of snuff, and laugh at frozen Vanka.... The young fir trees, covered with hoar frost, stood motionless, waiting to see which of them was to die. Wherever one looked, a hare flew like an arrow over the snowdrifts.... Grandfather could not refrain from shouting: "Hold him, hold him... hold him! Ah, the bob-tailed devil!"

When he had cut down the Christmas tree, grandfather used to drag it to the big house, and there set to work to decorate it.... The young lady, who was Vanka's favourite, Olga Ignatyevna, was the busiest of all. When Vanka's mother Pelageya was alive, and a servant in the big house, Olga Ignatyevna used to give him goodies, and having nothing better to do, taught him to read and write, to count up to a hundred, and even to dance a quadrille. When Pelageya died, Vanka had been transferred to the servants' kitchen to be with his grandfather, and from the kitchen to the shoemaker's in Moscow.

"Do come, dear grandfather," Vanka went on with his letter. "For Christ's sake, I beg you, take me away. Have pity on an unhappy orphan like me; here everyone knocks me about, and I am fearfully hungry; I can't tell you what misery it is, I am always crying. And the other day the master hit me on the head with a last, so that I fell down. My life is wretched, worse than any dog's.... I send greetings to Alyona, one-eyed Yegorka, and the coachman, and don't give my concertina to anyone. I remain, your grandson, Ivan Zhukov. Dear grandfather, do come."

Vanka folded the sheet of writing-paper twice, and put it into an envelope he had bought the day before for a kopeck.... After thinking a little, he dipped the pen and wrote the address: _To grandfather in the village._

Then he scratched his head, thought a little, and added: _Konstantin Makaritch._ Glad that he had not been prevented from writing, he put on his cap and, without putting on his little greatcoat, ran out into the street as he was in his shirt....

The shopmen at the butcher's, whom he had questioned the day before, told him that letters were put in post-boxes, and from the boxes were carried about all over the earth in mailcart with drunken drivers and ringing bells. Vanka ran to the nearest post-box, and thrust the precious letter in the slit....

An hour later, lulled by sweet hopes, he was sound asleep.... He dreamed of the stove. On the stove was sitting his grandfather, swinging his bare legs, and reading the letter to the cooks....

By the stove was Eel, wagging his tail.

THAT WRETCHED BOY

IVAN IVANICH LAPKIN, a pleasant looking young man, and Anna Zamblizky, a young girl with a little snub nose, walked down the sloping bank and sat down on the bench. The bench was close to the water's edge, among thick bushes of young willow. A heavenly spot! You sat down, and you were hidden from the world. Only the fish could see you and the catspaws which flashed over the water like lightning. The two young persons were equipped with rods, fish hooks, bags, tins of worms and everything else necessary. Once seated, they immediately began to fish.

"I am glad that we're left alone at last," said Lapkin, looking round. I've got a lot to tell you, Anna tremendous... when I saw you for the first time... you've got a nibble ... I understood then why I am alive, I knew where my idol was, to whom I can devote my honest, hard-working life... It must be a big one... it is biting... When I saw you for the first time in my life I fell in love passionately! Don't pull. Let it go on biting... Tell me, darling, tell me will you let me hope? No! I'm not worth it. I dare not even think of it may I hope for ... Pull!

Anna lifted her hand that held the rod pulled, cried out. A silvery green fish shone in the air.

"Goodness! it's a perch! Help quick! It's slipping off." The perch tore itself from the hook danced in the grass towards its native element and... leaped into the water.

But instead of the little fish that he was chasing, Lapkin quite by accident caught hold of Anna's hand quite by accident pressed it to his lips. She drew back, but it was too late; quite by accident their lips met and kissed; yes, it was an absolute accident! They kissed and kissed. Then came vows and assurances.... Blissful moments! But there is no such thing as absolute happiness in this life. If happiness itself does not contain a poison,

poison will enter in from without. Which happened this time. Suddenly, while the two were kissing, a laugh was heard. They looked at the river and were paralysed. The schoolboy Kolia, Anna's brother, was standing in the water, watching the young people and maliciously laughing.

"Ah ha! Kissing!" said he. "Right O, I'll tell Mother."

"I hope that you as a man of honour," Lapkin muttered, blushing. "It's disgusting to spy on us, it's loathsome to tell tales, it's rotten. As a man of honour..."

"Give me a shilling, then I'll shut up!" the man of honour retorted. "If you don't, I'll tell."

Lapkin took a shilling out of his pocket and gave it to Kolia, who squeezed it in his wet fist, whistled, and swam away. And the young people did not kiss any more just then.

Next day Lapkin brought Kolia some paints and a ball from town, and his sister gave him all her empty pill boxes. Then they had to present him with a set of studs like dogs' heads. The wretched boy enjoyed this game immensely, and to keep it going he began to spy on them. Wherever Lapkin and Anna went, he was there too. He did not leave them alone for a single moment.

"Beast!" Lapkin gnashed his teeth. "So young and yet such a full fledged scoundrel. What on earth will become of him later!"

During the whole of July the poor lovers had no life apart from him. He threatened to tell on them; he dogged them and demanded more presents. Nothing satisfied him finally he hinted at a gold watch. All right, they had to promise the watch.

Once, at table, when biscuits were being handed round, he burst out laughing and said to Lapkin : "Shall I let on? Ah ha!"

Lapkin blushed fearfully and instead of a biscuit he began to chew his table napkin. Anna jumped up from the table and rushed out of the room.

And this state of things went on until the end of August, up to the day when Lapkin at last proposed to Anna. Ah! What a happy day that was! When he had spoken to her parents and obtained their consent Lapkin rushed into the garden after Kolia. When he found him he nearly cried for joy and caught hold of the wretched boy by the ear. Anna, who was also looking for Kolia came running up and grabbed him by the other ear. You should have seen the happiness depicted on their faces while Kolia roared and begged them: "Darling, precious pets, I won't do it again. O-oh 0-oh! Forgive me!" And both of them confessed afterwards that during all the time they were in love with each other they never experienced such happiness, such overwhelming joy as during those moments when they pulled the wretched boy's ears.

'ANNA ON THE NECK'

I

AFTER the wedding they had not even light refreshments; the happy pair simply drank a glass of champagne, changed into their travelling things, and drove to the station. Instead of a gay wedding ball and supper, instead of music and dancing, they went on a journey to pray at a shrine a hundred and fifty miles away. Many people commended this, saying that Modest Alexeitch was a man high up in the service and no longer young, and that a noisy wedding might not have seemed quite suitable; and music is apt to sound dreary when a government official of fifty-two marries a girl who is only just eighteen. People said, too, that Modest Alexeitch, being a man of principle, had arranged this visit to the monastery expressly in order to make his young bride realize that even in marriage he put religion and morality above everything.

The happy pair were seen off at the station. The crowd of relations and colleagues in the service stood, with glasses in their hands, waiting for the train to start to shout "Hurrah!" and the bride's father, Pyotr Leontyitch, wearing a top-hat and the uniform of a teacher, already drunk and very pale, kept craning towards the window, glass in hand and saying in an imploring voice: "Anyuta! Anya, Anya! one word!"

Anna bent out of the window to him, and he whispered something to her, enveloping her in a stale smell of alcohol, blew into her ear —she could make out nothing—and made the sign of the cross over her face, her bosom, and her hands; meanwhile he was breathing in gasps and tears were shining in his eyes. And the schoolboys, Anna's brothers, Petya and Andrusha, pulled at his coat from behind, whispering in confusion: "Father, hush!... Father, that's enough...."

When the train started, Anna saw her father run a little way after the train, staggering and spilling his wine, and what a kind, guilty, pitiful face he had: "Hurra—ah!" he shouted.

The happy pair were left alone. Modest Alexeitch looked about the compartment, arranged their things on the shelves, and sat down, smiling, opposite his young wife. He was an official of medium height, rather stout and puffy, who looked exceedingly well nourished, with long whiskers and no moustache. His clean-shaven, round, sharply defined chin looked like the heel of a foot. The most characteristic point in his face was the absence of moustache, the bare, freshly shaven place, which gradually passed into the fat cheeks, quivering like jelly. His deportment was dignified, his movements were deliberate, his manner was soft.

"I cannot help remembering now one circumstance," he said, smiling. "When, five years ago, Kosorotov received the order of St. Anna of the second grade, and went to thank His Excellency, His Excellency expressed himself as follows: 'so now you have three Annas: one in your buttonhole and two on your neck.' And it must be explained that at that time Kosorotov's wife, a quarrelsome and frivolous person, had just returned to him, and that her name was Anna. I trust that when I receive the Anna of the second grade His Excellency will not have occasion to say the same thing to me."

He smiled with his little eyes. And she, too, smiled, troubled at the thought that at any moment this man might kiss her with his thick damp lips, and that she had no right to prevent his doing so. The soft movements of his fat person frightened her; she felt both fear and disgust. He got up, without haste took off the order from his neck, took off his coat and waistcoat, and put on his dressing-gown.

"That's better," he said, sitting down beside Anna.

Anna remembered what agony the wedding had been, when it had seemed to her that the priest, and the guests, and every one in church had been looking at her sorrowfully and asking why, why was she, such a sweet, nice girl, marrying such an elderly, uninteresting gentleman. Only that morning she was delighted that everything had been satisfactorily arranged, but at the time of the wedding, and now in the railway carriage, she felt cheated, guilty, and ridiculous. Here she had married a rich man and yet she had no money, her wedding-dress had been bought on credit, and when her father and brothers had been saying good-bye, she could see from their faces that they had not a farthing. Would they have any supper that day? And tomorrow? And for some reason it seemed to her that her father and the boys were sitting tonight hungry without her, and feeling the same misery as they had the day after their mother's funeral.

"Oh, how unhappy I am!" she thought. "Why am I so unhappy?"

With the awkwardness of a man with settled habits, unaccustomed to deal with women, Modest Alexeitch touched her on the waist and patted her on the shoulder, while she went on thinking about money, about her mother and her mother's death. When her mother died, her father, Pyotr Leontyitch, a teacher of drawing and writing in the high school, had taken to drink, impoverishment had followed, the boys had not had boots or galoshes, their father had been hauled up before the magistrate, the warrant officer had come and made an inventory of the furniture.... What a disgrace! Anna had had to look after her drunken father, darn her brothers' stockings, go to market, and when she was complimented on her youth, her beauty, and her elegant manners, it seemed to her that every one was looking at her cheap hat and the holes in her boots that were inked over. And at night there had been tears and a haunting dread that her father would soon, very soon, be dismissed from the school for his weakness, and that he would not survive it, but would die, too, like their mother. But ladies of their acquaintance had taken the matter in hand and looked about for a good match for Anna. This Modest Alexevitch, who was neither young nor good-looking but had money, was soon found. He had a hundred thousand in the bank and the family estate, which he had let on lease. He was a man of principle and stood well with His Excellency; it would be nothing to him, so they told Anna, to get a note from His Excellency to the directors of the high school, or even to the Education Commissioner, to prevent Pyotr Leontyitch from being dismissed.

While she was recalling these details, she suddenly heard strains of music which floated in at the window, together with the sound of voices. The train was stopping at a station. In the crowd beyond the platform an accordion and a cheap squeaky fiddle were being briskly played, and the sound of a military band came from beyond the villas and the tall birches and poplars that lay bathed in the moonlight; there must have been a dance in the place. Summer visitors and townspeople, who used to come out here by train in fine weather for a breath of fresh air, were parading up and down on the platform. Among them was the wealthy owner of all the summer villas—a tall, stout, dark man called Artynov. He had prominent eyes and looked like an Armenian. He wore a strange costume; his shirt was unbuttoned, showing his chest; he wore high boots with spurs, and a black cloak hung from his shoulders and dragged on the ground like a train. Two boar-hounds followed him with their sharp noses to the ground.

Tears were still shining in Anna's eyes, but she was not thinking now of her mother, nor of money, nor of her marriage; but shaking hands with schoolboys and officers she knew, she laughed gaily and said quickly: "How do you do? How are you?"

She went out on to the platform between the carriages into the moonlight, and stood so that they could all see her in her new splendid dress and hat.

"Why are we stopping here?" she asked.

"This is a junction. They are waiting for the mail train to pass."

Seeing that Artynov was looking at her, she screwed up her eyes coquettishly and began talking aloud in French; and because her voice sounded so pleasant, and because she heard music and the moon was reflected in the pond, and because Artynov, the notorious Don Juan and spoiled child of fortune, was looking at her eagerly and with curiosity, and because every one was in good spirits—she suddenly felt joyful, and when the train started and the officers of her acquaintance saluted her, she was humming the polka the strains of which reached her from the military band playing beyond the trees; and she returned to her compartment feeling as though it had been proved to her at the station that she would certainly be happy in spite of everything.

The happy pair spent two days at the monastery, then went back to town. They lived in a rent-free flat. When Modest Alexevitch had gone to the office, Anna played the piano, or shed tears of depression, or lay down on a couch and read novels or looked through fashion papers. At dinner Modest Alexevitch ate a great deal and talked about politics, about appointments, transfers, and promotions in the service, about the necessity of hard work, and said that, family life not being a pleasure but a duty, if you took care of the kopecks the roubles would take care of themselves, and that he put religion and morality before everything else in the world. And holding his knife in his fist as though it were a sword, he would say: "Every one ought to have his duties!"

And Anna listened to him, was frightened, and could not eat, and she usually got up from the table hungry. After dinner her husband lay down for a nap and snored loudly, while Anna went to see her own people. Her father and the boys looked at her in a peculiar way, as though just before she came in they had been blaming her for having married for money a tedious, wearisome man she did not love; her rustling skirts, her bracelets, and her general air of a married lady, offended them and made them uncomfortable. In her presence they felt a little embarrassed and did not know what to talk to her about; but yet they still loved her as before, and were not used to having dinner without her. She sat down with them to cabbage soup, porridge, and fried potatoes, smelling of mutton dripping. Pyotr Leontyitch filled his glass from the decanter with a trembling hand and drank it off hurriedly, greedily, with repulsion, then poured out a second glass and then a third. Petya and Andrusha, thin, pale boys with big eyes, would take the decanter and say desperately: "You mustn't, father.... Enough, father...."

And Anna, too, was troubled and entreated him to drink no more; and he would suddenly fly into a rage and beat the table with his fists: "I won't allow any one to dictate to me!" he would shout. "Wretched boys! wretched girl! I'll turn you all out!"

But there was a note of weakness, of good-nature in his voice, and no one was afraid of him. After dinner he usually dressed in his best. Pale, with a cut on his chin from shaving, craning his thin neck, he would stand for half an hour before the glass, prinking, combing his hair, twisting his black moustache, sprinkling himself with scent, tying his cravat in a bow; then he would put on his gloves and his top-hat, and go off to give his private lessons. Or if it was a holiday he would stay at home and paint, or play the harmonium, which wheezed and growled; he would try to wrest from it pure harmonious sounds and would sing to it; or would storm at the boys: "Wretches! Good-for-nothing boys! You have spoiled the instrument!"

In the evening Anna's husband played cards with his colleagues, who lived under the same roof in the government quarters. The wives of these gentlemen would come in—ugly, tastelessly dressed women, as coarse as cooks—and gossip would begin in the flat as tasteless and unattractive as the ladies themselves. Sometimes Modest Alexevitch would take Anna to the theatre. In the intervals he would never let her stir a step from his side, but walked about arm in arm with her through the corridors and the foyer. When he bowed to some one, he immediately whispered to Anna: "A civil councillor... visits at His Excellency's "; or, "A man of means... has a house of his own." When they passed the buffet Anna had a great longing for something sweet; she was fond of chocolate and apple cakes, but she had no money, and she did not like to ask her husband. He would take a pear, pinch it with his fingers, and ask uncertainly: "How much?"

"Twenty-five kopecks!"

"I say!" he would reply, and put it down; but as it was awkward to leave the buffet without buying anything, he would order some seltzer— water and drink the whole bottle himself, and tears would come into his eyes. And Anna hated him at such times.

And suddenly flushing crimson, he would say to her rapidly: "Bow to that old lady!"

"But I don't know her."

"No matter. That's the wife of the director of the local treasury! Bow, I tell you," he would grumble insistently. "Your head won't drop off."

Anna bowed and her head certainly did not drop off, but it was agonizing. She did everything her husband wanted her to, and was furious with herself for having let him deceive her like the veriest idiot. She had only married him for his money, and yet she had less money now than before her marriage. In old days her father would sometimes give her twenty kopecks, but now she had not a farthing.

To take money by stealth or ask for it, she could not; she was afraid of her husband, she trembled before him. She felt as though she had been afraid of him for years. In her childhood the director of the high school had always seemed the most impressive and terrifying force in the world, sweeping down like a thunderstorm or a steam-engine ready to crush her; another similar force of which the whole family talked, and of which they were for some reason afraid, was His Excellency; then there were a dozen others, less formidable, and among them the teachers at the high school, with shaven upper lips, stern, implacable; and now finally, there was Modest Alexeitch, a man of principle, who even resembled the director in the face. And in Anna's imagination all these forces blended together into one, and, in the form of a terrible, huge white bear, menaced the weak and erring such as her father. And she was afraid to say anything in opposition to her husband, and gave a forced smile, and tried to make a show of pleasure when she was coarsely caressed and defiled by embraces that excited her terror. Only once Pyotr Leontyitch had the temerity to ask for a loan of fifty roubles in order to pay some very irksome debt, but what an agony it had been!

"Very good; I'll give it to you," said Modest Alexeitch after a moment's thought; "but I warn you I won't help you again till you give up drinking. Such a failing is disgraceful in a man in the government service! I must remind you of the well-known fact that many capable people have been ruined by that passion, though they might possibly, with temperance, have risen in time to a very high."

And long-winded phrases followed: "inasmuch as...", "following upon which proposition...", "in view of the aforesaid contention..."; and Pyotr Leontyitch was in agonies of humiliation and felt an intense craving for alcohol.

And when the boys came to visit Anna, generally in broken boots and threadbare trousers, they, too, had to listen to sermons.

"Every man ought to have his duties!" Modest Alexeitch would say to them.

And he did not give them money. But he did give Anna bracelets, rings, and brooches, saying that these things would come in useful for a rainy day. And he often unlocked her drawer and made an inspection to see whether they were all safe.

II

Meanwhile winter came on. Long before Christmas there was an announcement in the local papers that the usual winter ball would take place on the twenty-ninth of December in the Hall of Nobility. Every evening after cards Modest Alexeitch was excitedly whispering with his colleagues' wives and glancing at Anna, and then paced up and down the room for a long while, thinking. At last, late one evening, he stood still, facing Anna, and said: "You ought to get yourself a ball dress. Do you understand? Only please consult Marya Grigoryevna and Natalya Kuzminishna."

And he gave her a hundred roubles. She took the money, but she did not consult any one when she ordered the ball dress; she spoke to no one but her father, and tried to imagine how her mother would have dressed for a ball. Her mother had always dressed in the latest fashion and had always taken trouble over Anna, dressing her elegantly like a doll, and had taught her to speak French and dance the mazurka superbly (she had been a governess for five years before her marriage). Like her mother, Anna could make a new dress out of an old one, clean gloves with benzine, hire jewels; and, like her mother, she knew how to screw up her eyes, lisp, assume

118

graceful attitudes, fly into raptures when necessary, and throw a mournful and enigmatic look into her eyes. And from her father she had inherited the dark colour of her hair and eyes, her highly-strung nerves, and the habit of always making herself look her best.

When, half an hour before setting off for the ball, Modest Alexeitch went into her room without his coat on, to put his order round his neck before her pier-glass, dazzled by her beauty and the splendour of her fresh, ethereal dress, he combed his whiskers complacently and said: "So that's what my wife can look like... so that's what you can look like! Anyuta!" he went on, dropping into a tone of solemnity, "I have made your fortune, and now I beg you to do something for mine. I beg you to get introduced to the wife of His Excellency! For God's sake, do! Through her I may get the post of senior reporting clerk!"

They went to the ball. They reached the Hall of Nobility, the entrance with the hall porter. They came to the vestibule with the hat-stands, the fur coats; footmen scurrying about, and ladies with low necks putting up their fans to screen themselves from the draughts. There was a smell of gas and of soldiers. When Anna, walking upstairs on her husband's arm, heard the music and saw herself full length in the looking-glass in the full glow of the lights, there was a rush of joy in her heart, and she felt the same presentiment of happiness as in the moonlight at the station. She walked in proudly, confidently, for the first time feeling herself not a girl but a lady, and unconsciously imitating her mother in her walk and in her manner. And for the first time in her life she felt rich and free. Even her husband's presence did not oppress her, for as she crossed the threshold of the hall she had guessed instinctively that the proximity of an old husband did not detract from her in the least, but, on the contrary, gave her that shade of piquant mystery that is so attractive to men. The orchestra was already playing and the dances had begun. After their flat Anna was overwhelmed by the lights, the bright colours, the music, the noise, and looking round the room, thought, "Oh, how lovely!" She at once distinguished in the crowd all her acquaintances, every one she had met before at parties or on picnics—all the officers, the teachers, the lawyers, the officials, the landowners, His Excellency, Artynov, and the ladies of the highest standing, dressed up and very décollettées, handsome and ugly, who had already taken up their positions in the stalls and pavilions of the charity bazaar, to begin selling things for the benefit of the poor. A huge officer in epaulettes—she had been introduced to him in Staro-Kievsky Street when she was a schoolgirl, but now she could not remember his name—seemed to spring from out of the ground, begging her for a waltz, and she flew away from her husband, feeling as though she were floating away in a sailing-boat in a violent storm, while her husband was left far away on the shore. She danced passionately, with fervour, a waltz, then a polka and a quadrille, being snatched by one partner as soon as she was left by another, dizzy with music and the noise, mixing Russian with French, lisping, laughing, and with no thought of her husband or anything else. She excited great admiration among the men—that was evident, and indeed it could not have been otherwise; she was breathless with excitement, felt thirsty, and convulsively clutched her fan. Pyotr Leontyitch, her father, in a crumpled dress-coat that smelt of benzine, came up to her, offering her a plate of pink ice.

"You are enchanting this evening," he said, looking at her rapturously, "and I have never so much regretted that you were in such a hurry to get married.... What was it for? I know you did it for our sake, but..." With a shaking hand he drew out a roll of notes and said: "I got the money for my lessons today, and can pay your husband what I owe him."

She put the plate back into his hand, and was pounced upon by some one and borne off to a distance. She caught a glimpse over her partner's shoulder of her father gliding over the floor, putting his arm round a lady and whirling down the ball-room with her.

"How sweet he is when he is sober!" she thought.

She danced the mazurka with the same huge officer; he moved gravely, as heavily as a dead carcase in a uniform, twitched his shoulders and his chest, stamped his feet very languidly—he felt fearfully disinclined to dance. She fluttered round him, provoking him by her beauty, her bare neck; her eyes glowed defiantly, her movements were passionate, while he became more and more indifferent, and held out his hands to her as graciously as a king.

"Bravo, bravo!" said people watching them.

But little by little the huge officer, too, broke out; he grew lively, excited, and, overcome by her fascination, was carried away and danced lightly, youthfully, while she merely moved her shoulders and looked slyly at him as though she were now the queen and he were her slave; and at that moment it seemed to her that the whole room was looking at them, and that everybody was thrilled and envied them. The huge officer had hardly had time to thank her for the dance, when the crowd suddenly parted and the men drew themselves up in a strange way, with their hands at their sides.

His Excellency, with two stars on his dress-coat, was walking up to her. Yes, His Excellency was walking straight towards her, for he was staring directly at her with a sugary smile, while he licked his lips as he always did when he saw a pretty woman.

"Delighted, delighted..." he began. "I shall order your husband to be clapped in a lock-up for keeping such a treasure hidden from us till now. I've come to you with a message from my wife," he went on, offering her his arm. "You must help us.... M-m-yes.... We ought to give you the prize for beauty as they do in America .... M-m-yes.... The Americans.... My wife is expecting you impatiently."

He led her to a stall and presented her to a middle-aged lady, the lower part of whose face was disproportionately large, so that she looked as though she were holding a big stone in her mouth.

"You must help us," she said through her nose in a sing-song voice. "All the pretty women are working for our charity bazaar, and you are the only one enjoying yourself. Why won't you help us?"

She went away, and Anna took her place by the cups and the silver samovar. She was soon doing a lively trade. Anna asked no less than a rouble for a cup of tea, and made the huge officer drink three cups. Artynov, the rich man with prominent eyes, who suffered from asthma, came up, too; he was not dressed in the strange costume in which Anna had seen him in the summer at the station, but wore a dress-coat like every one else. Keeping his eyes fixed on Anna, he drank a glass of champagne and paid a hundred roubles for it, then drank some tea and gave another hundred—all this without saying a word, as he was short of breath through asthma.... Anna invited purchasers and got money out of them, firmly convinced by now that her smiles and glances could not fail to afford these people great pleasure. She realized now that she was created exclusively for this noisy, brilliant, laughing life, with its music, its dancers, its adorers, and her old terror of a force that was sweeping down upon her and menacing to crush her seemed to her ridiculous: she was afraid of no one now, and only regretted that her mother could not be there to rejoice at her success.

Pyotr Leontyitch, pale by now but still steady on his legs, came up to the stall and asked for a glass of brandy. Anna turned crimson, expecting him to say something inappropriate (she was already ashamed of having such a poor and ordinary father); but he emptied his glass, took ten roubles out of his roll of notes, flung it down, and walked away with dignity without uttering a word. A little later she saw him dancing in the grand chain, and by now he was staggering and kept shouting something, to the great confusion of his partner; and Anna remembered how at the ball three years before he had staggered and shouted in the same way, and it had ended in the police-sergeant's taking him home to bed, and next day the director had threatened to dismiss him from his post. How inappropriate that memory was!

When the samovars were put out in the stalls and the exhausted ladies handed over their takings to the middle-aged lady with the stone in her mouth, Artynov took Anna on his arm to the hall where supper was served to all who had assisted at the bazaar. There were some twenty people at supper, not more, but it was very noisy. His Excellency proposed a toast: "In this magnificent dining-room it will be appropriate to drink to the success of the cheap dining-rooms, which are the object of today's bazaar."

The brigadier-general proposed the toast: "To the power by which even the artillery is vanquished," and all the company clinked glasses with the ladies. It was very, very gay.

When Anna was escorted home it was daylight and the cooks were going to market. Joyful, intoxicated, full of new sensations, exhausted, she undressed, dropped into bed, and at once fell asleep....

It was past one in the afternoon when the servant waked her and announced that M. Artynov had called. She dressed quickly and went down into the drawing-room. Soon after Artynov, His Excellency called to thank her for her assistance in the bazaar. With a sugary smile, chewing his lips, he kissed her hand, and asking her permission to come again, took his leave, while she remained standing in the middle of the drawing-room, amazed, enchanted, unable to believe that this change in her life, this marvellous change, had taken place so quickly; and at that moment Modest Alexeitch walked in... and he, too, stood before her now with the same ingratiating, sugary, cringingly respectful expression which she was accustomed to see on his face in the presence of the great and powerful; and with rapture, with indignation, with contempt, convinced that no harm would come to her from it, she said, articulating distinctly each word: "Be off, you blockhead!"

From this time forward Anna never had one day free, as she was always taking part in picnics, expeditions, performances. She returned home every day after midnight, and went to bed on the floor in the drawing-room, and afterwards used to tell every one, touchingly, how she slept under flowers. She needed a very great deal of money, but she was no longer afraid of Modest Alexeitch, and spent his money as though it were her own; and she did not ask, did not demand it, simply sent him in the bills. "Give bearer two hundred roubles," or "Pay one hundred roubles at once."

At Easter Modest Alexeitch received the Anna of the second grade.

When he went to offer his thanks, His Excellency put aside the paper he was reading and settled himself more comfortably in his chair.

"So now you have three Annas," he said, scrutinizing his white hands and pink nails— "one on your buttonhole and two on your neck."

Modest Alexeitch put two fingers to his lips as a precaution against laughing too loud and said: "Now I have only to look forward to the arrival of a little Vladimir. I make bold to beg your Excellency to stand godfather."

He was alluding to Vladimir of the fourth grade, and was already imagining how he would tell everywhere the story of this pun, so happy in its readiness and audacity, and he wanted to say something equally happy, but His Excellency was buried again in his newspaper, and merely gave him a nod.

And Anna went on driving about with three horses, going out hunting with Artynov, playing in one-act dramas, going out to supper, and was more and more rarely with her own family; they dined now alone. Pyotr Leontyitch was drinking more heavily than ever; there was no money, and the harmonium had been sold long ago for debt. The boys did not let him go out alone in the street now, but looked after him for fear he might fall down; and whenever they met Anna driving in Staro-Kievsky Street with a pair of horses and Artynov on the box instead of a coachman, Pyotr Leontyitch took off his top-hat, and was about to shout to her, but Petya and Andrusha took him by the arm, and said imploringly: "You mustn't, father. Hush, father!"

THE TWO VOLODYAS

"LET me; I want to drive myself! I' ll sit by the driver!" Sofya Lvovna said in a loud voice. "Wait a minute, driver; I'll get up on the box beside you."

She stood up in the sledge, and her husband, Vladimir Nikititch, and the friend of her childhood, Vladimir Mihalovitch, held her arms to prevent her falling. The three horses were galloping fast.

"I said you ought not to have given her brandy," Vladimir Nikititch whispered to his companion with vexation. "What a fellow you are, really!"

The Colonel knew by experience that in women like his wife, Sofya Lvovna, after a little too much wine, turbulent gaiety was followed by hysterical laughter and then tears. He was afraid that when they got home, instead of being able to sleep, he would have to be administering compresses and drops.

"Wo!" cried Sofya Lvovna. "I want to drive myself!"

She felt genuinely gay and triumphant. For the last two months, ever since her wedding, she had been tortured by the thought that she had married Colonel Yagitch from worldly motives and, as it is said, par dépit; but that evening, at the restaurant, she had suddenly become convinced that she loved him passionately. In spite of his fifty-four years, he was so slim, agile, supple, he made puns and hummed to the gipsies' tunes so charmingly. Really, the older men were nowadays a thousand times more interesting than the young. It seemed as though age and youth had changed parts. The Colonel was two years older than her father, but could there be any importance in that if, honestly speaking, there were infinitely more vitality, go, and freshness in him than in herself, though she was only twenty-three?

"Oh, my darling!" she thought. "You are wonderful!"

125

She had become convinced in the restaurant, too, that not a spark of her old feeling remained. For the friend of her childhood, Vladimir Mihalovitch, or simply Volodya, with whom only the day before she had been madly, miserably in love, she now felt nothing but complete indifference. All that evening he had seemed to her spiritless, torpid, uninteresting, and insignificant, and the sangfroid with which he habitually avoided paying at restaurants on this occasion revolted her, and she had hardly been able to resist saying, "If you are poor, you should stay at home." The Colonel paid for all.

Perhaps because trees, telegraph posts, and drifts of snow kept flitting past her eyes, all sorts of disconnected ideas came rushing into her mind. She reflected: the bill at the restaurant had been a hundred and twenty roubles, and a hundred had gone to the gipsies, and tomorrow she could fling away a thousand roubles if she liked; and only two months ago, before her wedding, she had not had three roubles of her own, and had to ask her father for every trifle. What a change in her life!

Her thoughts were in a tangle. She recalled, how, when she was a child of ten, Colonel Yagitch, now her husband, used to make love to her aunt, and every one in the house said that he had ruined her. And her aunt had, in fact, often come down to dinner with her eyes red from crying, and was always going off somewhere; and people used to say of her that the poor thing could find no peace anywhere. He had been very handsome in those days, and had an extraordinary reputation as a lady-killer. So much so that he was known all over the town, and it was said of him that he paid a round of visits to his adorers every day like a doctor visiting his patients. And even now, in spite of his grey hair, his wrinkles, and his spectacles, his thin face looked handsome, especially in profile.

Sofya Lvovna's father was an army doctor, and had at one time served in the same regiment with Colonel Yagitch. Volodya's father was an army doctor too, and he, too, had once been in the same regiment as her father and Colonel Yagitch. In spite of many amatory adventures, often very complicated and disturbing, Volodya had done splendidly at the university, and had taken a very good degree. Now he was specialising in foreign literature, and was said to be writing a thesis. He lived with his father, the army doctor, in the barracks, and had no means of his own, though he was thirty. As children Sofya and he had lived under the same roof, though in different flats. He often came to play with her, and they had dancing and French lessons together. But when he grew up into a graceful, remarkably handsome young man, she began to feel shy of him, and then fell madly in love with him, and had loved him right up to the time when she was married to Yagitch. He, too, had been renowned for his success with women almost from the age of fourteen, and the ladies who deceived their husbands on his account excused themselves by saying that he was only a boy. Some one had told a story of him lately that when he was a student living in lodgings so as to be near the university, it always happened if one knocked at his door, that one heard his footstep, and then a whispered apology: "Pardon, je ne suis pas setul." Yagitch was delighted with him, and blessed him as a worthy successor, as Derchavin blessed Pushkin; he appeared to be fond of him. They would play billiards or piquet by the hour together without uttering a word, if Yagitch drove out on any expedition he always took Volodya with him, and Yagitch was the only person Volodya initiated into the mysteries of his thesis. In earlier days, when Yagitch was rather younger, they had often been in the position of rivals, but they had never been jealous of one another. In the circle in which they moved Yagitch was nicknamed Big Volodya, and his friend Little Volodya.

Besides Big Volodya, Little Volodya, and Sofya Lvovna, there was a fourth person in the sledge—Margarita Alexandrovna, or, as every one called her, Rita, a cousin of Madame Yagitch—a very pale girl over thirty, with black eyebrows and a pince-nez, who was for ever smoking cigarettes, even in the bitterest frost, and who always had her knees and the front of her blouse covered with cigarette ash. She spoke through her nose, drawling every word, was of a cold temperament, could drink any amount of wine and liquor without being drunk, and used to tell scandalous anecdotes in a languid and tasteless way. At home she spent her days reading thick magazines, covering them with cigarette ash, or eating frozen apples.

"Sonia, give over fooling," she said, drawling. "It's really silly."

As they drew near the city gates they went more slowly, and began to pass people and houses. Sofya Lvovna subsided, nestled up to her husband, and gave herself up to her thoughts. Little Volodya sat opposite. By now her light-hearted and cheerful thoughts were mingled with gloomy ones. She thought that the man sitting opposite knew that she loved him, and no doubt he believed the gossip that she married the Colonel par dépit. She had never told him of her love; she had not wanted him to know, and had done her best to hide her feeling, but from her face she knew that he understood her perfectly—and her pride suffered. But what was most humiliating in her position was that, since her wedding, Volodya had suddenly begun to pay her attention, which he had never done before, spending hours with her, sitting silent or chattering about trifles; and even now in the sledge, though he did not talk to her, he touched her foot with his and pressed her hand a little. Evidently that was all he wanted, that she should be married; and it was evident that he despised her and that she only excited in him an interest of a special kind as though she were an immoral and disreputable woman. And when the feeling of triumph and love for her husband were mingled in her soul with humiliation and wounded pride, she was overcome by a spirit of defiance, and longed to sit on the box, to shout and whistle to the horses.

Just as they passed the nunnery the huge hundred-ton bell rang out. Rita crossed herself.

"Our Olga is in that nunnery," said Sofya Lvovna, and she, too, crossed herself and shuddered.

"Why did she go into the nunnery?" said the Colonel.

"Par dépit," Rita answered crossly, with obvious allusion to Sofya's marrying Yagitch. "Par dépit is all the fashion nowadays. Defiance of all the world. She was always laughing, a desperate flirt, fond of nothing but balls and young men, and all of a sudden off she went—to surprise every one!"

"That's not true," said Volodya, turning down the collar of his fur coat and showing his handsome face. "It wasn't a case of par dépit; it was simply horrible, if you like. Her brother Dmitri was sent to penal servitude, and they don't know where he is now. And her mother died of grief."

He turned up his collar again.

"Olga did well," he added in a muffled voice. "Living as an adopted child, and with such a paragon as Sofya Lvovna,—one must take that into consideration too!"

Sofya Lvovna heard a tone of contempt in his voice, and longed to say something rude to him, but she said nothing. The spirit of defiance came over her again; she stood up again and shouted in a tearful voice: "I want to go to the early service! Driver, back! I want to see Olga."

They turned back. The nunnery bell had a deep note, and Sofya Lvovna fancied there was something in it that reminded her of Olga and her life. The other church bells began ringing too. When the driver stopped the horses, Sofya Lvovna jumped out of the sledge and, unescorted and alone, went quickly up to the gate.

"Make haste, please!" her husband called to her. "It's late already."

She went in at the dark gateway, then by the avenue that led from the gate to the chief church. The snow crunched under her feet, and the ringing was just above her head, and seemed to vibrate through her whole being. Here was the church door, then three steps down, and an ante-room with ikons of the saints on both sides, a fragrance of juniper and incense, another door, and a dark figure opening it and bowing very low. The service had not yet begun. One nun was walking by the ikon-screen and lighting the candles on the tall standard candlesticks, another was lighting the chandelier. Here and there, by the columns and the side chapels, there stood black, motionless figures. "I suppose they must remain standing as they are now till the morning," thought Sofya Lvovna, and it seemed to her dark, cold, and dreary—drearier than a graveyard. She looked with a feeling of dreariness at the still, motionless figures and suddenly felt a pang at her heart. For some reason, in one short nun, with thin shoulders and a black kerchief on her head, she recognised Olga, though when Olga went into the nunnery she had been plump and had looked taller. Hesitating and extremely agitated, Sofya Lvovna went up to the nun, and looking over her shoulder into her face, recognised her as Olga.

"Olga!" she cried, throwing up her hands, and could not speak from emotion. "Olga!"

The nun knew her at once; she raised her eyebrows in surprise, and her pale, freshly washed face, and even, it seemed, the white headcloth that she wore under her wimple, beamed with pleasure.

"What a miracle from God!" she said, and she, too, threw up her thin, pale little hands.

Sofya Lvovna hugged her and kissed her warmly, and was afraid as she did so that she might smell of spirits.

"We were just driving past, and we thought of you," she said, breathing hard, as though she had been running. "Dear me! How pale you are! I... I'm very glad to see you. Well, tell me how are you? Are you dull?"

Sofya Lvovna looked round at the other nuns, and went on in a subdued voice: "There've been so many changes at home... you know, I'm married to Colonel Yagitch. You remember him, no doubt.... I am very happy with him."

"Well, thank God for that. And is your father quite well? "

"Yes, he is quite well. He often speaks of you. You must come and see us during the holidays, Olga, won't you?"

"I will come," said Olga, and she smiled. "I'll come on the second day."

Sofya Lvovna began crying, she did not know why, and for a minute she shed tears in silence, then she wiped her eyes and said: "Rita will be very sorry not to have seen you. She is with us too. And Volodya's here. They are close to the gate. How pleased they'd be if you'd come out and see them. Let's go out to them; the service hasn't begun yet."

"Let us," Olga agreed. She crossed herself three times and went out with Sofya Lvovna to the entrance.

"So you say you're happy, Sonitchka?" she asked when they came out at the gate.

"Very."

"Well, thank God for that."

The two Volodyas, seeing the nun, got out of the sledge and greeted her respectfully. Both were visibly touched by her pale face and her black monastic dress, and both were pleased that she had remembered them and come to greet them. That she might not be cold, Sofya Lvovna wrapped her up in a rug and put one half of her fur coat round her. Her tears had relieved and purified her heart, and she was glad that this noisy, restless, and, in reality, impure night should unexpectedly end so purely and serenely. And to keep Olga by her a little longer she suggested: "Let us take her for a drive! Get in, Olga; we'll go a little way."

The men expected the nun to refuse—saints don't dash about in three-horse sledges; but to their surprise, she consented and got into the sledge. And while the horses were galloping to the city gate all were silent, and only tried to make her warm and comfortable, and each of them was thinking of what she had been in the past and what she was now. Her face was now passionless, inexpressive, cold, pale, and transparent, as though there were water, not blood, in her veins. And two or three years ago she had been plump and rosy, talking about her suitors and laughing at every trifle.

Near the city gate the sledge turned back; when it stopped ten minutes later near the nunnery, Olga got out of the sledge. The bell had begun to ring more rapidly.

"The Lord save you," said Olga, and she bowed low as nuns do.

"Mind you come, Olga."

"I will, I will."

She went and quickly disappeared through the gateway. And when after that they drove on again, Sofya Lvovna felt very sad. Every one was silent. She felt dispirited and weak all over. That she should have made a nun get into a sledge and drive in a company hardly sober seemed to her now stupid, tactless, and almost sacrilegious. As the intoxication passed off, the desire to deceive herself passed away also. It was clear to her now that she did not love her husband, and never could love him, and that it all had been foolishness and nonsense. She had married him from interested motives, because, in the words of her school friends, he was madly rich, and because she was afraid of becoming an old maid like Rita, and because she was sick of her father, the doctor, and wanted to annoy Volodya.

If she could have imagined when she got married, that it would be so oppressive, so dreadful, and so hideous, she would not have consented to the marriage for all the wealth in the world. But now there was no setting it right. She must make up her mind to it.

They reached home. Getting into her warm, soft bed, and pulling the bed-clothes over her, Sofya Lvovna recalled the dark church, the smell of incense, and the figures by the columns, and she felt frightened at the thought that these figures would be standing there all the while she was asleep. The early service would be very, very long; then there would be "the hours," then the mass, then the service of the day.

"But of course there is a God—there certainly is a God; and I shall have to die, so that sooner or later one must think of one's soul, of eternal life, like Olga. Olga is saved now; she has settled all questions for herself.... But if there is no God? Then her life is wasted. But how is it wasted? Why is it wasted?"

And a minute later the thought came into her mind again: "There is a God; death must come; one must think of one's soul. If Olga were to see death before her this minute she would not be afraid. She is prepared. And the great thing is that she has already solved the problem of life for herself. There is a God... yes.... But is there no other solution except going into a monastery? To go into the monastery means to renounce life, to spoil it ...."

Sofya Lvovna began to feel rather frightened; she hid her head under her pillow.

"I mustn't think about it," she whispered. "I mustn't...."

Yagitch was walking about on the carpet in the next room with a soft jingle of spurs, thinking about something. The thought occurred to Sofya

Lvovna that this man was near and dear to her only for one reason—that his name, too, was Vladimir. She sat up in bed and called tenderly: "Volodya!"

"What is it?" her husband responded.

"Nothing."

She lay down again. She heard a bell, perhaps the same nunnery bell. Again she thought of the vestibule and the dark figures, and thoughts of God and of inevitable death strayed through her mind, and she covered her ears that she might not hear the bell. She thought that before old age and death there would be a long, long life before her, and that day by day she would have to put up with being close to a man she did not love, who had just now come into the bedroom and was getting into bed, and would have to stifle in her heart her hopeless love for the other young, fascinating, and, as she thought, exceptional man. She looked at her husband and tried to say good-night to him, but suddenly burst out crying instead. She was vexed with herself.

"Well, now then for the music!" said Yagitch.

She was not pacified till ten o'clock in the morning. She left off crying and trembling all over, but she began to have a splitting headache. Yagitch was in haste to go to the late mass, and in the next room was grumbling at his orderly, who was helping him to dress. He came into the bedroom once with the soft jingle of his spurs to fetch something, and then a second time wearing his epaulettes, and his orders on his breast, limping slightly from rheumatism; and it struck Sofya Lvovna that he looked and walked like a bird of prey.

She heard Yagitch ring the telephone bell.

"Be so good as to put me on to the Vassilevsky barracks," he said; and a minute later: "Vassilevsky barracks? Please ask Doctor Salimovitch to come to the telephone..." And a minute later: "With whom am I speaking? Is it you, Volodya? Delighted. Ask your father to come to us at once, dear boy; my wife is rather shattered after yesterday. Not at home, you say? H'm!... Thank you. Very good. I shall be much obliged... Merci."

Yagitch came into the bedroom for the third time, bent down to his wife, made the sign of the cross over her, gave her his hand to kiss (the women who had been in love with him used to kiss his hand and he had got into the habit of it), and saying that he should be back to dinner, went out.

At twelve o'clock the maid came in to announce that Vladimir Mihalovitch had arrived. Sofya Lvovna, staggering with fatigue and headache, hurriedly put on her marvellous new lilac dressing-gown trimmed with fur, and hastily did up her hair after a fashion. She was conscious of an inexpressible tenderness in her heart, and was trembling with joy and with fear that he might go away. She wanted nothing but to look at him.

Volodya came dressed correctly for calling, in a swallow-tail coat and white tie. When Sofya Lvovna came in he kissed her hand and expressed his genuine regret that she was ill. Then when they had sat down, he admired her dressing-gown.

"I was upset by seeing Olga yesterday," she said. "At first I felt it dreadful, but now I envy her. She is like a rock that cannot be shattered; there is no moving her. But was there no other solution for her, Volodya? Is burying oneself alive the only solution of the problem of life? Why, it's death, not life!"

At the thought of Olga, Volodya's face softened.

"Here, you are a clever man, Volodya," said Sofya Lvovna. "Show me how to do what Olga has done. Of course, I am not a believer and should not go into a nunnery, but one can do something equivalent. Life isn't easy for me," she added after a brief pause. "Tell me what to do.... Tell me something I can believe in. Tell me something, if it's only one word."

"One word? By all means: tararaboomdeeay."

"Volodya, why do you despise me?" she asked hotly. "You talk to me in a special, fatuous way, if you'll excuse me, not as one talks to one's friends and women one respects. You are so good at your work, you are fond of science; why do you never talk of it to me? Why is it? Am I not good enough?"

Volodya frowned with annoyance and said: "Why do you want science all of a sudden? Don't you perhaps want constitutional government? Or sturgeon and horse-radish?"

"Very well, I am a worthless, trivial, silly woman with no convictions. I have a mass, a mass of defects. I am neurotic, corrupt, and I ought to be despised for it. But you, Volodya, are ten years older than I am, and my husband is thirty years older. I've grown up before your eyes, and if you would, you could have made anything you liked of me—an angel. But you"—her voice quivered—"treat me horribly. Yagitch has married me in his old age, and you..."

"Come, come," said Volodya, sitting nearer her and kissing both her hands. "Let the Schopenhauers philosophise and prove whatever they like, while we'll kiss these little hands."

"You despise me, and if only you knew how miserable it makes me," she said uncertainly, knowing beforehand that he would not believe her. "And if you only knew how I want to change, to begin another life! I think of it with enthusiasm!" and tears of enthusiasm actually came into her eyes. "To be good, honest, pure, not to be lying; to have an object in life."

"Come, come, come, please don't be affected! I don't like it!" said Volodya, and an ill-humoured expression came into his face. "Upon my word, you might be on the stage. Let us behave like simple people."

To prevent him from getting cross and going away, she began defending herself, and forced herself to smile to please him; and again she began talking of Olga, and of how she longed to solve the problem of her life and to become something real.

"Ta-ra-ra-boomdee-ay," he hummed. "Ta-ra-ra-boom-dee-ay!"

And all at once he put his arm round her waist, while she, without knowing what she was doing, laid her hands on his shoulders and for a minute gazed with ecstasy, almost intoxication, at his clever, ironical face, his brow, his eyes, his handsome beard.

"You have known that I love you for ever so long," she confessed to him, and she blushed painfully, and felt that her lips were twitching with shame. "I love you. Why do you torture me?"

She shut her eyes and kissed him passionately on the lips, and for a long while, a full minute, could not take her lips away, though she knew it was unseemly, that he might be thinking the worse of her, that a servant might come in.

"Oh, how you torture me!" she repeated.

When half an hour later, having got all that he wanted, he was sitting at lunch in the dining-room, she was kneeling before him, gazing greedily into his face, and he told her that she was like a little dog waiting for a bit of ham to be thrown to it. Then he sat her on his knee, and dancing her up and down like a child, hummed: "Tara-raboom-dee-ay.... Tara-raboom-dee-ay."

And when he was getting ready to go she asked him in a passionate whisper: "When? Today? Where?" And held out both hands to his mouth as though she wanted to seize his answer in them.

"Today it will hardly be convenient," he said after a minute's thought. "Tomorrow, perhaps."

And they parted. Before dinner Sofya Lvovna went to the nunnery to see Olga, but there she was told that Olga was reading the psalter somewhere over the dead. From the nunnery she went to her father's and found that he, too, was out. Then she took another sledge and drove aimlessly about the streets till evening. And for some reason she kept thinking of the aunt whose eyes were red with crying, and who could find no peace anywhere.

And at night they drove out again with three horses to a restaurant out of town and listened to the gipsies. And driving back past the nunnery again, Sofya Lvovna thought of Olga, and she felt aghast at the thought that for the girls and women of her class there was no solution but to go on driving about and telling lies, or going into a nunnery to mortify the flesh.... And next day she met her lover, and again Sofya Lvovna drove about the town alone in a hired sledge thinking about her aunt.

A week later Volodya threw her over. And after that life went on as before, uninteresting, miserable, and sometimes even agonising. The Colonel and Volodya spent hours playing billiards and picquet, Rita told anecdotes in the same languid, tasteless way, and Sofya Lvovna went about alone in hired sledges and kept begging her husband to take her for a good drive with three horses.

Going almost every day to the nunnery, she wearied Olga, complaining of her unbearable misery, weeping, and feeling as she did so that she brought with her into the cell something impure, pitiful, shabby. And Olga repeated to her mechanically as though a lesson learnt by rote, that all this was of no consequence, that it would all pass and God would forgive her.

BETROTHED

I

IT was ten o'clock in the evening and the full moon was shining over the garden. In the Shumins' house an evening service celebrated at the request of the grandmother, Marfa Mihalovna, was just over, and now Nadya—she had gone into the garden for a minute—could see the table being laid for supper in the dining-room, and her grandmother bustling about in her gorgeous silk dress; Father Andrey, a chief priest of the cathedral, was talking to Nadya's mother, Nina Ivanovna, and now in the evening light through the window her mother for some reason looked very young; Andrey Andreitch, Father Andrey's son, was standing by listening attentively.

It was still and cool in the garden, and dark peaceful shadows lay on the ground. There was a sound of frogs croaking, far, far away beyond the town. There was a feeling of May, sweet May! One drew deep breaths and longed to fancy that not here but far away under the sky, above the trees, far away in the open country, in the fields and the woods, the life of spring was unfolding now, mysterious, lovely, rich and holy beyond the understanding of weak, sinful man. And for some reason one wanted to cry.

She, Nadya, was already twenty-three. Ever since she was sixteen she had been passionately dreaming of marriage and at last she was engaged to Andrey Andreitch, the young man who was standing on the other side of the window; she liked him, the wedding was already fixed for July 7, and yet there was no joy in her heart, she was sleeping badly, her spirits drooped.... She could hear from the open windows of the basement where the kitchen was the hurrying servants, the clatter of knives, the banging of the swing door; there was a smell of roast turkey and pickled cherries, and for some reason it seemed to her that it would be like that all her life, with no change, no end to it.

Some one came out of the house and stood on the steps; it was Alexandr Timofeitch, or, as he was always called, Sasha, who had come from Moscow ten days before and was staying with them. Years ago a distant relation of the grandmother, a gentleman's widow called Marya Petrovna, a thin, sickly little woman who had sunk into poverty, used to come to the house to ask for assistance. She had a son Sasha. It used for some reason to be said that he had talent as an artist, and when his mother died Nadya's grandmother had, for the salvation of her soul, sent him to the Komissarovsky school in Moscow; two years later he went into the school of painting, spent nearly fifteen years there, and only just managed to scrape through the leaving examination in the section of architecture. He did not set up as an architect, however, but took a job at a lithographer's. He used to come almost every year, usually very ill, to stay with Nadya's grandmother to rest and recover.

He was wearing now a frock-coat buttoned up, and shabby canvas trousers, crumpled into creases at the bottom. And his shirt had not been ironed and he had somehow all over a look of not being fresh. He was very thin, with big eyes, long thin fingers and a swarthy bearded face, and all the same he was handsome. With the Shumins he was like one of the family, and in their house felt he was at home. And the room in which he lived when he was there had for years been called Sasha's room. Standing on the steps he saw Nadya, and went up to her.

"It's nice here," he said.

"Of course it's nice, you ought to stay here till the autumn."

"Yes, I expect it will come to that. I dare say I shall stay with you till September."

He laughed for no reason, and sat down beside her.

"I'm sitting gazing at mother," said Nadya. "She looks so young from here! My mother has her weaknesses, of course," she added, after a pause, "but still she is an exceptional woman."

"Yes, she is very nice..." Sasha agreed. "Your mother, in her own way of course, is a very good and sweet woman, but... how shall I say? I went early this morning into your kitchen and there I found four servants sleeping on the floor, no bedsteads, and rags for bedding, stench, bugs, beetles... it is just as it was twenty years ago, no change at all. Well, Granny, God bless her, what else can you expect of Granny? But your mother speaks French, you know, and acts in private theatricals. One would think she might understand."

As Sasha talked, he used to stretch out two long wasted fingers before the listener's face.

"It all seems somehow strange to me here, now I am out of the habit of it," he went on. "There is no making it out. Nobody ever does anything. Your mother spends the whole day walking about like a duchess, Granny does nothing either, nor you either. And your Andrey Andreitch never does anything either."

Nadya had heard this the year before and, she fancied, the year before that too, and she knew that Sasha could not make any other criticism, and in old days this had amused her, but now for some reason she felt annoyed.

"That's all stale, and I have been sick of it for ages," she said and got up. "You should think of something a little newer."

He laughed and got up too, and they went together toward the house. She, tall, handsome, and well-made, beside him looked very healthy and smartly dressed; she was conscious of this and felt sorry for him and for some reason awkward.

"And you say a great deal you should not," she said. "You've just been talking about my Andrey, but you see you don't know him."

"My Andrey.... Bother him, your Andrey. I am sorry for your youth."

They were already sitting down to supper as the young people went into the dining-room. The grandmother, or Granny as she was called in the household, a very stout, plain old lady with bushy eyebrows and a little moustache, was talking loudly, and from her voice and manner of speaking it could be seen that she was the person of most importance in the house.

140

She owned rows of shops in the market, and the old-fashioned house with columns and the garden, yet she prayed every morning that God might save her from ruin and shed tears as she did so. Her daughter-in-law, Nadya's mother, Nina Ivanovna, a fair-haired woman tightly laced in, with a pince-nez, and diamonds on every finger, Father Andrey, a lean, toothless old man whose face always looked as though he were just going to say something amusing, and his son, Andrey Andreitch, a stout and handsome young man with curly hair looking like an artist or an actor, were all talking of hypnotism.

"You will get well in a week here," said Granny, addressing Sasha. "Only you must eat more. What do you look like!" she sighed. "You are really dreadful! You are a regular prodigal son, that is what you are."

"After wasting his father's substance in riotous living," said Father Andrey slowly, with laughing eyes. "He fed with senseless beasts."

"I like my dad," said Andrey Andreitch, touching his father on the shoulder. "He is a splendid old fellow, a dear old fellow."

Everyone was silent for a space. Sasha suddenly burst out laughing and put his dinner napkin to his mouth.

"So you believe in hypnotism?" said Father Andrey to Nina Ivanovna.

"I cannot, of course, assert that I believe," answered Nina Ivanovna, assuming a very serious, even severe, expression; "but I must own that there is much that is mysterious and incomprehensible in nature."

"I quite agree with you, though I must add that religion distinctly curtails for us the domain of the mysterious."

A big and very fat turkey was served. Father Andrey and Nina Ivanovna went on with their conversation. Nina Ivanovna's diamonds glittered on her fingers, then tears began to glitter in her eyes, she grew excited.

"Though I cannot venture to argue with you," she said, "you must admit there are so many insoluble riddles in life!"

"Not one, I assure you."

After supper Andrey Andreitch played the fiddle and Nina Ivanovna accompanied him on the piano. Ten years before he had taken his degree at the university in the Faculty of Arts, but had never held any post, had no definite work, and only from time to time took part in concerts for charitable objects; and in the town he was regarded as a musician.

Andrey Andreitch played; they all listened in silence. The samovar was boiling quietly on the table and no one but Sasha was drinking tea. Then when it struck twelve a violin string suddenly broke; everyone laughed, bustled about, and began saying good-bye.

After seeing her fiancé out, Nadya went upstairs where she and her mother had their rooms (the lower storey was occupied by the grandmother). They began putting the lights out below in the dining-room, while Sasha still sat on drinking tea. He always spent a long time over tea in the Moscow style, drinking as much as seven glasses at a time. For a long time after Nadya had undressed and gone to bed she could hear the servants clearing away downstairs and Granny talking angrily. At last everything was hushed, and nothing could be heard but Sasha from time to time coughing on a bass note in his room below.

II

When Nadya woke up it must have been two o'clock, it was beginning to get light. A watchman was tapping somewhere far away. She was not sleepy, and her bed felt very soft and uncomfortable. Nadya sat up in her bed and fell to thinking as she had done every night in May. Her thoughts were the same as they had been the night before, useless, persistent thoughts, always alike, of how Andrey Andreitch had begun courting her and had made her an offer, how she had accepted him and then little by little had come to appreciate the kindly, intelligent man. But for some reason now when there was hardly a month left before the wedding, she began to feel dread and uneasiness as though something vague and oppressive were before her.

"Tick-tock, tick-tock..." the watchman tapped lazily. "... Tick-tock."

Through the big old-fashioned window she could see the garden and at a little distance bushes of lilac in full flower, drowsy and lifeless from the cold; and the thick white mist was floating softly up to the lilac, trying to cover it. Drowsy rooks were cawing in the far-away trees.

"My God, why is my heart so heavy?"

Perhaps every girl felt the same before her wedding. There was no knowing! Or was it Sasha's influence? But for several years past Sasha had been repeating the same thing, like a copybook, and when he talked he seemed naïve and queer. But why was it she could not get Sasha out of her head? Why was it?

The watchman left off tapping for a long while. The birds were twittering under the windows and the mist had disappeared from the garden. Everything was lighted up by the spring sunshine as by a smile. Soon the whole garden, warm and caressed by the sun, returned to life, and dewdrops like diamonds glittered on the leaves and the old neglected garden on that morning looked young and gaily decked.

Granny was already awake. Sasha's husky cough began. Nadya could hear them below, setting the samovar and moving the chairs. The hours passed slowly, Nadya had been up and walking about the garden for a long while and still the morning dragged on.

At last Nina Ivanovna appeared with a tear-stained face, carrying a glass of mineral water. She was interested in spiritualism and homeopathy, read a great deal, was fond of talking of the doubts to which she was subject, and to Nadya it seemed as though there were a deep mysterious significance in all that.

Now Nadya kissed her mother and walked beside her.

"What have you been crying about, mother?" she asked.

"Last night I was reading a story in which there is an old man and his daughter. The old man is in some office and his chief falls in love with his daughter. I have not finished it, but there was a passage which made it hard to keep from tears," said Nina Ivanovna and she sipped at her glass. "I thought of it this morning and shed tears again."

"I have been so depressed all these days," said Nadya after a pause. "Why is it I don't sleep at night!"

"I don't know, dear. When I can't sleep I shut my eyes very tightly, like this, and picture to myself Anna Karenin moving about and talking, or something historical from the ancient world...."

Nadya felt that her mother did not understand her and was incapable of understanding. She felt this for the first time in her life, and it positively frightened her and made her want to hide herself; and she went away to her own room.

At two o'clock they sat down to dinner. It was Wednesday, a fast day, and so vegetable soup and bream with boiled grain were set before Granny.

To tease Granny Sasha ate his meat soup as well as the vegetable soup. He was making jokes all through dinner-time, but his jests were laboured and invariably with a moral bearing, and the effect was not at all amusing when before making some witty remark he raised his very long, thin, deathly-looking fingers; and when one remembered that he was very ill and would probably not be much longer in this world, one felt sorry for him and ready to weep.

After dinner Granny went off to her own room to lie down. Nina Ivanovna played on the piano for a little, and then she too went away.

"Oh, dear Nadya!" Sasha began his usual afternoon conversation, "if only you would listen to me! If only you would!"

She was sitting far back in an old-fashioned armchair, with her eyes shut, while he paced slowly about the room from corner to corner.

"If only you would go to the university," he said. "Only enlightened and holy people are interesting, it's only they who are wanted. The more of such people there are, the sooner the Kingdom of God will come on earth. Of your town then not one stone will be left, everything will he blown up from the foundations, everything will be changed as though by magic. And then there will be immense, magnificent houses here, wonderful gardens, marvellous fountains, remarkable people.... But that's not what matters most. What matters most is that the crowd, in our sense of the word, in the sense in which it exists now—that evil will not exist then, because every man will believe and every man will know what he is living for and no one will seek moral support in the crowd. Dear Nadya, darling girl, go away! Show them all that you are sick of this stagnant, grey, sinful life. Prove it to yourself at least!"

"I can't, Sasha, I'm going to be married."

"Oh nonsense! What's it for!"

They went out into the garden and walked up and down a little.

"And however that may be, my dear girl, you must think, you must realize how unclean, how immoral this idle life of yours is," Sasha went on. "Do understand that if, for instance, you and your mother and your grandmother do nothing, it means that someone else is working for you, you are eating up someone else's life, and is that clean, isn't it filthy?"

Nadya wanted to say "Yes, that is true"; she wanted to say that she understood, but tears came into her eyes, her spirits drooped, and shrinking into herself she went off to her room.

Towards evening Andrey Andreitch arrived and as usual played the fiddle for a long time. He was not given to much talk as a rule, and was fond of the fiddle, perhaps because one could be silent while playing. At eleven o'clock when he was about to go home and had put on his greatcoat, he embraced Nadya and began greedily kissing her face, her shoulders, and her hands.

"My dear, my sweet, my charmer," he muttered. "Oh how happy I am! I am beside myself with rapture!"

And it seemed to her as though she had heard that long, long ago, or had read it somewhere... in some old tattered novel thrown away long ago. In the dining-room Sasha was sitting at the table drinking tea with the saucer poised on his five long fingers; Granny was laying out patience; Nina Ivanovna was reading. The flame crackled in the ikon lamp and everything, it seemed, was quiet and going well. Nadya said good-night, went upstairs to her room, got into bed and fell asleep at once. But just as on the night before, almost before it was light, she woke up. She was not sleepy, there was an uneasy, oppressive feeling in her heart. She sat up with her head on her knees and thought of her fiancé and her marriage.... She for some reason remembered that her mother had not loved her father and now had nothing and lived in complete dependence on her mother-in-law, Granny. And however much Nadya pondered she could not imagine why she had hitherto seen in her mother something special and exceptional, how it was she had not noticed that she was a simple, ordinary, unhappy woman.

And Sasha downstairs was not asleep, she could hear him coughing. He is a queer, naïve man, thought Nadya, and in all his dreams, in all those marvellous gardens and wonderful fountains one felt there was something absurd. But for some reason in his naïveté, in this very absurdity there was something so beautiful that as soon as she thought of the possibility of going to the university, it sent a cold thrill through her heart and her bosom and flooded them with joy and rapture.

"But better not think, better not think..." she whispered. "I must not think of it."

"Tick-tock," tapped the watchman somewhere far away. "Tick-tock... tick-tock...."

III

In the middle of June Sasha suddenly felt bored and made up his mind to return to Moscow.

"I can't exist in this town," he said gloomily. "No water supply, no drains! It disgusts me to eat at dinner; the filth in the kitchen is incredible...."

"Wait a little, prodigal son!" Granny tried to persuade him, speaking for some reason in a whisper, "the wedding is to be on the seventh."

"I don't want to."

"You meant to stay with us until September!"

"But now, you see, I don't want to. I must get to work."

The summer was grey and cold, the trees were wet, everything in the garden looked dejected and uninviting, it certainly did make one long to get to work. The sound of unfamiliar women's voices was heard downstairs and upstairs, there was the rattle of a sewing machine in Granny's room, they were working hard at the trousseau. Of fur coats alone, six were provided for Nadya, and the cheapest of them, in Granny's words, had cost three hundred roubles! The fuss irritated Sasha; he stayed in his own room and was cross, but everyone persuaded him to remain, and he promised not to go before the first of July.

Time passed quickly. On St. Peter's day Andrey Andreitch went with Nadya after dinner to Moscow Street to look once more at the house which had been taken and made ready for the young couple some time before. It was a house of two storeys, but so far only the upper floor had been furnished. There was in the hall a shining floor painted and parqueted, there were Viennese chairs, a piano, a violin stand; there was a smell of paint. On the wall hung a big oil painting in a gold frame—a naked lady and beside her a purple vase with a broken handle.

"An exquisite picture," said Andrey Andreitch, and he gave a respectful sigh. "It's the work of the artist Shismatchevsky."

Then there was the drawing-room with the round table, and a sofa and easy chairs upholstered in bright blue. Above the sofa was a big photograph of Father Andrey wearing a priest's velvet cap and decorations. Then they went into the dining-room in which there was a sideboard; then into the bedroom; here in the half dusk stood two bedsteads side by side, and it looked as though the bedroom had been decorated with the idea that it would always be very agreeable there and could not possibly be anything else. Andrey Andreitch led Nadya about the rooms, all the while keeping his arm round her waist; and she felt weak and conscience-stricken. She hated all the rooms, the beds, the easy chairs; she was nauseated by the naked lady. It was clear to her now that she had ceased to love Andrey Andreitch or perhaps had never loved him at all; but how to say this and to whom to say it and with what object she did not understand, and could not understand, though she was thinking about it all day and all night....

He held her round the waist, talked so affectionately, so modestly, was so happy, walking about this house of his; while she saw nothing in it all but vulgarity, stupid, naïve, unbearable vulgarity, and his arm round her waist felt as hard and cold as an iron hoop. And every minute she was on the point of running away, bursting into sobs, throwing herself out of a window. Andrey Andreitch led her into the bathroom and here he touched a tap fixed in the wall and at once water flowed.

"What do you say to that?" he said, and laughed. "I had a tank holding two hundred gallons put in the loft, and so now we shall have water."

They walked across the yard and went out into the street and took a cab. Thick clouds of dust were blowing, and it seemed as though it were just going to rain.

"You are not cold?" said Andrey Andreitch, screwing up his eyes at the dust.

She did not answer.

"Yesterday, you remember, Sasha blamed me for doing nothing," he said, after a brief silence. "Well, he is right, absolutely right! I do nothing and can do nothing. My precious, why is it? Why is it that the very thought that I may some day fix a cockade on my cap and go into the government service is so hateful to me? Why do I feel so uncomfortable when I see a lawyer or a Latin master or a member of the Zemstvo? O Mother Russia! O Mother Russia! What a burden of idle and useless people you still carry! How many like me are upon you, long-suffering Mother!"

And from the fact that he did nothing he drew generalizations, seeing in it a sign of the times.

"When we are married let us go together into the country, my precious; there we will work! We will buy ourselves a little piece of land with a garden and a river, we will labour and watch life. Oh, how splendid that will be!"

He took off his hat, and his hair floated in the wind, while she listened to him and thought: "Good God, I wish I were home!"

When they were quite near the house they overtook Father Andrey.

"Ah, here's father coming," cried Andrey Andreitch, delighted, and he waved his hat. "I love my dad really," he said as he paid the cabman. "He's a splendid old fellow, a dear old fellow."

Nadya went into the house, feeling cross and unwell, thinking that there would be visitors all the evening, that she would have to entertain them, to smile, to listen to the fiddle, to listen to all sorts of nonsense, and to talk of nothing but the wedding.

Granny, dignified, gorgeous in her silk dress, and haughty as she always seemed before visitors, was sitting before the samovar. Father Andrey came in with his sly smile.

"I have the pleasure and blessed consolation of seeing you in health," he said to Granny, and it was hard to tell whether he was joking or speaking seriously.

IV

The wind was beating on the window and on the roof; there was a whistling sound, and in the stove the house spirit was plaintively and sullenly droning his song. It was past midnight; everyone in the house had gone to bed, but no one was asleep, and it seemed all the while to Nadya as though they were playing the fiddle below. There was a sharp bang; a shutter must have been torn off. A minute later Nina Ivanovna came in in her nightgown, with a candle.

"What was the bang, Nadya?" she asked.

Her mother, with her hair in a single plait and a timid smile on her face, looked older, plainer, smaller on that stormy night. Nadya remembered that quite a little time ago she had thought her mother an exceptional woman and had listened with pride to the things she said; and now she could not remember those things, everything that came into her mind was so feeble and useless.

In the stove was the sound of several bass voices in chorus, and she even heard "O-o-o my G-o-od!" Nadya sat on her bed, and suddenly she clutched at her hair and burst into sobs.

"Mother, mother, my own," she said. "If only you knew what is happening to me! I beg you, I beseech you, let me go away! I beseech you!"

"Where?" asked Nina Ivanovna, not understanding, and she sat down on the bedstead. "Go where?"

For a long while Nadya cried and could not utter a word.

"Let me go away from the town," she said at last. "There must not and will not be a wedding, understand that! I don't love that man... I can't even speak about him."

"No, my own, no!" Nina Ivanovna said quickly, terribly alarmed. "Calm yourself—it's just because you are in low spirits. It will pass, it often happens. Most likely you have had a tiff with Andrey; but lovers' quarrels always end in kisses!"

"Oh, go away, mother, oh, go away," sobbed Nadya.

"Yes," said Nina Ivanovna after a pause, "it's not long since you were a baby, a little girl, and now you are engaged to be married. In nature there is a continual transmutation of substances. Before you know where you are you will be a mother yourself and an old woman, and will have as rebellious a daughter as I have."

"My darling, my sweet, you are clever you know, you are unhappy," said Nadya. "You are very unhappy; why do you say such very dull, commonplace things? For God's sake, why?"

Nina Ivanovna tried to say something, but could not utter a word; she gave a sob and went away to her own room. The bass voices began droning in the stove again, and Nadya felt suddenly frightened. She jumped out of bed and went quickly to her mother. Nina Ivanovna, with tear-stained face, was lying in bed wrapped in a pale blue quilt and holding a book in her hands.

"Mother, listen to me!" said Nadya. "I implore you, do understand! If you would only understand how petty and degrading our life is. My eyes have been opened, and I see it all now. And what is your Andrey Andreitch?

Why, he is not intelligent, mother! Merciful heavens, do understand, mother, he is stupid!"

Nina Ivanovna abruptly sat up.

"You and your grandmother torment me," she said with a sob. "I want to live! to live," she repeated, and twice she beat her little fist upon her bosom. "Let me be free! I am still young, I want to live, and you have made me an old woman between you!"

She broke into bitter tears, lay down and curled up under the quilt, and looked so small, so pitiful, so foolish. Nadya went to her room, dressed, and sitting at the window fell to waiting for the morning. She sat all night thinking, while someone seemed to be tapping on the shutters and whistling in the yard.

In the morning Granny complained that the wind had blown down all the apples in the garden, and broken down an old plum tree. It was grey, murky, cheerless, dark enough for candles; everyone complained of the cold, and the rain lashed on the windows. After tea Nadya went into Sasha's room and without saying a word knelt down before an armchair in the corner and hid her face in her hands.

"What is it?" asked Sasha.

"I can't..." she said. "How I could go on living here before, I can't understand, I can't conceive! I despise the man I am engaged to, I despise myself, I despise all this idle, senseless existence."

"Well, well," said Sasha, not yet grasping what was meant. "That's all right... that's good."

"I am sick of this life," Nadya went on. "I can't endure another day here. Tomorrow I am going away. Take me with you for God's sake!"

For a minute Sasha looked at her in astonishment; at last he understood and was delighted as a child. He waved his arms and began pattering with his slippers as though he were dancing with delight.

"Splendid," he said, rubbing his hands. "My goodness, how fine that is!"

And she stared at him without blinking, with adoring eyes, as though spellbound, expecting every minute that he would say something important, something infinitely significant; he had told her nothing yet, but already it seemed to her that something new and great was opening before her which she had not known till then, and already she gazed at him full of expectation, ready to face anything, even death.

"I am going tomorrow," he said after a moment's thought. "You come to the station to see me off.... I'll take your things in my portmanteau, and I'll get your ticket, and when the third bell rings you get into the carriage, and we'll go off. You'll see me as far as Moscow and then go on to Petersburg alone. Have you a passport?"

"Yes."

"I can promise you, you won't regret it," said Sasha, with conviction. "You will go, you will study, and then go where fate takes you. When you turn your life upside down everything will be changed. The great thing is to turn your life upside down, and all the rest is unimportant. And so we will set off tomorrow?"

"Oh yes, for God's sake!"

It seemed to Nadya that she was very much excited, that her heart was heavier than ever before, that she would spend all the time till she went away in misery and agonizing thought; but she had hardly gone upstairs and lain down on her bed when she fell asleep at once, with traces of tears and a smile on her face, and slept soundly till evening.

V

A cab had been sent for. Nadya in her hat and overcoat went upstairs to take one more look at her mother, at all her belongings. She stood in her own room beside her still warm bed, looked about her, then went slowly in to her mother. Nina Ivanovna was asleep; it was quite still in her room. Nadya kissed her mother, smoothed her hair, stood still for a couple of minutes... then walked slowly downstairs.

It was raining heavily. The cabman with the hood pulled down was standing at the entrance, drenched with rain.

"There is not room for you, Nadya," said Granny, as the servants began putting in the luggage. "What an idea to see him off in such weather! You had better stop at home. Goodness, how it rains!"

Nadya tried to say something, but could not. Then Sasha helped Nadya in and covered her feet with a rug. Then he sat down beside her.

"Good luck to you! God bless you!" Granny cried from the steps. "Mind you write to us from Moscow, Sasha!"

"Right. Good-bye, Granny."

"The Queen of Heaven keep you!"

"Oh, what weather!" said Sasha.

It was only now that Nadya began to cry. Now it was clear to her that she certainly was going, which she had not really believed when she was saying good-bye to Granny, and when she was looking at her mother. Good-bye, town! And she suddenly thought of it all: Andrey, and his father and the new house and the naked lady with the vase; and it all no longer frightened her, nor weighed upon her, but was naïve and trivial and continually retreated further away. And when they got into the railway carriage and the train began to move, all that past which had been so big and serious shrank up into something tiny, and a vast wide future which till then had scarcely been noticed began unfolding before her. The rain pattered on the carriage windows, nothing could be seen but the green fields, telegraph posts with birds sitting on the wires flitted by, and joy made her hold her breath; she thought that she was going to freedom, going to study, and this was just like what used, ages ago, to be called going off to be a free Cossack.

She laughed and cried and prayed all at once.

"It's a-all right," said Sasha, smiling. "It's a-all right."

VI

Autumn had passed and winter, too, had gone. Nadya had begun to be very homesick and thought every day of her mother and her grandmother;

she thought of Sasha too. The letters that came from home were kind and gentle, and it seemed as though everything by now were forgiven and forgotten. In May after the examinations she set off for home in good health and high spirits, and stopped on the way at Moscow to see Sasha. He was just the same as the year before, with the same beard and unkempt hair, with the same large beautiful eyes, and he still wore the same coat and canvas trousers; but he looked unwell and worried, he seemed both older and thinner, and kept coughing, and for some reason he struck Nadya as grey and provincial.

"My God, Nadya has come!" he said, and laughed gaily. "My darling girl!"

They sat in the printing room, which was full of tobacco smoke, and smelt strongly, stiflingly of Indian ink and paint; then they went to his room, which also smelt of tobacco and was full of the traces of spitting; near a cold samovar stood a broken plate with dark paper on it, and there were masses of dead flies on the table and on the floor. And everything showed that Sasha ordered his personal life in a slovenly way and lived anyhow, with utter contempt for comfort, and if anyone began talking to him of his personal happiness, of his personal life, of affection for him, he would not have understood and would have only laughed.

"It is all right, everything has gone well," said Nadya hurriedly. "Mother came to see me in Petersburg in the autumn; she said that Granny is not angry, and only keeps going into my room and making the sign of the cross over the walls."

Sasha looked cheerful, but he kept coughing, and talked in a cracked voice, and Nadya kept looking at him, unable to decide whether he really were seriously ill or whether it were only her fancy.

"Dear Sasha," she said, "you are ill."

"No, it's nothing, I am ill, but not very..."

"Oh, dear!" cried Nadya, in agitation. "Why don't you go to a doctor? Why don't you take care of your health? My dear, darling Sasha," she said, and tears gushed from her eyes and for some reason there rose before her imagination Andrey Andreitch and the naked lady with the vase, and all her past which seemed now as far away as her childhood; and she began crying because Sasha no longer seemed to her so novel, so cultured, and so interesting as the year before. "Dear Sasha, you are very, very ill... I would do anything to make you not so pale and thin. I am so indebted to you! You can't imagine how much you have done for me, my good Sasha! In reality you are now the person nearest and dearest to me."

They sat on and talked, and now, after Nadya had spent a winter in Petersburg, Sasha, his works, his smile, his whole figure had for her a suggestion of something out of date, old-fashioned, done with long ago and perhaps already dead and buried.

"I am going down the Volga the day after tomorrow," said Sasha, "and then to drink koumiss. I mean to drink koumiss. A friend and his wife are going with me. His wife is a wonderful woman; I am always at her, trying to persuade her to go to the university. I want her to turn her life upside down."

After having talked they drove to the station. Sasha got her tea and apples; and when the train began moving and he waved his handkerchief at her, smiling, it could be seen even from his legs that he was very ill and would not live long.

Nadya reached her native town at midday. As she drove home from the station the streets struck her as very wide and the houses very small and squat; there were no people about, she met no one but the German piano-tuner in a rusty greatcoat. And all the houses looked as though they were covered with dust. Granny, who seemed to have grown quite old, but was as fat and plain as ever, flung her arms round Nadya and cried for a long time with her face on Nadya's shoulder, unable to tear herself away. Nina Ivanovna looked much older and plainer and seemed shrivelled up, but was still tightly laced, and still had diamonds flashing on her fingers.

"My darling," she said, trembling all over, "my darling!"

Then they sat down and cried without speaking. It was evident that both mother and grandmother realized that the past was lost and gone, never to return; they had now no position in society, no prestige as before, no right to invite visitors; so it is when in the midst of an easy careless life the police suddenly burst in at night and made a search, and it turns out that the head of the family has embezzled money or committed forgery—and goodbye then to the easy careless life for ever!

Nadya went upstairs and saw the same bed, the same windows with naïve white curtains, and outside the windows the same garden, gay and noisy, bathed in sunshine. She touched the table, sat down and sank into thought. And she had a good dinner and drank tea with delicious rich cream; but something was missing, there was a sense of emptiness in the rooms and the ceilings were so low. In the evening she went to bed, covered herself up and for some reason it seemed to her to be funny lying in this snug, very soft bed.

Nina Ivanovna came in for a minute; she sat down as people who feel guilty sit down, timidly, and looking about her.

"Well, tell me, Nadya," she enquired after a brief pause, "are you contented? Quite contented?"

"Yes, mother."

Nina Ivanovna got up, made the sign of the cross over Nadya and the windows.

"I have become religious, as you see," she said. "You know I am studying philosophy now, and I am always thinking and thinking.... And many things have become as clear as daylight to me. It seems to me that what is above all necessary is that life should pass as it were through a prism."

"Tell me, mother, how is Granny in health?"

"She seems all right. When you went away that time with Sasha and the telegram came from you, Granny fell on the floor as she read it; for three days she lay without moving. After that she was always praying and crying. But now she is all right again."

She got up and walked about the room.

"Tick-tock," tapped the watchman. "Tick-tock, tick-tock...."

"What is above all necessary is that life should pass as it were through a prism," she said; "in other words, that life in consciousness should be analyzed into its simplest elements as into the seven primary colours, and each element must be studied separately."

What Nina Ivanovna said further and when she went away, Nadya did not hear, as she quickly fell asleep.

May passed; June came. Nadya had grown used to being at home. Granny busied herself about the samovar, heaving deep sighs. Nina Ivanovna talked in the evenings about her philosophy; she still lived in the house like a poor relation, and had to go to Granny for every farthing. There were lots of flies in the house, and the ceilings seemed to become lower and lower. Granny and Nina Ivanovna did not go out in the streets for fear of meeting Father Andrey and Andrey Andreitch. Nadya walked about the garden and the streets, looked at the grey fences, and it seemed to her that everything in the town had grown old, was out of date and was only waiting either for the end, or for the beginning of something young and fresh. Oh, if only that new, bright life would come more quickly—that life in which one will be able to face one's fate boldly and directly, to know that one is right, to be light-hearted and free! And sooner or later such a life will come. The time will come when of Granny's house, where things are so arranged that the four servants can only live in one room in filth in the basement the time will come when of that house not a trace will remain, and it will be forgotten, no one will remember it. And Nadya's only entertainment was from the boys next door; when she walked about the garden they knocked on the fence and shouted in mockery: "Betrothed! Betrothed!"

A letter from Sasha arrived from Saratov. In his gay dancing handwriting he told them that his journey on the Volga had been a complete success, but that he had been taken rather ill in Saratov, had lost his voice, and had been for the last fortnight in the hospital. She knew what that meant, and she was overwhelmed with a foreboding that was like a conviction. And it vexed her that this foreboding and the thought of Sasha did not distress her so much as before. She had a passionate desire for life, longed to be in Petersburg, and her friendship with Sasha seemed now sweet but something far, far away! She did not sleep all night, and in the morning sat at the window, listening. And she did in fact hear voices below; Granny, greatly agitated, was asking questions rapidly. Then some one began crying.... When Nadya went downstairs Granny was standing in the corner, praying before the ikon and her face was tearful. A telegram lay on the table.

For some time Nadya walked up and down the room, listening to Granny's weeping; then she picked up the telegram and read it.

It announced that the previous morning Alexandr Timofeitch, or more simply, Sasha, had died at Saratov of consumption.

Granny and Nina Ivanovna went to the church to order a memorial service, while Nadya went on walking about the rooms and thinking. She recognized clearly that her life had been turned upside down as Sasha wished; that here she was, alien, isolated, useless and that everything here was useless to her; that all the past had been torn away from her and vanished as though it had been burnt up and the ashes scattered to the winds. She went into Sasha's room and stood there for a while.

"Good-bye, dear Sasha," she thought, and before her mind rose the vista of a new, wide, spacious life, and that life, still obscure and full of mysteries, beckoned her and attracted her.

She went upstairs to her own room to pack, and next morning said good-bye to her family, and full of life and high spirits left the town—as she supposed for ever.

IONITCH

I

WHEN visitors to the provincial town S— complained of the dreariness and monotony of life, the inhabitants of the town, as though defending themselves, declared that it was very nice in S—, that there was a library, a theatre, a club; that they had balls; and, finally, that there were clever, agreeable, and interesting families with whom one could make acquaintance. And they used to point to the family of the Turkins as the most highly cultivated and talented.

This family lived in their own house in the principal street, near the Governor's. Ivan Petrovitch Turkin himself—a stout, handsome, dark man with whiskers—used to get up amateur performances for benevolent objects, and used to take the part of an elderly general and cough very amusingly. He knew a number of anecdotes, charades, proverbs, and was fond of being humorous and witty, and he always wore an expression from which it was impossible to tell whether he were joking or in earnest. His wife, Vera Iosifovna—a thin, nice-looking lady who wore a pince-nez—used to write novels and stories, and was very fond of reading them aloud to her visitors. The daughter, Ekaterina Ivanovna, a young girl, used to play on the piano. In short, every member of the family had a special talent. The Turkins welcomed visitors, and good-humouredly displayed their talents with genuine simplicity. Their stone house was roomy and cool in summer; half of the windows looked into a shady old garden, where nightingales used to sing in the spring. When there were visitors in the house, there was a clatter of knives in the kitchen and a smell of fried onions in the yard— and that was always a sure sign of a plentiful and savoury supper to follow.

And as soon as Dmitri Ionitch Startsev was appointed the district doctor, and took up his abode at Dyalizh, six miles from S——, he, too, was told that as a cultivated man it was essential for him to make the acquaintance of the Turkins. In the winter he was introduced to Ivan Petrovitch in the street; they talked about the weather, about the theatre, about the cholera; an invitation followed. On a holiday in the spring—it was Ascension Day—after seeing his patients, Startsev set off for town in search of a little recreation and to make some purchases. He walked in a leisurely way (he had not yet set up his carriage), humming all the time: "'Before I'd drunk the tears from life's goblet....'"

In town he dined, went for a walk in the gardens, then Ivan Petrovitch's invitation came into his mind, as it were of itself, and he decided to call on the Turkins and see what sort of people they were.

"How do you do, if you please?" said Ivan Petrovitch, meeting him on the steps. "Delighted, delighted to see such an agreeable visitor. Come along; I will introduce you to my better half. I tell him, Verotchka," he went on, as he presented the doctor to his wife— "I tell him that he has no human right to sit at home in a hospital; he ought to devote his leisure to society. Oughtn't he, darling?"

"Sit here," said Vera Iosifovna, making her visitor sit down beside her. "You can dance attendance on me. My husband is jealous—he is an Othello; but we will try and behave so well that he will notice nothing."

"Ah, you spoilt chicken!" Ivan Petrovitch muttered tenderly, and he kissed her on the forehead. "You have come just in the nick of time," he said, addressing the doctor again. "My better half has written a 'hugeous' novel, and she is going to read it aloud today."

"Petit Jean," said Vera Iosifovna to her husband, "dites que l'on nous donne du th?"

Startsev was introduced to Ekaterina Ivanovna, a girl of eighteen, very much like her mother, thin and pretty. Her expression was still childish and her figure was soft and slim; and her developed girlish bosom, healthy and beautiful, was suggestive of spring, real spring.

Then they drank tea with jam, honey, and sweetmeats, and with very nice cakes, which melted in the mouth. As the evening came on, other visitors gradually arrived, and Ivan Petrovitch fixed his laughing eyes on each of them and said: "How do you do, if you please?"

Then they all sat down in the drawing-room with very serious faces, and Vera Iosifovna read her novel. It began like this: "The frost was intense...." The windows were wide open; from the kitchen came the clatter of knives and the smell of fried onions.... It was comfortable in the soft deep arm-chair; the lights had such a friendly twinkle in the twilight of the drawing-room, and at the moment on a summer evening when sounds of voices and laughter floated in from the street and whiffs of lilac from the yard, it was difficult to grasp that the frost was intense, and that the setting sun was lighting with its chilly rays a solitary wayfarer on the snowy plain. Vera Iosifovna read how a beautiful young countess founded a school, a hospital, a library, in her village, and fell in love with a wandering artist; she read of what never happens in real life, and yet it was pleasant to listen—it was comfortable, and such agreeable, serene thoughts kept coming into the mind, one had no desire to get up.

"Not badsome..." Ivan Petrovitch said softly.

And one of the visitors hearing, with his thoughts far away, said hardly audibly: "Yes... truly...."

One hour passed, another. In the town gardens close by a band was playing and a chorus was singing. When Vera Iosifovna shut her manuscript book, the company was silent for five minutes, listening to "Lutchina" being sung by the chorus, and the song gave what was not in the novel and is in real life.

"Do you publish your stories in magazines?" Startsev asked Vera Iosifovna.

"No," she answered. "I never publish. I write it and put it away in my cupboard. Why publish?" she explained. "We have enough to live on."

And for some reason every one sighed.

"And now, Kitten, you play something," Ivan Petrovitch said to his daughter.

The lid of the piano was raised and the music lying ready was opened. Ekaterina Ivanovna sat down and banged on the piano with both hands, and then banged again with all her might, and then again and again; her shoulders and bosom shook. She obstinately banged on the same notes, and it sounded as if she would not leave off until she had hammered the keys into the piano. The drawing-room was filled with the din; everything was resounding; the floor, the ceiling, the furniture.... Ekaterina Ivanovna was playing a difficult passage, interesting simply on account of its difficulty, long and monotonous, and Startsev, listening, pictured stones dropping down a steep hill and going on dropping, and he wished they would leave off dropping; and at the same time Ekaterina Ivanovna, rosy from the violent exercise, strong and vigorous, with a lock of hair falling over her forehead, attracted him very much. After the winter spent at Dyalizh among patients and peasants, to sit in a drawing-room, to watch this young, elegant, and, in all probability, pure creature, and to listen to these noisy, tedious but still cultured sounds, was so pleasant, so novel....

"Well, Kitten, you have played as never before," said Ivan Petrovitch, with tears in his eyes, when his daughter had finished and stood up. "Die, Denis; you won't write anything better."

All flocked round her, congratulated her, expressed astonishment, declared that it was long since they had heard such music, and she listened in silence with a faint smile, and her whole figure was expressive of triumph.

"Splendid, superb!"

"Splendid," said Startsev, too, carried away by the general enthusiasm. "Where have you studied?" he asked Ekaterina Ivanovna. "At the Conservatoire?"

"No, I am only preparing for the Conservatoire, and till now have been working with Madame Zavlovsky."

"Have you finished at the high school here?"

"Oh, no," Vera Iosifovna answered for her, "We have teachers for her at home; there might be bad influences at the high school or a boarding school, you know. While a young girl is growing up, she ought to be under no influence but her mother's."

"All the same, I'm going to the Conservatoire," said Ekaterina Ivanovna.

"No. Kitten loves her mamma. Kitten won't grieve papa and mamma."

"No, I'm going, I'm going," said Ekaterina Ivanovna, with playful caprice and stamping her foot.

And at supper it was Ivan Petrovitch who displayed his talents. Laughing only with his eyes, he told anecdotes, made epigrams, asked ridiculous riddles and answered them himself, talking the whole time in his extraordinary language, evolved in the course of prolonged practice in witticism and evidently now become a habit: "Badsome," "Hugeous," "Thank you most dumbly," and so on.

But that was not all. When the guests, replete and satisfied, trooped into the hall, looking for their coats and sticks, there bustled about them the footman Pavlusha, or, as he was called in the family, Pava—a lad of fourteen with shaven head and chubby cheeks.

"Come, Pava, perform!" Ivan Petrovitch said to him.

Pava struck an attitude, flung up his arm, and said in a tragic tone: "Unhappy woman, die!"

And every one roared with laughter.

"It's entertaining," thought Startsev, as he went out into the street.

He went to a restaurant and drank some beer, then set off to walk home to Dyalizh; he walked all the way singing: "'thy voice to me so languid and caressing....'"

On going to bed, he felt not the slightest fatigue after the six miles' walk. On the contrary, he felt as though he could with pleasure have walked another twenty.

"Not badsome," he thought, and laughed as he fell asleep.

II

Startsev kept meaning to go to the Turkins' again, but there was a great deal of work in the hospital, and he was unable to find free time. In this way more than a year passed in work and solitude. But one day a letter in a light blue envelope was brought him from the town.

Vera Iosifovna had been suffering for some time from migraine, but now since Kitten frightened her every day by saying that she was going away to the Conservatoire, the attacks began to be more frequent. All the doctors of the town had been at the Turkins'; at last it was the district doctor's turn. Vera Iosifovna wrote him a touching letter in which she begged him to come and relieve her sufferings. Startsev went, and after that he began to be often, very often at the Turkins'.... He really did something for Vera Iosifovna, and she was already telling all her visitors that he was a wonderful and exceptional doctor. But it was not for the sake of her migraine that he visited the Turkins' now....

It was a holiday. Ekaterina Ivanovna finished her long, wearisome exercises on the piano. Then they sat a long time in the dining-room, drinking tea, and Ivan Petrovitch told some amusing story. Then there was a ring and he had to go into the hall to welcome a guest; Startsev took advantage of the momentary commotion, and whispered to Ekaterina Ivanovna in great agitation: "For God's sake, I entreat you, don't torment me; let us go into the garden!"

She shrugged her shoulders, as though perplexed and not knowing what he wanted of her, but she got up and went.

"You play the piano for three or four hours," he said, following her; "then you sit with your mother, and there is no possibility of speaking to you. Give me a quarter of an hour at least, I beseech you."

Autumn was approaching, and it was quiet and melancholy in the old garden; the dark leaves lay thick in the walks. It was already beginning to get dark early.

"I haven't seen you for a whole week," Startsev went on, "and if you only knew what suffering it is! Let us sit down. Listen to me."

They had a favourite place in the garden; a seat under an old spreading maple. And now they sat down on this seat.

"What do you want?" said Ekaterina Ivanovna drily, in a matter-of-fact tone.

"I have not seen you for a whole week; I have not heard you for so long. I long passionately, I thirst for your voice. Speak."

She fascinated him by her freshness, the naive expression of her eyes and cheeks. Even in the way her dress hung on her, he saw something extraordinarily charming, touching in its simplicity and naive grace; and at the same time, in spite of this naivete, she seemed to him intelligent and developed beyond her years. He could talk with her about literature, about art, about anything he liked; could complain to her of life, of people, though it sometimes happened in the middle of serious conversation she would laugh inappropriately or run away into the house. Like almost all girls of her neighbourhood, she had read a great deal (as a rule, people read very little in S—, and at the lending library they said if it were not for the girls and the young Jews, they might as well shut up the library). This afforded Startsev infinite delight; he used to ask her eagerly every time what she had been reading the last few days, and listened enthralled while she told him.

"What have you been reading this week since I saw you last?" he asked now. "Do please tell me."

"I have been reading Pisemsky."

"What exactly?"

"'A Thousand Souls,'" answered Kitten. "And what a funny name Pisemsky had—Alexey Feofilaktitch!

"Where are you going?" cried Startsev in horror, as she suddenly got up and walked towards the house. "I must talk to you; I want to explain myself.... Stay with me just five minutes, I supplicate you!"

She stopped as though she wanted to say something, then awkwardly thrust a note into his hand, ran home and sat down to the piano again.

"Be in the cemetery," Startsev read, "at eleven o'clock tonight, near the tomb of Demetti."

"Well, that's not at all clever," he thought, coming to himself. "Why the cemetery? What for?"

It was clear: Kitten was playing a prank. Who would seriously dream of making an appointment at night in the cemetery far out of the town, when it might have been arranged in the street or in the town gardens? And was it in keeping with him—a district doctor, an intelligent, staid man to be sighing, receiving notes, to hang about cemeteries, to do silly things that even schoolboys think ridiculous nowadays? What would this romance lead to? What would his colleagues say when they heard of it? Such were Startsev's reflections as he wandered round the tables at the club, and at half-past ten he suddenly set off for the cemetery.

By now he had his own pair of horses, and a coachman called Panteleimon, in a velvet waistcoat. The moon was shining. It was still warm, warm as it is in autumn. Dogs were howling in the suburb near the slaughter-house. Startsev left his horses in one of the side-streets at the end of the town, and walked on foot to the cemetery.

"We all have our oddities," he thought. "Kitten is odd, too; and —who knows?—perhaps she is not joking, perhaps she will come"; and he abandoned himself to this faint, vain hope, and it intoxicated him.

He walked for half a mile through the fields; the cemetery showed as a dark streak in the distance, like a forest or a big garden. The wall of white stone came into sight, the gate.... In the moonlight he could read on the gate: "The hour cometh." Startsev went in at the little gate, and before anything else he saw the white crosses and monuments on both sides of the broad avenue, and the black shadows of them and the poplars; and for a long way round it was all white and black, and the slumbering trees bowed their branches over the white stones. It seemed as though it were lighter here than in the fields; the maple-leaves stood out sharply like paws on the yellow sand of the avenue and on the stones, and the inscriptions on the tombs could be clearly read. For the first moments Startsev was struck now by what he saw for the first time in his life, and what he would probably never see again; a world not like anything else, a world in which the moonlight was as soft and beautiful, as though slumbering here in its cradle, where there was no life, none whatever; but in every dark poplar, in every tomb, there was felt the presence of a mystery that promised a life peaceful, beautiful, eternal. The stones and faded flowers, together with the autumn scent of the leaves, all told of forgiveness, melancholy, and peace.

All was silence around; the stars looked down from the sky in the profound stillness, and Startsev's footsteps sounded loud and out of place, and only when the church clock began striking and he imagined himself dead, buried there for ever, he felt as though some one were looking at him, and for a moment he thought that it was not peace and tranquility, but stifled despair, the dumb dreariness of non-existence....

Demetti's tomb was in the form of a shrine with an angel at the top. The Italian opera had once visited S— and one of the singers had died; she had been buried here, and this monument put up to her. No one in the town remembered her, but the lamp at the entrance reflected the moonlight, and looked as though it were burning.

There was no one, and, indeed, who would come here at midnight? But Startsev waited, and as though the moonlight warmed his passion, he waited passionately, and, in imagination, pictured kisses and embraces. He sat near the monument for half an hour, then paced up and down the side avenues, with his hat in his hand, waiting and thinking of the many women and girls buried in these tombs who had been beautiful and fascinating, who had loved, at night burned with passion, yielding themselves to caresses. How wickedly Mother Nature jested at man's expense, after all! How humiliating it was to recognise it!

Startsev thought this, and at the same time he wanted to cry out that he wanted love, that he was eager for it at all costs. To his eyes they were not slabs of marble, but fair white bodies in the moonlight; he saw shapes hiding bashfully in the shadows of the trees, felt their warmth, and the languor was oppressive....

And as though a curtain were lowered, the moon went behind a cloud, and suddenly all was darkness. Startsev could scarcely find the gate—by now it was as dark as it is on an autumn night. Then he wandered about for an hour and a half, looking for the side-street in which he had left his horses.

"I am tired; I can scarcely stand on my legs," he said to Panteleimon.

And settling himself with relief in his carriage, he thought: "Och! I ought not to get fat!"

III

The following evening he went to the Turkins' to make an offer. But it turned out to be an inconvenient moment, as Ekaterina Ivanovna was in her own room having her hair done by a hair-dresser. She was getting ready to go to a dance at the club.

He had to sit a long time again in the dining-room drinking tea. Ivan Petrovitch, seeing that his visitor was bored and preoccupied, drew some notes out of his waistcoat pocket, read a funny letter from a German steward, saying that all the ironmongery was ruined and the plasticity was peeling off the walls.

"I expect they will give a decent dowry," thought Startsev, listening absent-mindedly.

After a sleepless night, he found himself in a state of stupefaction, as though he had been given something sweet and soporific to drink; there was fog in his soul, but joy and warmth, and at the same time a sort of cold, heavy fragment of his brain was reflecting: "Stop before it is too late! Is she the match for you? She is spoilt, whimsical, sleeps till two o'clock in the afternoon, while you are a deacon's son, a district doctor...."

"What of it?" he thought. "I don't care."

"Besides, if you marry her," the fragment went on, "then her relations will make you give up the district work and live in the town."

"After all," he thought, "if it must be the town, the town it must be.

They will give a dowry; we can establish ourselves suitably."

At last Ekaterina Ivanovna came in, dressed for the ball, with a low neck, looking fresh and pretty; and Startsev admired her so much, and went into such ecstasies, that he could say nothing, but simply stared at her and laughed.

She began saying good-bye, and he—he had no reason for staying now—got up, saying that it was time for him to go home; his patients were waiting for him.

"Well, there's no help for that," said Ivan Petrovitch. "Go, and you might take Kitten to the club on the way."

It was spotting with rain; it was very dark, and they could only tell where the horses were by Panteleimon's husky cough. The hood of the carriage was put up.

"I stand upright; you lie down right; he lies all right," said Ivan Petrovitch as he put his daughter into the carriage.

They drove off.

"I was at the cemetery yesterday," Startsev began. "How ungenerous and merciless it was on your part!..."

"You went to the cemetery?"

"Yes, I went there and waited almost till two o'clock. I suffered..."

"Well, suffer, if you cannot understand a joke."

Ekaterina Ivanovna, pleased at having so cleverly taken in a man who was in love with her, and at being the object of such intense love, burst out laughing and suddenly uttered a shriek of terror, for, at that very minute, the horses turned sharply in at the gate of the club, and the carriage almost tilted over. Startsev put his arm round Ekaterina Ivanovna's waist; in her fright she nestled up to him, and he could not restrain himself, and passionately kissed her on the lips and on the chin, and hugged her more tightly.

"That's enough," she said drily.

And a minute later she was not in the carriage, and a policeman near the lighted entrance of the club shouted in a detestable voice to

Panteleimon: "What are you stopping for, you crow? Drive on."

Startsev drove home, but soon afterwards returned. Attired in another man's dress suit and a stiff white tie which kept sawing at his neck and trying to slip away from the collar, he was sitting at midnight in the club drawing-room, and was saying with enthusiasm to Ekaterina Ivanovna.

"Ah, how little people know who have never loved! It seems to me that no one has ever yet written of love truly, and I doubt whether this tender, joyful, agonising feeling can be described, and any one who has once experienced it would not attempt to put it into words. What is the use of preliminaries and introductions? What is the use of unnecessary fine words? My love is immeasurable. I beg, I beseech you," Startsev brought out at last, "be my wife!"

"Dmitri Ionitch," said Ekaterina Ivanovna, with a very grave face, after a moment's thought—"Dmitri Ionitch, I am very grateful to you for the honour. I respect you, but..." she got up and continued standing, "but, forgive me, I cannot be your wife. Let us talk seriously. Dmitri Ionitch, you know I love art beyond everything in life. I adore music; I love it frantically; I have dedicated my whole life to it. I want to be an artist; I want fame, success, freedom, and you want me to go on living in this town, to go on living this empty, useless life, which has become insufferable to me. To become a wife—oh, no, forgive me! One must strive towards a lofty, glorious goal, and married life would put me in bondage for ever. Dmitri Ionitch" (she faintly smiled as she pronounced his name; she thought of "Alexey Feofilaktitch")—"Dmitri Ionitch, you are a good, clever, honourable man; you are better than any one...." Tears came into her eyes. "I feel for you with my whole heart, but... but you will understand...."

And she turned away and went out of the drawing-room to prevent herself from crying.

Startsev's heart left off throbbing uneasily. Going out of the club into the street, he first of all tore off the stiff tie and drew a deep breath. He was a little ashamed and his vanity was wounded— he had not expected a refusal—and could not believe that all his dreams, his hopes and yearnings, had led him up to such a stupid end, just as in some little play at an amateur performance, and he was sorry for his feeling, for that love of his, so sorry that he felt as though he could have burst into sobs or have violently belaboured Panteleimon's broad back with his umbrella.

For three days he could not get on with anything, he could not eat nor sleep; but when the news reached him that Ekaterina Ivanovna had gone away to Moscow to enter the Conservatoire, he grew calmer and lived as before.

Afterwards, remembering sometimes how he had wandered about the cemetery or how he had driven all over the town to get a dress suit, he stretched lazily and said: "What a lot of trouble, though!"

IV

Four years had passed. Startsev already had a large practice in the town. Every morning he hurriedly saw his patients at Dyalizh, then he drove in to see his town patients. By now he drove, not with a pair, but with a team of three with bells on them, and he returned home late at night. He had grown broader and stouter, and was not very fond of walking, as he was somewhat asthmatic. And Panteleimon had grown stout, too, and the broader he grew, the more mournfully he sighed and complained of his hard luck: he was sick of driving! Startsev used to visit various households and met many people, but did not become intimate with any one. The inhabitants irritated him by their conversation, their views of life, and even their appearance. Experience taught him by degrees that while he played cards or lunched with one of these people, the man was a peaceable, friendly, and even intelligent human being; that as soon as one talked of anything not eatable, for instance, of politics or science, he would be completely at a loss, or would expound a philosophy so stupid and ill-natured that there was nothing else to do but wave one's hand in despair and go away. Even when Startsev tried to talk to liberal citizens, saying, for instance, that humanity, thank God, was progressing, and that one day it would be possible to dispense with passports and capital punishment, the liberal citizen would look at him askance and ask him mistrustfully: "Then any one could murder any one he chose in the open street?" And when, at tea or supper, Startsev observed in company that one should work, and that one ought not to live without working, every one took this as a reproach, and began to get angry and argue aggressively. With all that, the inhabitants did nothing, absolutely nothing, and took no interest in anything, and it was quite impossible to think of anything to say. And Startsev avoided conversation, and confined himself to eating and playing _vint_; and when there was a family festivity in some household and he was invited to a meal, then he sat and ate in silence, looking at his plate.

And everything that was said at the time was uninteresting, unjust, and stupid; he felt irritated and disturbed, but held his tongue, and, because he sat glumly silent and looked at his plate, he was nicknamed in the town "the haughty Pole," though he never had been a Pole.

All such entertainments as theatres and concerts he declined, but he played _vint_ every evening for three hours with enjoyment. He had another diversion to which he took imperceptibly, little by little: in the evening he would take out of his pockets the notes he had gained by his practice, and sometimes there were stuffed in his pockets notes—yellow and green, and smelling of scent and vinegar and incense and fish oil—up to the value of seventy roubles; and when they amounted to some hundreds he took them to the Mutual Credit Bank and deposited the money there to his account.

He was only twice at the Turkins' in the course of the four years after Ekaterina Ivanovna had gone away, on each occasion at the invitation of Vera Iosifovna, who was still undergoing treatment for migraine. Every summer Ekaterina Ivanovna came to stay with her parents, but he did not once see her; it somehow never happened.

But now four years had passed. One still, warm morning a letter was brought to the hospital. Vera Iosifovna wrote to Dmitri Ionitch that she was missing him very much, and begged him to come and see them, and to relieve her sufferings; and, by the way, it was her birthday. Below was a postscript: "I join in mother's request.—K."

Startsev considered, and in the evening he went to the Turkins'.

"How do you do, if you please?" Ivan Petrovitch met him, smiling with his eyes only. "Bongjour."

Vera Iosifovna, white-haired and looking much older, shook Startsev's hand, sighed affectedly, and said: "You don't care to pay attentions to me, doctor. You never come and see us; I am too old for you. But now some one young has come; perhaps she will be more fortunate."

And Kitten? She had grown thinner, paler, had grown handsomer and more graceful; but now she was Ekaterina Ivanovna, not Kitten; she had lost the freshness and look of childish naivete? And in her expression and manners there was something new—guilty and diffident, as though she did not feel herself at home here in the Turkins' house.

"How many summers, how many winters!" she said, giving Startsev her hand, and he could see that her heart was beating with excitement; and looking at him intently and curiously, she went on: "How much stouter you are! You look sunburnt and more manly, but on the whole you have changed very little."

Now, too, he thought her attractive, very attractive, but there was something lacking in her, or else something superfluous—he could not himself have said exactly what it was, but something prevented him from feeling as before. He did not like her pallor, her new expression, her faint smile, her voice, and soon afterwards he disliked her clothes, too, the low chair in which she was sitting; he disliked something in the past when he had almost married her. He thought of his love, of the dreams and the hopes which had troubled him four years before—and he felt awkward.

They had tea with cakes. Then Vera Iosifovna read aloud a novel; she read of things that never happen in real life, and Startsev listened, looked at her handsome grey head, and waited for her to finish.

"People are not stupid because they can't write novels, but because they can't conceal it when they do," he thought.

"Not badsome," said Ivan Petrovitch.

Then Ekaterina Ivanovna played long and noisily on the piano, and when she finished she was profusely thanked and warmly praised.

"It's a good thing I did not marry her," thought Startsev.

She looked at him, and evidently expected him to ask her to go into the garden, but he remained silent.

"Let us have a talk," she said, going up to him. "How are you getting on? What are you doing? How are things? I have been thinking about you all these days," she went on nervously. "I wanted to write to you, wanted to come myself to see you at Dyalizh. I quite made up my mind to go, but afterwards I thought better of it. God knows what your attitude is towards me now; I have been looking forward to seeing you today with such emotion. For goodness' sake let us go into the garden."

They went into the garden and sat down on the seat under the old maple, just as they had done four years before. It was dark.

"How are you getting on?" asked Ekaterina Ivanovna.

"Oh, all right; I am jogging along," answered Startsev.

And he could think of nothing more. They were silent.

"I feel so excited!" said Ekaterina Ivanovna, and she hid her face in her hands. "But don't pay attention to it. I am so happy to be at home; I am so glad to see every one. I can't get used to it. So many memories! I thought we should talk without stopping till morning."

Now he saw her face near, her shining eyes, and in the darkness she looked younger than in the room, and even her old childish expression seemed to have come back to her. And indeed she was looking at him with naive curiosity, as though she wanted to get a closer view and understanding of the man who had loved her so ardently, with such tenderness, and so unsuccessfully; her eyes thanked him for that love. And he remembered all that had been, every minute detail; how he had wandered about the cemetery, how he had returned home in the morning exhausted, and he suddenly felt sad and regretted the past. A warmth began glowing in his heart.

"Do you remember how I took you to the dance at the club?" he asked. "It was dark and rainy then..."

The warmth was glowing now in his heart, and he longed to talk, to rail at life....

"Ech!" he said with a sigh. "You ask how I am living. How do we live here? Why, not at all. We grow old, we grow stout, we grow slack. Day after day passes; life slips by without colour, without expressions, without thoughts.... In the daytime working for gain, and in the evening the club, the company of card-players, alcoholic, raucous-voiced gentlemen whom I can't endure. What is there nice in it?"

"Well, you have work—a noble object in life. You used to be so fond of talking of your hospital. I was such a queer girl then; I imagined myself such a great pianist. Nowadays all young ladies play the piano, and I played, too, like everybody else, and there was nothing special about me. I am just such a pianist as my mother is an authoress. And of course I didn't understand you then, but afterwards in Moscow I often thought of you. I thought of no one but you. What happiness to be a district doctor; to help the suffering; to be serving the people! What happiness!" Ekaterina Ivanovna repeated with enthusiasm. "When I thought of you in Moscow, you seemed to me so ideal, so lofty...."

Startsev thought of the notes he used to take out of his pockets in the evening with such pleasure, and the glow in his heart was quenched.

He got up to go into the house. She took his arm.

"You are the best man I've known in my life," she went on. "We will see each other and talk, won't we? Promise me. I am not a pianist; I am not in error about myself now, and I will not play before you or talk of music."

When they had gone into the house, and when Startsev saw in the lamplight her face, and her sad, grateful, searching eyes fixed upon him, he felt uneasy and thought again: "It's a good thing I did not marry her then."

He began taking leave.

"You have no human right to go before supper," said Ivan Petrovitch as he saw him off. "It's extremely perpendicular on your part. Well, now, perform!" he added, addressing Pava in the hall.

Pava, no longer a boy, but a young man with moustaches, threw himself into an attitude, flung up his arm, and said in a tragic voice: "Unhappy woman, die!"

All this irritated Startsev. Getting into his carriage, and looking at the dark house and garden which had once been so precious and so dear, he thought of everything at once—Vera Iosifovna's novels and Kitten's noisy playing, and Ivan Petrovitch's jokes and Pava's tragic posturing, and thought if the most talented people in the town were so futile, what must the town be?

Three days later Pava brought a letter from Ekaterina Ivanovna.

"You don't come and see us—why?" she wrote to him. "I am afraid that you have changed towards us. I am afraid, and I am terrified at the very thought of it. Reassure me; come and tell me that everything is well. "

"I must talk to you.—Your E. I."

He read this letter, thought a moment, and said to Pava: "Tell them, my good fellow, that I can't come today; I am very busy. Say I will come in three days or so."

But three days passed, a week passed; he still did not go. Happening once to drive past the Turkins' house, he thought he must go in, if only for a moment, but on second thoughts... did not go in.

And he never went to the Turkins' again.

V

Several more years have passed. Startsev has grown stouter still, has grown corpulent, breathes heavily, and already walks with his head thrown back. When stout and red in the face, he drives with his bells and his team of three horses, and Panteleimon, also stout and red in the face with his thick beefy neck, sits on the box, holding his arms stiffly out before him as though they were made of wood, and shouts to those he meets: "Keep to the ri-i-ight!" it is an impressive picture; one might think it was not a mortal, but some heathen deity in his chariot. He has an immense practice in the town, no time to breathe, and already has an estate and two houses in the town, and he is looking out for a third more profitable; and when at the Mutual Credit Bank he is told of a house that is for sale, he goes to the house without ceremony, and, marching through all the rooms, regardless of half-dressed women and children who gaze at him in amazement and alarm, he prods at the doors with his stick, and says: "Is that the study? Is that a bedroom? And what's here?"

And as he does so he breathes heavily and wipes the sweat from his brow.

He has a great deal to do, but still he does not give up his work as district doctor; he is greedy for gain, and he tries to be in all places at once. At Dyalizh and in the town he is called simply "Ionitch": "Where is Ionitch off to?" or "Should not we call in Ionitch to a consultation?"

Probably because his throat is covered with rolls of fat, his voice has changed; it has become thin and sharp. His temper has changed, too: he has grown ill-humoured and irritable. When he sees his patients he is usually out of temper; he impatiently taps the floor with his stick, and shouts in his disagreeable voice: "Be so good as to confine yourself to answering my questions! Don't talk so much!"

He is solitary. He leads a dreary life; nothing interests him.

During all the years he had lived at Dyalizh his love for Kitten had been his one joy, and probably his last. In the evenings he plays _vint_ at the club, and then sits alone at a big table and has supper. Ivan, the oldest and most respectable of the waiters, serves him, hands him Lafitte No. 17, and every one at the club— the members of the committee, the cook and waiters—know what he likes and what he doesn't like and do their very utmost to satisfy him, or else he is sure to fly into a rage and bang on the floor with his stick.

As he eats his supper, he turns round from time to time and puts in his spoke in some conversation: "What are you talking about? Eh? Whom?"

And when at a neighbouring table there is talk of the Turkins, he asks: "What Turkins are you speaking of? Do you mean the people whose daughter plays on the piano?"

That is all that can be said about him.

And the Turkins? Ivan Petrovitch has grown no older; he is not changed in the least, and still makes jokes and tells anecdotes as of old. Vera Iosifovna still reads her novels aloud to her visitors with eagerness and touching simplicity. And Kitten plays the piano for four hours every day. She has grown visibly older, is constantly ailing, and every autumn goes to the Crimea with her mother. When Ivan Petrovitch sees them off at the station, he wipes his tears as the train starts, and shouts: "Good-bye, if you please."

And he waves his handkerchief.

THE BEAUTIES

I

I REMEMBER, when I was a high school boy in the fifth or sixth class, I was driving with my grandfather from the village of Bolshoe Kryepkoe in the Don region to Rostov-on-the-Don. It was a sultry, languidly dreary day of August. Our eyes were glued together, and our mouths were parched from the heat and the dry burning wind which drove clouds of dust to meet us; one did not want to look or speak or think, and when our drowsy driver, a Little Russian called Karpo, swung his whip at the horses and lashed me on my cap, I did not protest or utter a sound, but only, rousing myself from half-slumber, gazed mildly and dejectedly into the distance to see whether there was a village visible through the dust. We stopped to feed the horses in a big Armenian village at a rich Armenian's whom my grandfather knew. Never in my life have I seen a greater caricature than that Armenian. Imagine a little shaven head with thick overhanging eyebrows, a beak of a nose, long gray mustaches, and a wide mouth with a long cherry-wood chibouk sticking out of it. This little head was clumsily attached to a lean hunch-back carcass attired in a fantastic garb, a short red jacket, and full bright blue trousers. This figure walked straddling its legs and shuffling with its slippers, spoke without taking the chibouk out of its mouth, and behaved with truly Armenian dignity, not smiling, but staring with wide-open eyes and trying to take as little notice as possible of its guests.

There was neither wind nor dust in the Armenian's rooms, but it was just as unpleasant, stifling, and dreary as in the steppe and on the road. I remember, dusty and exhausted by the heat, I sat in the corner on a green box. The unpainted wooden walls, the furniture, and the floors colored with yellow ocher smelt of dry wood baked by the sun. Wherever I looked there were flies and flies and flies.... Grandfather and the Armenian were talking about grazing, about manure, and about oats.... I knew that they would be a good hour getting the samovar; that grandfather would be not less than an hour drinking his tea, and then would lie down to sleep for two or three hours; that I should waste a quarter of the day waiting, after which there would be again the heat, the dust, the jolting cart. I heard the muttering of the two voices, and it began to seem to me that I had been seeing the Armenian, the cupboard with the crockery, the flies, the windows with the burning sun beating on them, for ages and ages, and should only cease to see them in the far-off future, and I was seized with hatred for the steppe, the sun, the flies....

A Little Russian peasant woman in a kerchief brought in a tray of tea-things, then the samovar. The Armenian went slowly out into the passage and shouted: "Mashya, come and pour out tea! Where are you, Mashya?"

Hurried footsteps were heard, and there came into the room a girl of sixteen in a simple cotton dress and a white kerchief. As she washed the crockery and poured out the tea, she was standing with her back to me, and all I could see was that she was of a slender figure, barefooted, and that her little bare heels were covered by long trousers.

The Armenian invited me to have tea. Sitting down to the table, I glanced at the girl, who was handing me a glass of tea, and felt all at once as though a wind were blowing over my soul and blowing away all the impressions of the day with their dust and dreariness. I saw the bewitching features of the most beautiful face I have ever met in real life or in my dreams. Before me stood a beauty, and I recognized that at the first glance as I should have recognized lightning.

I am ready to swear that Masha—or, as her father called her, Mashya—was a real beauty, but I don't know how to prove it. It sometimes happens that clouds are huddled together in disorder on the horizon, and the sun hiding behind them colors them and the sky with tints of every possible shade—crimson, orange, gold, lilac, muddy pink; one cloud is like a monk, another like a fish, a third like a Turk in a turban. The glow of sunset enveloping a third of the sky gleams on the cross on the church, flashes on the windows of the manor house, is reflected in the river and the puddles, quivers on the trees; far, far away against the background of the sunset, a flock of wild ducks is flying homewards.... And the boy herding the cows, and the surveyor driving in his chaise over the dam, and the gentleman out for a walk, all gaze at the sunset, and every one of them thinks it terribly beautiful, but no one knows or can say in what its beauty lies.

I was not the only one to think the Armenian girl beautiful. My grandfather, an old man of seventy, gruff and indifferent to women and the beauties of nature, looked caressingly at Masha for a full minute, and asked: "Is that your daughter, Avert Nazaritch?"

"Yes, she is my daughter," answered the Armenian.

"A fine young lady," said my grandfather approvingly.

An artist would have called the Armenian girl's beauty classical and severe, it was just that beauty, the contemplation of which—God knows why!—inspires in one the conviction that one is seeing correct features; that hair, eyes, nose, mouth, neck, bosom, and every movement of the young body all go together in one complete harmonious accord in which nature has not blundered over the smallest line. You fancy for some reason that the ideally beautiful woman must have such a nose as Masha's, straight and slightly aquiline, just such great dark eyes, such long lashes, such a languid glance; you fancy that her black curly hair and eyebrows go with the soft white tint of her brow and cheeks as the green reeds go with the quiet stream. Masha's white neck and her youthful bosom were not fully developed, but you fancy the sculptor would need a great creative genius to mold them. You gaze, and little by little the desire comes over you to say to Masha something extraordinarily pleasant, sincere, beautiful, as beautiful as she herself was.

At first I felt hurt and abashed that Masha took no notice of me, but was all the time looking down; it seemed to me as though a peculiar atmosphere, proud and happy, separated her from me and jealously screened her from my eyes.

"That's because I am covered with dust," I thought, "am sunburnt, and am still a boy."

But little by little I forgot myself, and gave myself up entirely to the consciousness of beauty. I thought no more now of the dreary steppe, of the dust, no longer heard the buzzing of the flies, no longer tasted the tea, and felt nothing except that a beautiful girl was standing only the other side of the table.

I felt this beauty rather strangely. It was not desire, nor ecstacy, nor enjoyment that Masha excited in me, but a painful though pleasant sadness. It was a sadness vague and undefined as a dream. For some reason I felt sorry for myself, for my grandfather and for the Armenian, even for the girl herself, and I had a feeling as though we all four had lost something important and essential to life which we should never find again. My grandfather, too, grew melancholy; he talked no more about manure or about oats, but sat silent, looking pensively at Masha.

After tea my grandfather lay down for a nap while I went out of the house into the porch. The house, like all the houses in the Armenian village stood in the full sun; there was not a tree, not an awning, no shade. The Armenian's great courtyard, overgrown with goosefoot and wild mallows, was lively and full of gaiety in spite of the great heat. Threshing was going on behind one of the low hurdles which intersected the big yard here and there. Round a post stuck into the middle of the threshing-floor ran a dozen horses harnessed side by side, so that they formed one long radius. A Little Russian in a long waistcoat and full trousers was walking beside them, cracking a whip and shouting in a tone that sounded as though he were jeering at the horses and showing off his power over them.

"A-a-a, you damned brutes!... A-a-a, plague take you! Are you frightened?"

The horses, sorrel, white, and piebald, not understanding why they were made to run round in one place and to crush the wheat straw, ran unwillingly as though with effort, swinging their tails with an offended air.

The wind raised up perfect clouds of golden chaff from under their hoofs and carried it away far beyond the hurdle. Near the tall fresh stacks peasant women were swarming with rakes, and carts were moving, and beyond the stacks in another yard another dozen similar horses were running round a post, and a similar Little Russian was cracking his whip and jeering at the horses.

The steps on which I was sitting were hot; on the thin rails and here and there on the window-frames sap was oozing out of the wood from the heat; red ladybirds were huddling together in the streaks of shadow under the steps and under the shutters. The sun was baking me on my head, on my chest, and on my back, but I did not notice it, and was conscious only of the thud of bare feet on the uneven floor in the passage and in the rooms behind me. After clearing away the tea-things, Masha ran down the steps, fluttering the air as she passed, and like a bird flew into a little grimy outhouse—I suppose the kitchen—from which came the smell of roast mutton and the sound of angry talk in Armenian. She vanished into the dark doorway, and in her place there appeared on the threshold an old bent, red-faced Armenian woman wearing green trousers. The old woman was angry and was scolding someone. Soon afterwards Masha appeared in the doorway, flushed with the heat of the kitchen and carrying a big black loaf on her shoulder; swaying gracefully under the weight of the bread, she ran across the yard to the threshing-floor, darted over the hurdle, and, wrapt in a cloud of golden chaff, vanished behind the carts. The Little Russian who was driving the horses lowered his whip, sank into silence, and gazed for a minute in the direction of the carts. Then when the Armenian girl darted again by the horses and leaped over the hurdle, he followed her with his eyes, and shouted to the horses in a tone as though he were greatly disappointed: "Plague take you, unclean devils!"

And all the while I was unceasingly hearing her bare feet, and seeing how she walked across the yard with a grave, preoccupied face. She ran now down the steps, swishing the air about me, now into the kitchen, now to the threshing-floor, now through the gate, and I could hardly turn my head quickly enough to watch her.

And the oftener she fluttered by me with her beauty, the more acute became my sadness. I felt sorry both for her and for myself and for the Little Russian, who mournfully watched her every time she ran through the cloud of chaff to the carts. Whether it was envy of her beauty, or that I was regretting that the girl was not mine, and never would be, or that I was a stranger to her; or whether I vaguely felt that her rare beauty was accidental, unnecessary, and, like everything on earth, of short duration; or whether, perhaps, my sadness was that peculiar feeling which is excited in man by the contemplation of real beauty, God only knows.

The three hours of waiting passed unnoticed. It seemed to me that I had not had time to look properly at Masha when Karpo drove up to the river, bathed the horse, and began to put it in the shafts. The wet horse snorted with pleasure and kicked his hoofs against the shafts. Karpo shouted to it: "Ba—ack!" My grandfather woke up. Masha opened the creaking gates for us, we got into the chaise and drove out of the yard. We drove in silence as though we were angry with one another.

When, two or three hours later, Rostov and Nahitchevan appeared in the distance, Karpo, who had been silent the whole time, looked round quickly, and said: "A fine wench, that at the Armenian's."

And he lashed his horses.

II

Another time, after I had become a student, I was traveling by rail to the south. It was May. At one of the stations, I believe it was between Byelgorod and Harkov, I got out of the tram to walk about the platform.

The shades of evening were already lying on the station garden, on the platform, and on the fields; the station screened off the sunset, but on the topmost clouds of smoke from the engine, which were tinged with rosy light, one could see the sun had not yet quite vanished.

As I walked up and down the platform I noticed that the greater number of the passengers were standing or walking near a second-class compartment, and that they looked as though some celebrated person were in that compartment. Among the curious whom I met near this compartment I saw, however, an artillery officer who had been my fellow-traveler, an intelligent, cordial, and sympathetic fellow—as people mostly are whom we meet on our travels by chance and with whom we are not long acquainted.

"What are you looking at there?" I asked.

He made no answer, but only indicated with his eyes a feminine figure. It was a young girl of seventeen or eighteen, wearing a Russian dress, with her head bare and a little shawl flung carelessly on one shoulder; not a passenger, but I suppose a sister or daughter of the station-master. She was standing near the carriage window, talking to an elderly woman who was in the train. Before I had time to realize what I was seeing, I was suddenly overwhelmed by the feeling I had once experienced in the Armenian village.

The girl was remarkably beautiful, and that was unmistakable to me and to those who were looking at her as I was.

If one is to describe her appearance feature by feature, as the practice is, the only really lovely thing was her thick wavy fair hair, which hung loose with a black ribbon tied round her head; all the other features were either irregular or very ordinary. Either from a peculiar form of coquettishness, or from short-sightedness, her eyes were screwed up, her nose had an undecided tilt, her mouth was small, her profile was feebly and insipidly drawn, her shoulders were narrow and undeveloped for her age—and yet the girl made the impression of being really beautiful, and looking at her, I was able to feel convinced that the Russian face does not need strict regularity in order to be lovely; what is more, that if instead of her turn-up nose the girl had been given a different one, correct and plastically irreproachable like the Armenian girl's, I fancy her face would have lost all its charm from the change.

Standing at the window talking, the girl, shrugging at the evening damp, continually looking round at us, at one moment put her arms akimbo, at the next raised her hands to her head to straighten her hair, talked, laughed, while her face at one moment wore an expression of wonder, the next of horror, and I don't remember a moment when her face and body were at rest. The whole secret and magic of her beauty lay just in these tiny, infinitely elegant movements, in her smile, in the play of her face, in her rapid glances at us, in the combination of the subtle grace of her movements with her youth, her freshness, the purity of her soul that sounded in her laugh and voice, and with the weakness we love so much in children, in birds, in fawns, and in young trees.

It was that butterfly's beauty so in keeping with waltzing, darting about the garden, laughter and gaiety, and incongruous with serious thought, grief, and repose; and it seemed as though a gust of wind blowing over the platform, or a fall of rain, would be enough to wither the fragile body and scatter the capricious beauty like the pollen of a flower.

"So-o!..." the officer muttered with a sigh when, after the second bell, we went back to our compartment.

And what that "So-o" meant I will not undertake to decide.

Perhaps he was sad, and did not want to go away from the beauty and the spring evening into the stuffy train; or perhaps he, like me, was unaccountably sorry for the beauty, for himself, and for me, and for all the passengers, who were listlessly and reluctantly sauntering back to their compartments. As we passed the station window, at which a pale, red-haired telegraphist with upstanding curls and a faded, broad-cheeked face was sitting beside his apparatus, the officer heaved a sigh and said: "I bet that telegraphist is in love with that pretty girl. To live out in the wilds under one roof with that ethereal creature and not fall in love is beyond the power of man. And what a calamity, my friend! what an ironical fate, to be stooping, unkempt, gray, a decent fellow and not a fool, and to be in love with that pretty, stupid little girl who would never take a scrap of notice of you! Or worse still: imagine that telegraphist is in love, and at the same time married, and that his wife is as stooping, as unkempt, and as decent a person as himself."

On the platform between our carriage and the next the guard was standing with his elbows on the railing, looking in the direction of the beautiful girl, and his battered, wrinkled, unpleasantly beefy face, exhausted by sleepless nights and the jolting of the train, wore a look of tenderness and of the deepest sadness, as though in that girl he saw happiness, his own youth, soberness, purity, wife, children; as though he were repenting and feeling in his whole being that that girl was not his, and that for him, with his premature old age, his uncouthness, and his beefy face, the ordinary happiness of a man and a passenger was as far away as heaven....

The third bell rang, the whistles sounded, and the train slowly moved off. First the guard, the station-master, then the garden, the beautiful girl with her exquisitely sly smile, passed before our windows....

Putting my head out and looking back, I saw how, looking after the train, she walked along the platform by the window where the telegraph clerk was sitting, smoothed her hair, and ran into the garden. The station no longer screened off the sunset, the plain lay open before us, but the sun had already set and the smoke lay in black clouds over the green, velvety young corn. It was melancholy in the spring air, and in the darkening sky, and in the railway carriage.

The familiar figure of the guard came into the carriage, and he began lighting the candles.

KASHTANKA

I _Misbehaviour_

A YOUNG dog, a reddish mongrel, between a dachshund and a "yard-dog," very like a fox in face, was running up and down the pavement looking uneasily from side to side. From time to time she stopped and, whining and lifting first one chilled paw and then another, tried to make up her mind how it could have happened that she was lost.

She remembered very well how she had passed the day, and how, in the end, she had found herself on this unfamiliar pavement.

The day had begun by her master Luka Alexandritch's putting on his hat, taking something wooden under his arm wrapped up in a red handkerchief, and calling: "Kashtanka, come along!"

Hearing her name the mongrel had come out from under the work-table, where she slept on the shavings, stretched herself voluptuously and run after her master. The people Luka Alexandritch worked for lived a very long way off, so that, before he could get to any one of them, the carpenter had several times to step into a tavern to fortify himself. Kashtanka remembered that on the way she had behaved extremely improperly. In her delight that she was being taken for a walk she jumped about, dashed barking after the trains, ran into yards, and chased other dogs. The carpenter was continually losing sight of her, stopping, and angrily shouting at her. Once he had even, with an expression of fury in his face, taken her fox-like ear in his fist, smacked her, and said emphatically: "Pla-a-ague take you, you pest!"

After having left the work where it had been bespoken, Luka Alexandritch went into his sister's and there had something to eat and drink; from his sister's he had gone to see a bookbinder he knew; from the bookbinder's to a tavern, from the tavern to another crony's, and so on. In short, by the time Kashtanka found herself on the unfamiliar pavement, it was getting dusk, and the carpenter was as drunk as a cobbler. He was waving his arms and, breathing heavily, muttered: "In sin my mother bore me! Ah, sins, sins! Here now we are walking along the street and looking at the street lamps, but when we die, we shall burn in a fiery Gehenna...."

Or he fell into a good-natured tone, called Kashtanka to him, and said to her: "You, Kashtanka, are an insect of a creature, and nothing else. Beside a man, you are much the same as a joiner beside a cabinet-maker...."

While he talked to her in that way, there was suddenly a burst of music. Kashtanka looked round and saw that a regiment of soldiers was coming straight towards her. Unable to endure the music, which unhinged her nerves, she turned round and round and wailed. To her great surprise, the carpenter, instead of being frightened, whining and barking, gave a broad grin, drew himself up to attention, and saluted with all his five fingers. Seeing that her master did not protest, Kashtanka whined louder than ever, and dashed across the road to the opposite pavement.

When she recovered herself, the band was not playing and the regiment was no longer there. She ran across the road to the spot where she had left her master, but alas, the carpenter was no longer there. She dashed forward, then back again and ran across the road once more, but the carpenter seemed to have vanished into the earth. Kashtanka began sniffing the pavement, hoping to find her master by the scent of his tracks, but some wretch had been that way just before in new rubber galoshes, and now all delicate scents were mixed with an acute stench of india-rubber, so that it was impossible to make out anything.

Kashtanka ran up and down and did not find her master, and meanwhile it had got dark. The street lamps were lighted on both sides of the road, and lights appeared in the windows. Big, fluffy snowflakes were falling and painting white the pavement, the horses' backs and the cabmen's caps, and the darker the evening grew the whiter were all these objects. Unknown customers kept walking incessantly to and fro, obstructing her field of vision and shoving against her with their feet. (All mankind Kashtanka divided into two uneven parts: masters and customers; between them there was an essential difference: the first had the right to beat her, and the second she had the right to nip by the calves of their legs.) These customers were hurrying off somewhere and paid no attention to her.

When it got quite dark, Kashtanka was overcome by despair and horror. She huddled up in an entrance and began whining piteously. The long day's journeying with Luka Alexandritch had exhausted her, her ears and her paws were freezing, and, what was more, she was terribly hungry. Only twice in the whole day had she tasted a morsel: she had eaten a little paste at the bookbinder's, and in one of the taverns she had found a sausage skin on the floor, near the counter —that was all. If she had been a human being she would have certainly thought: "No, it is impossible to live like this! I must shoot myself ! "

II   _A Mysterious Stranger_

But she thought of nothing, she simply whined. When her head and back were entirely plastered over with the soft feathery snow, and she had sunk into a painful doze of exhaustion, all at once the door of the entrance clicked, creaked, and struck her on the side. She jumped up. A man belonging to the class of customers came out. As Kashtanka whined and got under his feet, he could not help noticing her. He bent down to her and asked: "Doggy, where do you come from? Have I hurt you? O, poor thing, poor thing.... Come, don't be cross, don't be cross.... I am sorry."

Kashtanka looked at the stranger through the snow-flakes that hung on her eyelashes, and saw before her a short, fat little man, with a plump, shaven face wearing a top hat and a fur coat that swung open.

"What are you whining for?" he went on, knocking the snow off her back with his fingers. "Where is your master? I suppose you are lost? Ah, poor doggy! What are we going to do now?"

Catching in the stranger's voice a warm, cordial note, Kashtanka licked his hand, and whined still more pitifully.

"Oh, you nice funny thing!" said the stranger. "A regular fox! Well, there's nothing for it, you must come along with me! Perhaps you will be of use for something.... Well!"

He clicked with his lips, and made a sign to Kashtanka with his hand, which could only mean one thing: "Come along!" Kashtanka went.

Not more than half an hour later she was sitting on the floor in a big, light room, and, leaning her head against her side, was looking with tenderness and curiosity at the stranger who was sitting at the table, dining. He ate and threw pieces to her.... At first he gave her bread and the green rind of cheese, then a piece of meat, half a pie and chicken bones, while through hunger she ate so quickly that she had not time to distinguish the taste, and the more she ate the more acute was the feeling of hunger.

"Your masters don't feed you properly," said the stranger, seeing with what ferocious greediness she swallowed the morsels without munching them. "And how thin you are! Nothing but skin and bones...."

Kashtanka ate a great deal and yet did not satisfy her hunger, but was simply stupefied with eating. After dinner she lay down in the middle of the room, stretched her legs and, conscious of an agreeable weariness all over her body, wagged her tail. While her new master, lounging in an easy-chair, smoked a cigar, she wagged her tail and considered the question, whether it was better at the stranger's or at the carpenter's. The stranger's surroundings were poor and ugly; besides the easy-chairs, the sofa, the lamps and the rugs, there was nothing, and the room seemed empty. At the carpenter's the whole place was stuffed full of things: he had a table, a bench, a heap of shavings, planes, chisels, saws, a cage with a goldfinch, a basin.... The stranger's room smelt of nothing, while there was always a thick fog in the carpenter's room, and a glorious smell of glue, varnish, and shavings. On the other hand, the stranger had one great superiority—he gave her a great deal to eat and, to do him full justice, when Kashtanka sat facing the table and looking wistfully at him, he did not once hit or kick her, and did not once shout: "Go away, damned brute!"

When he had finished his cigar her new master went out, and a minute later came back holding a little mattress in his hands.

"Hey, you dog, come here!" he said, laying the mattress in the corner near the dog. "Lie down here, go to sleep!"

Then he put out the lamp and went away. Kashtanka lay down on the mattress and shut her eyes; the sound of a bark rose from the street, and she would have liked to answer it, but all at once she was overcome with unexpected melancholy. She thought of Luka Alexandritch, of his son Fedyushka, and her snug little place under the bench.... She remembered on the long winter evenings, when the carpenter was planing or reading the paper aloud, Fedyushka usually played with her.... He used to pull her from under the bench by her hind legs, and play such tricks with her, that she saw green before her eyes, and ached in every joint. He would make her walk on her hind legs, use her as a bell, that is, shake her violently by the tail so that she squealed and barked, and give her tobacco to sniff .... The following trick was particularly agonising: Fedyushka would tie a piece of meat to a thread and give it to Kashtanka, and then, when she had swallowed it he would, with a loud laugh, pull it back again from her stomach, and the more lurid were her memories the more loudly and miserably Kashtanka whined.

But soon exhaustion and warmth prevailed over melancholy. She began to fall asleep. Dogs ran by in her imagination: among them a shaggy old poodle, whom she had seen that day in the street with a white patch on his eye and tufts of wool by his nose. Fedyushka ran after the poodle with a chisel in his hand, then all at once he too was covered with shaggy wool, and began merrily barking beside Kashtanka. Kashtanka and he goodnaturedly sniffed each other's noses and merrily ran down the street....

III   _New and Very Agreeable Acquaintances_

When Kashtanka woke up it was already light, and a sound rose from the street, such as only comes in the day-time. There was not a soul in the room. Kashtanka stretched, yawned and, cross and ill-humoured, walked about the room. She sniffed the corners and the furniture, looked into the passage and found nothing of interest there. Besides the door that led into the passage there was another door. After thinking a little Kashtanka scratched on it with both paws, opened it, and went into the adjoining room. Here on the bed, covered with a rug, a customer, in whom she recognised the stranger of yesterday, lay asleep.

"Rrrrr..." she growled, but recollecting yesterday's dinner, wagged her tail, and began sniffing.

She sniffed the stranger's clothes and boots and thought they smelt of horses. In the bedroom was another door, also closed. Kashtanka scratched at the door, leaned her chest against it, opened it, and was instantly aware of a strange and very suspicious smell. Foreseeing an unpleasant encounter, growling and looking about her, Kashtanka walked into a little room with a dirty wall-paper and drew back in alarm. She saw something surprising and terrible. A grey gander came straight towards her, hissing, with its neck bowed down to the floor and its wings outspread. Not far from him, on a little mattress, lay a white tom-cat; seeing Kashtanka, he jumped up, arched his back, wagged his tail with his hair standing on end and he, too, hissed at her. The dog was frightened in earnest, but not caring to betray her alarm, began barking loudly and dashed at the cat .... The cat arched his back more than ever, mewed and gave Kashtanka a smack on the head with his paw. Kashtanka jumped back, squatted on all four paws, and craning her nose towards the cat, went off into loud, shrill barks; meanwhile the gander came up behind and gave her a painful peck in the back. Kashtanka leapt up and dashed at the gander.

"What's this?" They heard a loud angry voice, and the stranger came into the room in his dressing-gown, with a cigar between his teeth. "What's the meaning of this? To your places!"

He went up to the cat, flicked him on his arched back, and said: "Fyodor Timofeyitch, what's the meaning of this? Have you got up a fight? Ah, you old rascal! Lie down!"

And turning to the gander he shouted: "Ivan Ivanitch, go home!"

The cat obediently lay down on his mattress and closed his eyes. Judging from the expression of his face and whiskers, he was displeased with himself for having lost his temper and got into a fight.

Kashtanka began whining resentfully, while the gander craned his neck and began saying something rapidly, excitedly, distinctly, but quite unintelligibly.

"All right, all right," said his master, yawning. "You must live in peace and friendship." He stroked Kashtanka and went on: "And you, redhair, don't be frightened.... They are capital company, they won't annoy you. Stay, what are we to call you? You can't go on without a name, my dear."

The stranger thought a moment and said: "I tell you what... you shall be Auntie.... Do you understand? Auntie!"

And repeating the word "Auntie" several times he went out. Kashtanka sat down and began watching. The cat sat motionless on his little mattress, and pretended to be asleep. The gander, craning his neck and stamping, went on talking rapidly and excitedly about something. Apparently it was a very clever gander; after every long tirade, he always stepped back with an air of wonder and made a show of being highly delighted with his own speech.... Listening to him and answering "R-r-r-r," Kashtanka fell to sniffing the corners. In one of the corners she found a little trough in which she saw some soaked peas and a sop of rye crusts. She tried the peas; they were not nice; she tried the sopped bread and began eating it. The gander was not at all offended that the strange dog was eating his food, but, on the contrary, talked even more excitedly, and to show his confidence went to the trough and ate a few peas himself.

IV _Marvels on a Hurdle_

A little while afterwards the stranger came in again, and brought a strange thing with him like a hurdle, or like the figure II. On the crosspiece on the top of this roughly made wooden frame hung a bell, and a pistol was also tied to it; there were strings from the tongue of the bell, and the trigger of the pistol. The stranger put the frame in the middle of the room, spent a long time tying and untying something, then looked at the gander and said: "Ivan Ivanitch, if you please!"

The gander went up to him and stood in an expectant attitude.

"Now then," said the stranger, "let us begin at the very beginning. First of all, bow and make a curtsey! Look sharp!"

Ivan Ivanitch craned his neck, nodded in all directions, and scraped with his foot.

"Right. Bravo.... Now die!"

The gander lay on his back and stuck his legs in the air. After performing a few more similar, unimportant tricks, the stranger suddenly clutched at his head, and assuming an expression of horror, shouted: "Help! Fire! We are burning!"

Ivan Ivanitch ran to the frame, took the string in his beak, and set the bell ringing.

The stranger was very much pleased. He stroked the gander's neck and said: "Bravo, Ivan Ivanitch! Now pretend that you are a jeweller selling gold and diamonds. Imagine now that you go to your shop and find thieves there. What would you do in that case?"

The gander took the other string in his beak and pulled it, and at once a deafening report was heard. Kashtanka was highly delighted with the bell ringing, and the shot threw her into so much ecstasy that she ran round the frame barking.

"Auntie, lie down!" cried the stranger; "be quiet!"

Ivan Ivanitch's task was not ended with the shooting. For a whole hour afterwards the stranger drove the gander round him on a cord, cracking a whip, and the gander had to jump over barriers and through hoops; he had to rear, that is, sit on his tail and wave his legs in the air. Kashtanka could not take her eyes off Ivan Ivanitch, wriggled with delight, and several times fell to running after him with shrill barks. After exhausting the gander and himself, the stranger wiped the sweat from his brow and cried: "Marya, fetch Havronya Ivanovna here!"

A minute later there was the sound of grunting. Kashtanka growled, assumed a very valiant air, and to be on the safe side, went nearer to the stranger. The door opened, an old woman looked in, and, saying something, led in a black and very ugly sow. Paying no attention to Kashtanka's growls, the sow lifted up her little hoof and grunted good-humouredly. Apparently it was very agreeable to her to see her master, the cat, and Ivan Ivanitch. When she went up to the cat and gave him a light tap on the stomach with her hoof, and then made some remark to the gander, a great deal of good-nature was expressed in her movements, and the quivering of her tail. Kashtanka realised at once that to growl and bark at such a character was useless.

The master took away the frame and cried. "Fyodor Timofeyitch, if you please!"

The cat stretched lazily, and reluctantly, as though performing a duty, went up to the sow.

"Come, let us begin with the Egyptian pyramid," began the master.

He spent a long time explaining something, then gave the word of command, "One... two... three!" At the word "three" Ivan Ivanitch flapped his wings and jumped on to the sow's back.... When, balancing himself with his wings and his neck, he got a firm foothold on the bristly back, Fyodor Timofeyitch listlessly and lazily, with manifest disdain, and with an air of scorning his art and not caring a pin for it, climbed on to the sow's back, then reluctantly mounted on to the gander, and stood on his hind legs. The result was what the stranger called the Egyptian pyramid. Kashtanka yapped with delight, but at that moment the old cat yawned and, losing his balance, rolled off the gander. Ivan Ivanitch lurched and fell off too. The stranger shouted, waved his hands, and began explaining something again. After spending an hour over the pyramid their indefatigable master proceeded to teach Ivan Ivanitch to ride on the cat, then began to teach the cat to smoke, and so on.

The lesson ended in the stranger's wiping the sweat off his brow and going away. Fyodor Timofeyitch gave a disdainful sniff, lay down on his mattress, and closed his eyes; Ivan Ivanitch went to the trough, and the pig was taken away by the old woman. Thanks to the number of her new impressions, Kashranka hardly noticed how the day passed, and in the evening she was installed with her mattress in the room with the dirty wall-paper, and spent the night in the society of Fyodor Timofeyitch and the gander.

V _Talent! Talent!_

A month passed.

Kashtanka had grown used to having a nice dinner every evening, and being called Auntie. She had grown used to the stranger too, and to her new companions. Life was comfortable and easy.

Every day began in the same way. As a rule, Ivan Ivanitch was the first to wake up, and at once went up to Auntie or to the cat, twisting his neck, and beginning to talk excitedly and persuasively, but, as before, unintelligibly. Sometimes he would crane up his head in the air and utter a long monologue. At first Kashtanka thought he talked so much because he was very clever, but after a little time had passed, she lost all her respect for him; when he went up to her with his long speeches she no longer wagged her tail, but treated him as a tiresome chatterbox, who would not let anyone sleep and, without the slightest ceremony, answered him with "R-r-r-r!"

Fyodor Timofeyitch was a gentleman of a very different sort. When he woke he did not utter a sound, did not stir, and did not even open his eyes. He would have been glad not to wake, for, as was evident, he was not greatly in love with life. Nothing interested him, he showed an apathetic and nonchalant attitude to everything, he disdained everything and, even while eating his delicious dinner, sniffed contemptuously.

When she woke Kashtanka began walking about the room and sniffing the corners. She and the cat were the only ones allowed to go all over the flat; the gander had not the right to cross the threshold of the room with the dirty wall-paper, and Hayronya Ivanovna lived somewhere in a little outhouse in the yard and made her appearance only during the lessons. Their master got up late, and immediately after drinking his tea began teaching them their tricks. Every day the frame, the whip, and the hoop were brought in, and every day almost the same performance took place. The lesson lasted three or four hours, so that sometimes Fyodor Timofeyitch was so tired that he staggered about like a drunken man, and Ivan Ivanitch opened his beak and breathed heavily, while their master became red in the face and could not mop the sweat from his brow fast enough.

The lesson and the dinner made the day very interesting, but the evenings were tedious. As a rule, their master went off somewhere in the evening and took the cat and the gander with him. Left alone, Auntie lay down on her little mattress and began to feel sad.

Melancholy crept on her imperceptibly and took possession of her by degrees, as darkness does of a room. It began with the dog's losing every inclination to bark, to eat, to run about the rooms, and even to look at things; then vague figures, half dogs, half human beings, with countenances attractive, pleasant, but incomprehensible, would appear in her imagination; when they came Auntie wagged her tail, and it seemed to her that she had somewhere, at some time, seen them and loved them. And as she dropped asleep, she always felt that those figures smelt of glue, shavings, and varnish.

When she had grown quite used to her new life, and from a thin, long mongrel, had changed into a sleek, well-groomed dog, her master looked at her one day before the lesson and said: "It's high time, Auntie, to get to business. You have kicked up your heels in idleness long enough. I want to make an artiste of you.... Do you want to be an artiste?"

And he began teaching her various accomplishments. At the first lesson he taught her to stand and walk on her hind legs, which she liked extremely. At the second lesson she had to jump on her hind legs and catch some sugar, which her teacher held high above her head. After that, in the following lessons she danced, ran tied to a cord, howled to music, rang the bell, and fired the pistol, and in a month could successfully replace Fyodor

Timofeyitch in the "Egyptian Pyramid." She learned very eagerly and was pleased with her own success; running with her tongue out on the cord, leaping through the hoop, and riding on old Fyodor Timofeyitch, gave her the greatest enjoyment. She accompanied every successful trick with a shrill, delighted bark, while her teacher wondered, was also delighted, and rubbed his hands.

"It's talent! It's talent!" he said. "Unquestionable talent! You will certainly be successful!"

And Auntie grew so used to the word talent, that every time her master pronounced it, she jumped up as if it had been her name.

VI   _An Uneasy Night_

Auntie had a doggy dream that a porter ran after her with a broom, and she woke up in a fright.

It was quite dark and very stuffy in the room. The fleas were biting. Auntie had never been afraid of darkness before, but now, for some reason, she felt frightened and inclined to bark. Her master heaved a loud sigh in the next room, then soon afterwards the sow grunted in her sty, and then all was still again. When one thinks about eating one's heart grows lighter, and Auntie began thinking how that day she had stolen the leg of a chicken from Fyodor Timofeyitch, and had hidden it in the drawing-room, between the cupboard and the wall, where there were a great many spiders' webs and a great deal of dust. Would it not be as well to go now and look whether the chicken leg were still there or not? It was very possible that her master had found it and eaten it. But she must not go out of the room before morning, that was the rule. Auntie shut her eyes to go to sleep as quickly as possible, for she knew by experience that the sooner you go to sleep the sooner the morning comes. But all at once there was a strange scream not far from her which made her start and jump up on all four legs. It was Ivan Ivanitch, and his cry was not babbling and persuasive as usual, but a wild, shrill, unnatural scream like the squeak of a door opening. Unable to distinguish anything in the darkness, and not understanding what was wrong, Auntie felt still more frightened and growled: "R-r-r...."

Some time passed, as long as it takes to eat a good bone; the scream was not repeated. Little by little Auntie's uneasiness passed off and she began to doze. She dreamed of two big black dogs with tufts of last year's coat left on their haunches and sides; they were eating out of a big basin some swill, from which there came a white steam and a most appetising smell; from time to time they looked round at Auntie, showed their teeth and growled: "We are not going to give you any!" But a peasant in a fur-coat ran out of the house and drove them away with a whip; then Auntie went up to the basin and began eating, but as soon as the peasant went out of the gate, the two black dogs rushed at her growling, and all at once there was again a shrill scream.

"K-gee! K-gee-gee!" cried Ivan Ivanitch.

Auntie woke, jumped up and, without leaving her mattress, went off into a yelping bark. It seemed to her that it was not Ivan Ivanitch that was screaming but someone else, and for some reason the sow again grunted in her sty.

Then there was the sound of shuffling slippers, and the master came into the room in his dressing-gown with a candle in his hand. The flickering light danced over the dirty wall-paper and the ceiling, and chased away the darkness. Auntie saw that there was no stranger in the room. Ivan Ivanitch was sitting on the floor and was not asleep. His wings were spread out and his beak was open, and altogether he looked as though he were very tired and thirsty. Old Fyodor Timofeyitch was not asleep either. He, too, must have been awakened by the scream.

"Ivan Ivanitch, what's the matter with you?" the master asked the gander. "Why are you screaming? Are you ill?"

The gander did not answer. The master touched him on the neck, stroked his back, and said: "You are a queer chap. You don't sleep yourself, and you don't let other people...."

When the master went out, carrying the candle with him, there was darkness again. Auntie felt frightened. The gander did not scream, but again she fancied that there was some stranger in the room. What was most dreadful was that this stranger could not be bitten, as he was unseen and had no shape. And for some reason she thought that something very bad would certainly happen that night. Fyodor Timofeyitch was uneasy too.

Auntie could hear him shifting on his mattress, yawning and shaking his head.

Somewhere in the street there was a knocking at a gate and the sow grunted in her sty. Auntie began to whine, stretched out her front-paws and laid her head down upon them. She fancied that in the knocking at the gate, in the grunting of the sow, who was for some reason awake, in the darkness and the stillness, there was something as miserable and dreadful as in Ivan Ivanitch's scream. Everything was in agitation and anxiety, but why? Who was the stranger who could not be seen? Then two dim flashes of green gleamed for a minute near Auntie. It was Fyodor Timofeyitch, for the first time of their whole acquaintance coming up to her. What did he want? Auntie licked his paw, and not asking why he had come, howled softly and on various notes.

"K-gee!" cried Ivan Ivanitch, "K-g-ee!"

The door opened again and the master came in with a candle. The gander was sitting in the same attitude as before, with his beak open, and his wings spread out, his eyes were closed.

"Ivan Ivanitch!" his master called him.

The gander did not stir. His master sat down before him on the floor, looked at him in silence for a minute, and said: "Ivan Ivanitch, what is it? Are you dying? Oh, I remember now, I remember!" he cried out, and clutched at his head. "I know why it is! It's because the horse stepped on you today! My God! My God!"

Auntie did not understand what her master was saying, but she saw from his face that he, too, was expecting something dreadful. She stretched out her head towards the dark window, where it seemed to her some stranger was looking in, and howled.

"He is dying, Auntie!" said her master, and wrung his hands. "Yes, yes, he is dying! Death has come into your room. What are we to do?"

Pale and agitated, the master went back into his room, sighing and shaking his head. Auntie was afraid to remain in the darkness, and followed her master into his bedroom. He sat down on the bed and repeated several times: "My God, what's to be done?"

Auntie walked about round his feet, and not understanding why she was wretched and why they were all so uneasy, and trying to understand, watched every movement he made. Fyodor Timofeyitch, who rarely left his little mattress, came into the master's bedroom too, and began rubbing himself against his feet. He shook his head as though he wanted to shake painful thoughts out of it, and kept peeping suspiciously under the bed.

The master took a saucer, poured some water from his wash-stand into it, and went to the gander again.

"Drink, Ivan Ivanitch!" he said tenderly, setting the saucer before him; "drink, darling."

But Ivan Ivanitch did not stir and did not open his eyes. His master bent his head down to the saucer and dipped his beak into the water, but the gander did not drink, he spread his wings wider than ever, and his head remained lying in the saucer.

"No, there's nothing to be done now," sighed his master. "It's all over. Ivan Ivanitch is gone!"

And shining drops, such as one sees on the window-pane when it rains, trickled down his cheeks. Not understanding what was the matter, Auntie and Fyodor Timofeyitch snuggled up to him and looked with horror at the gander.

"Poor Ivan Ivanitch!" said the master, sighing mournfully. "And I was dreaming I would take you in the spring into the country, and would walk with you on the green grass. Dear creature, my good comrade, you are no more! How shall I do without you now?"

It seemed to Auntie that the same thing would happen to her, that is, that she too, there was no knowing why, would close her eyes, stretch out her paws, open her mouth, and everyone would look at her with horror. Apparently the same reflections were passing through the brain of Fyodor Timofeyitch. Never before had the old cat been so morose and gloomy.

It began to get light, and the unseen stranger who had so frightened Auntie was no longer in the room. When it was quite daylight, the porter came in, took the gander, and carried him away. And soon afterwards the old woman came in and took away the trough.

Auntie went into the drawing-room and looked behind the cupboard: her master had not eaten the chicken bone, it was lying in its place among the dust and spiders' webs. But Auntie felt sad and dreary and wanted to cry. She did not even sniff at the bone, but went under the sofa, sat down there, and began softly whining in a thin voice.

VII   _An Unsuccessful Debut_

One fine evening the master came into the room with the dirty wall-paper, and, rubbing his hands, said: "Well...."

He meant to say something more, but went away without saying it. Auntie, who during her lessons had thoroughly studied his face and intonations, divined that he was agitated, anxious and, she fancied, angry. Soon afterwards he came back and said: "Today I shall take with me Auntie and Fyodor Timofeyitch. To-day, Auntie, you will take the place of poor Ivan Ivanitch in the 'Egyptian Pyramid.' Goodness knows how it will be! Nothing is ready, nothing has been thoroughly studied, there have been few rehearsals! We shall be disgraced, we shall come to grief!"

Then he went out again, and a minute later, came back in his fur-coat and top hat. Going up to the cat he took him by the fore-paws and put him inside the front of his coat, while Fyodor Timofeyitch appeared completely unconcerned, and did not even trouble to open his eyes. To him it was apparently a matter of absolute indifference whether he remained lying down, or were lifted up by his paws, whether he rested on his mattress or under his master's fur-coat.

"Come along, Auntie," said her master.

Wagging her tail, and understanding nothing, Auntie followed him. A minute later she was sitting in a sledge by her master's feet and heard him, shrinking with cold and anxiety, mutter to himself: "We shall be disgraced! We shall come to grief!"

The sledge stopped at a big strange-looking house, like a soup-ladle turned upside down. The long entrance to this house, with its three glass doors, was lighted up with a dozen brilliant lamps. The doors opened with a resounding noise and, like jaws, swallowed up the people who were moving to and fro at the entrance. There were a great many people, horses, too, often ran up to the entrance, but no dogs were to be seen.

The master took Auntie in his arms and thrust her in his coat, where Fyodor Timofeyirch already was. It was dark and stuffy there, but warm. For an instant two green sparks flashed at her; it was the cat, who opened his eyes on being disturbed by his neighbour's cold rough paws. Auntie licked his ear, and, trying to settle herself as comfortably as possible, moved uneasily, crushed him under her cold paws, and casually poked her head out from under the coat, but at once growled angrily, and tucked it in again. It seemed to her that she had seen a huge, badly lighted room, full of monsters; from behind screens and gratings, which stretched on both sides of the room, horrible faces looked out: faces of horses with horns, with long ears, and one fat, huge countenance with a tail instead of a nose, and two long gnawed bones sticking out of his mouth.

The cat mewed huskily under Auntie's paws, but at that moment the coat was flung open, the master said, "Hop!" and Fyodor Timofeyitch and Auntie jumped to the floor. They were now in a little room with grey plank walls; there was no other furniture in it but a little table with a looking-glass on it, a stool, and some rags hung about the corners, and instead of a lamp or candles, there was a bright fan-shaped light attached to a little pipe fixed in the wall. Fyodor Timofeyitch licked his coat which had been ruffled by Auntie, went under the stool, and lay down. Their master, still agitated and rubbing his hands, began undressing.... He undressed as he usually did at home when he was preparing to get under the rug, that is, took off everything but his underlinen, then he sat down on the stool, and, looking in the looking-glass, began playing the most surprising tricks with himself.... First of all he put on his head a wig, with a parting and with two tufts of hair standing up like horns, then he smeared his face thickly with something white, and over the white colour painted his eyebrows, his moustaches, and red on his cheeks. His antics did not end with that. After smearing his face and neck, he began putting himself into an extraordinary and incongruous costume, such as Auntie had never seen before, either in houses or in the street. Imagine very full trousers, made of chintz covered with big flowers, such as is used in working-class houses for curtains and covering furniture, trousers which buttoned up just under his armpits. One trouser leg was made of brown chintz, the other of bright yellow. Almost lost in these, he then put on a short chintz jacket, with a big scalloped collar, and a gold star on the back, stockings of different colours, and green slippers.

Everything seemed going round before Auntie's eyes and in her soul. The white-faced, sack-like figure smelt like her master, its voice, too, was the familiar master's voice, but there were moments when Auntie was tortured by doubts, and then she was ready to run away from the parti-coloured figure and to bark. The new place, the fan-shaped light, the smell, the transformation that had taken place in her master—all this aroused in her a vague dread and a foreboding that she would certainly meet with some horror such as the big face with the tail instead of a nose. And then, somewhere through the wall, some hateful band was playing, and from time to time she heard an incomprehensible roar. Only one thing reassured her—that was the imperturbability of Fyodor Timofeyitch. He dozed with the utmost tranquility under the stool, and did not open his eyes even when it was moved.

A man in a dress coat and a white waistcoat peeped into the little room and said: "Miss Arabella has just gone on. After her—you."

Their master made no answer. He drew a small box from under the table, sat down, and waited. From his lips and his hands it could be seen that he was agitated, and Auntie could hear how his breathing came in gasps.

"Monsieur George, come on!" someone shouted behind the door. Their master got up and crossed himself three times, then took the cat from under the stool and put him in the box.

"Come, Auntie," he said softly.

Auntie, who could make nothing out of it, went up to his hands, he kissed her on the head, and put her beside Fyodor Timofeyitch. Then followed darkness.... Auntie trampled on the cat, scratched at the walls of the box, and was so frightened that she could not utter a sound, while the box swayed and quivered, as though it were on the waves....

"Here we are again!" her master shouted aloud: "here we are again!"

Auntie felt that after that shout the box struck against something hard and left off swaying. There was a loud deep roar, someone was being slapped, and that someone, probably the monster with the tail instead of a nose, roared and laughed so loud that the locks of the box trembled. In response to the roar, there came a shrill, squeaky laugh from her master, such as he never laughed at home.

"Ha!" he shouted, trying to shout above the roar. "Honoured friends! I have only just come from the station! My granny's kicked the bucket and left me a fortune! There is something very heavy in the box, it must be gold, ha! ha! I bet there's a million here! We'll open it and look...."

The lock of the box clicked. The bright light dazzled Auntie's eyes, she jumped out of the box, and, deafened by the roar, ran quickly round her master, and broke into a shrill bark.

"Ha!" exclaimed her master. "Uncle Fyodor Timofeyitch! Beloved Aunt, dear relations! The devil take you!"

He fell on his stomach on the sand, seized the cat and Auntie, and fell to embracing them. While he held Auntie tight in his arms, she glanced round into the world into which fate had brought her and, impressed by its immensity, was for a minute dumbfounded with amazement and delight, then jumped out of her master's arms, and to express the intensity of her emotions, whirled round and round on one spot like a top. This new world was big and full of bright light; wherever she looked, on all sides, from floor to ceiling there were faces, faces, faces, and nothing else.

"Auntie, I beg you to sit down!" shouted her master. Remembering what that meant, Auntie jumped on to a chair, and sat down. She looked at her master. His eyes looked at her gravely and kindly as always, but his face, especially his mouth and teeth, were made grotesque by a broad immovable grin. He laughed, skipped about, twitched his shoulders, and made a show of being very merry in the presence of the thousands of faces. Auntie believed in his merriment, all at once felt all over her that those thousands of faces were looking at her, lifted up her fox-like head, and howled joyously.

"You sit there, Auntie," her master said to her, "while Uncle and I will dance the Kamarinsky."

Fyodor Timofeyitch stood looking about him indifferently, waiting to be made to do something silly. He danced listlessly, carelessly, sullenly, and one could see from his movements, his tail and his ears, that he had a profound contempt for the crowd, the bright light, his master and himself. When he had performed his allotted task, he gave a yawn and sat down.

"Now, Auntie!" said her master, "we'll have first a song, and then a dance, shall we?"

He took a pipe out of his pocket, and began playing. Auntie, who could not endure music, began moving uneasily in her chair and howled. A roar of applause rose from all sides. Her master bowed, and when all was still again, went on playing.... Just as he took one very high note, someone high up among the audience uttered a loud exclamation: "Auntie!" cried a child's voice, "why it's Kashtanka!"

"Kashtanka it is!" declared a cracked drunken tenor. "Kashtanka! Strike me dead, Fedyushka, it is Kashtanka. Kashtanka! here!"

Someone in the gallery gave a whistle, and two voices, one a boy's and one a man's, called loudly: "Kashtanka! Kashtanka!"

Auntie started, and looked where the shouting came from. Two faces, one hairy, drunken and grinning, the other chubby, rosy-cheeked and frightened-looking, dazed her eyes as the bright light had dazed them before.... She remembered, fell off the chair, struggled on the sand, then jumped up, and with a delighted yap dashed towards those faces. There was a deafening roar, interspersed with whistles and a shrill childish shout: "Kashtanka! Kashtanka!"

Auntie leaped over the barrier, then across someone's shoulders. She found herself in a box: to get into the next tier she had to leap over a high wall. Auntie jumped, but did not jump high enough, and slipped back down the wall. Then she was passed from hand to hand, licked hands and faces, kept mounting higher and higher, and at last got into the gallery....

Half an hour afterwards, Kashtanka was in the street, following the people who smelt of glue and varnish. Luka Alexandritch staggered and instinctively, taught by experience, tried to keep as far from the gutter as possible.

"In sin my mother bore me," he muttered. "And you, Kashtanka, are a thing of little understanding. Beside a man, you are like a joiner beside a cabinetmaker."

Fedyushka walked beside him, wearing his father's cap. Kashtanka looked at their backs, and it seemed to her that she had been following them for ages, and was glad that there had not been a break for a minute in her life.

She remembered the little room with dirty wall-paper, the gander, Fyodor Timofeyitch, the delicious dinners, the lessons, the circus, but all that seemed to her now like a long, tangled, oppressive dream.

MISERY

"To whom shall I tell my grief?"

THE twilight of evening. Big flakes of wet snow are whirling lazily about the street lamps, which have just been lighted, and lying in a thin soft layer on roofs, horses' backs, shoulders, caps. Iona Potapov, the sledge-driver, is all white like a ghost. He sits on the box without stirring, bent as double as the living body can be bent. If a regular snowdrift fell on him it seems as though even then he would not think it necessary to shake it off.... His little mare is white and motionless too. Her stillness, the angularity of her lines, and the stick-like straightness of her legs make her look like a halfpenny gingerbread horse. She is probably lost in thought. Anyone who has been torn away from the plough, from the familiar gray landscapes, and cast into this slough, full of monstrous lights, of unceasing uproar and hurrying people, is bound to think.

It is a long time since Iona and his nag have budged. They came out of the yard before dinnertime and not a single fare yet. But now the shades of evening are falling on the town. The pale light of the street lamps changes to a vivid color, and the bustle of the street grows noisier.

"Sledge to Vyborgskaya!" Iona hears. "Sledge!"

Iona starts, and through his snow-plastered eyelashes sees an officer in a military overcoat with a hood over his head.

"To Vyborgskaya," repeats the officer. "Are you asleep? To Vyborgskaya!"

In token of assent Iona gives a tug at the reins which sends cakes of snow flying from the horse's back and shoulders. The officer gets into the sledge. The sledge-driver clicks to the horse, cranes his neck like a swan, rises in his seat, and more from habit than necessity brandishes his whip.

The mare cranes her neck, too, crooks her stick-like legs, and hesitatingly sets of....

"Where are you shoving, you devil?" Iona immediately hears shouts from the dark mass shifting to and fro before him. "Where the devil are you going? Keep to the r-right!"

"You don't know how to drive! Keep to the right," says the officer angrily.

A coachman driving a carriage swears at him; a pedestrian crossing the road and brushing the horse's nose with his shoulder looks at him angrily and shakes the snow off his sleeve. Iona fidgets on the box as though he were sitting on thorns, jerks his elbows, and turns his eyes about like one possessed as though he did not know where he was or why he was there.

"What rascals they all are!" says the officer jocosely. "They are simply doing their best to run up against you or fall under the horse's feet. They must be doing it on purpose."

Iona looks as his fare and moves his lips.... Apparently he means to say something, but nothing comes but a sniff.

"What?" inquires the officer.

Iona gives a wry smile, and straining his throat, brings out huskily: "My son... er... my son died this week, sir."

"H'm! What did he die of?"

Iona turns his whole body round to his fare, and says: "Who can tell! It must have been from fever.... He lay three days in the hospital and then he died.... God's will."

"Turn round, you devil!" comes out of the darkness. "Have you gone cracked, you old dog? Look where you are going!"

"Drive on! drive on!..." says the officer. "We shan't get there till to-morrow going on like this. Hurry up!"

The sledge-driver cranes his neck again, rises in his seat, and with heavy grace swings his whip. Several times he looks round at the officer, but the latter keeps his eyes shut and is apparently disinclined to listen. Putting his fare down at Vyborgskaya, Iona stops by a restaurant, and again sits huddled up on the box.... Again the wet snow paints him and his horse white. One hour passes, and then another....

Three young men, two tall and thin, one short and hunchbacked, come up, railing at each other and loudly stamping on the pavement with their galoshes.

"Cabby, to the Police Bridge!" the hunchback cries in a cracked voice. "The three of us,... twenty kopecks!"

Iona tugs at the reins and clicks to his horse. Twenty kopecks is not a fair price, but he has no thoughts for that. Whether it is a rouble or whether it is five kopecks does not matter to him now so long as he has a fare.... The three young men, shoving each other and using bad language, go up to the sledge, and all three try to sit down at once. The question remains to be settled: Which are to sit down and which one is to stand? After a long altercation, ill-temper, and abuse, they come to the conclusion that the hunchback must stand because he is the shortest.

"Well, drive on," says the hunchback in his cracked voice, settling himself and breathing down Iona's neck. "Cut along! What a cap you've got, my friend! You wouldn't find a worse one in all Petersburg...."

"He-he!... he-he!..." laughs Iona. "It's nothing to boast of!"

"Well, then, nothing to boast of, drive on! Are you going to drive like this all the way? Eh? Shall I give you one in the neck?"

"My head aches," says one of the tall ones. "At the Dukmasovs' yesterday Vaska and I drank four bottles of brandy between us."

"I can't make out why you talk such stuff," says the other tall one angrily. "You lie like a brute."

"Strike me dead, it's the truth!..."

"It's about as true as that a louse coughs."

"He-he!" grins Iona. "Me-er-ry gentlemen!"

"Tfoo! the devil take you!" cries the hunchback indignantly. "Will you get on, you old plague, or won't you? Is that the way to drive? Give her one with the whip. Hang it all, give it her well."

Iona feels behind his back the jolting person and quivering voice of the hunchback. He hears abuse addressed to him, he sees people, and the feeling of loneliness begins little by little to be less heavy on his heart. The hunchback swears at him, till he chokes over some elaborately whimsical string of epithets and is overpowered by his cough. His tall companions begin talking of a certain Nadyezhda Petrovna. Iona looks round at them. Waiting till there is a brief pause, he looks round once more and says: "This week... er... my... er... son died!"

"We shall all die,..." says the hunchback with a sigh, wiping his lips after coughing. "Come, drive on! drive on! My friends, I simply cannot stand crawling like this! When will he get us there?"

"Well, you give him a little encouragement... one in the neck!"

"Do you hear, you old plague? I'll make you smart. If one stands on ceremony with fellows like you one may as well walk. Do you hear, you old dragon? Or don't you care a hang what we say?"

And Iona hears rather than feels a slap on the back of his neck.

"He-he!..." he laughs. "Merry gentlemen.... God give you health!"

"Cabman, are you married?" asks one of the tall ones.

"I? He he! Me-er-ry gentlemen. The only wife for me now is the damp earth.... He-ho-ho!.... The grave that is!... Here my son's dead and I am alive.... It's a strange thing, death has come in at the wrong door.... Instead of coming for me it went for my son...."

And Iona turns round to tell them how his son died, but at that point the hunchback gives a faint sigh and announces that, thank God! they have arrived at last. After taking his twenty kopecks, Iona gazes for a long while after the revelers, who disappear into a dark entry. Again he is alone and again there is silence for him.... The misery which has been for a brief space eased comes back again and tears his heart more cruelly than ever. With a look of anxiety and suffering Iona's eyes stray restlessly among the crowds moving to and fro on both sides of the street: can he not find among those thousands someone who will listen to him? But the crowds flit by heedless of him and his misery.... His misery is immense, beyond all bounds. If Iona's heart were to burst and his misery to flow out, it would flood the whole world, it seems, but yet it is not seen. It has found a hiding-place in such an insignificant shell that one would not have found it with a candle by daylight....

Iona sees a house-porter with a parcel and makes up his mind to address him.

"What time will it be, friend?" he asks.

"Going on for ten.... Why have you stopped here? Drive on!"

Iona drives a few paces away, bends himself double, and gives himself up to his misery. He feels it is no good to appeal to people. But before five minutes have passed he draws himself up, shakes his head as though he feels a sharp pain, and tugs at the reins.... He can bear it no longer.

"Back to the yard!" he thinks. "To the yard!"

And his little mare, as though she knew his thoughts, falls to trotting. An hour and a half later Iona is sitting by a big dirty stove. On the stove, on the floor, and on the benches are people snoring. The air is full of smells and stuffiness. Iona looks at the sleeping figures, scratches himself, and regrets that he has come home so early....

"I have not earned enough to pay for the oats, even," he thinks. "That's why I am so miserable. A man who knows how to do his work,... who has had enough to eat, and whose horse has had enough to eat, is always at ease...."

In one of the corners a young cabman gets up, clears his throat sleepily, and makes for the water-bucket.

"Want a drink?" Iona asks him.

"Seems so."

"May it do you good.... But my son is dead, mate.... Do you hear? This week in the hospital.... It's a queer business...."

Iona looks to see the effect produced by his words, but he sees nothing. The young man has covered his head over and is already asleep. The old man sighs and scratches himself.... Just as the young man had been thirsty for water, he thirsts for speech. His son will soon have been dead a week, and he has not really talked to anybody yet.... He wants to talk of it properly, with deliberation.... He wants to tell how his son was taken ill, how he suffered, what he said before he died, how he died.... He wants to describe the funeral, and how he went to the hospital to get his son's clothes. He still has his daughter Anisya in the country.... And he wants to talk about her too.... Yes, he has plenty to talk about now. His listener ought to sigh and exclaim and lament.... It would be even better to talk to women. Though they are silly creatures, they blubber at the first word.

"Let's go out and have a look at the mare," Iona thinks. "There is always time for sleep.... You'll have sleep enough, no fear...."

He puts on his coat and goes into the stables where his mare is standing. He thinks about oats, about hay, about the weather.... He cannot think about his son when he is alone.... To talk about him with someone is possible, but to think of him and picture him is insufferable anguish....

"Are you munching?" Iona asks his mare, seeing her shining eyes. "There, munch away, munch away.... Since we have not earned enough for oats, we will eat hay.... Yes,... I have grown too old to drive.... My son ought to be driving, not I.... He was a real cabman.... He ought to have lived...."

Iona is silent for a while, and then he goes on: "That's how it is, old girl.... Kuzma Ionitch is gone.... He said good-bye to me.... He went and died for no reason.... Now, suppose you had a little colt, and you were own mother to that little colt. ... And all at once that same little colt went and died.... You'd be sorry, wouldn't you?..."

The little mare munches, listens, and breathes on her master's hands. Iona is carried away and tells her all about it.

JOY

IT was twelve o'clock at night.

Mitya Kuldarov, with excited face and ruffled hair, flew into his parents' flat, and hurriedly ran through all the rooms. His parents had already gone to bed. His sister was in bed, finishing the last page of a novel. His schoolboy brothers were asleep.

"Where have you come from?" cried his parents in amazement. "What is the matter with you? "

"Oh, don't ask! I never expected it; no, I never expected it! It's... it's positively incredible!"

Mitya laughed and sank into an armchair, so overcome by happiness that he could not stand on his legs.

"It's incredible! You can't imagine! Look!"

His sister jumped out of bed and, throwing a quilt round her, went in to her brother. The schoolboys woke up.

"What's the matter? You don't look like yourself!"

"It's because I am so delighted, Mamma! Do you know, now all Russia knows of me! All Russia! Till now only you knew that there was a registration clerk called Dmitry Kuldarov, and now all Russia knows it! Mamma! Oh, Lord!"

Mitya jumped up, ran up and down all the rooms, and then sat down again.

"Why, what has happened? Tell us sensibly!"

"You live like wild beasts, you don't read the newspapers and take no notice of what's published, and there's so much that is interesting in the papers. If anything happens it's all known at once, nothing is hidden! How happy I am! Oh, Lord! You know it's only celebrated people whose names are published in the papers, and now they have gone and published mine!"

"What do you mean? Where?"

The papa turned pale. The mamma glanced at the holy image and crossed herself. The schoolboys jumped out of bed and, just as they were, in short nightshirts, went up to their brother.

"Yes! My name has been published! Now all Russia knows of me! Keep the paper, mamma, in memory of it! We will read it sometimes! Look!"

Mitya pulled out of his pocket a copy of the paper, gave it to his father, and pointed with his finger to a passage marked with blue pencil.

"Read it!"

The father put on his spectacles.

"Do read it!"

The mamma glanced at the holy image and crossed herself. The papa cleared his throat and began to read: "At eleven o'clock on the evening of the 29th of December, a registration clerk of the name of Dmitry Kuldarov..."

"You see, you see! Go on!"

"... a registration clerk of the name of Dmitry Kuldarov, coming from the beershop in Kozihin's buildings in Little Bronnaia in an intoxicated condition..."

"That's me and Semyon Petrovitch.... It's all described exactly! Go on! Listen!"

"... intoxicated condition, slipped and fell under a horse belonging to a sledge-driver, a peasant of the village of Durikino in the Yuhnovsky district, called Ivan Drotov. The frightened horse, stepping over Kuldarov and drawing the sledge over him, together with a Moscow merchant of the second guild called Stepan Lukov, who was in it, dashed along the street and was caught by some house-porters. Kuldarov, at first in an unconscious condition, was taken to the police station and there examined by the doctor. The blow he had received on the back of his head..."

"It was from the shaft, papa. Go on! Read the rest!"

"... he had received on the back of his head turned out not to be serious. The incident was duly reported. Medical aid was given to the injured man...."

"They told me to foment the back of my head with cold water. You have read it now? Ah! So you see. Now it's all over Russia! Give it here!"

Mitya seized the paper, folded it up and put it into his pocket.

"I'll run round to the Makarovs and show it to them.... I must show it to the Ivanitskys too, Natasya Ivanovna, and Anisim Vassilyitch.... I'll run! Good-bye!"

Mitya put on his cap with its cockade and, joyful and triumphant, ran into the street.

THE STUDENT

AT first the weather was fine and still. The thrushes were calling, and in the swamps close by something alive droned pitifully with a sound like blowing into an empty bottle. A snipe flew by, and the shot aimed at it rang out with a gay, resounding note in the spring air. But when it began to get dark in the forest a cold, penetrating wind blew inappropriately from the east, and everything sank into silence. Needles of ice stretched across the pools, and it felt cheerless, remote, and lonely in the forest. There was a whiff of winter.

Ivan Velikopolsky, the son of a sacristan, and a student of the clerical academy, returning home from shooting, walked all the time by the path in the water-side meadow. His fingers were numb and his face was burning with the wind. It seemed to him that the cold that had suddenly come on had destroyed the order and harmony of things, that nature itself felt ill at ease, and that was why the evening darkness was falling more rapidly than usual. All around it was deserted and peculiarly gloomy. The only light was one gleaming in the widows' gardens near the river; the village, over three miles away, and everything in the distance all round was plunged in the cold evening mist. The student remembered that, as he went out from the house, his mother was sitting barefoot on the floor in the entry, cleaning the samovar, while his father lay on the stove coughing; as it was Good Friday nothing had been cooked, and the student was terribly hungry. And now, shrinking from the cold, he thought that just such a wind had blown in the days of Rurik and in the time of Ivan the Terrible and Peter, and in their time there had been just the same desperate poverty and hunger, the same thatched roofs with holes in them, ignorance, misery, the same desolation around, the same darkness, the same feeling of oppression—all these had existed, did exist, and would exist, and the lapse of a thousand years would make life no better. And he did not want to go home.

The gardens were called the widows' because they were kept by two widows, mother and daughter. A camp fire was burning brightly with a crackling sound, throwing out light far around on the ploughed earth. The widow Vasilisa, a tall, fat old woman in a man's coat, was standing by and looking thoughtfully into the fire; her daughter Lukerya, a little pock-marked woman with a stupid-looking face, was sitting on the ground, washing a caldron and spoons. Apparently they had just had supper. There was a sound of men's voices; it was the labourers watering their horses at the river.

"Here you have winter back again," said the student, going up to the camp fire. "Good evening."

Vasilisa started, but at once recognized him and smiled cordially.

"I did not know you; God bless you," she said.

"You'll be rich."

They talked. Vasilisa, a woman of experience, who had been in service with the gentry, first as a wet-nurse, afterwards as a children's nurse, expressed herself with refinement, and a soft, sedate smile never left her face; her daughter Lukerya, a village peasant woman, who had been beaten by her husband, simply screwed up her eyes at the student and said nothing, and she had a strange expression like that of a deaf mute.

"At just such a fire the Apostle Peter warmed himself," said the student, stretching out his hands to the fire, "so it must have been cold then, too. Ah, what a terrible night it must have been, granny! An utterly dismal long night!"

He looked round at the darkness, shook his head abruptly and asked: "No doubt you have been at the reading of the Twelve Gospels?"

"Yes, I have," answered Vasilisa.

"If you remember at the Last Supper Peter said to Jesus, 'I am ready to go with Thee into darkness and unto death.' And our Lord answered him thus: 'I say unto thee, Peter, before the cock croweth thou wilt have denied Me thrice.' After the supper Jesus went through the agony of death in the garden and prayed, and poor Peter was weary in spirit and faint, his eyelids were heavy and he could not struggle against sleep. He fell asleep. Then you heard how Judas the same night kissed Jesus and betrayed Him to His tormentors. They took Him bound to the high priest and beat Him, while Peter, exhausted, worn out with misery and alarm, hardly awake, you know, feeling that something awful was just going to happen on earth, followed behind.... He loved Jesus passionately, intensely, and now he saw from far off how He was beaten..."

Lukerya left the spoons and fixed an immovable stare upon the student.

"They came to the high priest's," he went on; "they began to question Jesus, and meantime the labourers made a fire in the yard as it was cold, and warmed themselves. Peter, too, stood with them near the fire and warmed himself as I am doing. A woman, seeing him, said: 'He was with Jesus, too'—that is as much as to say that he, too, should be taken to be questioned. And all the labourers that were standing near the fire must have looked sourly and suspiciously at him, because he was confused and said: 'I don't know Him.' A little while after again someone recognized him as one of Jesus' disciples and said: 'thou, too, art one of them,' but again he denied it. And for the third time someone turned to him: 'Why, did I not see thee with Him in the garden today?' For the third time he denied it. And immediately after that time the cock crowed, and Peter, looking from afar off at Jesus, remembered the words He had said to him in the evening.... He remembered, he came to himself, went out of the yard and wept bitterly—bitterly. In the Gospel it is written: 'He went out and wept bitterly.' I imagine it: the still, still, dark, dark garden, and in the stillness, faintly audible, smothered sobbing..."

The student sighed and sank into thought. Still smiling, Vasilisa suddenly gave a gulp, big tears flowed freely down her cheeks, and she screened her face from the fire with her sleeve as though ashamed of her tears, and Lukerya, staring immovably at the student, flushed crimson, and her expression became strained and heavy like that of someone enduring intense pain.

The labourers came back from the river, and one of them riding a horse was quite near, and the light from the fire quivered upon him. The student said good-night to the widows and went on. And again the darkness was about him and his fingers began to be numb. A cruel wind was blowing, winter really had come back and it did not feel as though Easter would be the day after tomorrow.

Now the student was thinking about Vasilisa: since she had shed tears all that had happened to Peter the night before the Crucifixion must have some relation to her....

He looked round. The solitary light was still gleaming in the darkness and no figures could be seen near it now. The student thought again that if Vasilisa had shed tears, and her daughter had been troubled, it was evident that what he had just been telling them about, which had happened nineteen centuries ago, had a relation to the present—to both women, to the desolate village, to himself, to all people. The old woman had wept, not because he could tell the story touchingly, but because Peter was near to her, because her whole being was interested in what was passing in Peter's soul.

And joy suddenly stirred in his soul, and he even stopped for a minute to take breath. "The past," he thought, "is linked with the present by an unbroken chain of events flowing one out of another." And it seemed to him that he had just seen both ends of that chain; that when he touched one end the other quivered.

When he crossed the river by the ferry boat and afterwards, mounting the hill, looked at his village and towards the west where the cold crimson sunset lay a narrow streak of light, he thought that truth and beauty which had guided human life there in the garden and in the yard of the high priest had continued without interruption to this day, and had evidently always been the chief thing in human life and in all earthly life, indeed; and the feeling of youth, health, vigour—he was only twenty-two—and the inexpressible sweet expectation of happiness, of unknown mysterious happiness, took possession of him little by little, and life seemed to him enchanting, marvellous, and full of lofty meaning.

THE LADY WITH THE DOG

I

IT was said that a new person had appeared on the sea-front: a lady with a little dog. Dmitri Dmitritch Gurov, who had by then been a fortnight at Yalta, and so was fairly at home there, had begun to take an interest in new arrivals. Sitting in Verney's pavilion, he saw, walking on the sea-front, a fair-haired young lady of medium height, wearing a bérer; a white Pomeranian dog was running behind her.

And afterwards he met her in the public gardens and in the square several times a day. She was walking alone, always wearing the same béret, and always with the same white dog; no one knew who she was, and every one called her simply "the lady with the dog."

"If she is here alone without a husband or friends, it wouldn't be amiss to make her acquaintance," Gurov reflected.

He was under forty, but he had a daughter already twelve years old, and two sons at school. He had been married young, when he was a student in his second year, and by now his wife seemed half as old again as he. She was a tall, erect woman with dark eyebrows, staid and dignified, and, as she said of herself, intellectual. She read a great deal, used phonetic spelling, called her husband, not Dmitri, but Dimitri, and he secretly considered her unintelligent, narrow, inelegant, was afraid of her, and did not like to be at home. He had begun being unfaithful to her long ago—had been unfaithful to her often, and, probably on that account, almost always spoke ill of women, and when they were talked about in his presence, used to call them "the lower race."

It seemed to him that he had been so schooled by bitter experience that he might call them what he liked, and yet he could not get on for two days together without "the lower race." In the society of men he was bored and not himself, with them he was cold and uncommunicative; but when he was in the company of women he felt free, and knew what to say to them and how to behave; and he was at ease with them even when he was silent. In his appearance, in his character, in his whole nature, there was something attractive and elusive which allured women and disposed them in his favour; he knew that, and some force seemed to draw him, too, to them.

Experience often repeated, truly bitter experience, had taught him long ago that with decent people, especially Moscow people—always slow to move and irresolute—every intimacy, which at first so agreeably diversifies life and appears a light and charming adventure, inevitably grows into a regular problem of extreme intricacy, and in the long run the situation becomes unbearable. But at every fresh meeting with an interesting woman this experience seemed to slip out of his memory, and he was eager for life, and everything seemed simple and amusing.

One evening he was dining in the gardens, and the lady in the béret came up slowly to take the next table. Her expression, her gait, her dress, and the way she did her hair told him that she was a lady, that she was married, that she was in Yalta for the first time and alone, and that she was dull there.... The stories told of the immorality in such places as Yalta are to a great extent untrue; he despised them, and knew that such stories were for the most part made up by persons who would themselves have been glad to sin if they had been able; but when the lady sat down at the next table three paces from him, he remembered these tales of easy conquests, of trips to the mountains, and the tempting thought of a swift, fleeting love affair, a romance with an unknown woman, whose name he did not know, suddenly took possession of him.

He beckoned coaxingly to the Pomeranian, and when the dog came up to him he shook his finger at it. The Pomeranian growled: Gurov shook his finger at it again.

The lady looked at him and at once dropped her eyes.

"He doesn't bite," she said, and blushed.

"May I give him a bone?" he asked; and when she nodded he asked courteously, "Have you been long in Yalta?"

"Five days."

"And I have already dragged out a fortnight here."

There was a brief silence.

"Time goes fast, and yet it is so dull here!" she said, not looking at him.

"That's only the fashion to say it is dull here. A provincial will live in Belyov or Zhidra and not be dull, and when he comes here it's 'Oh, the dulness! Oh, the dust!' One would think he came from Grenada."

She laughed. Then both continued eating in silence, like strangers, but after dinner they walked side by side; and there sprang up between them the light jesting conversation of people who are free and satisfied, to whom it does not matter where they go or what they talk about. They walked and talked of the strange light on the sea: the water was of a soft warm lilac hue, and there was a golden streak from the moon upon it. They talked of how sultry it was after a hot day. Gurov told her that he came from Moscow, that he had taken his degree in Arts, but had a post in a bank; that he had trained as an opera-singer, but had given it up, that he owned two houses in Moscow.... And from her he learnt that she had grown up in Petersburg, but had lived in S— since her marriage two years before, that she was staying another month in Yalta, and that her husband, who needed a holiday too, might perhaps come and fetch her. She was not sure whether her husband had a post in a Crown Department or under the Provincial Council—and was amused by her own ignorance. And Gurov learnt, too, that she was called Anna Sergeyevna.

Afterwards he thought about her in his room at the hotel—thought she would certainly meet him next day; it would be sure to happen. As he got into bed he thought how lately she had been a girl at school, doing lessons like his own daughter; he recalled the diffidence, the angularity, that was still manifest in her laugh and her manner of talking with a stranger. This must have been the first time in her life she had been alone in surroundings in which she was followed, looked at, and spoken to merely from a secret motive which she could hardly fail to guess. He recalled her slender, delicate neck, her lovely grey eyes.

"There's something pathetic about her, anyway," he thought, and fell asleep.

II

A week had passed since they had made acquaintance. It was a holiday. It was sultry indoors, while in the street the wind whirled the dust round and round, and blew people's hats off. It was a thirsty day, and Gurov often went into the pavilion, and pressed Anna Sergeyevna to have syrup and water or an ice. One did not know what to do with oneself.

In the evening when the wind had dropped a little, they went out on the groyne to see the steamer come in. There were a great many people walking about the harbour; they had gathered to welcome some one, bringing bouquets. And two peculiarities of a well-dressed Yalta crowd were very conspicuous: the elderly ladies were dressed like young ones, and there were great numbers of generals.

Owing to the roughness of the sea, the steamer arrived late, after the sun had set, and it was a long time turning about before it reached the groyne. Anna Sergeyevna looked through her lorgnette at the steamer and the passengers as though looking for acquaintances, and when she turned to Gurov her eyes were shining. She talked a great deal and asked disconnected questions, forgetting next moment what she had asked; then she dropped her lorgnette in the crush.

The festive crowd began to disperse; it was too dark to see people's faces. The wind had completely dropped, but Gurov and Anna Sergeyevna still stood as though waiting to see some one else come from the steamer. Anna Sergeyevna was silent now, and sniffed the flowers without looking at Gurov.

"The weather is better this evening," he said. "Where shall we go now? Shall we drive somewhere?"

She made no answer.

Then he looked at her intently, and all at once put his arm round her and kissed her on the lips, and breathed in the moisture and the fragrance of the flowers; and he immediately looked round him, anxiously wondering whether any one had seen them.

"Let us go to your hotel," he said softly. And both walked quickly.

The room was close and smelt of the scent she had bought at the Japanese shop. Gurov looked at her and thought: "What different people one meets in the world!" From the past he preserved memories of careless, good-natured women, who loved cheerfully and were grateful to him for the happiness he gave them, however brief it might be; and of women like his wife who loved without any genuine feeling, with superfluous phrases, affectedly, hysterically, with an expression that suggested that it was not love nor passion, but something more significant; and of two or three others, very beautiful, cold women, on whose faces he had caught a glimpse of a rapacious expression—an obstinate desire to snatch from life more than it could give, and these were capricious, unreflecting, domineering, unintelligent women not in their first youth, and when Gurov grew cold to them their beauty excited his hatred, and the lace on their linen seemed to him like scales.

But in this case there was still the diffidence, the angularity of inexperienced youth, an awkward feeling; and there was a sense of consternation as though some one had suddenly knocked at the door. The attitude of Anna Sergeyevna—"the lady with the dog"—to what had happened was somehow peculiar, very grave, as though it were her fall so it seemed, and it was strange and inappropriate. Her face dropped and faded, and on both sides of it her long hair hung down mournfully; she mused in a dejected attitude like "the woman who was a sinner" in an old-fashioned picture.

"It's wrong," she said. "You will be the first to despise me now."

There was a water-melon on the table. Gurov cut himself a slice and began eating it without haste. There followed at least half an hour of silence.

Anna Sergeyevna was touching; there was about her the purity of a good, simple woman who had seen little of life. The solitary candle burning on the table threw a faint light on her face, yet it was clear that she was very unhappy.

"How could I despise you?" asked Gurov. "You don't know what you are saying."

"God forgive me," she said, and her eyes filled with tears. "It's awful."

"You seem to feel you need to be forgiven."

"Forgiven? No. I am a bad, low woman; I despise myself and don't attempt to justify myself. It's not my husband but myself I have deceived. And not only just now; I have been deceiving myself for a long time. My husband may be a good, honest man, but he is a flunkey! I don't know what he does there, what his work is, but I know he is a flunkey! I was twenty when I was married to him. I have been tormented by curiosity; I wanted something better. 'there must be a different sort of life,' I said to myself. I wanted to live! To live, to live!... I was fired by curiosity... you don't understand it, but, I swear to God, I could not control myself; something happened to me: I could not be restrained. I told my husband I was ill, and came here.... And here I have been walking about as though I were dazed, like a mad creature;... and now I have become a vulgar, contemptible woman whom any one may despise."

Gurov felt bored already, listening to her. He was irritated by the naive tone, by this remorse, so unexpected and inopportune; but for the tears in her eyes, he might have thought she was jesting or playing a part.

"I don't understand," he said softly. "What is it you want?"

She hid her face on his breast and pressed close to him.

"Believe me, believe me, I beseech you..." she said. "I love a pure, honest life, and sin is loathsome to me. I don't know what I am doing. Simple people say: 'The Evil One has beguiled me.' And I may say of myself now that the Evil One has beguiled me."

"Hush, hush!..." he muttered.

He looked at her fixed, scared eyes, kissed her, talked softly and affectionately, and by degrees she was comforted, and her gaiety returned; they both began laughing.

Afterwards when they went out there was not a soul on the sea-front. The town with its cypresses had quite a deathlike air, but the sea still broke noisily on the shore; a single barge was rocking on the waves, and a lantern was blinking sleepily on it.

They found a cab and drove to Oreanda.

"I found out your surname in the hall just now: it was written on the board—Von Diderits," said Gurov. "Is your husband a German?"

"No; I believe his grandfather was a German, but he is an Orthodox Russian himself."

At Oreanda they sat on a seat not far from the church, looked down at the sea, and were silent. Yalta was hardly visible through the morning mist; white clouds stood motionless on the mountain-tops. The leaves did not stir on the trees, grasshoppers chirruped, and the monotonous hollow sound of the sea rising up from below, spoke of the peace, of the eternal sleep awaiting us. So it must have sounded when there was no Yalta, no Oreanda here; so it sounds now, and it will sound as indifferently and monotonously when we are all no more. And in this constancy, in this complete indifference to the life and death of each of us, there lies hid, perhaps, a pledge of our eternal salvation, of the unceasing movement of life upon earth, of unceasing progress towards perfection. Sitting beside a young woman who in the dawn seemed so lovely, soothed and spellbound in these magical surroundings—the sea, mountains, clouds, the open sky— Gurov thought how in reality everything is beautiful in this world when one reflects: everything except what we think or do ourselves when we forget our human dignity and the higher aims of our existence.

A man walked up to them—probably a keeper—looked at them and walked away. And this detail seemed mysterious and beautiful, too. They saw a steamer come from Theodosia, with its lights out in the glow of dawn.

"There is dew on the grass," said Anna Sergeyevna, after a silence.

"Yes. It's time to go home."

They went back to the town.

Then they met every day at twelve o'clock on the sea-front, lunched and dined together, went for walks, admired the sea. She complained that she slept badly, that her heart throbbed violently; asked the same questions, troubled now by jealousy and now by the fear that he did not respect her sufficiently. And often in the square or gardens, when there was no one near them, he suddenly drew her to him and kissed her passionately. Complete idleness, these kisses in broad daylight while he looked round in dread of some one's seeing them, the heat, the smell of the sea, and the continual passing to and fro before him of idle, well-dressed, well-fed people, made a new man of him; he told Anna Sergeyevna how beautiful she was, how fascinating. He was impatiently passionate, he would not move a step away from her, while she was often pensive and continually urged him to confess that he did not respect her, did not love her in the least, and thought of her as nothing but a common woman. Rather late almost every evening they drove somewhere out of town, to Oreanda or to the waterfall; and the expedition was always a success, the scenery invariably impressed them as grand and beautiful.

They were expecting her husband to come, but a letter came from him, saying that there was something wrong with his eyes, and he entreated his wife to come home as quickly as possible. Anna Sergeyevna made haste to go.

"It's a good thing I am going away," she said to Gurov. "It's the finger of destiny!"

She went by coach and he went with her. They were driving the whole day. When she had got into a compartment of the express, and when the second bell had rung, she said: "Let me look at you once more... look at you once again. That's right."

She did not shed tears, but was so sad that she seemed ill, and her face was quivering.

"I shall remember you... think of you," she said. "God be with you; be happy. Don't remember evil against me. We are parting forever —it must be so, for we ought never to have met. Well, God be with you."

The train moved off rapidly, its lights soon vanished from sight, and a minute later there was no sound of it, as though everything had conspired together to end as quickly as possible that sweet delirium, that madness. Left alone on the platform, and gazing into the dark distance, Gurov listened to the chirrup of the grasshoppers and the hum of the telegraph wires, feeling as though he had only just waked up. And he thought, musing, that there had been another episode or adventure in his life, and it, too, was at an end, and nothing was left of it but a memory.... He was moved, sad, and conscious of a slight remorse. This young woman whom he would never meet again had not been happy with him; he was genuinely warm and affectionate with her, but yet in his manner, his tone, and his caresses there had been a shade of light irony, the coarse condescension of a happy man who was, besides, almost twice her age. All the time she had called him kind, exceptional, lofty; obviously he had seemed to her different from what he really was, so he had unintentionally deceived her....

Here at the station was already a scent of autumn; it was a cold evening.

"It's time for me to go north," thought Gurov as he left the platform. "High time!"

III

At home in Moscow everything was in its winter routine; the stoves were heated, and in the morning it was still dark when the children were having breakfast and getting ready for school, and the nurse would light the lamp for a short time. The frosts had begun already. When the first snow has fallen, on the first day of sledge-driving it is pleasant to see the white earth, the white roofs, to draw soft, delicious breath, and the season brings back the days of one's youth. The old limes and birches, white with hoar-frost, have a good-natured expression; they are nearer to one's heart than cypresses and palms, and near them one doesn't want to be thinking of the sea and the mountains.

Gurov was Moscow born; he arrived in Moscow on a fine frosty day, and when he put on his fur coat and warm gloves, and walked along Petrovka, and when on Saturday evening he heard the ringing of the bells, his recent trip and the places he had seen lost all charm for him. Little by little he became absorbed in Moscow life, greedily read three newspapers a day, and declared he did not read the Moscow papers on principle! He already felt a longing to go to restaurants, clubs, dinner-parties, anniversary celebrations, and he felt flattered at entertaining distinguished lawyers and artists, and at playing cards with a professor at the doctors' club. He could already eat a whole plateful of salt fish and cabbage.

In another month, he fancied, the image of Anna Sergeyevna would be shrouded in a mist in his memory, and only from time to time would visit him in his dreams with a touching smile as others did. But more than a month passed, real winter had come, and everything was still clear in his memory as though he had parted with Anna Sergeyevna only the day before. And his memories glowed more and more vividly. When in the evening stillness he heard from his study the voices of his children, preparing their lessons, or when he listened to a song or the organ at the restaurant, or the storm howled in the chimney, suddenly everything would rise up in his memory: what had happened on the groyne, and the early morning with the mist on the mountains, and the steamer coming from Theodosia, and the kisses. He would pace a long time about his room, remembering it all and smiling; then his memories passed into dreams, and in his fancy the past was mingled with what was to come. Anna Sergeyevna did not visit him in dreams, but followed him about everywhere like a shadow and haunted him. When he shut his eyes he saw her as though she were living before him, and she seemed to him lovelier, younger, tenderer than she was; and he imagined himself finer than he had been in Yalta. In the evenings she peeped out at him from the bookcase, from the fireplace, from the corner—he heard her breathing, the caressing rustle of her dress. In the street he watched the women, looking for some one like her.

He was tormented by an intense desire to confide his memories to some one. But in his home it was impossible to talk of his love, and he had no one outside; he could not talk to his tenants nor to any one at the bank. And what had he to talk of? Had he been in love, then? Had there been anything beautiful, poetical, or edifying or simply interesting in his relations with Anna Sergeyevna? And there was nothing for him but to talk vaguely of love, of woman, and no one guessed what it meant; only his wife twitched her black eyebrows, and said: "The part of a lady-killer does not suit you at all, Dimitri."

One evening, coming out of the doctors' club with an official with whom he had been playing cards, he could not resist saying:

"If only you knew what a fascinating woman I made the acquaintance of in Yalta!"

The official got into his sledge and was driving away, but turned suddenly and shouted: "Dmitri Dmitritch!"

"What?"

"You were right this evening: the sturgeon was a bit too strong!"

These words, so ordinary, for some reason moved Gurov to indignation, and struck him as degrading and unclean. What savage manners, what people! What senseless nights, what uninteresting, uneventful days! The rage for card-playing, the gluttony, the drunkenness, the continual talk always about the same thing. Useless pursuits and conversations always about the same things absorb the better part of one's time, the better part of one's strength, and in the end there is left a life grovelling and curtailed, worthless and trivial, and there is no escaping or getting away from it—just as though one were in a madhouse or a prison.

Gurov did not sleep all night, and was filled with indignation. And he had a headache all next day. And the next night he slept badly; he sat up in bed, thinking, or paced up and down his room. He was sick of his children, sick of the bank; he had no desire to go anywhere or to talk of anything.

In the holidays in December he prepared for a journey, and told his wife he was going to Petersburg to do something in the interests of a young friend—and he set off for S——. What for? He did not very well know himself. He wanted to see Anna Sergeyevna and to talk with her—to arrange a meeting, if possible.

He reached S—— in the morning, and took the best room at the hotel, in which the floor was covered with grey army cloth, and on the table was an inkstand, grey with dust and adorned with a figure on horseback, with its hat in its hand and its head broken off. The hotel porter gave him the necessary information: Von Diderits lived in a house of his own in Old Gontcharny Street—it was not far from the hotel: he was rich and lived in good style, and had his own horses; every one in the town knew him. The porter pronounced the name "Dridirits."

Gurov went without haste to Old Gontcharny Street and found the house. Just opposite the house stretched a long grey fence adorned with nails.

"One would run away from a fence like that," thought Gurov, looking from the fence to the windows of the house and back again.

He considered: today was a holiday, and the husband would probably be at home. And in any case it would be tactless to go into the house and upset her. If he were to send her a note it might fall into her husband's hands, and then it might ruin everything. The best thing was to trust to chance. And he kept walking up and down the street by the fence, waiting for the chance. He saw a beggar go in at the gate and dogs fly at him; then an hour later he heard a piano, and the sounds were faint and indistinct. Probably it was Anna Sergeyevna playing. The front door suddenly opened, and an old woman came out, followed by the familiar white Pomeranian. Gurov was on the point of calling to the dog, but his heart began beating violently, and in his excitement he could not remember the dog's name.

He walked up and down, and loathed the grey fence more and more, and by now he thought irritably that Anna Sergeyevna had forgotten him, and was perhaps already amusing herself with some one else, and that that was very natural in a young woman who had nothing to look at from morning till night but that confounded fence. He went back to his hotel room and sat for a long while on the sofa, not knowing what to do, then he had dinner and a long nap.

"How stupid and worrying it is!" he thought when he woke and looked at the dark windows: it was already evening. "Here I've had a good sleep for some reason. What shall I do in the night?"

He sat on the bed, which was covered by a cheap grey blanket, such as one sees in hospitals, and he taunted himself in his vexation: "So much for the lady with the dog... so much for the adventure .... You're in a nice fix...."

That morning at the station a poster in large letters had caught his eye. "The Geisha" was to be performed for the first time. He thought of this and went to the theatre.

"It's quite possible she may go to the first performance," he thought.

The theatre was full. As in all provincial theatres, there was a fog above the chandelier, the gallery was noisy and restless; in the front row the local dandies were standing up before the beginning of the performance, with their hands behind them; in the Governor's box the Governor's daughter, wearing a boa, was sitting in the front seat, while the Governor himself lurked modestly behind the curtain with only his hands visible; the orchestra was a long time tuning up; the stage curtain swayed. All the time the audience were coming in and taking their seats Gurov looked at them eagerly.

Anna Sergeyevna, too, came in. She sat down in the third row, and when Gurov looked at her his heart contracted, and he understood clearly that for him there was in the whole world no creature so near, so precious, and so important to him; she, this little woman, in no way remarkable, lost in a provincial crowd, with a vulgar lorgnette in her hand, filled his whole life now, was his sorrow and his joy, the one happiness that he now desired for himself, and to the sounds of the inferior orchestra, of the wretched provincial violins, he thought how lovely she was. He thought and dreamed.

A young man with small side-whiskers, tall and stooping, came in with Anna Sergeyevna and sat down beside her; he bent his head at every step and seemed to be continually bowing. Most likely this was the husband whom at Yalta, in a rush of bitter feeling, she had called a flunkey. And there really was in his long figure, his side-whiskers, and the small bald patch on his head, something of the flunkey's obsequiousness; his smile was sugary, and in his buttonhole there was some badge of distinction like the number on a waiter.

During the first interval the husband went away to smoke; she remained alone in her stall. Gurov, who was sitting in the stalls, too, went up to her and said in a trembling voice, with a forced smile: "Good-evening."

She glanced at him and turned pale, then glanced again with horror, unable to believe her eyes, and tightly gripped the fan and the lorgnette in her hands, evidently struggling with herself not to faint. Both were silent. She was sitting, he was standing, frightened by her confusion and not venturing to sit down beside her. The violins and the flute began tuning up. He felt suddenly frightened; it seemed as though all the people in the boxes were looking at them. She got up and went quickly to the door; he followed her, and both walked senselessly along passages, and up and down stairs, and figures in legal, scholastic, and civil service uniforms, all wearing badges, flitted before their eyes. They caught glimpses of ladies, of fur coats hanging on pegs; the draughts blew on them, bringing a smell of stale tobacco. And Gurov, whose heart was beating violently, thought: "Oh, heavens! Why are these people here and this orchestra!..."

And at that instant he recalled how when he had seen Anna Sergeyevna off at the station he had thought that everything was over and they would never meet again. But how far they were still from the end!

On the narrow, gloomy staircase over which was written "To the Amphitheatre," she stopped.

"How you have frightened me!" she said, breathing hard, still pale and overwhelmed. "Oh, how you have frightened me! I am half dead. Why have you come? Why?"

"But do understand, Anna, do understand..." he said hastily in a low voice. "I entreat you to understand...."

She looked at him with dread, with entreaty, with love; she looked at him intently, to keep his features more distinctly in her memory.

"I am so unhappy," she went on, not heeding him. "I have thought of nothing but you all the time; I live only in the thought of you. And I wanted to forget, to forget you; but why, oh, why, have you come?"

On the landing above them two schoolboys were smoking and looking down, but that was nothing to Gurov; he drew Anna Sergeyevna to him, and began kissing her face, her cheeks, and her hands.

"What are you doing, what are you doing!" she cried in horror, pushing him away. "We are mad. Go away today; go away at once.... I beseech you by all that is sacred, I implore you.... There are people coming this way!"

Some one was coming up the stairs.

"You must go away," Anna Sergeyevna went on in a whisper. "Do you hear, Dmitri Dmitritch? I will come and see you in Moscow. I have never been happy; I am miserable now, and I never, never shall be happy, never! Don't make me suffer still more! I swear I'll come to Moscow. But now let us part. My precious, good, dear one, we must part!"

She pressed his hand and began rapidly going downstairs, looking round at him, and from her eyes he could see that she really was unhappy. Gurov stood for a little while, listened, then, when all sound had died away, he found his coat and left the theatre.

IV

And Anna Sergeyevna began coming to see him in Moscow. Once in two or three months she left S—, telling her husband that she was going to consult a doctor about an internal complaint—and her husband believed her, and did not believe her. In Moscow she stayed at the Slaviansky Bazaar hotel, and at once sent a man in a red cap to Gurov. Gurov went to see her, and no one in Moscow knew of it.

Once he was going to see her in this way on a winter morning (the messenger had come the evening before when he was out). With him walked his daughter, whom he wanted to take to school: it was on the way. Snow was falling in big wet flakes.

"It's three degrees above freezing-point, and yet it is snowing," said Gurov to his daughter. "The thaw is only on the surface of the earth; there is quite a different temperature at a greater height in the atmosphere."

"And why are there no thunderstorms in the winter, father?"

He explained that, too. He talked, thinking all the while that he was going to see her, and no living soul knew of it, and probably never would know. He had two lives: one, open, seen and known by all who cared to know, full of relative truth and of relative falsehood, exactly like the lives of his friends and acquaintances; and another life running its course in secret. And through some strange, perhaps accidental, conjunction of circumstances, everything that was essential, of interest and of value to him, everything in which he was sincere and did not deceive himself, everything that made the kernel of his life, was hidden from other people; and all that was false in him, the sheath in which he hid himself to conceal the truth— such, for instance, as his work in the bank, his discussions at the club, his "lower race," his presence with his wife at anniversary festivities—all that was open. And he judged of others by himself, not believing in what he saw, and always believing that every man had his real, most interesting life under the cover of secrecy and under the cover of night. All personal life rested on secrecy, and possibly it was partly on that account that civilized man was so nervously anxious that personal privacy should be respected.

After leaving his daughter at school, Gurov went on to the Slaviansky Bazaar. He took off his fur coat below, went upstairs, and softly knocked at the door. Anna Sergeyevna, wearing his favourite grey dress, exhausted by the journey and the suspense, had been expecting him since the evening before. She was pale; she looked at him, and did not smile, and he had hardly come in when she fell on his breast. Their kiss was slow and prolonged, as though they had not met for two years.

"Well, how are you getting on there?" he asked. "What news?"

"Wait; I'll tell you directly.... I can't talk."

She could not speak; she was crying. She turned away from him, and pressed her handkerchief to her eyes.

"Let her have her cry out. I'll sit down and wait," he thought, and he sat down in an arm-chair.

Then he rang and asked for tea to be brought him, and while he drank his tea she remained standing at the window with her back to him. She was crying from emotion, from the miserable consciousness that their life was so hard for them; they could only meet in secret, hiding themselves from people, like thieves! Was not their life shattered?

"Come, do stop!" he said.

It was evident to him that this love of theirs would not soon be over, that he could not see the end of it. Anna Sergeyevna grew more and more attached to him. She adored him, and it was unthinkable to say to her that it was bound to have an end some day; besides, she would not have believed it!

He went up to her and took her by the shoulders to say something affectionate and cheering, and at that moment he saw himself in the looking-glass.

His hair was already beginning to turn grey. And it seemed strange to him that he had grown so much older, so much plainer during the last few years. The shoulders on which his hands rested were warm and quivering. He felt compassion for this life, still so warm and lovely, but probably already not far from beginning to fade and wither like his own. Why did she love him so much? He always seemed to women different from what he was, and they loved in him not himself, but the man created by their imagination, whom they had been eagerly seeking all their lives; and afterwards, when they noticed their mistake, they loved him all the same.

And not one of them had been happy with him. Time passed, he had made their acquaintance, got on with them, parted, but he had never once loved; it was anything you like, but not love.

And only now when his head was grey he had fallen properly, really in love—for the first time in his life.

Anna Sergeyevna and he loved each other like people very close and akin, like husband and wife, like tender friends; it seemed to them that fate itself had meant them for one another, and they could not understand why he had a wife and she a husband; and it was as though they were a pair of birds of passage, caught and forced to live in different cages. They forgave each other for what they were ashamed of in their past, they forgave everything in the present, and felt that this love of theirs had changed them both.

In moments of depression in the past he had comforted himself with any arguments that came into his mind, but now he no longer cared for arguments; he felt profound compassion, he wanted to be sincere and tender....

"Don't cry, my darling," he said. "You've had your cry; that's enough.... Let us talk now, let us think of some plan."

Then they spent a long while taking counsel together, talked of how to avoid the necessity for secrecy, for deception, for living in different towns and not seeing each other for long at a time. How could they be free from this intolerable bondage?

"How? How?" he asked, clutching his head. "How?"

And it seemed as though in a little while the solution would be found, and then a new and splendid life would begin; and it was clear to both of them that they had still a long, long road before them, and that the most complicated and difficult part of it was only just beginning.

SORROW

THE turner, Grigory Petrov, who had been known for years past as a splendid craftsman, and at the same time as the most senseless peasant in the Galtchinskoy district, was taking his old woman to the hospital. He had to drive over twenty miles, and it was an awful road. A government post driver could hardly have coped with it, much less an incompetent sluggard like Grigory. A cutting cold wind was blowing straight in his face. Clouds of snowflakes were whirling round and round in all directions, so that one could not tell whether the snow was falling from the sky or rising from the earth. The fields, the telegraph posts, and the forest could not be seen for the fog of snow. And when a particularly violent gust of wind swooped down on Grigory, even the yoke above the horse's head could not be seen. The wretched, feeble little nag crawled slowly along. It took all its strength to drag its legs out of the snow and to tug with its head. The turner was in a hurry. He kept restlessly hopping up and down on the front seat and lashing the horse's back.

"Don't cry, Matryona,..." he muttered. "Have a little patience. Please God we shall reach the hospital, and in a trice it will be the right thing for you.... Pavel Ivanitch will give you some little drops, or tell them to bleed you; or maybe his honor will be pleased to rub you with some sort of spirit—it'll... draw it out of your side. Pavel Ivanitch will do his best. He will shout and stamp about, but he will do his best.... He is a nice gentleman, affable, God give him health! As soon as we get there he will dart out of his room and will begin calling me names. 'How? Why so?' he will cry. 'Why did you not come at the right time? I am not a dog to be hanging about waiting on you devils all day. Why did you not come in the morning? Go away! Get out of my sight. Come again tomorrow.' And I shall say: 'Mr. Doctor! Pavel Ivanitch! Your honor!' Get on, do! plague take you, you devil! Get on!"

The turner lashed his nag, and without looking at the old woman went on muttering to himself: "'Your honor! It's true as before God.... Here's the Cross for you, I set off almost before it was light. How could I be here in time if the Lord.... The Mother of God... is wroth, and has sent such a snowstorm? Kindly look for yourself.... Even a first-rate horse could not do it, while mine—you can see for yourself—is not a horse but a disgrace.' And Pavel Ivanitch will frown and shout: 'We know you! You always find some excuse! Especially you, Grishka; I know you of old! I'll be bound you have stopped at half a dozen taverns!' And I shall say: 'Your honor! am I a criminal or a heathen? My old woman is giving up her soul to God, she is dying, and am I going to run from tavern to tavern! What an idea, upon my word! Plague take them, the taverns!' Then Pavel Ivanitch will order you to be taken into the hospital, and I shall fall at his feet.... 'Pavel Ivanitch! Your honor, we thank you most humbly! Forgive us fools and anathemas, don't be hard on us peasants! We deserve a good kicking, while you graciously put yourself out and mess your feet in the snow!' And Pavel Ivanitch will give me a look as though he would like to hit me, and will say: 'You'd much better not be swilling vodka, you fool, but taking pity on your old woman instead of falling at my feet. You want a thrashing!' 'You are right there—a thrashing, Pavel Ivanitch, strike me God! But how can we help bowing down at your feet if you are our benefactor, and a real father to us? Your honor! I give you my word,... here as before God,... you may spit in my face if I deceive you: as soon as my Matryona, this same here, is well again and restored to her natural condition, I'll make anything for your honor that you would like to order! A cigarette-case, if you like, of the best birchwood,... balls for croquet, skittles of the most foreign pattern I can turn.... I will make anything for you! I won't take a farthing from you. In Moscow they would charge you four roubles for such a cigarette-case, but I won't take a farthing.' The doctor will laugh and say: 'Oh, all right, all right.... I see! But it's a pity you are a drunkard....' I know how to manage the gentry, old girl. There isn't a gentleman I couldn't talk to. Only God grant we don't get off the road. Oh, how it is blowing! One's eyes are full of snow."

And the turner went on muttering endlessly. He prattled on mechanically to get a little relief from his depressing feelings. He had plenty of words on his tongue, but the thoughts and questions in his brain were even more numerous. Sorrow had come upon the turner unawares, unlooked-for, and unexpected, and now he could not get over it, could not recover himself. He had lived hitherto in unruffled calm, as though in drunken half-consciousness, knowing neither grief nor joy, and now he was suddenly aware of a dreadful pain in his heart. The careless idler and drunkard found himself quite suddenly in the position of a busy man, weighed down by anxieties and haste, and even struggling with nature.

The turner remembered that his trouble had begun the evening before. When he had come home yesterday evening, a little drunk as usual, and from long-established habit had begun swearing and shaking his fists, his old woman had looked at her rowdy spouse as she had never looked at him before. Usually, the expression in her aged eyes was that of a martyr, meek like that of a dog frequently beaten and badly fed; this time she had looked at him sternly and immovably, as saints in the holy pictures or dying people look. From that strange, evil look in her eyes the trouble had begun. The turner, stupefied with amazement, borrowed a horse from a neighbor, and now was taking his old woman to the hospital in the hope that, by means of powders and ointments, Pavel Ivanitch would bring back his old woman's habitual expression.

"I say, Matryona,..." the turner muttered, "if Pavel Ivanitch asks you whether I beat you, say, 'Never!' and I never will beat you again. I swear it. And did I ever beat you out of spite? I just beat you without thinking. I am sorry for you. Some men wouldn't trouble, but here I am taking you.... I am doing my best. And the way it snows, the way it snows! Thy Will be done, O Lord! God grant we don't get off the road.... Does your side ache, Matryona, that you don't speak? I ask you, does your side ache?"

It struck him as strange that the snow on his old woman's face was not melting; it was queer that the face itself looked somehow drawn, and had turned a pale gray, dingy waxen hue and had grown grave and solemn.

"You are a fool!" muttered the turner.... "I tell you on my conscience, before God,... and you go and... Well, you are a fool! I have a good mind not to take you to Pavel Ivanitch!"

The turner let the reins go and began thinking. He could not bring himself to look round at his old woman: he was frightened. He was afraid, too, of asking her a question and not getting an answer. At last, to make an end of uncertainty, without looking round he felt his old woman's cold hand. The lifted hand fell like a log.

"She is dead, then! What a business!"

And the turner cried. He was not so much sorry as annoyed. He thought how quickly everything passes in this world! His trouble had hardly begun when the final catastrophe had happened. He had not had time to live with his old woman, to show her he was sorry for her before she died. He had lived with her for forty years, but those forty years had passed by as it were in a fog. What with drunkenness, quarreling, and poverty, there had been no feeling of life. And, as though to spite him, his old woman died at the very time when he felt he was sorry for her, that he could not live without her, and that he had behaved dreadfully badly to her.

"Why, she used to go the round of the village," he remembered. "I sent her out myself to beg for bread. What a business! She ought to have lived another ten years, the silly thing; as it is I'll be bound she thinks I really was that sort of man.... Holy Mother! but where the devil am I driving? There's no need for a doctor now, but a burial. Turn back!"

Grigory turned back and lashed the horse with all his might. The road grew worse and worse every hour. Now he could not see the yoke at all. Now and then the sledge ran into a young fir tree, a dark object scratched the turner's hands and flashed before his eyes, and the field of vision was white and whirling again.

"To live over again," thought the turner.

He remembered that forty years ago Matryona had been young,

handsome, merry, that she had come of a well-to-do family. They had married her to him because they had been attracted by his handicraft. All the essentials for a happy life had been there, but the trouble was that, just as he had got drunk after the wedding and lay sprawling on the stove, so he had gone on without waking up till now. His wedding he remembered, but of what happened after the wedding—for the life of him he could remember nothing, except perhaps that he had drunk, lain on the stove, and quarreled. Forty years had been wasted like that.

The white clouds of snow were beginning little by little to turn gray. It was getting dusk.

"Where am I going?" the turner suddenly bethought him with a start. "I ought to be thinking of the burial, and I am on the way to the hospital.... It is as though I had gone crazy."

Grigory turned round again, and again lashed his horse. The little nag strained its utmost and, with a snort, fell into a little trot. The turner lashed it on the back time after time.... A knocking was audible behind him, and though he did not look round, he knew it was the dead woman's head knocking against the sledge. And the snow kept turning darker and darker, the wind grew colder and more cutting....

"To live over again!" thought the turner. "I should get a new lathe, take orders,... give the money to my old woman...."

And then he dropped the reins. He looked for them, tried to pick them up, but could not—his hands would not work....

"It does not matter," he thought, "the horse will go of itself, it knows the way. I might have a little sleep now.... Before the funeral or the requiem it would be as well to get a little rest...."

The turner closed his eyes and dozed. A little later he heard the horse stop; he opened his eyes and saw before him something dark like a hut or a haystack....

He would have got out of the sledge and found out what it was, but he felt overcome by such inertia that it seemed better to freeze than move, and he sank into a peaceful sleep.

He woke up in a big room with painted walls. Bright sunlight was streaming in at the windows. The turner saw people facing him, and his first feeling was a desire to show himself a respectable man who knew how things should be done.

"A requiem, brothers, for my old woman," he said. "The priest should be told...."

"Oh, all right, all right; lie down," a voice cut him short.

"Pavel Ivanitch!" the turner cried in surprise, seeing the doctor before him. "Your honor, benefactor!"

He wanted to leap up and fall on his knees before the doctor, but felt that his arms and legs would not obey him.

"Your honor, where are my legs, where are my arms!"

"Say good-bye to your arms and legs.... They've been frozen off. Come, come!... What are you crying for? You've lived your life, and thank God for it! I suppose you have had sixty years of it—that's enough for you!..."

"I am grieving.... Graciously forgive me! If I could have another five or six years!..."

"What for?"

"The horse isn't mine, I must give it back.... I must bury my old woman.... How quickly it is all ended in this world! Your honor, Pavel Ivanitch! A cigarette-case of birchwood of the best! I'll turn you croquet balls...."

The doctor went out of the ward with a wave of his hand. It was all over with the turner.